CHILDREN'S CLASSICS

Sherlock Holmes
Investigates

SIR ARTHUR CONAN DOYLE

Sherlock Holmes
Investigates

PARRAGON

Sherlock Holmes Investigates
A Parragon Classic

This is a Siena Book
Siena is an imprint of Parragon

"The Adventure of the Speckled Band" and "The Adventure of the Blue
Carbuncle" first published in
The Adventures of Sherlock Holmes, 1892;
"Silver Blaze", and "The Reigate Puzzle" first published in
Memoirs of Sherlock Holmes, 1984;
"The Adventure of the Dancing Men" and "The Adventure of the Sixth
Napoleons" first published in
The Return of Sherlock Holmes, 1905

This edition published in 1999 by
Parragon
13 Whiteladies Road
Clifton
Bristol BS8 1PB

Printed and bound in the UK

CONTENTS

The Adventure of the Speckled Band   1
The Adventure of the Blue Carbuncle   34
The Adventure of the Six Napoleons   94
The Adventure of the Dancing Men   122
Silver Blaze   134
The Reigate Puzzle   154

THE ADVENTURE OF
THE SPECKLED BAND

On glancing over my notes of the seventy odd cases in which I have during the last eight years studied the methods of my friend Sherlock Holmes, I find many tragic, some comic, a large number merely strange, but none commonplace; for, working as he did rather for the love of his art than for the acquirement of wealth, he refused to associate himself with any investigation which did not tend towards the unusual, and even the fantastic. Of all these varied cases, however, I cannot recall any which presented more singular features than that which was associated with the well-known Surrey family of the Roylotts of Stoke Moran. The events in question occurred in the early days of my association with Holmes, when we were sharing rooms as bachelors in Baker Street. It is possible that I might have placed them upon record before, but a promise of secrecy was made at the time, from which I have only been freed during the last month by the untimely death of the lady to whom the pledge was given. It is perhaps as well that the facts should now come to light, for I have reasons to know that there are widespread rumours as to the death of Dr Grimesby Roylott which tend to make the matter even more terrible than the truth.

It was early in April in the year '83 that I woke one

morning to find Sherlock Holmes standing, fully dressed, by the side of my bed. He was a late riser, as a rule, and as the clock on the mantelpiece showed me that it was only a quarter-past seven, I blinked up at him in some surprise, and perhaps just a little resentment, for I was myself regular in my habits.

'Very sorry to knock you up, Watson,' said he, 'but it's the common lot this morning. Mrs Hudson has been knocked up, she retorted upon me, and I on you.'

'What is it, then—a fire?'

'No; a client. It seems that a young lady has arrived in a considerable state of excitement, who insists upon seeing me. She is waiting now in the sitting-room. Now, when young ladies wander about the metropolis at this hour of the morning, and knock sleepy people up out of their beds, I presume that it is something very pressing which they have to communicate. Should it prove to be an interesting case, you would, I am sure, wish to follow it from the outset. I thought, at any rate, that I should call you and give you the chance.'

'My dear fellow, I would not miss it for anything.'

I had no keener pleasure than in following Holmes in his professional investigations, and in admiring the rapid deductions, as swift as intuitions, and yet always founded on a logical basis, with which he unravelled the problems which were submitted to him. I rapidly threw on my clothes and was ready in a few minutes to accompany my friend down to the sitting-room. A lady dressed in black and heavily veiled, who had been sitting in the window, rose as we entered.

'Good-morning, madam,' said Holmes cheerily. 'My name is Sherlock Holmes. This is my intimate friend and associate, Dr Watson, before whom you can speak as freely as before myself. Ha! I am glad to see that Mrs Hudson has had the good sense to light the fire. Pray draw up to it, and I shall order you a cup of hot coffee, for I observe that you are shivering.'

'It is not cold which makes me shiver,' said the woman in a low voice, changing her seat as requested.

'What, then?'

'It is fear, Mr Holmes. It is terror.' She raised her veil as she spoke, and we could see that she was indeed in a pitiable state of agitation, her face all drawn and grey, with restless, frightened eyes, like those of some haunted animal. Her features and figure were those of a woman of thirty, but her hair was shot with premature grey, and her expression was weary and haggard. Sherlock Holmes ran her over with one of his quick, all-comprehensive glances.

'You must not fear,' said he soothingly, bending forward and patting her forearm. 'We shall soon set matters right, I have no doubt. You have come in by train this morning, I see.'

'You know me, then?'

'No, but I observe the second half of a return ticket in the palm of your left glove. You must have started early, and yet you had a good drive in a dog-cart, along heavy roads, before you reached the station.'

The lady gave a violent start and stared in bewilderment at my companion.

'There is no mystery, my dear madam,' said he, smiling. 'The left arm of your jacket is spattered with mud in no less than seven places. The marks are perfectly fresh. There is no vehicle save a dog-cart which throws up mud in that way, and then only when you sit on the left-hand side of the driver.'

'Whatever your reasons may be, you are perfectly correct,' said she. 'I started from home before six, reached Leatherhead at twenty past, and came in by the first train to Waterloo. Sir, I can stand this strain no longer; I shall go mad if it continues. I have no one to turn to—none, save only one, who cares for me, and he, poor fellow, can be of little aid. I have heard of you, Mr Holmes; I have heard of you from Mrs Farintosh, whom you helped in the hour of her sore need. It was from her that I had your address. Oh, sir, do you not think that you could help me, too, and at least throw a little light through the dense darkness which surrounds me? At present it is out of my power to reward you for your services, but in a month or six weeks I shall be married, with the control of my own income, and then at least you shall not find me ungrateful.'

Holmes turned to his desk and, unlocking it, drew out a small case-book, which he consulted.

'Farintosh,' said he. 'Ah yes, I recall the case; it was concerned with an opal tiara. I think it was before your time, Watson. I can only say, madam, that I shall be happy to devote the same care to your case as I did to that of your friend. As to reward, my profession is its own reward; but you are at liberty to defray whatever expenses I may be put to, at the time which suits you best. And now I beg that you will lay, before us everything that may help us in forming an opinion upon the matter.'

'Alas!' replied our visitor, 'the very horror of my situation lies in the fact that my fears are so vague, and my suspicions depend so entirely upon small points, which might seem trivial to another, that even he to whom of all others I have a right to look for help and advice looks upon all that I tell him about it as the fancies of a nervous woman. He does not say so, but I can read it from his soothing answers and averted eyes. But I have heard, Mr Holmes, that you can see deeply into the manifold wickedness of the human heart. You may advise me how to walk amid the dangers which encompass me.'

'I am all attention, madam.'

'My name is Helen Stoner, and I am living with my stepfather, who is the last survivor of one of the oldest Saxon families in England, the Roylotts of Stoke Moran, on the western border of Surrey.'

Holmes nodded his head. 'The name is familiar to me,' said he.

'The family was at one time among the richest in England, and the estates extended over the borders into Berkshire in the north, and Hampshire in the west. In the last century, however, four successive heirs were of a dissolute and wasteful disposition, and the family ruin was eventually completed by a gambler in the days of the Regency. Nothing was left save a few acres of ground, and the two-hundred-year-old house, which is itself crushed under a heavy mortgage. The last squire dragged out his existence there, living the horrible life of an aristocratic pauper; but his only son, my stepfather, seeing that he must adapt himself to the new conditions, obtained an advance from a relative, which enabled him to take a medical degree and went out to Calcutta, where, by his professional skill and his force of character, he established a large practice. In a fit of anger, however, caused by some robberies which had been perpetrated in the house, he beat his native butler to death and narrowly escaped a capital sentence. As it was, he suffered a long term of imprisonment and afterwards returned to England a morose and disappointed man.

'When Dr Roylott was in India he married my mother, Mrs Stoner, the young widow of Major-General Stoner, of the Bengal Artillery. My sister Julia and I were twins, and we were only two years old at the time of my mother's re-marriage. She had a considerable sum of money—not less than £1000 a year—and this she bequeathed to Dr Roylott entirely while we resided with him, with a provision that a certain annual sum should be allowed to each of us in the event of our marriage. Shortly after our return to England my mother died—she was killed eight years ago in a railway accident near Crewe. Dr Roylott then abandoned his attempts to establish himself in practice in London and took us to live with him in the old ancestral house at Stoke Moran. The money which my mother had left was enough for all our wants, and there seemed to be no obstacle to our happiness.

'But a terrible change came over our stepfather about this time. Instead of making friends and exchanging visits with our neighbours, who had at first been overjoyed to see a Roylott of Stoke Moran back in the old family seat, he shut himself up in his house and seldom came out save to indulge in furious quarrels with whoever might cross his path. Violence of temper approaching to mania has been hereditary in the men of the family, and in my stepfather's case it had, I believe, been intensified by his long residence in the tropics. A series of disgraceful brawls took place, two of which ended in the police-court, until at last he became the terror of the village, and the folks would fly at his approach, for he is a man of immense strength, and absolutely uncontrollable in his anger.

'Last week he hurled the local blacksmith over a parapet into a stream, and it was only by paying over all the money which I could gather together that I was able to avert another public exposure. He had no friends at all save the wandering gypsies, and he would give these vagabonds leave to encamp upon the few acres of bramble-covered land which represent the family estate, and would accept in return the hospitality of their tents, wandering away with them sometimes for weeks on end. He has a passion also for Indian animals, which are sent over to him by a correspondent, and he has at this moment a cheetah and a baboon, which wander freely over his grounds and are feared by the villagers almost as much as their master.

'You can imagine from what I say that my poor sister Julia and I had no great pleasure in our lives. No servant would stay with us, and for a long time we did all the work of the house. She was but thirty at the time of her death, and yet her hair had already begun to whiten, even as mine has.'

'Your sister is dead, then?'

'She died just two years ago, and it is of her death that I wish to speak to you. You can understand that, living the life which I have described, we were little likely to see anyone of our own age and position. We had, however, an aunt, my mother's maiden sister, Miss Honoria Westphail, who lives near Harrow, and we were occasionally allowed to pay short visits at this lady's house. Julia went there at Christmas two years ago, and met there a half-pay major of marines, to whom she became engaged. My stepfather learned of the engagement when my sister returned and offered no objection to the marriage; but within a fortnight of the day which had been fixed for the wedding, the terrible event occurred which has deprived me of my only companion.'

Sherlock Holmes had been leaning back in his chair with his eyes closed and his head sunk in a cushion, but he half opened his lids now and glanced across at his visitor.

'Pray be precise as to details,' said he.

'It is easy for me to be so, for every event of that dreadful time is seared into my memory. The manor-house is, as I have already said, very old, and only one wing is now inhabited. The bedrooms in this wing are on the ground floor, the sitting-rooms being in the central block of the buildings. Of these bedrooms the first is Dr Roylott's, the second my sister's, and the third my own. There is no communication between them, but they all open out into the same corridor. Do I make myself plain?'

'Perfectly so.'

'The windows of the three rooms open out upon the lawn. The fatal night Dr Roylott had gone to his room early, though we knew that he had not retired to rest, for my sister was troubled by the smell of the strong Indian cigars which it was his custom to smoke. She left her room, therefore, and came into mine, where she sat for some time, chatting about her approaching wedding. At eleven o'clock she rose to leave me, but she paused at the door and looked back.

'"Tell me, Helen," said she, "have you ever heard anyone whistle in the dead of the night,"

'"Never," said I.

'"I suppose that you could not possibly whistle, yourself, in your sleep,"

'"Certainly not. But why,"

'"Because during the last few nights I have always, about three in the morning, heard a low, clear whistle. I am a light sleeper, and it has awakened me. I cannot tell where it came from—perhaps from the next room, perhaps from the lawn. I thought that I would just ask you whether you had heard it."

'"No, I have not. It must be those wretched gypsies in the plantation."

'"Very likely. And yet if it were on the lawn, I wonder that you did not hear it also."

'"Ah, but I sleep more heavily than you."

'"Well, it is of no great consequence, at any rate." She smiled back at me, closed my door, and a few moments later I heard her key turn in the lock."

'Indeed,' said Holmes. 'Was it your custom always to lock yourselves in at night?'

'Always.'

'And why?'

'I think that I mentioned to you that the doctor kept a cheetah and a baboon. We had no feeling of security unless our doors were locked.'

'Quite so. Pray proceed with your statement.'

'I could not sleep that night. A vague feeling of impending misfortune impressed me. My sister and I, you will recollect, were twins, and you know how subtle are the links which bind two souls which are so closely allied. It was a wild night. The wind was howling outside, and the rain was beating and splashing against the windows. Suddenly, amid all the hubbub of the gale, there burst forth the wild scream of a terrified woman. I knew that it was my sister's voice. I sprang from my bed, wrapped a shawl round me, and rushed into the corridor. As I opened my door I seemed to hear a low whistle, such as my sister described, and a few moments later a clanging sound, as if a mass of metal had fallen. As I ran down the passage, my sister's door was

9

unlocked, and revolved slowly upon its hinges. I stared at it horror-stricken, not knowing what was about to issue from it. By the light of the corridor-lamp I saw my sister appear at the opening, her face blanched with terror, her hands groping for help, her whole figure swaying to and fro like that of a drunkard. I ran to her and threw my arms round her, but at that moment her knees seemed to give way and she fell to the ground. She writhed as one who is in terrible pain, and her limbs were dreadfully convulsed. At first I thought that she had not recognized me, but as I bent over her she suddenly shrieked out in a voice which I shall never forget, "Oh, my God! Helen! It was the band! The speckled band," There was something else which she would fain have said, and she stabbed with her finger into the air in the direction of the doctor's room, but a fresh convulsion seized her and choked her words. I rushed out, calling loudly for my stepfather, and I met him hastening from his room in his dressing-gown. When he reached my sister's side she was unconscious, and though he poured brandy down her throat and sent for medical aid from the village, all efforts were in vain, for she slowly sank and died without having recovered her consciousness. Such was the dreadful end of my beloved sister.'

'One moment,' said Holmes; 'are you sure about this whistle and metallic sound? Could you swear to it?'

'That was what the county coroner asked me at the inquiry. It is my strong impression that I heard it, and yet, among the crash of the gale and the creaking of an old house, I may possibly have been deceived.'

'Was your sister dressed?'

'No, she was in her night-dress. In her right hand was

found the charred stump of a match, and in her left a match-box.'

'Showing that she had struck a light and looked about her when the alarm took place. That is important. And what conclusions did the coroner come to?'

'He investigated the case with great care, for Dr Roylott's conduct had long been notorious in the county, but he was unable to find any satisfactory cause of death. My evidence showed that the door had been fastened upon the inner side, and the windows were blocked by old-fashioned shutters with broad iron bars, which were secured every night. The walls were carefully sounded, and were shown to be quite solid all round, and the flooring was also thoroughly examined, with the same result. The chimney is wide, but is barred up by four large staples. It is certain, therefore, that my sister was quite alone when she met her end. Besides, there were no marks of any violence upon her.'

'How about poison?'

'The doctors examined her for it, but without success.'

'What do you think that this unfortunate lady died of, then?'

'It is my belief that she died of pure fear and nervous shock, though what it was that frightened her I cannot imagine.'

'Were there gypsies in the plantation at the time?'

'Yes, there are nearly always some there.'

'Ah, and what did you gather from this allusion to a band—a speckled band?'

'Sometimes I have thought that it was merely the wild talk of delirium, sometimes that it may have referred to some band of people, perhaps to these very gypsies in the plantation. I do not know whether the spotted handkerchiefs which so many of them wear over their heads might have suggested the strange adjective which she used.'

Holmes shook his head like a man who is far from being satisfied.

'These are very deep waters,' said he; 'pray go on with your narrative.'

'Two years have passed since then, and my life has been until lately lonelier than ever. A month ago, however, a dear friend, whom I have known for many years, has done me the honour to ask my hand in marriage. His name is Armitage—Percy Armitage—the second son of Mr Armitage, of Crane Water, near Reading. My stepfather has offered no opposition to the match, and we are to be married in the course of the spring. Two days ago some repairs were started in the west wing of the building, and my bedroom wall has been pierced, so that I have had to move into the chamber in which my sister died, and to sleep in the very bed in which she slept. Imagine, then, my thrill of terror when last night, as I lay awake, thinking over her terrible fate, I suddenly heard in the silence of the night the low whistle which had been the herald of her own death. I sprang up and lit the lamp, but nothing was to be seen in the room. I was too shaken to go to bed again, however, so I dressed, and as soon as it was daylight I slipped down, got a dog-cart at the Crown Inn, which is opposite, and drove to Leatherhead, from whence I have come on this morning with the one object of seeing you and asking your advice.'

'You have done wisely,' said my friend. 'But have you told me all?'

'Yes, all.'

'Miss Roylott, you have not. You are screening your stepfather.'

'Why, what do you mean?'

For answer Holmes pushed back the frill of black lace which fringed the hand that lay upon our visitor's knee. Five little livid spots, the marks of four fingers and a thumb, were printed upon the white wrist.

'You have been cruelly used,' said Holmes.

The lady coloured deeply and covered over her injured wrist. 'He is a hard man,' she said, 'and perhaps he hardly knows his own strength.'

There was a long silence, during which Holmes leaned his chin upon his hands and stared into the crackling fire.

'This is a very deep business,' he said at last. 'There are a thousand details which I should desire to know before I decide upon our course of action. Yet we have not a moment to lose. If we were to come to Stoke Moran today, would it be possible for us to see over these rooms without the knowledge of your stepfather?'

'As it happens, he spoke of coming into town today upon some most important business. It is probable that he will be away all day, and that there would be nothing to disturb you. We have a housekeeper now, but she is old and foolish, and I could easily get her out of the way.'

'Excellent. You are not averse to this trip, Watson?'

'By no means.'

'Then we shall both come. What are you going to do yourself?'

'I have one or two things which I would wish to do now that I am in town. But I shall return by the twelve o'clock train, so as to be there in time for your coming.'

'And you may expect us early in the afternoon. I have

13

myself some small business matters to attend to. Will you not wait and breakfast?'

'No, I must go. My heart is lightened already since I have confided my trouble to you. I shall look forward to seeing you again this afternoon.' She dropped her thick black veil over her face and glided from the room.

'And what do you think of it all, Watson?' asked Sherlock Holmes, leaning back in his chair.

'It seems to me to be a most dark and sinister business.'

'Dark enough and sinister enough.'

'Yet if the lady is correct in saying that the flooring and walls are sound, and that the door, window, and chimney are impassable, then her sister must have been undoubtedly alone when she met her mysterious end.'

'What becomes, then, of these nocturnal whistles, and what of the very peculiar words of the dying woman?'

'I cannot think.'

'When you combine the ideas of whistles at night, the presence of a band of gypsies who are on intimate terms with this old doctor, the fact that we have every reason to believe that the doctor has an interest in preventing his stepdaughter's marriage, the dying allusion to a band, and, finally, the fact that Miss Helen Stoner heard a metallic clang, which might have been caused by one of those metal bars that secured the shutters falling back into its place, I think that there is good ground to think that the mystery may be cleared along those lines.'

'But what, then, did the gypsies do?'

'I cannot imagine.'

'I see many objections to any such theory.'

'And so do I. It is precisely for that reason that we are going to Stoke Moran this day. I want to see whether the objections are fatal, or if they may be explained away. But what in the name of the devil!'

The ejaculation had been drawn from my companion by the fact that our door had been suddenly dashed open, and that a huge man had framed himself in the aperture. His costume was a peculiar mixture of the professional and of the agricultural, having a black top-hat, a long frock-coat, and a pair of high gaiters, with a hunting-crop swinging in his hand. So tall was he that his hat actually brushed the cross bar of the doorway, and his breadth seemed to span it across from side to side. A large face, seared with a thousand wrinkles, burned yellow with the sun, and marked with every evil passion, was turned from one to the other of us, while his deep-set, bile-shot eyes, and his high, thin, fleshless nose, gave him somewhat the resemblance to a fierce old bird of prey.

'Which of you is Holmes?' asked this apparition.

'My name, sir; but you have the advantage of me,' said my companion quietly.

'I am Dr Grimesby Roylott, of Stoke Moran.'

'Indeed, Doctor,' said Holmes blandly. 'Pray take a seat.'

'I will do nothing of the kind. My stepdaughter has been here. I have traced her. What has she been saying to you?'

'It is a little cold for the time of the year,' said Holmes.

'What has she been saying to you?' screamed the old man furiously.

'But I have heard that the crocuses promise well,' continued my companion imperturbably.

'Ha! You put me off, do you?' said our new visitor, taking a step forward and shaking his hunting-crop. 'I know you, you scoundrel! I have heard of you before. You are Holmes, the meddler.'

My friend smiled.

'Holmes, the busybody!'

His smile broadened.

'Holmes, the Scotland Yard Jack-in-office!'

Holmes chuckled heartily. 'Your conversation is most entertaining,' said he. 'When you go out close the door, for there is a decided draught.'

'I will go when I have said my say. Don't you dare to meddle with my affairs. I know that Miss Stoner has been here. I traced her! I am a dangerous man to fall foul of! See here.' He stepped swiftly forward, seized the poker, and bent it into a curve with his huge brown hands.

'See that you keep yourself out of my grip,' he snarled, and hurling the twisted poker into the fireplace he strode out of the room.

'He seems a very amiable person,' said Holmes, laughing. 'I am not quite so bulky, but if he had remained I might have shown him that my grip was not much more feeble than his own.' As he spoke he picked up the steel poker and, with a sudden effort, straightened it out again.

'Fancy his having the insolence to confound me with the official detective force! This incident gives zest to our investigation, however, and I only trust that our little friend will not suffer from her imprudence in allowing this brute to trace her. And now, Watson, we shall order breakfast, and afterwards I shall walk down to Doctors' Commons, where I hope to get some data which may help us in this matter.'

It was nearly one o'clock when Sherlock Holmes returned

from his excursion. He held in his hand a sheet of blue paper, scrawled over with notes and figures.

'I have seen the will of the deceased wife,' said he. 'To determine its exact meaning I have been obliged to work out the present prices of the investments with which it is concerned. The total income, which at the time of the wife's death was little short of £1100, is now, through the fall in agricultural prices, not more than £750. Each daughter can claim an income of £250, in case of marriage. It is evident, therefore, that if both girls had married, this beauty would have had a mere pittance, while even one of them would cripple him to a very serious extent. My morning's work has not been wasted, since it has proved that he has the very strongest motives for standing in the way of anything of the sort. And now, Watson, this is too serious for dawdling, especially as the old man is aware that we are interesting ourselves in his affairs; so if you are ready, we shall call a cab and drive to Waterloo. I should be very much obliged if you would slip your revolver into your pocket. An Eley's No. 2 is an excellent argument with gentlemen who can twist steel pokers into knots. That and a toothbrush are, I think, all that we need.'

At Waterloo we were fortunate in catching a train for Leatherhead, where we hired a trap at the station inn and drove for four or five miles through the lovely Surrey lanes. It was a perfect day, with a bright sun and a few fleecy clouds in the heavens. The trees and wayside hedges were just throwing out their first green shoots, and the air was full of the pleasant smell of the moist earth. To me at least there was a strange contrast between the sweet promise of the spring and this sinister quest upon which we were engaged. My companion sat in the front of the trap, his arms folded, his hat pulled down over his eyes, and his chin sunk upon his breast, buried in the deepest thought. Suddenly, however, he started, tapped me on the shoulder, and pointed over the meadows.

'Look there!' said he.

A heavily timbered park stretched up in a gentle slope, thickening into a grove at the highest point. From amid the branches there jutted out the grey gables and high roof-tree of a very old mansion.

'Stoke Moran?' said he.

'Yes, sir, that be the house of Dr Grimesby Roylott,' remarked the driver.

'There is some building going on there,' said Holmes; 'that is where we are going.'

'There's the village,' said the driver, pointing to a cluster of roofs some distance to the left; 'but if you want to get to the house, you'll find it shorter to get over this stile, and so by the foot-path over the fields. There it is, where the lady is walking.'

'And the lady, I fancy, is Miss Stoner,' observed Holmes, shading his eyes. 'Yes, I think we had better do as you suggest.'

We got off, paid our fare, and the trap rattled back on its way to Leatherhead.

'I thought it as well,' said Holmes as we climbed the stile, 'that this fellow should think we had come here as architects, or on some definite business. It may stop his gossip. Good-afternoon, Miss Stoner. You see that we have been as good as our word.'

Our client of the morning had hurried forward to meet us with a face which spoke her joy. 'I have been waiting so eagerly for you,' she cried, shaking hands with us warmly. 'All has turned out splendidly. Dr Roylott has gone to town, and it is unlikely that he will be back before evening.'

'We have had the pleasure of making the doctor's acquaintance,' said Holmes, and in a few words he sketched out what had occurred. Miss Stoner turned white to the lips as she listened.

'Good heavens!' she cried, 'he has followed me, then.'

'So it appears.'

'He is so cunning that I never know when I am safe from him. What will he say when he returns?'

'He must guard himself, for he may find that there is someone more cunning than himself upon his track. You must lock yourself up from him tonight. If he is violent, we shall take you away to your aunt's at Harrow. Now, we must make the best use of our time, so kindly take us at once to the rooms which we are to examine.'

The building was of grey, lichen-blotched stone, with a high central portion and two curving wings, like the claws of a crab, thrown out on each side. In one of these wings the windows were broken and blocked with wooden boards, while the roof was partly caved in, a picture of ruin. The central portion was in little better repair, but the right-hand block was comparatively modern, and the blinds in the windows, with the blue smoke curling up from the chimneys, showed that this was where the family resided. Some scaffolding had been erected against the end wall, and the stone-work had been broken into, but there were no signs of any workmen at the moment of our visit. Holmes walked slowly up and down the ill-trimmed lawn and examined with deep attention the outsides of the windows.

'This, I take it, belongs to the room in which you used

to sleep, the centre one to your sister's, and the one next to the main building to Dr Roylott's chamber?'

'Exactly so. But I am now sleeping in the middle one.'

'Pending the alterations, as I understand. By the way, there does not seem to be any very pressing need for repairs at that end wall.'

'There were none. I believe that it was an excuse to move me from my room.'

'Ah! that is suggestive. Now, on the other side of this narrow wing runs the corridor from which these three rooms open. There are windows in it, of course?'

'Yes, but very small ones. Too narrow for anyone to pass through.'

'As you both locked your doors at night, your rooms were unapproachable from that side. Now, would you have the kindness to go into your room and bar your shutters?'

Miss Stoner did so, and Holmes, after a careful examination through the open window, endeavoured in every way to force the shutter open, but without success. There was no slit through which a knife could be passed to raise the bar. Then with his lens he tested the hinges, but they were of solid iron, built firmly into the massive masonry. 'Hum!' said he, scratching his chin in some perplexity, 'my theory certainly presents some difficulties. No one could pass these shutters if they were bolted. Well, we shall see if the inside throws any light upon the matter.'

A small side door led into the whitewashed corridor from which the three bedrooms opened. Holmes refused to examine the third chamber, so we passed at once to the second, that in which Miss Stoner was now sleeping, and in which her sister had met with her fate. It was a homely little room, with a low ceiling and a gaping fireplace, after the fashion of old country-houses. A brown chest of drawers stood in one corner, a narrow white-counterpaned bed in another, and a dressing-table on the left-hand side of the window. These articles, with two small wickerwork chairs, made up all the furniture in the room save for a square of Wilton carpet in the centre. The boards round and the panelling of the walls were of brown, worm-eaten oak, so old and discoloured that it may have dated from the original building of the house. Holmes 'drew one of the chairs into a corner and sat silent, while his eyes travelled round and round and up and down, taking in every detail of the apartment.

'Where does the bell communicate with?' he asked at last, pointing to a thick bell-rope which hung down beside the bed, the tassel actually lying upon the pillow.

'It goes to the housekeeper's room.'

'It looks newer than the other things?'

'Yes, it was only put there a couple of years ago.'

'Your sister asked for it, I suppose?'

'No, I never heard of her using it. We used always to get what we wanted for ourselves.'

'Indeed, it seemed unnecessary to put so nice a bell-pull there. You will excuse me for a few minutes while I satisfy myself as to this floor.' He threw himself down upon his face with his lens in his hand and crawled swiftly backward and forward, examining minutely the cracks between the boards. Then he did the same with the woodwork with which the chamber was panelled. Finally he walked over to the bed and spent some time in staring at it and in running his eye up and down the wall. Finally he took the bell-rope in his hand and gave it a brisk tug.

'Why, it's a dummy,' said he.

'Won't it ring?'

'No, it is not even attached to a wire. This is very interesting. You can see now that it is fastened to a hook just above where the little opening for the ventilator is.'

'How very absurd! I never noticed that before.'

'Very strange!' muttered Holmes, pulling at the rope. 'There are one or two very singular points about this room. For example, what a fool a builder must be to open a ventilator into another room, when, with the same trouble, he might have communicated with the outside air!'

'That is also quite modern,' said the lady.

'Done about the same time as the bell-rope?' remarked Holmes.

'Yes, there were several little changes carried out about that time.'

'They seem to have been of a most interesting character—dummy bell-ropes, and ventilators which do not ventilate. With your permission, Miss Stoner, we shall now carry our researches into the inner apartment.'

Dr Grimesby Roylott's chamber was larger than that of his stepdaughter, but was as plainly furnished. A camp-bed, a small wooden shelf full of books, mostly of a technical character, an armchair beside the bed, a plain wooden chair against the wall, a round table, and a large iron safe were the principal things which met the eye. Holmes walked slowly round and examined each and all of them with the keenest interest.

'What's in here?' he asked, tapping the safe.

'My stepfather's business papers.'

'Oh!. You have seen inside, then?'

'Only once, some years ago. I remember that it was full of papers.'

'There isn't a cat in it, for example?'

'No. What a strange idea!'

'Well, look at this!' He took up a small saucer of milk which stood on the top of it.

'No; we don't keep a cat. But there is a cheetah and a baboon.'

'Ah, yes, of course! Well, a cheetah is just a big cat, and yet a saucer of milk does not go very far in satisfying its wants, I daresay. There is one point which I should wish to determine.' He squatted down in front of the wooden chair and examined the seat of it with the greatest attention.

'Thank you. That is quite settled,' said he, rising and putting his lens in his pocket. 'Hello! Here is something interesting!'

The object which had caught his eye was a small dog lash hung on one corner of the bed. The lash, however, was curled upon itself and tied so as to make a loop of whipcord.

'What do you make of that, Watson?'

'It is a common enough lash. But I don't know why it should be tied.'

'That is not quite so common, is it? Ah, me! it's a wicked world, and when a clever man turns his brains to crime it is the worst of all. I think that I have seen enough now, Miss Stoner, and with your permission we shall walk out upon the lawn.'

I had never seen my friend's face so grim or his brow so dark as it was when we turned from the scene of this investigation. We had walked several times up and down the lawn, neither Miss Stoner nor myself liking to break in upon his thoughts before he roused himself from his reverie.

'It is very essential, Miss Stoner,' said he, 'that you should absolutely follow my advice in every respect.'

'I shall most certainly do so.'

'The matter is too serious for any hesitation. Your life may depend upon your compliance.'

'I assure you that I am in your hands.'

'In the first place, both my friend and I must spend the night in your room.'

Both Miss Stoner and I gazed at him in astonishment.

'Yes, it must be so. Let me explain. I believe that that is the village inn over there?'

'Yes, that is the Crown.'

'Very good. Your windows would be visible from there?'

'Certainly.'

'You must confine yourself to your room, on pretence of a headache, when your stepfather comes back. Then when you hear him retire for the night, you must open the shutters of your window, undo the hasp, put your lamp there as a signal to us, and then withdraw quietly with everything which you are likely to want into the room which you used to occupy. I have no doubt that, in spite of the repairs, you could manage there for one night.'

'Oh, yes, easily.'

'The rest you will leave in our hands.'

'But what will you do?'

'We shall spend the night in your room, and we shall investigate the cause of this noise which has disturbed you.'

'I believe, Mr Holmes, that you have already made up your mind,' said Miss Stoner, laying her hand upon my companion's sleeve.

'Perhaps I have.'

'Then, for pity's sake, tell me what was the cause of my sister's death.'

'I should prefer to have clearer proofs before I speak.'

'You can at least tell me whether my own thought is correct, and if she died from some sudden fright.'

'No, I do not think so. I think that there was probably some more tangible cause. And now, Miss Stoner, we must leave you, for if Dr Roylott returned and saw us our journey would be in vain. Goodbye, and be brave, for if you will do what I have told you you may rest assured that we shall soon drive away the dangers that threaten you.'

Sherlock Holmes and I had no difficulty in engaging a bedroom and sitting-room at the Crown Inn. They were on the upper floor, and from our window we could command a view of the avenue gate, and of the inhabited wing of Stoke Moran Manor House. At dusk we saw Dr Grimesby Roylott drive past, his huge form looming up beside the little figure of the lad who drove him. The boy had some slight difficulty in undoing the heavy iron gates, and we heard the hoarse roar of the doctor's voice and saw the fury with which he shook his clinched fists at him. The trap drove on, and a few minutes later we saw a sudden light spring up among the trees as the lamp was lit in one of the sitting-rooms.

'Do you know, Watson,' said Holmes as we sat together in the gathering darkness, 'I have really some scruples as to taking you tonight. There is a distinct element of danger.'

'Can I be of assistance?'

'Your presence might be invaluable.'

'Then I shall certainly come.'

'It is very kind of you.'

'You speak of danger. You have evidently seen more in these rooms than was visible to me.'

'No, but I fancy that I may have deduced a little more. I imagine that you saw all that I did.'

'I saw nothing remarkable save the bell-rope, and what purpose that could answer I confess is more than I can imagine.'

'You saw the ventilator, too?'

'Yes, but I do not think that it is such a very unusual thing to have a small opening between two rooms. It was so small that a rat could hardly pass through.'

'I knew that we should find a ventilator before ever we came to Stoke Moran.'

'My dear Holmes!'

'Oh, yes, I did. You remember in her statement she said that her sister could smell Dr Roylott's cigar. Now, of course that suggested at once that there must be a communication between the two rooms. It could only be a small one, or it would have been remarked upon at the coroner's inquiry. I deduced a ventilator.'

'But what harm can there be in that?'

'Well, there is at least a curious coincidence of dates. A ventilator is made, a cord is hung, and a lady who sleeps in the bed dies. Does not that strike you?'

'I cannot as yet see any connection.'

'Did you observe anything very peculiar about that bed?'

'No.'

'It was clamped to the floor. Did you ever see a bed fastened like that before?'

'I cannot say that I have.'

'The lady could not move her bed. It must always be in the same relative position to the ventilator and to the rope—or so we may call it, since it was clearly never meant for a bell-pull.'

'Holmes,' I cried, 'I seem to see dimly what you are hinting at. We are only just in time to prevent some subtle and horrible crime.'

'Subtle enough and horrible enough. When a doctor does go wrong he is the first of criminals. He has nerve and he has knowledge. Palmer and Pritchard were among the heads of their profession. This man strikes even deeper, but I think, Watson, that we shall be able to strike deeper still. But we shall have horrors enough before the night is over; for goodness' sake let us have a quiet pipe and turn our minds for a few hours to something more cheerful.'

About nine o'clock the light among the trees was extinguished, and all was dark in the direction of the Manor House. Two hours passed slowly away, and then, suddenly, just at the stroke of eleven, a single bright light shone out right in front of us.

'That is our signal,' said Holmes, springing to his feet; 'it comes from the middle window.'

As we passed out he exchanged a few words with the landlord, explaining that we were going on a late visit to an acquaintance, and that it was possible that we might spend the night there. A moment later we were out on the dark road, a chill wind blowing in our faces, and one yellow light twinkling in front of us through the gloom to guide us on our sombre errand.

There was little difficulty in entering the grounds, for unrepaired breaches gaped in the old park wall. Making our way among the trees, we reached the lawn, crossed it, and were about to enter through the window when out from a clump of laurel bushes there darted what seemed to be a hideous and distorted child, who threw itself upon the grass with writhing limbs and then ran swiftly across the lawn into the darkness.

'My God!' I whispered; 'did you see it?'

Holmes was for the moment as startled as I. His hand closed like a vice upon my wrist in his agitation. Then he broke into a low laugh and put his lips to my ear.

'It is a nice household,' he murmured. 'That is the baboon.'

I had forgotten the strange pets which the doctor affected. There was a cheetah, too; perhaps we might find it upon our shoulders at any moment. I confess that I felt easier in my mind when, after following Holmes's example and slipping off my shoes, I found myself inside the bedroom. My companion noiselessly closed the shutters, moved the lamp on to the table, and cast his eyes round the room. All was as we had seen it in the daytime. Then creeping up to me and making a trumpet of his hand, he whispered into my ear again so gently that it was all that I could do to distinguish the words:

'The least sound would be fatal to our plans.'

I nodded to show that I had heard.

'We must sit without light. He would see it through the ventilator.'

I nodded again.

'Do not go asleep; your very life may depend upon it. Have your pistol ready in case we should need it. I will sit on the side of the bed, and you in that chair.'

I took out my revolver and laid it on the corner of the table.

Holmes had brought up a long thin cane, and this he

placed upon the bed beside him. By it he laid the box of matches and the stump of a candle. Then he turned down the lamp, and we were left in darkness.

How shall I ever forget that dreadful vigil? I could not hear a sound, not even the drawing of a breath, and yet I knew that my companion sat open-eyed, within a few feet of me, in the same state of nervous tension in which I was myself. The shutters cut off the least ray of light, and we waited in absolute darkness. From outside came the occasional cry of a night-bird, and once at our very window a long-drawn catlike whine, which told us that the cheetah was indeed at liberty. Far away we could hear the deep tones of the parish clock, which boomed out every quarter of an hour. How long they seemed, those quarters! Twelve struck, and one and two and three, and still we sat waiting silently for whatever might befall.

Suddenly there was the momentary gleam of a light up in the direction of the ventilator, which vanished immediately, but was succeeded by a strong smell of burning oil and heated metal. Someone in the next room had lit a dark-lantern. I heard a gentle sound of movement, and then all was silent once more, though the smell grew stronger. For half an hour I sat with straining ears. Then suddenly another sound became audible—a very gentle, soothing sound, like that of a small jet of steam escaping continually from a kettle. The instant that we heard it, Holmes sprang from the bed, struck a match, and lashed furiously with his cane at the bell-pull.

'You see it, Watson?' he yelled. 'You see it?'

But I saw nothing. At the moment when Holmes struck the light I heard a low, clear whistle, but the sudden glare flashing into my weary eyes made it impossible for me to tell what it was at which my friend lashed so savagely.

I could, however, see that his face was deadly pale and filled with horror and loathing.

He had ceased to strike and was gazing up at the ventilator when suddenly there broke from the silence of the night the most horrible cry to which I have ever listened. It swelled up louder and louder, a hoarse yell of pain and fear and anger all mingled in the one dreadful shriek. They say that away down in the village, and even in the distant parsonage, that cry raised the sleepers from their beds. It struck cold to our hearts, and I stood gazing at Holmes, and he at me, until the last echoes of it had died away into the silence from which it rose.

'What can it mean?' I gasped.

'It means that it is all over,' Holmes answered. 'And perhaps, after all, it is for the best. Take your pistol, and we will enter Dr Roylott's room.'

With a grave face he lit the lamp and led the way down the corridor. Twice he struck at the chamber door without any reply from within. Then he turned the handle and entered, I at his heels, with the cocked pistol in my hand.

It was a singular sight which met our eyes. On the table stood a dark-lantern with the shutter half open, throwing a brilliant beam of light upon the iron safe, the door of which was ajar. Beside this table, on the wooden chair, sat Dr Grimesby Roylott, clad in a long grey dressing-gown, his bare ankles protruding beneath, and his feet thrust into red heelless Turkish slippers. Across his lap lay the short stock with the long lash which we had noticed during the day. His chin was cocked upward and his eyes were fixed in a dreadful, rigid stare at the corner of the ceiling. Round his brow he had a peculiar yellow band, with brownish speckles, which seemed to be bound tightly round his head. As we entered he made neither sound nor motion.

'The band! the speckled band!' whispered Holmes.

I took a step forward. In an instant his strange headgear began to move, and there reared itself from among his hair the squat diamond-shaped head and puffed neck of a loathsome serpent.

'It is a swamp adder!' cried Holmes; 'the deadliest snake in India. He has died within ten seconds of being bitten. Violence does, in truth, recoil upon the violent, and the schemer falls into the pit which he digs for another. Let us thrust this creature back into its den, and we can then remove Miss Stoner to some place of shelter and let the county police know what has happened.'

As he spoke he drew the dog-whip swiftly from the dead man's lap, and throwing the noose round the reptile's neck he drew it from its horrid perch and, carrying it at arm's length, threw it into the iron safe, which he closed upon it.

Such are the true facts of the death of Dr Grimesby Roylott, of Stoke Moran. It is not necessary that I should prolong a narrative which has already run to too great a length by telling how we broke the sad news to the terrified girl, how we conveyed her by the morning train to the care of her good aunt at Harrow, of how the slow process of official inquiry came to the conclusion that the doctor met his fate while indiscreetly playing with a dangerous pet. The little which I had yet to learn of the case was told me by Sherlock Holmes as we travelled back next day.

'I had,' said he, 'come to an entirely erroneous conclusion which shows, my dear Watson, how dangerous it always is to reason from insufficient data. The presence of the gypsies, and the use of the word "band", which was used by the poor girl, no doubt to explain the appearance which she had caught a hurried glimpse of by the light of her match, were sufficient to put me upon an entirely wrong scent. I can only claim the merit that I instantly reconsidered my position when, however, it became clear to me that whatever danger threatened an occupant of the room could not come either from the window or the door. My attention was speedily drawn, as I have already remarked to you, to this ventilator, and to the bell-rope which hung down to the bed. The discovery that this was a dummy, and that the bed was clamped to the floor, instantly gave rise to the suspicion that the rope was there as a bridge for something passing through the hole and coming to the bed. The idea of a snake instantly occurred to me, and when I coupled it with my knowledge that the doctor was furnished with a supply of creatures from India, I felt that I was probably on the right track. The idea of using a form of poison which could not possibly be discovered by any chemical test was just such a one as would occur to a clever and ruthless man who had had an Eastern training. The rapidity with which such a poison would take effect would also, from his point of view, be an advantage. It would be a sharp-eyed coroner, indeed, who could distinguish the two little dark punctures which would show where the poison fangs had done their work. Then I thought of the whistle. Of course he must recall the snake before the morning light revealed it to the victim. He had trained it, probably by the use of the milk which we saw, to return to him when summoned. He would put it through this ventilator at the hour that he thought best, with the certainty that it would crawl down the rope and land on the bed. It might or might not bite the occupant, perhaps she might escape every night for a week, but sooner or later she must fall a victim.

'I had come to these conclusions before ever I had entered his room. An inspection of his chair showed me that he had been in the habit of standing on it, which of course would be necessary in order that he should reach the ventilator. The sight of the safe, the saucer of milk, and the loop of whipcord were enough to finally dispel any doubts which may have remained. The metallic clang heard by Miss Stoner was obviously caused by her stepfather hastily closing the door of his safe upon its terrible occupant. Having once made up my mind, you know the steps which I took in order to put the matter to the proof. I heard the creature hiss as I have no doubt that you did also, and I instantly lit the light and attacked it.'

'With the result of driving it through the ventilator.'

'And also with the result of causing it to turn upon its master at the other side. Some of the blows of my cane came home and roused its snakish temper, so that it flew upon the first person it saw. In this way I am no doubt indirectly responsible for Dr Grimesby Roylott's death, and I cannot say that it is likely to weigh very heavily upon my conscience.'

THE ADVENTURE OF
THE BLUE CARBUNCLE

I had called upon my friend Sherlock Holmes upon the second morning after Christmas, with the intention of wishing him the compliments of the season. He was lounging upon the sofa in a purple dressing-gown, a pipe-rack within his reach upon the right, and a pile of crumpled morning papers, evidently newly studied, near at hand. Beside the couch was a wooden chair, and on the angle of the back hung a very seedy and disreputable hard-felt hat, much the worse for wear, and cracked in several places. A lens and a forceps lying upon the seat of the chair suggested that the hat had been suspended in this manner for the purpose of examination.

'You are engaged,' said I; 'perhaps I interrupt you.'

'Not at all. I am glad to have a friend with whom I can discuss my results. The matter is a perfectly trivial one'—he jerked his thumb in the direction of the old hat—'but there are points in connection with it which are not entirely devoid of interest and even of instruction.'

I seated myself in his armchair and warmed my hands before his crackling fire, for a sharp frost had set in, and the windows were thick with the ice crystals. 'I suppose,' I remarked, 'that, homely as it looks, this thing has some deadly story linked on to it—that it is the clue which will guide you in the solution of some mystery and the punishment of some crime.'

'No, no. No crime,' said Sherlock Holmes, laughing. 'Only one of those whimsical little incidents which will happen when you have four million human beings all jostling each other within the space of a few square miles. Amid the action and reaction of so dense a swarm of humanity, every possible combination of events may be expected to take place, and many a little problem will be presented which may be striking and bizarre without being criminal. We have already had experience of such.'

'So much so,' I remarked, 'that of the last six cases which I have added to my notes, three have been entirely free of any legal crime.'

'Precisely. You allude to my attempt to recover the Irene Adler papers, to the singular case of Miss Mary Sutherland, and to the adventure of the man with the twisted lip. Well, I have no doubt that this small matter will fall into the same innocent category. You know Peterson, the commissionaire?'

'Yes.'

'It is to him that this trophy belongs.'

'It is his hat.'

'No, no; he found it. Its owner is unknown. I beg that you will look upon it not as a battered billycock but as an intellectual problem. And, first, as to how it came here. It arrived upon Christmas morning, in company with a good fat goose, which is, I have no doubt, roasting at this moment in front of Peterson's fire. The facts are these: about four o'clock on Christmas morning, Peterson, who, as you know, is a very honest fellow, was returning from some small jollification and was making his way homeward down Tottenham Court Road. In front of him he saw, in the gaslight, a tallish man, walking with a slight stagger, and carrying a white goose slung over his shoulder. As he reached the corner of Goodge Street, a row broke out between this stranger and a little knot of roughs. One of the latter knocked off the man's hat, on which he raised his stick to defend himself and, swinging it over his head, smashed the shop window behind him. Peterson had rushed forward to protect the stranger from his assailants; but the man, shocked at having broken the window, and seeing an official-looking person in uniform rushing towards him, dropped his goose, took to his heels, and vanished amid the labyrinth of small streets which lie at the back of Tottenham Court Road. The roughs had also fled at the appearance of Peterson, so that he was left in possession of the field of battle, and also of the spoils of victory in the shape of this battered hat and a most unimpeachable Christmas goose.'

'Which surely he restored to their owner?'

'My dear fellow, there lies the problem. It is true that "For Mrs Henry Baker" was printed upon a small card which was tied to the bird's left leg, and it is also true that the initials "H.B." are legible upon the lining of this hat; but as there are some thousands of Bakers, and some hundreds of Henry Bakers in this city of ours, it is not easy to restore lost property to any one of them.'

'What, then, did Peterson do?'

'He brought round both hat and goose to me on Christmas morning, knowing that even the smallest problems are of interest to me. The goose we retained until this morning, when there were signs that, in spite of the slight frost, it would be well that it should be eaten without unnecessary delay. Its finder has carried it off, therefore, to fulfil the ultimate destiny of a goose, while I continue to retain the hat of the unknown gentleman who lost his Christmas dinner.'

'Did he not advertise?'

'No.'

'Then, what clue could you have as to his identity?'

'Only as much as we can deduce.'

'From his hat?'

'Precisely.'

'But you are joking. What can you gather from this old battered felt?'

'Here is my lens. You know my methods. What can you gather yourself as to the individuality of the man who has worn this article?'

I took the tattered object in my hands and turned it over rather ruefully. It was a very ordinary black hat of the usual round shape, hard and much the worse for wear. The lining had been of red silk, but was a good deal discoloured. There was no maker's name; but, as Holmes had remarked, the initials 'H.B.' were scrawled upon one side. It was pierced in the brim for a hat-securer, but the elastic was missing. For the rest, it was cracked, exceedingly dusty, and spotted in several places, although there seemed to have been some attempt to hide the discoloured patches by smearing them with ink.

'I can see nothing,' said I, handing it back to my friend.

'On the contrary, Watson, you can see everything. You fail, however, to reason from what you see. You are too timid in drawing your inferences.'

'Then, pray tell me what it is that you can infer from this hat?'

He picked it up and gazed at it in the peculiar introspective fashion which was characteristic of him. 'It is perhaps less suggestive than it might have been,' he remarked, 'and yet there are a few inferences which are very distinct, and a few others which represent at least a strong balance of probability. That the man was highly intellectual is of course obvious upon the face of it, and also that he was fairly well-to-do within the last three years, although he has now fallen upon evil days. He had foresight, but has less now than formerly, pointing to a moral retrogression, which, when taken with the decline of his fortunes, seems to indicate some evil influence, probably drink, at work upon him. This may account also for the obvious fact that his wife has ceased to love him.'

'My dear Holmes!'

'He has, however, retained some degree of self-respect,' he continued, disregarding my remonstrance. 'He is a man who leads a sedentary life, goes out little, is out of training entirely, is middle-aged, has grizzled hair which he has had cut within the last few days, and which he anoints with lime-cream. These are the more patent facts which are to be deduced from his hat. Also, by the way, that it is extremely improbable that he has gas laid on in his house.'

'You are certainly joking, Holmes.'

'Not in the least. Is it possible that even now, when I give you these results, you are unable to see how they are attained?'

'I have no doubt that I am very stupid, but I must confess that I am unable to follow you. For example, how did you deduce that this man was intellectual?'

For answer Holmes clapped the hat upon his head. It

came right over the forehead and settled upon the bridge of his nose. 'It is a question of cubic capacity,' said he; 'a man with so large a brain must have something in it.'

'The decline of his fortunes, then?'

'This hat is three years old. These flat brims curled at the edge came in then. It is a hat of the very best quality. Look at the band of ribbed silk and the excellent lining. If this man could afford to buy so expensive a hat three years ago, and has had no hat since, then he has assuredly gone down in the world.'

'Well, that is clear enough, certainly. But how about the foresight and the moral retrogression?'

Sherlock Holmes laughed. 'Here is the foresight,' said he, putting his finger upon the little disc and loop of the hat-securer. 'They are never sold upon hats. If this man ordered one, it is a sign of a certain amount of foresight, since he went out of his way to take this precaution against the wind. But since we see that he has broken the elastic and has not troubled to replace it, it is obvious that he has less foresight now than formerly, which is a distinct proof of a weakening nature. On the other hand, he has endeavoured to conceal some of these stains upon the felt by daubing them with ink, which is a sign that he has not entirely lost his self-respect.'

'Your reasoning is certainly plausible.'

'The further points, that he is middle-aged, that his hair is grizzled, that it has been recently cut, and that he uses lime-cream, are all to be gathered from a close examination of the lower part of the lining. The lens discloses a large number of hair-ends, clean cut by the scissors of the barber. They all appear to be adhesive, and there is a distinct odour of lime-cream. This dust, you will observe, is not the gritty, grey dust of the street but the fluffy brown dust of the house, showing that it has been hung up indoors most of the time; while the marks of moisture upon the inside are proof positive that the wearer perspired very freely, and could therefore, hardly be in the best of training.'

'But his wife—you said that she had ceased to love him.'

'This hat has not been brushed for weeks. When I see you, my dear Watson, with a week's accumulation of dust upon your hat, and when your wife allows you to go out in such a state, I shall fear that you also have been unfortunate enough to lose your wife's affection.'

'But he might be a bachelor.'

'Nay, he was bringing home the goose as a peace-offering to his wife. Remember the card upon the bird's leg.'

'You have an answer to everything. But how on earth do you deduce that the gas is not laid on in his house?'

'One tallow stain, or even two, might come by chance; but when I see no less than five, I think that there can be little doubt that the individual must be brought into frequent contact with burning tallow—walks upstairs at night probably with his hat in one hand and a guttering candle in the other. Anyhow, he never got tallow-stains from a gas-jet. Are you satisfied?'

'Well, it is very ingenious,' said I, laughing; 'but since, as you said just now, there has been no crime committed, and no harm done save the loss of a goose, all this seems to be rather a waste of energy.'

Sherlock Holmes had opened his mouth to reply, when the door flew open, and Peterson, the commissionaire, rushed into the apartment with flushed cheeks and the face of a man who is dazed with astonishment.

'The goose, Mr Holmes! The goose, sir!' he gasped.

'Eh? What of it, then? Has it returned to life and flapped off through the kitchen window?' Holmes twisted himself round upon the sofa to get a fairer view of the man's excited face.

'See here, sir! See what my wife found in its crop!' He held out his hand and displayed upon the centre of the palm a brilliantly scintillating blue stone, rather smaller than a bean in size, but of such purity and radiance that it twinkled like an electric point in the dark hollow of his hand.

Sherlock Holmes sat up with a whistle. 'By Jove, Peterson!' said he, 'this is treasure trove indeed. I suppose you know what you have got?'

'A diamond, sir? A precious stone. It cuts into glass as though it were putty.'

'It's more than a precious stone. It is *the* precious stone.'

'Not the Countess of Morcar's blue carbuncle!' I ejaculated.

'Precisely so. I ought to know its size and shape, seeing that I have read the advertisement about it in *The Times* every day lately. It is absolutely unique, and its value can only be conjectured, but the reward offered of £1000 is certainly not within a twentieth part of the market price.'

'A thousand pounds! Great Lord of mercy!' The commissionaire plumped down into a chair and stared from one to the other of us.

'That is the reward, and I have reason to know that there are sentimental considerations in the background which would induce the Countess to part with half her fortune if she could but recover the gem.'

41

'It was lost, if I remember aright, at the Hotel Cosmopolitan,' I remarked.

'Precisely so, on December 22nd, just five days ago. John Horner, a plumber, was accused of having abstracted it from the lady's jewel-case. The evidence against him was so strong that the case has been referred to the Assizes. I have some account of the matter here, I believe.' He rummaged amid his newspapers, glancing over the dates, until at last he smoothed one out, doubled it over, and read the following paragraph:

'Hotel Cosmopolitan Jewel Robbery. John Horner, 26, plumber, was brought up upon the charge of having upon the 22nd inst., abstracted from the jewel-case of the Countess of Morcar the valuable gem known as the blue carbuncle. James Ryder, upper-attendant at the hotel, gave his evidence to the effect that he had shown Horner up to the dressing-room of the Countess of Morcar upon the day of the robbery in order that he might solder the second bar of the grate, which was loose. He had remained with Horner some little time, but had finally been called away. On returning, he found that Horner had disappeared, that the bureau had been forced open, and that the small morocco casket in which, as it afterwards transpired, the Countess was accustomed to keep her jewel, was lying empty upon the dressing-table. Ryder instantly gave the alarm, and Horner was arrested the same evening; but the stone could not be found either upon his person or in his rooms. Catherine Cusack, maid to the Countess, deposed to having heard Ryder's cry of dismay on discovering the robbery, and to having rushed into the room, where she found matters as described by the last witness. Inspector Bradstreet, B division, gave evidence as to the arrest of Horner, who struggled frantically, and protested his innocence in the strongest terms. Evidence of a previous conviction for robbery having been given against the prisoner, the magistrate refused to deal summarily with the offence, but referred it to the Assizes. Horner, who had shown signs of intense emotion during the proceedings, fainted away at the conclusion and was carried out of court.'

'Hum! So much for the police-court,' said Holmes thoughtfully, tossing aside the paper. 'The question for us now to solve is the sequence of events leading from a rifled jewel-case at one end to the crop of a goose in Tottenham Court Road at the other. You see, Watson, our little deductions have suddenly assumed a much more important and less innocent aspect. Here is the stone; the stone came from the goose, and the goose came from Mr Henry Baker, the gentleman with the bad hat and all the other characteristics with which I have bored you. So now we must set ourselves very seriously to finding this gentleman and ascertaining what part he has played in this little mystery. To do this, we must try the simplest means first, and these lie undoubtedly in an advertisement in all the evening papers. If this fail, I shall have recourse to other methods.'

'What will you say?'

'Give me a pencil and that slip of paper. Now, then:

'Found at the corner of Goodge Street, a goose and a black felt hat. Mr Henry Baker can have the same by applying at 6.30 this evening at 221B, Baker Street.

That is clear and concise.'

'Very. But will he see it?'

'Well, he is sure to keep an eye on the papers, since, to a poor man, the loss was a heavy one. He was clearly so scared by his mischance in breaking the window and by the approach of Peterson that he thought of nothing but flight, but since then he must have bitterly regretted the impulse which caused him to drop his bird. Then, again, the introduction of his name will cause him to see it, for everyone who knows him will direct his attention to it. Here you are, Peterson, run down to the advertising agency and have this put in the evening papers.'

'In which, sir?'

'Oh, in the *Globe, Star, Pall Mall, St James's, Evening News Standard, Echo,* and any others that occur to you.'

'Very well, sir. And this stone?'

'Ah, yes, I shall keep the stone. Thank you. And, I say, Peterson, just buy a goose on your way back and leave it here with me, for we must have one to give to this gentleman in place of the one which your family is now devouring.'

When the commissionaire had gone, Holmes took up the stone and held it against the light. 'It's a bonny thing,' said he. 'Just see how it glints and sparkles. Of course it is a nucleus and focus of crime. Every good stone is. They are the devil's pet baits. In the larger and older jewels every facet may stand for a bloody deed. This stone is not yet twenty years old. It was found in the banks of the Amoy River in southern China and is remarkable in having every characteristic of the carbuncle, save that it is blue in shade instead of ruby red. In spite of its youth, it has already a sinister history. There have been two murders, a vitriol-throwing, a suicide, and several robberies brought about for the sake of this forty-grain weight of crystallized charcoal. Who would think that so pretty a toy would be a purveyor to the gallows and the prison? I'll lock it up in my strong box now and drop a line to the Countess to say that we have it.'

'Do you think that this man Horner is innocent?'

'I cannot tell.'

'Well, then, do you imagine that this other one, Henry Baker, had anything to do with the matter?'

'It is, I think, much more likely that Henry Baker is an absolutely innocent man, who had no idea that the bird which he was carrying was of considerably more value than if it were made of solid gold. That, however, I shall determine by a very simple test if we have an answer to our advertisement.'

'And you can do nothing until then?'

'Nothing.'

'In that case I shall continue my professional round. But I shall come back in the evening at the hour you have mentioned, for I should like to see the solution of so tangled a business.'

'Very glad to see you. I dine at seven. There is a woodcock, I believe. By the way, in view of recent occurrences, perhaps I ought to ask Mrs Hudson to examine its crop.'

I had been delayed at a case, and it was a little after half-past six when I found myself in Baker Street once more. As I approached the house I saw a tall man in a Scotch bonnet with a coat which was buttoned up to his chin waiting outside in the bright semicircle which was thrown from the fanlight. Just as I arrived the door was opened, and we were shown up together to Holmes's room.

'Mr Henry Baker, I believe,' said he, rising from his armchair and greeting his visitor with the easy air of geniality which he could so readily assume. 'Pray take this chair by the fire, Mr Baker. It is a cold night, and I observe that your circulation is more adapted for summer than for winter. Ah, Watson, you have just come at the right time. Is that your hat, Mr Baker?'

'Yes, sir, that is undoubtedly my hat.'

He was a large man with rounded shoulders, a massive head, and a broad, intelligent face, sloping down to a pointed beard of grizzled brown. A touch of red in nose and cheeks, with a slight tremor of his extended hand, recalled Holmes's surmise as to his habits. His rusty black frock-coat was buttoned right up in front, with the collar turned up, and his lank wrists protruded from his sleeves without a sign of cuff or shirt. He spoke in a slow staccato fashion, choosing his words with care, and gave the impression generally of a man of learning and letters who had had ill-usage at the hands of fortune.

'We have retained these things for some days,' said Holmes, 'because we expected to see an advertisement from you giving your address. I am at a loss to know now why you did not advertise.'

Our visitor gave a rather shame-faced laugh. 'Shillings have not been so plentiful with me as they once were,' he remarked. 'I had no doubt that the gang of roughs who assaulted me had carried off both my hat and the bird. I did not care to spend more money in a hopeless attempt at recovering them.'

'Very naturally. By the way, about the bird, we were compelled to eat it.'

'To eat it!' Our visitor half rose from his chair in his excitement.

'Yes, it would have been of no use to anyone had we not done so. But I presume that this other goose upon the sideboard, which is about the same weight and perfectly fresh, will answer your purpose equally well?'

'Oh, certainly, certainly,' answered Mr Baker with a sigh of relief.

'Of course, we still have the feathers, legs, crop, and so on of your own bird, so if you wish— '

The man burst into a hearty laugh. 'They might be useful to me as relics of my adventure,' said he, 'but beyond that I can hardly see what use the *disjecta membra* of my late acquaintance are going to be to me. No, sir, I think that, with your permission, I will confine my attentions to the excellent bird which I perceive upon the sideboard.'

Sherlock Holmes glanced sharply across at me with a slight shrug of his shoulders.

'There is your hat, then, and there your bird,' said he. 'By the way, would it bore you to tell me where you got the other one from? I am somewhat of a fowl fancier, and I have seldom seen a better grown goose.'

'Certainly, sir,' said Baker, who had risen and tucked his newly gained property under his arm. 'There are a few of us who frequent the Alpha Inn, near the Museum—we are to be found in the Museum itself during the day, you understand. This year our good host, Windigate by name, instituted a goose club, by which, on consideration of some few pence every week, we were each to receive a bird at Christmas. My pence were duly paid, and the rest is familiar to you. I am much indebted to you, sir, for a Scotch bonnet is fitted neither to my years nor my gravity.' With a comical pomposity of manner he bowed solemnly to both of us and strode off upon his way.

'So much for Mr Henry Baker,' said Holmes when he

had closed the door behind him. 'It is quite certain that he knows nothing whatever about the matter. Are you hungry, Watson?'

'Not particularly.'

'Then I suggest that we turn our dinner into a supper and follow up this clue while it is still hot.'

'By all means.'

It was a bitter night, so we drew on our ulsters and wrapped cravats about our throats. Outside, the stars were shining coldly in a cloudless sky, and the breath of the passers-by blew out into smoke like so many pistol shots. Our footfalls rang out crisply and loudly as we swung through the doctors' quarter, Wimpole Street, Harley Street, and so through Wigmore Street into Oxford Street. In a quarter of an hour we were in Bloomsbury at the Alpha Inn, which is a small public-house at the corner of one of the streets which runs down into Holborn. Holmes pushed open the door of the private bar and ordered two glasses of beer from the ruddy-faced, white-aproned landlord.

'Your beer should be excellent if it is as good as your geese,' said he.

'My geese!' the man seemed surprised.

'Yes. I was speaking only half an hour ago to Mr Henry Baker, who was a member of your goose club.'

'Ah! yes, I see. But you see, sir, them's not *our* geese.'

'Indeed! Whose, then?'

'Well, I got the two dozen from a salesman in Covent Garden.'

'Indeed? I know some of them. Which was it?'

'Breckinridge is his name.'

'Ah! I don't know him. Well, here's your good health, landlord, and prosperity to your house. Good-night.'

'Now for Mr Breckinridge,' he continued, buttoning up his coat as we came out into the frosty air. 'Remember, Watson, that though we have so homely a thing as a goose at one end of this chain, we have at the other a man who will certainly get seven years' penal servitude unless we can establish his innocence. It is possible that our inquiry may but confirm his guilt; but, in any case, we have a line of investigation which has been missed by the police, and which a singular chance has placed in our hands. Let us follow it out to the bitter end. Faces to the south, then, and quick march!'

We passed across Holborn, down Endell Street, and so through a zigzag of slums to Covent Garden Market. One of the largest stalls bore the name of Breckinridge upon it, and the proprietor, a horsy-looking man, with a sharp face and trim side-whiskers, was helping a boy to put up the shutters.

'Good-evening. It's a cold night,' said Holmes.

The salesman nodded and shot a questioning glance at my companion.

'Sold out of geese, I see,' continued Holmes, pointing at the bare slabs of marble.

'Let you have five hundred tomorrow morning.'

'That's no good.'

'Well, there are some on the stall with the gas-flare.'

'Ah, but I was recommended to you.'

'Who by?'

'The landlord of the Alpha.'

'Oh, yes; I sent him a couple of dozen.'

'Fine birds they were, too. Now where did you get them from?'

To my surprise the question provoked a burst of anger from the salesman.

'Now, then, mister,' said he, with his head cocked and his arms akimbo, 'what are you driving at? Let's have it straight, now.'

'It is straight enough. I should like to know who sold you the geese which you supplied to the Alpha.'

'Well, then, I shan't tell you. So now!'

'Oh, it is a matter of no importance; but I don't know why you should be so warm over such a trifle.'

'Warm! You'd be as warm, maybe, if you were as pestered as I am. When I pay good money for a good article there should be an end of the business; but it's 'Where are the geese?' and 'Who did you sell the geese to?' and 'What will you take for the geese?' One would think they were the only geese in the world, to hear the fuss that is made over them.'

'Well, I have no connection with any other people who have been making inquiries,' said Holmes carelessly. 'If you won't tell us the bet is off, that is all. But I'm always ready to back my opinion on a matter of fowls, and I have a fiver on it that the bird I ate is country bred.'

'Well, then, you've lost your fiver, for it's town bred,' snapped the salesman.

'It's nothing of the kind.'

'I say it is.'

'I don't believe it.'

'D'you think you know more about fowls than I, who have handled them ever since I was a nipper? I tell you, all those birds that went to the Alpha were town bred.'

'You'll never persuade me to believe that.'

'Will you bet, then?'

'It's merely taking your money, for I know that I am right. But I'll have a sovereign on with you, just to teach you not to be obstinate.'

The salesman chuckled grimly. 'Bring me the books, Bill,' said he.

The small boy brought round a small thin volume and a great greasy-backed one, laying them out together beneath the hanging lamp.

'Now then, Mr Cocksure,' said the salesman, 'I thought that I was out of geese, but before I finish you'll find that there is still one left in my shop. You see this little book?'

'Well?'

'That's the list of the folk from whom I buy. D'you see? Well, then, here on this page are the country folk, and the numbers after their names are where their accounts are in the big ledger. Now, then! You see this other page in red ink? Well, that is a list of my town suppliers. Now, look at that third name. Just read it out to me.'

'Mrs Oakshott, 117, Brixton Road—249,' read Holmes.

'Quite so. Now turn that up in the ledger.'

Holmes turned to the page indicated. 'Here you are, "Mrs Oakshott, 117, Brixton Road, egg and poultry supplier."'

'Now, then, what's the last entry?'

'"December 22nd. Twenty-four geese at 7s. 6d."'

'Quite so. There you are. And underneath?'

'"Sold to Mr Windigate of the Alpha, at 12s."'

'What have you to say now?'

Sherlock Holmes looked deeply chagrined. He drew a sovereign from his pocket and threw it down upon the slab, turning away with the air of a man whose disgust is too deep for words. A few yards off he stopped under a lamp-post and laughed in the hearty, noiseless fashion which was peculiar to him.

'When you see a man with whiskers of that cut and the

"Pink" un protruding out of his pocket, you can always draw him by a bet,' said he. 'I daresay that if I had put £100 down in front of him, that man would not have given me such complete information as was drawn from him by the idea that he was doing me on a wager. Well, Watson, we are, I fancy, nearing the end of our quest, and the only point which remains to be determined is whether we should go on to this Mrs Oakshott tonight, or whether we should reserve it for tomorrow. It is clear from what that surly fellow said that there are others besides ourselves who are anxious about the matter, and I should—'

His remarks were suddenly cut short by a loud hubbub which broke out from the stall which we had just left. Turning round we saw a little rat-faced fellow standing in the centre of the circle of yellow light which was thrown by the swinging lamp, while Breckinridge, the salesman, framed in the door of his stall, was shaking his fists fiercely at the cringing figure.

'I've had enough of you and your geese,' he shouted. 'I wish you were all at the devil together. If you come pestering me any more with your silly talk I'll set the dog at you. You bring Mrs Oakshott here and I'll answer her, but what have you to do with it? Did I buy the geese off you?'

'No; but one of them was mine all the same,' whined the little man.

'Well, then, ask Mrs Oakshott for it.'

'She told me to ask you.'

'Well, you can ask the King of Proosia, for all I care. I've had enough of it. Get out of this!' He rushed fiercely forward, and the inquirer flitted away into the darkness.

'Ha! this may save us a visit to Brixton Road,' whispered Holmes. 'Come with me, and we will see what is to be made of this fellow.' Striding through the scattered knots of people who lounged round the flaring stalls, my companion speedily overtook the little man and touched him upon the shoulder. He sprang round, and I could see in the gas-light that every vestige of colour had been driven from his face.

'Who are you, then? What do you want?' he asked in a quavering voice.

'You will excuse me,' said Holmes blandly, 'but I could not help overhearing the questions which you put to the salesman just now. I think that I could be of assistance to you.'

'You? Who are you? How could you know anything of the matter?'

'My name is Sherlock Holmes. It is my business to know what other people don't know.'

'But you can know nothing of this?'

'Excuse me, I know everything of it. You are endeavouring to trace some geese which were sold by Mrs Oakshott, of Brixton Road, to a salesman named Breckinridge, by him in turn to Mr Windigate, of the Alpha, and by him to his club, of which Mr Henry Baker is a member.'

'Oh, sir, you are the very man whom I have longed to meet,' cried the little fellow with outstretched hands and quivering fingers. 'I can hardly explain to you how interested I am in this matter.'

Sherlock Holmes hailed a four-wheeler which was passing. 'In that case we had better discuss it in a cosy room rather than in this wind-swept market-place,' said he. 'But pray tell me, before we go farther, who it is that I have the pleasure of assisting.'

The man hesitated for an instant. 'My name is John Robinson,' he answered with a sidelong glance.

'No, no; the real name,' said Holmes sweetly. 'It is always awkward doing business with an alias.'

A flush sprang to the white cheeks of the stranger. 'Well, then,' said he, 'my real name is James Ryder.'

'Precisely so. Head attendant at the Hotel Cosmopolitan. Pray step into the cab, and I shall soon be able to tell you everything which you would wish to know.'

The little man stood glancing from one to the other of us with half-frightened, half-hopeful eyes, as one who is not sure whether he is on the verge of a windfall or of a catastrophe. Then he stepped into the cab, and in half an hour we were back in the sitting-room at Baker Street. Nothing had been said during our drive, but the high, thin breathing of our new companion, and the claspings and unclaspings of his hands, spoke of the nervous tension within him.

'Here we are!' said Holmes cheerily as we filed into the room. 'The fire looks very seasonable in this weather. You look cold, Mr Ryder. Pray take the basket-chair. I will just put on my slippers before we settle this little matter of yours. Now, then! You want to know what became of those geese?'

'Yes, sir.'

'Or rather, I fancy, of that goose. It was one bird, I imagine, in which you were interested—white, with a black bar across the tail.'

Ryder quivered with emotion. 'Oh, sir,' he cried, 'can you tell me where it went to?'

'It came here.'

'Here?'

'Yes, and a most remarkable bird it proved. I don't

wonder that you should take an interest in it. It laid an egg after it was dead—the bonniest, brightest little blue egg that ever was seen. I have it here in my museum.'

Our visitor staggered to his feet and clutched the mantelpiece with his right hand. Holmes unlocked his strong-box and held up the blue carbuncle, which shone out like a star, with a cold, brilliant, many-pointed radiance. Ryder stood glaring with a drawn face, uncertain whether to claim or to disown it.

'The game's up, Ryder,' said Holmes quietly. 'Hold up, man, or you'll be into the fire! Give him an arm back into his chair, Watson. He's not got blood enough to go in for felony with impunity. Give him a dash of brandy. So! Now he looks a little more human. What a shrimp it is, to be sure!'

For a moment he had staggered and nearly fallen, but the brandy brought a tinge of colour into his cheeks, and he sat staring with frightened eyes at his accuser.

'I have almost every link in my hands, and all the proofs which I could possibly need, so there is little which you need tell me. Still, that little may as well be cleared up to make the case complete. You had heard, Ryder, of this blue stone of the Countess of Morcar's?'

'It was Catherine Cusack who told me of it,' said he in a crackling voice.

'I see—her ladyship's waiting-maid. Well, the temptation of sudden wealth so easily acquired was too much for you, as it has been for better men before you; but you were not very scrupulous in the means you used. It seems to me, Ryder, that there is the making of a very pretty villain in you. You knew that this man Horner, the plumber, had been concerned in some such matter before, and that suspicion would rest the more readily upon him. What did you do, then? You made some small job in my lady's room—you and your confederate Cusack—and you managed that he should be the man sent for. Then, when he had left, you rifled the jewel-case, raised the alarm, and had this unfortunate man arrested. You then—'

Ryder threw himself down suddenly upon the rug and clutched at my companion's knees. 'For God's sake, have mercy!' he shrieked. 'Think of my father! of my mother! It would break their hearts. I never went wrong before! I never will again. I swear it. I'll swear it on a Bible. Oh, don't bring it into court! For Christ's sake, don't!'

'Get back into your chair!' said Holmes sternly. 'It is very well to cringe and crawl now, but you thought little enough of this poor Horner in the dock for a crime of which he knew nothing.'

'I will fly, Mr Holmes. I will leave the country, sir. Then the charge against him will break down.'

'Hum! We will talk about that. And now let us hear a true account of the next act. How came the stone into the goose, and how came the goose into the open market? Tell us the truth, for there lies your only hope of safety.'

Ryder passed his tongue over his parched lips. 'I will tell you it just as it happened, sir,' said he. 'When Horner had been arrested, it seemed to me that it would be best for me to get away with the stone at once, for I did not know at what moment the police might not take it into their heads to search me and my room. There was no place about the hotel where it would be safe. I went out, as if on some commissions, and I made for my sister's house. She had married a man named Oakshott, and lived in Brixton Road, where she fattened fowls for the market. All the way there every man I met seemed to me to be a policeman or a detective; and, for all that it was a cold night, the sweat was pouring down my face before I came to the Brixton Road. My sister asked me what was the matter, and why I was so pale; but I told her that I had been upset by the jewel robbery at the hotel. Then I went into the back yard and smoked a pipe, and wondered what it would be best to do.

'I had a friend once called Maudsley, who went to the bad, and had just been serving his time in Pentonville. One day he had met me, and fell into talk about the ways of thieves, and how they could get rid of what they stole. I knew that he would be true to me, for I knew one or two things about him; so I made up my mind to go right on to Kilburn, where he lived, and take him into my confidence. He would show me how to turn the stone into money. But how to get to him in safety? I thought of the agonies I had gone through in coming from the hotel. I might at any moment be seized and searched, and there would be the stone in my waistcoat pocket. I was leaning against the wall at the time and looking at the geese which were waddling about round my feet, and suddenly an idea came into my head which showed me how I could beat the best detective that ever lived.

'My sister had told me some weeks before that I might have the pick of her geese for a Christmas present, and I knew that she was always as good as her word. I would take my goose now, and in it I would carry my stone to Kilburn. There was a little shed in the yard, and behind this I drove one of the birds —a fine big one, white, with a barred tail. I caught it, and, prying its bill open, I thrust the stone down its throat as far as my finger could reach. The bird gave a gulp, and I felt the stone pass along its gullet and down into its crop. But the creature flapped

57

and struggled, and out came my sister to know what was the matter. As I turned to speak to her the brute broke loose and fluttered off among the others.

'"Whatever were you doing with that bird, Jem," says she.

'"Well," said I, "you said you'd give me one for Christmas, and I was feeling which was the fattest."

'"Oh," says she, "we've set yours aside for you—Jem's bird, we call it. It's the big white one over yonder. There's twenty-six of them, which makes one for you, and one for us, and two dozen for the market."

'"Thank you, Maggie," says I; "but if it is all the same to you, I'd rather have that one I was handling just now."

'"The other is a good three pound heavier," said she, "and we fattened it expressly for you."

'"Never mind. I'll have the other, and I'll take it now," said I.

'"Oh, just as you like," said she, a little huffed. "Which is it you want, then?"

'"That white one with the barred tail, right in the middle of the flock."

'"Oh, very well. Kill it and take it with you."

'Well, I did what she said, Mr Holmes, and I carried the bird all the way to Kilburn. I told my pal what I had done, for he was a man that it was easy to tell a thing like that to. He laughed until he choked, and we got a knife and opened the goose. My heart turned to water, for there was no sign of the stone, and I knew that some terrible mistake had occurred. I left the bird, rushed back to my sister's, and hurried into the back yard. There was not a bird to be seen there.

'"Where are they all, Maggie?" I cried.

'"Gone to the dealer's, Jem."

'"Which dealer's?"

'"Breckinridge, of Covent Garden."

'"But was there another with a barred tail?" I asked, "the same as the one I chose?"

'"Yes, Jem; there were two barred-tailed ones, and I could never tell them apart."

'Well, then, of course I saw it all, and I ran off as hard as my feet would carry me to this man Breckinridge; but he had sold the lot at once, and not one word would he tell me as to where they had gone. You heard him yourselves tonight. Well, he has always answered me like that. My sister thinks that I am going mad. Sometimes I think that I am myself. And now—and now I am myself a branded thief, without ever having touched the wealth for which I sold my character. God help me! God help me!' He burst into convulsive sobbing, with his face buried in his hands.

There was a long silence, broken only by his heavy breathing, and by the measured tapping of Sherlock Holmes's finger-tips upon the edge of the table. Then my friend rose and threw open the door.

'Get out!' said he.

'What, sir! Oh, Heaven bless you!'

'No more words. Get out!'

And no more words were needed. There was a rush, a clatter upon the stairs, the bang of a door, and the crisp rattle of running footfalls from the street.

'After all, Watson,' said Holmes, reaching up his hand for his clay pipe, 'I am not retained by the police to supply their deficiencies. If Horner were in danger it would be another thing; but this fellow will not appear against him, and the case must collapse. I suppose that I am commuting a felony, but it is just possible that

I am saving a soul. This fellow will not go wrong again; he is too terribly frightened. Send him to jail now, and you make him a jail-bird for life. Besides, it is the season of forgiveness. Chance has put in our way a most singular and whimsical problem, and its solution is its own reward. If you will have the goodness to touch the bell, Doctor, we will begin another investigation, in which also a bird will be the chief feature.'

SILVER BLAZE

'I am afraid, Watson, that I shall have to go,' said Holmes as we sat down together to our breakfast one morning.

'Go! Where to?'

'To Dartmoor; to King's Pyland.'

I was not surprised. Indeed, my only wonder was that he had not already been mixed up in this extraordinary case, which was the one topic of conversation through the length and breadth of England. For a whole day my companion had rambled about the room with his chin upon his chest and his brows knitted, charging and recharging his pipe with the strongest black tobacco, and absolutely deaf to any of my questions or remarks. Fresh editions of every paper had been sent up by our news agent, only to be glanced over and tossed down into a corner. Yet, silent as he was, I knew perfectly well what it was over which he was brooding. There was but one problem before the public which could challenge his powers of analysis, and that was the singular disappearance of the favourite for the Wessex Cup, and the tragic murder of its trainer. When, therefore, he suddenly announced his intention of setting out for the scene of the drama, it was only what I had both expected and hoped for.

'I should be most happy to go down with you if I should not be in the way,' said I.

'My dear Watson, you would confer a great favour

upon me by coming. And I think that your time will not be misspent, for there are points about the case which promise to make it an absolutely unique one. We have, I think, just time to catch our train at Paddington, and I will go further into the matter upon our journey. You would oblige me by bringing with you your very excellent field-glass.'

And so it happened that an hour or so later I found myself in the corner of a first-class carriage flying along en route for Exeter, while Sherlock Holmes, with his sharp, eager face framed in his ear-flapped travelling-cap, dipped rapidly into the bundle of fresh papers which he had procured at Paddington. We had left Reading far behind us before he thrust the last one of them under the seat and offered me his cigar-case.

'We are going well,' said he, looking out of the window and glancing at his watch. 'Our rate at present is fifty-three and a half miles an hour.'

'I have not observed the quarter-mile posts,' said I.

'Nor have I. But the telegraph posts upon this line are sixty yards apart, and the calculation is a simple one. I presume that you have looked into this matter of the murder of John Straker and the disappearance of Silver Blaze?'

'I have seen what the *Telegraph* and the *Chronicle* have to say.'

'It is one of those cases where the art of the reasoner should be used rather for the sifting of details than for the acquiring of fresh evidence. The tragedy has been so uncommon, so complete, and of such personal importance to so many people that we are suffering from a plethora of surmise, conjecture, and hypothesis. The difficulty is to detach the framework of fact—of absolute undeniable fact—from the embellishments of theorists and reporters. Then, having established ourselves upon this sound basis, it is our duty to see what inferences may be drawn and what are the special points upon which the whole mystery turns. On Tuesday evening I received telegrams from both Colonel Ross, the owner of the horse, and from Inspector Gregory, who is looking after the case, inviting my co-operation.'

'Tuesday evening!' I exclaimed. 'And this is Thursday morning. Why didn't you go down yesterday?'

'Because I made a blunder, my dear Watson—which is, I am afraid, a more common occurrence than anyone would think who only knew me through your memoirs. The fact is that I could not believe it possible that the most remarkable horse in England could long remain concealed, especially in so sparsely inhabited a place as the north of Dartmoor. From hour to hour yesterday I expected to hear that he had been found, and that his abductor was the murderer of John Straker. When, however, another morning had come and I found that beyond the arrest of young Fitzroy Simpson nothing had been done, I felt that it was time for me to take action. Yet in some ways I feel that yesterday has not been wasted.'

'You have formed a theory, then?'

'At least I have got a grip of the essential facts of the case. I shall enumerate them to you, for nothing clears up a case so much as stating it to another person, and I can hardly expect your co-operation if I do not show you the position from which we start.'

I lay back against the cushions, puffing at my cigar, while Holmes, leaning forward, with his long, thin forefinger checking off the points upon the palm of his left hand, gave me a sketch of the events which had led to our journey.

'Silver Blaze,' said he, 'is from the Somomy stock and holds as brilliant a record as his famous ancestor. He is now in his fifth year and has brought in turn each of the prizes of the turf to Colonel Ross, his fortunate owner. Up to the time of the catastrophe he was the first favourite for the Wessex Cup, the betting being three to one on him. He has always, however, been a prime favourite with the racing public and has never yet disappointed them, so that even at those odds enormous sums of money have been laid upon him. It is obvious, therefore, that there were many people who had the strongest interest in preventing Silver Blaze from being there at the fall of the flag next Tuesday.

'The fact was, of course, appreciated at King's Pyland, where the colonel's training-stable is situated. Every precaution was taken to guard the favourite. The trainer, John Straker, is a retired jockey who rode in Colonel Ross's colours before he became too heavy for the weighing-chair. He has served the colonel for five years as jockey and for seven as trainer, and has always shown himself to be a zealous and honest servant. Under him were three lads, for the establishment was a small one, containing only four horses in all. One of these lads sat up each night in the stable, while the others slept in the loft. All three bore excellent characters. John Straker, who is a married man, lived in a small villa about two hundred yards from the stables. He has no children, keeps one maidservant, and is comfortably off. The country round is very lonely, but about half a mile to the north there is a small cluster of villas which have been built by a Tavistock contractor for the use of invalids and others who may wish to enjoy the pure Dartmoor air. Tavistock itself lies two miles to the west, while across the moor, also about two miles distant, is the larger training establishment of Mapleton, which belongs to Lord Backwater and is managed by Silas Brown. In every other direction the moor is a complete wilderness, inhabited only by a few roaming gypsies. Such was the general situation last Monday night when the catastrophe occurred.

'On that evening the horses had been exercised and watered as usual, and the stables were locked up at nine o'clock. Two of the lads walked up to the trainer's house, where they had supper in the kitchen, while the third, Ned Hunter, remained on guard. At a few minutes after nine the maid, Edith Baxter, carried down to the stables his supper, which consisted of a dish of curried mutton. She took no liquid, as there was a water-tap in the stables, and it was the rule that the lad on duty should drink nothing else. The maid carried a lantern with her, as it was very dark and the path ran across the open moor.

'Edith Baxter was within thirty yards of the stables when a man appeared out of the darkness and called to her to stop. As she stepped into the circle of yellow light thrown by the lantern she saw that he was a person of gentlemanly bearing, dressed in a grey suit of tweeds, with a cloth cap. He wore gaiters and carried a heavy stick with a knob to it. She was most impressed, however, by the extreme pallor of his face and by the nervousness of his manner. His age, she thought, would be rather over thirty than under it.

'"Can you tell me where I am?" he asked. "I had almost made up my mind to sleep on the moor when I saw the light of your lantern."

'"You are close to the King's Pyland training stables," said she.

'"Oh, indeed! What a stroke of luck!" he cried. "I understand that a stable-boy sleeps there alone every night. Perhaps that is his supper which you are carrying to him. Now I am sure that you would not be too proud to earn the price of a new dress, would you?" He took a piece of white paper folded up out of his waistcoat pocket. "See that the boy has this tonight, and you shall have the prettiest frock that money can buy."

'"She was frightened by the earnestness of his manner and ran past him to the window through which she was accustomed to hand the meals. It was already opened, and Hunter was seated at the small table inside. She had begun to tell him of what had happened when the stranger came up again.

'"Good-evening," said he, looking through the window. "I wanted to have a word with you." The girl has sworn that as he spoke she noticed the corner of the little paper packet protruding from his closed hand.

'"What business have you here?" asked the lad.

'"It's business that may put something into your pocket," said the other. "You've two horses in for the Wessex Cup—Silver Blaze and Bayard. Let me have the straight tip and you won't be a loser. Is it a fact that at the weights Bayard could give the other a hundred yards in five furlongs, and that the stable have put their money on him?"

'"So, you're one of those damned touts!" cried the lad. "I'll show you how we serve them in King's Pyland." He sprang up and rushed across the stable to unloose the dog. The girl fled away to the house, but as she ran she looked back and saw that the stranger was leaning through the window. A minute later, however, when Hunter rushed out with the hound he was gone, and though he ran all round the buildings he failed to find any trace of him.'

'One moment,' I asked. 'Did the stable-boy, when he ran out with the dog, leave the door unlocked behind him?'

'Excellent, Watson, excellent!' murmured my companion. 'The importance of the point struck me so forcibly that I sent a special wire to Dartmoor yesterday to clear the matter up. The boy locked the door before he left it. The window, I may add, was not large enough for a man to get through.

'Hunter waited until his fellow-grooms had returned, when he sent a message to the trainer and told him what had occurred. Straker was excited at hearing the account, although he does not seem to have quite realized its true significance. It left him, however, vaguely uneasy, and Mrs Straker, waking at one in the morning, found that he was dressing. In reply to her inquiries, he said that he could not sleep on account of his anxiety about the horses, and that he intended to walk down to the stables to see that all was well. She begged him to remain at home, as she could hear the rain pattering against the window, but in spite of her entreaties he pulled on his large mackintosh and left the house.

'Mrs Straker awoke at seven in the morning to find that her husband had not yet returned. She dressed herself hastily, called the maid, and set off for the stables. The door was open; inside, huddled together upon a chair, Hunter was sunk in a state of absolute stupor, the favourite's stall was empty, and there were no signs of his trainer.

'The two lads who slept in the chaff-cutting loft above the harness-room were quickly aroused. They had heard nothing during the night, for they are both sound sleepers. Hunter was obviously under the influence of some powerful drug, and as no sense could be got out of him, he was left to sleep it off while the two lads and the two women ran out in search of the absentees. They still had hopes that the trainer had for some reason taken out the horse for early exercise, but on ascending the knoll near the house, from which all the neighbouring moors were visible, they not only could see no signs of the missing favourite, but they perceived something which warned them that they were in the presence of a tragedy.

'About a quarter of a mile from the stables John Straker's overcoat was flapping from a furze-bush. Immediately beyond there was a bowl-shaped depression in the moor, and at the bottom of this was found the dead body of the unfortunate trainer. His head had been shattered by a savage blow from some heavy weapon, and he was wounded in the thigh, where there was a long, clean cut, inflicted evidently by some very sharp instrument. It was clear, however, that Straker had defended himself vigorously against his assailants, for in his right hand he held a small knife, which was clotted with blood up to the handle, while in his left he clasped a red and black silk cravat, which was recognized by the maid as having been worn on the preceding evening by the stranger who had visited the stables. Hunter, on recovering from his stupor, was also quite positive as to the ownership of the cravat. He was equally certain that the same stranger had, while standing at the window, drugged his curried mutton, and so deprived the stables of their watchman. As to the missing horse, there were abundant proofs in the mud which lay at the bottom of the fatal hollow that he had been there at the time of the struggle. But from that morning he has disappeared, and although a large reward has been offered, and all the gypsies of Dartmoor are on the alert, no news has come of him. Finally, an analysis has shown that the remains of his supper left by the stable-lad contained an appreciable quantity of powdered opium, while the people at the house partook of the same dish on the same night without any ill effect.

'Those are the main facts of the case, stripped of all surmise, and stated as baldly as possible. I shall now recapitulate what the police have done in the matter.

'Inspector Gregory, to whom the case has been committed, is an extremely competent officer. Were he but gifted with imagination he might rise to great heights in his profession. On his arrival he promptly found and arrested the man upon whom suspicion naturally rested. There was little difficulty in finding him, for he inhabited one of those villas which I have mentioned. His name, it appears, was Fitzroy Simpson. He was a man of excellent birth and education, who had squandered a fortune upon the turf, and who lived now by doing a little quiet and genteel book-making in the sporting clubs of London. An examination of his betting-book shows that bets to the amount of five thousand pounds had been registered by him against the favourite. On being arrested he volunteered the statement that he had come down to Dartmoor in the hope of getting some information about the King's Pyland horses, and also about Desborough, the second favourite, which was in charge of Silas Brown at the Mapleton stables. He did not attempt to deny that he had acted as described upon the evening before, but declared that he had no sinister designs and had simply wished to obtain first-hand information. When confronted with his cravat he turned very pale and was utterly unable to account for its presence in the hand of the murdered man. His wet clothing showed that he had been out in the storm of the night before, and his stick, which was a penang-lawyer weighted with lead, was just such a weapon as might, by repeated blows, have inflicted the terrible injuries to which the trainer had succumbed. On the other hand, there was no wound upon his person, while the state of Straker's knife would show that one at least of his assailants must bear his mark upon him. There you have it all in a nutshell, Watson, and if you can give me any light I shall be infinitely obliged to you.'

I had listened with the greatest interest to the statement which Holmes, with characteristic clearness, had laid before me. Though most of the facts were familiar to me, I had not sufficiently appreciated their relative importance, nor their connection to each other.

'Is it not possible,' I suggested, 'that the incised wound upon Straker may have been caused by his own knife in the convulsive struggles which follow any brain injury?'

'It is more than possible; it is probable,' said Holmes. 'In that case one of the main points in favour of the accused disappears.'

'And yet,' said I, 'even now I fail to understand what the theory of the police can be.'

'I am afraid that whatever theory we state has very grave objections to it,' returned my companion. 'The police imagine, I take it, that this Fitzroy Simpson, having drugged the lad, and having in some way obtained a duplicate key, opened the stable door and took out the horse, with the intention, apparently, of kidnapping him altogether. His bridle is missing, so that Simpson must have put this on. Then, having left the door open behind him, he was leading the horse away over the moor when he was either met or overtaken by the trainer. A row naturally ensued. Simpson beat out the trainer's brains with his heavy stick without receiving any injury from the small knife which Straker used in self-defence, and then the thief either led the horse on to some secret hiding-place, or else it may have bolted during the struggle, and be now wandering out on the moors. That is the case as it appears to the police, and improbable as it is, all other explanations are more improbable still. However, I shall very quickly test the matter when I am once upon the spot, and until then I cannot really see how we can get much further than our present position.'

It was evening before we reached the little town of Tavistock, which lies, like the boss of a shield, in the middle of the huge circle of Dartmoor. Two gentlemen were awaiting us in the station—the one a tall, fair man with lion-like hair and beard and curiously penetrating light blue eyes; the other a small, alert person, very neat and dapper, in a frock-coat and gaiters, with trim little side-whiskers and an eyeglass. The latter was Colonel Ross, the well-known sportsman; the other, Inspector Gregory; a man who was rapidly making his name in the English detective service.

'I am delighted that you have come down, Mr Holmes,' said the colonel. 'The inspector here has done all that could possibly be suggested, but I wish to leave no stone unturned in trying to avenge poor Straker and in recovering my horse.'

'Have there been any fresh developments?' asked Holmes.

'I am sorry to say that we have made very little progress,' said the inspector. 'We have an open carriage outside, and as you would no doubt like to see the place before the light fails, we might talk it over as we drive.'

A minute later we were all seated in a comfortable landau and were rattling through the quaint old Devonshire city. Inspector Gregory was full of his case and poured out a stream of remarks, while Holmes threw in an occasional question or interjection. Colonel Ross leaned back with his arms folded and his hat tilted over his eyes, while I listened with interest to the dialogue of the two detectives. Gregory was formulating his theory, which was almost exactly what Holmes had foretold in the train.

'The net is drawn pretty close round Fitzroy Simpson,' he remarked, 'and I believe myself that he is our man. At the same time I recognize that the evidence is purely circumstantial, and that some new development may upset it.'

'How about Straker's knife?'

'We have quite come to the conclusion that he wounded himself in his fall.'

'My friend Dr Watson made that suggestion to me as we came down. If so, it would tell against this man Simpson.'

'Undoubtedly. He has neither a knife nor any sign of a wound. The evidence against him is certainly very strong. He had a great interest in the disappearance of the favourite. He lies under suspicion of having poisoned the stable-boy; he was undoubtedly out in the storm; he was armed with a heavy stick, and his cravat was found in the dead man's hand. I really think we have enough to go before a jury.'

Holmes shook his head. 'A clever counsel would tear it

all to rags,' said he. 'Why should he take the horse out of the stable? If he wished to injure it, why could he not do it there? Has a duplicate key been found in his possession? What chemist sold him the powdered opium? Above all, where could he, a stranger to the district, hide a horse, and such a horse as this? What is his own explanation as to the paper which he wished the maid to give to the stable-boy?'

'He says that it was a ten-pound note. One was found in his purse. But your other difficulties are not so formidable as they seem. He is not a stranger to the district. He has twice lodged at Tavistock in the summer. The opium was probably brought from London. The key, having served its purpose, would be hurled away. The horse may be at the bottom of one of the pits or old mines upon the moor.'

'What does he say about the cravat?'

'He acknowledges that it is his and declares that he has lost it. But a new element has been introduced into the case which may account for his leading the horse from the stable.'

Holmes pricked up his ears.

'We have found traces which show that a party of gypsies encamped on Monday night within a mile of the spot where the murder took place. On Tuesday they were gone. Now, presuming that there was some under-standing between Simpson and these gypsies, might he not have been leading the horse to them when he was overtaken, and may they not have him now?'

'It is certainly possible.'

'The moor is being scoured for these gypsies. I have also examined every stable and outhouse in Tavistock, and for a radius of ten miles.'

'There is another training-stable quite close, I understand?'

'Yes, and that is a factor which we must certainly not neglect. As Desborough, their horse, was second in the betting, they had an interest in the disappearance of the favourite. Silas Brown, the trainer, is known to have had large bets upon the event, and he was no friend to poor Straker. We have, however, examined the stables, and there is nothing to connect him with the affair.'

'And nothing to connect this man Simpson with the interests of the Mapleton stables?'

'Nothing at all.'

Holmes leaned back in the carriage, and the conversation ceased. A few minutes later our driver pulled up at a neat little red-brick villa with overhanging eaves which stood by the road. Some distance off, across a paddock, lay a long grey-tiled outbuilding. In every other direction the low curves of the moor, bronze-coloured from the fading ferns, stretched away to the sky-line, broken only by the steeples of Tavistock, and by a cluster of houses away to the westward which marked the Mapleton stables. We all sprang out with the exception of Holmes, who continued to lean back with his eyes fixed upon the sky in front of him, entirely absorbed in his own thoughts. It was only when I touched his arm that he roused himself with a violent start and stepped out of the carriage.

'Excuse me,' said he, turning to Colonel Ross, who had looked at him in some surprise. 'I was day-dreaming.' There was a gleam in his eyes and a suppressed excitement in his manner which convinced me, used as I was to his ways, that his hand was upon a clue, though I could not imagine where he had found it.

'Perhaps you would prefer at once to go on to the scene of the crime, Mr Holmes?' said Gregory.

'I think that I should prefer to stay here a little and go into one or two questions of detail. Straker was brought back here, I presume?'

'Yes, he lies upstairs. The inquest is tomorrow.'

'He has been in your service some years, Colonel Ross?'

'I have always found him an excellent servant.'

'I presume that you made an inventory of what he had in his pockets at the time of his death, Inspector?'

'I have the things themselves in the sitting-room if you would care to see them.'

'I should be very glad.' We all filed into the front room and sat round the central table while the inspector unlocked a square tin box and laid a small heap of things before us. There was a box of vestas, two inches of tallow candle, an A D P brier-root pipe, a pouch of sealskin with half an ounce of long-cut Cavendish, a silver watch with a gold chain, five sovereigns in gold, an aluminum pencil-case, a few papers, and an ivory-handled knife with a very delicate, inflexible blade marked Weiss & Co., London.

'This is a very singular knife,' said Holmes, lifting it up and examining it minutely. 'I presume, as I see bloodstains upon it, that it is the one which was found in the dead man's grasp. Watson, this knife is surely in your line?'

'It is what we call a cataract knife,' said I.

'I thought so. A very delicate blade devised for very delicate work. A strange thing for a man to carry with him upon a rough expedition, especially as it would not shut in his pocket.'

'The tip was guarded by a disc of cork which we found beside his body,' said the inspector. 'His wife tells us that the knife had lain upon the dressing-table, and that he had picked it up as he left the room. It was a poor weapon, but perhaps the best that he could lay his hands on at the moment.'

'Very possibly. How about these papers?'

'Three of them are receipted hay-dealers' accounts. One of them is a letter of instructions from Colonel Ross. This other is a milliner's account for thirty-seven pounds fifteen made out by Madame Lesurier, of Bond Street, to William Derbyshire. Mrs Straker tells us that Derbyshire was a friend of her husband's, and that occasionally his letters were addressed here.'

'Madame Derbyshire had somewhat expensive tastes,' remarked Holmes, glancing down the account. 'Twenty two guineas is rather heavy for a single costume. However, there appears to be nothing more to learn, and we may now go down to the scene of the crime."

As we emerged from the sitting-room a woman, who had been waiting in the passage, took a step forward and laid her hand upon the inspector's sleeve. Her face was haggard and thin and eager, stamped with the print of a recent horror.

'Have you got them? Have you found them?' she panted.

'No, Mrs Straker. But Mr Holmes here has come from London to help us, and we shall do all that is possible.'

'Surely I met you in Plymouth at a garden-party some little time ago, Mrs Straker?' said Holmes.

'No, sir; you are mistaken.'

'Dear me! Why, I could have sworn to it. You wore

a costume of dove-coloured silk with ostrich-feather trimming.'

'I never had such a dress, sir,' answered the lady.

'Ah, that quite settles it,' said Holmes. And with an apology he followed the inspector outside. A short walk across the moor took us to the hollow in which the body had been found. At the brink of it was the furze-bush upon which the coat had been hung.

'There was no wind that night, I understand,' said Holmes.

'None, but very heavy rain.'

'In that case the overcoat was not blown against the furze-bush, but placed there.'

'Yes, it was laid across the bush.'

'You fill me with interest. I perceive that the ground has been trampled up a good deal. No doubt many feet have been here since Monday night.'

'A piece of matting has been laid here at the side, and we have all stood upon that.'

'Excellent.'

'In this bag I have one of the boots which Straker wore, one of Fitzroy Simpson's shoes, and a cast horseshoe of Silver Blaze.'

'My dear Inspector, you surpass yourself!' Holmes took the bag, and, descending into the hollow, he pushed the matting into a more central position. Then stretching himself upon his face and leaning his chin upon his hands, he made a careful study of the trampled mud in front of him. 'Hullo!' said he suddenly. 'What's this?' It was a wax vesta, half burned, which was so coated with mud that it looked at first like a little chip of wood.

'I cannot think how I came to overlook it,' said the inspector with an expression of annoyance.

'It was invisible, buried in the mud. I only saw it because I was looking for it.'

'What! you expected to find it?'

'I thought it not unlikely.'

He took the boots from the bag and compared the impressions of each of them with marks upon the ground. Then he clambered up to the rim of the hollow and crawled about among the ferns and bushes.

'I am afraid that there are no more tracks,' said the inspector. 'I have examined the ground very carefully for a hundred yards in each direction.'

'Indeed!' said Holmes, rising. 'I should not have the impertinence to do it again after what you say. But I should like to take a little walk over the moor before it grows dark that I may know my ground tomorrow, and I think that I shall put this horseshoe into my pocket for luck.'

Colonel Ross, who had shown some signs of impatience at my companion's quiet and systematic method of work, glanced at his watch. 'I wish you would come back with me, Inspector,' said he. 'There are several points on which I should like your advice, and especially as to whether we do not owe it to the public to remove our horse's name from the entries for the cup.'

'Certainly not,' cried Holmes with decision. 'I should let the name stand.'

The colonel bowed. 'I am very glad to have had your opinion, sir,' said he. 'You will find us at poor Straker's house when you have finished your work, and we can drive together into Tavistock.'

He turned back with the inspector, while Holmes and I walked slowly across the moor. The sun was beginning to sink behind the stable of Mapleton, and the long, sloping plain in front of us was tinged with gold, deepening into rich, ruddy browns where the faded ferns and brambles caught the evening light. But the glories of the landscape were all wasted upon my companion, who was sunk in the deepest thought.

'It's this way, Watson,' said he at last. 'We may leave the question of who killed John Straker for the instant and confine ourselves to finding out what has become of the horse. Now, supposing that he broke away during or after the tragedy, where could he have gone to? The horse is a very gregarious creature. If left to himself his instincts would have been either to return to King's Pyland or go over to Mapleton. Why should he run wild upon the moor? He would surely have been seen by now. And why should gypsies kidnap him? These people always clear out when they hear of trouble, for they do not wish to be pestered by the police. They could not hope to sell such a horse. They would run a great risk and gain nothing by taking him. Surely that is clear.'

'Where is he, then?'

'I have already said that he must have gone to King's Pyland or to Mapleton. He is not at King's Pyland. Therefore he is at Mapleton. Let us take that as a working hypothesis and see what it leads us to. This part of the moor, as the inspector remarked, is very hard and dry. But it falls away towards Mapleton, and you can see from here that there is a long hollow over yonder, which must have been very wet on Monday night. If our supposition is correct, then the horse must have crossed that, and there is the point where we should look for his tracks.'

We had been walking briskly during this conversation, and a few more minutes brought us to the hollow in question. At Holmes's request I walked down the bank to the right, and he to the left, but I had not taken fifty paces before I heard him give a shout and saw him waving his hand to me. The track of a horse was plainly outlined in the soft earth in front of him, and the shoe which he took from his pocket exactly fitted the impression.

'See the value of imagination,' said Holmes. 'It is the one quality which Gregory lacks. We imagined what might have happened, acted upon the supposition, and find ourselves justified. Let us proceed.'

We crossed the marshy bottom and passed over a quarter of a mile of dry, hard turf. Again the ground sloped, and again we came on the tracks. Then we lost them for half a mile, but only to pick them up once more quite close to Mapleton. It was Holmes who saw them first, and he stood pointing with a look of triumph upon his face. A man's track was visible beside the horse's.

'The horse was alone before,' I cried.

'Quite so. It was alone before. Hullo, what is this?'

The double track turned sharp off and took the direction of King's Pyland. Holmes whistled, and we both followed along after it. His eyes were on the trail, but I happened to look a little to one side and saw to my surprise the same tracks coming back again in the opposite direction.

'One for you, Watson,' said Holmes when I pointed it out. 'You have saved us a long walk, which would have brought us back on our own traces. Let us follow the return track.'

We had not to go far. It ended at the paving of asphalt which led up to the gates of the Mapleton stables. As we approached, a groom ran out from them.

'We don't want any loiterers about here,' said he.

'I only wished to ask a question,' said Holmes, with his finger and thumb in his waistcoat pocket. 'Should I be too early to see your master, Mr Silas Brown, if I were to call at five o'clock to-morrow morning?'

'Bless you, sir, if anyone is about he will be, for he is always the first stirring. But here he is, sir, to answer your questions for himself. No, sir, no, it is as much as my place is worth to let him see me touch your money. Afterwards, if you like.'

As Sherlock Holmes replaced the half-crown which he had drawn from his pocket, a fierce-looking elderly man strode out from the gate with a hunting-crop swinging in his hand.

'What's this, Dawson!' he cried. 'No gossiping! Go about your business! And you, what the devil do you want here?'

'Ten minutes' talk with you, my good sir,' said Holmes in the sweetest of voices.

'I've no time to talk to every gadabout. We want no strangers here. Be off, or you may find a dog at your heels.'

Holmes leaned forward and whispered something in the trainer's ear. He started violently and flushed to the temples.

'It's a lie!' he shouted. 'An infernal lie!'

'Very good. Shall we argue about it here in public or talk it over in your parlour?'

'Oh, come in if you wish to.'

Holmes smiled. 'I shall not keep you more than a few minutes, Watson,' said he. 'Now, Mr Brown, I am quite at your disposal.'

It was twenty minutes, and the reds had all faded into greys before Holmes and the trainer reappeared. Never

81

have I seen such a change as had been brought about in Silas Brown in that short time. His face was ashy pale, beads of perspiration shone upon his brow, and his hands shook until the hunting-crop wagged like a branch in the wind. His bullying, overbearing manner was all gone too, and he cringed along at my companion's side like a dog with its master.

'Your instructions will be done. It shall all be done,' said he.

'There must be no mistake,' said Holmes, looking round at him. The other winced as he read the menace in his eyes.

'Oh, no, there shall be no mistake. I shall be there. Should I change it first or not?'

Holmes thought a little and then burst out laughing. 'No, don't,' said he, 'I shall write to you about it. No tricks, now, or—'

'Oh, you can trust me, you can trust me!'

'Yes, I think I can. Well, you shall hear from me tomorrow.' He turned upon his heel, disregarding the trembling hand which the other held out to him, and we set off for King's Pyland.

'A more perfect compound of the bully, coward, and sneak than Master Silas Brown I have seldom met with,' remarked Holmes as we trudged along together.

'He has the horse, then?'

'He tried to bluster out of it, but I described to him so exactly what his actions had been upon that morning that he is convinced that I was watching him. Of course you observed the peculiarly square toes in the impressions, and that his own boots exactly corresponded to them. Again, of course no subordinate would have dared to do such a thing. I described to him how, when according to his custom he was the first down, he perceived a strange horse wandering over the moor. How he went out to it, and his astonishment at recognizing, from the white forehead which has given the favourite its name, that chance had put in his power the only horse which could beat the one upon which he had put his money. Then I described how his first impulse had been to lead him back to King's Pyland, and how the devil had shown him how he could hide the horse until the race was over, and how he had led it back and concealed it at Mapleton. When I told him every detail he gave it up and thought only of saving his own skin.'

'But his stables had been searched?'

'Oh, an old horse-faker like him has many a dodge.'

'But are you not afraid to leave the horse in his power now, since he has every interest of injuring it?'

'My dear fellow, he will guard it as the apple of his eye. He knows that his only hope of mercy is to produce it safe.'

'Colonel Ross did not impress me as a man who would be likely to show much mercy in any case.'

'The matter does not rest with Colonel Ross. I follow my own methods and tell as much or as little as I choose. That is the advantage of being unofficial. I don't know whether you observed it, Watson, but the colonel's manner has been just a trifle cavalier to me. I am inclined now to have a little amusement at his expense. Say nothing to him about the horse.'

'Certainly not without your permission.'

'And of course this is all quite a minor point compared to the question of who killed John Straker.'

'And you will devote yourself to that?'

'On the contrary, we both go back to London by the night train.'

I was thunderstruck by my friend's words. We had only been a few hours in Devonshire, and that he should give up an investigation which he had begun so brilliantly was quite incomprehensible to me. Not a word more could I draw from him until we were back at the trainer's house. The colonel and the inspector were awaiting us in the parlour.

'My friend and I return to town by the night-express,' said Holmes. 'We have had a charming little breath of your beautiful Dartmoor air.'

The inspector opened his eyes, and the colonel's lip curled in a sneer.

'So you despair of arresting the murderer of poor Straker,' said he.

Holmes shrugged his shoulders. 'There are certainly grave difficulties in the way,' said he. 'I have every hope, however, that your horse will start upon Tuesday, and I beg that you will have your jockey in readiness. Might I ask for a photograph of Mr John Straker?'

The inspector took one from an envelope and handed it to him.

'My dear Gregory, you anticipate all my wants. If I might ask you to wait here for an instant, I have a question which I should like to put to the maid.'

'I must say that I am rather disappointed in our London consultant,' said Colonel Ross bluntly as my friend left the room. 'I do not see that we are any further than when he came.'

'At least you have his assurance that your horse will run,' said I.

'Yes, I have his assurance,' said the colonel with a

shrug of his shoulders. 'I should prefer to have the horse.'

I was about to make some reply in defence of my friend when he entered the room again.

'Now, gentlemen,' said he, 'I am quite ready for Tavistock.'

As we stepped into the carriage one of the stable-lads held the door open for us. A sudden idea seemed to occur to Holmes, for he leaned forward and touched the lad upon the sleeve.

'You have a few sheep in the paddock,' he said. 'Who attends to them?'

'I do, sir.'

'Have you noticed anything amiss with them of late?'

'Well, sir, not of much account, but three of them have gone lame, sir.'

I could see that Holmes was extremely pleased, for he chuckled and rubbed his hands together.

'A long shot, Watson, a very long shot,' said he, pinching my arm. 'Gregory, let me recommend to your attention this singular epidemic among the sheep. Drive on, coachman!'

Colonel Ross still wore an expression which showed the poor opinion which he had formed of my companion's ability, but I saw by the inspector's face that his attention had been keenly aroused.

'You consider that to be important?' he asked.

'Exceedingly so.'

'Is there any point to which you would wish to draw my attention?'

'To the curious incident of the dog in the night-time.'

'The dog did nothing in the night-time.'

'That was the curious incident,' remarked Sherlock Holmes.

Four days later Holmes and I were again in the train, bound for Winchester to see the race for the Wessex Cup. Colonel Ross met us by appointment outside the station, and we drove in his drag to the course beyond the town. His face was grave, and his manner was cold in the extreme.

'I have seen nothing of my horse,' said he.

'I suppose that you would know him when you saw him?' asked Holmes.

The colonel was very angry. 'I have been on the turf for twenty years and never was asked such a question as that before,' said he. 'A child would know Silver Blaze with his white forehead and his mottled off-foreleg.'

'How is the betting?'

'Well, that is the curious part of it. You could have got fifteen to one yesterday, but the price has become shorter and shorter, until you can hardly get three to one now.'

'Hum!' said Holmes. 'Somebody knows something, that is clear.'

As the drag drew up in the enclosure near the grandstand I glanced at the card to see the entries.

Wessex Plate [it ran] 50 sovs. each h ft with 1000 sovs. added, for four and five year olds. Second, £300. Third, £200. New course (one mile and five furlongs).

1. Mr Heath Newton's The Negro. Red cap. Cinnamon jacket.
2. Colonel Wardlaw's Pugilist. Pink cap. Blue and black jacket.
3. Lord Backwater's Desborough. Yellow cap and sleeves.

4. Colonel Ross's Silver Blaze. Black cap. Red jacket.
5. Duke of Balmoral's Iris. Yellow and black stripes.
6. Lord Singleford's Rasper. Purple cap. Black sleeves.

'We scratched our other one and put all hopes on your word,' said the colonel. 'Why, what is that? Silver Blaze favourite?'

'Five to four against Silver Blaze!' roared the ring. 'Five to four against Silver Blaze! Five to fifteen against Desborough! Five to four on the field!'

'There are the numbers up,' I cried. 'They are all six there.'

'All six there? Then my horse is running,' cried the colonel in great agitation. 'But I don't see him. My colours have not passed.'

'Only five have passed. This must be he.'

As I spoke a powerful bay horse swept out from the weighing enclosure and cantered past us, bearing on its back the well-known black and red of the colonel.

'That's not my horse,' cried the owner. 'That beast has not a white hair upon its body. What is this that you have done, Mr Holmes?'

'Well, well, let us see how he gets on,' said my friend imperturbably. For a few minutes he gazed through my field-glass. 'Capital! An excellent start!' he cried suddenly. 'There they are, coming round the curve!'

From our drag we had a superb view as they came up the straight. The six horses were so close together that a carpet could have covered them, but halfway up the yellow of the Mapleton stable showed to the front. Before they reached us, however, Desborough's bolt was shot, and the colonel's horse, coming away with a rush, passed the post a good six lengths before its rival, the Duke of Balmoral's Iris making a bad third.

'It's my race, anyhow,' gasped the colonel, passing his hand over his eyes. 'I confess that I can make neither head nor tail of it. Don't you think that you have kept up your mystery long enough, Mr Holmes?'

'Certainly, Colonel, you shall know everything. Let us all go round and have a look at the horse together. Here he is,' he continued as we made our way into the weighing enclosure, where only owners and their friends find admittance. 'You have only to wash his face and his leg in spirits of wine, and you will find that he is the same old Silver Blaze as ever.'

'You take my breath away!'

'I found him in the hands of a faker and took the liberty of running him just as he was sent over.'

'My dear sir, you have done wonders. The horse looks very fit and well. It never went better in its life. I owe you a thousand apologies for having doubted your ability. You have done me a great service by recovering my horse. You would do me a greater still if you could lay your hands on the murderer of John Straker.'

'I have done so,' said Holmes quietly.

The colonel and I stared at him in amazement. 'You have got him! Where is he, then?'

'He is here.'

'Here! Where?'

'In my company at the present moment.'

The colonel flushed angrily. 'I quite recognize that I am under obligations to you, Mr Holmes,' said he, 'but I must regard what you have just said as either a very bad joke or an insult.'

Sherlock Holmes laughed. 'I assure you that I have not

associated you with the crime, Colonel,' said he. 'The real murderer is standing immediately behind you.' He stepped past and laid his hand upon the glossy neck of the thoroughbred.

'The horse!' cried both the colonel and myself.

'Yes, the horse. And it may lessen his guilt if I say that it was done in self-defence, and that John Straker was a man who was entirely unworthy of your confidence. But there goes the bell, and as I stand to win a little on this next race, I shall defer a lengthy explanation until a more fitting time.'

We had the corner of a Pullman car to ourselves that evening as we whirled back to London, and I fancy that the journey was a short one to Colonel Ross as well as to myself as we listened to our companion's narrative of the events which had occurred at the Dartmoor training stables upon that Monday night, and the means by which he had unravelled them.

'I confess,' said he, 'that any theories which I had formed from the newspaper reports were entirely erroneous. And yet there were indications there, had they not been overlaid by other details which concealed their true import. I went to Devonshire with the conviction that Fitzroy Simpson was the true culprit, although, of course, I saw that the evidence against him was by no means complete. It was while I was in the carriage, just as we reached the trainer's house, that the immense significance of the curried mutton occurred to me. You may remember that I was distrait and remained sitting after you had all alighted. I was marvelling in my own mind how I could possibly have overlooked so obvious a clue.'

'I confess', said the colonel, 'that even now I cannot see how it helps us.'

'It was the first link in my chain of reasoning. Powdered opium is by no means tasteless. The flavour is not disagreeable, but it is perceptible. Were it mixed with any ordinary dish the eater would undoubtedly detect it and would probably eat no more. A curry was exactly the medium which would disguise this taste. By no possible supposition could this stranger, Fitzroy Simpson, have caused curry to be served in the trainer's family that night, and it is surely too monstrous a coincidence to suppose that he happened to come along with powdered opium upon the very night when a dish happened to be served which would disguise the flavour. That is unthinkable. Therefore Simpson becomes eliminated from the case, and our attention centres upon Straker and his wife, the only two people who could have chosen curried mutton for supper that night. The opium was added after the dish was set aside for the stable-boy, for the others had the same for supper with no ill effects. Which of them, then, had access to that dish without the maid seeing them?

'Before deciding that question I had grasped the significance of the silence of the dog, for one true inference invariably suggests others. The Simpson incident had shown me that a dog was kept in the stables, and yet, though someone had been in and had fetched out a horse, he had not barked enough to arouse the two lads in the loft. Obviously the midnight visitor was someone whom the dog knew well.

'I was already convinced, or almost convinced, that John Straker went down to the stables in the dead of the night and took out Silver Blaze. For what purpose? For a dishonest one, obviously, or why should he drug his own stable-boy? And yet I was at a loss to know why. There have been cases before now where trainers have made sure of great sums of money by laying against their own horses through agents and then preventing them from winning by fraud. Sometimes it is a pulling jockey. Sometimes it is some surer and subtler means. What was it here? I hoped that the contents of his pockets might help me to form a conclusion.

'And they did so. You cannot have forgotten the singular knife which was found in the dead man's hand, a knife which certainly no sane man would choose for a weapon. It was, as Dr Watson told us, a form of knife which is used for the most delicate operations known in surgery. And it was to be used for a delicate operation that night. You must know, with your wide experience of turf matters, Colonel Ross, that it is possible to make a slight nick upon the tendons of a horse's ham, and to do it subcutaneously, so as to leave absolutely no trace. A horse so treated would develop a slight lameness, which would be put down to a strain in exercise or a touch of rheumatism, but never to foul play.'

'Villain! Scoundrel!' cried the colonel.

'We have here the explanation of why John Straker wished to take the horse out on to the moor. So spirited a creature would have certainly roused the soundest of sleepers when it felt the prick of the knife. It was absolutely necessary to do it in the open air.'

'I have been blind!' cried the colonel. 'Of course that was why he needed the candle and struck the match.'

'Undoubtedly. But in examining his belongings I was fortunate enough to discover not only the method of the crime but even its motives. As a man of the world,

Colonel, you know that men do not carry other people's bills about in their pockets. We have most of us quite enough to do to settle our own. I at once concluded that Straker was leading a double life and keeping a second establishment. The nature of the bill showed that there was a lady in the case, and one who had expensive tastes. Liberal as you are with your servants, one can hardly expect that they can buy twenty-guinea walking dresses for their ladies. I questioned Mrs Straker as to the dress without her knowing it, and, having satisfied myself that it had never reached her, I made a note of the milliner's address and felt that by calling there with Straker's photograph I could easily dispose of the mythical Derbyshire.

'From that time on all was plain. Straker had led out the horse to a hollow where his light would be invisible. Simpson in his flight had dropped his cravat, and Straker had picked it up—with some idea, perhaps, that he might use it in securing the horse's leg. Once in the hollow, he had got behind the horse and had struck a light; but the creature, frightened at the sudden glare, and with the strange instinct of animals feeling that some mischief was intended, had lashed out, and the steel shoe had struck Straker full on the forehead. He had already, in spite of the rain, taken off his overcoat in order to do his delicate task, and so, as he fell, his knife gashed his thigh. Do I make it clear?'

'Wonderful!' cried the colonel. 'Wonderful! You might have been there!'

'My final shot was, I confess, a very long one. It struck me that so astute a man as Straker would not undertake this delicate tendon-nicking without a little practice. What could he practise on? My eyes fell upon the sheep, and I asked a question which, rather to my surprise, showed that my surmise was correct.

'When I returned to London I called upon the milliner, who had recognized Straker as an excellent customer of the name of Derbyshire, who had a very dashing wife, with a strong partiality for expensive dresses. I have no doubt that this woman had plunged him over head and ears in debt, and so led him into this miserable plot.'

'You have explained all but one thing,' cried the colonel. 'Where was the horse?'

'Ah, it bolted, and was cared for by one of your neighbours. We must have an amnesty in that direction, I think. This is Clapham Junction, if I am not mistaken, and we shall be in Victoria in less than ten minutes. If you care to smoke a cigar in our rooms, Colonel, I shall be happy to give you any other details which might interest you.'

THE ADVENTURE OF
THE SIX NAPOLEONS

It was no very unusual thing for Mr Lestrade, of Scotland
Yard, to look in upon us of an evening, and his visits
were welcome to Sherlock Holmes, for they enabled
him to keep in touch with all that was going on at
the police headquarters. In return for the news which
Lestrade would bring, Holmes was always ready to listen
with attention to the details of any case upon which
the detective was engaged, and was able occasionally,
without any active interference, to give some hint or
suggestion drawn from his own vast knowledge and
experience.

On this particular evening, Lestrade had spoken of the
weather and the newspapers. Then he had fallen silent,
puffing thoughtfully at his cigar. Holmes looked keenly
at him.

'Anything remarkable on hand?' he asked.

'Oh, no, Mr Holmes—nothing very particular.'

'Then tell me about it.'

Lestrade laughed.

'Well, Mr Holmes, there is no use denying that there
is something on my mind. And yet it is such an absurd
business, that I hesitated to bother you about it. On
the other hand, although it is trivial, it is undoubtedly
queer, and I know that you have a taste for all that is

out of the common. But, in my opinion, it comes more in Dr Watson's line than ours.'

'Disease?' said I.

'Madness, anyhow. And a queer madness, too. You wouldn't think there was anyone living at this time of day who had such a hatred of Napoleon the First that he would break any image of him that he could see.'

Holmes sank back in his chair.

'That's no business of mine,' said he.

'Exactly. That's what I said. But then, when the man commits burglary in order to break images which are not his own, that brings it away from the doctor and on to the policeman.'

Holmes sat up again.

'Burglary! This is more interesting. Let me hear the details.'

Lestrade took out his official notebook and refreshed his memory from its pages.

'The first case reported was four days ago,' said he. 'It was at the shop of Morse Hudson, who has a place for the sale of pictures and statues in the Kennington Road. The assistant had left the front shop for an instant, when he heard a crash, and hurrying in he found a plaster bust of Napoleon, which stood with several other works of art upon the counter, lying shivered into fragments. He rushed out into the road, but, although several passers-by declared that they had noticed a man run out of the shop, he could neither see anyone nor could he find any means of identifying the rascal. It seemed to be one of those senseless acts of hooliganism which occur from time to time, and it was reported to the constable on the beat as such. The plaster cast was not worth more than a few shillings, and the whole affair appeared to be too childish for any particular investigation.

'The second case, however, was more serious, and also more singular. It occurred only last night.

'In Kennington Road, and within a few hundred yards of Morse Hudson's shop, there lives a well-known medical practitioner, named Dr Barnicot, who has one of the largest practices upon the south side of the Thames. His residence and principal consulting-room is at Kennington Road, but he has a branch surgery and dispensary at Lower Brixton Road, two miles away. This Dr Barnicot is an enthusiastic admirer of Napoleon, and his house is full of books, pictures, and relics of the French Emperor. Some little time ago he purchased from Morse Hudson two duplicate plaster casts of the famous head of Napoleon by the French sculptor, Devine. One of these he placed in his hall in the house at Kennington Road, and the other on the mantelpiece of the surgery at Lower Brixton. Well, when Dr Barnicot came down this morning he was astonished to find that his house had been burgled during the night, but that nothing had been taken save the plaster head from the hall. It had been carried out and had been dashed savagely against the garden wall, under which its splintered fragments were discovered.'

Holmes rubbed his hands.

'This is certainly very novel,' said he.

'I thought it would please you. But I have not got to the end yet. Dr Barnicot was due at his surgery at twelve o'clock, and you can imagine his amazement when, on arriving there, he found that the window had been opened in the night, and that the broken pieces of his second bust were strewn all over the room. It had been smashed to atoms where it stood. In neither case were there any signs which could give us a clue as to the criminal or lunatic who had done the mischief. Now, Mr Holmes, you have got the facts.'

'They are singular, not to say grotesque,' said Holmes. 'May I ask whether the two busts smashed in Dr Barnicot's rooms were the exact duplicates of the one which was destroyed in Morse Hudson's shop?'

'They were taken from the same mould.'

'Such a fact must tell against the theory that the man who breaks them is influenced by any general hatred of Napoleon. Considering how many hundreds of statues of the great Emperor must exist in London, it is too much to suppose such a coincidence as that a promiscuous iconoclast should chance to begin upon three specimens of the same bust.'

'Well, I thought as you do,' said Lestrade. 'On the other hand, this Morse Hudson is the purveyor of busts in that part of London, and these three were the only ones which had been in his shop for years. So, although, as you say, there are many hundreds of statues in London, it is very probable that these three were the only ones in that district. Therefore, a local fanatic would begin with them. What do you think, Dr Watson?'

'There are no limits to the possibilities of monomania,' I answered. 'There is the condition which the modern French psychologists have called the "*idée fixe*", which may be trifling in character, and accompanied by complete sanity in every other way. A man who had read deeply about Napoleon, or who had possibly received some hereditary family injury through the great war, might conceivably form such an *idée fixe* and under its influence be capable of any fantastic outrage."

'That won't do, my dear Watson,' said Holmes, shaking

his head, 'for no amount of *idée fixe* would enable your interesting monomaniac to find out where these busts were situated.'

'Well, how do *you* explain it?'

'I don't attempt to do so. I would only observe that there is a certain method in the gentleman's eccentric proceedings. For example, in Dr Barnicot's hall, where a sound might arouse the family, the bust was taken outside before being broken, whereas in the surgery, where there was less danger of an alarm, it was smashed where it stood. The affair seems absurdly trifling, and yet I dare call nothing trivial when I reflect that some of my most classic cases have had the least promising commencement. You will remember, Watson, how the dreadful business of the Abernetty family was first brought to my notice by the depth which the parsley had sunk into the butter upon a hot day. I can't afford, therefore, to smile at your three broken busts, Lestrade, and I shall be very much obliged to you if you will let me hear of any fresh development of so singular a chain of events.'

The development for which my friend had asked came in a quicker and an infinitely more tragic form than he could have imagined. I was still dressing in my bedroom next morning, when there was a tap at the door and Holmes entered, a telegram in his hand. He read it aloud:

'Come instantly, 131 Pitt Street, Kensington.

LESTRADE."

'What is it, then?' I asked.

'Don't know—may be anything. But I suspect it is

the sequel of the story of the statues. In that case our friend the image-breaker has begun operations in another quarter of London. There's coffee on the table, Watson, and I have a cab at the door.'

In half an hour we had reached Pitt Street, a quiet little backwater just beside one of the briskest currents of London life. No. 131 was one of a row, all flat-chested, respectable, and most unromantic dwellings. As we drove up, we found the railings in front of the house lined by a curious crowd. Holmes whistled.

'By George! it's attempted murder at the least. Nothing less will hold the London message-boy. There's a deed of violence indicated in that fellow's round shoulders and outstretched neck. What's this, Watson? The top steps swilled down and the other ones dry. Footsteps enough, anyhow! Well, well, there's Lestrade at the front window, and we shall soon know all about it.'

The official received us with a very grave face and showed us into a sitting-room, where an exceedingly unkempt and agitated elderly man, clad in a flannel dressing-gown, was pacing up and down. He was introduced to us as the owner of the house—Mr Horace Harker, of the Central Press Syndicate.

'It's the Napoleon bust business again,' said Lestrade. 'You seemed interested last night, Mr Holmes, so I thought perhaps you would be glad to be present now that the affair has taken a very much graver turn.'

'What has it turned to, then?'

'To murder. Mr Harker, will you tell these gentlemen exactly what has occurred?'

The man in the dressing-gown turned upon us with a most melancholy face.

'It's an extraordinary thing,' said he, 'that all my life I

have been collecting other people's news, and now that a real piece of news has come my own way I am so confused and bothered that I can't put two words together. If I had come in here as a journalist, I should have interviewed myself and had two columns in every evening paper. As it is, I am giving away valuable copy by telling my story over and over to a string of different people, and I can make no use of it myself. However, I've heard your name, Mr Sherlock Holmes, and if you'll only explain this queer business, I shall be paid for my trouble in telling you the story.'

Holmes sat down and listened.

'It all seems to centre round that bust of Napoleon which I bought for this very room about four months ago. I picked it up cheap from Harding Brothers, two doors from the High Street Station. A great deal of my journalistic work is done at night, and I often write until the early morning. So it was today. I was sitting in my den, which is at the back of the top of the house, about three o'clock, when I was convinced that I heard some sounds downstairs. I listened, but they were not repeated, and I concluded that they came from outside. Then suddenly, about five minutes later, there came a most horrible yell—the most dreadful sound, Mr Holmes, that ever I heard. It will ring in my ears as long as I live. I sat frozen with horror for a minute or two. Then I seized the poker and went downstairs. When I entered this room I found the window wide open, and I at once observed that the bust was gone from the mantelpiece. Why any burglar should take such a thing passes my understanding, for it was only a plaster cast and of no real value whatever.

'You can see for yourself that anyone going out through that open window could reach the front doorstep by taking a long stride. This was clearly what the burglar had done, so I went round and opened the door. Stepping out into the dark, I nearly fell over a dead man, who was lying there. I ran back for a light, and there was the poor fellow, a great gash in his throat and the whole place swimming in blood. He lay on his back, his knees drawn up, and his mouth horribly open. I shall see him in my dreams. I had just time to blow on my police-whistle, and then I must have fainted, for I knew nothing more until I found the policeman standing over me in the hall.'

'Well, who was the murdered man?' asked Holmes.

'There's nothing to show who he was,' said Lestrade. 'You shall see the body at the mortuary, but we have made nothing of it up to now. He is a tall man, sunburned, very powerful, not more than thirty. He is poorly dressed, and yet does not appear to be a labourer. A horn-handled clasp knife was lying in a pool of blood beside him. Whether it was the weapon which did the deed, or whether it belonged to the dead man, I do not know. There was no name on his clothing, and nothing in his pockets save an apple, some string, a shilling map of London, and a photograph. Here it is.'

It was evidently taken by a snapshot from a small camera. It represented an alert, sharp-featured simian man, with thick eyebrows and a very peculiar projection of the lower part of the face, like the muzzle of a baboon.

'And what became of the bust?' asked Holmes, after a careful study of this picture.

'We had news of it just before you came. It has been found in the front garden of an empty house in Campden House Road. It was broken into fragments. I am going round now to see it. Will you come?'

'Certainly. I must just take one look round.' He examined the carpet and the window. 'The fellow had either very long legs or was a most active man,' said he. 'With an area beneath, it was no mean feat to reach that window-ledge and open that window. Getting back was comparatively simple. Are you coming with us to see the remains of your bust, Mr Harker?'

The disconsolate journalist had seated himself at a writing-table.

'I must try and make something of it,' said he, 'though I have no doubt that the first editions of the evening papers are out already with full details. It's like my luck! You remember when the stand fell at Doncaster? Well, I was the only journalist in the stand, and my journal the only one that had no account of it, for I was too shaken to write it. And now I'll be too late with a murder done on my own doorstep.'

As we left the room, we heard his pen travelling shrilly over the foolscap.

The spot where the fragments of the bust had been found was only a few hundred yards away. For the first time our eyes rested upon this presentment of the great emperor, which seemed to raise such frantic and destructive hatred in the mind of the unknown. It lay scattered, in splintered shards, upon the grass. Holmes picked up several of them and examined them carefully. I was convinced, from his intent face and his purposeful manner, that at last he was upon a clue.

'Well?' asked Lestrade.

Holmes shrugged his shoulders.

'We have a long way to go yet,' said he. 'And yet—and yet—well, we have some suggestive facts to act upon. The possession of this trifling bust was worth more, in the eyes of this strange criminal, than a human life. This is one point. Then there is the singular fact that he did not break it in the house, or immediately outside the house, if to break it was his sole object.'

'He was rattled and bustled by meeting this other fellow. He hardly knew what he was doing.'

'Well, that's likely enough. But I wish to call your attention very particularly to the position of this house, in the garden of which the bust was destroyed.'

Lestrade looked about him.

'It was an empty house, and so he knew that he would not be disturbed in the garden.'

'Yes, but there is another empty house farther up the street which he must have passed before he came to this one. Why did he not break it there, since it is evident that every yard that he carried it increased the risk of someone meeting him?'

'I give it up,' said Lestrade.

Holmes pointed to the street lamp above our heads.

'He could see what he was doing here, and he could not there. That was his reason.'

'By Jove! that's true,' said the detective. 'Now that I come to think of it, Dr Barnicot's bust was broken not far from his red lamp. Well, Mr Holmes, what are we to do with that fact?'

'To remember it—to docket it. We may come on something later which will bear upon it. What steps do you propose to take now, Lestrade?'

'The most practical way of getting at it, in my opinion, is to identify the dead man. There should be no difficulty about that. When we have found who he is and who his associates are, we should have a good start in learning what he was doing in Pitt Street last night, and who it was who met him and killed him on the doorstep of Mr Horace Harker. Don't you think so?'

'No doubt; and yet it is not quite the way in which I should approach the case.'

'What would you do then?'

'Oh, you must not let me influence you in any way. I suggest that you go on your line and I on mine. We can compare notes afterwards, and each will supplement the other.'

'Very good,' said Lestrade.

'If you are going back to Pitt Street, you might see Mr Horace Harker. Tell him for me that I have quite made up my mind, and that it is certain that a dangerous homicidal lunatic, with Napoleonic delusions, was in his house last night. It will be useful for his article.'

Lestrade stared.

'You don't seriously believe that?'

Holmes smiled.

'Don't I? Well, perhaps I don't. But I am sure that it will interest Mr Horace Harker and the subscribers of the Central Press Syndicate. Now, Watson, I think that we shall find that we have a long and rather complex day's work before us. I should be glad, Lestrade, if you could make it convenient to meet us at Baker Street at six o'clock this evening. Until then I should like to keep this photograph, found in the dead man's pocket. It is possible that I may have to ask your company and assistance upon a small expedition which will have to be undertaken tonight, if my chain of reasoning should prove to be correct. Until then goodbye and good luck!'

Sherlock Holmes and I walked together to the High Street, where we stopped at the shop of Harding Brothers, whence the bust had been purchased. A young assistant informed us that Mr Harding would be absent until afternoon, and that he was himself a newcomer, who could give us no information. Holmes's face showed his disappointment and annoyance.

'Well, well, we can't expect to have it all our own way, Watson,' he said, at last. 'We must come back in the afternoon, if Mr Harding will not be here until then. I am, as you have no doubt surmised, endeavouring to trace these busts to their source, in order to find if there is not something peculiar which may account for their remarkable fate. Let us make for Mr Morse Hudson, of the Kennington Road, and see if he can throw any light upon the problem.'

A drive of an hour brought us to the picture-dealer's establishment. He was a small, stout man with a red face and a peppery manner.

'Yes, sir. On my very counter, sir,' said he. 'What we pay rates and taxes for I don't know, when any ruffian can come in and break one's goods. Yes, sir, it was I who sold Dr Barnicot his two statues. Disgraceful, sir! A Nihilist plot—that's what I make it. No one but an anarchist would go about breaking statues. Red republicans—that's what I call 'em. Who did I get the statues from? I don't see what that has to do with it. Well, if you really want to know, I got them from Gelder & Co., in Church Street, Stepney. They are a well-known house in the trade, and have been this twenty years. How many had I? Three—two and one are three—two of Dr Barnicot's, and one smashed in broad daylight on my own counter. Do I know that photograph? No, I don't. Yes, I do, though. Why, it's Beppo. He was a kind of Italian piece-work man, who made himself useful in the shop. He could carve a bit, and gild and frame, and do

105

odd jobs. The fellow left me last week, and I've heard nothing of him since. No, I don't know where he came from nor where he went to. I had nothing against him while he was here. He was gone two days before the bust was smashed.'

'Well, that's all we could reasonably expect from Morse Hudson,' said Holmes, as we emerged from the shop. 'We have this Beppo as a common factor, both in Kennington and in Kensington, so that is worth a tenmile drive. Now, Watson, let us make for Gelder & Co., of Stepney, the source and origin of the busts. I shall be surprised if we don't get some help down there.'

In rapid succession we passed through the fringe of fashionable London, hotel London, theatrical London, literary London, commercial London, and, finally, maritime London, till we came to a riverside city of a hundred thousand souls, where the tenement houses swelter and reek with the outcasts of Europe. Here, in a broad thoroughfare, once the abode of wealthy City merchants, we found the sculpture works for which we searched. Outside was a considerable yard full of monumental masonry. Inside was a large room in which fifty workers were carving or moulding. The manager, a big blond German, received us civilly and gave a clear answer to all Holmes's questions. A reference to his books showed that hundreds of casts had been taken from a marble copy of Devine's head of Napoleon, but that the three which had been sent to Morse Hudson a year or so before had been half of a batch of six, the other three being sent to Harding Brothers, of Kensington. There was no reason why those six should be different from any of the other casts. He could suggest no possible cause why anyone should wish to destroy them—in fact, he laughed at the idea. Their wholesale price was six shillings, but the retailer would get twelve or more. The cast was taken in two moulds from each side of the face, and then these two profiles of plaster of Paris were joined together to make the complete bust. The work was usually done by Italians, in the room we were in. When finished, the busts were put on a table in the passage to dry, and afterwards stored. That was all he could tell us.

But the production of the photograph had a remarkable effect upon the manager. His face flushed with anger, and his brows knotted over his blue Teutonic eyes.

'Ah, the rascal!' he cried. 'Yes, indeed, I know him very well. This has always been a respectable establishment, and the only time that we have ever had the police in it was over this very fellow. It was more than a year ago now. He knifed another Italian in the street, and then he came to the works with the police on his heels, and he was taken here. Beppo was his name—his second name I never knew. Serve me right for engaging a man with such a face. But he was a good workman—one of the best.'

'What did he get?'

'The man lived and he got off with a year. I have no doubt he is out now, but he has not dared to show his nose here. We have a cousin of his here, and I daresay he could tell you where he is.'

'No, no,' cried Holmes, 'not a word to the cousin—not a word, I beg of you. The matter is very important, and the farther I go with it, the more important it seems to grow. When you referred in your ledger to the sale of those casts I observed that the date was June 3rd of last year. Could you give me the date when Beppo was arrested?'

'I could tell you roughly by the pay-list,' the manager

answered. 'Yes,' he continued, after some turning over of pages, 'he was paid last on May 20th.'

'Thank you,' said Holmes. 'I don't think that I need intrude upon your time and patience any more.' With a last word of caution that he should say nothing as to our researches, we turned our faces westwards once more.

The afternoon was far advanced before we were able to snatch a hasty luncheon at a restaurant. A news-bill at the entrance announced 'Kensington Outrage. Murder by a Madman', and the contents of the paper showed that Mr Horace Harker had got his account into print after all. Two columns were occupied with a highly sensational and flowery rendering of the whole incident. Holmes propped it against the cruet-stand and read it while he ate. Once or twice he chuckled.

'This is all right, Watson,' said he. 'Listen to this:

"It is satisfactory to know that there can be no difference of opinion upon this case, since Mr Lestrade, one of the most experienced members of the official force, and Mr Sherlock Holmes, the well-known consulting expert, have each come to the conclusion that the grotesque series of incidents, which have ended in so tragic a fashion, arise from lunacy rather than from deliberate crime. No explanation save mental aberration can cover the facts."

The Press, Watson, is a most valuable institution, if you only know how to use it. And now, if you have quite finished, we will hark back to Kensington and see what the manager of Harding Brothers has to say on the matter.'

The founder of that great emporium proved to be a

brisk, crisp little person, very dapper and quick, with a clear head and a ready tongue.

'Yes, sir, I have already read the account in the evening papers. Mr Horace Harker is a customer of ours. We supplied him with the bust some months ago. We ordered three busts of that sort from Gelder & Co., of Stepney. They are all sold now. To whom? Oh, I daresay by consulting our sales book we could very easily tell you. Yes, we have the entries here. One to Mr Harker you see, and one to Mr Josiah Brown, of Laburnum Lodge, Laburnum Vale, Chiswick, and one to Mr Sandeford, of Lower Grove Road, Reading. No, I have never seen this face which you show me in the photograph. You would hardly forget it, would you, sir, for I've seldom seen an uglier. Have we any Italians on the staff? Yes, sir, we have several among our workpeople and cleaners. I daresay they might get a peep at that sales book if they wanted to. There is no particular reason for keeping a watch upon that book. Well, well, it's a very strange business, and I hope that you will let me know if anything comes of your inquiries."

Holmes had taken several notes during Mr Harding's evidence, and I could see that he was thoroughly satisfied by the turn which affairs were taking. He made no remark, however, save that, unless we hurried, we should be late for our appointment with Lestrade. Sure enough, when we reached Baker Street the detective was already there, and we found him pacing up and down in a fever of impatience. His look of importance showed that his day's work had not been in vain.

'Well?' he asked. 'What luck, Mr Holmes?'

'We have had a very busy day, and not entirely a wasted one,' my friend explained. 'We have seen both the retailers and also the wholesale manufacturers. I can trace each of the busts now from the beginning.'

'The busts!' cried Lestrade. 'Well, well, you have your own methods, Mr Sherlock Holmes, and it is not for me to say a word against them, but I think I have done a better day's work than you. I have identified the dead man.'

'You don't say so?'

'And found a cause for the crime.'

'Splendid!'

'We have an inspector who makes a specialty of Saffron Hill and the Italian Quarter. Well, this dead man had some Catholic emblem round his neck, and that, along with his colour, made me think he was from the South. Inspector Hill knew him the moment he caught sight of him. His name is Pietro Venucci, from Naples, and he is one of the greatest cut-throats in London. He is connected with the Mafia, which, as you know, is a secret political society, enforcing its decrees by murder. Now, you see how the affair begins to clear up. The other fellow is probably an Italian also, and a member of the Mafia. He has broken the rules in some fashion. Pietro is set upon his track. Probably the photograph we found in his pocket is the man himself, so that he may not knife the wrong person. He dogs the fellow, he sees him enter a house, he waits outside for him, and in the scuffle he receives his own death-wound. How is that, Mr Sherlock Holmes?'

Holmes clapped his hands approvingly.

'Excellent, Lestrade, excellent!' he cried. 'But I didn't quite follow your explanation of the destruction of the busts.'

'The busts! You never can get those busts out of your head. After all, that is nothing; petty larceny, six months at the most. It is the murder that we are really investigating, and I tell you that I am gathering all the threads into my hands.'

'And the next stage?'

'Is a very simple one. I shall go down with Hill to the Italian Quarter, find the man whose photograph we have got, and arrest him on the charge of murder. Will you come with us?'

'I think not. I fancy we can attain our end in a simpler way. I can't say for certain, because it all depends—well, it all depends upon a factor which is completely outside our control. But I have great hopes—in fact, the betting is exactly two to one—that if you will come with us tonight I shall be able to help you to lay him by the heels.'

'In the Italian Quarter?'

'No, I fancy Chiswick is an address which is more likely to find him. If you will come with me to Chiswick tonight, Lestrade, I'll promise to go to the Italian Quarter with you tomorrow, and no harm will be done by the delay. And now I think that a few hours' sleep would do us all good, for I do not propose to leave before eleven o'clock, and it is unlikely that we shall be back before morning. You'll dine with us, Lestrade, and then you are welcome to the sofa until it is time for us to start. In the meantime, Watson, I should be glad if you would ring for an express messenger, for I have a letter to send and it is important that it should go at once.'

Holmes spent the evening in rummaging among the files of the old daily papers with which one of our lumber-rooms was packed. When at last he descended, it was with triumph in his eyes, but he said nothing to either of us as to the result of his researches. For my own part, I had followed step by step the methods by which he had traced the various windings of this complex case, and, though I could not yet perceive the goal which we would reach, I understood clearly that Holmes expected this grotesque criminal to make an attempt upon the two remaining busts, one of which, I remembered, was at Chiswick. No doubt the object of our journey was to catch him in the very act, and I could not but admire the cunning with which my friend had inserted a wrong clue in the evening paper, so as to give the fellow the idea that he could continue his scheme with impunity. I was not surprised when Holmes suggested that I should take my revolver with me. He had himself picked up the loaded hunting-crop, which was his favourite weapon.

A four-wheeler was at the door at eleven, and in it we drove to a spot at the other side of Hammersmith Bridge. Here the cabman was directed to wait. A short walk brought us to a secluded road fringed with pleasant houses, each standing in its own grounds. In the light of a street lamp we read 'Laburnum Villa' upon the gate-post of one of them. The occupants had evidently retired to rest, for all was dark save for a fanlight over the hall door, which shed a single blurred circle on to the garden path. The wooden fence which separated the grounds from the road threw a dense black shadow upon the inner side, and here it was that we crouched.

'I fear that you'll have a long wait,' Holmes whispered. 'We may thank our stars that it is not raining. I don't think we can even venture to smoke to pass the time. However, it's a two to one chance that we get something to pay us for our trouble.'

It proved, however, that our vigil was not to be so long as Holmes had led us to fear, and it ended in a very sudden and singular fashion. In an instant, without the least sound to warn us of his coming, the garden gate swung open, and a lithe, dark figure, as swift and active as an ape, rushed up the garden path. We saw it whisk past the light thrown from over the door and disappear against the black shadow of the house. There was a long pause, during which we held our breath, and then a very gentle creaking sound came to our ears. The window was being opened. The noise ceased, and again there was a long silence. The fellow was making his way into the house. We saw the sudden flash of a dark lantern inside the room. What he sought was evidently not there, for again we saw the flash through another blind, and then through another.

'Let us get to the open window. We will nab him as he climbs out,' Lestrade whispered.

But before we could move, the man had emerged again. As he came out into the glimmering patch of light, we saw that he carried something white under his arm. He looked stealthily all around him. The silence of the deserted street reassured him. Turning his back upon us he laid down his burden, and the next instant there was the sound of a sharp tap, followed by a clatter and rattle. The man was so intent upon what he was doing that he never heard our steps as we stole across the grass plot. With the bound of a tiger Holmes was on his back, and an instant later Lestrade and I had him by either wrist, and the handcuffs had been fastened. As we turned him over I saw a hideous, sallow face, with writhing, furious features, glaring up at us, and I knew that it was indeed the man of the photograph whom we had secured.

But it was not our prisoner to whom Holmes was giving his attention. Squatted on the doorstep, he was engaged in most carefully examining that which the man had brought from the house. It was a bust of Napoleon, like the one which we had seen that morning, and it had been broken into similar fragments. Carefully Holmes held each separate shard to the light, but in no way did it differ from any other shattered piece of plaster. He had just completed his examination when the hall lights flew up, the door opened, and the owner of the house, a jovial, rotund figure in shirt and trousers, presented himself.

'Mr Josiah Brown, I suppose?' said Holmes.

'Yes, sir; and you, no doubt, are Mr Sherlock Holmes? I had the note which you sent by the express messenger, and I did exactly what you told me. We locked every door on the inside and awaited developments. Well, I'm very glad to see that you have got the rascal. I hope, gentlemen, that you will come in and have some refreshment.'

However, Lestrade was anxious to get his man into safe quarters, so within a few minutes our cab had been summoned and we were all four upon our way to London. Not a word would our captive say, but he glared at us from the shadow of his matted hair, and once, when my hand seemed within his reach, he snapped at it like a hungry wolf. We stayed long enough at the police-station to learn that a search of his clothing revealed nothing save a few shillings and a long sheath knife, the handle of which bore copious traces of recent blood.

'That's all right,' said Lestrade, as we parted. "Hill knows all these gentry, and he will give a name to him. You'll find that my theory of the Mafia will work out all right. But I'm sure I am exceedingly obliged to you, Mr Holmes, for the workmanlike way in which you laid hands upon him. I don't quite understand it all yet.'

'I fear it is rather too late an hour for explanations,' said

Holmes. "Besides, there are one or two details which are not finished off, and it is one of these cases which are worth working out to the very end. If you will come round once more to my rooms at six o'clock tomorrow, I think I shall be able to show you that even now you have not grasped the entire meaning of this business, which presents some features which make it absolutely original in the history of crime. If ever I permit you to chronicle any more of my little problems, Watson, I foresee that you will enliven your pages by an account of the singular adventure of the Napoleonic busts.'

When we met again next evening, Lestrade was furnished with much information concerning our prisoner. His name, it appeared, was Beppo, second name unknown. He was a well-known ne'er-do-well among the Italian colony. He had once been a skilful sculptor and had earned an honest living, but he had taken to evil courses and had twice already been in jail—once for a petty theft, and once, as we had already heard, for stabbing a fellow-countryman. He could talk English perfectly well. His reasons for destroying the busts were still unknown, and he refused to answer any questions upon the subject, but the police had discovered that these same busts might very well have been made by his own hands, since he was engaged in this class of work at the establishment of Gelder & Co. To all this information, much of which we already knew, Holmes listened with polite attention, but I, who knew him so well, could clearly see that his thoughts were elsewhere, and I detected a mixture of mingled uneasiness and expectation beneath that mask which he was wont to assume. At last he started in his chair, and his eyes brightened. There had been a ring at the bell. A minute later we heard steps upon the stairs, and an elderly red-faced man with grizzled side-whiskers was ushered in. In his right hand he carried an old-fashioned carpet-bag, which he placed upon the table.

'Is Mr Sherlock Holmes here?'

My friend bowed and smiled. "Mr Sandeford, of Reading, I suppose?' said he.

'Yes, sir, I fear that I am a little late, but the trains were awkward. You wrote to me about a bust that is in my possession.'

'Exactly.'

"I have your letter here. You said, "I desire to possess a copy of Devine's Napoleon, and am prepared to pay you ten pounds for the one which is in your possession." Is that right?'

'Certainly.'

'I was very much surprised at your letter, for I could not imagine how you knew that I owned such a thing.'

'Of course you must have been surprised, but the explanation is very simple. Mr Harding, of Harding Brothers, said that they had sold you their last copy, and he gave me your address.'

'Oh, that was it, was it? Did he tell you what I paid for it?'

'No, he did not.'

'Well, I am an honest man, though not a very rich one. I only gave fifteen shillings for the bust, and I think you ought to know that before I take ten pounds from you.'

'I am sure the scruple does you honour, Mr Sandeford. But I have named that price, so I intend to stick to it.'

'Well, it is very handsome of you, Mr Holmes. I brought the bust up with me, as you asked me to do. Here it is!' He opened his bag, and at last we saw placed upon our table a complete specimen of that bust which we had already seen more than once in fragments.

Holmes took a paper from his pocket and laid a ten-pound note upon the table.

'You will kindly sign that paper, Mr Sandeford, in the presence of these witnesses. It is simply to say that you transfer every possible right that you ever had in the bust to me. I am a methodical man, you see, and you never know what turn events might take afterwards. Thank you, Mr Sandeford; here is your money, and I wish you a very good evening.'

When our visitor had disappeared, Sherlock Holmes's movements were such as to rivet our attention. He began by taking a clean white cloth from a drawer and laying it over the table. Then he placed his newly acquired bust in the centre of the cloth. Finally, he picked up his hunting-crop and struck Napoleon a sharp blow on the top of the head. The figure broke into fragments, and Holmes bent eagerly over the shattered remains. Next instant, with a loud shout of triumph he held up one splinter, in which a round, dark object was fixed like a plum in a pudding.

'Gentlemen,' he cried, 'let me introduce you to the famous black pearl of the Borgias.'

Lestrade and I sat silent for a moment, and then, with a spontaneous impulse, we both broke out clapping, as at the well-wrought crisis of a play. A flush of colour sprang to Holmes's pale cheeks, and he bowed to us like the master dramatist who receives the homage of his audience. It was at such moments that for an instant he ceased to be a reasoning machine, and betrayed his human love for admiration and applause. The same singularly proud and reserved nature which turned away with disdain from popular notoriety was capable of being moved to its depths by spontaneous wonder and praise from a friend.

'Yes, gentlemen,' said he, 'it is the most famous pearl now existing in the world, and it has been my good fortune, by a connected chain of inductive reasoning, to trace it from the Prince of Colonna's bedroom at the Dacre Hotel, where it was lost, to the interior of this, the last of the six busts of Napoleon which were manufactured by Gelder & Co., of Stepney. You will remember, Lestrade, the sensation caused by the disappearance of this valuable jewel, and the vain efforts of the London police to recover it. I was myself consulted upon the case, but I was unable to throw any light upon it. Suspicion fell upon the maid of the Princess, who was an Italian, and it was proved that she had a brother in London, but we failed to trace any connection between them. The maid's name was Lucretia Venucci, and there is no doubt in my mind that this Pietro who was murdered two nights ago was the brother. I have been looking up the dates in the old files of the paper, and I find that the disappearance of the pearl was exactly two days before the arrest of Beppo, for some crime of violence—an event which took place in the factory of Gelder & Co., at the very moment when these busts were being made. Now you clearly see the sequence of events, though you see them, of course, in the inverse order to the way in which they presented themselves to me. Beppo had the pearl in his possession. He may have stolen it from Pietro, he may have been Pietro's confederate, he may have been the go-between of Pietro and his sister. It is of no consequence to us which is the correct solution.

'The main fact is that he *had* the pearl, and at that

moment, when it was on his person, he was pursued by the police. He made for the factory in which he worked, and he knew that he had only a few minutes in which to conceal this enormously valuable prize, which would otherwise be found on him when he was searched. Six plaster casts of Napoleon were drying in the passage. One of them was still soft. In an instant Beppo, a skilful workman, made a small hole in the wet plaster, dropped in the pearl, and with a few touches covered over the aperture once more. It was an admirable hiding-place. No one could possibly find it. But Beppo was condemned to a year's imprisonment, and in the meanwhile his six busts were scattered over London. He could not tell which contained his treasure. Only by breaking them could he see. Even shaking would tell him nothing, for as the plaster was wet it was probable that the pearl would adhere to it—as, in fact, it had done. Beppo did not despair, and he conducted his search with considerable ingenuity and perseverance. Through a cousin who works with Gelder, he found out the retail firms who had bought the busts. He managed to find employment with Morse Hudson, and in that way tracked down three of them. The pearl was not there. Then, with the help of some Italian employé, he succeeded in finding out where the other three busts had gone. The first was at Harker's. There he was dogged by his confederate, who held Beppo responsible for the loss of the pearl, and he stabbed him in the scuffle which followed.'

'If he was his confederate, why should he carry his photograph?' I asked.

'As a means of tracing him, if he wished to inquire about him from any third person. That was the obvious reason. Well, after the murder I calculated that Beppo

119

would probably hurry rather than delay his movements. He would fear that the police would read his secret, and so he hastened on before they should get ahead of him. Of course, I could not say that he had not found the pearl in Harker's bust. I had not even concluded for certain that it was the pearl, but it was evident to me that he was looking for something, since he carried the bust past the other houses in order to break it in the garden which had a lamp overlooking it. Since Harker's bust was one in three, the chances were exactly as I told you—two to one against the pearl being inside it. There remained two busts, and it was obvious that he would go for the London one first. I warned the inmates of the house, so as to avoid a second tragedy, and we went down, with the happiest results. By that time, of course, I knew for certain that it was the Borgia pearl that we were after. The name of the murdered man linked the one event with the other. There only remained a single bust—the Reading one—and the pearl must be there. I bought it in your presence from the owner—and there it lies.'

We sat in silence for a moment.

'Well,' said Lestrade, 'I've seen you handle a good many cases, Mr Holmes, but I don't know that I ever knew a more workmanlike one than that. We're not jealous of you at Scotland Yard. No, sir, we are very proud of you, and if you come down tomorrow, there's not a man, from the oldest inspector to the youngest constable, who wouldn't be glad to shake you by the hand.'

'Thank you!' said Holmes. 'Thank you!' and as he turned away, it seemed to me that he was more nearly moved by the softer human emotions than I had ever seen him. A moment later he was the cold and practical thinker once more. 'Put the pearl in the safe, Watson,' said he, 'and get out the papers of the Conk-Singleton forgery case. Goodbye, Lestrade. If any little problem comes your way, I shall be happy, if I can, to give you a hint or two as to its solution.'

THE ADVENTURE OF
THE DANCING MEN

Holmes had been seated for some hours in silence with his long, thin back curved over a chemical vessel in which he was brewing a particularly malodorous product. His head was sunk upon his breast, and he looked from my point of view like a strange, lank bird, with dull grey plumage and a black top-knot.

'So, Watson,' said he, suddenly, 'you do not propose to invest in South African securities?'

I gave a start of astonishment. Accustomed as I was to Holmes's curious faculties, this sudden intrusion into my most intimate thoughts was utterly inexplicable.

'How on earth do you know that?' I asked.

He wheeled round upon his stool, with a steaming test-tube in his hand, and a gleam of amusement in his deep-set eyes.

'Now, Watson, confess yourself utterly taken aback,' said he.

'I am.'

'I ought to make you sign a paper to that effect.'

'Why?'

'Because in five minutes you will say that it is all so absurdly simple.'

'I am sure that I shall say nothing of the kind.'

'You see, my dear Watson'—he propped his test-tube

in the rack, and began to lecture with the air of a professor addressing his class—'it is not really difficult to construct a series of inferences, each dependent upon its predecessor and each simple in itself. If, after doing so, one simply knocks out all the central inferences and presents one's audience with the starting-point and the conclusion, one may produce a startling, though possibly a meretricious, effect. Now, it was not really difficult, by an inspection of the groove between your left forefinger and thumb, to feel sure that you did *not* propose to invest your small capital in the gold fields.'

'I see no connection.'

'Very likely not; but I can quickly show you a close connection. Here are the missing links of the very simple chain: 1. You had chalk between your left finger and thumb when you returned from the club last night. 2. You put chalk there when you play billiards, to steady the cue. 3. You never play billiards except with Thurston. 4. You told me, four weeks ago, that Thurston had an option on some South African property which would expire in a month, and which he desired you to share with him. 5. Your check book is locked in my drawer, and you have not asked for the key. 6. You do not propose to invest your money in this manner.'

'How absurdly simple!' I cried.

'Quite so!' said he, a little nettled. 'Every problem becomes very childish when once it is explained to you. Here is an unexplained one. See what you can make of that, friend Watson.' He tossed a sheet of paper upon the table, and turned once more to his chemical analysis.

I looked with amazement at the absurd hieroglyphics upon the paper.

'Why, Holmes, it is a child's drawing,' I cried.

'Oh, that's your idea!'

'What else should it be?'

'That is what Mr Hilton Cubitt, of Riding Thorpe Manor, Norfolk, is very anxious to know. This little conundrum came by the first post, and he was to follow by the next train. There's a ring at the bell, Watson. I should not be very much surprised if this were he.'

A heavy step was heard upon the stairs, and an instant later there entered a tall, ruddy, clean-shaven gentleman, whose clear eyes and florid cheeks told of a life led far from the fogs of Baker Street. He seemed to bring a whiff of his strong, fresh, bracing, east-coast air with him as he entered. Having shaken hands with each of us, he was about to sit down, when his eye rested upon the paper with the curious markings, which I had just examined and left upon the table.

'Well, Mr Holmes, what do you make of these?' he cried. 'They told me that you were fond of queer mysteries, and I don't think you can find a queerer one than that. I sent the paper on ahead, so that you might have time to study it before I came.'

'It is certainly rather a curious production,' said Holmes. 'At first sight it would appear to be some childish prank. It consists of a number of absurd little figures dancing across the paper upon which they are drawn. Why should you attribute any importance to so grotesque an object?'

'I never should, Mr Holmes. But my wife does. It is frightening her to death. She says nothing, but I can see terror in her eyes. That's why I want to sift the matter to the bottom.'

Holmes held up the paper so that the sunlight shone

full upon it. It was a page torn from a notebook. The markings were done in pencil, and ran in this way:

Holmes examined it for some time, and then, folding it carefully up, he placed it in his pocketbook.

'This promises to be a most interesting and unusual case,' said he. 'You gave me a few particulars in your letter, Mr Hilton Cubitt, but I should be very much obliged if you would kindly go over it all again for the benefit of my friend, Dr Watson.'

'I'm not much of a story-teller,' said our visitor, nervously clasping and unclasping his great, strong hands. 'You'll just ask me anything that I don't make clear. I'll begin at the time of my marriage last year, but I want to say first of all that, though I'm not a rich man, my people have been at Riding Thorpe for a matter of five centuries, and there is no better known family in the county of Norfolk. Last year I came up to London for the Jubilee, and I stopped at a boardinghouse in Russell Square, because Parker, the vicar of our parish, was staying in it. There was an American young lady there—Patrick was the name—Elsie Patrick. In some way we became friends, until before my month was up I was as much in love as man could be. We were quietly married at a registry office, and we returned to Norfolk a married couple. You'll think it very mad, Mr Holmes, that a man of a good old family should marry a wife in this fashion, knowing nothing of her past or of her people, but if you saw her and knew her, it would help you to understand.

'She was very straight about it, was Elsie. I can't say that she did not give me every chance of getting out of it if I wished to do so. 'I have had some very disagreeable associations in my life,' said she, 'I wish to forget all about them. I would rather never allude to the past, for it is very painful to me. If you take me, Hilton, you will take a woman who has nothing that she need be personally ashamed of; but you will have to be content with my word for it, and to allow me to be silent as to all that passed up to the time when I became yours. If these conditions are too hard, then go back to Norfolk, and leave me to the lonely life in which you found me.' It was only the day before our wedding that she said those very words to me. I told her that I was content to take her on her own terms, and I have been as good as my word.

'Well, we have been married now for a year, and very happy we have been. But about a month ago, at the end of June, I saw for the first time signs of trouble. One day my wife received a letter from America. I saw the American stamp. She turned deadly white, read the letter, and threw it into the fire. She made no allusion to it afterwards, and I made none, for a promise is a promise, but she has never known an easy hour from that moment. There is always a look of fear upon her face—a look as if she were waiting and expecting. She would do better to trust me. She would find that I was her best friend. But until she speaks, I can say nothing. Mind you, she is a truthful woman, Mr Holmes, and whatever trouble there may have been in her past life it has been no fault of hers. I am only a simple Norfolk squire, but there is not a man in England who ranks his family honour more highly than I do. She knows it well, and she knew it well before she married me. She would never bring any stain upon it—of that I am sure.

'Well, now I come to the queer part of my story. About a week ago—it was the Tuesday of last week—I found on one of the window-sills a number of absurd little dancing figures like these upon the paper. They were scrawled with chalk. I thought that it was the stable-boy who had drawn them, but the lad swore he knew nothing about it. Anyhow, they had come there during the night. I had them washed out, and I only mentioned the matter to my wife afterwards. To my surprise, she took it very seriously, and begged me if any more came to let her see them. None did come for a week, and then yesterday morning I found this paper lying on the sundial in the garden. I showed it to Elsie, and down she dropped in a dead faint. Since then she has looked like a woman in a dream, half dazed, and with terror always lurking in her eyes. It was then that I wrote and sent the paper to you, Mr Holmes. It was not a thing that I could take to the police, for they would have laughed at me, but you will tell me what to do. I am not a rich man, but if there is any danger threatening my little woman, I would spend my last copper to shield her."

He was a fine creature, this man of the old English soil – simple, straight, and gentle, with his great, earnest, blue eyes and broad, comely face. His love for his wife and his trust in her shone in his features. Holmes had listened to his story with the utmost attention, and now he sat for some time in silent thought.

'Don't you think, Mr Cubitt,' said he, at last, 'that your best plan would be to make a direct appeal to your wife, and to ask her to share her secret with you?'

Hilton Cubitt shook his massive head.

'A promise is a promise, Mr Holmes. If Elsie wished to tell me she would. If not, it is not for me to force her confidence. But I am justified in taking my own line—and I will.'

'Then I will help you with all my heart. In the first place, have you heard of any strangers being seen in your neighbourhood?'

'No.'

'I presume that it is a very quiet place. Any fresh face would cause comment?'

'In the immediate neighbourhood, yes. But we have several small watering-places not very far away. And the farmers take in lodgers.'

'These hieroglyphics have evidently a meaning. If it is a purely arbitrary one, it may be impossible for us to solve it. If, on the other hand, it is systematic, I have no doubt that we shall get to the bottom of it. But this particular sample is so short that I can do nothing, and the facts which you have brought me are so indefinite that we have no basis for an investigation. I would suggest that you return to Norfolk, that you keep a keen lookout, and that you take an exact copy of any fresh dancing men which may appear. It is a thousand pities that we have not a reproduction of those which were done in chalk upon the window-sill. Make a discreet inquiry also as to any strangers in the neighbourhood. When you have collected some fresh evidence, come to me again. That is the best advice which I can give you, Mr Hilton Cubitt. If there are any pressing fresh developments, I shall be always ready to run down and see you in your Norfolk home.'

The interview left Sherlock Holmes very thoughtful,

and several times in the next few days I saw him take his slip of paper from his notebook and look long and earnestly at the curious figures inscribed upon it. He made no allusion to the affair, however, until one afternoon a fortnight or so later. I was going out when he called me back.

'You had better stay here, Watson.'

'Why?'

'Because I had a wire from Hilton Cubitt this morning. You remember Hilton Cubitt, of the dancing men? He was to reach Liverpool Street at one-twenty. He may be here at any moment. I gather from this wire that there have been some new incidents of importance.'

We had not long to wait, for our Norfolk squire came straight from the station as fast as a hansom could bring him. He was looking worried and depressed, with tired eyes and a lined forehead.

'It's getting on my nerves, this business, Mr Holmes,' said he, as he sank, like a wearied man, into an armchair. 'It's bad enough to feel that you are surrounded by unseen, unknown folk, who have some kind of design upon you, but when, in addition to that, you know that it is just killing your wife by inches, then it becomes as much as flesh and blood can endure. She's wearing away under it—just wearing away before my eyes.'

'Has she said anything yet?'

'No, Mr Holmes, she has not. And yet there have been times when the poor girl has wanted to speak, and yet could not quite bring herself to take the plunge. I have tried to help her, but I daresay I did it clumsily, and scared her from it. She has spoken about my old family, and our reputation in the county, and our pride in our unsullied honour, and I always felt it was leading to the point, but somehow it turned off before we got there.'

'But you have found out something for yourself?'

'A good deal, Mr Holmes. I have several fresh dancing-men pictures for you to examine, and, what is more important, I have seen the fellow.'

'What, the man who draws them?'

'Yes, I saw him at his work. But I will tell you everything in order. When I got back after my visit to you, the very first thing I saw next morning was a fresh crop of dancing men. They had been drawn in chalk upon the black wooden door of the tool-house, which stands beside the lawn in full view of the front windows. I took an exact copy, and here it is.' He unfolded a paper and laid it upon the table. Here is a copy of the hieroglyphics:

'Excellent!' said Holmes. 'Excellent! Pray continue.'

'When I had taken the copy, I rubbed out the marks, but, two mornings later, a fresh inscription had appeared. I have a copy of it here':

Holmes rubbed his hands and chuckled with delight.

'Our material is rapidly accumulating,' said he.

'Three days later a message was left scrawled upon paper, and placed under a pebble on the sundial. Here it is. The characters are, as you see, exactly the same as the last one. After that I determined to lie in wait, so I got out my revolver and I sat up in my study, which overlooks the lawn and garden. About two in the morning I was seated by the window, all being dark save for the moonlight outside, when I heard steps behind me, and there was my wife in her dressing-gown. She implored me to come to bed. I told her frankly that I wished to see who it was who played such absurd tricks upon us. She answered that it was some senseless practical joke, and that I should not take any notice of it.

'"If it really annoys you, Hilton, we might go and travel, you and I, and so avoid this nuisance."

'"What, be driven out of our own house by a practical joker," said I. "Why, we should have the whole county laughing at us."

'"Well, come to bed," said she, "and we can discuss it in the morning."

'Suddenly, as she spoke, I saw her white face grow whiter yet in the moonlight, and her hand tightened upon my shoulder. Something was moving in the shadow of the tool-house. I saw a dark, creeping figure which crawled round the corner and squatted in front of the door. Seizing my pistol, I was rushing out, when my wife threw her arms round me and held me with convulsive strength. I tried to throw her off, but she clung to me most desperately. At last I got clear, but by the time I had opened the door and reached the house the creature was gone. He had left a trace of his presence, however, for there on the door was the very same arrangement of dancing men which had already twice appeared, and which I have copied on that paper. There was no other sign of the fellow anywhere, though I ran all the time, for when I examined the door again in the morning, he had scrawled some more of his pictures under the line which I had already seen.'

'Have you that fresh drawing?'

'Yes, it is very short, but I made a copy of it, and here it is.'

Again he produced a paper. The new dance was in this form:

𝕏🏃🏃𝕏

'Tell me,' said Holmes—and I could see by his eyes that he was much excited—'was this a mere addition to the first or did it appear to be entirely separate?'

'It was on a different panel of the door.'

'Excellent! This is far the most important of all for our purpose. It fills me with hopes. Now, Mr Hilton Cubitt, please continue your most interesting statement.'

'I have nothing more to say, Mr Holmes, except that I was angry with my wife that night for having held me back when I might have caught the skulking rascal. She said that she feared that I might come to harm. For an instant it had crossed my mind that perhaps what she really feared was that *he* might come to harm, for I could not doubt that she knew who this man was, and what he meant by these strange signals. But there is a tone in my wife's voice, Mr Holmes, and a look in her eyes which forbid doubt, and I am sure that it was indeed my own safety that was in her mind. There's the whole case, and now I want your advice as to what I ought to do. My own inclination is to put half a dozen of my farm lads in the shrubbery, and when this fellow comes again to give him such a hiding that he will leave us in peace for the future.'

'I fear it is too deep a case for such simple remedies,' said Holmes. 'How long can you stay in London?'

'I must go back today. I would not leave my wife alone all night for anything. She is very nervous, and begged me to come back.'

'I daresay you are right. But if you could have stopped, I might possibly have been able to return with you in a day or two. Meanwhile you will leave me these papers, and I think that it is very likely that I shall be able to pay you a visit shortly and to throw some light upon your case.'

Sherlock Holmes preserved his calm professional manner until our visitor had left us, although it was easy for me, who knew him so well, to see that he was profoundly excited. The moment that Hilton Cubitt's broad back had disappeared through the door my comrade rushed to the table, laid out all the slips of paper containing dancing men in front of him, and threw himself into an intricate and elaborate calculation. For two hours I watched him as he covered sheet after sheet of paper with figures and letters, so completely absorbed in his task that he had evidently forgotten my presence. Sometimes he was making progress and whistled and sang at his work; sometimes he was puzzled, and would sit for long spells with a furrowed brow and a vacant eye. Finally he sprang from his chair with a cry of satisfaction, and walked up and down the room rubbing his hands together. Then he wrote a long telegram upon a cable form. 'If my answer to this is as I hope, you will have a very pretty case to add to your collection, Watson,' said he. 'I expect that we shall be able to go down to Norfolk tomorrow, and to take our friend some very definite news as to the secret of his annoyance.'

I confess that I was filled with curiosity, but I was aware that Holmes liked to make his disclosures at his own time and in his own way, so I waited until it should suit him to take me into his confidence.

But there was a delay in that answering telegram, and two days of impatience followed, during which Holmes pricked up his ears at every ring of the bell. On the evening of the second there came a letter from Hilton Cubitt. All was quiet with him, save that a long inscription had appeared that morning upon the pedestal of the sundial. He enclosed a copy of it, which is here reproduced:

Holmes bent over this grotesque frieze for some minutes, and then suddenly sprang to his feet with an exclamation of surprise and dismay. His face was haggard with anxiety.

'We have let this affair go far enough,' said he. 'Is there a train to North Walsham tonight?'

I turned up the timetable. The last had just gone.

'Then we shall breakfast early and take the very first in the morning,' said Holmes. 'Our presence is most urgently needed. Ah! here is our expected cablegram. One moment, Mrs Hudson, there may be an answer. No, that is quite as I expected. This message makes it even more essential that we should not lose an hour in letting Hilton Cubitt know how matters stand, for it is a singular and a dangerous web in which our simple Norfolk squire is entangled.'

So, indeed, it proved, and as I come to the dark conclusion of a story which had seemed to me to be only childish and bizarre, I experience once again the dismay and horror with which I was filled. Would that I had some brighter ending to communicate to my readers, but these are the chronicles of fact, and I must follow to their dark crisis the strange chain of events which for some days made Riding Thorpe Manor a household word through the length and breadth of England.

We had hardly alighted at North Walsham, and mentioned the name of our destination, when the stationmaster hurried towards us. 'I suppose that you are the detectives from London?' said he.

A look of annoyance passed over Holmes's face.

'What makes you think such a thing?'

'Because Inspector Martin from Norwich has just passed through. But maybe you are the surgeons. She's not dead—or wasn't by last accounts. You may be in time to save her yet—though it be for the gallows.'

Holmes's brow was dark with anxiety.

'We are going to Riding Thorpe Manor,' said he, 'but we have heard nothing of what has passed there.'

'It's a terrible business,' said the stationmaster. 'They are shot, both Mr Hilton Cubitt and his wife. She shot him and then herself—so the servants say. He's dead and her life is despaired of. Dear, dear, one of the oldest families in the county of Norfolk, and one of the most honoured.'

Without a word Holmes hurried to a carriage, and during the long seven miles' drive he never opened his mouth. Seldom have I seen him so utterly despondent. He had been uneasy during all our journey from town, and I had observed that he had turned over the morning papers with anxious attention, but now this sudden realization of his worst fears left him in a blank melancholy. He leaned

135

back in his seat, lost in gloomy speculation. Yet there was much around to interest us, for we were passing through as singular a countryside as any in England, where a few scattered cottages represented the population of today, while on every hand enormous square-towered churches bristled up from the flat green landscape and told of the glory and prosperity of old East Anglia. At last the violet rim of the German Ocean appeared over the green edge of the Norfolk coast, and the driver pointed with his whip to two old brick and timber gables which projected from a grove of trees. 'That's Riding Thorpe Manor,' said he.

As we drove up to the porticoed front door, I observed in front of it, beside the tennis lawn, the black toolhouse and the pedestalled sundial with which we had such strange associations. A dapper little man, with a quick, alert manner and a waxed moustache, had just descended from a high dog-cart. He introduced himself as Inspector Martin, of the Norfolk Constabulary, and he was considerably astonished when he heard the name of my companion.

'Why, Mr Holmes, the crime was only committed at three this morning. How could you hear of it in London and get to the spot as soon as I?'

'I anticipated it. I came in the hope of preventing it.'

'Then you must have important evidence, of which we are ignorant, for they were said to be a most united couple.'

'I have only the evidence of the dancing men,' said Holmes. 'I will explain the matter to you later. Meanwhile, since it is too late to prevent this tragedy, I am very anxious that I should use the knowledge which I possess in order to ensure that justice be done. Will you associate me in your investigation, or will you prefer that I should act independently?'

'I should be proud to feel that we were acting together, Mr Holmes,' said the inspector, earnestly.

'In that case I should be glad to hear the evidence and to examine the premises without an instant of unnecessary delay.'

Inspector Martin had the good sense to allow my friend to do things in his own fashion, and contented himself with carefully noting the results. The local surgeon, an old, white-haired man, had just come down from Mrs Hilton Cubitt's room, and he reported that her injuries were serious, but not necessarily fatal. The bullet had passed through the front of her brain, and it would probably be some time before she could regain consciousness. On the question of whether she had been shot or had shot herself, he would not venture to express any decided opinion. Certainly the bullet had been discharged at very close quarters. There was only the one pistol found in the room, two barrels of which had been emptied. Mr Hilton Cubitt had been shot through the heart. It was equally conceivable that he had shot her and then himself, or that she had been the criminal, for the revolver lay upon the floor midway between them.

'Has he been moved?' asked Holmes.

'We have moved nothing except the lady. We could not leave her lying wounded upon the floor.'

'How long have you been here, Doctor?'

'Since four o'clock.'

'Anyone else?'

'Yes, the constable here.'

'And you have touched nothing?'

'Nothing.'

'You have acted with great discretion. Who sent for you?'

'The housemaid, Saunders.'

'Was it she who gave the alarm?'

'She and Mrs King, the cook.'

'Where are they now?'

'In the kitchen, I believe.'

'Then I think we had better hear their story at once.'

The old hall, oak-panelled and high-windowed, had been turned into a court of investigation. Holmes sat in a great, old-fashioned chair, his inexorable eyes gleaming out of his haggard face. I could read in them a set purpose to devote his life to this quest until the client whom he had failed to save should at last be avenged. The trim Inspector Martin, the old, grey-headed country doctor, myself, and a stolid village policeman made up the rest of that strange company.

The two women told their story clearly enough. They had been aroused from their sleep by the sound of an explosion, which had been followed a minute later by a second one. They slept in adjoining rooms, and Mrs King had rushed in to Saunders. Together they had descended the stairs. The door of the study was open, and a candle was burning upon the table. Their master lay upon his face in the centre of the room. He was quite dead. Near the window his wife was crouching, her head leaning against the wall. She was horribly wounded, and the side of her face was red with blood. She breathed heavily, but was incapable of saying anything. The passage, as well as the room, was full of smoke and the smell of powder. The window was certainly shut and fastened upon the inside. Both women were positive upon the point. They had at once sent for the doctor and for the constable. Then, with the aid of the groom and the stable-boy, they had conveyed their injured mistress to her room. Both she and her husband had occupied the bed. She was clad in her dress—he in his dressing-gown, over his night-clothes. Nothing had been moved in the study. So far as they knew, there had never been any quarrel between husband and wife. They had always looked upon them as a very united couple.

These were the main points of the servants' evidence. In answer to Inspector Martin, they were clear that every door was fastened upon the inside, and that no one could have escaped from the house. In answer to Holmes, they both remembered that they were conscious of the smell of powder from the moment that they ran out of their rooms upon the top floor. 'I commend that fact very carefully to your attention,' said Holmes to his professional colleague. 'And now I think that we are in a position to undertake a thorough examination of the room.'

The study proved to be a small chamber, lined on three sides with books, and with a writing-table facing an ordinary window, which looked out upon the garden. Our first attention was given to the body of the unfortunate squire, whose huge frame lay stretched across the room. His disordered dress showed that he had been hastily aroused from sleep. The bullet had been fired at him from the front, and had remained in his body, after penetrating the heart. His death had certainly been instantaneous and painless. There was no powder-marking either upon his dressing-gown or on his hands. According to the country surgeon, the lady had stains upon her face, but none upon her hand.

'The absence of the latter means nothing, though its presence may mean everything,' said Holmes. 'Unless the powder from a badly fitting cartridge happens to spurt backward, one may fire many shots without leaving a sign. I would suggest that Mr Cubitt's body may now be removed. I suppose, Doctor, you have not recovered the bullet which wounded the lady?'

'A serious operation will be necessary before that can be done. But there are still four cartridges in the revolver. Two have been fired and two wounds inflicted, so that each bullet can be accounted for.'

'So it would seem,' said Holmes. 'Perhaps you can account also for the bullet which has so obviously struck the edge of the window?'

He had turned suddenly, and his long, thin finger was pointing to a hole which had been drilled right through the lower window-sash, about an inch above the bottom.

'By George!' cried the inspector. 'How ever did you see that?'

'Because I looked for it.'

'Wonderful!' said the country doctor. 'You are certainly right, sir. Then a third shot has been fired, and therefore a third person must have been present. But who could that have been, and how could he have got away?'

'That is the problem which we are now about to solve,' said Sherlock Holmes. 'You remember, Inspector Martin, when the servants said that on leaving their room they were at once conscious of a smell of powder, I remarked that the point was an extremely important one?'

'Yes, sir; but I confess I did not quite follow you.'

'It suggested that at the time of the firing, the window as well as the door of the room had been open. Otherwise the fumes of powder could not have been blown so rapidly through the house. A draught in the room was necessary for that. Both door and window were only open for a very short time, however.'

'How do you prove that?'

'Because the candle was not guttered.'

'Capital!' cried the inspector. 'Capital!'

'Feeling sure that the window had been open at the time of the tragedy, I conceived that there might have been a third person in the affair, who stood outside this opening and fired through it. Any shot directed at this person might hit the sash. I looked, and there, sure enough, was the bullet mark!'

'But how came the window to be shut and fastened?'

'The woman's first instinct would be to shut and fasten the window. But, hallo! what is this?'

It was a lady's handbag which stood upon the study table—a trim little handbag of crocodile-skin and silver. Holmes opened it and turned the contents out. There were twenty fifty-pound notes of the Bank of England, held together by an india-rubber band—nothing else.

'This must be preserved, for it will figure in the trial,' said Holmes, as he handed the bag with its contents to the inspector. 'It is now necessary that we should try to throw some light upon this third bullet, which has clearly, from the splintering of the wood, been fired from inside the room. I should like to see Mrs King, the cook, again. You said, Mrs King, that you were awakened by a *loud* explosion. When you said that, did you mean that it seemed to you to be louder than the second one?'

'Well, sir, it wakened me from my sleep, so it is hard to judge. But it did seem very loud.'

'You don't think that it might have been two shots fired almost at the same instant?'

'I am sure I couldn't say, sir.'

141

'I believe that it was undoubtedly so. I rather think, Inspector Martin, that we have now exhausted all that this room can teach us. If you will kindly step round with me, we shall see what fresh evidence the garden has to offer.'

A flower-bed extended up to the study window, and we all broke into an exclamation as we approached it. The flowers were trampled down, and the soft soil was imprinted all over with footmarks. Large, masculine feet they were, with peculiarly long, sharp toes. Holmes hunted about among the grass and leaves like a retriever after a wounded bird. Then, with a cry of satisfaction, he bent forward and picked up a little brazen cylinder.

'I thought so,' said he; 'the revolver had an ejector, and here is the third cartridge. I really think, Inspector Martin, that our case is almost complete.'

The country inspector's face had shown his intense amazement at the rapid and masterful progress of Holmes's investigation. At first he had shown some disposition to assert his own position, but now he was overcome with admiration, and ready to follow without question wherever Holmes led.

'Whom do you suspect?' he asked.

'I'll go into that later. There are several points in this problem which I have not been able to explain to you yet. Now that I have got so far, I had best proceed on my own lines, and then clear the whole matter up once and for all.'

'Just as you wish, Mr Holmes, so long as we get our man.'

'I have no desire to make mysteries, but it is impossible at the moment of action to enter into long and complex explanations. I have the threads of this affair all in my

142

hand. Even if this lady should never recover consciousness, we can still reconstruct the events of last night, and ensure that justice be done. First of all, I wish to know whether there is any inn in this neighbourhood known as "Elrige's"?'

The servants were cross-questioned, but none of them had heard of such a place. The stable-boy threw a light upon the matter by remembering that a farmer of that name lived some miles off, in the direction of East Ruston.

'Is it a lonely farm?'

'Very lonely, sir.'

'Perhaps they have not heard yet of all that happened here during the night?'

'Maybe not, sir.'

Holmes thought for a little, and then a curious smile played over his face.

'Saddle a horse, my lad,' said he. 'I shall wish you to take a note to Elrige's Farm.'

He took from his pocket the various slips of the dancing men. With these in front of him, he worked for some time at the study-table. Finally he handed a note to the boy, with directions to put it into the hands of the person to whom it was addressed, and especially to answer no questions of any sort which might be put to him. I saw the outside of the note, addressed in straggling, irregular characters, very unlike Holmes's usual precise hand. It was consigned to Mr Abe Slaney, Elrige's Farm, East Ruston, Norfolk.

'I think, Inspector,' Holmes remarked, 'that you would do well to telegraph for an escort, as, if my calculations prove to be correct, you may have a particularly dangerous prisoner to convey to the county jail. The boy who takes this note could no doubt forward your telegram. If there is an afternoon train to town, Watson, I think we should do well to take it, as I have a chemical analysis of some interest to finish, and this investigation draws rapidly to a close.'

When the youth had been dispatched with the note, Sherlock Holmes gave his instructions to the servants. If any visitor were to call asking for Mrs Hilton Cubitt, no information should be given as to her condition, but he was to be shown at once into the drawing-room. He impressed these points upon them with the utmost earnestness. Finally he led the way into the drawing-room, with the remark that the business was now out of our hands, and that we must while away the time as best we might until we could see what was in store for us. The doctor had departed to his patients, and only the inspector and myself remained.

'I think that I can help you to pass an hour in an interesting and profitable manner,' said Holmes, drawing his chair up to the table, and spreading out in front of him the various papers upon which were recorded the antics of the dancing men. 'As to you, friend Watson, I owe you every atonement for having allowed your natural curiosity to remain so long unsatisfied. To you, Inspector, the whole incident may appeal as a remarkable professional study. I must tell you, first of all, the interesting circumstances connected with the previous consultations which Mr Hilton Cubitt has had with me in Baker Street.' He then shortly recapitulated the facts which have already been recorded. 'I have here in front of me these singular productions, at which one might smile, had they not proved themselves to be the forerunners of so terrible a tragedy. I am fairly familiar with all forms of secret writings, and am myself the author of a trifling monograph upon the subject, in which I analyse one hundred and sixty separate ciphers, but I confess that this is entirely new to me. The object of those who invented the system has apparently been to conceal that these characters convey a message, and to give the idea that they are the mere random sketches of children.

'Having once recognized, however, that the symbols stood for letters, and having applied the rules which guide us in all forms of secret writings, the solution was easy enough. The first message submitted to me was so short that it was impossible for me to do more than to say, with some confidence, that the symbol ⚹ stood for E. As you are aware, E is the most common letter in the English alphabet, and it predominates to so marked an extent that even in a short sentence one would expect to find it most often. Out of fifteen symbols in the first message, four were the same, so it was reasonable to set this down as E. It is true that in some cases the figure was bearing a flag, and in some cases not, but it was probable, from the way in which the flags were distributed, that they were used to break the sentence up into words. I accepted this as a hypothesis, and noted that E was represented by ⚹

'But now came the real difficulty of the inquiry. The order of the English letters after E is by no means well marked, and any preponderance which may be shown in an average of a printed sheet may be reversed in a single short.sentence. Speaking roughly, T, A, O, I, N, S, H, R, D, and L are the numerical order in which letters occur; but T, A, O, and I are very nearly abreast of each other,

145

and it would be an endless task to try each combination until a meaning was arrived at. I therefore waited for fresh material. In my second interview with Mr Hilton Cubitt he was able to give me two other short sentences and one message, which appeared—since there was no flag—to be a single word. Here are the symbols. Now, in the single word I have already got the two E's coming second and fourth in a word of five letters. It might be 'sever', or 'lever', or 'never'. There can be no question that the latter as a reply to an appeal is far the most probable, and the circumstances pointed to its being a reply written by the lady. Accepting it as correct, we are now able to say that the symbols 〵〵 stand respectively for N, V, and R.

'Even now I was in considerable difficulty, but a happy thought put me in possession of several other letters. It occurred to me that if these appeals came, as I expected, from someone who had been intimate with the lady in her early life, a combination which contained two E's with three letters between might very well stand for the name 'ELSIE'. On examination I found that such a combination formed the termination of the message which was three times repeated. It was certainly some appeal to 'Elsie'. In this way I had got my L, S, and I. But what appeal could it be? There were only four letters in the word which preceded 'Elsie', and it ended in E. Surely the word must be 'COME'. I tried all other four letters ending in E, but could find none to fit the case. So now I was in possession of C, O, and M and I was in a position to attack the first message once more, dividing it into words and putting dots for each symbol which was still unknown. So treated, it worked out in this fashion:

. M . ERE .. E SL . NE.

'Now the first letter *can* only be A, which is a most useful discovery, since it occurs no fewer than three times in this short sentence, and the H is also apparent in the second word. Now it becomes:

AM HERE A . E SLANE.

Or, filling in the obvious vacancies in the name:

AM HERE ABE SLANEY.

I had so many letters now that I could proceed with considerable confidence to the second message, which worked out in this fashion:

A . ELRI . ES.

Here I could only make sense by putting T and G for the missing letters, and supposing that the name was that of some house or inn at which the writer was staying.'

Inspector Martin and I had listened with the utmost interest to the full and clear account of how my friend had produced results which had led to so complete a command over our difficulties.

'What did you do then, sir?' asked the inspector.

'I had every reason to suppose that this Abe Slaney was an American, since Abe is an American contraction, and since a letter from America had been the starting-point of all the trouble. I had also every cause to think that there was some criminal secret in the matter. The lady's allusions to her past, and her refusal to take her husband into her confidence, both pointed in that direction. I therefore cabled to my friend, Wilson Hargreave, of the New York Police Bureau, who has more than once made use of my knowledge of London crime. I asked him whether the name of Abe Slaney was known to him. Here is his reply: 'The most dangerous crook in Chicago'. On the very evening upon which I had his answer, Hilton Cubitt sent me the last message from Slaney. Working with known letters, it took this form:

ELSIE . RE . ARE TO MEET THY GO.

The addition of a P and a D completed a message which showed me that the rascal was proceeding from persuasion to threats, and my knowledge of the crooks of Chicago prepared me to find that he might very rapidly put his words into action. I at once came to Norfolk with my friend and colleague, Dr Watson, but, unhappily, only in time to find that the worst had already occurred.'

'It is a privilege to be associated with you in the handling of a case,' said the inspector, warmly. 'You will excuse me, however, if I speak frankly to you. You are only answerable to yourself, but I have to answer to my superiors. If this Abe Slaney, living at Elrige's, is indeed the murderer, and if he has made his escape while I am seated here, I should certainly get into serious trouble.'

'You need not be uneasy. He will not try to escape.'

'How do you know?'

'To fly would be a confession of guilt.'

'Then let us go to arrest him.'

'I expect him here every instant.'

'But why should he come?'

'Because I have written and asked him.'

148

'But this is incredible, Mr Holmes! Why should he come because you have asked him? Would not such a request rather rouse his suspicions and cause him to fly?'

'I think I have known how to frame the letter,' said Sherlock Holmes. 'In fact, if I am not very much mistaken, here is the gentleman himself coming up the drive.'

A man was striding up the path which led to the door. He was a tall, handsome, swarthy fellow, clad in a suit of grey flannel, with a Panama hat, a bristling black beard, and a great, aggressive hooked nose, and flourishing a cane as he walked. He swaggered up the path as if the place belonged to him, and we heard his loud, confident peal at the bell.

'I think, gentlemen,' said Holmes, quietly, 'that we had best take up our position behind the door. Every precaution is necessary when dealing with such a fellow. You will need your handcuffs, Inspector. You can leave the talking to me.'

We waited in silence for a minute—one of those minutes which one can never forget. Then the door opened and the man stepped in. In an instant Holmes clapped a pistol to his head, and Martin slipped the handcuffs over his wrists. It was all done so swiftly and deftly that the fellow was helpless before he knew that he was attacked. He glared from one to the other of us with a pair of blazing black eyes. Then he burst into a bitter laugh.

'Well, gentlemen, you have the drop on me this time. I seem to have knocked up against something hard. But I came here in answer to a letter from Mrs Hilton Cubitt. Don't tell me that she is in this? Don't tell me that she helped to set a trap for me?'

'Mrs Hilton Cubitt was seriously injured, and is at death's door.'

The man gave a hoarse cry of grief, which rang through the house.

'You're crazy!' he cried, fiercely. 'It was he that was hurt, not she. Who would have hurt little Elsie? I may have threatened her—God forgive me!—but I would not have touched a hair of her pretty head. Take it back—you! Say that she is not hurt!'

'She was found, badly wounded, by the side of her dead husband.'

He sank with a deep groan on to the settee, and buried his face in his manacled hands. For five minutes he was silent. Then he raised his face once more, and spoke with the cold composure of despair.

'I have nothing to hide from you, gentlemen,' said he. 'If I shot the man he had his shot at me, and there's no murder in that. But if you think I could have hurt that woman, then you don't know either me or her. I tell you, there was never a man in this world loved a woman more than I loved her. I had a right to her. She was pledged to me years ago. Who was this Englishman that he should come between us? I tell you that I had the first right to her, and that I was only claiming my own.'

'She broke away from your influence when she found the man that you are,' said Holmes sternly. 'She fled from America to avoid you, and she married an honourable gentleman in England. You dogged her and followed her and made her life a misery to her, in order to induce her to abandon the husband whom she loved and respected in order to fly with you, whom she feared and hated. You have ended by bringing about the death of a noble man and driving his wife to suicide. That is your record in this business, Mr Abe Slaney, and you will answer for it to the law.'

150

'If Elsie dies, I care nothing what becomes of me,' said the American. He opened one of his hands, and looked at a note crumpled up in his palm. 'See here, mister,' he cried, with a gleam of suspicion in his eyes, 'you're not trying to scare me over this, are you? If the lady is hurt as bad as you say, who was it that wrote this note?' He tossed it forward on to the table.

'I wrote it, to bring you here.'

'You wrote it? There was no one on earth outside the Joint who knew the secret of the dancing men. How came you to write it?'

'What one man can invent another can discover,' said Holmes. 'There is a cab coming to convey you to Norwich, Mr Slaney. But, meanwhile, you have time to make some small reparation for the injury you have wrought. Are you aware that Mrs Hilton Cubitt has herself lain under grave suspicion of the murder of her husband, and that it was only my presence here, and the knowledge which I happened to possess, which has saved her from the accusation? The least that you owe her is to make it clear to the whole world that she was in no way, directly or indirectly, responsible for his tragic end.'

'I ask nothing better,' said the American. 'I guess the very best case I can make for myself is the absolute naked truth.'

'It is my duty to warn you that it will be used against you,' cried the inspector, with the magnificent fair play of the British criminal law.

Slaney shrugged his shoulders.

'I'll chance that,' said he. 'First of all, I want you gentlemen to understand that I have known this lady since she was a child. There were seven of us in a gang in Chicago, and Elsie's father was the boss of the Joint. He was a clever man, was old Patrick. It was he who invented that writing, which would pass as a child's scrawl unless you just happened to have the key to it. Well, Elsie learned some of our ways, but she couldn't stand the business, and she had a bit of honest money of her own, so she gave us all the slip and got away to London. She had been engaged to me, and she would have married me, I believe, if I had taken over another profession, but she would have nothing to do with anything on the cross. It was only after her marriage to this Englishman that I was able to find out where she was. I wrote to her, but got no answer. After that I came over, and, as letters were no use, I put my messages where she could read them.

'Well, I have been here a month now. I lived in that farm, where I had a room down below, and could get in and out every night, and no one the wiser. I tried all I could to coax Elsie away. I knew that she read the messages, for once she wrote an answer under one of them. Then my temper got the better of me, and I began to threaten her. She sent me a letter then, imploring me to go away, and saying that it would break her heart if any scandal should come upon her husband. She said that she would come down when her husband was asleep at three in the morning, and speak with me through the end window, if I would go away afterwards and leave her in peace. She came down and brought money with her, trying to bribe me to go. This made me mad, and I caught her arm and tried to pull her through the window. At that moment in rushed the husband with his revolver in his hand. Elsie had sunk down upon the floor, and we were face to face. I was heeled also, and I held up my gun to scare him off and let me get away. He fired and missed me. I pulled off almost at the same instant, and down he

152

dropped. I made away across the garden, and as I went I heard the window shut behind me. That's God's truth, gentlemen, every word of it; and I heard no more about it until that lad came riding up with a note which made me walk in here, like a jay, and give myself into your hands.'

A cab had driven up whilst the American had been talking. Two uniformed policemen sat inside. Inspector Martin rose and touched his prisoner on the shoulder.

'It is time for us to go.'

'Can I see her first?'

'No, she is not conscious. Mr Sherlock Holmes, I only hope that, if ever again I have an important case, I shall have the good fortune to have you by my side.'

We stood at the window and watched the cab drive away. As I turned back, my eye caught the pellet of paper which the prisoner had tossed upon the table. It was the note with which Holmes had decoyed him.

'See if you can read it, Watson,' said he, with a smile.

It contained no word, but this little line of dancing men:

'If you use the code which I have explained,' said Holmes, 'you will find that it simply means "Come here at once." I was convinced that it was an invitation which he would not refuse, since he could never imagine that it could come from anyone but the lady. And so, my dear Watson, we have ended by turning the dancing men to good when they have so often been the agents of evil, and I think that I have fulfilled my promise of giving you something unusual for your notebook. Three-forty is our train, and I fancy we should be back in Baker Street for dinner.'

Only one word of epilogue. The American, Abe Slaney, was condemned to death at the winter assizes at Norwich, but his penalty was changed to penal servitude in consideration of mitigating circumstances, and the certainty that Hilton Cubitt had fired the first shot. Of Mrs Hilton Cubitt I only know that I have heard she recovered entirely, and that she still remains a widow, devoting her whole life to the care of the poor and to the administration of her husband's estate.

THE REIGATE PUZZLE

It was some time before the health of my friend Mr
Sherlock Holmes recovered from the strain caused by
his immense exertions in the spring of '87. The whole
question of the Netherland-Sumatra Company and of the
colossal schemes of Baron Maupertuis are too recent in
the minds of the public, and are too intimately concerned
with politics and finance to be fitting subjects for this
series of sketches. They led, however, in an indirect
fashion to a singular and complex problem which gave
my friend an opportunity of demonstrating the value of
a fresh weapon among the many with which he waged
his lifelong battle against crime.

On referring to my notes I see that it was upon the
fourteenth of April that I received a telegram from
Lyons which informed me that Holmes was lying ill
in the Hotel Dulong. Within twenty-four hours I was
in his sick-room and was relieved to find that there
was nothing formidable in his symptoms. Even his
iron constitution, however, had broken down under the
strain of an investigation which had extended over two
months, during which period he had never worked less
than fifteen hours a day and had more than once, as he
assured me, kept to his task for five days at a stretch.
Even the triumphant issue of his labours could not save
him from reaction after so terrible an exertion, and at a

time when Europe was ringing with his name and when his room was literally ankle-deep with congratulatory telegrams I found him a prey to the blackest depression. Even the knowledge that he had succeeded where the police of three countries had failed, and that he had outmanoeuvred at every point the most accomplished swindler in Europe, was insufficient to rouse him from his nervous prostration.

Three days later we were back in Baker Street together; but it was evident that my friend would be much the better for a change, and the thought of a week of springtime in the country was full of attractions to me also. My old friend, Colonel Hayter, who had come under my professional care in Afghanistan, had now taken a house near Reigate in Surrey and had frequently asked me to come down to him upon a visit. On the last occasion he had remarked that if my friend would only come with me he would be glad to extend his hospitality to him also. A little diplomacy was needed, but when Holmes understood that the establishment was a bachelor one, and that he would be allowed the fullest freedom, he fell in with my plans and a week after our return from Lyons we were under the colonel's roof. Hayter was a fine old soldier who had seen much of the world, and he soon found, as I had expected, that Holmes and he had much in common.

On the evening of our arrival we were sitting in the colonel's gun-room after dinner, Holmes stretched upon the sofa, while Hayter and I looked over his little armory of Eastern weapons.

'By the way,' said he suddenly, 'I think I'll take one of these pistols upstairs with me in case we have an alarm.'

'An alarm!' said I.

'Yes, we've had a scare in this part lately. Old Acton, who is one of our county magnates, had his house broken into last Monday. No great damage done, but the fellows are still at large.'

'No clue?' asked Holmes, cocking his eye at the colonel.

'None as yet. But the affair is a petty one, one of our little country crimes, which must seem too small for your attention, Mr Holmes, after this great international affair.'

Holmes waved away the compliment, though his smile showed that it had pleased him.

'Was there any feature of interest?'

'I fancy not. The thieves ransacked the library and got very little for their pains. The whole place was turned upside down, drawers burst open, and presses ransacked, with the result that an odd volume of Pope's *Homer*, two plated candlesticks, an ivory letter-weight, a small oak barometer, and a ball of twine are all that have vanished.'

'What an extraordinary assortment!' I exclaimed.

'Oh, the fellows evidently grabbed hold of everything they could get.'

Holmes grunted from the sofa.

'The county police ought to make something of that,' said he; 'why, it is surely obvious that—'

But I held up a warning finger.

'You are here for a rest, my dear fellow. For heaven's sake don't get started on a new problem when your nerves are all in shreds.'

Holmes shrugged his shoulders with a glance of comic resignation towards the colonel, and the talk drifted away into less dangerous channels.

It was destined, however, that all my professional caution should be wasted, for next morning the problem obtruded itself upon us in such a way that it was impossible to ignore it, and our country visit took a turn which neither of us could have anticipated. We were at breakfast when the colonel's butler rushed in with all his propriety shaken out of him.

'Have you heard the news, sir?' he gasped. 'At the Cunningham's, sir!'

'Burglary!' cried the colonel, with his coffee-cup in mid-air.

'Murder!'

The colonel whistled. 'By Jove!' said he. 'Who's killed, then? The JP or his son?'

'Neither, sir. It was William the coachman. Shot through the heart, sir, and never spoke again.'

'Who shot him, then?'

'The burglar, sir. He was off like a shot and got clean away. He'd just broke in at the pantry window when William came on him and met his end in saving his master's property.'

'What time?'

'It was last night, sir, somewhere about twelve.'

'Ah, then, we'll step over afterwards,' said the colonel, coolly settling down to his breakfast again. 'It's a baddish business,' he added when the butler had gone; 'he's our leading man about here, is old Cunningham, and a very decent fellow too. He'll be cut up over this, for the man has been in his service for years and was a good servant. It's evidently the same villains who broke into Acton's.'

'And stole that very singular collection,' said Holmes thoughtfully.

'Precisely.'

'Hum! It may prove the simplest matter in the world, but all the same at first glance this is just a little curious, is it not? A gang of burglars acting in the country might be expected to vary the scene of their operations, and not to crack two cribs in the same district within a few days. When you spoke last night of taking precautions I remember that it passed through my mind that this was probably the last parish in England to which the thief or thieves would be likely to turn their attention—which shows that I have still much to learn.'

'I fancy it's some local practitioner,' said the colonel. 'In that case, of course, Acton's and Cunningham's are just the places he would go for, since they are far the largest about here.'

'And richest?'

'Well, they ought to be, but they've had a lawsuit for some years which has sucked the blood out of both of them, I fancy. Old Acton has some claim on half Cunningham's estate, and the lawyers have been at it with both hands.'

'If it's a local villain there should not be much difficulty in running him down,' said Holmes with a yawn. 'All right, Watson, I don't intend to meddle.'

'Inspector Forrester, sir,' said the butler, throwing open the door.

The official, a smart, keen-faced young fellow, stepped into the room. 'Good-morning, Colonel,' said he. 'I hope I don't intrude, but we hear that Mr Holmes of Baker Street is here.'

The colonel waved his hand towards my friend, and the inspector bowed.

'We thought that perhaps you would care to step across, Mr Holmes.'

'The fates are against you, Watson,' said he, laughing. 'We were chatting about the matter when you came in, Inspector. Perhaps you can let us have a few details.' As he leaned back in his chair in the familiar attitude I knew that the case was hopeless.

'We had no clue in the Acton affair. But here we have plenty to go on, and there's no doubt it is the same party in each case. The man was seen.'

'Ah!'

'Yes, sir. But he was off like a deer after the shot that killed poor William Kirwan was fired. Mr Cunningham saw him from the bedroom window, and Mr Alec Cunningham saw him from the back passage. It was quarter to twelve when the alarm broke out. Mr Cunningham had just got into bed, and Mr Alec was smoking a pipe in his dressing-gown. They both heard William, the coachman, calling for help, and Mr Alec ran down to see what was the matter. The back door was open, and as he came to the foot of the stairs he saw two men wrestling together outside. One of them fired a shot, the other dropped, and the murderer rushed across the garden and over the hedge. Mr Cunningham, looking out of his bedroom, saw the fellow as he gained the road, but lost sight of him at once. Mr Alec stopped to see if he could help the dying man, and so the villain got clean away. Beyond the fact that he was a middle-sized man and dressed in some dark stuff, we have no personal clue; but we are making energetic inquiries, and if he is a stranger we shall soon find him out.'

'What was this William doing there? Did he say anything before he died?'

'Not a word. He lives at the lodge with his mother, and as he was a very faithful fellow we imagine that he walked up to the house with the intention of seeing that all was right there. Of course this Acton business has put everyone on their guard. The robber must have just burst open the door—the lock has been forced—when William came upon him.'

'Did William say anything to his mother before going out?'

'She is very old and deaf, and we can get no information from her. The shock has made her half-witted, but I understand that she was never very bright. There is one very important circumstance, however. Look at this!'

He took a small piece of torn paper from a notebook and spread it out upon his knee.

'This was found between the finger and thumb of the dead man. It appears to be a fragment torn from a larger sheet. You will observe that the hour mentioned upon it is the very time at which the poor fellow met his fate. You see that this murderer might have torn the rest of the sheet from him or he might have taken this fragment from the murderer. It reads almost as though it were an appointment.'

Holmes took up the scrap of paper, a facsimile of which is here reproduced.

'Presuming that it is an appointment,' continued the

inspector, 'it is of course a conceivable theory that this William Kirwan, though he had the reputation of being an honest man, may have been in league with the thief. He may have met him there, may even have helped him to break in the door, and then they may have fallen out between themselves.'

'This writing is of extraordinary interest,' said Holmes, who had been examining it with intense concentration. 'These are much deeper waters than I had thought.' He sank his head upon his hands, while the inspector smiled at the effect which his case had had upon the famous London specialist.

'Your last remark,' said Holmes presently, 'as to the possibility of there being an understanding between the burglar and the servant, and this being a note of appointment from one to the other, is an ingenious and not entirely impossible supposition. But this writing opens up—' He sank his head into his hands again and remained for some minutes in the deepest thought. When he raised his face again I was surprised to see that his cheek was tinged with colour, and his eyes as bright as before his illness. He sprang to his feet with all his old energy.

'I'll tell you what,' said he, 'I should like to have a quiet little glance into the details of this case. There is something in it which fascinates me extremely. If you will permit me, Colonel, I will leave my friend Watson and you, and I will step round with the inspector to test the truth of one or two little fancies of mine. I will be with you again in half an hour.'

An hour and a half had elapsed before the inspector returned alone.

'Mr Holmes is walking up and down in the field

outside,' said he. 'He wants us all four to go up to the house together.'

'To Mr Cunningham's?'

'Yes, sir.'

'What for?'

The inspector shrugged his shoulders. 'I don't quite know, sir. Between ourselves, I think Mr Holmes has not quite got over his illness yet. He's been behaving very queerly, and he is very much excited.'

'I don't think you need alarm yourself,' said I. 'I have usually found that there was method in his madness.'

'Some folk might say there was madness in his method,' muttered the inspector. 'But he's all on fire to start, Colonel, so we had best go out if you are ready.'

We found Holmes pacing up and down in the field, his chin sunk upon his breast, and his hands thrust into his trousers pockets.

'The matter grows in interest,' said he. 'Watson, your country trip has been a distinct success. I have had a charming morning.'

'You have been up to the scene of the crime, I understand,' said the colonel.

'Yes, the inspector and I have made quite a little reconnaissance together.'

'Any success?'

'Well, we have seen some very interesting things. I'll tell you what we did as we walk. First of all, we saw the body of this unfortunate man. He certainly died from a revolver wound as reported.'

'Had you doubted it, then?'

'Oh, it is as well to test everything. Our inspection was not wasted. We then had an interview with Mr Cunningham and his son, who were able to point out the exact spot where the murderer had broken through the garden-hedge in his flight. That was of great interest.'

'Naturally.'

'Then we had a look at this poor fellow's mother. We could get no information from her, however, as she is very old and feeble.'

'And what is the result of your investigations?'

'The conviction that the crime is a very peculiar one. Perhaps our visit now may do something to make it less obscure. I think that we are both agreed, Inspector, that the fragment of paper in the dead man's hand, bearing, as it does, the very hour of his death written upon it, is of extreme importance.'

'It should give a clue, Mr Holmes.'

'It *does* give a clue. Whoever wrote that note was the man who brought William Kirwan out of his bed at that hour. But where is the rest of that sheet of paper?'

'I examined the ground carefully in the hope of finding it,' said the inspector.

'It was torn out of the dead man's hand. Why was someone so anxious to get possession of it? Because it incriminated him. And what would he do with it? Thrust it into his pocket, most likely, never noticing that a corner of it had been left in the grip of the corpse. If we could get the rest of that sheet it is obvious that we should have gone a long way towards solving the mystery.'

'Yes, but how can we get at the criminal's pocket before we catch the criminal?'

'Well, well, it was worth thinking over. Then there is another obvious point. The note was sent to William. The man who wrote it could not have taken it; otherwise, of course, he might have delivered his own message by word of mouth. Who brought the note, then? Or did it come through the post?'

'I have made inquiries,' said the inspector. 'William received a letter by the afternoon post yesterday. The envelope was destroyed by him.'

'Excellent!' cried Holmes, clapping the inspector on the back. 'You've seen the postman. It is a pleasure to work with you. Well, here is the lodge, and if you will come up, Colonel, I will show you the scene of the crime.'

We passed the pretty cottage where the murdered man had lived and walked up an oak-lined avenue to the fine old Queen Anne house, which bears the date of Malplaquet upon the lintel of the door. Holmes and the inspector led us round it until we came to the side gate, which is separated by a stretch of garden from the hedge which lines the road. A constable was standing at the kitchen door.

'Throw the door open, officer,' said Holmes. 'Now, it was on those stairs that young Mr Cunningham stood and saw the two men struggling just where we are. Old Mr Cunningham was at that window—the second on the left—and he saw the fellow get away just to the left of that bush. So did the son. They are both sure of it on account of the bush. Then Mr Alec ran out and knelt beside the wounded man. The ground is very hard, you see, and there are no marks to guide us.' As he spoke two men came down the garden path, from round the angle of the house. The one was an elderly man, with a strong, deep-lined, heavy-eyed face; the other a dashing young fellow, whose bright, smiling expression and showy dress were in strange contrast with the business which had brought us there.

'Still at it, then?' said he to Holmes. 'I thought you

Londoners were never at fault. You don't seem to be so very quick, after all.'

'Ah, you must give us a little time,' said Holmes good-humouredly.

'You'll want it,' said young Alec Cunningham. 'Why, I don't see that we have any clue at all.'

'There's only one,' answered the inspector. 'We thought that if we could only find—Good heavens, Mr Holmes! what is the matter?'

My poor friend's face had suddenly assumed the most dreadful expression. His eyes rolled upward, his features writhed in agony, and with a suppressed groan he dropped on his face upon the ground. Horrified at the suddenness and severity of the attack, we carried him into the kitchen, where he lay back in a large chair and breathed heavily for some minutes. Finally, with a shamefaced apology for his weakness, he rose once more.

'Watson would tell you that I have only just recovered from a severe illness,' he explained. 'I am liable to these sudden nervous attacks.'

'Shall I send you home in my trap?' asked old Cunningham.

'Well, since I am here, there is one point on which I should like to feel sure. We can very easily verify it.'

'What is it?'

'Well, it seems to me that it is just possible that the arrival of this poor fellow William was not before, but after, the entrance of the burglar into the house. You appear to take it for granted that although the door was forced the robber never got in.'

'I fancy that is quite obvious,' said Mr Cunningham gravely. 'Why, my son Alec had not yet gone to bed, and he would certainly have heard anyone moving about.'

'Where was he sitting?'

'I was smoking in my dressing-room.'

'Which window is that?'

'The last on the left, next my father's.'

'Both of your lamps were lit, of course?'

'Undoubtedly.'

'There are some very singular points here,' said Holmes, smiling. 'Is it not extraordinary that a burglar—and a burglar who had some previous experience—should deliberately break into a house at a time when he could see from the lights that two of the family were still afoot?'

'He must have been a cool hand.'

'Well, of course, if the case were not an odd one we should not have been driven to ask you for an explanation,' said young Mr Alec. 'But as to your ideas that the man had robbed the house before William tackled him, I think it a most absurd notion. Wouldn't we have found the place disarranged and missed the things which he had taken?'

'It depends on what the things were,' said Holmes. 'You must remember that we are dealing with a burglar who is a very peculiar fellow, and who appears to work on lines of his own. Look, for example, at the queer lot of things which he took from Acton's—what was it?—a ball of string, a letter-weight, and I don't know what other odds and ends.'

'Well, we are quite in your hands, Mr Holmes,' said old Cunningham. 'Anything which you or the inspector may suggest will most certainly be done.'

'In the first place,' said Holmes, 'I should like you to

offer a reward—coming from yourself, for the officials may take a little time before they would agree upon the sum, and these things cannot be done too promptly. I have jotted down the form here, if you would not mind signing it. Fifty pounds was quite enough, I thought.'

'I would willingly give five hundred,' said the JP, taking the slip of paper and the pencil which Holmes handed to him. 'This is not quite correct, however,' he added, glancing over the document.

'I wrote it rather hurriedly.'

'You see you begin, "Whereas, at about a quarter to one on Tuesday morning an attempt was made", and so on. It was at a quarter to twelve, as a matter of fact.'

I was pained at the mistake, for I knew how keenly Holmes would feel any slip of the kind. It was his specialty to be accurate as to fact, but his recent illness had shaken him, and this one little incident was enough to show me that he was still far from being himself. He was obviously embarrassed for an instant, while the inspector raised his eyebrows, and Alec Cunningham burst into a laugh. The old gentleman corrected the mistake, however, and handed the paper back to Holmes.

'Get it printed as soon as possible,' he said; 'I think your idea is an excellent one.'

Holmes put the slip of paper carefully away into his pocketbook.

'And now,' said he, 'it really would be a good thing that we should all go over the house together and make certain that this rather erratic burglar did not, after all, carry anything away with him.'

Before entering, Holmes made an examination of the door which had been forced. It was evident that a chisel or strong knife had been thrust in, and the lock forced back with it. We could see the marks in the wood where it had been pushed in.

'You don't use bars, then?' he asked.

'We have never found it necessary.'

'You don't keep a dog?'

'Yes, but he is chained on the other side of the house.'

'When do the servants go to bed?'

'About ten.'

'I understand that William was usually in bed also at that hour?'

'Yes.'

'It is singular that on this particular night he should have been up. Now, I should be very glad if you would have the kindness to show us over the house, Mr Cunningham.'

A stone-flagged passage, with the kitchens branching away from it, led by a wooden staircase directly to the first floor of the house. It came out upon the landing opposite to a second more ornamental stair which came up from the front hall. Out of this landing opened the drawing-room and several bedrooms, including those of Mr Cunningham and his son. Holmes walked slowly, taking keen note of the architecture of the house. I could tell from his expression that he was on a hot scent, and yet I could not in the least imagine in what direction his inferences were leading him.

'My good sir,' said Mr Cunningham, with some impatience, 'this is surely very unnecessary. That is my room at the end of the stairs, and my son's is the one beyond it. I leave it to your judgement whether it was possible for the thief to have come up here without disturbing us.'

'You must try round and get on a fresh scent, I fancy,' said the son with a rather malicious smile.

'Still, I must ask you to humour me a little further. I should like, for example, to see how far the windows of the bedrooms command the front. This, I understand, is your son's room'—he pushed open the door—'and that, I presume is the dressing-room in which he sat smoking when the alarm was given. Where does the window of that look out to?' He stepped across the bedroom, pushed open the door, and glanced round the other chamber.

'I hope that you are satisfied now?' said Mr Cunningham tartly.

'Thank you, I think I have seen all that I wished.'

'Then if it is really necessary we can go into my room.'

'If it is not too much trouble.'

The JP shrugged his shoulders and led the way into his own chamber, which was a plainly furnished and commonplace room. As we moved across it in the direction of the window, Holmes fell back until he and I were the last of the group. Near the foot of the bed stood a dish of oranges and a carafe of water. As we passed it Holmes, to my unutterable astonishment, leaned over in front of me and deliberately knocked the whole thing over. The glass smashed into a thousand pieces and the fruit rolled about into every corner of the room.

'You've done it now, Watson,' said he coolly. 'A pretty mess you've made of the carpet.'

I stooped in some confusion and began to pick up the fruit, understanding for some reason my companion desired me to take the blame upon myself. The others did the same and set the table on its legs again.

'Hullo!' cried the inspector, 'where's he got to?'

Holmes had disappeared.

'Wait here an instant,' said young Alec Cunningham.

'The fellow is off his head, in my opinion. Come with me, father, and see where he has got to!'

They rushed out of the room, leaving the inspector, the colonel, and me staring at each other.

''Pon my word, I am inclined to agree with Master Alec,' said the official. 'It may be the effect of this illness, but it seems to me that—'

His words were cut short by a sudden scream of 'Help! Help! Murder!' With a thrill I recognized the voice as that of my friend. I rushed madly from the room on to the landing. The cries, which had sunk down into a hoarse, inarticulate shouting, came from the room which we had first visited. I dashed in, and on into the dressing-room beyond. The two Cunninghams were bending over the prostrate figure of Sherlock Holmes, the younger clutching his throat with both hands, while the elder seemed to be twisting one of his wrists. In an instant the three of us had torn them away from him, and Holmes staggered to his feet, very pale and evidently greatly exhausted.

'Arrest these men, Inspector,' he gasped.

'On what charge?'

'That of murdering their coachman, William Kirwan.'

The inspector stared about him in bewilderment. 'Oh, come now, Mr Holmes,' said he at last, 'I'm sure you don't really mean to—'

'Tut, man, look at their faces!' cried Holmes curtly.

Never certainly have I seen a plainer confession of guilt upon human countenances. The older man seemed numbed and dazed, with a heavy, sullen expression upon his strongly marked face. The son, on the other hand, had dropped all that jaunty, dashing style which had characterized him, and the ferocity of a dangerous wild beast gleamed in his dark eyes and distorted his handsome features. The inspector said nothing, but, stepping to the door, he blew his whistle. Two of his constables came at the call.

'I have no alternative, Mr Cunningham,' said he. 'I trust that this may all prove to be an absurd mistake, but you can see that—Ah, would you? Drop it!' He struck out with his hand, and a revolver which the younger man was in the act of cocking clattered down upon the floor.

'Keep that,' said Holmes, quietly putting his foot upon it; 'you will find it useful at the trial. But this is what we really wanted.' He held up a little crumpled piece of paper.

'The remainder of the sheet!' cried the inspector.

'Precisely.'

'And where was it?'

'Where I was sure it must be. I'll make the whole matter clear to you presently. I think, Colonel, that you and Watson might return now, and I will be with you again in an hour at the furthest. The inspector and I must have a word with the prisoners, but you will certainly see me back at luncheon time.'

Sherlock Holmes was as good as his word, for about one o'clock he rejoined us in the colonel's smoking-room. He was accompanied by a little elderly gentleman, who was introduced to me as the Mr Acton whose house had been the scene of the original burglary.

'I wished Mr Acton to be present while I demonstrated this small matter to you,' said Holmes, 'for it is natural that he should take a keen interest in the details. I am afraid, my dear Colonel, that you must regret the hour that you took in such a stormy petrel as I am.'

'On the contrary,' answered the colonel warmly, 'I consider it the greatest privilege to have been permitted to study your methods of working. I confess that they quite surpass my expectations, and that I am utterly unable to account for your result. I have not yet seen the vestige of a clue.'

'I am afraid that my explanation may disillusion you, but it has always been my habit to hide none of my methods, either from my friend Watson or from anyone who might take an intelligent interest in them. But, first, as I am rather shaken by the knocking about which I had in the dressing-room, I think that I shall help myself to a dash of your brandy, Colonel. My strength has been rather tried of late.'

'I trust you had no more of those nervous attacks.'

Sherlock Holmes laughed heartily. 'We will come to that in its turn,' said he. 'I will lay an account of the case before you in its due order, showing you the various points which guided me in my decision. Pray interrupt me if there is any inference which is not perfectly clear to you.

'It is of the highest importance in the art of detection to be able to recognize, out of a number of facts, which are incidental and which vital. Otherwise your energy and attention must be dissipated instead of being concentrated. Now, in this case there was not the slightest doubt in my mind from the first that the key of the whole matter must be looked for in the scrap of paper in the dead man's hand.

'Before going into this, I would draw your attention to the fact that, if Alec Cunningham's narrative was correct, and if the assailant, after shooting William Kirwan, had *instantly* fled, then it obviously could not be he who tore

173

the paper from the dead man's hand. But if it was not he, it must have been Alec Cunningham himself, for by the time that the old man had descended several servants were upon the scene. The point is a simple one, but the inspector had overlooked it because he had started with the supposition that these county magnates had had nothing to do with the matter. Now, I make a point of never having any prejudices, and of following docilely wherever fact may lead me, and so, in the very first stage of the investigation, I found myself looking a little askance at the part which had been played by Mr Alec Cunningham.

'And now I made a very careful examination of the corner of paper which the inspector had submitted to us. It was at once clear to me that it formed part of a very remarkable document. Here it is. Do you not now observe something very suggestive about it?'

'It has a very irregular look,' said the colonel.

'My dear sir,' cried Holmes, 'there cannot be the least doubt in the world that it has been written by two persons doing alternate words. When I draw your attention to the strong t's of 'at' and 'to', and ask you to compare them with the weak ones of 'quarter' and 'twelve' you will instantly recognize the fact. A very brief analysis of these four words would enable you to say with the utmost confidence that the 'learn' and the 'maybe' are written in the stronger hand, and the 'what' in the weaker.'

'By Jove, it's as clear as day!' cried the colonel. 'Why on earth should two men write a letter in such a fashion?'

'Obviously the business was a bad one, and one of the men who distrusted the other was determined that, whatever was done, each should have an equal hand in it. Now, of the two men, it is clear that the one who wrote the 'at' and 'to' was the ringleader.'

'How do you get at that?'

'We might deduce it from the mere character of the one hand as compared with the other. But we have more assured reasons than that for supposing it. If you examine this scrap with attention you will come to the conclusion that the man with the stronger hand wrote all his words first, leaving blanks for the other to fill up. These blanks were not always sufficient, and you can see that the second man had a squeeze to fit his 'quarter' in between the 'at' and the 'to', showing that the latter were already written. The man who wrote all his words first is undoubtedly the man who planned the affair.'

'Excellent!' cried Mr Acton.

'But very superficial,' said Holmes. 'We come now, however, to a point which is of importance. You may not be aware that the deduction of a man's age from his writing is one which has been brought to considerable accuracy by experts. In normal cases one can place a man in his true decade with tolerable confidence. I say normal cases, because ill-health and physical weakness reproduce the signs of old age, even when the invalid is a youth. In this case, looking at the bold, strong hand of the one, and the rather broken-backed appearance of the other, which still retains its legibility although the t's have begun to lose their crossing, we can say that the one was a young man and the other was advanced in years without being positively decrepit.'

'Excellent!' cried Mr Acton again.

'There is a further point, however, which is subtler and of greater interest. There is something in common between these hands. They belong to men who are

175

blood-relatives. It may be most obvious to you in the Greek *e*'s, but to me there are many small points which indicate the same thing. I have no doubt at all that a family mannerism can be traced in these two specimens of writing. I am only, of course, giving you the leading results now of my examination of the paper. There were twenty-three other deductions which would be of more interest to experts than to you. They all tend to deepen the impression upon my mind that the Cunninghams, father and son, had written this letter.

'Having got so far, my next step was, of course, to examine into the details of the crime, and to see how far they would help us. I went up to the house with the inspector and saw all that was to be seen. The wound upon the dead man was, as I was able to determine with absolute confidence, fired from a revolver at the distance of something over four yards. There was no powder-blackening on the clothes. Evidently, therefore, Alec Cunningham had lied when he said that the two men were struggling when the shot was fired. Again, both father and son agreed as to the place where the man escaped into the road. At that point, however, as it happens, there is a broadish ditch, moist at the bottom. As there were no indications of boot-marks about this ditch, I was absolutely sure not only that the Cunninghams had again lied but that there had never been any unknown man upon the scene at all.

'And now I have to consider the motive of this singular crime. To get at this, I endeavoured first of all to solve the reason of the original burglary at Mr Acton's. I understood, from something which the colonel told us, that a lawsuit had been going on between you, Mr Acton, and the Cunninghams. Of course, it instantly occurred to me that they had broken into your library with the intention of getting at some document which might be of importance in the case.'

'Precisely so,' said Mr Acton. 'There can be no possible doubt as to their intentions. I have the clearest claim upon half of their present estate, and if they could have found a single paper—which, fortunately, was in the strong-box of my solicitors—they would undoubtedly have crippled our case.'

'There you are,' said Holmes, smiling. 'It was a dangerous, reckless attempt in which I seem to trace the influence of young Alec. Having found nothing, they tried to divert suspicion by making it appear to be an ordinary burglary, to which end they carried off whatever they could lay their hands upon. That is all clear enough, but there was much that was still obscure. What I wanted, above all, was to get the missing part of that note. I was certain that Alec had torn it out of the dead man's hand, and almost certain that he must have thrust it into the pocket of his dressing-gown. Where else could he have put it? The only question was whether it was still there. It was worth an effort to find out, and for that object we all went up to the house.

'The Cunninghams joined us, as you doubtless remember, outside the kitchen door. It was, of course, of the very first importance that they should not be reminded of the existence of this paper, otherwise they would naturally destroy it without delay. The inspector was about to tell them the importance which we attached to it when, by the luckiest chance in the world, I tumbled down in a sort of fit and so changed the conversation.'

'Good heavens!' cried the colonel, laughing, 'do you

If you will only come round
to the east gate you will
will very much surprise you and
be of the greatest service to you and also
to Annie Morrison. But say nothing to anyone
upon the matter

mean to say all our sympathy was wasted and your fit an imposture?'

'Speaking professionally, it was admirably done,' cried I, looking in amazement at this man who was forever confounding me with some new phase of his astuteness.

'It is an art which is often useful,' said he. 'When I recovered I managed, by a device which had perhaps some little merit of ingenuity, to get old Cunningham to write the word "twelve", so that I might compare it with the "twelve" upon the paper.'

'Oh, what an ass I have been!' I exclaimed.

'I could see that you were commiserating me over my weakness,' said Holmes, laughing. 'I was sorry to cause you the sympathetic pain which I know that you felt. We then went upstairs together, and, having entered the room and seen the dressing-gown hanging up behind the door, I contrived, by upsetting a table, to engage their attention for the moment and slipped back to examine the pockets. I had hardly got the paper, however—which was, as I had expected, in one of them—when the two Cunninghams were on me, and would, I verily believe, have murdered me then and there but for your prompt and friendly aid. As it is, I feel that young man's grip on my throat now, and the father has twisted my wrist round in the effort to get the paper out of my hand. They saw that I must know all about it, you see, and the sudden change from absolute security to complete despair made them perfectly desperate.

'I had a little talk with old Cunningham afterwards as to the motive of the crime. He was tractable enough, though his son was a perfect demon, ready to blow out his own or anybody else's brains if he could have got to his revolver. When Cunningham saw that the case against him was so strong he lost all heart and made a clean breast of everything. It seems that William had secretly followed his two masters on the night when they made their raid upon Mr Acton's and, having thus got them into his power, proceeded, under threats of exposure, to levy blackmail upon them. Mr Alec, however, was a dangerous man to play games of that sort with. It was a stroke of positive genius on his part to see in the burglary scare which was convulsing the countryside an opportunity of plausibly getting rid of the man whom he feared. William was decoyed up and shot, and had they only got the whole of the note and paid a little more attention to detail in their accessories, it is very possible that suspicion might never have been aroused.'

'And the note?' I asked.

Sherlock Holmes placed the subjoined paper before us.

'It is very much the sort of thing that I expected,' said he. 'Of course, we do not yet know what the relations may have been between Alec Cunningham, William Kirwan, and Annie Morrison. The result shows that the trap was skilfully baited. I am sure that you cannot fail to be delighted with the traces of heredity shown in the *p*'s and in the tails of the *g*'s. The absence of the *i*-dots in the old man's writing is also most characteristic. Watson, I think our quiet rest in the country has been a distinct success, and I shall certainly return much invigorated to Baker Street tomorrow.'

Tom Brown's Schooldays

THOMAS HUGHES

Tom Brown's Schooldays

PARRAGON

Tom Brown's Schooldays
A Parragon Classic

This is a Siena Book
Siena is an imprint of Parragon

First published in 1857

This edition published in 1999 by
Parragon
13 Whiteladies Road
Clifton
Bristol BS8 1PB

Printed and bound in the UK

PART ONE

CHAPTER 1

THE BROWN FAMILY

'I'm the Poet of White Horse Vale, Sir,
With liberal notions under my cap.'
—*Ballad*

The Browns have become illustrious by the pen of Thackeray and the pencil of Doyle, within the memory of the young gentlemen who are now matriculating at the Universities. Notwithstanding the well-merited but late fame which has now fallen upon them, any one at all acquainted with the family must feel, that much has yet to be written and said before the British nation will be properly sensible of how much of its greatness it owes to the Browns. For centuries, in their quiet, dogged, homespun way, they have been subduing the earth in most English counties, and leaving their mark in American forests and Australian uplands. Wherever the fleets and armies of England have won renown, there stalwart sons of the Browns have done yeomen's work. With the yew bow and cloth-yard shaft at Cressy and Agincourt—with the brown bill and pike under the brave Lord Willoughby—with culverin and demi-culverin against Spaniards and Dutchmen—with hand-grenade and sabre, and musket and bayonet, under Rodney and St Vincent, Wolfe and Moore, Nelson and Wellington, they have carried their lives in their hands; getting hard knocks and hard work in plenty, which was on the whole what they looked for, and the best thing for them; and little praise or pudding, which indeed they, and most of us, are better without. Talbots and Stanleys, St Maurs, and such-like folk, have led armies and made laws time out of mind; but those noble families would be somewhat astounded—if the accounts ever came to be fairly taken—to find how small their work for England has been by the side of that of the Browns.

These latter, indeed, have until the present generation rarely

1

been sung by poet, or chronicled by sage. They have wanted their 'sacer vates', having been too solid to rise to the top by themselves, and not having been largely gifted with the talent of catching hold of, and holding on tight to, whatever good things happened to be going—the foundation of the fortunes of so many noble families. But the world goes on its way, and the wheel turns, and the wrongs of the Browns, like other wrongs, seem in a fair way to get righted. And this present writer having for many years of his life been a devout Brown-worshipper, and moreover having the honour of being nearly connected with an eminently respectable branch of the great Brown family, is anxious, so far as in him lies, to help the wheel over, and throw his stone on to the pile.

However, gentle reader, or simple reader, whichever you may be, lest you should be led to waste your precious time upon these pages, I make so bold as at once to tell you the sort of folk you'll have to meet and put up with, if you and I are to jog on comfortably together. You shall hear at once what sort of folk the Browns are, at least my branch of them; and then if you don't like the sort, why, cut the concern at once, and let you and I cry quits before either of us can grumble at the other.

In the first place, the Browns are a fighting family. One may question their wisdom, or wit, or beauty, but about their fight there can be no question. Wherever hard knocks of any kind, visible or invisible, are going, there the Brown who is nearest must shove in his carcase. And these carcases for the most part answer very well to the characteristic propensity; they are a square-headed and snake-necked generation, broad in the shoulder, deep in the chest, and thin in the flank, carrying no lumber. Then for clanship, they are as bad as Highlanders; it is amazing the belief they have in one another. With them there is nothing like the Browns, to the third and fourth generation. 'Blood is thicker than water,' is one of their pet sayings. They can't be happy unless they are always meeting one another. Never were such people for family gatherings, which, were you a stranger or sensitive, you might think had better not have been gathered together. For during the whole time of their being together they luxuriate in telling one another their minds on whatever subject turns up; and their minds are wonderfully antagonist, and all their opinions are downright beliefs. Till you've been among them some time and understand them, you can't think but that they are quarrelling. Not a bit of it; they love and respect one another ten times the more after a good set family arguing bout, and go back, one to his curacy, another to his chambers, and another to his regiment, freshened for work, and more than ever convinced that the Browns are the height of company.

This family training too, combined with their turn for combativeness, makes them eminently quixotic. They can't let anything alone which they think going wrong. They must speak their mind about it, annoying all easy-going folk; and spend their time and money in having a tinker at it, however hopeless the job. It is an impossibility to a Brown to leave the most disreputable lame dog on the other side of a stile. Most other folk get tired of such work. The old Browns, with red faces, white whiskers, and bald heads, go on believing and fighting to a green old age. They have always a crotchet going, till the old man with the scythe reaps and garners them away for troublesome old boys as they are.

And the most provoking thing is, that no failures knock them up, or make them hold their hands, or think you, or me, or other sane people in the right. Failures slide off them like July rain off a duck's back feathers. Jem and his whole family turn out bad, and cheat them one week, and the next they are doing the same thing for Jack; and when he goes to the tread-mill, and his wife and children to the workhouse, they will be on the look-out for Bill to take his place.

However, it is time for us to get from the general to the particular; so, leaving the great army of Browns, who are scattered over the whole empire on which the sun never sets, and whose general diffusion I take to be the chief cause of that empire's stability, let us at once fix our attention upon the small nest of Browns in which our hero was hatched, and which dwelt in that portion of the Royal county of Berks which is called the Vale of White Horse.

Most of you have probably travelled down the Great Western Railway as far as Swindon. Those of you who did so with their eyes open, have been aware, soon after leaving the Didcot station, of a fine range of chalk hills running parallel with the railway on the left-hand side as you go down, and distant some two or three miles, more or less, from the line. The highest point in the range is the White Horse Hill, which you come in front of just before you stop at the Shrivenham station. If you love English scenery and have a few hours to spare, you can't do better, the next time you pass, than stop at the Farringdon-road or Shrivenham station, and make your way to that highest point. And those who care for the vague old stories that haunt countrysides all about England, will not, if they are wise, be content with only a few hours' stay; for glorious as the view is, the neighbourhood is yet more interesting for its relics of bygone times. I only know two English neighbourhoods thoroughly, and in each, within a circle of five miles, there is enough of interest and beauty to last any reasonable man his life. I believe this to be the case almost throughout the country, but each has its special attraction, and none can be richer than the one I am speaking of and going to introduce you to very particularly; for on this subject I must be prosy; so those that don't care for England in detail may skip the chapter.

Oh young England! young England! You who are born into these racing railroad times, when there's a Great Exhibition, or some monster sight, every year; and you can get over a couple of thousand miles of ground for three pound ten, in a five weeks' holiday; why don't you know more of your own birthplaces? You're all in the ends of the earth, it seems to me, as soon as you get your necks out of the educational collar, for Midsummer holidays, long vacations, or what not. Going round Ireland with a return ticket, in a fortnight; dropping your copies of Tennyson on the tops of Swiss mountains; or pulling down the Danube in Oxford racing boats. And when you get home for a quiet fortnight, you turn the steam off, and lie on your backs in the paternal garden, surrounded by the last batch of books from Mudie's library, and half bored to death. Well, well! I know it has its good side. You all patter French more or less, and perhaps German; you have seen men and cities, no doubt, and have your opinions, such as they are, about schools of painting, high art, and all that; have seen the pictures at Dresden and the Louvre, and know the taste of sour krout. All I say is, you don't know your own lanes and woods and fields. Though you may be choke full of science, not one in twenty of you knows where to find the wood-sorrel, or bee-orchis, which grow in the next wood, or on the down three miles off, or what the bog-bean and wood-sage are good for. And as for the country legends, the stories of the old gable-ended farm-houses, the place where the last skirmish was fought in the civil wars, where the parish Butts stood, where the last highwayman turned to bay, where the last ghost was laid by the parson, they're gone out of date altogether.

Now in my time, when we got home by the old coach, which

put us down at the cross-roads with our boxes the first day of the holidays, and had been driven off by the family coachman, singing 'Dulce domum' at the top of our voices, there we were, fixtures, till black Monday came round. We had to cut out our own amusements within a walk or a ride of home. And so we got to know all the country folk, and their ways and songs and stories, by heart; and went over the fields, and woods, and hills, again and again, till we made friends of them all. We were Berkshire, or Gloucestershire, or Yorkshire boys, and you're young cosmopolites, belonging to all counties and no countries. No doubt it's all right, I dare say it is. This is the day of large views and glorious humanity, and all that; but I wish backsword play hadn't gone out in the Vale of White Horse, and that that confounded Great Western hadn't carried away Alfred's Hill to make an embankment.

But to return to the said Vale of White Horse, the country in which the first scenes of this true and interesting story are laid. As I said, the Great Western now runs right through it, and it is a land of large rich pastures, bounded by ox-fences, and covered with fine hedgerow timber, with here and there a nice little gorse or spinney, where abideth poor Charley, having no other cover to which to betake himself for miles and miles, when pushed out some fine November morning by the Old Berkshire. Those who have been there and well mounted, only know how he and the staunch little pack who dash after him—heads high and sterns low, with a breast-high scent—can consume the ground at such times. There being little plough-land, and few woods, the Vale is only an average sporting country, except for hunting. The villages are straggling, queer, old-fashioned places, the houses being dropped down without the least regularity, in nooks and out-of-the-way corners, by the sides of shadowy lanes and footpaths, each with its patch of garden. They are built chiefly of good grey stone and thatched; though I see that within the last year or two the red-brick cottages are multiplying, for the Vale is beginning to manufacture largely both brick and tiles. There are lots of waste ground by the side of the roads in every village, amounting often to village greens, where feed the pigs and ganders of the people; and these roads are old-fashioned, homely roads, very dirty and badly made, and hardly endurable in winter, but still pleasant jog-trot roads running through the great pasture lands, dotted here and there with little clumps of thorns, where the sleek kine are feeding, with no fence on either side of them, and a gate at the end of each field, which makes you get out of your gig (if you keep one), and gives you a chance of looking about you every quarter of a mile.

One of the moralists whom we sat under in my youth—was it the great Richard Swiveller, or Mr Stiggins?—says, 'we are born in a vale, and must take the consequences of being found in such a situation.' These consequences, I for one am ready to encounter. I pity people who weren't born in a vale. I don't mean a flat country, but a vale: that is, a flat country bounded by hills. The having your hill *always* in view if you choose to turn towards him, that's the essence of a vale. There he is for ever in the distance, your friend and companion; you never lose him as you do in hilly districts.

And then what a hill is the White Horse hill! There it stands right up above all the rest, nine hundred feet above the sea, and the boldest, bravest shape for a chalk hill that you ever saw. Let us go up to the top of him, and see what is to be found there. Aye, you may well wonder, and think it odd you never heard of this before; but, wonder or not, as you please, there are hundreds of such things lying about England, which wiser folk than you know nothing of, and care nothing for. Yes, it's a magnificent Roman camp, and no mistake, with gates, and ditch, and mounds, all as complete as it was twenty years after the strong old rogues left it. Here, right up on the highest point, from which they say you can see eleven counties, they trenched round all the table-land, some twelve or fourteen acres, as was their custom, for they couldn't bear anybody to overlook them, and made their eyrie. The ground falls away rapidly on all sides. Was there ever such turf in the whole world? You sink up to your ankles at every step, and yet the spring of it is delicious. There is always a breeze in the 'camp', as it is called, and here it lies, just as the Romans left it, except that cairn on the east side, left by Her Majesty's corps of Sappers and Miners the other day, when they and the Engineer officer had finished their sojourn there, and their surveys for the Ordnance Map of Berkshire. It is altogether a place that you won't forget—a place to open a man's soul and make him prophesy, as he looks down on that great Vale spread out as the garden of the Lord before him, and wave on wave of the mysterious downs behind; and to the right and left the chalk hills running away into the distance, along which he can trace for miles the old Roman road, 'the Ridgeway' ('the Rudge' as

6

the country folk call it), keeping straight along the highest back of the hills—such a place as Balak brought Balaam to, and told him to prophesy against the people in the valley beneath. And he could not, neither shall you, for they are a people of the Lord who abide there.

And now we leave the camp, and descend towards the west, and are on the Ash-down. We are treading on heroes. It is sacred ground for Englishmen, more sacred than all but one or two fields where their bones lie whitening. For this is the actual place where our Alfred won his great battle, the battle of Ash–down ('Aescendum' in the chroniclers) which broke the Danish power, and made England a Christian land. The Danes held the camp and the slope where we are standing—the whole crown of the hill in fact. 'The heathen had beforehand seized the higher ground,' as old Asser says, having wasted everything behind them from London, and being just ready to burst down on the fair vale, Alfred's own birthplace and heritage. And up the heights came the Saxons, as they did at the Alma. 'The Christians led up their line from the lower ground. There stood also on that same spot a single thorn tree, marvellous stumpy (which we ourselves with our very own eyes have seen).' Bless the old chronicler! does he think nobody ever saw the 'single thorn tree' but himself? Why, there it stands to this very day, just on the edge of the slope, and I saw it not three weeks since; an old single thorn tree, 'marvellous stumpy'. At least if it isn't the same tree, it ought to have been, for it's just in the place where the battle must have been won or lost—'around which, as I was saying, the two lines of foemen came together in battle with a huge shout. And in this place, one of the two Kings of the heathen, and five of his earls fell down and died, and many thousands of the heathen side in the same place'.* After which crowning mercy, the pious King, that there might never be wanting a sign and a memorial to the countryside, carved out on the northern side of the chalk hill,

---

* 'Pagani editiorem locum præoccupaverant. Christiani ab inferiori loco aciem dirigebant. Erat quoque in eodem loco unica spinosa arbor, brevis admodum (quam nos ipsi nostris propriis oculis vidimus). Circa quam ergo hostiles inter se acies cum ingenti clamore hostiliter conveniunt. Quo in loco alter de duobus Paganorum regibus et quinque comites occisi occubuerunt, et multa millia Paganæ partis in eodem loco. Cecidit illic ergo Bœgsceg Rex, et Sidroc ille senex comes, et Sidroc junior comes, et Obsbern comes, &c.'—*Annales Rerum Gestarum Ælfredi Magni, Auctore Asserio, Recensuit Franciscus Wise.* Oxford. 1722, p. 23.

under the camp, where it is almost precipitous, the great Saxon white horse, which he who will may see from the railway, and which gives its name to the vale, over which it has looked these thousand years and more.

Right down below the White Horse is a curious deep and broad gully called 'the Manger', into one side of which the hills fall with a series of the most lovely sweeping curves, known as 'the Giant's Stairs'; they are not a bit like stairs, but I never saw anything like them anywhere else, with their short green turf, and tender bluebells, and gossamer and thistledown gleaming in the sun, and the sheep-paths running along their sides like ruled lines.

The other side of the Manger is formed by the Dragon's Hill, a curious little round self-confident fellow, thrown forward from the range, and utterly unlike everything round him. On this hill, some deliverer of mankind, St George, the country folk used to tell me, killed a dragon. Whether it were St George, I cannot say, but surely a dragon was killed there, for you may see the marks yet where his blood ran down, and more by token the place where it ran down is the easiest way up the hillside.

Passing along the Ridgeway to the west for about a mile, we come to a little clump of young beech and firs, with a growth of thorn and privet underwood. Here you may find nests of the strong down partridge and peewit, but take care that the keeper isn't down upon you; and in the middle of it is an old cromlech, a huge flat stone raised on seven or eight others, and led up to by a path, with large single stones set up on each side. This is Wayland Smith's cave, a place of classic fame now; but as Sir Walter has touched it, I may as well let it alone, and refer you to Kenilworth for the legend.

The thick deep wood which you see in the hollow, about a mile off, surrounds Ashdown Park, built by Inigo Jones. Four broad alleys are cut through the wood from circumference to centre, and each leads to one face of the house. The mystery of the downs hangs about house and wood, as they stand there alone, so unlike all around, with the green slopes, studded with great stones just about this part, stretching away on all sides. It was wise Lord Craven, I think, who pitched his tent there.

Passing along the Ridgeway to the east, we soon come to

cultivated land. The downs, strictly so called, are no more; Lincolnshire farmers have been imported, and the long fresh slopes are sheep-walks no more, but grow famous turnips and barley. One of these improvers lives over there at the 'Seven Barrows' farm, another mystery of the great downs. There are the barrows still, solemn and silent, like ships in the calm sea, the sepulchres of some sons of men. But of whom? It is three miles from the White Horse, too far for the slain of Ashdown to be buried there—who shall say what heroes are waiting there? But we must get down into the vale again, and so away by the Great Western Railway to town, for time and the printer's devil press, and it is a terrible long and slippery descent, and a shocking bad road. At the bottom, however, there is a pleasant public, whereat we must really take a modest quencher, for the down air is provocative of thirst. So we pull up under an old oak which stands before the door.

'What is the name of your hill, landlord?'

'Blawing STWUN Hill, sir, to be sure.'

[READER. '*Sturm?*'

AUTHOR. '*Stone*, stupid: the Blowing *Stone*.']

'And of your house? I can't make out the sign.'

'Blawing Stwun, Sir,' says the landlord, pouring out his old ale from a Toby Philpot jug, with a melodious crash, into the long-necked glass.

'What queer names,' say we, sighing at the end of our draught, and holding out the glass to be replenished.

'Be'ant queer at all, as I can see, Sir,' says mine host, handing back our glass, 'seeing as this here is the Blawing Stwun his self,' putting his hand on a square lump of stone, some three feet and a half high, perforated with two or three queer holes, like petrified antediluvian rat-holes, which lies there close under the oak, under our very nose. We are more than ever puzzled, and drink our second glass of ale, wondering what will come next. 'Like to hear un, sir?' says mine host, setting down Toby Philpot on the tray, and resting both hands on the 'Stwun'. We are ready for anything; and he, without waiting for a reply, applies his mouth to one of the rat-holes. Something must come out of it, if he doesn't burst. Good heavens! I hope he has no apoplectic tendencies. Yes, here it comes, sure enough, a gruesome sound between a moan and a roar, and spreads itself way over the valley, and up the hillside, and into the woods at the back of the house, a ghost-like awful voice. 'Um do say, sir,' says mine host, rising purple-faced, while the moan is still coming out of the Stwun, 'as they used in old times to warn the countryside, by blawing the Stwun when the enemy was comin'——and as how folks could make un heered then for seven mile round; leastways, so I've heered lawyer Smith say and he knows a smart sight about them old times.' We can scarcely swallow lawyer Smith's seven miles, but could the blowing of the stone have been a summons, a sort of sending the fiery cross round the neighbourhood in the old times? What old times? Who knows? We pay for our beer, and are thankful.

'And what's the name of the village just below, landlord?'

'Kingstone Lisle, sir.'

'Fine plantations you've got here?'

'Yes, sir, the Squire's 'mazin fond of trees and such like.'

'No wonder. He's got some real beauties to be fond of. Good day, landlord.'

'Good day, sir, and a pleasant ride to 'e.'

And now, my boys, you whom I want to get for readers, have you had enough? Will you give in at once, and say you're convinced, and let me begin my story, or will you have more of it? Remember, I've only been over a little bit of the hillside yet, what you could ride round easily on your ponies in an hour. I'm only just come down into the vale, by Blowing Stone Hill, and if I once begin about the vale, what's to stop me? You'll have to hear all about Wantage, the birthplace of Alfred, and Farringdon, which held out so long for Charles the First (the vale was near Oxford, and dreadfully malignant; full of Throgmortons, Puseys, and Pyes, and such like, and their brawny retainers). Did you ever read Thomas Ingoldsby's 'Legend of Hamilton Tighe'? If you haven't, you ought to have. Well, Farringdon is where he lived, before he went to sea; his real name was Hamden Pye, and the Pyes were the great folk at Farringdon. Then there's Pusey. You've heard of the Pusey horn, which King Canute gave to the Puseys of that day, and which the gallant old Squire, lately gone to his rest (whom Berkshire freeholders turned out of last Parliament, to their eternal disgrace, for voting according to his conscience), used to bring out on high days, holidays, and bonfire nights. And the splendid old Cross church at Uffington, the Uffingas town—how the whole countryside teems with Saxon names and memories! And the old moated grange at Compton, nestled close under the hillside, where twenty Marianas may have lived, with its bright water-lilies in the moat, and its yew walk, 'the Cloister walk', and its peerless terraced gardens. There they all are, and twenty things besides, for those who care about them, and have eyes. And these are the sort of things you may find, I believe, every one of you, in any common English country neighbourhood.

Will you look for them under your own noses, or will you not? Well, well; I've done what I can to make you, and if you will go gadding over half Europe now every holidays, I can't help it. I was born and bred a west-country man, thank God! a Wessex man, a citizen of the noblest Saxon kingdom of Wessex, a regular 'Angular Saxon', the very soul of me 'ad scriptus glebae'. There's nothing like the old countryside for me, and no music like the twang of the real old Saxon tongue, as one gets it fresh from the veritable chaw in the White Horse Vale: and I say with 'Gaarge Ridler', the old west-country yeoman,

> Throo aall the waarld owld Gaarge would bwoast
> Commend me to merry owld England mwoast:
> While vools gwoes praating vur and nigh,
> We stwops at whum, my dog and I.

Here at any rate lived and stopped at home, Squire Brown, J.P. for the County of Berks, in a village near the foot of the White Horse range. And here he dealt out justice and mercy in a rough way, and begat sons and daughters, and hunted the fox, and grumbled at the badness of the roads and the times. And his wife dealt out stockings, and calico shirts, and smock frocks, and comforting drinks to the old folks with the 'rheumatiz', and good counsel to all; and kept the coal and clothes clubs going, for yule tide, when the bands of mummers came round, dressed out in ribbons and coloured paper caps, and stamped round the Squire's kitchen, repeating in true sing-song vernacular the legend of St George and his fight, and the tenpound Doctor, who plays his part at healing the Saint—a relic I believe of the old middle-age mysteries. It was the first dramatic representation which greeted the eyes of little Tom, who was brought down into the kitchen by his nurse to witness it, at the mature age of three years. Tom was the eldest child of his parents, and from his earliest babyhood exhibited the

11

family characteristics in great strength. He was a hearty strong boy from the first, given to fighting with and escaping from his nurse, and fraternizing with all the village boys, with whom he made expeditions all round the neighbourhood. And here, in the quiet old-fashioned country village, under the shadow of the everlasting hills, Tom Brown was reared, and never left it till he went first to school when nearly eight years of age—for in those days change of air twice a-year was not thought absolutely necessary for the health of all her Majesty's lieges.

I have been credibly informed, and am inclined to believe, that the various Boards of Directors of Railway Companies, those gigantic jobbers and bribers, while quarrelling about everything else, agreed together some ten years back to buy up the learned profession of Medicine, body and soul. To this end they set apart several millions of money, which they continually distribute judiciously amongst the Doctors, stipulating only this one thing, that they shall prescribe change of air to every patient who can pay, or borrow money to pay, a railway fare, and see their prescription carried out. If it be not for this, why is it that none of us can be well at home for a year together? It wasn't so twenty years ago—not a bit of it. The Browns didn't go out of the county once in five years. A visit to Reading or Abingdon twice a year, at Assizes or Quarter Sessions, which the Squire made on his horse with a pair of saddlebags containing his wardrobe—a stay of a day or two at some country neighbour's—or an expedition to a county ball, or the yeomanry review—made up the sum of the Brown locomotion in most years. A stray Brown from some distant county dropped in every now and then; or from Oxford, on grave nag, an old don, contemporary of the Squire; and were looked upon by the Brown household and the villagers with the same sort of feeling with which we now regard a man who has crossed the Rocky mountains, or launched a boat on the great Lake in Central Africa. The White Horse Vale, remember, was traversed by no great road; nothing but country parish roads, and these very bad. Only one coach ran there, and this one only from Wantage to London, so that the western part of the vale was without regular means of moving on, and certainly didn't seem to want them. There was the canal, by the way, which supplied the countryside with coal, and up and down which continually went the long barges, with the big black men lounging by the side of the horses along the towing-path, and the women in bright coloured handkerchiefs standing in the sterns steering. Standing I say, but you could never see whether they were standing or sitting, all but their heads and shoulders being out of sight in the cosy little cabins which occupied some eight feet of the stern, and which Tom Brown pictured to himself as the most desirable of residences. His nurse told him that those goodnatured-looking women were in the constant habit of enticing children into the barges, and taking them up to London and selling them, which Tom wouldn't believe, and which made him resolve as soon as possible to accept the oft-proffered invitation of these sirens to 'young Master', to come in and have a ride. But as yet the nurse was too much for Tom.

Yet why should I after all abuse the gadabout propensities of my countrymen? We are a vagabond nation now, that's certain, for better for worse. I am a vagabond; I have been away from home no less than five distinct times in the last year. The Queen sets us the example—we are moving on from top to bottom. Little dirty Jack, who abides in Clement's Inn gateway, and blacks my boots for a penny, takes his month's hop-picking every year as a matter of course. Why shouldn't he? I'm delighted at it. I love vagabonds, only I prefer poor to rich ones—couriers and ladies' maids, imperials and travelling carriages are an abomination unto me—I cannot away with them. But for dirty Jack, and every good fellow who, in the words of the capital French song, moves about,

> Comme le limaçon,
> Portant tout son bagage,
> Ses meubles, sa maison,

on his own back, why, good luck to them, and many a merry road-side adventure, and steaming supper in the chimney corners of road-side inns, Swiss châlets, Hottentot kraals, or wherever else they like to go. So having succeeded in contradicting myself in my first chapter (which gives me great hopes that you will all go on, and think me a good fellow notwithstanding my crotchets). I shall here shut up for the present, and consider my ways; having resolved to 'sar' it out', as we say in the Vale, 'holus-bolus' just as it comes, and then you'll probably get the truth out of me.

CHAPTER 2

THE VEAST

'And the King commandeth and forbiddeth, that from henceforth neither fairs nor markets be kept in Churchyards, for the honour of the Church.'
—STATUTES: 13 *Edw. 1.* Stat. II. cap. VI.

As that venerable and learned poet (whose voluminous works we all think it the correct thing to admire and talk about, but don't read often), most truly says, 'the child is father to the man'; *a fortiori*, therefore, he must be father to the boy. So, as we are going at any rate to see Tom Brown through his boyhood, supposing we never get any further (which, if you show a proper sense of the value of this history, there is no knowing but what we may), let us have a look at the life and environments of the child, in the quiet country village to which we were introduced in the last chapter.

Tom, as has been already said, was a robust and combative urchin, and at the age of four began to struggle against the yoke and authority of his nurse. That functionary was a good-hearted, tearful, scatterbrained girl, lately taken by Tom's mother, Madam Brown, as she was called, from the village school to be trained as nurserymaid. Madam Brown was a rare trainer of servants, and spent herself freely in the profession; for profession it was, and gave her more trouble by half than many people take to earn a good income. Her servants were known and sought after for miles round. Almost all the girls who attained a certain place in the village school were taken by her, one or two at a time, as housemaids, laundrymaids, nursery maids, or kitchen-maids, and after a year or two's drilling, were started in life amongst the neighbouring families, with good principles and wardrobes. One of the results of this system was the perpetual despair of Mrs Brown's cook and own maid, who no sooner had a notable girl made to their hands, than Missus was sure to find a good place for her and send her off, taking in fresh importations from the school. Another was, that the house was always full of young girls, with clean shining faces; who broke plates and scorched linen, but made an atmosphere of cheerful homely life about the place, good for every one who came within its influence. Mrs Brown loved young people, and in fact human creatures in general, above plates and linen. They were more like a lot of elder children than servants, and felt to her more as a mother or aunt than as a mistress.

Tom's nurse was one who took in her instruction very slowly—she seemed to have two left hands and no head; and so Mrs Brown kept her on longer than usual, that she might expend her awkwardness and forgetfulness upon those who would not judge and punish her too strictly for them.

Charity Lamb was her name. It had been the immemorial habit of the village, to christen children either by Bible names, or by those of the cardinal and other virtues; so that one was for ever hearing in the village-street, or on the green, shrill sounds of, 'Prudence! Prudence! thee cum' out o' the gutter'; or 'Mercy! drat the girl, what bist thee a doin' wi' little Faith?' and there were Ruths, Rachels, Keziahs, in every corner. The same with the boys; they were Benjamins, Jacobs, Noahs, Enochs. I suppose the custom has come down from Puritan times—there it is at any rate, very strong still in the Vale.

Well, from early morn till dewy eve, when she had it out of him in the cold tub before putting him to bed, Charity and Tom were pitted against one another. Physical power was as yet on the side of Charity, but she hadn't a chance with him wherever head-work was wanted. This war of independence began every morning before breakfast, when Charity escorted her charge to a neighbouring farmhouse which supplied the Browns, and where, by his mother's wish, Master Tom went to drink whey, before breakfast. Tom had no sort of objection to whey, but he had a decided liking for curds, which were forbidden as unwholesome, and there was seldom a morning that he did not manage to secure a handful of hard curds, in defiance of Charity and of the farmer's wife. The latter good soul was a gaunt angular woman, who, with an old black bonnet on the top of her head, the strings dangling about her shoulders, and her gown tucked through her pocket-holes, went clattering about the dairy, cheese-room, and yard, in high pattens. Charity was some sort of niece of the old lady's, and was consequently free of the

15

farmhouse and garden, into which she could not resist going for the purposes of gossip and flirtation with the heir apparent, who was a dawdling fellow, never out at work as he ought to have been. The moment Charity had found her cousin, or any other occupation, Tom would slip away; and in a minute shrill cries would be heard from the dairy, 'Charity, Charity, thee lazy huzzy, where bist?' and Tom would break cover, hands and mouth full of curds, and take refuge on the shaky surface of the great muck reservoir in the middle of the yard, disturbing the repose of the great pigs. Here he was in safety, as no grown person could follow without getting over their knees; and the luckless Charity, while her aunt scolded her from the dairy-door, for being 'allus hankering about arter our Willum, instead of minding Master Tom', would descend from threats to coaxing, to lure Tom out of the muck, which was rising over his shoes and would soon tell a tale on his stockings, for which she would be sure to catch it from missus's maid.

Tom had two abettors in the shape of a couple of old boys, Noah and Benjamin by name, who defended him from Charity, and expended much time upon his education. They were both of them retired servants of former generations of the Browns. Noah Crooke was a keen dry old man of almost ninety, but still able to totter about. He talked to Tom quite as if he were one of his own family, and indeed had long completely identified the Browns with himself. In some remote age he had been the attendant of a Miss Brown, and had conveyed her about the country on a pillion. He had a little round picture of the identical grey horse, caparisoned with the identical pillion, before which he used to do a sort of fetish worship, and abuse turn-pike-roads and carriages. He wore an old full-bottomed wig, the gift of some dandy old Brown whom he had valeted in the middle of last century, which habiliment Master Tom looked upon with considerable respect, not to say fear; and indeed his whole feeling towards Noah was strongly tainted with awe; and when the old gentleman was gathered to his fathers, Tom's lamentation over him was not unaccompanied by a certain joy at having seen the last of the wig: 'Poor old Noah, dead and gone,' said he, 'Tom Brown so sorry! Put him in the coffin, wig and all.'

But old Benjy was young Master's real delight and refuge. He was a youth by the side of Noah, scarce seventy years old. A cheery, humorous, kind-hearted old man, full of sixty years of vale gossip, and of all sorts of helpful ways for young and old, but above all

16

for children. It was he who bent the first pin, with which Tom extracted his first stickleback out of 'pebbly brook', the little stream which ran through the village. The first stickleback was a splendid fellow, with fabulous red and blue gills. Tom kept him in a small basin until the day of his death, and became a fisherman from that day. Within a month from the taking of the first stickleback, Benjy had carried off our hero to the canal in defiance of Charity, and between them, after a whole afternoon's popjoying, they had caught three or four small coarse fish and a perch, averaging perhaps two and a half ounces each, which Tom bore home in rapture to his mother as a precious gift and she received like a true mother with equal rapture, instructing the cook nevertheless, in a private interview, not to prepare the same for the Squire's dinner. Charity had appealed against old Benjy in the meantime, representing the dangers of the canal banks; but Mrs Brown, seeing the boy's inaptitude for female guidance, had decided in Benjy's favour, and from thenceforth the old man was Tom's dry nurse. And as they sat by the canal watching their little green-and-white float, Benjy would instruct him in the doings of deceased Browns. How his grandfather, in the early days of the great war, when there was much distress and crime in the Vale, and the magistrates had been threatened by the mob, had ridden in with a big stick in his hand, and held the Petty Sessions by himself. How his great uncle, the Rector, had encountered and laid the last ghost, who had frightened the old women, male and female, of the parish out of their senses, and who turned out to be the blacksmith's apprentice, disguised in drink and a white sheet. It was Benjy too who saddled Tom's first pony, and instructed him in the mysteries of horsemanship, teaching him to throw his weight back and keep his hand low; and who stood chuckling outside the door of the girls' school, when Tom rode his little Shetland into the cottage and round the table, where the old dame and her pupils were seated at their work.

Benjy himself was come of a family distinguished in the Vale for their prowess in all athletic games. Some half-dozen of his brothers and kinsmen had gone to the wars, of whom only one had survived to come home, with a small pension, and three bullets in different parts of his body; he had shared Benjy's cottage till his death, and had left him his old dragoon's sword and pistol, which hung over the mantelpiece, flanked by a pair of heavy single-sticks with which Benjy himself had won renown long ago as an old gamester, against the picked men of Wiltshire and Somersetshire, in many a good bout at the revels and pastimes of the country-side. For he had been a famous backsword man in his young days, and a good wrestler at elbow and collar.

Backswording and wrestling were the most serious holiday pursuits of the Vale—those by which men attained fame—and each village had its champion. I suppose that on the whole, people were less worked then than they are now; at any rate they seemed to have more time and energy for the old pastimes. The great times for backswording came round once a-year in each village, at the feast. The Vale 'veasts' were not common statute feasts, but much more ancient business. They are literally, so far as one can ascertain, feasts of the dedication, i.e. they were first established in the Church-yard on the day on which the village Church was opened for public worship, which was on the wake or festival of the patron Saint, and have been held on the same day in every year since that time.

There was no longer any remembrance of why the 'veast' had been instituted, but nevertheless it had a pleasant and almost sacred character of its own. For it was then that all the children of the village, wherever they were scattered, tried to get home for a holiday to visit their fathers and mothers and friends, bringing with them their wages or some little gift from up the country for the old folk. Perhaps for a day or two before, but at any rate on 'veast day' and the day after, in our village, you might see strapping healthy young men and women from all parts of the country going round from house to house in their best clothes, and finishing up with a call on Madam Brown, whom they would consult as to putting out their earnings to the best advantage, or how to expend the same best for the benefit of the old folk. Every household, however poor, managed to raise a 'feast-cake' and bottle of ginger or raisin wine, which stood on the cottage table ready for all comers, and not unlikely to make them remember feast-time—for feast-cake is very solid, and full of huge raisins. Moreover feast-time was the day of reconciliation for the parish. If Job Higgins and Noah Freeman hadn't spoken for the last six months, their 'old women' would be sure to get it patched up by that day. And though there was a good deal of drinking and low vice in the booths of an evening, it was pretty well confined to those who would have been doing the like, 'veast or no veast', and on the whole, the effect was humanizing and Christian. In fact, the only reason why this is not the case still, is that gentlefolk and farmers have taken to other amusements, and have as usual forgotten the poor. They don't attend the feasts themselves, and call them disreputable, whereupon the steadiest of the poor leave them also, and they become what they are called. Class amusements, be they for dukes or plough-boys, always become nuisances and curses to a country. The true charm of cricket and hunting is, that they are still more or less sociable and universal; there's a place for every man who will come and take his part.

No one in the village enjoyed the approach of 'veast day' more than Tom, in the year in which he was taken under old Benjy's tutelage. The feast was held in a large green field at the lower end of the village. The road to Farringdon ran along one side of it, and the brook by the side of the road; and above the brook was another large gentle sloping pasture-land, with a footpath running down it from the churchyard; and the old church, the originator of all the mirth, towered up with its grey walls and lancet windows, overlooking and sanctioning the whole, though its own share therein had been forgotten. At the point where the footpath crossed the brook and road, and entered on the field where the feast was held, was a long low road-side inn, and on the opposite side of the field was a large white thatched farmhouse, where dwelt an old sporting farmer, a great promoter of the revels.

Past the old church and down the footpath, pottered the old man and the child hand in hand early on the afternoon of the day before the feast, and wandered all round the ground, which was already being occupied by the 'cheap Jacks', with their green covered carts and marvellous assortment of wares, and the booths of more legitimate small traders with their tempting arrays of fairings and eatables! and penny peep-shows and other shows, containing pink-eyed ladies, and dwarfs, and boa-constrictors, and wild Indians. But the object of most interest to Benjy, and of course to his pupil also, was the stage of rough planks some four feet high, which was being put up by the village carpenter for the back-swording and wrestling; and after surveying the whole tenderly, old Benjy led his charge away to the road-side inn, where he ordered a glass of ale and a long pipe for himself, and discussed these unwonted luxuries on the bench outside in the soft autumn evening with mine host, another old servant of the Browns, and speculated with him on the likelihood of a good show of old gamesters to contend for the morrow's prizes, and told tales of the gallant bouts of forty years back, to which Tom listened with all his ears and eyes.

But who shall tell the joy of the next morning, when the church bells were ringing a merry peal, and old Benjy appeared in the servants' hall, resplendent in a long blue coat and brass buttons, and a pair of old yellow buckskins and top-boots, which he had cleaned for and inherited from Tom's grandfather; a stout thorn-stick in his hand, and a nosegay of pinks and lavender in his button-hole, and led away Tom in his best clothes, and two new shillings in his breeches pockets? Those two, at any rate, look like enjoying the day's revel.

They quicken their pace when they get into the churchyard, for already they see the field thronged with country folk, the men in clean white smocks or velveteen or fustian coats, with rough plush waistcoats of many colours, and the women in the beautiful long scarlet cloak, the usual outdoor dress of west-country women in those days, and which often descended in families from mother to daughter, or in new-fashioned stuff shawls, which, if they would but believe it, don't become them half so well. The air resounds with the pipe and tabor, and the drums and trumpets of the showmen shouting at the doors of their caravans, over which tremendous pictures of the wonders to be seen within hang temptingly; while through all rises the shrill 'root-too-too-too' of Mr Punch, and the unceasing panpipe of his satellite.

'Lawk a' massey, Mr Benjamin,' cries a stout motherly woman in a red cloak, as they enter the field, 'be that you? Well I never! you do look purely. And how's the Squire, and Madam, and the family?'

Benjy graciously shakes hands with the speaker, who has left our village for some years, but has come over for Veast-day on a visit to an old gossip—and gently indicates the heir apparent of the Browns.

'Bless his little heart! I must gi' un a kiss. Here, Susannah, Susannah!' cries she, raising herself from the embrace, 'come and see Mr Benjamin and young Master Tom. You minds our Sukey, Mr Benjamin, she be growed a rare slip of a wench since you seen her, tho' her'll be sixteen come Martinmas. I do aim to take her to see Madam to get her a place.'

And Sukey comes bouncing away from a knot of old school-fellows, and drops a curtsey to Mr Benjamin. And elders come up from all parts to salute Benjy, and girls who have been Madam's pupils to kiss Master Tom. And they carry him off to load him with fairings; and he returns to Benjy, his hat and coat covered with ribands, and his pockets crammed with wonderful boxes which open upon ever new boxes and boxes, and popguns, and trumpets, and apples, and gilt ginger-bread from the stall of Angel Heavens, sole vendor thereof, whose booth groans with kings and queens, and elephants, and prancing steeds, all gleaming with gold. There was more gold on Angel's cakes than there is ginger in those of this degenerate age. Skilled diggers might yet make a fortune in the churchyards of the Vale, by carefully washing the dust of the consumers of Angel's gingerbread. Alas! he is with his namesakes, and his receipts have, I fear, died with him.

And then they inspect the penny peep-show, at least Tom does, while old Benjy stands outside and gossips, and walks up the steps, and enters the mysterious doors of the pink-eyed lady, and the Irish Giant, who do not by any means come up to their pictures; and the boa will not swallow his rabbit, but there the rabbit is waiting to be swallowed—and what can you expect for tuppence? We are easily pleased in the Vale. Now there is a rush of the crowd, and a tinkling bell is heard, and shouts of laughter; and Master Tom mounts on Benjy's shoulders and beholds a jingling match in all its glory. The games are begun, and this is the opening of them. It is a quaint game, immensely amusing to look at, and as I don't know whether it is used in your counties, I had better describe it. A large roped ring is made, into which are introduced a dozen or so of big boys and young men who mean to play; these are carefully blinded and turned loose into the ring, and then a man is introduced not blindfolded, with a bell hung round his neck, and his two hands tied behind him. Of course every time he moves, the bell must ring, as he has no hand to hold it, and so the dozen blindfolded men have to catch him. This they cannot always manage if he is a lively fellow, but half of them always rush into the arms of the other half, or drive their heads together, or tumble over; and then the crowd laughs vehemently, and invents nicknames for them on the spur of the moment, and they, if they be choleric, tear off the handkerchiefs which blind them, and not unfrequently pitch into one another, each thinking that the other must have run against

21

him on purpose. It is great fun to look at a jingling match certainly, and Tom shouts and jumps on old Benjy's shoulders at the sight, until the old man feels weary and shifts him to the strong young shoulders of the groom who has just got down to the fun.

And now, while they are climbing the pole in another part of the field, and muzzling in a flour-tub in another, the old farmer whose house, as has been said, overlooks the field, and who is master of the revels, gets up the steps on to the stage, and announces to all whom it may concern that a half-sovereign in money will be forthcoming for the old gamester who breaks most heads; to which the Squire and he have added a new hat.

The amount of the prize is sufficient to stimulate the men of the immediate neighbourhood, but not enough to bring any very high talent from a distance; so, after a glance or two a tall fellow, who is a down shepherd, chucks his hat on to the stage and climbs up the steps, looking rather sheepish. The crowd of course first cheer, and then chaff as usual, as he picks up his hat and begins handling the sticks to see which will suit him.

'Wooy, Willum Smith, thee canst plaay wi' he arra daay,' says his companion to the blacksmith's apprentice, a stout young fellow of nineteen or twenty. Willum's sweetheart is in the 'veast' somewhere, and has strictly enjoined him not to get his head broke at backswording, on pain of her highest displeasure; but as she is not to be seen (the women pretend not to like to see the back-sword play, and keep away from the stage) and his hat is decidedly getting old, he chucks it on to the stage, and follows himself, hoping that he will only have to break other people's heads, or that after all Rachel won't really mind.

Then follows the greasy cap lined with fur of a half-gipsy, poaching, loafing fellow, who travels the Vale not for much good, I fancy:

> Full twenty times was Peter feared
> For once that Peter was respected

in fact. And then three or four other hats, including the glossy castor of Joe Willis, the self-elected and would-be champion of the neighbourhood, a well-to-do young butcher of twenty-eight or thereabouts, and a great strapping fellow with his full allowance of bluster. This is a capital show of gamesters, considering the amount

22

of the prize; so while they are picking their sticks and drawing their lots, I think I must tell you as shortly as I can how the noble old game of backsword is played; for it is sadly gone out of late, even in the Vale, and may be you have never seen it.

The weapon is a good stout ash-stick with a large basket handle, heavier and somewhat shorter than a common singlestick. The players are called 'old gamesters'—why I can't tell you—and their object is simply to break one another's heads: for the moment that blood runs an inch anywhere above the eyebrow, the old gamester to whom it belongs is beaten, and has to stop. A very slight blow with the sticks will fetch blood, so that it is by no means a punishing pastime, if the men don't play on purpose, and savagely, at the body and arms of their adversaries. The old gamester going into action only takes off his hat and coat, and arms himself with a stick; he then loops the fingers of his left-hand in a handkerchief or strap which he fastens round his left leg, measuring the length, so that when he draws it tight with his left elbow in the air, that elbow shall just reach as high as his crown. Thus you see, so long as he chooses to keep his left elbow up, regardless of cuts, he has a perfect guard for the left side of his head. Then he advances his right hand above and in front of his head, holding his stick across so that its point projects an inch or two over his left elbow, and thus his whole head is completely guarded, and he faces his man armed in like manner, and they stand some three feet apart, often nearer, and feint, and strike, and return at one another's heads, until one cries 'hold', or blood flows; in the first case they are allowed a minute's time, and go on again; in the latter, another pair of gamesters are called on. If good men are playing, the quickness of the returns is marvellous; you hear the rattle like that a boy makes drawing his stick along palings, only heavier, and the closeness of the men in action to one another gives it a strange interest, and makes a spell at backswording a very noble sight.

They are all suited now with sticks, and Joe Willis and the gipsy man have drawn first lot. So the rest lean against the rails of the stage, and Joe and the dark man meet in the middle, the boards having been strewed with sawdust; Joe's white shirt and spotless drab breeches and boots contrasting with the gipsy's coarse blue shirt and dirty green velveteen breeches and leather gaiters. Joe is evidently turning up his nose at the other, and half insulted at having to break his head.

The gipsy is a tough active fellow, but not very skilful with his weapon, so that Joe's weight and strength tell in a minute; he is too heavy metal for him: whack, whack, whack, come his blows, breaking down the gipsy's guard, and threatening to reach his head every moment. There it is at last—'Blood, blood!' shout the spectators as a thin stream oozes out slowly from the roots of his hair, and the umpire calls to them to stop. The gipsy scowls at Joe under his brows in no pleasant manner, while Master Joe swaggers about, and makes attitudes, and thinks himself, and shows that he thinks himself, the greatest man in the field.

Then follow several stout sets-to between the other candidates for the new hat, and at last come the shepherd and Willum Smith. This is the crack set-to of the day. They are both in famous wind, and there is no crying 'hold'; the shepherd is an old hand and up to all the dodges; he tries them one after another, and very nearly gets at Willum's head by coming in near, and playing over his guard at the half-stick, but somehow Willum blunders through, catching the stick on his shoulders, neck, sides, every now and then, anywhere but on his head, and his returns are heavy and straight, and he is the youngest gamester and a favourite in the parish, and his gallant stand brings down shouts and cheers, and the knowing ones think he'll win if he keeps steady, and Tom on the groom's shoulders holds his hands together, and can hardly breathe for excitement.

Alas for Willum! his sweetheart getting tired of female companionship has been hunting the booths to see where he can have got to, and now catches sight of him on the stage in full combat. She flushes and turns pale; her old aunt catches hold of her, saying, 'Bless'ee, child, doan't 'ee go a'nigst it'; but she breaks away and runs towards the stage calling his name. Willum keeps up his guard stoutly, but glances for a moment towards the voice. No guard will do it, Willum, without the eye. The shepherd steps round and strikes, and the point of his stick just grazes Willum's forehead, fetching off the skin, and the blood flows, and the umpire cries 'Hold', and poor Willum's chance is up for the day. But he takes it very well, and puts on his old hat and coat, and goes down to be scolded by his sweetheart, and led away out of mischief. Tom hears him say coaxingly as he walks off—

'Now doan't'ee, Rachel! I wouldn't ha' done it, only I wanted

24

summut to buy'ee a fairing wi', and I be as vlush o' money as a twod o' veathers.'

'Thee mind what I tells'ee,' rejoins Rachel saucily, 'and doan't'ee kep blethering about fairings.' Tom resolves in his heart to give Willum the remainder of his two shillings after the backswording.

Joe Willis has all the luck today. His next bout ends in an easy victory, while the shepherd has a tough job to break his second head; and when Joe and the shepherd meet, and the whole circle expect and hope to see him get a broken crown, the shepherd slips in the first round and falls against the rails, hurting himself so that the old farmer will not let him go on, much as he wishes to try; and that impostor Joe (for he is certainly not the best man) struts and swaggers about the stage the conquering gamester, though he hasn't had five minutes' really trying play.

Joe takes the new hat in his hand, and puts the money into it, and then as if a thought strikes him, and he doesn't think his victory quite acknowledged down below, walks to each face of the stage, and looks down, shaking the money, and chaffing, as how he'll stake hat and money and another half-sovereign 'agin any gamester as hasn't played already'. Cunning Joe! he thus gets rid of Willum and the shepherd, who is quite fresh again.

No one seems to like the offer, and the umpire is just coming down, when a queer old hat, something like a Doctor of Divinity's shovel, is chucked on to the stage, and an elderly quiet man steps out, who has been watching the play, saying he should like to cross a stick wi' the prodigalish young chap.

The crowd cheer and begin to chaff Joe, who turns up his nose and swaggers across to the sticks. 'Imp'dent old wosbird!' says he, 'I'll break the bald head on un to the truth.'

The old boy is very bald certainly, and the blood will show fast enough if you can touch him, Joe.

He takes off his long-flapped coat, and stands up in a long-flapped waistcoat, which Sir Roger de Coverley might have worn when it was new, picks out a stick, and is ready for Master Joe, who loses no time but begins his old game, whack, whack, whack, trying to break down the old man's guard by sheer strength. But it won't do—he catches every blow close by the basket, and though he is rather stiff in his returns, after a minute walks Joe about the stage, and is clearly a staunch old gamester. Joe now comes in, and making the most of his height, tries to get over the old man's guard at half-stick, by which he takes a smart blow in the ribs and another on the elbow and nothing more. And now he loses wind and begins to puff, and the crowd laugh: 'Cry "hold", Joe—thee'st met thy match!' Instead of taking good advice and getting his wind, Joe loses his temper, and strikes at the old man's body.

'Blood, blood!' shout the crowd, 'Joe's head's broke!'

Who'd have thought it? How did it come? That body-blow left Joe's head unguarded for a moment, and with one turn of the wrist the old gentleman has picked a neat little bit of skin off the middle of his forehead, and though he won't believe it, and hammers on for three more blows despite of the shouts, is then convinced by the blood trickling into his eye. Poor Joe is sadly crestfallen, and fumbles in his pocket for the other half-sovereign, but the old gamester won't have it. 'Keep thy money, man, and gi's thy hand,' says he, and they shake hands; but the old gamester gives the new hat to the shepherd, and, soon after, the half-sovereign to Willum, who thereout decorates his sweetheart with ribbons to his heart's content.

'Who can a be?' 'Wur do a cum from?' ask the crowd. And it soon flies about that the old west-country champion, who played a tie with Shaw the Life-guardsman at 'Vizes' twenty years before, has broken Joe Willis's crown for him.

How my country fair is spinning out! I see I must skip the wrestling, and the boys jumping in sacks, and rolling wheel-barrows blindfolded; and the donkey-race, and the fight which arose thereout, marring the otherwise peaceful 'veast'; and the frightened scurrying away of the female feast-goers, and descent of Squire Brown, summoned by the wife of one of the combatants to stop it: which he wouldn't start to do till he had got on his top-boots. Tom is carried away by old Benjy dog-tired and surfeited with pleasure, as the evening comes on and the dancing begins in the booths; and though Willum and Rachel in her new ribbons and many another good lad and lass don't come away just yet, but have a good step out, and enjoy it, and get no harm thereby, yet we, being sober folk, will just stroll away up through the churchyard, and by the old yewtree; and get a quiet dish of tea and a parle with our gossips, as the steady ones of our village do, and so to bed.

That's the fair true sketch, as far as it goes, of one of the larger village feasts in the Vale of Berks, when I was a little boy. They are much altered for the worse, I am told. I haven't been at one these twenty years, but I have been at the statute fairs in some west-country towns, where servants are hired, and greater abominations cannot be found. What village feasts have come to, I fear, in many cases, may be read in the pages of Yeast (though I never saw one so bad—thank God!)

Do you want to know why? It is because, as I said before, gentlefolk and farmers have left off joining or taking an interest in them. They don't either subscribe to the prizes, or go down and enjoy the fun.

Is this a good or a bad sign? I hardly know. Bad, sure enough, if it only arises from the further separation of classes consequent on twenty years of buying cheap and selling dear, and its accompanying over-work; or because our sons and daughters have their hearts in London Club-life, or so called Society, instead of in the old English home duties; because farmers' sons are apeing fine gentlemen, and farmers' daughters caring more to make bad foreign music than good English cheeses. Good, perhaps, if it be that the time for the old 'veast' has gone by, that it is no longer the healthy sound expression of English country holiday-making; that, in fact, we as a nation have got beyond it, and are in a transition state, feeling for and soon likely to find some better substitute.

Only I have just got this to say before I quit the text. Don't let reformers of any sort think that they are going really to lay hold of the working boys and young men of England by any educational grapnel whatever, which hasn't some bona fide equivalent for the games of the old country 'veast' in it; something to put in the place of the backsswording and wrestling and racing; something to try the muscles of men's bodies, and the endurance of their hearts, and to make them rejoice in their strength. In all the new-fangled comprehensive plans which I see, this is all left out; and the consequence is, that your great Mechanics' Institutes end in intellectual priggism, and your Christian Young Men's Societies in religious Pharisaism.

Well, well, we must bide our time. Life isn't all beer and skittles—but beer and skittles, or something better of the same sort, must form a good part of every Englishman's education. If I could only drive this into the heads of you rising Parliamentary Lords, and young swells who 'have your ways made for you', as the saying is—you, who frequent palaver houses and West-end clubs, waiting always ready to strap yourselves on to the back of poor dear old John, as soon as the present used-up lot (your fathers and uncles) who sit there on the great Parliamentary-majorities' pack-saddle, and make belief they're guiding him with their red-tape bridle, tumble, or have to be lifted off!

I don't think much of you yet—I wish I could; though you do go talking and lecturing up and down the country to crowded audiences, and are busy with all sorts of philanthropic intellectualism, and circulating libraries and museums, and Heaven only knows what besides; and try to make us think, through newspaper reports, that you are, even as we, of the working classes. But, bless your hearts, we 'ain't so green', though lots of us of all sorts toady you enough certainly, and try to make you think so.

I'll tell you what to do now: instead of all this trumpeting and fuss, which is only the old Parliamentary-majority dodge over again—just you go each of you (you've plenty of time for it, if you'll only give up t'other line) and quietly make three or four friends, real friends, among us. You'll find a little trouble in getting at the right sort, because such birds don't come lightly to your lure—but found they may be. Take, say, two out of the professions, lawyer, parson, doctor—which you will; one out of trade, and three or four out of the working classes, tailors, engineers, carpenters, engravers—there's plenty of choice. Let them be men of your own ages, mind, and ask them to your homes; introduce them to your wives, and sisters, and get introduced to theirs: give them good dinners, and talk to them about what is really at the bottom of your hearts, and box, and run, and row with them, when you have a chance. Do all this honestly as man to man, and by the time you come to ride old John, you'll be able to do something more than sit on his back, and may feel his mouth with some stronger bridle than a red-tape one.

Ah, if you only would! But you have got too far out of the right rut, I fear. Too much over-civilization, and the deceitfulness of riches. It is easier for a camel to go through the eye of a needle. More's the pity. I never came across but two of you, who could value a man wholly and solely for what was in him; who thought themselves verily and indeed of the same flesh and blood as John Jones the attorney's clerk, and Bill Smith the costermonger, and could act as if they thought so.

28

CHAPTER 3

SUNDRY WARS AND ALLIANCES

Poor old Benjy! the 'rheumatiz' has much to answer for all through English countrysides, but it never played a scurvier trick than in laying thee by the heels, when thou wast yet in a green old age. The enemy, which had long been carrying on a sort of border warfare, and trying his strength against Benjy's on the battlefield of his hands and legs, now, mustering all his forces, began laying siege to the citadel, and over-running the whole country. Benjy was seized in the back and loins; and though he made strong and brave fight, it was soon clear enough that all which could be beaten of poor old Benjy, would have to give in before long.

It was as much as he could do now, with the help of his big stick and frequent stops, to hobble down to the canal with Master Tom, and bait his hook for him, and sit and watch his angling, telling him quaint old country stories; and when Tom had no sport, and detecting a rat some hundred yards or so off along the bank would rush off with Toby the turnspit terrier, his other faithful companion, in bootless pursuit, he might have tumbled in and been drowned twenty times over before Benjy could have got near him.

Cheery and unmindful of himself as Benjy was, this loss of locomotive power bothered him greatly. He had got a new object in his old age, and was just beginning to think himself useful again in the world. He feared much too lest Master Tom should fall back again into the hands of Charity and the women. So he tried everything he could think of to get set up. He even went an expedition to the dwelling of one of those queer mortals, who—say what we will, and reason how we will—do cure simple people of diseases of one kind or another without the aid of physic; and so get to themselves the reputation of using charms, and inspire for themselves and their dwellings great respect, not to say fear, amongst a simple folk such as the dwellers in the Vale of White Horse. Where this power, or whatever else it may be, descends upon the shoulders of a man whose ways are not straight, he becomes a nuisance to the neighbourhood; a receiver of stolen goods, giver of love-potions, and deceiver of silly women; the avowed enemy of law and order, of justices of the peace, head boroughs, and gamekeepers. Such a man in fact as was recently caught tripping, and deservedly dealt with by the Leeds justices, for seducing a girl who had come to him to get back a faithless lover, and has been convicted of bigamy since then. Sometimes however they are of quite a different stamp, men who pretend to nothing, and are with difficulty persuaded to exercise their occult arts in the simplest cases.

Of this latter sort was old farmer Ives, as he was called, the 'wise man' to whom Benjy resorted (taking Tom with him as usual), in the early spring of the year next after the feast described in the last chapter. Why he was called 'farmer' I cannot say, unless it be that he was the owner of a cow, a pig or two, and some poultry, which he maintained on about an acre of land enclosed from the middle of a wild common, on which probably his father had squatted before lords of manors looked as keenly after their rights as they do now. Here he had lived no one knew how long, a solitary man. It was often rumoured that he was to be turned out and his cottage pulled down, but somehow it never came to pass; and his pigs and cow went grazing on the common, and his geese hissed at the passing children and at the heels of the horse of my lord's steward, who often rode by with a covetous eye on the enclosure, still unmolested. His dwelling was some miles from our village; so Benjy, who was half ashamed of his errand, and wholly unable to walk there, had to exercise much ingenuity to get the means of transporting himself and Tom thither without exciting suspicion. However, one fine May morning he managed to borrow the old blind pony of our friend the publican, and Tom persuaded Madam Brown to give him a holiday to spend with old Benjy, and to lend them the squire's light cart, stored with bread and cold meat and a bottle of ale. And so the two in high glee started behind old Dobbin, and jogged along the deep rutted plashy roads, which had not been mended after their winter's wear, towards the dwelling of the wizard. About noon they passed the gate which opened on to the large common, and old Dobbin toiled slowly up the hill, while Benjy pointed out a little deep dingle on the left, out of which welled a tiny stream. As they crept up the hill the tops of a few birch-trees came in sight, and blue smoke curling up through their delicate light boughs; and then the little white thatched home and patch of enclosed ground of farmer Ives, lying cradled in the dingle, with the gay gorse common rising behind and on both sides; while in front, after traversing a gentle slope, the eye might travel for miles and miles over the rich vale. They now left the main road and struck into a green track over the common marked lightly with wheel and horseshoe, which led down into the dingle and stopped at the rough gate of farmer Ives. Here they found the farmer, an iron-grey old man, with a bushy eyebrow and strong aquiline nose, busied in one of his vocations. He was a horse and cow doctor, and was tending a sick beast which had been sent up to be cured. Benjy hailed him as an old friend, and he returned the greeting cordially enough, looking however hard for a moment both at Benjy and Tom, to see whether there was more in their visit than appeared at first sight. It was a work of some difficulty and danger for Benjy to reach the ground, which however he managed to do without mishap; and then he devoted himself to unharnessing Dobbin, and turning him out for a graze ('a run' one could not say of that virtuous steed) on the common. This done, he extricated the cold provisions from the cart, and they entered the farmer's wicket; and he, shutting up the knife with which he was taking maggots out of the cow's back and sides, accompanied them towards the cottage. A big old lurcher got up slowly from the door-stone, stretching first one hind leg and then the other, and taking Tom's caresses and the presence of Toby, who kept however at a respectful distance, with equal indifference.

'Us be cum to pay'e a visit. I've a been long minded to do't for old sake's sake, only I vinds I dwont get about now as I'd used to't. I be so plaguy bad wi' th' rumatiz in my back.' Benjy paused in hopes of drawing the farmer at once on the subject of his ailments without futher direct application.

'Ah, I see as you bean't quite so lissom as you was,' replied the farmer with a grim smile, as he lifted the latch of his door; 'we bean't so young as we was, nother on us, wuss luck.'

The farmer's cottage was very like those of the better class of peasantry in general. A snug chimney corner with two seats, and a small carpet on the hearth, an old flint gun and a pair of spurs over the fireplace, a dresser with shelves on which some bright pewter plates and crockeryware were arranged, an old walnut table, a few chairs and settles, some framed samplers, and an old print or two, and a bookcase with some dozen volumes on the walls, a rack with flitches of bacon, and other stores fastened to the ceiling, and you have the best part of the furniture. No sign of occult art is to be seen, unless the bundles of dried herbs hanging to the rack and in the ingle, and the row of labelled phials on one of the shelves, betoken it.

Tom played about with some kittens who occupied the hearth, and with a goat who walked demurely in at the open door, while their host and Benjy spread the table for dinner—and was soon engaged in conflict with the cold meat, to which he did much honour. The two old men's talk was of old comrades and their deeds, mute inglorious Miltons of the Vale, and of the doings of thirty years back—which didn't interest him much, except when they spoke of the making of the canal, and then indeed he began to listen with all his ears; and learned to his no small wonder that his dear and wonderful canal had not been there always—was not in fact so old as Benjy or farmer Ives, which caused a strange commotion in his small brain.

After dinner Benjy called attention to a wart which Tom had on the knuckles of his hand, and which the family doctor had been trying his skill on without success, and begged the farmer to charm it away. Farmer Ives looked at it, muttered something or another over it, and cut some notches in a short stick, which he handed to Benjy, giving him instructions for cutting it down on certain days, and cautioning Tom not to meddle with the wart for a fortnight. And then they strolled out and sat on a bench in the sun with their pipes, and the pigs came up and grunted sociably and let Tom scratch them; and the farmer, seeing how he liked animals, stood up and held his arms in the air and gave a call, which brought a flock of pigeons wheeling and dashing through the birch-trees. They settled down in clusters on the farmer's arms and shoulders, making love to him and scrambling over one another's backs to get to his face; and then he threw them all off, and they fluttered about close by, and lighted on him again and again when he held up his arms. All the creatures about the place were clean and fearless, quite unlike their relations elsewhere; and Tom begged to be taught how to make all the pigs and cows and poultry in our village tame, at which the farmer only gave one of his grim chuckles.

It wasn't till they were just ready to go, and old Dobbin was harnessed, that Benjy broached the subject of his rheumatism again, detailing his symptoms one by one. Poor old boy! He hoped the farmer could charm it away as easily as he could Tom's wart, and was ready with equal faith to put another notched stick into his other pocket, for the cure of his own ailments. The physician shook his head, but nevertheless produced a bottle and handed it to Benjy with instructions for use. 'Not as 't'll do'e much good—leastways I be afeard not,' shading his eyes with his hand and looking up at them in the cart; 'there's only one thing as I knows on, as'll cure old folk like you and I o' th' rhumatis.'

'Wot be that then, farmer?' inquired Benjy.

'Churchyard mould,' said the old iron-grey man with another chuckle. And so they said their goodbyes and went their ways home. Tom's wart was gone in a fortnight, but not so Benjy's rheumatism, which laid him by the heels more and more. And though Tom still spent many an hour with him, as he sat on a bench in the sunshine, or by the chimney corner when it was cold, he soon had to seek elsewhere for his regular companions.

Tom had been accustomed often to accompany his mother in her visits to the cottages, and had thereby made acquaintance with many of the village boys of his own age. There was Job Rudkin, son of widow Rudkin, the most bustling woman in the parish. How she could ever have had such a stolid boy as Job for a child, must always remain a mystery. The first time Tom went to their cottage with his mother, Job was not indoors, but he entered soon after, and stood with both hands in his pockets staring at Tom. Widow Rudkin, who would have had to cross Madam to get at young Hopeful—a breach of good manners of which she was wholly incapable—began a series of pantomime signs, which only puzzled him, and at last, unable to contain herself longer, burst out with, 'Job! Job! where's thy cap?'

'What! beant'e on ma' head, mother?' replied Job, slowly extricating one hand from a pocket and feeling for the article in question; which he found on his head sure enough, and left there, to his mother's horror and Tom's great delight.

Then there was poor Jacob Dodson the half-witted boy, who ambled about cheerfully, undertaking messages and little helpful odds and ends for every one, which however poor Jacob managed always hopelessly to embrangle. Everything came to pieces in his hands, and nothing would stop in his head. They nicknamed him Jacob Doodle-calf.

But above all there was Harry Winburn, the quickest and best boy in the parish. He might be a year older than Tom, but was very little bigger, and he was the Crichton of our village boys. He could wrestle and climb and run better than all the rest, and learned all that the schoolmaster could teach him faster than that worthy at all liked. He was a boy to be proud of, with his curly brown hair, keen grey eye, straight active figure, and little ears and hands and feet, 'as fine as a lord's', as Charity remarked to Tom one day, talking as usual great nonsense. Lords' hands and ears and feet are just as ugly as other folks' when they are children, as any one may convince themselves if they like to look. Tight boots and gloves, and doing nothing with them, I allow make a difference by the time they are twenty.

Now that Benjy was laid on the shelf, and his young brothers were still under petticoat government, Tom, in search of companions, began to cultivate the village boys generally more and more. Squire Brown, be it said, was a true blue Tory to the backbone, and believed honestly that the powers which be were ordained of God, and that loyalty and steadfast obedience were men's first duties. Whether it were in consequence or in spite of his political creed, I do not mean to give an opinion, though I have one; but certain it is, that he held therewith divers social principles not generally supposed to be true blue in colour. Foremost of these, and the one which the Squire loved to propound above all others, was the belief that a man is to be valued wholly and solely for that which he is in himself, for that which stands up in the four fleshly walls of him, apart from clothes, rank, fortune, and all externals whatsoever. Which belief I take to be a wholesome corrective of all political opinions, and, if held sincerely, to make all opinions equally harmless, whether they be blue, red, or green. As a necessary corollary to this belief, Squire Brown held further that it didn't matter a straw whether his son associated with lords' sons or ploughmen's sons, provided they were brave and honest. He himself had played football and gone bird's-nesting with the farmers whom he met at vestry and the labourers who tilled their fields, and so had his father and grandfather with their progenitors. So he encouraged Tom in his intimacy with the boys of the village, and forwarded it by all means in his power, and gave them the run of a close for a playground, and provided bats and balls and a football for their sports.

Our village was blessed amongst other things with a well-endowed school. The building stood by itself, apart from the master's house, on an angle of ground where three roads met; an old grey stone building with a steep roof and mullioned windows. On one of the opposite angles stood Squire Brown's stables and kennel, with their backs to the road, over which towered a great elm tree; on the third stood the village carpenter and wheelwright's large open shop, and his house and the schoolmaster's, with long low eaves under which the swallows built by scores.

The moment Tom's lessons were over, he would now get him down to this corner by the stables, and watch till the boys came out of school. He prevailed on the groom to cut notches for him in the bark of the elm, so that he could climb into the lower branches, and there he would sit watching the school door, and speculating on the possibility of turning the elm into a dwelling-place for himself and friends after the manner of the Swiss Family Robinson. But the school hours were long and Tom's patience short, so that soon he began to descend into the street, and go and peep in at the school door and the wheelwright's shop, and look out for something to while away the time. Now the wheelwright was a choleric man, and one fine afternoon, returning from a short absence, found Tom occupied with one of his pet adzes, the edge of which was fast vanishing under our hero's care. A speedy flight saved Tom from all but one sound cuff on the ears, but he resented this unjustifiable interruption of his first essays at carpentering, and still more the further proceedings of the wheelwright, who cut a switch and hung it over the door of his workshop, threatening to use it upon Tom if he came within twenty yards of his gate. So Tom, to retaliate, commenced a war upon the swallows who dwelt under the wheelwright's eaves, whom he harassed with sticks and stones, and being fleeter of foot than his enemy, escaped all punishment, and kept him in perpetual anger. Moreover his presence about the school door began to incense the master, as the boys in that neighbourhood neglected their lessons in consequence; and more than once he issued into the porch, rod in hand, just as Tom beat a hasty retreat. And he and the wheelwright, laying their heads together, resolved to acquaint the Squire with Tom's afternoon occupations; but in order to do it with effect, determined to take him captive and lead him away to judgement fresh from his evil doings. This they would have found some difficulty in doing, had

Tom continued the war single-handed, or rather single-footed, for he would have taken to the deepest part of Pebbly Brook to escape them; but like other active powers, he was ruined by his alliances. Poor Jacob Doodle-calf could not go to school with the other boys, and one fine afternoon, about three o'clock (the school broke up at four), Tom found him ambling about the street, and pressed him into a visit to the school-porch. Jacob, always ready to do what he was asked, consented, and the two stole down to the school together. Tom first reconnoitred the wheelwright's shop, and seeing no signs of activity, thought all safe in that quarter, and ordered at once an advance of all his troops upon the school-porch. The door of the school was ajar, and the boys seated on the nearest bench at once recognized and opened a correspondence with the invaders. Tom waxing bold, kept putting his head into the school and making faces at the master when his back was turned. Poor Jacob, not in the least comprehending the situation, and in high glee at finding himself so near the school, which he had never been allowed to enter, suddenly, in a fit of enthusiasm, pushed by Tom, and ambling three steps into the school, stood there, looking round him and nodding with a self-approving smile. The master, who was stooping over a boy's slate, with his back to the door, became aware of something unusual, and turned quickly round. Tom rushed at Jacob, and began dragging him back by his smock-frock, and the master made at them, scattering forms and boys in his career. Even now they might have escaped, but that in the porch, barring retreat, appeared the crafty wheelwright, who had been watching all their proceedings. So they were seized, the school dismissed, and Tom and Jacob led away to Squire Brown as lawful prize, the boys following to the gate in groups, and speculating on the result.

The Squire was very angry at first, but the interview, by Tom's pleading, ended in a compromise. Tom was not to go near the school till three o'clock, and only then if he had done his own lessons well, in which case he was to be the bearer of a note to the master from Squire Brown, and the master agreed in such case to release ten or twelve of the best boys an hour before the time of breaking up, to go off and play in the close. The wheelwright's adzes and swallows were to be for ever respected; and that hero and the master withdrew to the servants' hall, to drink the Squire's health, well satisfied with their day's work.

The second act of Tom's life may now be said to have begun.

The war of independence had been over for some time: none of the women now, not even his mother's maid, dared offer to help him in dressing or washing. Between ourselves, he had often at first to run to Benjy in an unfinished state of toilet; Charity and the rest of them seemed to take delight in putting impossible buttons and ties in the middle of his back; but he would have gone without nether integuments altogether, sooner than have had recourse to female valeting. He had a room to himself, and his father gave him sixpence a week pocket-money. All this he had achieved by Benjy's advice and assistance. But now he had conquered another step in life, the step which all real boys so long to make; he had got amongst his equals in age and strength, and could measure himself with other boys; he lived with those whose pursuits and wishes and ways were the same in kind as his own.

The little governess who had lately been installed in the house found her work grow wondrously easy, for Tom slaved at his lessons in order to make sure of his note to the school-master. So there were very few days in the week in which Tom and the village boys were not playing in their close by three o'clock. Prisoner's base, rounders, high-cock-a-lorum, cricket, football, he was soon initiated into the delights of them all; and though most of the boys were older than himself, he managed to hold his own very well. He was naturally active and strong, and quick of eye and hand, and had the advantage of light shoes and well-fitting dress, so that in a short time he could run and jump and climb with any of them.

They generally finished their regular games half-an-hour or so before tea-time, and then began trials of skill and strength in many ways. Some of them would catch the Shetland pony who was turned out in the field, and get two or three together on his back, and the little rogue, enjoying the fun, would gallop off for fifty yards and then turn round, or stop short and shoot them on to the turf, and then graze quietly on till he felt another load; others played peg-top or marbles, while a few of the bigger ones stood up for a bout at wrestling. Tom at first only looked on at this pastime, but it had peculiar attractions for him, and he could not long keep out of it. Elbow and collar wrestling as practised in the western counties was, next to backswording, the way to fame for the youth of the Vale; and all the boys knew the rules of it, and were more or less expert. But Job Rudkin and Harry Winburn were the stars, the former stiff and sturdy, with legs like small towers, the latter pliant as india-rubber, and quick as lightning. Day after day they stood foot to foot, and offered first one hand and then the other, and grappled and closed and swayed and strained, till a well-aimed crook of the heel or thrust of the loin took effect, and a fair back-fall ended the matter. And Tom watched with all his eyes, and first challenged one of the less scientific, and threw him; and so one by one wrestled his way up to the leaders.

Then indeed for months he had a poor time of it; it was not long indeed before he could manage to keep his legs against Job, for that hero was slow of offence, and gained his victories chiefly by allowing others to throw themselves against his immoveable legs and loins. But Harry Winburn was undeniably his master; from the first clutch of hands when they stood up, down to the last trip which sent him on to his back on the turf, he felt that Harry knew more and could do more than he. Luckily Harry's bright unconsciousness, and Tom's natural good temper, kept them from ever quarrelling; and so Tom worked on and on, and trod more and more nearly on Harry's heels, and at last mastered all the dodges and falls except one. This one was Harry's own particular invention and pet; he scarcely ever used it except when hard pressed, but then out it came, and as sure as it did, over went poor Tom. He thought about that fall at his meals, in his walks, when he lay awake in bed, in his dreams—but all to no purpose; until Harry one day in his open way suggested to him how he thought it should be met, and in a week from that time the boys were equal, save only the slight difference of strength in Harry's favour, which some extra ten months of age gave. Tom had often afterwards reason to be thankful for that early drilling, and above all for having mastered Harry Winburn's fall.

Besides their home games, on Saturdays the boys would wander all over the neighbourhood; sometimes to the downs, or up to the camp, where they cut their initials out in the springy turf, and watched the hawks soaring, and the 'peert' bird, as Harry Winburn called the grey plover, gorgeous in his wedding feathers; and so home, racing down the Manger with many a roll among the thistles, or through Uffington-wood to watch the fox cubs playing in the green rides; sometimes to Rosy Brook, to cut long whispering reeds which grew there to make pan-pipes of; sometimes to Moor Mills, where was a piece of old forest land, with short browsed turf and tufted brambly thickets stretching under the oaks, amongst which rumour declared that a raven, last of his race, still lingered;

or to the sand-hills, in vain quest of rabbits; and birds'-nesting, in the season, anywhere and everywhere.

The few neighbours of the Squire's own rank every now and then would shrug their shoulders as they drove or rode by a party of boys with Tom in the middle, carrying along bulrushes or whispering reeds, or great bundles of cowslip and meadow-sweet, or young starlings or magpies, or other spoil of wood, brook, or meadow: and Lawyer Red-tape might mutter to Squire Straightback at the Board, that no good would come of the young Browns, if they were let run wild with all the dirty village boys, whom the best farmers' sons even would not play with. And the Squire might reply with a shake of his head, that *his* sons only mixed with their equals, and never went into the village without the governess or a footman. But luckily Squire Brown was full as stiff-backed as his neighbours, and so went on his own way; and Tom and his younger brothers, as they grew up, went on playing with the village boys without the idea of equality or inequality (except in wrestling, running, and climbing) ever entering their heads, as it doesn't till it's put there by Jack Nastys or fine ladies' maids.

I don't mean to say it would be the case in all villages, but it certainly was so in this one; the village boys were full as manly and honest, and certainly purer than those in a higher rank; and Tom got more harm from his equals in his first fortnight at a private-school, where he went when he was nine years old, than he had from his village friends from the day he left Charity's apron-strings.

Great was the grief amongst the village school-boys when Tom drove off with Squire, one August morning, to meet the coach on his way to school. Each of them had given him some little present of the best that he had, and his small private box was full of peg-tops, white marbles (called 'alley-taws' in the Vale), screws, birds' eggs, whip-cord, jews-harps, and other miscellaneous boys' wealth. Poor Jacob Doodle-calf, in floods of tears, had pressed upon him with spluttering earnestness his lame pet hedgehog (he had always some poor broken-down beast or bird by him); but this Tom had been obliged to refuse by the Squire's order. He had given them all a great tea under the big elm in their playground, for which Madam Brown had supplied the biggest cake ever seen in our village; and Tom was really as sorry to leave them as they to lose him, but his sorrow was not unmixed with the pride and excitement of making a new step in life.

And this feeling carried him through his first parting with his mother better than could have been expected. Their love was as fair and whole as human love can be, perfect self-sacrifice on the one side, meeting a young and true heart on the other. It is not within the scope of my book, however, to speak of family relations, or I should have much to say on the subject of English mothers—aye, and of English fathers, and sisters, and brothers too.

Neither have I room to speak of our private schools: what I have to say is about public schools, those much abused and much delauded institutions peculiar to England. So we must hurry through Master Tom's year at a private school as fast as we can.

It was a fair average specimen, kept by a gentleman, with another gentleman as second master; but it was little enough of the real work they did—merely coming into school when lessons were prepared and all ready to be heard. The whole discipline of the school out of lesson hours was in the hands of the two ushers, one of whom was always with the boys in their playground, in the school, at meals—in fact at all times and everywhere, till they were fairly in bed at night.

Now the theory of private schools is (or was) constant supervision out of school; therein differing fundamentally from that of public schools.

It may be right or wrong; but if right, this supervision surely ought to be the especial work of the headmaster, the responsible person. The object of all schools is not to ram Latin and Greek into boys, but to make them good English boys, good future citizens; and by far the most important part of that work must be done, or not done, out of school hours. To leave it therefore in the hands of inferior men is just giving up the highest and hardest part of the work of education. Were I a private schoolmaster, I should say, let who will hear the boys their lessons, but let me live with them when they are at play and rest.

The two ushers at Tom's first school were not gentlemen, and very poorly educated, and were only driving their poor trade of usher to get such living as they could out of it. They were not bad men, but had little heart for their work, and of course were bent on making it as easy as possible. One of the methods by which they endeavoured to accomplish this, was by encouraging tale-bearing, which had become a frightfully common vice in the school in consequence, and had sapped all the foundations of school morality. Another was by favouring grossly the biggest boys, who alone could have given them much trouble; whereby those young gentlemen became most abominable tyrants, oppressing the little boys in all the small mean ways which prevail in private schools.

Poor little Tom was made dreadfully unhappy in his first week, by a catastrophe which happened to his first letter home. With huge labour he had, on the very evening of his arrival, managed to fill two sides of a sheet of letter-paper with assurances of his love for dear mamma, his happiness at school, and his resolves to do all she would wish. This missive, with the help of the boy who sat at the desk next him, also a new arrival, he managed to fold successfully; but this done, they were sadly put to it for means of sealing. Envelopes were then unknown, they had no wax, and dared not disturb the stillness of the evening school-room by getting up and going to ask the usher for some. At length Tom's friend, being of an ingenious turn of mind, suggested sealing with ink, and the letter was accordingly stuck down with a blob of ink, and duly handed by Tom, on his way to bed, to the housekeeper to be posted. It was not till four days afterwards that that good dame sent for him, and produced the precious letter and some wax, saying, 'Oh, Master Brown, I forgot to tell you before, but your letter isn't sealed.' Poor Tom took the wax in silence and sealed his letter, with a huge lump rising in his throat during the process, and then ran away to a quiet corner of the playground, and burst into an agony of tears. The idea of his mother waiting day after day for the letter he had promised her at once, and perhaps thinking him forgetful of her, when he had done all in his power to make good his promise, was as bitter a grief as any which he had to undergo for many a long year. His wrath then was proportionately violent when he was aware of two boys, who stopped close by him, and one of whom, a fat gaby of a fellow, pointed at him and called him 'Young mammy-sick!' Whereupon Tom arose, and giving vent thus to his grief and shame and rage, smote his derider on the nose, and made it bleed—which sent that young worthy howling to the usher, who reported Tom for violent and unprovoked assault and battery. Hitting in the face was a felony punishable with flogging, other hitting only a misdemeanour—a distinction not altogether clear in principle. Tom however escaped the penalty by pleading 'primum tempus'; and having written a second letter to his mother, enclosing some forget-me-nots, which he picked on their first half-holiday walk, felt quite happy again, and began to enjoy vastly a good deal of his new life.

These half-holiday walks were the great events of the week. The whole fifty boys started after dinner with one of the ushers for Hazeldown, which was distant some mile or so from the school. Hazeldown measured some three miles round, and in the neighbourhood were several woods full of all manner of birds and butterflies. The usher walked slowly round the down with such boys as liked to accompany him; the rest scattered in all directions, being only bound to appear again when the usher had completed his round, and accompany him home. They were forbidden however to go anywhere except on the down and into the woods, the village being especially prohibited, where huge bulls-eyes and unctuous toffy might be procured in exchange for coin of the realm.

Various were the amusements to which the boys then betook themselves. At the entrance of the down there was a steep hillock, like the barrows of Tom's own downs. This mound was the weekly scene of terrific combats, at a game called by the queer name of 'mud-patties'. The boys who played divided into sides under different leaders, and one side occupied the mound. Then, all parties having provided themselves with many sods of turf, cut with their bread-and-cheese knives, the side which remained at the bottom proceeded to assault the mound, advancing up on all sides under cover of a heavy fire of turfs, and then struggling for victory with the occupants, which was theirs as soon as they could, even for a moment, clear the summit, when they in turn became the besieged. It was a good rough dirty game, and of great use in counteracting the sneaking tendencies of the school. Then others of the boys spread over the down, looking for the holes of humble-bees and mice, which they dug up without mercy, often (I regret to say) killing and skinning the unlucky mice, and (I do not regret to say) getting well stung by the humble-bees. Others went after butterflies and birds' eggs in their seasons; and Tom found on Hazeldown, for the first time, the beautiful little blue butterfly with golden spots on his wings, which he had never seen on his own downs, and dug out his first sand-martin's nest. This latter achievement resulted in a flogging, for the sand-martins built in a high bank close to the village, consequently out of bounds; but one of the bolder spirits of the school, who never could be happy unless he was doing something to which risk attached, easily persuaded Tom to break bounds and visit the martins' bank. From whence it being only a step to the toffy shop, what could be more simple than to go on there and fill their pockets; or what more certain than that on their return, a distribution of treasure having been made, the usher should shortly detect the forbidden smell of bulls-eyes, and, a search ensuing, discover the state of the breeches-pockets of Tom and his ally?

This ally of Tom's was indeed a desperate hero in the sight of the boys, and feared as one who dealt in magic or something approaching thereto. Which reputation came to him in this wise. The boys went to bed at eight, and of course consequently lay awake in the dark for an hour or two, telling ghost-stories by turns. One night, when it came to his turn, and he had dried up their souls by his story, he suddenly declared that he would make a fiery hand appear on the door; and to the astonishment and terror of the boys in his room, a hand, or something like it, in pale light, did then and there appear. The fame of this exploit having spread to the other rooms, and being discredited there, the young necromancer declared that the same wonder would appear in all the rooms in turn, which it accordingly did; and the whole circumstances having been privately reported to one of the ushers as usual, that functionary, after listening about at the doors of the rooms, by a sudden descent caught the performer in his night-shirt, with a box of phosphorus in his guilty hand. Lucifer-matches and all the present facilities for getting acquainted with fire were then unknown; the very name of phosphorus had something diabolic in it to the boy-mind; so Tom's ally, at the cost of a sound flogging, earned what many older folk covet much—the very decided fear of most of his companions.

He was a remarkable boy, and by no means a bad one. Tom stuck to him till he left, and got into many scrapes by so doing. But he was the great opponent of the tale-bearing habits of the school, and the open enemy of the ushers; and so worthy of all support.

Tom imbibed a fair amount of Latin and Greek at the school, but somehow on the whole it didn't suit him, or he it, and in the holidays he was constantly working the Squire to send him at once to a public school. Great was his joy then, when in the middle of his third half-year, in October, 183–, a fever broke out in the village, and the master having himself slightly sickened of it, the whole of the boys were sent off at a day's notice to their respective homes.

The Squire was not quite so pleased as Master Tom to see that young gentleman's brown merry face appear at home, some two months before the proper time, for Christmas holidays; and so after putting on his thinking cap, he retired to his study and wrote several letters, the result of which was, that one morning at the breakfast-table, about a fortnight after Tom's return, he addressed his wife with—'My dear, I have arranged that Tom shall go to Rugby at once, for the last six weeks of this half-year, instead of wasting them, riding and loitering about home. It is very kind of the Doctor to allow it. Will you see that his things are all ready by Friday, when I shall take him up to town, and send him down the next day by himself.'

Mrs Brown was prepared for the announcement, and merely suggested a doubt whether Tom were yet old enough to travel by himself. However, finding both father and son against her on this point, she gave in like a wise woman, and proceeded to prepare Tom's kit for his launch into a public school.

CHAPTER 4

THE STAGE COACH

'Let the steam-pot hiss till it's hot,
Give me the speed of the Tantivy trot.
Vulgar Coaching Song—Author Unknown.'

'Now, sir, time to get up if you please. Tally-ho coach for Leicester'll be round in half-an-hour, and don't wait for nobody.' So spake the boots of the Peacock Inn, Islington, at half-past two o'clock on the morning of a day in the early part of November, 183–, giving Tom at the same time a shake by the shoulder, and then putting down a candle and carrying off his shoes to clean.

Tom and his father had arrived in town from Berkshire the day before, and finding, on inquiry, that the Birmingham coaches which ran from the city did not pass through Rugby, but deposited their passengers at Dunchurch, a village three miles distant on the main road, where said passengers had to wait for the Oxford and Leicester coach in the evening, or to take a post-chaise—had resolved that Tom should travel down by the Tally-ho, which diverged from the main road and passed through Rugby itself. And as the Tally-ho was an early coach, they had driven out to the Peacock to be on the road.

Tom had never been in London, and would have liked to have stopped at the Belle Savage, where they had been put down by the Star, just at dusk, that he might have gone roving about those endless, mysterious, gaslit streets, which, with their glare and hum and moving crowds, excited him so that he couldn't talk even. But as soon as he found that the Peacock arrangement would get him to Rugby by twelve o'clock in the day, whereas otherwise he wouldn't be there till the evening, all other plans melted away; his one absorbing aim being to become a public school boy as fast as possible, and six hours sooner or later seeming to him of the most alarming importance.

Tom and his father had alighted at the Peacock, at about seven in the evening; and having heard with unfeigned joy the paternal order at the bar of steaks and oyster sauce for supper in half-an-hour, and seen his father seated cosily by the bright fire in the coffee-room, with the paper in his hand—Tom had run out to see about him, had wondered at all the vehicles passing and repassing, and had fraternized with the boots and ostler, from whom he ascertained that the Tally-ho was a tip-top goer, ten miles an hour including stoppages, and so punctual, that all the road set their clocks by her.

Then being summoned to supper, he had regaled himself in one of the bright little boxes of the Peacock coffee-room, on the beef-steak and unlimited oyster-sauce, and brown stout (tasted then for the first time—a day to be marked for ever by Tom with a white stone); had at first attended to the excellent advice which his father was bestowing on him from over his glass of steaming brandy and water, and then begun nodding, from the united effects of the stout, the fire, and the lecture. Till the Squire observing Tom's state, and remembering that it was nearly nine o'clock, and that the Tally-ho left at three, sent the little fellow off to the chambermaid, with a shake of the hand (Tom having stipulated in the morning before starting, that kissing should now cease between them) and a few parting words.

'And now, Tom my boy,' said the Squire, 'remember you are going, at your own earnest request, to be chucked into this great school, like a young bear with all your troubles before you—earlier than we should have sent you perhaps. If schools are what they were in my time, you'll see a great many cruel blackguard things done, and hear a deal of foul bad talk. But never fear. You tell the truth, keep a brave and kind heart, and never listen to or say anything you wouldn't have your mother and sister hear, and you'll never feel ashamed to come home, or we to see you.'

The allusion to his mother made Tom feel rather chokey, and he would have liked to have hugged his father well, if it hadn't been for the recent stipulation.

As it was, he only squeezed his father's hand, and looked bravely up and said, 'I'll try, father.'

'I know you will, my boy. Is your money all safe?'

'Yes,' said Tom, diving into one pocket to make sure.

'And your keys?' said the Squire.

'All right,' said Tom, diving into the other pocket.

'Well then, good-night. God bless you! I'll tell Boots to call you, and be up to see you off.'

Tom was carried off by the chambermaid in a brown study, from which he was roused in a clean little attic, by that buxom person calling him a little darling, and kissing him as she left the room; which indignity he was too much surprised to resent. And still thinking of his father's last words, and the look with which they were spoken, he knelt down and prayed, that come what might, he might never bring shame or sorrow on the dear folk at home.

Indeed the Squire's last words deserved to have their effect, for they had been the result of much anxious thought. All the way up to London he had pondered what he should say to Tom by way of parting advice; something that the boy could keep in his head ready for use. By way of assisting meditation, he had even gone the length of taking out his flint and steel, and tinder, and hammering away for a quarter of an hour till he had manufactured a light for a long Trichinopoli cheroot, which he silently puffed; to the no small wonder of Coachee, who was an old friend, and an institution on the Bath road; and who always expected a talk on the prospects and doings, agricultural and social, of the whole county when he carried the Squire.

To condense the Squire's meditation, it was somewhat as follows:

46

'I won't tell him to read his Bible, and love and serve God; if he don't do that for his mother's sake and teaching, he won't for mine. Shall I go into the sort of temptations he'll meet with? No, I can't do that. Never do for an old fellow to go into such things with a boy. He won't understand me. Do him more harm than good, ten to one. Shall I tell him to mind his work, and say he's sent to school to make himself a good scholar? Well, but he isn't sent to school for that—at any rate not for that mainly. I don't care a straw for Greek particles, or the digamma, no more does his mother. What is he sent to school for? Well, partly because he wanted so to go. If he'll only turn out a brave, helpful, truth-telling Englishman, and a gentleman, and a Christian, that's all I want,' thought the Squire; and upon this view of the case framed his last words of advice to Tom, which were well enough suited to his purpose.

For they were Tom's first thoughts as he tumbled out of bed at the summons of Boots, and proceeded rapidly to wash and dress himself. At ten minutes to three he was down in the coffee-room in his stockings, carrying his hat-box, coat, and comforter in his hand; and there he found his father nursing a bright fire, and a cup of hot coffee and a hard biscuit on the table.

'Now then, Tom, give us your things here, and drink that; there's nothing like starting warm, old fellow.'

Tom addressed himself to the coffee, and prattled away while he worked himself into his shoes and his great-coat, well warmed through; a Petersham coat with velvet collar, made tight after the abominable fashion of those days. And just as he is swallowing his last mouthful, winding his comforter round his throat, and tucking the ends into the breast of his coat, the horn sounds. Boots looks in and says, 'Tally-ho, sir;' and they hear the ring and the rattle of the four fast trotters and the town-made drag, as it dashes up to the Peacock.

'Anything for us, Bob?' says the burly guard, dropping down from behind, and slapping himself across the chest.

'Young genl'm'n, Rugby; three parcels, Leicester; hamper o' game, Rugby,' answers ostler.

'Tell young gent to look alive,' says guard, opening the hindboot and shooting in the parcels after examining them by the lamps. 'Here, shove the portmanteau up a-top—I'll fasten him presently. Now then, sir, jump up behind.'

'Good-bye, father—my love at home.' A last shake of the hand.

Up goes Tom, the guard catching his hat-box and holding on with one hand, while with the other he claps the horn to his mouth. Toot, toot, toot! the ostler lets go their heads, the four bays plunge at the collar, and away goes the Tally-ho into the darkness, forty-five seconds from the time they pulled up; Ostler, Boots, and the Squire, stand looking after them under the Peacock lamp.

'Sharp work!' says the Squire, and goes in again to his bed, the coach being well out of sight and hearing.

Tom stands up on the coach and looks back at his father's figure as long as he can see it, and then the guard having disposed of his luggage comes to an anchor, and finishes his buttonings and other preparations for facing the three hours before dawn; no joke for those who minded cold, on a fast coach in November, in the reign of his late Majesty.

I sometimes think that you boys of this generation are a deal tenderer fellows than we used to be. At any rate you're much more comfortable travellers, for I see every one of you with his rug or plaid, and other dodges for preserving the caloric, and most of you going in those fuzzy, dusty, padded first-class carriages. It was another affair altogether, a dark ride on the top of the Tally-ho, I can tell you, in a tight Petersham coat, and your feet dangling six inches from the floor. Then you knew what cold was, and what it was to be without legs, for not a bit of feeling had you in them after the first half-hour. But it had its pleasures, the old dark ride. First there was the consciousness of silent endurance, so dear to every Englishman—of standing out against something, and not giving in. Then there was the music of the rattling harness, and the ring of the horses' feet on the hard road, and the glare of the two bright lamps through the steaming hoar-frost, over the leaders' ears, into the darkness; and the cheery toot of the guard's horn, to warn some drowsy pikeman or the ostler at the next change; and the looking forward to daylight—and last but not least, the delight of returning sensation in your toes.

Then the break of dawn and the sunrise, where can they be ever seen in perfection but from a coach roof? You want motion and change and music to see them in their glory; not the music of singing-men and singing-women, but good silent music, which sets itself in your own head, the accompaniment of work and getting over the ground.

The Tally-ho is past St Alban's, and Tom is enjoying the ride, though half frozen. The guard, who is alone with him on the back of the coach, is silent, but has muffled Tom's feet up in straw, and put the end of an oat-sack over his knees. The darkness has driven him inwards, and he has gone over his little past life, and thought of all his doings and promises, and of his mother and sister, and his father's last words; and has made fifty good resolutions, and means to bear himself like a brave Brown as he is, though a young one. Then he has been forward into the mysterious boy-future, speculating as to what sort of a place Rugby is, and what they do there, and calling up all the stories of public schools which he has heard from big boys in the holidays. He is chock full of hope and life, notwithstanding the cold, and kicks his heels against the back-board, and would like to sing, only he doesn't know how his friend the silent guard might take it.

And now the dawn breaks at the end of the fourth stage, and the coach pulls up at a little road-side inn with huge stables behind. There is a bright fire gleaming through the red curtains of the bar-window, and the door is open. The coachman catches his whip into a double thong, and throws it to the ostler; the steam of the horses rises straight up into the air. He has put them along over the last two miles, and is two minutes before his time; he rolls down from the box and into the inn. The guard rolls off behind. 'Now, sir,' says he to Tom, 'you just jump down, and I'll give you a drop of something to keep the cold out.'

Tom finds a difficulty in jumping, or indeed in finding the top of the wheel with his feet, which may be in the next world for all he feels; so the guard picks him off the coach-top, and sets him on his legs, and they stump off into the bar, and join the coachman and the other outside passengers.

Here a fresh-looking barmaid serves them each with a glass of early purl as they stand before the fire, coachman and guard exchanging business remarks. The purl warms the cockles of Tom's heart and makes him cough.

'Rare tackle that, sir, of a cold morning,' says the coachman, smiling; 'Time's up.' They are out again and up; coachee the last, gathering the reins into his hands and talking to Jem the ostler about the mare's shoulder, and then swinging himself up on to the box—the horses dashing off in a canter before he falls into his seat. Toot-toot-tootle-too goes the horn, and away they are again, five-and-thirty miles on their road (nearly half-way to

49

Rugby, thinks Tom), and the prospect of breakfast at the end of the stage.

And now they begin to see, and the early life of the countryside comes out; a market cart or two, men in smock-frocks going to their work pipe in mouth, a whiff of which is no bad smell this bright morning. The sun gets up, and the mist shines like silver gauze. They pass the hounds jogging along to a distant meet, at the heels of the huntsman's hack, whose face is about the colour of the tails of his old pink, as he exchanges greetings with coachman and guard. Now they pull up at a lodge, and take on board a well muffled up sportsman, with his gun-case and carpet-bag. An early up-coach meets them, and the coachmen gather up their horses, and pass one another with the accustomed lift of the elbow, each team doing eleven miles an hour, with a mile to spare behind if necessary. And here comes breakfast.

'Twenty minutes here, gentlemen,' says the coachman, as they pull up at half-past seven at the inn door.

Have we not endured nobly this morning, and is not this a worthy reward for much endurance? There is the low dark wainscoted room hung with sporting prints; the hat-stand (with a whip or two standing up in it belonging to bagmen who are still snug in bed), by the door; the blazing fire, with the quaint old glass over the mantelpiece, in which is stuck a large card with the list of the meets for the week of the county hounds. The table covered with the whitest of cloths and of china, and bearing a pigeon-pie, ham, round of cold boiled beef cut from a mammoth ox, and the great loaf of household bread on a wooden trencher. And here comes in the stout head waiter, puffing under a tray of hot viands; kidneys and a steak, transparent rashers and poached eggs, buttered toast and muffins, coffee and tea, all smoking hot. The table can never hold it all; the cold meats are removed to the sideboard, they were only put on for show and to give us an appetite. And now fall on, gentlemen all. It is a well-known sporting-house, and the breakfasts are famous. Two or three men in pink, on their way to the meet, drop in, and are very jovial and sharp-set, as indeed we all are.

'Tea or coffee, sir?' says head waiter, coming round to Tom.

'Coffee, please,' says Tom, with his mouth full of muffin and kidney; coffee is a treat to him, tea is not.

Our coachman, I perceive, who breakfasts with us, is a cold beef man. He also eschews hot potations, and addicts himself to a tankard of ale, which is brought him by the barmaid. Sportsman looks on approvingly, and orders a ditto for himself.

Tom has eaten kidney and pigeon pie, and imbibed coffee, till his little skin is as tight as a drum; and then has the further pleasure of paying head waiter out of his own purse, in a dignified manner, and walks out before the inn door to see the horses put to. This is done leisurely and in a highly-finished manner by the ostlers, as if they enjoyed the not being hurried. Coachman comes out with his way-bill, and puffing a fat cigar which the sportsman has given him. Guard emerges from the tap, where he prefers breakfasting, licking round a tough-looking doubtful cheroot, which you might tie round your finger, and three whiffs of which would knock any one else out of time.

The pinks stand about the inn door lighting cigars and waiting to see us start, while their hacks are led up and down the market-place on which the inn looks. They all know our sportsman, and we feel a reflected credit when we see him chatting and laughing with them.

'Now, sir, please,' says the coachman; 'all the rest of the passengers are up; the guard is locking the hind boot.'

'A good run to you,' says the sportsman to the pinks, and is by the coachman's side in no time.

'Let 'em go, Dick!' The ostlers fly back, drawing off the cloths from their glossy loins, and away we go through the market-place and down the High Street, looking in at the first-floor windows, and seeing several worthy burgesses shaving thereat; while all the shopboys who are cleaning the windows, and housemaids who are doing the steps, stop and look pleased as we rattle past, as if we were a part of their legitimate morning's amusement. We clear the town, and are well out between the hedgerows again as the town clock strikes eight.

The sun shines almost warmly, and breakfast has oiled all springs and loosened all tongues. Tom is encouraged by a remark or two of the guard's between the puffs of his oily cheroot, and besides is getting tired of not talking. He is too full of his destination to talk about anything else; and so asks the guard if he knows Rugby.

'Goes through it every day of my life. Twenty minutes afore twelve down—ten o'clock up.'

'What sort of a place is it, please?' says Tom.

Guard looks at him with a comical expression. 'Werry out-o'-the-way place, sir; no paving to streets, nor no lighting. 'Mazin' big horse and cattle fair in autumn—lasts a week—just over now. Takes town a week to get clean after it. Fairish hunting country. But slow place, sir, slow place; off the main road you see—only three coaches a-day, and one on 'em a two-oss wan, more like a hearse nor a coach—Regulator—comes from Oxford. Young genl'm'n at school calls her Pig and Whistle, and goes up to college by her (six miles an hour) when they goes to enter. Belong to school, sir?'

'Yes,' says Tom, not unwilling for a moment that the guard should think him an old boy. But then having some qualms as to the truth of the assertion, and seeing that if he were to assume the character of an old boy he couldn't go on asking the questions he wanted, added—'that is to say, I'm on my way there. I'm a new boy.'

The guard looked as if he knew this quite as well as Tom.

'You're werry late, sir,' says the guard; 'ony six weeks to-day to the end of the half.' Tom assented. 'We takes up fine loads this day six weeks, and Monday and Tuesday arter. Hopes we shall have the pleasure of carrying you back.'

Tom said he hoped they would; but he thought within himself that his fate would probably be the Pig and Whistle.

'It pays uncommon cert'nly,' continues the guard. 'Werry free with their cash is the young genl'm'n. But, Lor' bless you, we gets into such rows all 'long the road, what wi' their pea-shooters, and long whips, and hollering, and upsetting every one as comes by; I'd a sight sooner carry one or two on 'em, sir, as I may be a carryin' of you now, than a coach-load.'

'What do they do with the pea-shooters?' inquires Tom.

'Do wi' 'em! why, peppers every one's faces as we comes near, 'cept the young gals, and breaks windows wi' them too, some on 'em shoots so hard. Now 'twas just here last June, as we was a driving up the first-day boys, they was mendin' a quarter-mile of road, and there was a lot of Irish chaps, reg'lar roughs, a breaking stones. As we comes up, "Now, boys," says young gent on the box (smart young fellow and desper't reckless), "here's fun! let the Pats have it about the ears." "God's sake, sir," says Bob (that's my mate the coachman), "don't go for to shoot at 'em, they'll knock us off the coach." "Damme, Coachee," says young my lord, "you ain't afraid; hoora, boys! let 'em have it." "Hoora," sings out the others,

52

and fills their mouths chock full of peas to last the whole line. Bob seeing as 'twas to come, knocks his hat over his eyes, hollers to his 'osses, and shakes 'em up, and away we goes up to the line on 'em, twenty miles an hour. The Pats begins to hoora too, thinking it was a runaway, and first lot on 'em stands grinnin' and wavin' their old hats as we comes abreast on 'em; and then you'd ha' laughed to see how took aback and choking savage they looked, when they gets the peas a stinging all over 'em. But bless you, the laugh weren't all of our side, sir, by a long way. We was going fast, and they was so took aback, that they didn't take what was up till we was half-way up the line. Then 'twas "look out all", surely. They howls all down the line fit to frighten you, some on 'em runs arter us and tries to clamber up behind, only we hits 'em over the fingers and pulls their hands off; one as had had it very sharp act'ly runs right at the leaders, as though he'd ketch 'em by the heads, ony luck'ly for him he misses his tip, and comes over a heap o' stones first. The rest picks up stones, and gives it us right away till we gets out of shot, the young gents holding out werry manful with the pea-shooters and such stones as lodged on us, and a pretty many there was too. Then Bob picks hisself up again, and looks at young gent on box werry solemn. Bob'd had a rum un in the ribs, which'd like to ha' knocked him off the box, or made him drop the reins. Young gent on box picks hisself up, and so does we all, and looks round to count damage. Box's head cut open and his hat gone; 'nother young gent's hat gone: mine knocked in at the side, and not one on us as wasn't black and blue somewheres or another, most on 'em all over. Two pound ten to pay for damage to paint, which they subscribed for there and then, and give Bob and me an extra half-sovereign each; but I wouldn't go down that line again not for twenty half-sovereigns.' And the guard shook his head slowly, and got up and blew a clear brisk toot, toot.

'What fun!' said Tom, who could scarcely contain his pride at this exploit of his future schoolfellows. He longed already for the end of the half that he might join them.

' 'Taint such good fun though, sir, for the folk as meets the coach, nor for we who has to go back with it next day. Them Irishers last summer had all got stones ready for us, and was all but letting drive, and we'd got two reverend gents aboard too. We pulled up at the beginning of the line, and pacified them, and we're never going to carry no more pea-shooters, unless they promises not to

53

fire when there's a line of Irish chaps a stone-breaking.' The guard stopped and pulled away at his cheroot, regarding Tom benignantly the while.

'Oh, don't stop! Tell us something more about the pea-shooting.'

'Well, there'd like to have been a pretty piece of work over it at Bicester, a while back. We was six mile from the town, when we meets an old square-headed grey-haired yeoman chap, a jogging along quite quiet. He looks up at the coach, and just then a pea hits him on the nose, and some catches his cob behind and makes him dance up on his hind legs. I see'd the old boy's face flush and look plaguy awkward, and I thought we was in for somethin' nasty.

'He turns his cob's head, and rides quietly after us just out of shot. How that ere cob did step! we never shook him off not a dozen yards in the six miles. At first the young gents were werry lively on him; but afore we got in, seeing how steady the old chap come on, they was quite quiet, and laid their heads together what they should do. Some was for fighting, some for axing his pardon. He rides into the town close after us, comes up when we stops, and says the two as shot at him must come before a magistrate; and a great crowd comes round, and we couldn't get the osses to. But the young 'uns they all stand by one another, and says all or none must go, and as how they'd fight it out, and have to be carried. Just as 'twas getting serious, and the old boy and the mob was going to pull 'em off the coach, one little fellow jumps up and says, "Here—I'll stay—I'm only going three miles further. My father's name's Davis, he's known about here, and I'll go before the magistrate with this gentleman." "What! be thee parson Davis' son," says the old boy. "Yes," says the young 'un. "Well, I be mortal sorry to meet thee in such company, but for thy father's sake and thine (for thee bi'st a brave young chap) I'll say no more about it." Didn't the boys cheer him, and the mob cheered the young chap—and then one of the biggest gets down, and begs his pardon werry gentlemanly for all the rest, saying as they all had been plaguy vexed from the first, but didn't like to ax his pardon till then, 'cause they felt they hadn't ought to shirk the consequences of their joke. And then they all got down, and shook hands with the old boy, and asked him to all parts of the country, to their homes, and we drives off twenty minutes behind time, with cheering and hollering as if we was county members. But, Lor' bless you, sir,' says the guard, smacking his hand down on his knee and looking full into Tom's face, 'ten minutes after they was all as bad as ever.'

Tom showed such undisguised and open-mouthed interest in his narrations, that the old guard rubbed up his memory, and launched out into a graphic history of all the performances of the boys, on the roads for the last twenty years. Off the road he couldn't go; the exploit must have been connected with horses or vehicles to hang in the old fellow's head. Tom tried him off his own ground once or twice, but found he knew nothing beyond, and so let him have his head, and the rest of the road bowled easily away; for old Blow-hard (as the boys called him) was a dry old file, with much kindness and humour, and a capital spinner of a yarn when he had broken the neck of his day's work, and got plenty of ale under his belt.

What struck Tom's youthful imagination most, was the desperate and lawless character of most of the stories. Was the guard hoaxing him? He couldn't help hoping that they were true. It's very odd how almost all English boys love danger; you can get ten to join a game, or climb a tree, or swim a stream, when there's a chance of breaking their limbs or getting drowned, for one who'll stay on level ground, or in his depth, or play quoits or bowls.

The guard had just finished an account of a desperate fight which had happened at one of the fairs between the drovers and the farmers with their whips, and the boys with cricket-bats and wickets, which arose out of a playful but objectionable practice of the boys of going round to the public-houses and taking the linch-pins out of the wheels of the gigs, and was moralizing upon the way in which the Doctor, 'a terrible stern man he'd heard tell,' had come down upon several of the performers, 'sending three on 'em off next morning, each in a pochay with a parish constable,' when they turned a corner and neared the milestone, the third from Rugby. By the stone two boys stood, their jackets buttoned tight, waiting for the coach.

'Look here, sir,' says the guard, after giving a sharp toot-toot, 'there's two on 'em, out and out runners they be. They comes out about twice or three times a-week, and spirts a mile alongside of us.'

And as they came up, sure enough, away went the two boys along the footpath, keeping up with the horses; the first a light clean made fellow going on springs, the other stout and round-shouldered, labouring in his pace but going as dogged as a bull-terrier.

Old Blow-hard looked on admiringly. 'See how beautiful that there un holds hisself together, and goes from his hips, sir,' said he; 'he's a "mazin' fine runner. Now many coachmen as drives a first-rate team'd put it on, and try and pass 'em. But Bob, sir, bless you, he's tender-hearted; he'd sooner pull in a bit if he see'd 'em gettin' beat. I do b'lieve too as that there un'd sooner break his heart than let us go by him afore next milestone.'

At the second milestone the boys pulled up short, and waved their hats to the guard, who had his watch out and shouted '4.56,' thereby indicating that the mile had been done in four seconds under five minutes. They passed several more parties of boys, all of them objects of the deepest interest to Tom, and came in sight of the town at ten minutes before twelve. Tom fetched a long breath, and thought he had never spent a pleasanter day. Before he went to bed he had quite settled that it must be the greatest day he should ever spend, and didn't alter his opinion for many a long year—if he has yet.

<hr />

CHAPTER 5

RUGBY AND FOOTBALL

'—Foot and eye opposed
In dubious strife.'
—*Scott*.

'And so here's Rugby, sir, at last, and you'll be in plenty of time for dinner at the Schoolhouse, as I tell'd you,' said the old guard, pulling his horn out of its case, and tootle-tooing away; while the coachman shook up his horses, and carried them along the side of the school close, round Dead-man's corner, past the school gates, and down the High Street, to the Spread Eagle; the wheelers in a spanking trot, and leaders cantering, in a style which would not have disgraced 'Cherry Bob', 'ramping, stamping, tearing, swearing Billy Harwood', or any other of the old coaching heroes.

Tom's heart beat quick as he passed the great school field or close, with its noble elms, in which several games at football were going on, and tried to take in at once the long line of grey buildings, beginning with the chapel, and ending with the Schoolhouse, the residence of the headmaster, where the great flag was lazily waving from the highest round tower. And he began already to be proud of being a Rugby boy, as he passed the school gates, with the oriel window above, and saw the boys standing there, looking as if the town belonged to them, and nodding in a familiar manner to the coachman, as if any one of them would be quite equal to getting on the box, and working the team down street as well as he.

One of the young heroes however ran out from the rest, and scrambled up behind; where, having righted himself, and nodded to the guard, with 'How do, Jem?' he turned short round to Tom, and, after looking him over for a minute, began—

'I say, you fellow, is your name Brown?'

'Yes,' said Tom, in considerable astonishment; glad however to have lighted on some one already who seemed to know him.

'Ah, I thought so; you know my old aunt, Miss East, she lives somewhere down your way in Berkshire. She wrote to me that you were coming today, and asked me to give you a lift.'

Tom was somewhat inclined to resent the patronizing air of his new friend, a boy of just about his own height and age, but gifted with the most transcendent coolness and assurance, which Tom felt to be aggravating and hard to bear, but couldn't for the life of him help admiring and envying—especially when young my lord begins hectoring two or three long loafing fellows, half porter, half stableman, with a strong touch of the blackguard; and in the end arranges with one of them, nicknamed Cooey, to carry Tom's luggage up to the Schoolhouse for sixpence.

'And heark'ee, Cooey, it must be up in ten minutes, or no more jobs from me. Come along, Brown.' And away swaggers the young potentate, with his hands in his pockets, and Tom at his side.

'All right, sir,' says Cooey, touching his hat, with a leer and a wink at his comrades.

'Hullo tho',' says East, pulling up, and taking another look at Tom, 'this'll never do—haven't you got a hat?—we never wear caps here. Only the louts wear caps. Bless you, if you were to go into the quadrangle with that thing on, I—don't know what'd happen.' The very idea was quite beyond young Master East, and he looked unutterable things.

Tom thought his cap a very knowing affair, but confessed that he had a hat in his hat-box; which was accordingly at once extracted from the hind boot and Tom equipped in his go-to-meeting roof, as his new friend called it. But this didn't quite suit his fastidious taste in another minute, being too shiny; so, as they walk up the town, they dive into Nixon's the hatter's, and Tom is arrayed, to his utter astonishment, and without paying for it, in a regulation cat-skin at seven-and-sixpence; Nixon undertaking to send the best hat up to the matron's room, Schoolhouse, in half-an-hour.

'You can send in a note for a tile on Monday, and make it all right, you know,' said Mentor; 'we're allowed two seven-and-sixers a half, besides what we bring from home.'

Tom by this time began to be conscious of his new social position and dignities, and to luxuriate in the realized ambition of being a public school boy at last, with a vested right of spoiling two seven-and-sixers in half a year.

'You see,'—said his friend, as they strolled up towards the school gates, in explanation of his conduct—'a great deal depends on how a fellow cuts up at first. If he's got nothing odd about him, and answers straightforward, and holds his head up, he gets on. Now you'll do very well as to rig, all but that cap. You see I'm doing the handsome thing by you, because my father knows yours; besides, I want to please the old lady. She gave me half-a-sov this half, and perhaps'll double it next, if I keep in her good books.'

There's nothing for candour like a lower-school boy, and East was a genuine specimen—frank, hearty, and good-natured, well satisfied with himself and his position, and chock full of life and spirits, and all the Rugby prejudices and traditions which he had been able to get together, in the long course of one half year, during which he had been at the Schoolhouse.

And Tom, notwithstanding his bumptiousness, felt friends with him at once, and began sucking in all his ways and prejudices, as fast as he could understand them.

East was great in the character of cicerone; he carried Tom through the great gates, where were only two or three boys. These satisfied themselves with the stock questions—'You fellow, what's your name? Where do you come from? How old are you? Where do you board? and, What form are you in?'—and so they passed on through the quadrangle and a small courtyard, upon which looked down a lot of little windows (belonging, as his guide informed him,

58

to some of the Schoolhouse studies) into the matron's room, where East introduced Tom to that dignitary; made him give up the key of his trunk, that the matron might unpack his linen, and told the story of the hat and of his own presence of mind: upon the relation whereof, the matron laughingly scolded him, for the coolest new boy in the house; and East, indignant at the accusation of newness, marched Tom off into the quadrangle, and began showing him the schools, and examining him as to his literary attainments; the result of which was a prophecy that they would be in the same form, and could do their lessons together.

'And now come in and see my study; we shall have just time before dinner; and afterwards, before calling over, we'll do the close.'

Tom followed his guide through the Schoolhouse hall, which opens into the quadrangle. It is a great room thirty feet long and eighteen high, or thereabouts, with two great tables running the whole length, and two large fireplaces at the side, with blazing fires in them, at one of which some dozen boys were standing and lounging, some of whom shouted to East to stop; but he shot through with his convoy, and landed him in the long dark passages, with a large fire at the end of each, upon which the studies opened. Into one of these, in the bottom passage, East bolted with our hero, slamming and bolting the door behind them, in case of pursuit from the hall, and Tom was for the first time in a Rugby boy's citadel.

He hadn't been prepared for separate studies, and was not a little astonished and delighted with the palace in question.

It wasn't very large certainly, being about six feet long by four broad. It couldn't be called light, as there were bars and a grating to the window; which little precautions were necessary in the studies on the ground-floor looking out into the close, to prevent the exit of small boys after locking-up, and the entrance of contraband articles. But it was uncommonly comfortable to look at, Tom thought. The space under the window at the further end was occupied by a square table covered with a reasonably clean and whole red and blue check tablecloth; a hard-seated sofa covered with red stuff occupied one side, running up to the end, and making a seat for one, or by sitting close, for two, at the table; and a good stout wooden chair afforded a seat to another boy, so that three could sit and work together. The walls were wainscoted half-way up, the wainscot being covered with green baize, the remainder with a bright-patterned paper, on which hung three or four prints, of dog's heads, Grimaldi winning the Aylesbury steeple-chase, Amy Robsart, the reigning Waverley beauty of the day, and Tom Crib in a posture of defence, which did no great credit to the science of that hero, if truly represented. Over the door were a row of hat-pegs, and on each side bookcases with cupboards at the bottom; shelves and cupboards being filled indiscriminately with school-books, a cup or two, a mousetrap, and brass sticks, leather straps, a fustian bag, and some curious-looking articles, which puzzled Tom not a little, until his friend explained that they were climbing irons, and showed their use. A cricket bat and small fishing-rod stood up in one corner.

This was the residence of East and another boy in the same form, and had more interest for Tom than Windsor Castle, or any other residence in the British Isles. For was he not about to become the joint owner of a similar home, the first place which he could call his own? One's own—what a charm there is in the words! How long it takes boy and man to find out their worth! how fast most of us hold on to them! faster and more jealously, the nearer we are to the general home, into which we can take nothing, but must go naked as we came into the world. When shall we learn that he who multiplieth possessions multiplieth troubles, and that the one single use of things which we call our own, is that they may be his who hath need of them?

'And shall I have a study like this too?' said Tom.

'Yes, of course, you'll be chummed with some fellow on Monday, and you can sit here till then.'

'What nice places!'

'They're well enough,' answered East patronizingly, 'only uncommon cold at nights sometimes. Gower, that's my chum, and I make a fire with paper on the floor after supper generally, only that makes it so smoky.'

'But there's a big fire out in the passage,' said Tom.

'Precious little good we get of that tho',' said East; 'Jones the praepostor has the study at the fire end, and he has rigged up an iron rod and green baize curtain across the passage, which he draws at night, and sits there with his door open, so he gets all the fire, and hears if we come out of our studies after eight, or make a noise. However, he's taken to sitting in the fifth-form room lately, so we do get a bit of fire now sometimes; only keep a sharp

60

look-out that he don't catch you behind his curtain when he comes down—that's all.'

A quarter past one now struck, and the bell began tolling for dinner, so they went into the hall and took their places, Tom at the very bottom of the second table next to the praepostor (who sat at the end to keep order there), and East a few places higher. And now Tom for the first time saw his future schoolfellows in a body. In they came, some hot and ruddy from football or long walks, some pale and chilly from hard reading in their studies, some from loitering over the fire at the pastrycook's, dainty mortals, bringing with them pickles and saucebottles to help them with their dinners. And a great big bearded man, whom Tom took for a master, began calling over the names, while the great joints were being rapidly carved on a third table in the corner by the old verger and the housekeeper. Tom's turn came last, and meanwhile he was all eyes, looking first with awe at the great man who sat close to him, and was helped first, and who read a hard-looking book all the time he was eating; and when he got up and walked off to the fire, at the small boys around him, some of whom were reading, and the rest talking in whispers to one another, or stealing one another's bread, or shooting pellets, or digging their forks through the tablecloth. However, notwithstanding his curiosity, he managed to make a capital dinner by the time the big man called 'Stand up!' and said grace.

As soon as dinner was over, and Tom had been questioned by such of his neighbours as were curious as to his birth, parentage, education, and other like matters, East, who evidently enjoyed his new dignity of patron and mentor, proposed having a look at the close, which Tom, athirst for knowledge, gladly assented to, and they went out through the quadrangle and past the big fives' court, into the great playground.

'That's the chapel you see,' said East, 'and there just behind it is the place for fights; you see it's most out of the way of the masters, who all live on the other side and don't come by here after first lesson or callings-over. That's when the fights come off. And all this part where we are is the little-side ground, right up to the trees, and on the other side of the trees is the big-side ground, where the great matches are played. And there's the island in the furthest corner; you'll know that well enough next half, when there's island fagging. I say, it's horrid cold, let's have a run across,' and away went East, Tom close behind him. East was evidently putting his best foot foremost, and Tom, who was mighty proud of his running, and not a little anxious to show his friend that although a new boy he was no milksop, laid himself down to work in his very best style. Right across the close they went, each doing all he knew, and there wasn't a yard between them when they pulled up at the island moat.

'I say,' said East, as soon as he got his wind, looking with much increased respect at Tom, 'you ain't a bad scud, not by no means. Well, I'm as warm as toast now.'

'But why do you wear white trousers in November?' said Tom. He had been struck by this peculiarity in the costume of almost all the Schoolhouse boys.

'Why, bless us, don't you know?—No, I forgot. Why to-day's the Schoolhouse match. Our house plays the whole of the School at football. And we all wear white trousers, to show 'em we don't care for hacks. You're in luck to come to-day. You just will see a match; and Brooke's going to let me play in quarters. That's more than he'll do for any other lower-school boy, except James, and he's fourteen.'

'Who's Brooke?'

. 'Why, that big fellow who called over at dinner, to be sure. He's cock of the School, and head of the Schoolhouse side, and the best kick and charge in Rugby.'

'Oh, but do show me where they play. And tell me about it. I love football so and I've played all my life. Won't Brooke let me play?'

'Not he,' said East, with some indignation; 'why you don't know the rules—you'll be a month learning them. And then it's no joke playing-up in a match, I can tell you. Quite another thing from your private school games. Why, there's been two collar-bones broken this half, and a dozen fellows lamed. And last year a fellow had his leg broken.'

Tom listened with the profoundest respect to this chapter of accidents, and followed East across the level ground till they came to a sort of gigantic gallows of two poles eighteen feet high, fixed upright in the ground some fourteen feet apart, with a cross bar running from one to the other at the height of ten feet or thereabouts.

'This is one of the goals,' said East, 'and you see the other, across there, right opposite, under the Doctor's wall. Well, the match is for the best of three goals; whichever side kicks two goals wins: and it won't do, you see, just to kick the ball through these posts, it must go over the cross bar; any height'll do, so long as it's between the posts. You'll have to stay in goal to touch the ball when it rolls behind the posts, because if the other side touch it they have a try at goal. Then we fellows in quarters, we play just about in front of goal here, and have to turn the ball and kick it back, before the big fellows on the other side can follow it up. And in front of us all the big fellows play, and that's where the scrummages are mostly.'

Tom's respect increased as he struggled to make out his friend's technicalities, and the other set to work to explain the mysteries of 'off your side', 'drop-kicks', 'punts', 'places', and the other intricacies of the great science of football.

'But how do you keep the ball between the goals?' said he; 'I can't see why it mightn't go right down to the chapel.'

'Why, that's out of play,' answered East. 'You see this gravel walk running down all along this side of the playing-ground, and the line of elms opposite on the other? Well, they're the bounds. As soon as the ball gets past them, it's in touch, and out of play. And then whoever first touches it, has to knock it straight out amongst the players-up, who make two lines with a space between them, every fellow going on his own side. Ain't there just fine scrummages then! and the three trees you see there which come out into the play, that's a tremendous place when the ball hangs there, for you get thrown against the trees, and that's worse than any hack.'

Tom wondered within himself as they strolled back again towards the fives' court, whether the matches were really such break-neck affairs as East represented, and whether, if they were, he should ever get to like them and play-up well.

He hadn't long to wonder, however, for next minute East cried out, 'Hurra! here's the punt-about—come along and try your hand at a kick.' The punt-about is the practice ball, which is just brought out and kicked about anyhow from one boy to another before callings-over and dinner, and at other odd times. They joined the boys who had brought it out, all small School-house fellows, friends of East; and Tom had the pleasure of trying his skill, and performed very creditably, after first driving his foot three inches into the ground, and then nearly kicking his leg into the air, in vigorous efforts to accomplish a drop-kick after the manner of East.

Presently more boys and bigger came out, and boys from other houses on their way to calling-over, and more balls were sent for. The crowd thickened as three o'clock approached; and when the hour struck, one hundred and fifty boys were hard at work. Then the balls were held, the master of the week came down in cap and gown to calling-over, and the whole school of three hundred boys swept into the big school to answer to their names.

'I may come in, mayn't I?' said Tom, catching East by the arm, and longing to feel one of them.

'Yes, come along, nobody'll say anything. You won't be so eager to get into calling-over after a month,' replied his friend; and they marched into the big school together, and up to the further end, where that illustrious form, the lower fourth, which had the honour of East's patronage for the time being, stood.

The master mounted into the high desk by the door, and one of the praepostors of the week stood by him on the steps, the other three marching up and down the middle of the school with their canes, calling out 'Silence, silence!' The sixth form stood close by the door on the left, some thirty in number, mostly great big grown men, as Tom thought, surveying them from a distance with awe. The fifth form behind them, twice their number and not quite so big. These on the left; and on the right the lower fifth, shell, and all the junior forms in order, while up the middle marched the three praepostors.

Then the praepostor who stands by the master calls out the names, beginning with the sixth form, and as he calls, each boy answers 'here' to his name, and walks out. Some of the sixth stop at the door to turn the whole string of boys into the close; it is a great match day, and every boy in the school, will-he nill-he, must be there. The rest of the sixth go forwards into the close, to see that no one escapes by any of the side gates.

To-day however being the Schoolhouse match, none of the Schoolhouse praepostors stay by the door to watch for truants of their side; there is *carte blanche* to the Schoolhouse fags to go where they like; 'They trust to our honour,' as East proudly informs Tom; 'they know very well that no Schoolhouse boy would cut the match. If he did, we'd very soon cut him, I can tell you.'

The master of the week being short-sighted, and the praepostors of the week small and not well up to their work, the lower school boys employ the ten minutes which elapse before their names are called, in pelting one another vigorously with acorns, which fly about in all directions. The small praepostors dash in every now and then, and generally chastise some quiet, timid boy who is equally afraid of acorns and canes, while the principal performers get dexterously out of the way; and so calling-over rolls on somehow, much like the big world, punishments lighting on wrong shoulders, and matters going generally in a queer, cross-grained way, but the end coming somehow, which is after all the great point. And now the master of the week has finished, and locked up the big school; and the praepostors of the week come out, sweeping the last remnant of the school fags—who had been loafing about the corners by the fives' court, in hopes of a chance of bolting—before them into the close.

'Hold the punt-about!' 'To the goals!' are the cries, and all stray balls are impounded by the authorities; and the whole mass of boys moves up towards the two goals, dividing as they go into three bodies That little band on the left, consisting of from fifteen to twenty boys, Tom amongst them, who are making for the goal under the Schoolhouse wall, are the Schoolhouse boys who are not to play-up, and have to stay in goal. The larger body moving to the island goal, are the school-boys in a like predicament. The great mass in the middle are the players-up, both sides mingled together; they are hanging their jackets, and all who mean real work, their hats, waistcoats, neck-handkerchiefs, and braces, on the railings round the small trees; and there they go by twos and threes up to their respective grounds. There is none of the colour and tastiness of get-up, you will perceive, which lends such a life to the present game at Rugby, making the dullest and worst fought match a pretty sight. Now each house has its own uniform of cap and jersey, of some lively colour: but at the time we are speaking of, plush caps have not yet come in, or uniforms of any sort, except the Schoolhouse white trousers, which are abominably cold today: let us get to work, bare-headed and girded with our plain leather straps—but we mean business, gentlemen.

And now that the two sides have fairly sundered, and each occupies its own ground, and we get a good look at them, what absurdity is this? You don't mean to say that those fifty or sixty boys in white trousers, many of them quite small, are going to play that huge mass opposite? Indeed I do, gentlemen; they're going to try at any rate, and won't make such a bad fight of it either, mark my word; for hasn't old Brooke won the toss, with his lucky halfpenny, and got choice of goals and kick-off? The new ball you may see lie there quite by itself, in the middle, pointing towards the school or island goal; in another minute it will be well on its way there. Use that minute in remarking how the Schoolhouse side is drilled. You will see in the first place, that the sixth-form boy, who has the charge of goal, has spread his force (the goal-keepers) so as to occupy the whole space behind the goal-posts, at distances of about five yards apart; a safe and well kept goal is the foundation of all good play. Old Brooke is talking to the captain of quarters; and now he moves away; see how that youngster spreads his men (the light brigade) carefully over the ground, half-way between their own goal and the body of their own players-up (the heavy brigade). These again play in several bodies; there is young Brooke and the bull-dogs—mark them well—they are 'the fighting brigade', the 'die-hards', larking about at leap-frog to keep themselves warm, and playing tricks on one another. And on each side of old Brooke, who is now standing in the middle of the ground and just going to kick-off, you see a separate wing of players-up, each with a boy of acknowledged prowess to look to—here Warner, and there Hedge; but over all is old Brooke, absolute as he of Russia, but wisely and bravely ruling over willing and worshipping subjects, a true football king. His face is earnest and careful as he glances a last time over his array, but full of pluck and hope, the sort of look I hope to see in my general when I go out to fight.

The School side is not organized in the same way. The goalkeepers are all in lumps, any-how and no-how; you can't distinguish between the players-up and the boys in quarters, and there is divided leadership, but with such odds in strength and weight it must take more than that to hinder them from winning, and so their leaders seem to think, for they let the players-up manage themselves.

But now look, there is a slight move forward of the Schoolhouse wings; a shout of 'Are you ready?' and loud affirmative reply. Old Brooke takes half-a-dozen quick steps, and away goes the ball spinning towards the School goal; seventy yards before it touches ground and at no point above twelve or fifteen feet high, a model kick-off; and the Schoolhouse cheer and rush on; the ball is returned, and they meet it and drive it back amongst the masses of the School already in motion. Then the two sides close, and you can see nothing for minutes but a swaying crowd of boys, at one point violently agitated. That is where the ball is, and there are the keen players to be met, and the glory and the hard knocks to be got: you hear the dull thud thud of the ball, and the shouts of 'Off your side', 'Down with him', 'Put him over', 'Bravo'. This is what we call a scrummage, gentlemen, and the first scrummage in a School-house match is no joke in the consulship of Plancus.

But see! it has broken, the ball is driven out on the Schoolhouse side, and the rush of the School carries it past the Schoolhouse players-up. 'Look out in quarters,' Brooke's and twenty other voices ring out; no need to call tho', the School-house captain of quarters has caught it on the bound, dodges the foremost Schoolboys, who are heading the rush, and sends it back with a good drop-kick well into the enemies' country. And then follows rush upon rush, and scrummage upon scrummage, the ball now driven through into the Schoolhouse quarters, and now into the School goal; for the Schoolhouse have not lost the advantage which the kick-off and a slight wind gave them at the outset, and are slightly 'penning' their adversaries. You say, you don't see much in it all; nothing but a struggling mass of boys, and a leather ball, which seems to excite them all to great fury, as a red rag does a bull. My dear sir, a battle would look much the same to you, except that the boys would be men, and the balls iron; but a battle would be worth your looking at for all that, and so is a football match. You can't be expected to appreciate the delicate strokes of play, the turns by which a game is lost and won—it takes an old player to do that, but the broad philosophy of football you can understand if you will. Come along with me a little nearer, and let us consider it together.

The ball has just fallen again where the two sides are thickest, and they close rapidly around it in a scrummage; it must be driven through now by force or skill, till it flies out on one side or the other. Look how differently the boys face it. Here come two of the bull-dogs, bursting through the outsiders; in they go, straight to the heart of the scrummage, bent on driving that ball out on the opposite side. That is what they mean to do. My sons, my sons! you are too hot; you have gone past the ball, and must struggle now right through the scrummage, and get round and back again to your own side, before you can be of any further use. Here comes young Brooke; he goes in as straight as you, but keeps his head, and backs and bends, holding himself still behind the ball, and driving it furiously when he gets the chance. Take a leaf out of his book, you young chargers. Here comes Speedicut, and Flashman the Schoolhouse bully, with shouts and great action. Won't you two come up to young Brooke, after locking-up, by the Schoolhouse fire, with 'Old fellow, wasn't that just a splendid scrummage by the three trees!' But he knows you, and so do we. You don't really want to drive that ball through that scrummage, chancing all hurt for the glory of the Schoolhouse—but to make us think that's what you want—a vastly different thing; and fellows of your kidney will never go through more than the skirts of a scrummage, where it's all push and no kicking. We respect boys who keep out of it, and don't sham going in; but you—we had rather not say what we think of you.

Then the boys who are bending and watching on the outside, mark them—they are most useful players, the dodgers; who seize on the ball the moment it rolls out from amongst the chargers, and away with it across to the opposite goal; they seldom go into the scrummage, but must have more coolness than the chargers: as endless as are boys' characters, so are their ways of facing or not facing a scrummage at football.

Three-quarters of an hour are gone; first winds are failing, and weight and numbers beginning to tell. Yard by yard the Schoolhouse have been driven back, contesting every inch of ground. The bull-dogs are the colour of mother earth from shoulder to ankle, except young Brooke, who has a marvellous knack of keeping his legs. The Schoolhouse are being penned in their turn, and now the ball is behind their goal, under the Doctor's wall. The Doctor and some of his family are there looking on, and seem as anxious as any boy for the success of the Schoolhouse. We get a minute's breathing time before old Brooke kicks out, and he gives the word to play strongly for touch, by the three trees. Away goes the ball, and the bull-dogs after it, and in another minute there is a shout of 'In touch', 'Our ball'. Now's your time, old Brooke, while your men are still fresh. He stands with the ball in his hand, while the two sides form in deep lines opposite one another: he must strike it straight out between them. The lines are thickest close to him, but young Brooke and two or three of his men are shifting up further, where the opposite line is weak. Old Brooke strikes it out straight and strong, and it falls opposite his brother. Hurra! that rush has taken it right through the School line, and away past the three trees, far into their quarters, and young

Brooke and the bull-dogs are close upon it. The School leaders rush back shouting 'Look out in goal,' and strain every nerve to catch him, but they are after the fleetest foot in Rugby. There they go straight for the School goal-posts, quarters scattering before them. One after another the bull-dogs go down, but young Brooke holds on. 'He is down.' No! a long stagger, but the danger is past; that was the shock of Crew, the most dangerous of dodgers. And now he is close to the School goal, the ball not three yards before him. There is a hurried rush of the School fags to the spot, but no one throws himself on the ball, the only chance, and young Brooke has touched it right under the School goal-posts.

The School leaders come up furious, and administer toco to the wretched fags nearest at hand; they may well be angry, for it is all Lombard-street to a china orange that the Schoolhouse kick a goal with the ball touched in such a good place. Old Brooke of course will kick it out, but who shall catch and place it? Call Crab Jones. Here he comes, sauntering along with a straw in his mouth, the queerest, coolest fish in Rugby: if he were tumbled into the moon this minute, he would just pick himself up without taking his hands out of his pockets or turning a hair. But it is a moment when the boldest charger's heart beats quick. Old Brooke stands with the ball under his arm motioning the School back; he will not kick-out till they are all in goal, behind the posts; they are all edging forwards, inch by inch, to get nearer for the rush at Crab Jones, who stands there in front of old Brooke to catch the ball. If they can reach and destroy him before he catches, the danger is over; and with one and same rush they will carry it right away to the Schoolhouse goal. Fond hope! It is kicked out and caught beautifully. Crab strikes his heel into the ground, to mark the spot where the ball was caught, beyond which the School line may not advance; but there they stand, five deep, ready to rush the moment the ball touches the ground. Take plenty of room! don't give the rush a chance of reaching you! place it true and steady! Trust Crab Jones—he has made a small hole with his heel for the ball to lie on, by which he is resting on one knee, with his eye on old Brooke. 'Now!' Crab places the ball at the word, old Brooke kicks, and it rises slowly and truly as the School rush forward.

Then a moment's pause, while both sides look up at the spinning ball. There it flies, straight between the two posts, some five feet above the cross-bar, an unquestioned goal; and a shout of real genuine joy rings out from the Schoolhouse players-up, and a faint echo of it comes over the close from the goal-keepers under the Doctor's wall. A goal in the first hour—such a thing hasn't been done in the Schoolhouse match this five years.

'Over!' is the cry: the two sides change goals, and the Schoolhouse goal-keepers come threading their way across through the masses of the School; the most openly triumphant of them, amongst whom is Tom, a Schoolhouse boy of two hours' standing, getting their ears boxed in the transit. Tom indeed is excited beyond measure, and it is all the sixth-form boy, kindest and safest of goal-keepers, has been able to do, to keep him from rushing out whenever the ball has been near their goal. So he holds him by his side, and instructs him in the science of touching.

At this moment Griffith, the itinerant vendor of oranges from Hill Morton, enters the close with his heavy baskets; there is a rush of small boys upon the little pale-faced man, the two sides mingling together subdued by the great Goddess Thirst, like the English and French by the streams in the Pyrenees. The leaders are past oranges and apples, but some of them visit their coats, and apply innocent-looking ginger-beer bottles to their mouths. It is no ginger-beer though I fear, and will do you no good. One short mad rush, and then a stitch in the side, and no more honest play; that's what comes of those bottles.

But now Griffith's baskets are empty, the ball is placed again midway, and the School are going to kick off. Their leaders have sent their lumber into goal, and rated the rest soundly, and one hundred and twenty picked players-up are there, bent on retrieving the game. They are to keep the ball in front of the Schoolhouse goal, and then to drive it in by sheer strength and weight. They mean heavy play and no mistake, and so old Brooke sees; and places Crab Jones in quarters just before the goal, with four or five picked players, who are to keep the ball away to the sides, where a try at goal, if obtained, will be less dangerous than in front. He himself, and Warner and Hedge, who have saved themselves till now, will lead the charges.

'Are you ready?' 'Yes.' And away comes the ball kicked high in the air, to give the School time to rush on and catch it as it falls. And here they are amongst us. Meet them like Englishmen, you Schoolhouse boys, and charge them home. Now is the time to show what mettle is in you—and there shall be a warm seat

70

by the hall fire, and honour, and lots of bottled beer to-night, for him who does his duty in the next half-hour. And they are well met. Again and again the cloud of their players-up gathers before our goal, and comes threatening on, and Warner or Hedge, with young Brooke and the relics of the bull-dogs, break through and carry the ball back; and old Brooke ranges the field like Job's war-horse, the thickest scrummage parts asunder before his rush, like the waves before a clipper's bows; his cheery voice rings over the field, and his eye is everywhere. And if these miss the ball, and it rolls dangerously in front of our goal, Crab Jones and his men have seized it and sent it away towards the sides with the unerring drop-kick. This is worth living for; the whole sum of school-boy existence gathered up into one straining, struggling half-hour, a half-hour worth a year of common life.

The quarter to five has struck, and the play slackens for a minute before goal; but there is Crew, the artful dodger, driving the ball in behind our goal, on the island side, where our quarters are weakest. Is there no one to meet him? Yes! look at little East! the ball is just at equal distances between the two, and they rush together, the young man of seventeen and the boy of twelve, and kick it at the same moment. Crew passes on without a stagger; East is hurled forward by the shock, and plunges on his shoulder, as if he would bury himself in the ground; but the ball rises straight into the air, and falls behind Crew's back, while the 'bravos' of the Schoolhouse attest the pluckiest charge of all that hard-fought day. Warner picks East up lame and half stunned, and he hobbles back into goal, conscious of having played the man.

And now the last minutes are come, and the School gather for their last rush every boy of the hundred and twenty who has a run left in him. Reckless of the defence of their own goal, on they come across the level big-side ground, the ball well down amongst them, straight for our goal, like the column of the old guard up the slope at Waterloo. All former charges have been child's play to this. Warner and Hedge have met them, but still on they come. The bull-dogs rush in for the last time; they are hurled over or carried back, striving hand, foot, and eyelids. Old Brooke comes sweeping round the skirts of the play, and turning short round, picks out the very heart of the scrummage, and plunges in. It wavers for a moment—he has the ball! No, it has passed him, and his voice rings out clear over the advancing tide, 'Look out in goal.' Crab Jones catches it for a moment; but before he can kick, the rush is upon him and passes over him; and he picks himself up behind them with his straw in his mouth, a little dirtier, but as cool as ever.

The ball rolls slowly in behind the Schoolhouse goal, not three yards in front of a dozen of the biggest School players-up.

There stand the Schoolhouse praepostor, safest of goalkeepers, and Tom Brown by his side, who has learned his trade by this time. Now is your time, Tom. The blood of all the Browns is up, and the two rush in together, and throw themselves on the ball, under the very feet of the advancing column; the praepostor on his hands and knees arching his back, and Tom all along on his face. Over them topple the leaders of the rush, shooting over the back of the praepostor, but falling flat on Tom, and knocking all the wind out of his small carcase. 'Our ball,' says the praepostor, rising with his prize, 'but get up there, there's a little fellow under you.' They are hauled and roll off him, and Tom is discovered a motionless body.

Old Brooke picks him up. 'Stand back, give him air,' he says; and then feeling his limbs, adds, 'No bones broken. How do you feel, young 'un?'

'Hah-hah,' gasps Tom as his wind comes back, 'pretty well, thank you—all right.'

'Who is he?' says Brooke. 'Oh, it's Brown, he's a new boy; I know him,' says East, coming up.

'Well, he is a plucky youngster, and will make a player,' says Brooke.

And five o'clock strikes. 'No side' is called, and the first day of the Schoolhouse match is over.

CHAPTER 6

AFTER THE MATCH

'—Some food we had.'—Shakespeare.
ἦς πότυς ἁδύς. —THEOCR *Id*.

As the boys scattered away from the ground, and East leaning on

Tom's arm, and limping along, was beginning to consider what luxury they should go and buy for tea to celebrate that glorious victory, the two Brookes came striding by. Old Brooke caught sight of East, and stopped; put his hand kindly on his shoulder and said, 'Bravo, youngster, you played famously; not much the matter, I hope?'

'No, nothing at all,' said East, 'only a little twist from that charge.'

'Well, mind and get all right for next Saturday;' and the leader passed on, leaving East better for those few words than all the opodeldoc in England would have made him, and Tom ready to give one of his ears for as much notice. Ah! light words of those whom we love and honour, what a power ye are, and how carelessly wielded by those who can use you! Surely for these things also God will ask an account.

'Tea's directly after locking-up, you see,' said East, hobbling along as fast as he could, 'so you come along down to Sally Harrowell's; that's our Schoolhouse tuck shop—she bakes such stunning murphies, we'll have a penn'orth each for tea; come along, or they'll all be gone.'

Tom's new purse and money burnt in his pocket; he wondered, as they toddled through the quadrangle and along the street, whether East would be insulted if he suggested further extravagance, as he had not sufficient faith in a pennyworth of potatoes. At last he blurted out—

'I say, East, can't we get something else besides potatoes? I've got lots of money, you know.'

'Bless us, yes, I forgot,' said East, 'you've only just come. You see all my tin's been gone this twelve weeks, it hardly ever lasts beyond the first fortnight; and our allowances were all stopped this morning for broken windows, so I haven't got a penny. I've got a tick at Sally's, of course; but then I hate running it high, you see, towards the end of the half, 'cause one has to shell out for it all directly one comes back, and that's a bore.'

Tom didn't understand much of this talk, but seized on the fact that East had no money, and was denying himself some little pet luxury in consequence. 'Well what shall I buy?' said he, 'I'm uncommon hungry.'

'I say,' said East, stopping to look at him and rest his leg, 'you're a trump, Brown. I'll do the same by you next half. Let's

73

have a pound of sausages then, that's the best grub for tea I know of.'

'Very well,' said Tom, as pleased as possible, 'where do they sell them?'

'Oh, over here, just opposite'; and they crossed the street and walked into the cleanest little front room of a small house, half parlour, half shop, and bought a pound of most particular sausages; East talking pleasantly to Mrs Porter while she put them in paper, and Tom doing the paying part.

From Porter's they adjourned to Sally Harrowell's, where they found a lot of Schoolhouse boys waiting for the roast potatoes, and relating their own exploits in the day's match at the top of their voices. The street opened at once into Sally's kitchen, a low brick-floored room, with large recess for fire, and chimney-corner seats. Poor little Sally, the most goodnatured and much enduring of womankind, was bustling about with a napkin in her hand, from her own oven to those of the neighbours' cottages, up the yard at the back of her house. Stumps, her husband, a short easy-going shoemaker, with a beery humorous eye and ponderous calves, who lived mostly on his wife's earnings, stood in a corner of the room, exchanging shots of the roughest description of repartee with every boy in turn. 'Stumps, you lout, you've had too much beer again today.' ' 'Twasn't of your paying for then.'—'Stumps's calves are running down into his ankles, they want to get to grass.' 'Better be doing that, than gone altogether like yours,' &c. &c. Very poor stuff it was, but it served to make time pass; and every now and then Sally arrived in the middle with a smoking tin of potatoes, which was cleared off in a few seconds, each boy as he seized his lot running off to the house with 'Put me down two penn'orth, Sally'; 'Put down three penn'orth between me and Davis,' &c. How she ever kept the accounts so straight as she did, in her head, and on her slate, was a perfect wonder.

East and Tom got served at last, and started back for the School-house just as the locking-up bell began to ring; East on the way recounting the life and adventures of Stumps, who was a character. Amongst his other small avocations, he was the hind carrier of a sedan-chair, the last of its race, in which the Rugby ladies still went out to tea, and in which, when he was fairly harnessed and carrying a load, it was the delight of small and mischievous boys to follow him and whip his calves. This was too much for the temper even of Stumps, and he would pursue his tormentors in a vindictive and apoplectic manner when released, but was easily pacified by twopence to buy beer with.

The lower-school boys of the Schoolhouse, some fifteen in number, had tea in the lower-fifth school, and were presided over by the old verger or head-porter. Each boy had a quarter of a loaf of bread and pat of butter, and as much tea as he pleased, and there was scarcely one who didn't add to this some further luxury, such as baked potatoes, a herring, sprats, or something of the sort; but few, at this period of the half-year, could live up to a pound of Porter's sausages, and East was in great magnificence upon the strength of theirs. He had produced a toasting-fork from his study, and set Tom to toast the sausages, while he mounted guard over their butter and potatoes; ''cause,' as he explained, 'you're a new boy, and they'll play you some trick and get our butter, but you can toast just as well as I.' So Tom, in the midst of three or four more urchins similarly employed, toasted his face and the sausages at the same time before the huge fire, till the latter cracked; when East from his watch-tower shouted that they were done, and then the feast proceeded, and the festive cups of tea were filled and emptied, and Tom imparted of the sausages in small bits to many neighbours, and thought he had never tasted such good potatoes or seen such jolly boys. They on their parts waived all ceremony, and pegged away at the sausages and potatoes, and remembering Tom's performance in goal, voted East's new crony a brick. After tea, and while the things were being cleared away, they gathered round the fire, and the talk on the match still went on; and those who had them to show, pulled up their trousers and showed the hacks they had received in the good cause.

They were soon however all turned out of the school, and East conducted Tom up to his bedroom, that he might get on clean things and wash himself before singing.

'What's singing?' said Tom, taking his head out of his basin, where he had been plunging it in cold water.

'Well, you are jolly green,' answered his friend from a neighbouring basin. 'Why the last six Saturdays of every half, we sing of course: and this is the first of them. No first lesson to do, you know, and lie in bed tomorrow morning.'

'But who sings?'

'Why everybody, of course; you'll see soon enough. We begin

75

directly after supper, and sing till bed-time. It ain't such good fun now tho' as in the summer half, 'cause then we sing in the little fives' court, under the library you know. We take out tables, and the big boys sit round, and drink beer; double allowance on Saturday nights; and we cut about the quadrangle between the songs, and it looks like a lot of robbers in a cave. And the louts come and pound at the great gates, and we pound back again, and shout at them. But this half we only sing in the hall. Come along down to my study.'

Their principal employment in the study was to clear out East's table, removing the drawers and ornaments and tablecloth, for he lived in the bottom passage, and his table was in requisition for the singing.

Supper came in due course at seven o'clock, consisting of bread and cheese and beer, which was all saved for the singing; and directly afterwards the fags went to work to prepare the hall. The Schoolhouse hall, as has been said, is a great long high room, with two large fires on one side, and two large ironbound tables, one running down the middle, and the other along the wall opposite the fireplaces. Around the upper fire the fags placed the tables in the form of a horse-shoe, and upon them the jugs with the Saturday night's allowance of beer. Then the big boys began to drop in and take their seats, bringing with them bottled beer and song-books; for although they all knew the songs by heart, it was the thing to have an old manuscript book descended from some departed hero, in which they were all carefully written out.

The sixth-form boys had not yet appeared; so to fill up the gap, an interesting and time-honoured ceremony was gone through. Each new boy was placed on the table in turn, and made to sing a solo, under the penalty of drinking a large mug of salt and water if he resisted or broke down. However, the new boys all sing like nightingales tonight, and the salt water is not in requisition; Tom as his part performing the old west-country song of 'the leather Bottèl' with considerable applause. And at the half-hour down come the sixth and fifth form boys, and take their places at the tables, which are filled up by the next biggest boys, the rest, for whom there is no room at table, standing round outside.

The glasses and mugs are filled, and then the fugleman strikes up the old sea song—

A wet sheet and a flowing sea,
And a wind that follows fast, &c.,

which is the invariable first song in the School-house, and all the seventy voices join in, not mindful of harmony, but bent on noise, which they attain decidedly—but the general effect isn't bad. And then follow 'The British Grenadiers', 'Billy Taylor'. 'The siege of Seringapatam', 'Three jolly postboys', and other vociferous songs in rapid succession, including the 'Chesapeake and Shannon', a song lately introduced in honour of old Brooke; and when they come to the words—

Brave Broke he waved his sword, crying, Now, my
   lads, aboard,
And we'll stop their playing Yankee-doodle-dandy oh!

you expect the roof to come down. The sixth and fifth know that 'brave Broke' of the Shannon was no sort of relation to our old Brooke. The fourth form are uncertain in their belief, but for the most part hold that old Brooke *was* a midshipman then, on board his uncle's ship. And the lower school never doubt for a moment that it was our old Brooke who led the boarders, in what capacity they care not a straw. During the pauses the bottled-beer corks fly rapidly, and the talk is fast and merry, and the big boys, at least all of them who have a fellow-feeling for dry throats, hand their mugs over their shoulders to be emptied by the small ones who stand round behind.

Then Warner, the head of the house, gets up and wants to speak, but he can't, for every boy knows what's coming; and the big boys who sit at the tables pound them and cheer; and the small boys who stand behind pound one another, and cheer, and rush about the hall cheering. Then silence being made, Warner reminds them of the old Schoolhouse custom of drinking the healths, on the first night of singing, of those who are going to leave at the end of the half. 'He sees that they know what he is going to say already—(loud cheers)—and so won't keep them, but only ask them to treat the toast as it deserves. It is, the head of the eleven, the head of big-side football, their leader on this glorious day—Pater Brooke!'

And away goes the pounding and cheering again, becoming deafening when old Brooke gets on his legs: till, a table having broken down, and a gallon or so of beer been upset, and all throats getting dry, silence ensues, and the hero speaks, leaning his hands on the table, and bending a little forwards. No action, no tricks of oratory; plain, strong and straight, like his play.

'Gentlemen of the Schoolhouse! I am very proud of the way in which you have received my name, and I wish I could say all I should like in return. But I know I shan't. However, I'll do the best I can to say what seems to me ought to be said by a fellow who's just going to leave, and who has spent a good slice of his life here. Eight years it is, and eight such years as I can never hope to have again. So now I hope you'll all listen to me—(loud cries of "that we will")—for I'm going to talk seriously. You're bound to listen to me, for what's the use of calling me "pater", and all that, if you won't mind what I say? And I'm going to talk seriously, because I feel so. It's a jolly time, too, getting to the end of the half, and a goal kicked by us first day—(tremendous applause)—after one of the hardest and fiercest day's play I can remember in eight years—(frantic shoutings). The school played splendidly too, I will say, and kept it up to the last. That last charge of theirs would have carried away a house. I never thought to see anything again of old Crab there, except little pieces, when I saw him tumbled over by it—(laughter and shouting, and great slapping on the back of Jones by the boys nearest him). Well, but we beat 'em—(cheers). Aye, but why did we beat 'em? answer me that—(shouts of "your play"). Nonsense. 'Twasn't the wind and kick-off either—that wouldn't do it. 'Twasn't because we've half-a-dozen of the best players in the school, as we have. I wouldn't change Warner, and Hedge, and Crab, and the young 'un, for any six on their side—(violent cheers). But half-a-dozen fellows can't keep it up for two hours against two hundred. Why is it, then? I'll tell you what I think. It's because we've more reliance on one another, more of a house feeling, more fellowship than the school can have. Each of us knows and can depend on his next hand man better—that's why we beat 'em today. We've union, they've division—there's the secret—(cheers). But how's this to be kept up? How's it to be improved? That's the question. For I take it, we're all in earnest about beating the school, whatever else we care about. I know I'd sooner win two Schoolhouse matches running than get the Balliol scholarship any day—(frantic cheers).

'Now, I'm as proud of the house as any one. I believe it's the best house in the school, out-and-out—(cheers). But it's a long way from what I want to see it. First, there's a deal of bullying going on. I know it well. I don't pry about and interfere; that only makes it more underhand, and encourages the small boys to come to us with their fingers in their eyes telling tales, and so we should be worse off than ever. It's very little kindness for the sixth to meddle generally—you youngsters, mind that. You'll be all the better football players for learning to stand it, and to take your own parts, and fight it through. But depend on it, there's nothing breaks up a house like bullying. Bullies are cowards, and one coward makes many; so good-bye to the Schoolhouse match if bullying gets ahead here. (Loud applause from the small boys, who look meaningly at Flashman and other boys at the tables.) Then there's fuddling about in the public-house, and drinking bad spirits, and punch, and such rot-gut stuff. That won't make good drop-kicks or chargers of you, take my word for it. You get plenty of good beer here, and that's enough for you; and drinking isn't fine or manly, whatever some of you may think of it.

'One other thing I must have a word about. A lot of you think and say, for I've heard you, "There's this new Doctor hasn't been here so long as some of us, and he's changing all the old customs. Rugby, and the Schoolhouse especially, are going to the dogs. Stand up for the good old ways, and down with the Doctor," Now I'm as fond of old Rugby customs and ways as any of you, and I've been here longer than any of you, and I'll give you a word of advice in time, for I shouldn't like to see any of you getting sacked. "Down with the Doctor"s' easier said than done. You'll find him pretty tight on his perch, I take it, and an awkwardish customer to handle in that line. Besides now, what customs has he put down? There was the good old custom of taking the linchpins out of the farmer's and bagmen's gigs at the fairs and a cowardly blackguard custom it was. We all know what came of it, and no wonder the Doctor objected to it. But, come now, any of you, name a custom that he has put down.'

'The hounds', calls out a fifth-form boy, clad in a green cut-away with brass buttons and cord trousers, the leader of the sporting interest, and reputed a great rider and keen hand generally.

'Well, we had six or seven mangey harriers and beagles belonging to the house, I'll allow, and had had them for years, and that the Doctor put them down. But what good ever came of them? Only rows with all the keepers for ten miles round; and big-side Hare and Hounds is better fun ten times over. What else?'

No answer.

'Well, I won't go on. Think it over for yourselves: you'll find, I believe, that he don't meddle with any one that's worth keeping. And mind now, I say again, look out for squalls, if you will go your own way, and that way ain't the Doctor's, for it'll lead to grief. You all know that I'm not the fellow to back a master through thick and thin. If I saw him stopping football, or cricket, or bathing, or sparring, I'd be as ready as any fellow to stand up about it. But he don't—he encourages them; didn't you see him out today for half-an-hour watching us? (Loud cheers for the Doctor.) And he's a strong true man, and a wise one too, and a public-school man too. (Cheers.) And so let's stick to him, and talk no more rot, and drink his health as the head of the house. (Loud cheers.) And now I've done blowing up, and very glad I am to have done. But it's a solemn thing to be thinking of leaving a place which one has lived in and loved for eight years; and if one can say a word for the good of the old house at such a time, why it should be said, whether bitter or sweet. If I hadn't been proud—I shouldn't be blowing you up. And now let's get to singing. But before I sit down I must give you a toast to be drunk with three-times-three and all the honours. It's a toast which I hope every one of us, wherever he may go hereafter, will never fail to drink when he thinks of the brave bright days of his boyhood. It's a toast which should bind us all together, and to those who've gone before, and who'll come after us here. It is the dear old Schoolhouse—the best house of the best school in England!'

My dear boys, old and young, you who have belonged, or do belong, to other schools and other houses, don't begin throwing my poor little book about the room, and abusing me and it, and vowing you'll read no more when you get to this point. I allow you've provocation for it. But, come now—would you, any of you, give a fig for a fellow who didn't believe in, and stand up for his own house and his own school? You know you wouldn't. Then don't object to my cracking up the old School-house, Rugby. Haven't I a right to do it, when I'm taking all the trouble of writing this true history for all your benefits. If you ain't satisfied, go and write the history of your own houses in your own times, and say all you know for your own schools and houses, provided it's true, and I'll read it without abusing you.

The last few words hit the audience in their weakest place; they had been not altogether enthusiastic at several parts of old Brooke's speech; but 'the best house of the best school in England' was too much for them all, and carried even the sporting and drinking interests off their legs into rapturous applause, and (it is to be hoped) resolutions to lead a new life and remember old Brooke's words; which however they didn't altogether do, as will appear hereafter.

But it required all old Brooke's popularity to carry down parts of his speech; especially that relating to the Doctor. For there are no such bigoted holders by established forms and customs, be they never so foolish or meaningless, as English school-boys, at least as the school-boy of our generation. We magnified into heroes every boy who had left, and looked upon him with awe and reverence, when he revisited the place a year or so afterwards, on his way to or from Oxford or Cambridge; and happy was the boy who remembered him, and sure of an audience as he expounded what he used to do and say, though it were sad enough stuff to make angels, not to say headmasters, weep.

We looked upon every trumpery little custom and habit which had obtained in the school as though it had been a law of the Medes and Persians, and regarded the infringement or variation of it as a sort of sacrilege. And the Doctor, than whom no man or boy had a stronger liking for old school customs, which were good and sensible, had, as has already been hinted, come into most decided collision with several which were neither the one or the other. And as old Brooke had said, when he came into collision with boys or customs, there was nothing for them but to give in or take themselves off; because what he said had to be done, and no mistake about it. And this was beginning to be pretty clearly understood; the boys felt that there was a strong man over them, who would have things his own way; and hadn't yet learned that he was a wise and loving man also. His personal character and influence had not had time to make itself felt, except by a very few of the bigger boys with whom he came more directly in contact; and he was looked upon with great fear and dislike by the great majority even of his own house. For he had found school, and school-house, in a state of monstrous licence and misrule, and was still employed in the necessary but unpopular work of setting up order with a strong hand.

However, as has been said, old Brooke triumphed, and the boys cheered him, and then the Doctor. And then more songs came, and the healths of the other boys about to leave, who each made a speech, one flowery, another maudlin, a third prosy, and so on, which are not necessary to be here recorded.

Half-past nine struck in the middle of the performance of 'Auld Lang Syne', a most obstreperous proceeding; during which there was an immense amount of standing with one foot on the table, knocking mugs together and shaking hands, without which accompaniments it seems impossible for the youth of Britain to take part in that famous old song. The underporter of the School-house entered during the performance, bearing five or six long wooden candlesticks, with lighted dips in them, which he proceeded to stick into their holes in such part of the great tables as he could get at; and then stood outside the ring till the end of the song, when he was hailed with shouts.

'Bill, you old muff, the half-hour hasn't struck.'

'Here, Bill, drink some cocktail', 'Sing us a song, old boy', 'Don't you wish you may get the table?' Bill drank the proffered cocktail not unwillingly, and putting down the empty glass remonstrated, 'Now, gentlemen, there's only ten minutes to prayers, and we must get the hall straight.'

Shouts of 'No, no!' and a violent effort to strike up 'Billy Taylor's' for the third time. 'Now then, lend a hand, you youngsters, and get the tables back, clear away the jugs and glasses. Bill's right. Open the windows, Warner.' The boy addressed, who sat by the long ropes, proceeded to pull up the great windows, and let in a clear fresh rush of night air, which made the candles flicker and gutter, and the fires roar. The circle broke up, each collaring his own jug, glass and songbook; Bill pounced on the big table, and began to rattle it away to its place outside the buttery-door. The lower-passage boys carried off their small tables aided by their friends, while above all, standing on the great hall-table, a knot of untiring sons of harmony made night doleful by a prolonged performance of 'God save the King'. His Majesty King William IV then reigned over us, a monarch deservedly popular amongst the boys addicted to melody, to whom he was chiefly known from the beginning of that excellent, if slightly vulgar song in which they much delighted—

Come neighbours all, both great and small,
   Perform your duties here,
And loudly sing 'live Billy our King,'
   For bating the tax upon beer.

Others of the more learned in songs also celebrated his praises in a sort of ballad, which I take to have been written by some Irish loyalist. I have forgotten all but the chorus, which ran

God save our good King William,
   be his name for ever blest,
He's the father of all his people,
   and the guardian of all the rest.

In truth we were loyal subjects in those days, in a rough way. I trust that our successors make as much of Her present Majesty, and, having regard to the greater refinement of the times, have adopted or written other songs equally hearty, but more civilized, in her honour.

Then the quarter to ten struck, and the prayer-bell rang. The sixth and fifth form boys ranged themselves in their school order along the wall, on either side of the great fires, the middle fifth and upper school boys round the long table in the middle of the hall, and the lower school boys round the upper part of the second long table, which ran down the side of the hall furthest from the fires. Here Tom found himself at the bottom of all, in a state of mind and body not at all fit for prayers, as he thought; and so tried hard to make himself serious, but couldn't, for the life of him, do anything but repeat in his head the choruses of some of the songs, and stare at all the boys opposite, wondering at the brilliancy of their waistcoats, and speculating what sort of fellows they were. The steps of the head-porter are heard on the stairs, and a light gleams at the door. 'Hush!' from the fifth-form boys who stand there, and then in strides the Doctor, cap on head, book in one hand, and gathering up his gown in the other. He walks up the middle, and takes his post by Warner, who begins calling over the names. The Doctor takes no notice of anything, but quietly turns over his book and finds the place, and then stands, cap in hand and finger in book, looking straight before his nose. He knows better than any one when to look, and when to see nothing; tonight is singing night, and there's been lots of noise and no harm done; nothing but beer drunk, and nobody the worse for it; though some of them do look hot and excited. So the Doctor sees nothing, but fascinates Tom in a horrible manner as he stands there, and reads out the Psalm in that deep, ringing, searching voice of his. Prayers are over, and Tom still stares open-mouthed after the Doctor's retiring figure, when he feels a pull at his sleeve, and turning round sees East.

'I say, were you ever tossed in a blanket?'

'No,' said Tom; 'why?'

''Cause there'll be tossing tonight most likely, before the sixth come up to bed. So if you funk, you just come along and hide, or else they'll catch you and toss you.'

'Were you ever tossed? Does it hurt?' inquired Tom.

'Oh yes, bless you, a dozen times,' said East, as he hobbled along by Tom's side upstairs. 'It don't hurt unless you fall on the floor. But most fellows don't like it.'

They stopped at the fireplace in the top passage, where were a crowd of small boys whispering together, and evidently unwilling to go up into the bed-rooms. In a minute, however, a study door opened and a sixth-form boy came out, and off they all scuttled up the stairs, and then noiselessly dispersed to their different rooms. Tom's heart beat rather quick as he and East reached their room, but he had made up his mind. 'I shan't hide, East,' said he.

'Very well, old fellow,' replied East, evidently pleased; 'no more shall I—they'll be here for us directly.'

The room was a great big one with a dozen beds in it, but not a boy that Tom could see, except East and himself. East pulled off his coat and waistcoat, and then sat on the bottom of his bed, whistling, and pulling off his boots; Tom followed his example.

A noise and steps are heard in the passage, the door opens, and in rush four or five great fifth-form boys, headed by Flashman in his glory.

Tom and East slept in the further corner of the room, and were not seen at first.

'Gone to ground, eh?' roared Flashman; 'push 'em out then, boys! look under the beds:' and he pulled up the little white curtain of the one nearest him. 'Who-o-op,' he roared, pulling away at the leg of a small boy, who held on tight to the leg of the bed, and sung out lustily for mercy.

'Here, lend a hand, one of you, and help me pull out this young howling brute. Hold your tongue, sir, or I'll kill you.'

'Oh, please, Flashman, please, Walker, don't toss me! I'll fag for you, I'll do anything, only don't toss me.'

'You be hanged,' said Flashman, lugging the wretched boy along, "twon't hurt you,—you! Come along, boys, here he is.'

'I say, Flashey,' sung out another of the big boys, 'drop that; you heard what old Pater Brooke said tonight. I'll be hanged if we'll toss any one against their will——no more bullying. Let him go, I say.'

Flashman, with a oath and a kick, released his prey, who rushed headlong under his bed again, for fear they should change their minds, and crept along underneath the other beds, till he got under that of the sixth-form boy, which he knew they daren't disturb.

'There's plenty of youngsters don't care about it,' said Walker. 'Here, here's Scud East—you'll be tossed, won't you, young un?' Scud was East's nickname, or Black, as we called it, gained by his fleetness of foot.

'Yes,' said East, 'if you like, only mind my foot.'

'And here's another who didn't hide. Hullo! new boy; what's your name, sir?'

'Brown.'

'Well, Whitey Brown, you don't mind being tosted?'

'No,' said Tom, setting his teeth.

'Come along then, boys,' sung out Walker, and away they all went, carrying along Tom and East, to the intense relief of four or five other small boys, who crept out from under the beds and behind them.

'What a trump Scud is!' said one. 'They won't come back here now.'

'And that new boy too; he must be a good plucked one.'

'Ah, wait till he's been tossed on to the floor; see how he'll like it then!'

Meantime the procession went down the passage to Number 7, the largest room, and the scene of tossing, in the middle of which was a great open space. Here they joined other parties of the bigger boys, each with a captive or two, some willing to be tossed, some sullen, and some frightened to death. At Walker's suggestion all who were afraid were let off, in honour of Brooke's speech.

Then a dozen big boys seized hold of a blanket dragged from one of the beds. 'In with Scud, quick, there's no time to lose.' East was chucked into the blanket. 'Once, twice, thrice, and away!' up he went like a shuttlecock, but not quite up to the ceiling.

'Now, boys, with a will,' cried Walker, 'once, twice, thrice, and away!' This time he went clean up, and kept himself from touching the ceiling with his hand, and so again, a third time, when he was turned out, and up went another boy. And then came Tom's turn. He lay quite still by East's advice, and didn't dislike the 'once, twice, thrice'; but the 'away' wasn't so pleasant. They were in good wind now, and sent him slap up to the ceiling first time, against which his knees came rather sharply. But the moment's pause before descending was the rub, the feeling of utter helplessness, and of leaving his whole inside behind him sticking to the ceiling. Tom was very near shouting to be set down, when he found himself back in the blanket, but thought of East, and didn't; and so took his three tosses without a kick or a cry, and was called a young trump for his pains.

He and East, having earned it, stood now looking on. No catastrophe happened, as all the captives were cool hands, and didn't struggle. This didn't suit Flashman. What your real bully likes in tossing, is when the boys kick and struggle, or hold on to the side of the blanket, and so get pitched bodily on to the floor; it's no fun to him when no one is hurt or frightened.

'Let's toss two of them together, Walker,' suggested he. 'What a cursed bully you are, Flashey!' rejoined the other. 'Up with another one.'

And so no two boys were tossed together, the peculiar hardship of which is, that it's too much for human nature to lie still then and share troubles; and so the wretched pair of small boys struggle in the air which shall fall a-top in the descent, to the no small risk of both falling out of the blanket, and the huge delight of brutes like Flashman.

But now there's a cry that the praepostor of the room is coming; so the tossing stops, and all scatter to their different rooms; and Tom is left to turn in, with the first day's experience of a public school to meditate upon.

CHAPTER 7

SETTLING TO THE COLLAR

Say Giles, "'Tis mortal hard to go,
But if so be's I must:
I means to follow arter he
As goes hisself the fust.'
—*Ballad.*

Everybody, I suppose, knows the dreamy delicious state in which one lies, half asleep, half awake, while consciousness begins to return, after a sound night's rest in a new place which we are glad to be in, following upon a day of unwonted excitement and exertion. There are few pleasanter pieces of life. The worst of it is that they last such a short time; for, nurse them as you will, by lying perfectly passive in mind and body, you can't make more than five minutes or so of them. After which time, the stupid, obtrusive, wakeful entity which we call 'I', as impatient as he is stiff-necked, spite of our teeth will force himself back again, and take possession of us down to our very toes.

It was in this state that Master Tom lay at half-past seven on the morning following the day of his arrival, and from his clean little white bed watched the movements of Bogle (the generic name by which the successive shoeblacks of the Schoolhouse were known), as he marched round from bed to bed, collecting the dirty shoes and boots, and depositing clean ones in their places.

There he lay, half doubtful as to where exactly in the universe he was, but conscious that he had made a step in life which he had been anxious to make. It was only just light as he looked lazily out of the wide windows, and saw the tops of the great elms, and the rooks circling about, and cawing remonstrances to the lazy ones of their commonwealth, before starting in a body for the neighbouring ploughed fields. The noise of the room-door closing behind Bogle, as he made his exit with the shoe-basket under his arm, roused

87

him thoroughly, and he sat up in bed and looked round the room. What in the world could be the matter with his shoulders and loins? He felt as if he had been severely beaten all down his back, the natural results of his performance at his first match. He drew up his knees and rested his chin on them, and went over all the events of yesterday, rejoicing in his new life, what he had seen of it, and all that was to come.

Presently one or two of the other boys roused themselves, and began to sit up and talk to one another in low tones. Then East, after a roll or two, came to an anchor also, and, nodding to Tom, began examining his ankle.

'What a pull,' said he, 'that it's lie-in-bed, for I shall be as lame as a tree, I think.'

It was Sunday morning, and Sunday lectures had not yet been established; so that nothing but breakfast intervened between bed and eleven o'clock chapel—a gap by no means easy to fill up: in fact, though received with the correct amount of grumbling, the first lecture instituted by the Doctor shortly afterwards, was a great boon to the School. It was lie-in-bed, and no one was in a hurry to get up, especially in rooms where the sixth-form boy was a good-tempered fellow, as was the case in Tom's room, and allowed the small boys to talk and laugh, and do pretty much what they pleased, so long as they didn't disturb him. His bed was a bigger one than the rest, standing in the corner by the fireplace, with washing-stand and large basin by the side, where he lay in state with his white curtains tucked in so as to form a retiring place: an awful subject of contemplation to Tom, who slept nearly opposite, and watched the great man rouse himself and take a book from under his pillow and begin reading, leaning his head on his hand and turning his back to the room. Soon, however, a noise of striving urchins arose, and muttered encouragements from the neighbouring boys, of—'Go it Tadpole!' 'Now, young Green!' 'Haul away his blanket!' 'Slipper him on the hands!' Young Green and little Hall, commonly called Tadpole, from his great black head and thin legs, slept side-by-side far away by the door, and were for ever playing one another tricks, which usually ended, as on this morning, in open and violent collision: and now, unmindful of all order and authority, there they were each hauling away at the other's bed-clothes with one hand, and with the other, armed with a slipper, belabouring whatever portion of the body of his adversary came within reach.

'Hold that noise, up in the corner,' called out the praepostor, sitting up and looking round his curtains; and the Tadpole and young Green sank down into their disordered beds, and then, looking at his watch, added, 'Hullo, past eight!—whose turn for hot water?'

(Where the praepostor was particular in his ablutions, the fags in his room had to descend in turn to the kitchen, and beg or steal hot water for him; and often the custom extended further, and two boys went down every morning to get a supply for the whole room.)

'East's and Tadpole's,' answered the senior fag, who kept the rota.

'I can't go,' said East, 'I'm dead lame.'

'Well, be quick, some of you, that's all,' said the great man, as he turned out of bed, and putting on his slippers, went out into the great passage which runs the whole length of the bedrooms, to get his Sunday habiliments out of his portmanteau.

'Let me go for you,' said Tom to East, 'I should like it.'

'Well, thank'ee, that's a good fellow. Just pull on your trousers, and take your jug and mine. Tadpole will show you the way.'

And so Tom and Tadpole, in nightshirts and trousers, started off downstairs, and through 'Thos's hole', as the little buttery, where candles and beer and bread and cheese were served out at night, was called; across the Schoolhouse court, down a long passage, and into the kitchen; where, after some parley with the stalwart, handsome cook, who declared that she had filled a dozen jugs already, they got their hot water, and returned with all speed and great caution. As it was, they narrowly escaped capture by some privateers from the fifth-form rooms, who were on the look-out for the hot-water convoys, and pursued them up to the very door of their room, making them spill half their load in the passage. 'Better than going down again, tho',' as Tadpole remarked, 'as we should have had to do, if those beggars had caught us.'

By the time that the calling-over bell rang, Tom and his new comrades were all down, dressed in their best clothes, and he had the satisfaction of answering 'here' to his name for the first time, the praepostor of the week having put it in at the bottom of his list. And then came breakfast, and a saunter about the close and town with East, whose lameness only became severe when any fagging had to be done. And so they whiled away the time until morning chapel.

It was a fine November morning, and the close soon became alive with boys of all ages, who sauntered about on the grass, or walked round the gravel-walk, in parties of two or three. East, still doing the cicerone, pointed out all the remarkable characters to Tom as they passed: Osbert, who could throw a cricket-ball from the little-side ground over the rook trees to the Doctor's wall; Gray, who had got the Balliol scholarship, and, what East evidently thought of much more importance, a half-holiday for the School by his success; Thorne, who had run ten miles in two minutes over the hour; Black, who had held his own against the cock of the town in the last row with the louts; and many more heroes, who then and there walked about and were worshipped, all trace of whom has long since vanished from the scene of their fame; and the fourth-form boy, who reads their names rudely cut out on the old hall tables, or painted upon the big-side cupboard (if hall tables and big-side cupboard still exist), wonders what manner of boys they were. It will be the same with you who wonder, my sons, whatever your prowess may be, in cricket, or scholarship, or football. Two or three years more or less, and then the steadily advancing, blessed wave will pass over your names as it has passed over ours. Nevertheless play your games and do your work manfully—see only that that be done, and let the remembrance of it take care of itself.

The chapel-bell began to ring at a quarter to eleven, and Tom got in early and took his place in the lowest row, and watched all the other boys come in and take their places, filling row after row; and tried to construe the Greek text which was inscribed over the door with the slightest possible success, and wondered which of the masters, who walked down the chapel and took their seats in the exalted boxes at the end, would be his lord. And then came the closing of the doors, and the Doctor in his robes, and the service, which however didn't impress him much, for his feeling of wonder and curiosity was too strong. And the boy on one side of him was scratching his name on the oak panelling in front, and he couldn't help watching to see what the name was, and whether it was well scratched: and the boy on the other side went to sleep and kept falling against him; and on the whole, though many boys even in that part of the School were serious and attentive, the general atmosphere was by no means devotional; and when he got out into the close again, he didn't feel at all comfortable, or as if he had been to church.

But at afternoon chapel it was quite another thing. He had spent the time after dinner in writing home to his mother, and so was in a better frame of mind; and his first curiosity was over, and he could attend more to the service. As the hymn after the prayers was being sung and the chapel was getting a little dark, he was beginning to feel that he had been really worshipping. And then came that great event in his, as in every Rugby boy's life of that day—the first sermon from the Doctor.

More worthy pens than mine have described that scene. The oak pulpit standing out by itself above the School seats. The tall gallant form, the kindling eye, the voice, now soft as the low notes of a flute, now clear and stirring as the call of the light infantry bugle, of him who stood there Sunday after Sunday, witnessing and pleading for his Lord, the King of righteousness and love and glory, with whose spirit he was filled, and in whose power he spoke. The long lines of young faces rising tier above tier down the whole length of the chapel, from the little boy's who had just left his mother to the young man's who was going out next week into the great world rejoicing in his strength. It was a great and solemn sight, and never more so than at this time of year, when the only lights in the chapel were in the pulpit and at the seats of the praepostors of the week, and the soft twilight stole over the rest of the chapel, deepening into darkness in the high gallery behind the organ.

But what was it after all which seized and held these three hundred boys, dragging them out of themselves, willing or unwilling, for twenty minutes, on Sunday afternoons? True, there always were boys scattered up and down the School, who in heart and head were worthy to hear and able to carry away the deepest and wisest words there spoken. But these were a minority always, generally a very small one, often so small a one as to be countable on the fingers of your hand. What was it that moved and held us, the rest of the three hundred reckless childish boys, who feared the Doctor with all our hearts, and very little besides in heaven or earth; who thought more of our sets in the School than of the Church of Christ, and put the traditions of Rugby and the public opinion of boys in our daily life above the laws of God? We couldn't enter into half that we heard; we hadn't the knowledge of our own hearts or the knowledge of one another; and little enough of the faith, hope, and love needed to that end. But we listened, as all boys in their better moods will listen (aye and men too for the matter of that), to a man who we felt to be with all his heart and soul and strength striving against whatever was mean and unmanly and unrighteous in our little world. It was not the cold clear voice of one giving advice and warning from serene heights to those who were struggling and sinning below, but the warm living voice of one who was fighting for us and by our sides, and calling on us to help him and ourselves and one another. And so, wearily and little by little, but surely and steadily on the whole, was brought home to the young boy, for the first time, the meaning of his life: that it was no fool's or sluggard's paradise into which he had wandered by chance, but a battlefield ordained from of old, where there are no spectators, but the youngest must take his side, and the stakes are life and death. And he who roused this consciousness in them, showed them at the same time, by every word he spoke in the pulpit, and by his whole daily life, how that battle was to be fought; and stood there before them their fellow-soldier and the captain of their band. The true sort of captain too for a boys' army, one who had no misgivings and gave no uncertain word of command, and, let who would yield or make truce, would fight the fight out (so every boy felt) to the last gasp and the last drop of blood. Other sides of his character might take hold of and influence boys here and there, but it was this thoroughness and undaunted courage which more than anything else won his way to the hearts of the great mass of those on whom he left his mark, and made them believe first in him, and then in his Master.

It was this quality above all others which moved such boys as our hero, who had nothing whatever remarkable about him except excess of boyishness; by which I mean animal life in its fullest measure, good nature and honest impulses, hatred of injustice and meanness, and thoughtlessness enough to sink a three-decker. And so, during the next two years, in which it was more than doubtful whether he would get good or evil from the School, and before any steady purpose or principle grew up in him, whatever his week's sins and shortcomings might have been, he hardly ever left the chapel on Sunday evenings without a serious resolve to stand by and follow the Doctor, and a feeling that it was only cowardice (the incarnation of all other sins in such a boy's mind) which hindered him from doing so with all his heart.

The next day Tom was duly placed in the third form, and began his lessons in a corner of the big School. He found the work very easy, as he had been well grounded and knew his grammar by heart, and as he had no intimate companion to make him idle (East and his other Schoolhouse friends being in the lower fourth, the form above him), soon gained golden opinions from his master, who said he was placed too low, and should be put out at the end of the half-year. So all went well with him in school, and he wrote the most flourishing letters home to his mother, full of his own success and the unspeakable delights of a public school.

In the house, too, all went well. The end of the half-year was drawing near, which kept everybody in a good humour, and the house was ruled well and strongly by Warner and Brooke. True, the general system was rough and hard, and there was bullying in nooks and corners, bad signs for the future; but it never got further, or dared show itself openly, stalking about the passages and hall and bedrooms, and making the life of the small boys a continual fear.

Tom, as a new boy, was of right excused fagging for the first month, but in his enthusiasm for his new life this privilege hardly pleased him; and East and others of his young friends discovering this, kindly allowed him to indulge his fancy, and take their turns at night fagging and cleaning studies. These were the principal duties of the fags in the house. From supper until nine o'clock, three fags taken in order stood in the passages, and answered any praepostor who called Fag, racing to the door, the last comer having to do the work. This consisted generally of going to the buttery for beer and bread and cheese (for the great men did not sup with the rest, but had each his own allowance in his study or the fifth-form room), cleaning candlesticks, and putting in new candles, toasting cheese, bottling beer, and carrying messages about the house; and Tom, in the first blush of his hero-worship, felt it a high privilege to receive orders from, and be the bearer of the supper of old Brooke. And besides this night-work, each praepostor had three or four fags specially allotted to him, of whom he was supposed to be the guide, philosopher, and friend, and who in return for these good offices had to clean out his study every morning by turns, directly after first lesson and before he returned from breakfast. And the pleasure of seeing the great men's studies, and looking at their pictures, and peeping into their books, made Tom a ready substitute for any boy who was too lazy to do his own work. And so he soon gained the character of a good-natured willing fellow, who was ready to do a turn for any one.

In all the games too he joined with all his heart, and soon became well versed in all the mysteries of football by continued practice at the Schoolhouse little-side, which played daily.

The only incident worth recording here, however, was his first run at Hare-and-hounds. On the last Tuesday but one of the half-year, he was passing through the hall after dinner when he was hailed with shouts from Tadpole and several other fags seated at one of the long tables, the chorus of which was. 'Come and help us tear up scent.'

Tom approached the table in obedience to the mysterious summons, always ready to help, and found the party engaged in tearing up old newspapers, copybooks, and magazines into small pieces, with which they were filling four large canvas bags.

'It's the turn of our house to find scent for big-side Hare-and-hounds,' explained Tadpole; 'tear away, there's no time to lose before calling-over.'

'I think it's a great shame,' said another small boy, 'to have such a hard run for the last day.'

'Which run is it?' said Tadpole.

'Oh, the Barby run, I hear,' answered the other, 'nine miles at least, and hard ground; no chance of getting in at the finish, unless you're a first-rate scud.'

'Well, I'm going to have a try,' said Tadpole; 'it's the last run of the half, and if a fellow gets in at the end, big-side stands ale and bread and cheese, and a bowl of punch; and the Cock's such a famous place for ale.'

'I should like to try too,' said Tom.

'Well then, leave your waistcoat behind, and listen at the door, after calling-over, and you'll hear where the meet is.'

After calling-over, sure enough, there were two boys at the door, calling out 'Big-side Hare-and-hounds meet at White Hall,' and Tom having girded himself with leather strap, and left all superfluous clothing behind, set off for White Hall, an old gable-ended house some quarter of a mile from the town, with East, whom he had persuaded to join, notwithstanding his prophecy that they would never get in, as it was the hardest run of the year.

At the meet they found some forty or fifty boys, and Tom felt sure, from having seen many of them run at football, that he and East were more likely to get in than they.

After a few minutes waiting, two well-known runners, chosen for the hares, buckled on the four bags filled with scent, compared their

94

watches with those of young Brooke and Thorne, and started off at a long slinging trot across the fields in the direction of Barby.

Then the hounds clustered round Thorne, who explained shortly, 'they're to have six minutes' law. We run into the Cock, and every one who comes in within a quarter of an hour of the hares'll be counted, if he has been round Barby church.' Then came a minute's pause or so, and then the watches are pocketed, and the pack is led through the gateway into the field which the hares had first crossed. Here they break into a trot, scattering over the field to find the first traces of the scent which the hares throw out as they go along. The old hounds make straight for the likely points, and in a minute a cry of 'forward' comes from one of them, and the whole pack quickening their pace make for the spot, while the boy who hit the scent first, and the two or three nearest to him, are over the first fence, and making play along the hedgerow in the long grass-field beyond. The rest of the pack rush at the gap already made and scramble through, jostling one another. 'Forward' again, and before they are half through; the pace quickens into a sharp run, the tail hounds all straining to get up with the lucky leaders. They are gallant hares, and the scent lies thick right across another meadow and into a ploughed field, where the pace begins to tell; then over a good wattle with a ditch on the other side, and down a large pasture studded with old thorns, which slopes down to the first brook; the great Leicestershire sheep charge away across the field as the pack comes racing down the slope. The brook is a small one, and the scent lies right ahead up the opposite slope, and as thick as ever not a turn or a check to favour the tail hounds, who strain on, now trailing in a long line, many a youngster beginning to drag his legs heavily and feel his heart beat like a hammer, and the bad plucked ones thinking that after all it isn't worth while to keep it up.

Tom, East, and the Tadpole, had a good start, and are well up for such young hands, and after rising the slope and crossing the next field, find themselves up with the leading hounds who have over-run the scent and are trying back; they have come a mile and a half in about eleven minutes, a pace which shows that it is the last day. About twenty-five of the original starters only show here, the rest having already given in; the leaders are busy making casts into the fields on the left and right, and the others get their second winds.

Then comes the cry of 'forward' again, from young Brooke, from the extreme left, and the pack settles down to work again steadily

95

and doggedly, the whole keeping pretty well together. The scent though still good is not so thick; there is no need of that, for in this part of the run everyone knows the line which must be taken, and so there are no casts to be made, but good downright running and fencing to be done. All who are now up mean coming in, and they come to the foot of Barby Hill without losing more than two or three more of the pack. This last straight two miles and a half is always a vantage ground for the hounds, and the hares know it well; they are generally viewed on the side of Barby Hill, and all eyes are on the look-out for them today. But not a sign of them appears, so now will be the hard work for the hounds, and there is nothing for it but to cast about for the scent, for it is now the hares' turn, and they may baffle the pack dreadfully in the next two miles.

Ill fares it now with our youngsters that they are Schoolhouse boys, and so follow young Brooke, for he takes the wide casts round to the left conscious of his own powers, and loving the hard work. For if you would consider for a moment, you small boys, you would remember that the Cock, where the run ends, and the good ale will be going, lies far out to the right on the Dunchurch road, so that every cast you take to the left is so much extra work. And at this stage of the run, when the evening is closing in already, no one remarks whether you run a little cunning or not, so you should stick to those crafty hounds who keep edging away to the right, and not follow a prodigal like young Brooke, whose legs are twice as long as yours and of cast-iron, wholly indifferent to two or three miles more or less. However they struggle after him, sobbing and plunging along, Tom and East pretty close, and Tadpole, whose big head begins to pull him down, some thirty yards behind.

Now comes a brook, with stiff clay banks, from which they can hardly drag their legs, and they hear faint cries for help from the wretched Tadpole, who has fairly stuck fast. But they have too little run left in themselves to pull up for their own brothers. Three fields more, and another check, and then 'forward' called away to the extreme right.

The two boys' souls die within them; they can never do it. Young Brooke thinks so too, and says kindly, 'You'll cross a lane after next field, keep down it, and you'll hit the Dunchurch road below the Cock,' and then steams away for the run in, in which he's sure to be first, as if he were just starting. They struggle on across the next field, the 'forwards' getting fainter and fainter, and then ceasing. The whole hunt is out of earshot, and all hope of coming in is over.

'Hang it all!' broke out East, as soon as he had got wind enough, pulling off his hat and mopping at his face, all spattered with dirt and lined with sweat, from which went up a thick steam into the still cold air. 'I told you how it would be. What a thick I was to come. Here we are dead beat, and yet I know we're close to the run in, if we knew the country.'

'Well,' said Tom, mopping away, and gulping down his disappointment, 'it can't be helped. We did our best any how. Hadn't we better find this lane, and go down it as young Brooke told us?'

'I suppose so—nothing else for it,' grunted East. 'If ever I go out last day again,' growl—growl—growl.

So they tried back slowly and sorrowfully, and found the lane, and went limping down it, plashing in the cold puddly ruts, and beginning to feel how the run had taken it out of them. The evening closed in fast, and clouded over, dark, cold, and dreary.

'I say, it must be locking-up, I should think,' remarked East, breaking the silence, 'it's so dark.'

'What if we're late?' said Tom.

'No tea, and sent up to the Doctor,' answered East. The thought didn't add to their cheerfulness. Presently a faint halloo was heard from an adjoining field. They answered it and stopped, hoping for some competent rustic to guide them, when over a gate some twenty yards ahead crawled the wretched Tadpole, in a state of collapse; he had lost a shoe in the brook, and been groping after it up to his elbows in the stiff wet clay, and a more miserable creature in the shape of a boy has seldom been seen.

The sight of him, notwithstanding, cheered them, for he was some degrees more wretched than they. They also cheered him, as he was now no longer under the dread of passing his night alone in the fields. And so in better heart, the three plashed painfully down the never-ending lane. At last it widened, just as utter darkness set in, and they came out on to a turnpikeroad, and there paused bewildered, for they had lost all bearings, and knew not whether to turn to the right or left.

Luckily for them they had not to decide, for lumbering along the road, with one lamp lighted, and two spavined horses in the shafts, came a heavy coach, which after a moment's suspense they recognized as the Oxford coach, the redoubtable Pig and Whistle.

It lumbered slowly up, and the boys mustering their last run, caught it as it passed, and began scrambling up behind, in which exploit East missed his footing and fell flat on his nose along the road. Then the others hailed the old scarecrow of a coachman, who pulled up and agreed to take them in for a shilling; so there they sat on the back seat, drubbing with their heels, and their teeth chattering with cold, and jogged into Rugby some forty minutes after locking-up.

Five minutes afterwards, three small limping shivering figures steal along through the Doctor's garden, and into the house by the servants' entrance (all the other gates have been closed long since), where the first thing they light upon in the passage is old Thomas, ambling along, candle in one hand and keys in the other.

He stops and examines their condition with a grim smile. 'Ah! East, Hall, and Brown, late for locking-up. Must go up to the Doctor's study at once.'

'Well but, Thomas, mayn't we go and wash first? You can put down the time, you know.'

'Doctor's study d'rectly you come in—that's the orders,' replied old Thomas, motioning towards the stairs at the end of the passage which led up into the Doctor's house; and the boys turned ruefully down it, not cheered by the old verger's muttered remark, 'What a pickle they boys be in!' Thomas referred to their faces and habiliments, but they construed it as indicating the Doctor's state of mind. Upon the short flight of stairs they pause to hold counsel.

'Who'll go in first?' inquires Tadpole.

'You—you're the senior,' answered East.

'Catch me—look at the state I'm in,' rejoined Hall, showing the arms of his jacket. 'I must get behind you two.'

'Well, but look at me,' said East, indicating the mass of clay behind which he was standing; 'I'm worse than you, two to one; you might grow cabbages on my trousers.'

'That's all down below, and you can keep your legs behind the sofa,' said Hall.

'Here, Brown, you're the show-figure—you must lead.'

'But my face is all muddy,' argued Tom.

'Oh, we're all in one boat for that matter; but come on, we're only making it worse dawdling here.'

'Well, just give us a brush then,' said Tom; and they began trying to rub off the superfluous dirt from each other's jackets, but it was not dry enough, and the rubbing made it worse; so in despair they pushed through the swing-door at the head of the stairs, and found themselves in the Doctor's hall.

'That's the library door,' said East in a whisper, pushing Tom forwards. The sound of merry voices and laughter came from within, and his first hesitating knock was unanswered. But at the second, the Doctor's voice said 'Come in,' and Tom turned the handle, and he, with the others behind him, sidled into the room.

The Doctor looked up from his task; he was working away with a great chisel at the bottom of a boy's sailing boat, the lines of which he was no doubt fashioning on the model of one of Nicias' galleys. Round him stood three or four children; the candles burnt brightly on a large table at the further end, covered with books and papers, and a great fire threw a ruddy glow over the rest of the room. All looked so kindly, and homely, and comfortable, that the boys took heart in a moment, and Tom advanced from behind the shelter of the great sofa. The Doctor nodded to the children, who went out, casting curious and amused glances at the three young scarecrows.

'Well, my little fellows,' began the Doctor, drawing himself up, with his back to the fire, the chisel in one hand and his coat-tails in the other, and his eye twinkling as he looked them over; 'what makes you so late?'

'Please, sir, we've been out big-side Hare-and-hounds, and lost our way.'

'Hah! you couldn't keep up, I suppose?'

'Well, sir,' said East, stepping out, and not liking that the Doctor should think lightly of his running powers, 'we got round Barby all right, but then—'

'Why, what a state you're in, my boy,' interrupted the Doctor, as the pitiful condition of East's garments was fully revealed to him.

'That's the fall I got, sir, in the road,' said East, looking down at himself; 'the Old Pig came by—'

'The what?' said the Doctor.

'The Oxford coach, sir,' explained Hall.

'Hah! yes, the Regulator,' said the Doctor.

'And I tumbled on my face, trying to get up behind,' went on East.

'You're not hurt, I hope?' said the Doctor.

'Oh no, sir.'

'Well now, run upstairs, all three of you, and get clean things on, and then tell the housekeeper to give you some tea. You're too young to try such long runs. Let Warner know I've seen you. Good night.'

'Good night, sir.' And away scuttled the three boys in high glee.

'What a brick, not to give us even twenty lines to learn,' said the Tadpole, as they reached their bedroom; and in half-an-hour afterwards they were sitting by the fire in the housekeeper's room at a sumptuous tea, with cold meat, 'twice as good a grub as we should have got in the hall,' as the Tadpole remarked with a grin, his mouth full of buttered toast. All their grievances were forgotten, and they were resolving to go out the first big-side next half, and thinking Hare-and-hounds the most delightful of games.

A day or two afterwards the great passage outside the bedrooms was cleared of the boxes and portmanteaus, which went down to be packed by the matron, and great games of chariot-racing, and cock-fighting, and bolstering, went on in the vacant space, the sure sign of a closing half-year.

Then came the making up of parties for the journey home, and Tom joined a party who were to hire a coach, and post with four horses to Oxford.

Then the last Saturday, on which the Doctor came round to each form to give out the prizes, and hear the masters' last reports of how they and their charges had been conducting themselves; and Tom, to his huge delight, was praised, and got his remove into the lower fourth, in which all his Schoolhouse friends were.

On the next Tuesday morning, at four o'clock, hot coffee was going on in the housekeeper's and matron's rooms; boys wrapped in great-coats and mufflers were swallowing hasty mouthfuls, rushing about, tumbling over luggage, and asking questions all at once of the matron; outside the School-gates were drawn up several chaises and the four-horse coach which Tom's party had chartered, the post-boys in their best jackets and breeches, and a cornopean-player, hired for the occasion, blowing away 'A southerly wind and a cloudy sky', waking all peaceful inhabitants half-way down the High Street.

Every minute the bustle and hubbub increased, porters staggered about with boxes and bags, the cornopean played louder. Old Thomas sat in his den with a great yellow bag by his side, out of which he was paying journey-money to each boy, comparing by the light of a solitary dip the dirty crabbed little list in his own handwriting with the Doctor's list, and the amount of his cash; his head was on one side, his mouth screwed up, and his spectacles dim from early toil. He had prudently locked the door and carried on his operations solely through the window, or he would have been driven wild and lost all his money.

'Thomas, do be quick, we shall never catch the Highflyer at Dunchurch.'

'That's your money, all right, Green.'

'Hullo, Thomas, the Doctor said I was to have two-pound-ten; you've only given me two pound.'—I fear that Master Green is not confining himself strictly to truth—Thomas turns his head more on one side than ever, and spells away at the dirty list—Green is forced away from the window.

'Here, Thomas, never mind him, mine's thirty shillings.' 'And mine too,' 'and mine,' shouted others.

One way or another, the party to which Tom belonged all got packed and paid, and sallied out to the gates, the cornopean playing frantically 'Drops of brandy', in allusion probably to the slight potations in which the musician and postboys had been already indulging. All luggage was carefully stowed away inside the coach and in the front and hind boots, so that not a hat-box was visible outside. Five or six small boys with pea-shooters and the cornopean player got up behind; in front the big boys, mostly smoking, not for pleasure, but because they are now gentlemen at large—and this is the most correct public method of notifying the fact.

'Robinson's coach will be down the road in a minute, it has gone up to Bird's to pick up—we'll wait till they're close and make a race of it,' says the leader. 'Now, boys, half-a-sovereign apiece if you beat 'em into Dunchurch by one hundred yards.'

'All right, sir,' shouted the grinning post-boys.

Down comes Robinson's coach in a minute or two, with a rival cornopean, and away go the two vehicles, horses galloping, boys cheering, horns playing loud. There is a special Providence over school-boys as well as sailors, or they must have upset twenty times in the first five miles; sometimes actually abreast of one another, and the boys on the roofs exchanging volleys of peas, now nearly running over a post-chaise which had started before them, now half-way up a bank, now with a wheel-and-a-half over a yawning ditch; and all this in a dark morning, with nothing but their own lamps to guide them. However, it's all over at last, and they have run over nothing but an old pig in Southam Street; the last peas are distributed in the Corn Market at Oxford, where they arrive between eleven and twelve, and sit down to a sumptuous breakfast at the Angel, which they are made to pay for accordingly. Here the party breaks up, all going now different ways; and Tom orders out a chaise and pair as grand as a lord, tho' he has scarcely five shillings left in his pocket, and more than twenty miles to get home.

'Where to, sir?'

'Red Lion, Farringdon,' says Tom, giving hostler a shilling.

'All right, sir. Red Lion, Jem,' to the post-boy, and Tom rattles away towards home. At Farringdon, being known to the innkeeper, he gets that worthy to pay for the Oxford horses, and forward him in another chaise at once; and so the gorgeous young gentleman arrives at the paternal mansion, and Squire Brown looks rather blue at having to pay two-pound ten-shillings for the posting expenses from Oxford. But the boy's intense joy at getting home, and the wonderful health he is in, and the good character he brings, and the brave stories he tells of Rugby, its doings and delights, soon mollify the Squire, and three happier people didn't sit down to dinner that day in England (it is the boy's first dinner at six o'clock at home, great promotion already), than the Squire and his wife, and Tom Brown, at the end of his first half-year at Rugby.

CHAPTER 8

THE WAR OF INDEPENDENCE

'They are slaves who will not choose
Hatred, scoffing, and abuse,
Rather than in silence shrink
From the truth they needs must think:
They are slaves who dare not be
In the right with two or three.'
    —LOWELL, *Stanzas on Freedom*.

The lower fourth form in which Tom found himself at the

beginning of the next half-year was the largest form in the lower school, and numbered upwards of forty boys. Young gentlemen of all ages, from nine to fifteen, were to be found there, who expended such part of their energies as was devoted to Latin and Greek, upon a book of Livy, the Bucolics of Virgil, and the Hecuba of Euripides, which were ground out in small daily portions. The driving of this unlucky lower-fourth must have been grievous work to the unfortunate master, for it was the most unhappily constituted of any in the School. Here stuck the great stupid boys, who for the life of them could never master the accidence; the objects alternately of mirth and terror to the youngsters, who were daily taking them up, and laughing at them in lesson, and getting kicked by them for so doing in play-hours. There were no less than three unhappy fellows in tail coats, with incipient down on their chins, whom the Doctor and the master of the form were always endeavouring to hoist into the upper school, but whose parsing and construing resisted the most well-meant shoves. Then came the mass of the form, boys of eleven and twelve, the most mischievous and reckless age of British youths, of whom East and Tom Brown were fair specimens. As full of tricks as monkeys, and of excuses as Irish women, making fun of their master, one another, and their lessons, Argus himself would have been puzzled to keep an eye on them; and as for making them steady or serious for half-an-hour together it was simply hopeless. The remainder of the form consisted of young prodigies of nine and ten, who were going up the school at the rate of a form a half-year, all boys' hands and wits being against them in their progress. It would have been one man's work to see that the precocious youngsters had fair play; and as the master had a good deal besides to do, they hadn't, and were for ever being shoved down three or four places, their verses stolen, their books inked, their jackets whitened, and their lives otherwise made a burden to them.

The lower fourth, and all the forms below it, were heard in the great school, and were not trusted to prepare their lessons before coming in, but were whipped into school three-quarters of an hour before the lesson began by their respective masters, and there scattered about on the benches, with dictionary and grammar, hammered out their twenty lines of Virgil or Euripides in the midst of Babel. The masters of the lower school walked up and down the great school together during this three-quarters of an hour, or sat in their desks reading or looking over copies, and keeping such order as was possible. But the lower fourth was just now an overgrown form, too large for any one man to attend to properly, and consequently the elysium or ideal form of the young scapegraces, who formed the staple of it.

Tom, as has been said, had come up from the third with a good character, but the temptations of the lower fourth soon proved too strong for him, and he rapidly fell away, and became as unmanageable as the rest. For some weeks indeed he succeeded in maintaining the appearance of steadiness, and was looked upon favourably by his new master, whose eyes were first opened by the following little incident.

Besides the desk which the master himself occupied, there was another large unoccupied desk in the corner of the great school, which was untenanted. To rush and seize upon this desk, which was ascended by three steps, and held four boys, was the great object of ambition of the lower fourthers; and the contentions for the occupation of it bred such disorder, that at last the master forbade its use altogether. This of course was a challenge to the more adventurous spirits to occupy it, and as it was capacious enough for two boys to lie hid there completely, it was seldom that it remained empty notwithstanding the veto. Small holes were cut in the front, through which the occupants watched the masters as they walked up and down, and as lesson time approached, one boy at a time stole out and down the steps, as the masters' backs were turned, and mingled with the general crowd on the forms below. Tom and East had successfully occupied the desk some half-dozen times, and were grown so reckless that they were in the habit of playing small games with fives'-balls inside, when the masters were at the other end of the big school. One day, as ill-luck would have it, the game became more exciting than usual, and the ball slipped through East's fingers, and rolled slowly down the steps and out into the middle of the school, just as the masters turned in their walk and faced round upon the desk. The young delinquents watched their master through the look-out holes march slowly down the school straight upon their retreat, while all the boys in the neighbourhood of course stopped their work to look on: and not only were they ignominiously drawn out, and caned over the hand then and there, but their characters for steadiness were gone from that time. However, as they only shared the fate of some three-fourths of the rest of the form, this did not weigh heavily upon them.

In fact, the only occasions on which they cared about the matter, were the monthly examinations, when the Doctor came round to examine their form, for one long awful hour, in the work which they had done in the preceding month. The second monthly examination came round soon after Tom's fall, and it was with anything but lively anticipations that he and the other lower-fourth boys came into prayers on the morning of the examination-day.

Prayers and calling-over seemed twice as short as usual, and before they could get construes of a tithe of the hard passages marked in the margin of their books, they were all seated round, and the Doctor was standing in the middle, talking in whispers to the master. Tom couldn't hear a word which passed, and never lifted his eyes from his book; but he knew by a sort of magnetic instinct that the Doctor's under lip was coming out, and his eye beginning to burn, and his gown getting gathered up more and more tightly in his left hand. The suspense was agonizing, and Tom knew that he was sure on such occasions to make an example of the Schoolhouse boys. 'If he would only begin,' thought Tom, 'I shouldn't mind.'

At last the whispering ceased, and the name which was called out was not Brown. He looked up for a moment, but the Doctor's face was too awful; Tom wouldn't have met his eye for all he was worth, and buried himself in his book again.

The boy who was called up first was a clever merry School-house boy, one of their set: he was some connection of the Doctor's, and a great favourite, and ran in and out of his house as he liked, and so was selected for the first victim.

'Triste lupus stabulis,' began the luckless youngster, and stammered through some eight or ten lines.

'There, that will do,' said the Doctor, 'now construe.'

On common occasions the boy could have construed the passage well enough probably, but now his head was gone.

'Triste lupus, the sorrowful wolf,' he began.

A shudder ran through the whole form, and the Doctor's wrath fairly boiled over; he made three steps up to the construer, and gave him a good box on the ear. The blow was not a hard one, but the boy was so taken by surprise that he started back; the form caught the back of his knees, and over he went on to the floor behind. There was a dead silence over the whole School; never before and never again while Tom was at school did the Doctor strike a boy in lesson. The provocation must have been great. However, the victim had saved his form for that occasion, for the Doctor turned to the top bench, and put on the best boys for the rest of the hour; and though, at the end of the lesson he gave them all such a rating as they did not forget, this terrible field-day passed over without any severe visitations in the shape of punishments or floggings. Forty young scapegraces expressed their thanks to the 'sorrowful wolf' in their different ways before second lesson.

But a character for steadiness once gone is not easily recovered, as Tom found, and for years afterwards he went up the School without it, and the masters' hands were against him, and his against them. And he regarded them, as a matter of course, as his natural enemies.

Matters were not so comfortable either in the house as they had been, for old Brooke left at Christmas, and one or two others of the sixth-form boys at the following Easter. Their rule had been rough, but strong and just in the main, and a higher standard was beginning to be set up; in fact there had been a short foretaste of the good time which followed some years later. Just now, however, all threatened to return into darkness and chaos again. For the new praepostors were either small young boys, whose cleverness had carried them up to the top of the School, while in strength of body and character, they were not yet fit for a share in the government; or else big fellows of the wrong sort, boys whose friendships and tastes had a downward tendency, who had not caught the meaning of their position and work, and felt none of its responsibilities. So under this no-government the Schoolhouse began to see bad times. The big fifth-form boys, who were a sporting and drinking set, soon began to usurp power, and to fag the little boys as if they were praepostors and to bully and oppress any who showed signs of resistance. The bigger sort of sixth-form boys just described soon made common cause with the fifth, while the smaller sort, hampered by their colleagues' desertion to the enemy, could not make head against them. So the fags were without their lawful masters and protecters, and ridden over rough-shod by a set of boys whom they were not bound to obey, and whose only right over them stood in their bodily powers; and, as old Brooke had prophesied, the house by degrees broke up into small sets and parties, and lost the strong feeling of fellowship which he set so much store by, and with it much of the prowess in games, and the lead in all school matters, which he had done so much to keep up.

In no place in the world has individual character more weight than at a public school. Remember this, I beseech you, all you boys who are getting into the upper forms. Now is the time in all your lives probably when you may have more wide influence for good or evil on the society you live in, than you ever can have again. Quit yourselves like men then; speak up, and strike out if necessary for whatsoever is true, and manly, and lovely, and of good report; never try to be popular, but only to do your duty and help others to do theirs, and you may leave the tone of feeling in the school higher than you found it, and so be doing good which no living soul can measure to generations of your countrymen yet unborn. For boys follow one another in herds like sheep, for good or evil; they hate thinking, and have rarely any settled principles. Every school indeed has its own traditionary standard of right and wrong, which cannot be transgressed with impunity, marking certain things as low and blackguard, and certain others as lawful and right. This standard is ever varying, though it changes only slowly, and little by little; and, subject only to such standard, it is the leading boys for the time being who give the tone to all the rest, and make the school either a noble institution for the training of Christian Englishmen, or a place where a young boy will get more evil than he would if he were turned out to make his way in London streets, or anything between these two extremes.

The change for the worse in the School-house, however, didn't press very heavily on our youngsters for some time; they were in a good bedroom, where slept the only praepostor left who was able to keep thorough order, and their study was in his passage; so, though they were fagged more or less, and occasionally kicked or cuffed by the bullies, they were on the whole well off; and the fresh brave school-life, so full of games, adventures, and good fellowship, so ready at forgetting, so capacious at enjoying, so bright at forecasting, out-weighed a thousandfold their troubles with the master of their form, and the occasional ill-usage of the big boys in the house. It wasn't till some year or so after the events recorded above, that the praepostor of their room and passage left. None of the other sixth-form boys would move into their passage, and, to the disgust and indignation of Tom and East, one morning after breakfast they were seized upon by Flashman, and made to carry down his books and furniture into the unoccupied study which he had taken. From this time they began to feel the weight of the tyranny of Flashman and his friends, and, now that trouble had come home to their own doors, began to look out for sympathizers and partners amongst the rest of the fags; and meetings of the oppressed began to be held, and murmurs to arise, and plots to be laid, as to how they should free themselves and be avenged on their enemies.

While matters were in this state, East and Tom were one evening sitting in their study. They had done their work for first lesson, and Tom was in a brown study, brooding like a young William Tell upon the wrongs of fags in general, and his own in particular.

'I say, Scud,' said he at last, rousing himself to snuff the candle, 'what right have the fifth-form boys to fag us as they do?'

'No more right than you have to fag them,' answered East, without looking up from an early number of Pickwick, which was just coming out, and which he was luxuriously devouring, stretched on his back on the sofa.

Tom relapsed into his brown study, and East went on reading and chuckling. The contrast of the boys' faces would have given infinite amusement to a looker-on, the one so solemn and big with mighty purpose, the other radiant and bubbling over with fun.

'Do you know, old fellow, I've been thinking it over a good deal,' began Tom again.

'Oh yes, I know, fagging you are thinking of. Hang it all, but listen here, Tom—here's fun. Mr Winkle's horse—'

'And I've made up my mind,' broke in Tom, 'that I won't fag except for the sixth.'

'Quite right too, my boy,' cried East, putting his finger in the place and looking up; 'but a pretty peck of troubles you'll get into, if you're going to play that game. However, I'm all for a strike myself if we can get others to join—it's getting too bad.'

'Can't we get some sixth-form fellow to take it up?' asked Tom.

'Well, perhaps we might; Morgan would interfere, I think. 'Only,' added East, after a moment's pause, 'you see we should have to tell him about it, and that's against School principles. Don't you remember what old Brooke said about learning to take our own parts?'

'Ah, I wish old Brooke were back again—it was all right in his time.'

'Why yes, you see then the strongest and best fellows were in the sixth, and the fifth-form fellows were afraid of them, and they kept

108

good order; but now our sixth-form fellows are too small, and the fifth don't care for them, and do what they like in the house.'

'And so we get a double set of masters,' cried Tom indignantly; 'the lawful ones, who are responsible to the Doctor at any rate, and the unlawful—the tyrants, who are responsible to nobody.'

'Down with the tyrants!' cried East; 'I'm all for law and order, and hurra for a revolution.'

'I shouldn't mind if it were only for young Brooke now,' said Tom, 'he's such a good-hearted gentlemanly fellow, and ought to be in the sixth—I'd do anything for him. But that blackguard Flashman, who never speaks to one without a kick or an oath—'

'The cowardly brute,' broke in East, 'how I hate him. And he knows it too, he knows that you and I think him a coward. What a bore that he's got a study in this passage: don't you hear them now at supper in his den? Brandy punch going, I'll bet. I wish the Doctor would come out and catch him. We must change our study as soon as we can.'

'Change or no change, I'll never fag for him again,' said Tom, thumping the table.

'Fa-a-a-ag,' sounded along the passage from Flashman's study. The two boys looked at one another in silence. It had struck nine. so the regular night-fags had left duty, and they were the nearest to the supper-party. East sat up, and began to look comical, as he always did under difficulties.

'Fa-a-a-ag,' again. No answer.

'Here, Brown! East! you cursed young skulks,' roared out Flashman, coming to his open door, 'I know you're in—no shirking.'

Tom stole to their door, and drew the bolts as noiselessly as he could; East blew out the candle. 'Barricade the first,' whispered he. 'Now, Tom, mind, no surrender.'

'Trust me for that,' said Tom between his teeth.

In another minute they heard the supper-party turn out and come down the passage to their door. They held their breaths, and heard whispering, of which they only made out Flashman's words, 'I know the young brutes are in.'

Then came summonses to open, which being unanswered, the assault commenced: luckily the door was a good strong oak one, and resisted the united weight of Flashman's party. A pause followed, and they heard a besieger remark, 'They're in safe enough—don't you see how the door holds at top and bottom? so the bolts must be drawn. We should have forced the lock long ago.' East gave Tom a nudge, to call attention to this scientific remark.

Then came attacks on particular panels, one of which at last gave way to the repeated kicks; but it broke inwards, and the broken piece got jammed across, the door being lined with green-baize, and couldn't easily be removed from outside; and the besieged, scorning further concealment, strengthened their defences by pressing the end of their sofa against the door. So, after one or two more ineffectual efforts, Flashman & Co. retired, vowing vengeance in no mild terms.

The first danger over, it only remained for the besieged to effect a safe retreat, as it was now near bed-time. They listened intently, and heard the supper party resettle themselves, and then gently drew back first one bolt and then the other. Presently the convivial noises began again steadily. 'Now then stand by for a run,' said East, throwing the door wide open and rushing into the passage, closely followed by Tom. They were too quick to be caught, but Flashman was on the look-out, and sent an empty pickle-jar whizzing after them, which narrowly missed Tom's head, and broke into twenty pieces at the end of the passage. 'He wouldn't mind killing one if he wasn't caught,' said East, as they turned the corner.

There was no pursuit, so the two turned into the hall, where they found a knot of small boys round the fire. Their story was told—the war of independence had broken out—who would join the revolutionary forces? Several others present bound themselves not to fag for the fifth form at once. One or two only edged off, and left rebels. What else could they do? 'I've a good mind to go to the Doctor straight,' said Tom.

'That'll never do—don't you remember the levy of the School last half?' put in another.

In fact, that solemn assembly, a levy of the School, had been held, at which the captain of the School had got up, and, after premising that several instances had occurred of matters having been reported to the masters, that this was against public morality and School tradition; that a levy of the sixth had been held on the subject, and they had resolved that the practice must be stopped at once; had given out that any boy, in whatever form, who should thenceforth appeal to a master, without having first gone to some praepostor and laid the case before him, should be thrashed publicly, and sent to Coventry.

'Well, then, let's try the sixth. Try Morgan,' suggested another. 'No use.'—'Blabbing won't do,' was the general feeling.

'I'll give you fellows a piece of advice,' said a voice from the end of the hall. They all turned round with a start, and the speaker got up from a bench on which he had been lying unobserved, and gave himself a shake; he was a big loose-made fellow, with huge limbs which had grown too far through his jacket and trousers. 'Don't you go to anybody at all—you just stand out; say you won't fag—they'll soon get tired of licking you. I've tried it on years ago with their forerunners.'

'No! did you?—tell us how it was,' cried a chorus of voices, as they clustered round him.

'Well, just as it is with you. The fifth form would fag us, and I and some more struck, and we beat 'em. The good fellows left off directly, and the bullies who kept on soon got afraid.'

'Was Flashman here then?'

'Yes! and a dirty little snivelling, sneaking fellow he was too. He never dared join us, and used to toady the bullies by offering to fag for them, and peaching against the rest of us.'

'Why wasn't he cut then?' said East.

'Oh, toadies never get cut, they're too useful. Besides, he has no end of great hampers from home, with wine and game in them; so he toadied and fed himself into favour.'

The quarter-to-ten bell now rang, and the small boys went off upstairs, still consulting together, and praising their new counsellor, who stretched himself out on the bench before the Hall fire again. There he lay, a very queer specimen of boyhood, by name Diggs, and familiarly called "the Mucker". He was young for his size, and a very clever fellow, nearly at the top of the fifth. His friends at home, having regard, I suppose, to his age, and not to his size and place in the school, hadn't put him into tails; and even his jackets were always too small; and he had a talent for destroying clothes, and making himself look shabby. He wasn't on terms with Flashman's set, who sneered at his dress and ways behind his back, which he knew, and revenged himself by asking Flashman the most disagreeable questions, and treating him familiarly whenever a crowd of boys were round them. Neither was he intimate with any of the other bigger boys, who were warned off by his oddnesses, for he was a very queer fellow; besides, amongst other failings, he had that of impecuniosity in a remarkable degree. He brought as

111

much money as other boys to school, but got rid of it in no time, no one knew how. And then, being also reckless, borrowed from any one, and when his debts accumulated and creditors pressed, would have an auction in the Hall of everything he possessed in the world, selling even his school-books, candlestick, and study table. For weeks after one of these auctions, having rendered his study uninhabitable, he would live about in the fifth-form room and Hall, doing his verses on old letter-backs and odd scraps of paper, and learning his lessons no one knew how. He never meddled with any little boy, and was popular with them, though they all looked on him with a sort of compassion, and called him 'poor Diggs', not being able to resist appearances, or to disregard wholly even the sneers of their enemy Flashman. However, he seemed equally indifferent to the sneers of big boys and the pity of small ones, and lived his own queer life with much apparent enjoyment to himself. It is necessary to introduce Diggs thus particularly, as he not only did Tom and East good service in their present warfare, as is about to be told, but soon afterwards, when he got into the sixth, chose them for his fags, and excused them from study-fagging, thereby earning unto himself eternal gratitude from them, and all who are interested in their history.

And seldom had small boys more need of a friend, for the morning after the siege the storm burst upon the rebels in all its violence. Flashman laid wait, and caught Tom before second lesson, and receiving a point blank 'No' when told to fetch his hat, seized him and twisted his arm, and went through the other methods of torture in use: 'He couldn't make me cry tho',' as Tom said triumphantly to the rest of the rebels, 'and I kicked his shins well, I know.' And soon it crept out that a lot of the fags were in league, and Flashman excited his associates to join him in bringing the young vagabonds to their senses; and the house was filled with constant chasings, and sieges, and lickings of all sorts; and in return, the bullies' beds were pulled to pieces, and drenched with water, and their names written up on the walls with every insulting epithet which the fag invention could furnish. The war in short raged fiercely; but soon, as Diggs had told them, all the better fellows in the fifth gave up trying to fag them, and public feeling began to set against Flashman and his two or three intimates, and they were obliged to keep their doings secret, but being thorough bad fellows, missed no opportunity of torturing in private. Flashman was an adept in all ways, but above all in the power of saying cutting and cruel things, and could often bring tears to the eyes of boys in this way, which all the thrashings in the world wouldn't have wrung from them.

And as his operations were being cut short in other directions, he now devoted himself chiefly to Tom and East, who lived at his own door, and would force himself into their study whenever he found a chance, and sit there, sometimes alone, sometimes with a companion, interrupting all their work, and exulting in the evident pain which every now and then he could see he was inflicting on one or the other.

The storm had cleared the air for the rest of the house, and a better state of things now began than there had been since old Brooke had left: but an angry dark spot of thunder cloud still hung over the end of the passage, where Flashman's study and that of East and Tom lay.

He felt that they had been the first rebels, and that the rebellion had been to a great extent successful; but what above all stirred the hatred and bitterness of his heart against them, was that in the frequent collisions which there had been of late, they had openly called him coward and sneak—the taunts were too true to be forgiven. While he was in the act of thrashing them, they would roar out instances of his funking at football or shirking some encounter with a lout of half his own size. These things were all well enough known in the house, but to have his disgrace shouted out by small boys, to feel that they despised him, to be unable to silence them by any amount of torture, and to see the open laugh and sneer of his own associates (who were looking on, and took no trouble to hide their scorn from him, though they neither interfered with his bullying or lived a bit the less intimately with him), made him beside himself. Come what might, he would make those boys' lives miserable. So the strife settled down into a personal affair between Flashman and our youngsters; a war to the knife to be fought out in the little cockpit at the end of the bottom passage.

Flashman, be it said, was about seventeen years old, and big and strong of his age. He played well at all games where pluck wasn't much wanted, and managed generally to keep up appearances where it was; and having a bluff off-hand manner, which passed for heartiness and considerable power of being pleasant when he liked, went down with the school in general for a good fellow enough. Even in the Schoolhouse, by dint of his command of money, the constant supply of good things which he kept up, and his adroit toadyism, he had managed to make himself not only tolerated but rather popular amongst his own contemporaries; although young Brooke scarcely spoke to him, and one or two others of the right sort showed their opinions of him whenever a chance offered. But the wrong sort happened to be in the ascendant just now, and so Flashman was a formidable enemy for small boys. This soon became plain enough. Flashman left no slander unspoken, and no deed undone, which could in any way hurt his victims, or isolate them from the rest of the house. One by one most of the other rebels fell away from them, while Flashman's cause prospered, and several other fifth-form boys began to look black at them and ill-treat them as they passed about the house. By keeping out of bounds, or at all events out of the house and quadrangle, all day, and carefully barring themselves in at night, East and Tom managed to hold on without feeling very miserable; but it was as much as they could do. Greatly were they drawn then towards old Diggs, who, in an uncouth way, began to take a good deal of notice of them, and once or twice came to their study when Flashman was there, who immediately decamped in consequence. The boys thought that Diggs must have been watching.

When therefore, about this time, an auction was one night pronounced to take place in the Hall, at which, amongst the superfluities of other boys, all Diggs' Penates for the time being were going to the hammer, East and Tom laid their heads together, and resolved to devote their ready cash (some four shillings sterling) to redeem such articles as that sum would cover. Accordingly they duly attended to bid, and Tom became the owner of two lots of Diggs' things—lot 1, price one-and-threepence, consisting (as the auctioneer remarked) of a 'valuable assortment of old metals,' in the shape of a mouse-trap, a cheese-toaster without a handle, and a saucepan: lot 2, of a villainous dirty tablecloth and green-baize curtain: while East, for one-and-sixpence, purchased a leather paper-case, with a lock but no key, once handsome, but now much the worse for wear. But they had still the point to settle, of how to get Diggs to take the things without hurting his feelings. This they solved by leaving them in his study, which was never locked, when he was out. Diggs, who had attended the auction, remembered who had bought the lots, and came to their study soon after,

114

and sat silent for some time, cracking his great red finger-joints. Then he laid hold of their verses, and began looking over and altering them, and at last got up, and turning his back to them, said, 'You're uncommon good-hearted little beggars, you two—I value that paper-case, my sister gave it me last holidays—I won't forget;' and so tumbled out into the passage, leaving them somewhat embarrassed, but not sorry that he knew what they had done.

The next morning was Saturday, the day on which the allowances of one shilling a-week were paid, an important event to spendthrift youngsters; and great was the disgust amongst the small fry, to hear that all the allowances had been impounded for the Derby lottery. That great event in the English year, the Derby, was celebrated at Rugby in those days by many lotteries. It was not an improving custom, I own, gentle reader, and led to making books and betting and other objectionable results; but when our great Houses of Palaver think it right to stop the nation's business on that day, and many of the members bet heavily themselves, can you blame us boys for following the example of our betters?—at any rate we did follow it. First there was the great School lottery, where the first prize was six or seven pounds; then each house had one or more separate lotteries. These were all nominally voluntary, no boy being compelled to put in his shilling who didn't choose to do so: but besides Flashman, there were three or four other fast sporting young gentlemen in the Schoolhouse, who considered subscription a matter of duty and necessity, and so, to make their duty come easy to the small boys, quietly secured the allowances in a lump when given out for distribution, and kept them. It was no use grumbling—so many fewer tartlets and apples were eaten and fives'-balls bought on that Saturday; and after locking-up, when the money would otherwise have been spent, consolation was carried to many a small boy, by the sound of the night-fags shouting along the passages, 'Gentlemen sportsmen of the Schoolhouse, the lottery's going to be drawn in the Hall.' It was pleasant to be called a gentleman sportsman—also to have a chance of drawing a favourite horse.

The Hall was full of boys, and at the head of one of the long tables stood the sporting interest, with a hat before them, in which were the tickets folded up. One of them then began calling out the list of the house; each boy as his name was called drew a ticket from the hat and opened it; and most of the bigger boys, after drawing left the Hall directly to go back to their studies or the fifth-form room. The sporting interest had all drawn blanks, and they were sulky accordingly; neither of the favourites had yet been drawn, and it had come down to the upper fourth. So now, as each small boy came up and drew his ticket, it was seized and opened by Flashman, or some other of the standers-by. But no great favourite is drawn until it comes to the Tadpole's turn, and he shuffles up and draws, and tries to make off, but is caught, and his ticket is opened like the rest.

'Here you are! Wanderer! the third favourite,' shouts the opener.

'I say, just give me my ticket, please,' remonstrates Tadpole.

'Hullo, don't be in a hurry,' breaks in Flashman; 'what'll you sell Wanderer for now?'

'I don't want to sell,' rejoins Tadpole.

'Oh, don't you! Now listen, you young fool—you don't know anything about it; the horse is no use to you. He won't win, but I want him as a hedge. Now I'll give you half-a-crown for him.' Tadpole holds out, but between threats and cajoleries at length sells half for one-shilling-and-sixpence, about a fifth of its fair market value; however he is glad to realize anything, and as he wisely remarks. 'Wanderer mayn't win, and the tizzy is safe any how.'

East presently comes up and draws a blank. Soon after comes Tom's turn; his ticket like the others is seized and opened. 'Here you are then,' shouts the opener, holding it up, 'Harkaway! By Jove, Flashey, your young friend's in luck.'

'Give me the ticket,' says Flashman with an oath, leaning across the table with open hand and his face black with rage.

'Wouldn't you like it?' replies the opener, not a bad fellow at the bottom, and no admirer of Flashman's. 'Here, Brown, catch hold,' and he hands the ticket to Tom, who pockets it; whereupon Flashman makes for the door at once, that Tom and the ticket may not escape, and there keeps watch until the drawing is over and all the boys are gone except the sporting set of five or six, who stay to compare books, make bets, and so on, Tom, who doesn't choose to move while Flashman is at the door, and East, who stays by his friend, anticipating trouble.

The sporting set now gathered round Tom. Public opinion wouldn't allow them actually to rob him of his ticket, but any

116

humbug or intimidation by which he could be driven to sell the whole or part at an under-value was lawful.

'Now, young Brown, come, what'll you sell me Harkaway for? I hear he isn't going to start. I'll give you five shillings for him,' begins the boy who had opened the ticket. Tom, remembering his good deed, and moreover in his forlorn state wishing to make a friend, is about to accept the offer, when another cries out, 'I'll give you seven shillings.' Tom hesitated, and looked from one to the other.

'No, no!' said Flashman, pushing in, 'leave me to deal with him; we'll draw lots for it afterwards. Now, sir, you know me—you'll sell Harkaway to us for five shillings, or you'll repent it.'

'I won't sell a bit of him,' answered Tom shortly.

'You hear that now!' said Flashman, turning to the others. 'He's the coxiest young blackguard in the house—I always told you so. We're to have all the trouble and risk of getting up the lotteries for the benefit of such fellows as he.'

Flashman forgets to explain what risk they ran, but he speaks to willing ears. Gambling makes boys selfish and cruel as well as men.

'That's true—we always draw blanks,' cries one. 'Now, sir, you shall sell half at any rate.'

'I won't,' said Tom, flushing up to his hair, and lumping them all in his mind with his sworn enemy.

'Very well then, let's roast him,' cried Flashman, and catches hold of Tom by the collar: one or two boys hesitate, but the rest join in. East seizes Tom's arm and tries to pull him away, but is knocked back by one of the boys, and Tom is dragged along struggling. His shoulders are pushed against the mantelpiece, and he is held by main force before the fire, Flashman drawing his trousers tight by way of extra torture. Poor East, in more pain even than Tom, suddenly thinks of Diggs, and darts off to find him. 'Will you sell now for ten shillings?' says one boy who is relenting.

Tom only answers by groans and struggles.

'I say, Flashey, he has had enough,' says the same boy, dropping the arm he holds.

'No, no, another turn'll do it,' answers Flashman. But poor Tom is done already, turns deadly pale, and his head falls forward on his breast, just as Diggs in frantic excitement rushes into the hall with East at his heels.

'You cowardly brutes!' is all he can say, as he catches Tom from

117

them and supports him to the Hall table. 'Good God! he's dying. Here, get some cold water—run for the housekeeper.'

Flashman and one or two others slink away; the rest, ashamed and sorry, bend over Tom or run for water, while East darts off for the housekeeper. Water comes, and they throw it on his hands and face, and he begins to come to. 'Mother!'—the words came feebly and slowly—'it's very cold tonight.' Poor old Diggs is blubbering like a child. 'Where am I?' goes on Tom, opening his eyes. 'Ah! I remember now,' and he shut his eyes again and groaned.

'I say,' is whispered, 'we can't do any good, and the housekeeper will be here in a minute,' and all but one steal away; he stays with Diggs, silent and sorrowful, and fans Tom's face.

The housekeeper comes in with strong salts, and Tom soon recovers enough to sit up. There is a smell of burning; she examines his clothes, and looks up inquiringly. The boys are all silent.

'How did he come so?' No answer.

'There's been some bad work here,' she adds, looking very serious, 'and I shall speak to the Doctor about it.' Still no answer.

'Hadn't we better carry him to the sick-room?' suggests Diggs.

'Oh, I can walk now,' says Tom; and supported by East and the housekeeper, goes to the sick-room. The boy who held his ground is soon amongst the rest, who are all in fear of their lives. 'Did he peach?' 'Does she know about it?'

'Not a word—he's a staunch little fellow.' And pausing a moment he adds, 'I'm sick of this work: what brutes we've been.'

Meantime Tom is stretched on the sofa in the housekeeper's room, with East by his side, while she gets wine and water and other restoratives.

'Are you much hurt, dear old boy?' whispers East.

'Only the back of my legs,' answers Tom. They are indeed badly scorched, and part of his trousers burnt through. But soon he is in bed with cold bandages. At first he feels broken, and thinks of writing home and getting taken away; and the verse of a hymn he had learned years ago sings through his head, and he goes to sleep, murmuring—

Where the wicked cease from troubling,
and the weary are at rest.

But after a sound night's rest, the old boy-spirit comes back again. East comes in reporting that the whole house is with him, and he forgets everything except their old resolve, never to be beaten by that bully Flashman.

Not a word could the housekeeper extract from either of them, and though the Doctor knew all that she knew that morning, he never knew any more.

I trust and believe that such scenes are not possible now at school, and that lotteries and betting-books have gone out; but I am writing of schools as they were in our time, and must give the evil with the good.

CHAPTER 9

A CHAPTER OF ACCIDENTS

'Wherein I [speak] of most disastrous chances,
Of moving accidents by flood and field,
Of hair-breadth 'scapes.'
                                        —*Shakespeare.*

When Tom came back into school after a couple of days in the sick-room, he found matters much changed for the better, as East had led him to expect. Flashman's brutality had disgusted most even of his intimate friends, and his cowardice had once more been made plain to the House; for Diggs had encountered him on the morning after the lottery, and after high words on both sides had struck him, and the blow was not returned. However, Flashey was not unused to this sort of thing, and had lived through as awkward affairs before, and, as Diggs had said, fed and toadied himself back into favour again. Two or three of the boys who had helped to roast Tom came up and begged his pardon, and thanked him for not telling anything. Morgan sent for him, and was inclined to take the matter up warmly, but Tom begged him not to do it; to which he agreed, on Tom's promising to come to him at once in future—a promise which I regret to say he didn't keep. Tom kept Harkaway all to himself, and won the second prize in the lottery, some thirty shillings, which he and East contrived to spend in about three days, in the purchase of pictures for their study, two new bats and a cricket-ball, all the best that could be got, and a supper of sausages, kidneys, and beef-steak pies to all the rebels. Light come, light go; they wouldn't have been comfortable with money in their pockets in the middle of the half.

The embers of Flashman's wrath, however, were still smouldering, and burst out every now and then in sly blows and taunts, and they both felt that they hadn't quite done with him yet. It wasn't long, however, before the last act of that drama came, and with it, the end of bullying for Tom and East at Rugby. They now often stole out into the Hall at nights, incited thereto, partly by the hope of finding Diggs there and having a talk with him, partly by the excitement of doing something which was against rules; for, sad to say, both of our youngsters, since their loss of character for steadiness in their form, had got into the habit of doing things which were forbidden, as a matter of adventure; just in the same way, I should fancy, as men fall into smuggling, and for the same sort of reasons. Thoughtlessness in the first place. It never occurred to them to consider why such and such rules were laid down, the reason was nothing to them, and they only looked upon rules as a sort of challenge from the rule-makers, which it would be rather bad pluck in them not to accept; and then again, in the lower parts of the school they hadn't enough to do. The work of the form they could manage to get through pretty easily, keeping a good enough place to get their regular yearly remove; and not having much ambition beyond this, their whole superfluous steam was available for games and scrapes. Now one rule of the House which it was a daily pleasure of all such boys to break, was that after supper all fags, except the three on duty in the passages, should remain in their own studies until nine o'clock; and if caught about the passages or hall, or in one another's studies, they were liable to punishments or caning. The rule was stricter than its observance, for most of the sixth spent their evenings in the fifthform room, where the library was, and the lessons were learnt in common. Every now and then, however, a praepostor would be seized with a fit of district visiting, and would make a tour of the passages and hall, and the fags' studies. Then, if the owner were entertaining a friend or two, the first kick at the door and ominous 'open here', had the effect of the shadow of a hawk over a chicken-yard; every one cut to cover—one small boy diving under the sofa, another under the table, while the owner would hastily pull down a book or two and open them, and cry out in a meek voice, 'Hullo, who's there?' casting an anxious eye round, to see that no protruding leg or elbow could betray the hidden boys. 'Open, sir, directly, it's Snooks.' 'Oh, I'm very sorry, I didn't know it was you, Snooks;' and then, with well-feigned zeal, the door would be opened, young hopeful praying that that beast Snooks mightn't have heard the scuffle caused by his coming. If a study was empty, Snooks proceeded to draw the passage and hall to find the truants.

Well, one evening, in forbidden hours, Tom and East were in the Hall. They occupied the seats before the fire nearest the door, while Diggs sprawled as usual before the further fire. He was busy with a copy of verses, and East and Tom were chatting together in whispers by the light of the fire, and splicing a favourite old fives' bat which had sprung. Presently a step came down the bottom passage; they listened a moment, assured themselves that it wasn't a praepostor, and then went on with their work, and the door swung open, and in walked Flashman. He didn't see Diggs, and thought it a good chance to keep his hand in; and as the boys didn't move for him, struck one of them, to make them get out of his way.

'What's that for?' growled the assaulted one.

'Because I choose. You've no business here—go to your study.'

'You can't send us.'

'Can't I? Then I'll thrash you if you stay,' said Flashman, savagely.

'I say, you two,' said Diggs from the end of the Hall, rousing up and resting himself on his elbow, 'you'll never get rid of that fellow till you lick him. Go in at him, both of you—I'll see fair play.'

Flashman was taken aback, and retreated two steps. East looked at Tom. 'Shall we try?' said he. 'Yes,' said Tom, desperately. So the two advanced on Flashman with clenched fists and beating hearts. They were about up to his shoulder, but tough boys of their age and in perfect training; while he, though strong and big, was in poor condition from his monstrous habits of stuffing and want of exercise. Coward as he was, however, Flashman couldn't swallow such an insult as this; besides, he was confident of having easy work, and so faced the boys, saying, 'You impudent young blackguards!'—Before he could finish his abuse they rushed in on him, and began pummeling at all of him which they could reach.

He hit out wildly and savagely, but the full force of his blows didn't tell, they were too near him. It was long odds though in point of strength, and in another minute Tom went spinning backwards over a form, and Flashman turned to demolish East with a savage grin. But now Diggs jumped down from the table on which he had seated himself. 'Stop there,' shouted he, 'the round's over—half-minute time allowed.'

'What the — is it to you?' faltered Flashman, who began to lose heart.

'I'm going to see fair, I tell you,' said Diggs with a grin, and snapping his great red fingers; ''tain't fair for you to be fighting one of them at a time. Are you ready, Brown? Time's up.'

The small boys rushed in again. Closing they saw was their best chance, and Flashman was wilder and more flurried than ever: he caught East by the throat and tried to force him back on the iron-bound table; Tom grasped his waist, and remembering the old throw he had learned in the Vale from Harry Winburn, crooked his leg inside Flashman's, and threw his whole weight forward. The three tottered for a moment, and then over they went on to the floor, Flashman striking his head against a form in the fall.

The two youngsters sprang to their legs, but he lay there still. They began to be frightened. Tom stooped down, and then cried out, scared out of his wits, 'He's bleeding awfully; come here, East, Diggs—he's dying!'

'Not he,' said Diggs, getting leisurely off the table; 'it's all sham, he's only afraid to fight it out.'

East was as frightened as Tom. Diggs lifted Flashman's head, and he groaned.

'What's the matter?' shouted Diggs.

'My skull's fractured,' sobbed Flashman.

'Oh, let me run for the housekeeper,' cried Tom. 'What shall we do?'

'Fiddlesticks! it's nothing but the skin broken,' said the relentless Diggs, feeling his head. 'Cold water and a bit of rag's all he'll want.'

'Let me go,' said Flashman, surlily, sitting up; 'I don't want your help.'

'We're really very sorry,' began East.

'Hang your sorrow,' answered Flashman, holding his handkerchief to the place; 'you shall pay for this, I can tell you, both of you.' And he walked out of the Hall.

'He can't be very bad,' said Tom with a deep sigh, much relieved to see his enemy march so well.

'Not he,' said Diggs, 'and you'll see you won't be troubled with him any more. But, I say, your head's broken too—your collar is covered with blood.'

'Is it though?' said Tom, putting up his hand, 'I didn't know it.'

'Well, mop it up, or you'll have your jacket spoilt. And you have got a nasty eye, Scud; you'd better go and bathe it well in cold water.'

'Cheap enough too, if we've done with our old friend Flashy,' said East, as they made off upstairs to bathe their wounds.

They had done with Flashman in one sense, for he never laid finger on either of them again; but whatever harm a spiteful heart and venomous tongue could do them, he took care should be done. Only throw dirt enough, and some of it is sure to stick; and so it was with the fifth form and the bigger boys in general, with whom he associated more or less, and they not at all, Flashman managed to get Tom and East into disfavour, which did not wear off for some time after the author of it had disappeared from the School world. This event, much prayed for by the small fry in general, took place a few months after the above encounter. One fine summer evening Flashman had been regaling himself on gin-punch, at Brownsover; and having exceeded his usual limits, started home uproarious. He fell in with a friend or two coming back from bathing, proposed a glass of beer, to which they assented, the weather being hot, and they thirsty souls, and unaware of the quantity of drink which Flashman had already on board. The short result was, that Flashy became beastly drunk; they tried to get him along, but couldn't, so they chartered a hurdle and two men to carry him. One of the masters came upon them, and they naturally enough fled. The flight of the rest raised the master's suspicions, and the good angel of the fags incited him to examine the freight, and after examination, to convoy the hurdle himself up to the School-house; and the Doctor, who had long had his eye on Flashman, arranged for his withdrawal next morning.

The evil that men, and boys too, do, lives after them: Flashman was gone, but our boys, as hinted above, still felt the effects of his hate. Besides, they had been the movers of the strike against unlawful fagging. The cause was righteous, the result had been triumphant to a great extent; but the best of the fifth, even those who had never fagged the small boys, or had given up the practice cheerfully, couldn't help feeling a small grudge against the first rebels. After all, their form had been defied; on just grounds, no doubt, so just indeed, that they had at once acknowledged the wrong, and remained passive in the strife: had they sided with Flashman and his set, the rebels must have given way at once. They couldn't help, on the whole, being glad that they had so acted, and that the resistance had been successful against such of their own form as had shown fight; they felt that law and order had gained thereby, but the ringleaders they couldn't quite pardon at once. 'Confoundedly coxy those young rascals will get if we don't mind,' was the general feeling.

So it is, and must be always, my dear boys. If the Angel Gabriel were to come down from Heaven, and head a successful rise against the most abominable and unrighteous vested interest which this poor old world groans under, he would most certainly lose his character for many years, probably for centuries, not only with upholders of said vested interest, but with the respectable mass of the people whom he had delivered. They wouldn't ask him to dinner, or let their names appear with his in the papers; they would be very careful how they spoke of him in the Palaver or at their clubs. What can we expect then, when we have only poor gallant blundering men like Kossuth, Garibaldi, Mazzini, and righteous causes which do not triumph in their hands; men who have holes enough in their armour, God knows, easy to be hit by respectabilities sitting in their lounging chairs, and having large balances at their bankers? But you are brave gallant boys, who hate easy-chairs, and have no balances or bankers. You only want to have your heads set straight to take the right side: so bear in mind that majorities, especially respectable ones, are nine times out of ten in the wrong; and that if you see man or boy striving earnestly on the weak side, however wrong-headed or blundering he may be, you are not to go and join the cry against him. If you can't join him and help him, and make him wiser, at any rate remember that he has found something in the world which he will fight and suffer for, which is just what you have got to do for yourselves, and so think and speak of him tenderly.

So East and Tom, the Tadpole, and one or two more, became a sort of young Ishmaelites, their hands against everyone, and everyone's hand against them. It has been already told how they got to war with the masters and the fifth form, and with the sixth it was much the same. They saw the praepostors cowed by or joining with the fifth, and shirking their own duties, so they didn't respect them, and rendered no willing obedience. It had been one thing to clear out studies for sons of heroes like old Brooke, but was quite another to do the like for Snooks and Green, who had never faced a good scrummage at football, and couldn't keep the passages in order at night. So they only slurred through their fagging just well enough to escape a licking, and not always that, and got the character of sulky, unwilling fags. In the fifth-form room, after supper, when such matters were often discussed and arranged, their names were for ever coming up.

'I say, Green,' Snooks began one night, 'isn't that new boy, Harrison, your fag?'

'Yes, why?'

'Oh, I know something of him at home, and should like to excuse him—will you swop?'

'Who will you give me?'

'Well, let's see, there's Willis, Johnson—No, that won't do. Yes, I have it—there's young East, I'll give you him.'

'Don't you wish you may get it?' replied Green. 'I'll tell you what I'll do—I'll give you two for Willis, if you like.'

'Who then?' asks Snooks.

'Hall and Brown.'

'Wouldn't have 'em at a gift.'

'Better than East though, for they ain't quite so sharp,' said Green, getting up and leaning his back against the mantelpiece—he wasn't a bad fellow, and couldn't help not being able to put down the unruly fifth form. His eye twinkled as he went on, 'Did I ever tell you how the young vagabond sold me last half?'

'No—how?'

'Well, he never half cleaned my study out, only just stuck the candlesticks in the cupboard, and swept the crumbs on to the floor. So at last I was mortal angry and had him up, made him go through the whole performance under my eyes: the dust the young scamp made nearly choked me, and showed that he hadn't swept the carpet before. Well, when it was all finished, "Now, young gentleman," says I, "mind, I expect this to be done every morning, floor swept, tablecloth taken off and shaken, and everything dusted." "Very well," grunts he. Not a bit of it though—I was quite sure in a day or two that he never took the tablecloth off even. So I laid a trap for him: I tore up some paper and put half-a-dozen bits on my table one night, and the cloth over them, as usual. Next morning, after breakfast, up I came, pulled off the cloth, and sure enough there was the paper, which fluttered down on to the floor. I was in a towering rage. "I've got you now," thought I, and sent for him, while I got out my cane. Up he came as cool as you please, with his hands in his pockets. "Didn't I tell you to shake my tablecloth every morning," roared I. "Yes," says he. "Did you do it this morning," "Yes." "You young liar! I put these pieces of paper on the table last night, and if you'd taken the tablecloth off you'd have seen them, so I'm going to give you a good licking." Then my youngster takes one hand out of his pocket, and just stoops down and picks up two of the bits of paper, and holds them out to me. There was written on each in great round text, "Harry East, his mark." The young rogue had found my trap out, taken away my paper and put some of his there, every bit ear-marked. I'd a great mind to lick him for his impudence, but after all one has no right to be laying traps, so I didn't. Of course I was at his mercy till the end of the half, and in his weeks my study was so frowsy, I couldn't sit in it.'

'They spoil one's things so, too,' chimed in a third boy. 'Hall and Brown were night-fags last week: I called fag, and gave them my candlesticks to clean; away they went, and didn't appear again. When they'd had time enough to clean them three times over, I went out to look after them. They weren't in the passages, so down I went into the Hall, where I heard music, and there I found them sitting on the table, listening to Johnson who was playing the flute, and my candlesticks stuck between the bars well into the fire, red-hot, clean spoiled; they've never stood straight since, and I must get some more. However, I gave them both a good licking, that's one comfort.'

Such were the sort of scrapes they were always getting into: and so, partly by their own faults, partly from circumstances, partly from the faults of others, they found themselves outlaws, ticket-of-leave men, or what you will in that line; in short, dangerous parties, and lived the sort of hand-to-mouth, wild, reckless life which such parties generally have to put up with. Nevertheless, they never quite lost favour with young Brooke, who was now the cock of the house, and just getting into the sixth, and Diggs stuck to them like a man, and gave

126

them store of good advice, by which they never in the least profited.

And even after the house mended, and law and order had been restored, which soon happened after young Brooke and Diggs got into the sixth, they couldn't easily or at once return into the paths of steadiness, and many of the old wild out-of-bounds habits stuck to them as firmly as ever. While they had been quite little boys, the scrapes they got into in the School hadn't much mattered to any one; but now they were in the upper school, all wrong-doers from which were sent up straight to the Doctor at once: so they began to come under his notice; and as they were sort of leaders in a small way amongst their own contemporaries, his eye, which was everywhere, was upon them.

It was a toss-up whether they turned out well or ill, and so they were just the boys who caused most anxiety to such a master. You have been told of the first occasion on which they were sent up to the Doctor, and the remembrance of it was so pleasant that they had much less fear of him than most boys of their standing had. 'It's all his look,' Tom used to say to East, 'that frightens fellows: don't you remember, he never said anything to us my first half-year, for being an hour late for locking-up?'

The next time that Tom came before him, however, the interview was of a very different kind. It happened just about the time at which we have now arrived, and was the first of a series of scrapes into which our hero managed now to tumble.

The river Avon at Rugby is a slow and not very clear stream, in which chub, dace, roach and other coarse fish are (or were) plentiful enough, together with a fair sprinkling of small jack, but no fish worth sixpence either for sport or food. It is, however, a capital river for bathing, as it has many nice small pools and several good reaches for swimming, all within about a mile of one another, and at an easy twenty minutes' walk from the school. This mile of water is rented, or used to be rented, for bathing purposes, by the Trustees of the School, for the boys. The footpath to Brownsover crosses the river by 'the Planks', a curious old single-plank bridge, running for fifty or sixty yards into the flat meadows on each side of the river—for in the winter there are frequent floods. Above the Planks were the bathing places for the smaller boys; Sleath's, the first bathing place where all new boys had to begin, until they had proved to the bathing men (three steady individuals who were paid to attend daily through the summer to prevent accidents) that they could swim pretty decently, when they were allowed to go on to Anstey's, about one-hundred-and-fifty yards below. Here there was a hole about six feet deep and twelve feet across, over which the puffing urchins struggled to the opposite side, and thought no small-beer of themselves for having been out of their depths. Below the Planks came larger and deeper holes, the first of which was Wratislaw's,—and the last Swift's, a famous hole ten or twelve feet deep in parts, and thirty yards across, from which there was a fine swimming reach right down to the Mill. Swift's was reserved for the sixth and fifth forms, and had a spring-board and two sets of steps: the others had one set of steps each, and were used indifferently by all the lower boys, though each house addicted itself more to one hole than to another. The Schoolhouse at this time affected Wratislaw's hole, and Tom and East, who had learnt to swim like fishes, were to be found there as regular as the clock through the summer, always twice, and often three times a day.

Now the boys either had, or fancied they had, a right also to fish at their pleasure over the whole of this part of the river, and would not understand that the right (if any) only extended to the Rugby side. As ill luck would have it, the gentleman who owned the opposite bank, after allowing it for some time without interference, had ordered his keepers not to let the boys fish on his side; the consequence of which had been, that there had been first wranglings and then fights between the keepers and boys; and so keen had the quarrel become, that the landlord and his keepers, after a ducking had been inflicted on one of the latter, and a fierce fight ensued thereon, had been up to the great School at calling-over to identify the delinquents, and it was all the Doctor himself and five or six masters could do to keep the peace. Not even his authority could prevent the hissing, and so strong was the feeling, that the four praepostors of the week walked up the school with their canes, shouting s-s-s-s-i-lenc-c-c-c-e at the top of their voices. However, the chief offenders for the time were flogged and kept in bounds, but the victorious party had brought a nice hornet's nest about their ears. The landlord was hissed at the School gates as he rode past, and when he charged his horse at the mob of boys and tried to thrash them with his whip, was driven back by cricket bats and wickets, and pursued with pebbles and fives' balls; while the wretched keepers' lives were a burthen to them, from having to watch the waters so closely.

The Schoolhouse boys of Tom's standing, one and all, as a protest against this tyranny and cutting short of their lawful amusements, took to fishing in all ways, and especially by means of night-lines. The little tackle-maker at the bottom of the town would soon have made his fortune had the rage lasted, and several of the barbers began to lay in fishing tackle. The boys had this great advantage over their enemies, that they spent a large portion of the day in nature's garb by the river side, and so when tired of swimming, would get out on the other side and fish, or set night-lines till the keeper hove in sight, and then plunge in and swim back and mix with the other bathers, and the keepers were too wise to follow across the stream.

While things were in this state, one day Tom and three or four others were bathing at Wratislaw's, and had, as a matter of course, been taking up and re-setting night-lines. They had all left the water, and were sitting or standing about at their toilettes, in all costumes from a shirt upwards, when they were aware of a man in a velveteen shooting-coat approaching from the other side. He was a new keeper, so they didn't recognize or notice him, till he pulled up right opposite, and began:

'I see'd some of you young gentlemen over this side a fishing just now.'

'Hullo, who are you? What business is that of yours, old Velveteens?'

'I'm the new under-keeper, and master's told me to keep a sharp look-out on all o' you young chaps. And I tells 'ee I means business, and you'd better keep on your own side, or we shall fall out.'

'Well, that's right, Velveteens—speak out, and let's know your mind at once.'

'Look here, old boy,' cried East, holding up a miserable coarse fish or two and a small jack, 'would you like to smell 'em and see which bank they lived under?'

'I'll give you a bit of advice, keeper,' shouted Tom, who was sitting in his shirt paddling with his feet in the river; 'you'd better go down there to Swift's where the big boys are, they're beggars at setting lines, and'll put you up to a wrinkle or two for catching the five-pounders.' Tom was nearest to the keeper, and that officer, who was getting angry at the chaff, fixed his eyes on our hero, as if

129

to take a note of him for future use. Tom returned his gaze with a steady stare, and then broke into a laugh, and struck into the middle of a favourite Schoolhouse song—

> As I and my companions
> Were setting of a snare,
> The gamekeeper was watching us,
> For him we did not care:
> For we can wrestle and fight, my boys,
> And jump out anywhere.
> For it is my delight of a likely night,
> In the season of the year.

The chorus was taken up by the other boys with shouts of laughter, and the keeper turned away with a grunt, but evidently bent on mischief. The boys thought no more of the matter.

But now came on the may-fly season; the soft hazy summer weather lay sleepily along the rich meadows by Avon side, and the green and grey flies flickered with their graceful lazy up and down flight over the reeds and the water and the meadows, in myriads upon myriads. The may-flies must surely be the lotuseaters of the ephemerae; the happiest, laziest, carelessest fly that dances and dreams out his few hours of sunshiny life by English rivers.

Every pitiful little coarse fish in the Avon was on the alert for the flies, and gorging his wretched carcase with hundreds daily, the gluttonous rogues! and every lover of the gentle craft was out to avenge the poor may-flies.

So one fine Thursday afternoon, Tom having borrowed East's new rod, started by himself to the river. He fished for some time with small success, not a fish would rise at him; but as he prowled along the bank he was presently aware of mighty ones feeding in a pool on the opposite side, under the shade of a huge willow-tree. The stream was deep here, but some fifty yards below was a shallow, for which he made off hot-foot; and forgetting landlords, keepers, solemn prohibitions of the Doctor, and everything else, pulled up his trousers, plunged across, and in three minutes was creeping along on all fours towards the clump of willows.

It isn't often that great chub, or any other coarse fish, are in earnest about anything, but just then they were thoroughly bent on feeding, and in half-an-hour Master Tom had deposited three thumping fellows at the foot of the giant willow. As he was baiting for a fourth pounder, and just going to throw in again, he became aware of a man coming up the bank not one hundred yards off. Another look told him that it was the under-keeper. Could he reach the shallow before him? No, not carrying his rod. Nothing for it but the tree, so Tom laid his bones to it, shinning up as fast as he could, and dragging up his rod after him. He had just time to reach and crouch along upon a huge branch some ten feet up, which stretched out over the river, when the keeper arrived at the clump. Tom's heart beat fast as he came under the tree; two steps more and he would have passed, when, as ill-luck would have it, the gleam on the scales of the dead fish caught his eye, and he made a dead point at the foot of the tree. He picked up the fish one by one; his eye and touch told him that they had been alive and feeding within the hour. Tom crouched lower along the branch, and heard the keeper beating the clump. 'If I could only get the rod hidden,' thought he, and began gently shifting it to get it alongside him; 'willow-trees don't throw out straight hickory shoots twelve feet long, with no leaves, worse luck.' Alas! the keeper catches the rustle, and then a sight of the rod, and then of Tom's hand and arm.

'Oh, be up ther', be 'ee?' says he, running under the tree. 'Now you come down this minute.'

'Tree'd at last,' thinks Tom, making no answer, and keeping as close as possible, but working away at the rod, which he takes to pieces: 'I'm in for it, unless I can starve him out.' And then he begins to meditate getting along the branch for a plunge, and scramble to the other side; but the small branches are so thick, and the opposite bank so difficult, that the keeper will have lots of time to get round by the ford before he can get out, so he gives that up. And now he hears the keeper beginning to scramble up the trunk. That will never do; so he scrambles himself back to where his branch joins the trunk, and stands with lifted rod.

'Hullo, Velveteens, mind your fingers if you come any higher.'

The keeper stops and looks up, and then with a grin says, 'Oh! be you, be it, young measter? Well, here's luck. Now I tells 'ee to come down at once, and 't'll be best for 'ee.'

'Thank'ee, Velveteens, I'm very comfortable,' said Tom, shortening the rod in his hand, and preparing for battle.

'Werry well, please yourself,' says the keeper, descending however to the ground again, and taking his seat on the bank; 'I bean't

131

in no hurry, so you med' take yer time. I'll larn 'ee to gee honest folk names afore I've done with 'ee.'

'My luck as usual,' thinks Tom; 'what a fool I was to give him a black. If I'd called him "keeper" now I might get off. The return match is all his way.'

The keeper quietly proceeded to take out his pipe, fill, and light it, keeping an eye on Tom, who now sat disconsolately across the branch, looking at keeper—a pitiful sight for men and fishes. The more he thought of it the less he liked it. 'It must be getting near second calling-over,' thinks he. Keeper smokes on stolidly. 'If he takes me up, I shall be flogged safe enough. I can't sit here all night. Wonder if he'll rise at silver.'

'I say, keeper,' said he meekly, 'let me go for two bob?'

'Not for twenty neither,' grunts his persecutor.

And so they sat on till long past second calling-over, and the sun came slanting in through the willow branches, and telling of locking-up near at hand.

'I'm coming down, keeper,' said Tom at last with a sigh, fairly tired out. 'Now what are you going to do?'

'Walk 'ee up to School, and give 'ee over to the Doctor; them's my orders,' says Velveteens, knocking the ashes out of his fourth pipe, and standing up and shaking himself.

'Very good,' said Tom; 'but hands off, you know. I'll go with you quietly, so no collaring or that sort of thing.'

Keeper looked at him a minute—'Werry good,' said he at last; and so Tom descended, and wended his way drearily by the side of the keeper up to the Schoolhouse, where they arrived just at locking-up. As they passed the School-gates, the Tadpole and several others, who were standing there, caught the state of things, and rushed out, crying 'rescue'; but Tom shook his head, so they only followed to the Doctor's gate, and went back sorely puzzled.

How changed and stern the Doctor seemed from the last time that Tom was up there, as the keeper told the story, not omitting to state how Tom had called him blackguard names. 'Indeed, sir,' broke in the culprit, 'it was only Velveteens.' The Doctor only asked one question.

'You know the rule about the banks, Brown?'

'Yes, sir.'

'Then wait for me tomorrow, after first lesson.'

'I thought so,' muttered Tom.

'And about the rod, sir?' went on the keeper; 'Master's told we as we might have all the rods—'

'Oh, please sir,' broke in Tom, 'the rod isn't mine.' The Doctor looked puzzled, but the keeper, who was a good-hearted fellow, and melted at Tom's evident distress, gave up his claim. Tom was flogged next morning, and a few days afterwards met Velveteens, and presented him with half-a-crown for giving up the rod claim, and they became sworn friends: and I regret to say that Tom had many more fish from under the willow that may-fly season, and was never caught again by Velveteens.

It wasn't three weeks before Tom, and now East by his side, were again in the awful presence. This time, however, the Doctor was not so terrible. A few days before, they had been fagged at fives to fetch the balls that went off the Court. While standing watching the game, they saw five or six nearly new balls hit on to the top of the School. 'I say, Tom,' said East, when they were dismissed, 'couldn't we get those balls somehow?'

'Let's try, any how.'

So they reconnoitred the walls carefully, borrowed a coal hammer from old Stumps, bought some big nails, and after one or two attempts, scaled the Schools, and possessed themselves of huge quantities of fives' balls. The place pleased them so much that they spent all their spare time there, scratching and cutting their names on the top of every tower; and at last, having exhausted all other places, finished up with inscribing H. EAST, T. BROWN, on the minute-hand of the great clock. In the doing of which, they held the minute hand, and disturbed the clock's economy. So next morning, when masters and boys came trooping down to prayers, and entered the quadrangle, the injured minute-hand was indicating three minutes to the hour. They all pulled up, and took their time. When the hour struck doors were closed, and half the school late. Thomas being set to make inquiry, discovers their names on the minute-hand, and reports accordingly; and they are sent for, a knot of their friends making derisive and pantomimic allusions to what their fate will be, as they walk off.

But the Doctor, after hearing their story, doesn't make much of it, and only gives them thirty lines of Homer to learn by heart, and a lecture on the likelihood of such exploits ending in broken bones.

Alas! almost the next day was one of the great fairs in the town; and as several rows and other disagreeable accidents had of late taken place on these occasions, the Doctor gives out, after prayers in the morning, that no boy is to go down into the town. Wherefore East and Tom, for no earthly pleasure except that of doing what they are told not to do, start away, after second lesson, and making a short circuit through the fields, strike a back lane which leads into the town, go down it, and run plump upon one of the masters as they emerge into the High Street. The master in question, though a very clever, is not a righteous man: he has already caught several of his own pupils, and gives them lines to learn, while he sends East and Tom, who are not his pupils, up to the Doctor; who, on learning that they had been at prayers in the morning, flogs them soundly.

The flogging did them no good at the time, for the injustice of their captor was rankling in their minds; but it was just the end of the half, and on the next evening but one Thomas knocks at their door, and says the Doctor wants to see them. They look at one another in silent dismay. What can it be now? Which of their countless wrong-doings can he have heard of officially? However, it's no use delaying, so up they go to the study. There they find the Doctor, not angry, but very grave. 'He has sent for them to speak very seriously, before they go home. They have each been flogged several times in the half-year for direct and wilful breaches of rules. This cannot go on. They are doing no good to themselves or others, and now they are getting up in the School, and have influence. They seem to think that rules are made capriciously, and for the pleasure of the master; but this is not so, they are made for the good of the whole School, and must and shall be obeyed. Those who thoughtlessly or wilfully break them will not be allowed to stay at the School. He should be sorry if they had to leave, as the School might do them both much good, and wishes them to think very seriously in the holidays over what he has said. Good night.'

And so the two hurry off horribly scared: the idea of having to leave has never crossed their minds, and is quite unbearable.

As they go out, they meet at the door old Holmes, a sturdy cherry praepostor of another house, who goes in to the Doctor; and they hear his genial hearty greeting of the newcomer, so different to their own reception, as the door closes, and return to their study with heavy hearts, and tremendous resolves to break no more rules.

Five minutes afterwards the master of their form, a late arrival and a model young master, knocks at the Doctor's study-door. 'Come in!' and as he enters the Doctor goes on to Holmes—'you see I do not know anything of the case officially, and if I take any notice of it at all, I must publicly expel the boy. I don't wish to do that, for I think there is some good in him. There's nothing for it but a good sound thrashing.' He paused to shake hands with the master, which Holmes does also, and then prepares to leave.

'I understand. Good night, sir.'

'Good night, Holmes. And remember,' added the Doctor, emphasizing the words, 'a good sound thrashing before the whole house.'

The door closed on Holmes, and the Doctor, in answer to the puzzled look of his lieutenant, explained shortly. 'A gross case of bullying. Wharton, the head of the house, is a very good fellow, but slight and weak, and severe physical pain is the only way to deal with such a case; so I have asked Holmes to take it up. He is very careful and trustworthy, and has plenty of strength. I wish all the sixth had as much. We must have it here, if we are to keep order at all.'

Now I don't want any wiseacres to read this book; but if they should, of course they will prick up their long ears, and howl, or rather bray, at the above story. Very good, I don't object; but what I have to add for you boys is this, that Holmes called a levy of his house after breakfast next morning, made them a speech on the case of bullying in question, and then gave the bully a 'good sound thrashing'; and that years afterwards, that boy sought out Holmes, and thanked him, saying it had been the kindest act which had ever been done upon him, and the turning point in his character; and a very good fellow he became, and a credit to his school.

After some other talk between them, the Doctor said, 'I want to speak to you about two boys in your form, East and Brown; I have just been speaking to them. What do you think of them?'

'Well, they are not hard workers, and very thoughtless and full of spirits—but I can't help liking them, I think they are sound good fellows at the bottom.'

'I'm glad of it. I think so too. But they make me very uneasy. They are taking the lead a good deal amongst the fags in my house, for they are very active bold fellows. I should be sorry to lose them, but I shan't let them stay if I don't see them gaining character and manliness. In another year they may do great harm to all the younger boys.'

'Oh, I hope you won't send them away,' pleaded their master.

'Not if I can help it. But now I never feel sure, after any

half-holiday, that I shan't have to flog one of them next morning for some foolish thoughtless scrape. I quite dread seeing either of them.'

They were both silent for a minute. Presently the Doctor began again:

'They don't feel that they have any duty or work to do in the School, and how is one to make them feel it?'

'I think if either of them had some little boy to take care of, it would steady them. Brown is the most reckless of the two, I should say; East wouldn't get into so many scrapes without him.'

'Well,' said the Doctor, with something like a sigh, 'I'll think of it.' And they went on to talk of other subjects.

PART TWO

'I [hold] it truth, with him who sings
To one clear harp in divers tones,
That men may rise on stepping-stones
Of their dead selves to higher things.'
—TENNYSON

CHAPTER 1

HOW THE TIDE TURNED

'Once to every man and nation, comes the moment to decide,
In the strife of Truth with falsehood, for the good or evil side:

Then it is the brave man chooses, while the coward stands aside.
Doubting in his abject spirit, till his Lord is crucified.'
—LOWELL

The turning point in our hero's school career had now come, and the manner of it was as follows. On the evening of the first day of the next half-year, Tom, East, and another Schoolhouse boy, who had just been dropped at the Spread Eagle by the old Regulator, rushed into the matron's room in high spirits, such as all real boys are in when they first get back, however fond they may be of home.

'Well, Mrs Wixie,' shouted one, seizing on the methodical active little dark-eyed woman, who was busy stowing away the linen of the boys who had already arrived into their several pigeon-holes, 'here we are again you see, as jolly as ever. Let us help you put the things away.'

'And, Mary,' cried another (she was called indifferently by either name), 'who's come back? Has the Doctor made old Jones leave? How many new boys are there?'

'Am I and East to have Gray's study? You know you promised to get it for us if you could,' shouted Tom.

'And am I to sleep in Number 4?' roared East.

'How's old Sam, and Bogle, and Sally?'

'Bless the boys!' cries Mary, at last getting in a word, 'why you'll shake me to death. There, now do go away up to the housekeeper's room and get your suppers; you know I haven't time to talk—you'll find plenty more in the house. Now, Master East, do let those things alone—you're mixing up three new boys' things.' And she rushed at East, who escaped round the open trunks holding up a prize.

'Hullo, look here, Tommy,' shouted he, 'here's fun!' and he brandished above his head some pretty little night-caps, beautifully made and marked, the work of loving fingers in some distant country home. The kind mother and sisters, who sewed that delicate stitching with aching hearts, little thought of the trouble they might be bringing on the young head for which they were meant. The little matron was wiser, and snatched the caps from East before he could look at the name on them.

'Now, Master East, I shall be very angry if you don't go,' said she; 'there's some capital cold beef and pickles upstairs, and I won't have you old boys in my room first night.'

'Hurrah for the pickles! Come along, Tommy, come along, Smith. We shall find out who the young Count is, I'll be bound: I hope he'll sleep in my room. Mary's always vicious first week.'

As the boys turned to leave the room, the matron touched Tom's arm, and said, 'Master Brown, please stop a minute, I want to speak to you.'

'Very well, Mary. I'll come in a minute, East; don't finish the pickles—'

'Oh, Master Brown,' went on the little matron when the rest had gone, 'you're to have Gray's study, Mrs Arnold says. And she wants you to take in this young gentleman. He's a new boy and thirteen years old, tho' he don't look it. He's very delicate, and has never been from home before. And I told Mrs Arnold I thought you'd be kind to him, and see that they don't bully him at first. He's put into your form, and I've given him the bed next to yours in Number 4; so East can't sleep there this half.'

Tom was rather put about by this speech. He had got the double study which he coveted, but here were conditions attached which greatly moderated his joy. He looked across the room, and in the far corner of the sofa was aware of a slight pale boy, with large blue eyes and light fair hair, who seemed ready to shrink through the floor. He saw at a glance that the little stranger was just the boy whose first half-year at a public school would be misery to himself if he were left alone, or constant anxiety to any one who meant to see him through his troubles. Tom was too honest to take in the youngster and then let him shift for himself; and if he took him as his chum instead of East, where were all his pet plans of having a bottled-beer cellar under his window, and making night-lines and slings, and plotting expeditions to Brownsover Mills and Caldecott's Spinney? East and he had made up their minds to get this study, and then every night from locking-up till then they would be together, to talk about fishing, drink bottled-beer, read Maryatt's novels, and sort birds' eggs. And this new boy would most likely never go out of the close, and would be afraid of wet feet, and always getting laughed at, and called Molly, or Jenny, or some derogatory feminine nickname.

The matron watched him for a moment, and saw what was passing in his mind, and so, like a wise negotiator, threw in an appeal to his warm heart. 'Poor little fellow,' said she in almost a whisper, 'his father's dead, and he's got no brothers. And his mamma, such a kind sweet lady, almost broke her heart at leaving him this morning; and she said one of his sisters was like to die of decline, and so—'

'Well, well,' burst in Tom, with something like a sigh at the effort, 'I suppose I must give up East. Come along, young'un. What's your name? We'll go and have some supper, and then I'll show you our study.'

'His name's George Arthur,' said the matron, walking up to him with Tom, who grasped his little delicate hand as the proper preliminary to making a chum of him, and felt as if he could have blown him away. 'I've had his books and things put into the study, which his mamma has had new papered, and the sofa covered, and new green-baize curtains over the door,' (the diplomatic matron threw this in, to show that the new boy was contributing largely to the partnership comforts). 'And Mrs Arnold told me to say,' she added, 'that she should like you both to come up to tea with her. You know the way, Master Brown, and the things are just gone up, I know.'

Here was an announcement for Master Tom! He was to go up to tea the first night, just as if he were a sixth or fifth form boy, and of importance in the school world, instead of the most reckless young scapegrace amongst the fags. He felt himself lifted on to a higher moral and social platform at once. Nevertheless, he couldn't give up without a sigh the idea of the jolly supper in the housekeeper's room with East and the rest, and a rush round to all the studies of his friends afterwards, to pour out the deeds and wonders of the holidays, to plot fifty plans for the coming half-year, and to gather news of who had left, and what new boys had come, who had got who's study, and where the new praepostors slept. However, Tom consoled himself with thinking that he couldn't have done all this with the new boy at his heels, and so marched off along the passages to the Doctor's private house with his young charge in tow, in monstrous good humour with himself and all the world.

It is needless, and would be impertinent to tell, how the two young boys were received in that drawing-room. The lady who presided there is still living, and has carried with her to her peaceful home in the North the respect and love of all those who ever felt and shared that gentle and high-bred hospitality. Aye, many is the brave heart now doing its work and bearing its load in country curacies, London chambers, under the Indian sun, and in Australian towns and clearings, which looks back with fond and grateful memory to that Schoolhouse drawing-room, and dates much of its highest and best training to the lessons learnt there.

Besides Mrs Arnold and one or two of the elder children, there were one of the younger masters, young Brooke, who was now in the sixth and had succeeded to his brother's position and influence, and another sixth-form boy there, talking together before the fire. The master and young Brooke, now a great strapping fellow six feet high, eighteen years old, and powerful as a coalheaver, nodded kindly to Tom to his intense glory, and then went on talking; the other did not notice them. The hostess, after a few kind words, which led the boys at once and insensibly to feel at their ease, and to begin talking to one another, left them with her own children while she finished a letter. The young ones got on fast and well, Tom holding forth about a prodigious pony he had been riding out hunting, and hearing stories of the winter glories of the lakes, when tea came in, and immediately after the Doctor himself.

How frank, and kind, and manly, was his greeting to the party by the fire; it did Tom's heart good to see him and young Brooke shake hands, and look one another in the face; and he didn't fail to remark, that Brooke was nearly as tall, and quite as broad as the Doctor. And his cup was full, when in another moment his master turned to him with another warm shake of the hand, and, seemingly oblivious of all the late scrapes which he had been getting into, said, 'Ah, Brown, you here! I hope you left your father and all well at home?'

'Yes, sir, quite well.'

'And this is the little fellow who is to share your study. Well, he doesn't look as we should like to see him. He wants some Rugby air, and cricket. And you must take him some good long walks, to Bilton Grange, and Caldecott's Spinney, and show him what a little pretty country we have about here.'

Tom wondered if the Doctor knew that his visits to Bilton Grange were for the purpose of taking rooks' nests (a proceeding strongly discountenanced by the owner thereof), and those to Caldecott's Spinney were prompted chiefly by the conveniences for setting night-lines. What didn't the Doctor know? And what a noble use he always made of it. He almost resolved to abjure rook-pies and night-lines for ever. The tea went merrily off, the Doctor now talking of holiday doings, and then of the prospects of the half-year, what chance there was for the Balliol scholarship, whether the eleven would be a good one. Everybody was at his ease, and everybody felt that he, young as he might be, was of some use in the little School world, and had a work to do there.

Soon after tea the Doctor went off to his study, and the young boys a few minutes afterwards took their leave, and went out of the private door which led from the Doctor's house into the middle passage.

At the fire, at the further end of the passage, was a crowd of boys in loud talk and laughter. There was a sudden pause when the door opened, and then a great shout of greeting, as Tom was recognized marching down the passage.

'Hullo, Brown, where do you come from?'

'Oh, I've been to tea with the Doctor,' says Tom with great dignity.

'My eye!' cried East. 'Oh! so that's why Mary called you back, and you didn't come to supper. You lost something—that beef and pickles was no end good.'

'I say, young fellow,' cried Hall, detecting Arthur and catching him by the collar, 'what's your name? Where do you come from? How old are you?'

Tom saw Arthur shrink back and look scared as all the group turned to him, but thought it best to let him answer, just standing by his side to support in case of need.

'Arthur, sir. I come from Devonshire.'

'Don't call me "sir", you young muff. How old are you?'

'Thirteen.'

'Can you sing?'

The poor boy was trembling and hesitating. Tom struck in—'You be hanged, Tadpole. He'll have to sing, whether he can or not, Saturday twelve weeks, and that's long enough off yet.'

'Do you know him at home, Brown?'

'No; but he's my chum in Gray's old study, and it's near prayer time, and I haven't had a look at it yet. Come along, Arthur.'

Away went the two, Tom longing to get his charge safe under cover, where he might advise him on his deportment.

'What a queer chum for Tom Brown,' was the comment at the fire; and it must be confessed so thought Tom himself, as he lighted his candle, and surveyed the new green-baize curtains, and the carpet and sofa, with much satisfaction.

'I say, Arthur, what a brick your mother is to make us so cosy. But look here now, you must answer straight up when the fellows speak to you, and don't be afraid. If you're afraid, you'll get bullied. And don't you say you can sing; and don't you ever talk about home, or your mother and sisters.'

Poor little Arthur looked ready to cry.

'But please,' said he, 'mayn't I talk about—about home to you?'

'Oh, yes, I like it. But don't talk to boys you don't know, or they'll call you home-sick, or mamma's darling, or some such stuff. What a jolly desk! is that yours? And what stunning binding! why, your school-books look like novels.'

And Tom was soon deep in Arthur's goods and chattels, all new and good enough for a fifth-form boy, and hardly thought of his friends outside, till the prayer-bell rang.

I have already described the Schoolhouse prayers; they were the same on the first night as on the other nights, save for the gaps caused by the absence of those boys who came late, and the line of new boys who stood all together at the further table—of all sorts and sizes, like young bears with all their troubles to come, as Tom's father had said to him when he was in the same position. He thought of it as he looked at the line, and poor little slight Arthur standing with them, and as he was leading him upstairs to Number 4, directly after prayers, and showing him his bed. It was a huge high airy room, with two large windows looking on to the School close. There were twelve beds in the room. The one in the furthest corner by the fireplace, occupied by the sixth-form boy who was responsible for the discipline of the room, and the rest by boys in the lower-fifth and other junior forms, all fags (for the fifth-form boys, as has been said, slept in rooms by themselves). Being fags, the eldest of them was not more than about sixteen years old, and were all bound to be up and in bed by ten; the sixth-form boys came to bed from ten to a quarter-past (at which time the old verger came round to put the candles out), except when they sat up to read.

Within a few minutes therefore of their entry, all the other boys who slept in Number 4 had come up. The little fellows went quietly to their own beds, and began undressing and talking to one another in whispers; while the elder, amongst whom was Tom, sat chatting about on one another's beds, with their jackets and waistcoats off. Poor little Arthur was overwhelmed with the novelty of his position. The idea of sleeping in the room with strange boys had clearly never crossed his mind before, and was as painful as it was strange to him. He could hardly bear to take his jacket off; however, presently, with an effort, off it came, and then he paused and looked at Tom, who was sitting at the bottom of his bed talking and laughing.

'Please, Brown,' he whispered, 'may I wash my face and hands?'

'Of course, if you like,' said Tom, staring; 'that's your wash-hand-stand, under the window, second from your bed. You'll have to go down for more water in the morning if you use it all.' And on he went with his talk, while Arthur stole timidly from between the beds out to his wash-hand-stand, and began his ablutions, thereby drawing for a moment on himself the attention of the room.

On went the talk and laughter. Arthur finished his washing and undressing, and put on his night-gown. He then looked round more nervously than ever. Two or three of the little boys were already in bed, sitting up with their chins on their knees. The light burned clear, the noise went on. It was a trying moment for the poor little lonely boy; however, this time he didn't ask Tom what he might or might not do, but dropped on his knees by his bedside, as he had done every day from his childhood, to open his heart to Him who heareth the cry and beareth the sorrows of the tender child, and the strong man in agony.

Tom was sitting at the bottom of his bed unlacing his boots, so that his back was towards Arthur, and he didn't see what had happened, and looked up in wonder at the sudden silence. Then two or three boys laughed and sneered, and a big brutal fellow, who was standing in the middle of the room, picked up a slipper, and shied it at the kneeling boy, calling him a snivelling young shaver. Then Tom saw the whole, and the next moment the boot he had just pulled off flew straight at the head of the bully, who had just time to throw up his arm and catch it on his elbow.

'Confound you, Brown, what's that for?' roared he, stamping with pain.

'Never mind what I mean,' said Tom, stepping on to the floor, every drop of blood in his body tingling; 'if any fellow wants the other boot, he knows how to get it.'

What would have been the result is doubtful, for at this moment the sixth-form boy came in, and not another word could be said. Tom and the rest rushed into bed and finished their unrobing there, and the old verger, as punctual as the clock, had put out the candle in another minute, and toddled on to the next room, shutting their door with his usual 'Good-night, genl'm'n.'

There were many boys in the room by whom that little scene was taken to heart before they slept. But sleep seemed to have deserted the pillow of poor Tom. For some time his excitement, and the flood of memories which chased one another through his brain, kept him from thinking or resolving. His head throbbed, his heart leapt, and he could hardly keep himself from springing out of bed and rushing about the room. Then the thought of his own mother came across him, and the promise he had made at her knee, years ago, never to forget to kneel by his bedside, and give himself up to his Father, before he laid his head on the pillow, from which it might never rise; and he lay down gently and cried as if his heart would break. He was only fourteen years old.

It was no light act of courage in those days, my dear boys, for a little fellow to say his prayers publicly, even at Rugby. A few years later, when Arnold's manly piety had begun to leaven the school, the tables turned; before he died, in the Schoolhouse at least, and I believe in the other houses, the rule was the other way. But poor Tom had come to school in other times. The first few nights after he came he did not kneel down because of the noise, but sat up in bed till the candle was out, and then stole out and said his prayers, in fear lest some one should find him out. So did many another poor little fellow. Then he began to think that he might just as well say his prayers in bed, and then that it didn't matter whether he was kneeling, or sitting, or lying down. And so it had come to pass with Tom, as with all who will not confess their Lord before men; and for the last year he had probably not said his prayers in earnest a dozen times.

Poor Tom! the first and bitterest feeling which was like to break his heart, was the sense of his own cowardice. The vice of all others which he loathed was brought in and burned in on his own soul. He had lied to his mother, to his conscience, to his God. How could he bear it? And then the poor little weak boy, whom he had pitied and almost scorned for his weakness, had done that which he, braggart as he was, dared not do. The first dawn of comfort came to him in swearing to himself that he would stand by that boy through thick and thin, and cheer him, and help him, and bear his burthens, for the good deed done that night. Then he resolved to write home next day and tell his mother all, and what a coward her son had been. And then peace came to him as he resolved, lastly, to bear his testimony next morning. The morning would be harder than the night to begin with, but he felt that he could not afford to let one chance slip. Several times he faltered, for the devil showed him first, all his old friends calling him 'Saint' and 'Squaretoes', and a dozen hard names, and whispered to him that his motives would be misunderstood, and he would only be left alone with the new boy; whereas it was his duty to keep all means of influence, that he might do good to the largest number. And then came the more subtle temptation, 'Shall I not be showing myself braver than others by doing this? Have I any right to begin it now? Ought I not rather to pray in my own study, letting other boys know that I do so, and trying to lead them to it, while in public at least I should go on as I have done?' However, his good angel was too strong that night, and he turned on his side and slept, tired of trying to reason, but resolved to follow the impulse which had been so strong, and in which he had found peace.

Next morning he was up and washed and dressed, all but his jacket and waistcoat, just as the ten minutes' bell began to ring, and then in the face of the whole room knelt down to pray. Not five words could he say—the bell mocked him; he was listening for every whisper in the room—what were they all thinking of him? He was ashamed to go on kneeling, ashamed to rise from his knees. At last, as it were from his inmost heart, a still small voice seemed to breathe forth the words of the publican, 'God be merciful to me a sinner!' He repeated them over and over, clinging to them as for his life, and rose from his knees comforted and humbled, and ready to face the whole world. It was not needed: two other boys besides Arthur had already followed his example, and he went down to the great School with a glimmering of another lesson in his heart—the lesson that he who has conquered his own coward spirit has conquered the whole outward world; and that other one which the old prophet learnt in the cave in Mount Horeb, when he hid his face, and the still small voice asked, 'What doest thou here, Elijah?' that however we may fancy ourselves alone on the side of good, the King and Lord of men is nowhere without his witnesses; for in every society, however seemingly corrupt and godless, there are those who have not bowed the knee to Baal.

He found too how greatly he had exaggerated the effect to be produced by his act. For a few nights there was a sneer or a laugh when he knelt down, but this passed off soon, and one by one all the other boys but three or four followed the lead. I fear that this was in some measure owing to the fact, that Tom could probably have thrashed any boy in the room except the praepostor; at any rate, everybody knew that he would try upon very slight provocation, and didn't choose to run the risk of a hard fight because Tom Brown had taken a fancy to say his prayers. Some of the small boys of Number 4 communicated the new state of things to their chums, and in several other rooms the poor little fellows tried it on; in one instance or so, where the praepostor heard of it and interfered very decidedly, with partial success; but in the rest, after a short struggle, the confessors were bullied or laughed down, and the old state of things went on for some time longer. Before either Tom Brown or Arthur left the Schoolhouse, there was no room in which it had not become the regular custom. I trust it is so still, and that the old heathen state of things has gone out for ever.

CHAPTER 2

THE NEW BOY

'And Heaven's rich instincts in him grew,
As effortless as woodland nooks
Send violets up and paint them blue.'
—LOWELL

I do not mean to recount all the little troubles and annoyances which thronged upon Tom at the beginning of this half-year, in his new character of bear-leader to a gentle little boy straight from home. He seemed to himself to have become a new boy again, without any of the long-suffering and meekness indispensable for supporting that character with moderate success. From morning till night he had the feeling of responsibility on his mind, and even if he left Arthur in their study or in the close for an hour, was never at ease till he had him in sight again. He waited for him at the doors of the school after every lesson and every calling-over; watched that no tricks were played him, and none but the regulation questions asked; kept his eyes on his plate at dinner and breakfast, to see that no unfair depredations were made upon his viands; in short, as East remarked, cackled after him like a hen with one chick.

Arthur took a long time thawing too, which made it all the harder work; was sadly timid; scarcely ever spoke unless Tom spoke to him first; and, worst of all, would agree with him in everything, the hardest thing in the world for a Brown to bear. He got quite angry sometimes, as they sat together of a night in their study, at this provoking habit of agreement, and was on the point of breaking out a dozen times with a lecture upon the propriety of a fellow having a will of his own and speaking out; but managed to restrain himself by the thought that it might only frighten Arthur, and the remembrance of the lesson he had learnt from him on his first night at Number 4. Then he would resolve to sit still, and not say a word till Arthur began; but he was always beat at that game, and had presently to begin talking in despair, fearing lest Arthur might think he was vexed at something if he didn't, and dog-tired of sitting tongue-tied.

It was hard work! but Tom had taken it up, and meant to stick to it, and go through with it, so as to satisfy himself; in which resolution he was much assisted by the chaffing of East and his other old friends, who began to call him 'dry-nurse', and otherwise to break their small wit on him. But when they took other ground, as they did every now and then, Tom was sorely puzzled.

'Tell you what, Tommy,' East would say, 'you'll spoil young hopeful with too much coddling. Why can't you let him go about by himself and find his own level? He'll never be worth a button, if you go on keeping him under your skirts.'

'Well, but he ain't fit to fight his own way yet; I'm trying to get him to it every day—but he's very odd. Poor little beggar! I can't make him out a bit. He ain't a bit like anything I've ever seen or heard of—he seems all over nerves; anything you say seems to hurt him like a cut or a blow.'

'That sort of boy's no use here,' said East, 'he'll only spoil. Now, I'll tell you what you do, Tommy. Go and get a nice large band-box made, and put him in with plenty of cotton-wool, and a pap-bottle, labelled 'With care—this side up', and send him back to mamma.'

'I think I shall make a hand of him though,' said Tom, smiling, 'say what you will. There's something about him, every now and then, which shows me he's got pluck somewhere in him. That's the only thing after all that'll wash, ain't it, old Scud? But how to get at it and bring it out?'

Tom took one hand out of his breeches-pocket and stuck it in his back hair for a scratch, giving his hat a tilt over his nose, his one method of invoking wisdom. He stared at the ground with a ludicrously puzzled look, and presently looked up and met East's eyes. That young gentleman slapped him on the back, and then put his arm round his shoulder, as they strolled through the quadrangle together. 'Tom,' said he, 'blest if you ain't the best old fellow ever was—I do like to see you go into a thing. Hang it, I wish I could take things as you do—but I never can get higher than a joke. Everything's a joke. If I was going to be flogged next minute, I should be in a blue funk, but I couldn't help laughing at it for the life of me.'

'Brown and East, you go and fag for Jones on the great fives'-court.'

'Hullo, tho', that's past a joke,' broke out East, springing at the young gentleman who addressed them and catching him by the collar. 'Here, Tommy, catch hold of him t'other side before he can holla.'

The youth was seized, and dragged struggling out of the quadrangle into the Schoolhouse hall. He was one of the miserable little pretty white-handed curly-headed boys, petted and pampered by some of the big fellows, who wrote their verses for them, taught them to drink and use bad language, and did all they could to spoil them for everything* in this world and the next. One of the avocations in which these young gentlemen took particular delight, was in going about and getting fags for their protectors, when those heroes were playing any game. They carried about pencil and paper with them, putting down the names of all the boys they sent, always sending five times as many as were wanted, and getting all those thrashed who didn't go. The present youth belonged to a house which was very jealous of the Schoolhouse, and always picked out Schoolhouse fags when he could find them. However, this time he'd got the wrong sow by the ear. His captors slammed the great door of the hall, and East put his back against it, while Tom gave the prisoner a shake-up, took away his list, and stood him up on the floor, while he proceeded leisurely to examine that document.

'Let me out, let me go!' screamed the boy in a furious passion. 'I'll go and tell Jones this minute and he'll give you both the — thrashing you ever had.'

---

* A kind and wise critic, an old Rugbeian, notes here in the margin: The 'small friend system was not so utterly bad from 1841–1847.' Before that, too, there were many noble friendships between big and little boys, but I can't strike out the passage; many boys will know why it is left in.

'Pretty little dear,' said East, patting the top of his hat; 'hark how he swears, Tom. Nicely brought-up young man, ain't he I don't think.'

'Let me alone, — you!' roared the boy, foaming with rage and kicking at East who quietly tripped him up, and deposited him on the floor in a place of safety.

'Gently, young fellow,' said he; ''tain't improving for little whippersnappers like you to be indulging in blasphemy; so you stop that, or you'll get something you won't like.'

'I'll have you both licked when I get out, that I will,' rejoined the boy, beginning to snivel.

'Two can play at that game, mind you,' said Tom, who had finished his examination of the list. 'Now you just listen here. We've just come across the fives'-court, and Jones has four fags there already, two more than he wants. If he'd wanted us to change, he'd have stopped us himself. And here, you little blackguard, you've got seven names down on your list besides ours, and five of them Schoolhouse.' Tom walked up to him and jerked him on to his legs; he was by this time whining like a whipped puppy.

'Now just listen to me. We ain't going to fag for Jones. If you tell him you've sent us, we'll each of us give you such a thrashing as you'll remember.' And Tom tore up the list and threw the pieces into the fire.

'And mind you too,' said East, 'don't let me catch you again sneaking about the Schoolhouse, and picking up our fags. You haven't got the sort of hide to take a sound licking kindly,' and he opened the door and sent the young gentleman flying into the quadrangle, with a parting kick.

'Nice boy, Tommy,' said East, shoving his hands in his pockets and strolling to the fire.

'Worst sort we breed,' responded Tom, following his example. 'Thank goodness, no big fellow ever took to petting me.'

'You'd never have been like that,' said East. 'I should like to have him put in a museum. Christian young gentleman, nineteenth century, highly educated. Stir him up with the long pole, Jack, and hear him swear like a drunken sailor. He'd make a respectable public open its eyes, I think.'

'Think he'll tell Jones?' said Tom.

'No,' said East. 'Don't care if he does.'

'Nor I,' said Tom. And they went back to talk about Arthur.

The young gentleman had brains enough not to tell Jones, reasoning that East and Brown, who were noted as some of the toughest fags in the school, wouldn't care three straws for any licking Jones might give them, and would be likely to keep their words as to passing it on with interest.

After the above conversation, East came a good deal to their study, and took notice of Arthur; and soon allowed to Tom that he was a thorough little gentleman, and would get over his shyness all in good time; which much comforted our hero. He felt every day, too, the value of having an object in his life, something that drew him out of himself; and, it being the dull time of the year, and no games going about which he much cared, was happier than he had ever yet been at school, which was saying a great deal.

The time which Tom allowed himself away from his charge, was from locking-up till supper-time. During this hour or hour-and-a-half he used to take his fling, going round to the studies of all his acquaintance, sparring or gossiping in the hall, now jumping the old iron-bound tables, or carving a bit of his name on them, then joining in some chorus of merry voices; in fact, blowing off his steam, as we should now call it.

This process was so congenial to his temper, and Arthur showed himself so pleased at the arrangement, that it was several weeks before Tom was ever in their study before supper. One evening, however, he rushed in to look for an old chisel, or some corks, or other article essential to his pursuit for the time being, and while rummaging about in the cupboards, looked up for a moment, and was caught at once by the figure of poor little Arthur. The boy was sitting with his elbows on the table, and his head leaning on his hands, and before him an open book, on which his tears were falling fast. Tom shut the door at once, and sat down on the sofa by Arthur, putting his arm round his neck.

'Why, young 'un! what's the matter?' said he, kindly; 'you ain't unhappy, are you?'

'Oh no, Brown,' said the little boy, looking up with the great tears in his eyes, 'you are so kind to me, I'm very happy.'

'Why don't you call me Tom? lots of boys do that I don't like half so much as you. What are you reading, then? Hang it, you must come about with me and not mope yourself,' and Tom cast down his eyes on the book, and saw it was the Bible. He was silent for a minute, and thought to himself, 'Lesson Number 2, Tom Brown,' and then said gently—

'I'm very glad to see this, Arthur, and ashamed that I don't read the Bible more myself. Do you read it every night before supper while I'm out?'

'Yes.'

'Well, I wish you'd wait till afterwards, and then we'd read together. But, Arthur, why does it make you cry?'

'Oh, it isn't that I'm unhappy. But at home, while my father was alive, we always read the lessons after tea; and I love to read them over now, and try to remember what he said about them. I can't remember all, and I think I scarcely understand a great deal of what I do remember. But it all comes back to me so fresh, that I can't help crying sometimes to think I shall never read them again with him.'

Arthur had never spoken of his home before, and Tom hadn't encouraged him to do so, as his blundering school-boy reasoning made him think that Arthur would be softened and less manly for thinking of home. But now he was fairly interested, and forgot all about chisels and bottled beer; while with very little encouragement Arthur launched into his home history, and the prayer-bell put them both out sadly when it rang to call them to the hall.

From this time Arthur constantly spoke of his home, and above all, of his father, who had been dead about a year, and whose memory Tom soon got to love and reverence almost as much as his own son did.

Arthur's father had been the clergyman of a parish in the Midland Counties, which had risen into a large town during the war, and upon which the hard years which followed had fallen with a fearful weight. The trade had been half ruined: and then came the old sad story, of masters reducing their establishments, men turned off and wandering about, hungry and wan in body, and fierce in soul, from the thought of wives and children starving at home, and the last sticks of furniture going to the pawn-shop. Children taken from school, and lounging about the dirty streets and courts, too listless almost to play, and squalid in rags and misery. And then the fearful struggle between the employers and men; lowerings of wages, strikes, and the long course of oft-repeated crime, ending every now and then with a riot, a fire, and the county yeomanry. There is no need here to dwell upon such tales; the Englishman into whose soul they have not sunk deep, is not worthy the name: you English boys for whom this book is meant (God bless your bright faces and kind hearts!) will learn it all soon enough.

Into such a parish and state of society, Arthur's father had been thrown at the age of twenty-five, a young married parson, full of faith, hope, and love. He had battled with it like a man, and had lots of fine Utopian ideas about the perfectibility of mankind, glorious humanity, and such like knocked out of his head; and a real wholesome Christian love for the poor struggling, sinning men, of whom he felt himself one, and with and for whom he spent fortune, and strength, and life, driven into his heart. He had battled like a man, and gotten a man's reward. No silver teapots or salvers, with flowery inscriptions, setting forth his virtues and the appreciation of a genteel parish; no fat living or stall, for which he never looked, and didn't care; no sighs and praises of comfortable dowagers and well got-up young women, who worked him slippers, sugared his tea, and adored him as 'a devoted man'; but a manly respect, wrung from the unwilling souls of men who fancied his order their natural enemies; the fear and hatred of every one who was false or unjust in the district, were he master or man; and the blessed sight of women and children daily becoming more human and more homely, a comfort to themselves and to their husbands and fathers.

These things of course took time, and had to be fought for with toil and sweat of brain and heart, and with the life-blood poured out. All that, Arthur had laid his account to give, and took as a matter of course; neither pitying himself, or looking on himself as a martyr, when he felt the wear and tear making him feel old before his time, and the stifling air of fever dens telling on his health. His wife seconded him in everything. She had been rather fond of society, and much admired and run after before her marriage; and the London world to which she had belonged pitied poor Fanny Evelyn when she married the young clergyman, and went to settle in that smoky hole Turley, a very nest of Chartism and Atheism, in a part of the county which all the decent families had had to leave for years. However, somehow or other she didn't seem to care. If her husband's living had been amongst green fields and near pleasant neighbours, she would have liked it better, that she never pretended to deny. But there they were: the air wasn't bad after all; the people were very good sort of people, civil to you if you were civil to them, after the first brush; and they didn't expect to work miracles, and convert them all off-hand into model Christians. So he and she went quietly among the folk, talking to and treating them just as they would have done people of their own rank. They didn't feel that they were doing anything out of the common way, and so were perfectly natural, and had none of that condescension or consciousness of manner, which so outrages the independent poor. And thus they gradually won respect and confidence; and after sixteen years he was looked up to by the whole neighbourhood as the just man, the man to whom masters and men could go in their strikes, and all in their quarrels and difficulties, and by whom the right and true word would be said without fear or favour. And the women had come round to take her advice, and go to her as a friend in all their troubles; while the children all worshipped the very ground she trod on.

They had three children, two daughters and a son, little Arthur, who came between his sisters. He had been a very delicate boy from his childhood; they thought he had a tendency to consumption, and so he had been kept at home and taught by his father, who had made a companion of him, and from whom he had gained good scholarship, and a knowledge of and interest in many subjects which boys in general never come across till they are many years older.

Just as he reached his thirteenth year, and his father had settled that he was strong enough to go to school, and, after much debating with himself, had resolved to send him there, a desperate typhus-fever broke out in the town: most of the other clergy, and almost all the doctors ran away; the work fell with tenfold weight on those who stood to their work. Arthur and his wife both caught the fever, of which he died in a few days, and she recovered, having been able to nurse him to the end, and store up his last words. He was sensible to the last, and calm and happy, leaving his wife and children with fearless trust for a few years in the hands of the Lord and Friend, who had lived and died for him, and for whom he, to the best of his power, had lived and died. His widow's mourning was deep and gentle; she was more affected by the request of the Committee of a Freethinking club, established in the town by some of the factory hands (which he had striven against with might and main, and nearly suppressed), that some of their number might be allowed to help bear the coffin, than by anything else. Two of them were chosen, who with six other labouring men, his own fellow-workmen and friends, bore him to his grave—a man who had fought the Lord's fight even unto the death. The shops were closed and the factories shut that day in the parish, yet no master stopped the day's wages; but for many a year afterwards the townsfolk felt the want of that brave, hopeful, loving parson, and his wife, who had lived to teach them mutual forbearance and helpfulness, and had *almost* at last given them a glimpse of what this old world would be, if people would live for God and each other, instead of for themselves.

What has all this to do with our story? Well, my dear boys, let a fellow go on his own way, or you won't get anything out of him worth having. I must show you what sort of a man it was who had begotten and trained little Arthur, or else you won't believe in him, which I am resolved you shall do; and you won't see how he, the timid weak boy, had points in him from which the bravest and strongest recoiled, and made his presence and example felt from the first on all sides, unconsciously to himself, and without the least attempt at proselytizing. The spirit of his father was in him, and the Friend to whom his father had left him did not neglect the trust.

After supper that night, and almost nightly for years afterwards, Tom and Arthur, and by degrees East occasionally, and sometimes one, sometimes another, of their friends, read a chapter of the Bible together, and talked it over afterwards. Tom was at first utterly astonished, and almost shocked, at the sort of way in which Arthur read the book, and talked about the men and women whose lives were there told. The first night they happened to fall on the chapters about the famine in Egypt, and Arthur began talking about Joseph as if he were a living statesman; just as he might have talked about Lord Grey and the Reform Bill; only that they were much more living realities to him. The book was to him, Tom saw, the most vivid and delightful history of real people, who might do right or wrong, just like any one who was walking about in Rugby—the Doctor, or the masters, or the sixth-form boys. But the astonishment soon passed off, the scales seemed to drop from his eyes, and the book became at once and for ever to him the great human and divine book, and the men and women, whom he had looked upon as something quite different from himself, became his friends and counsellors.

For our purposes, however, the history of one night's reading will be sufficient, which must be told here, now we are on the subject, though it didn't happen till a year afterwards, and long after the events recorded in the next chapter of our story.

Arthur, Tom, and East were together one night, and read the story of Naaman coming to Elisha to be cured of his leprosy. When the chapter was finished, Tom shut his Bible with a slap.

'I can't stand that fellow Naaman,' said he, 'after what he'd seen and felt, going back and bowing himself down in the house of Rimmon, because his effeminate scoundrel of a master did it. I wonder Elisha took the trouble to heal him. How he must have despised him.'

'Yes, there you go off as usual, with a shell on your head,' struck in East, who always took the opposite side to Tom; half from love of argument, half from conviction. 'How do you know he didn't think better of it? how do you know his master was a scoundrel? His letter don't look like it, and the book don't say so.'

'I don't care,' rejoined Tom; 'why did Naaman talk about bowing down then if he didn't mean to do it? He wasn't likely to get more in earnest when he got back to Court, and away from the Prophet.'

'Well but, Tom,' said Arthur, 'look what Elisha says to him, "Go in peace." He wouldn't have said that if Naaman had been in the wrong.'

'I don't see that that means more than saying, "You're not the man I took you for."'

'No, no, that won't do at all,' said East; 'read the words fairly, and take men as you find them. I like Naaman, and think he was a very fine fellow.'

'I don't,' said Tom positively.

'Well, I think East is right,' said Arthur; 'I can't see but what it's right to do the best you can, though it mayn't be the best absolutely. Every man isn't born to be a martyr.'

'Of course, of course,' said East; 'but he's on one of his pet hobbies. How often have I told you, Tom, that you must drive a nail where it'll go.'

'And how often have I told you,' rejoined Tom, 'that it'll always

155

go where you want, if you only stick to it and hit hard enough. I hate half-measures and compromises.'

'Yes, he's a whole-hog man, is Tom. Must have the whole animal, hair and teeth, claws and tail,' laughed East. 'Sooner have no bread any day, than half the loaf.'

'I don't know,' said Arthur, 'it's rather puzzling; but ain't most right things got by proper compromises, I mean where the principle isn't given up?'

'That's just the point,' said Tom; 'I don't object to a compromise, where you don't give up your principle.'

'Not you,' said East laughingly. 'I know him of old, Arthur, and you'll find him out some day. There isn't such a reasonable fellow in the world, to hear him talk. He never wants anything but what's right and fair; only when you come to settle what's right and fair, it's everything that he wants, and nothing that you want. And that's his idea of a compromise. Give me the Brown compromise when I'm on his side.'

'Now, Harry,' said Tom, 'no more chaff—I'm serious. Look here—this is what makes my blood tingle;' and he turned over the pages of his Bible and read, 'Shadrach, Meshach, and Abednego answered and said to the king, "O Nebuchadnezzar, we are not careful to answer thee in this matter. If it *be* so, our God whom we serve is able to deliver us from the burning fiery furnace, and He will deliver us out of thine hand, O king. But *if not*, be it known unto thee, O king, that we will not serve thy gods, nor worship the golden image which thou hast set up."' He read the last verse twice, emphasizing the nots, and dwelling on them as if they gave him actual pleasure, and were hard to part with.

They were silent a minute, and then Arthur said, 'Yes, that's a glorious story, but it don't prove your point, Tom, I think. There are times when there is only one way, and that the highest, and then the men are found to stand in the breach.'

'There's always a highest way, and it's always the right one,' said Tom. 'How many times has the Doctor told us that in his sermons in the last year. I should like to know?'

'Well, you ain't going to convince us, is he, Arthur? No Brown compromise to-night,' said East, looking at his watch. 'But it's past eight, and we must go to first lesson. What a bore.'

So they took down their books and fell to work; but Arthur didn't forget, and thought long and often over the conversation.

CHAPTER 3

ARTHUR MAKES A FRIEND

'Let Nature be your teacher
Sweet is the lore which Nature brings;
Our meddling intellect
Mis-shapes the beauteous forms of things,
We murder to dissect—
Enough of science and of Art;
Close up those barren leaves,
Come forth, and bring with you a heatt
That watches and receives.'
                                        —WORDSWORTH

About six weeks after the beginning of the half, as Tom and Arthur were sitting one night before supper beginning their verses, Arthur suddenly stopped, and looked up, and said, 'Tom, do you know anything of Martin?'

'Yes,' said Tom, taking his hand out of his back hair, and delighted to throw his Gradus ad Parnassum on to the sofa; 'I know him pretty well. He's a very good fellow, but as mad as a hatter. He's called madman, you know. And never was such a fellow for getting all sorts of rum things about him. He tamed two snakes last half, and used to carry them about in his pocket, and I'll be bound he's got some hedgehogs and rats in his cupboard now, and no one knows what besides.'

'I should like very much to know him,' said Arthur; 'he was next to me in the form today, and he'd lost his book and looked over mine, and he seemed so kind and gentle, that I liked him very much.'

'Ah, poor old madman, he's always losing his books,' said Tom, 'and getting called up and floored because he hasn't got them.'

'I like him all the better,' said Arthur.

'Well, he's great fun, I can tell you,' said Tom, throwing himself

157

back on the sofa and chuckling at the remembrance. 'We had such a game with him one day last half. He had been kicking up horrid stinks for some time in his study, till I suppose some fellow told Mary, and she told the Doctor. Any how, one day a little before dinner, when he came down from the library, the Doctor, instead of going home, came striding into the Hall. East and I and five or six other fellows were at the fire, and preciously we stared, for he don't come in like that once a-year, unless it's a wet day and there's a fight in the Hall. "East," says he, "just come and show me Martin's study." "Oh, here's a game," whispered the rest of us, and we all cut upstairs after the Doctor, East leading. As we got into the New Row, which was hardly wide enough to hold the Doctor and his gown, click, click, click, we heard in the old madman's den. Then that stopped all of a sudden, and the bolts went to like fun: the madman knew East's step, and thought there was going to be a siege.

' "It's the Doctor, Martin. He's here and wants to see you," sings out East.

'Then the bolts went back slowly, and the door opened, and there was the old madman standing, looking precious scared; his jacket off, his shirt-sleeves up to his elbows, and his long skinny arms all covered with anchors and arrows and letters, tattooed in with gunpowder like a sailor-boy's, and a stink fit to knock you down coming out. 'Twas all the Doctor could do to stand his ground, and East and I, who were looking in under his arms, held our noses tight. The old magpie was standing on the window-sill, all his feathers drooping, and looking disgusted and half-poisoned.

' "What can you be about, Martin," says the Doctor; "you really mustn't go on in this way—you're a nuisance to the whole passage."

' "Please, Sir, I was only mixing up this powder, there isn't any harm in it;" and the madman seized nervously on his pestle-and-mortar, to show the Doctor the harmlessness of his pursuits, and went off pounding: click, click, click; he hadn't given six clicks before, puff! up went the whole into a great blaze, away went the pestle-and-mortar across the study, and back we tumbled into the passage. The magpie fluttered down into the court, swearing, and the madman danced out, howling, with his fingers in his mouth. The Doctor caught hold of him, and called to us to fetch some water. "There, you silly fellow," said he, quite

158

pleased though to find he wasn't much hurt, "you see you don't know the least what you are doing with all these things; and now, mind, you must give up practising chemistry by yourself." Then he took hold of his arm and looked at it, and I saw he had to bite his lip, and his eyes twinkled; but he said, quite grave, "Here, you see, you've been making all these foolish marks on yourself, which you can never get out, and you'll be very sorry for it in a year or two: now come down to the housekeeper's room, and let us see if you are hurt." And away went the two, and we all stayed and had a regular turn-out of the den, till Martin came back with his hand bandaged and turned us out. However, I'll go and see what he's after, and tell him to come in after prayers to supper.' And away went Tom to find the boy in question, who dwelt in a little study by himself in New Row.

The aforesaid Martin, whom Arthur had taken such a fancy for, was one of those unfortunates, who were at that time of day (and are, I fear, still) quite out of their places at a public-school. If we knew how to use our boys, Martin would have been seized upon and educated as a natural philosopher. He had a passion for birds, beasts, and insects, and knew more of them and their habits than any one in Rugby; except perhaps the Doctor, who knew everything. He was also an experimental chemist on a small scale, and had made unto himself an electric machine, from which it was his greatest pleasure and glory to administer small shocks to any small boys who were rash enough to venture into his study. And this was by no means an adventure free from excitement; for, besides the probability of a snake dropping on to your head or twining lovingly up your leg, or a rat getting into your breeches-pocket in search of food, there was the animal and chemical odour to be faced, which always hung about the den, and the chances of being blown up in some of the many experiments which Martin was always trying, with the most wondrous results in the shape of explosions and smells that mortal boy ever heard of. Of course, poor Martin, in consequence of his pursuits, had become an Ishmaelite in the house. In the first place, he half-poisoned all his neighbours, and they in turn were always on the look-out to pounce upon any of his numerous live-stock, and drive him frantic by enticing his pet old magpie out of his window into a neighbouring study, and making the disreputable old bird drunk on toast soaked in beer and sugar. Then Martin, for his sins, inhabited a study looking into a small court some ten feet across, the window of which was completely commanded by those of the studies opposite in the sick-room row, these latter being at a slightly higher elevation. East, and another boy of an equally tormenting and ingenious turn of mind, now lived exactly opposite, and had expended huge pains and time in the preparation of instruments of annoyance for the behoof of Martin and his live colony. One morning an old basket made its appearance, suspended by a short cord outside Martin's window, in which was deposited an amateur nest containing four young hungry jackdaws, the pride and glory of Martin's life for the time being, and which he was currently asserted to have hatched upon his own person. Early in the morning and late at night he was to be seen half out of window, administering to the varied wants of his callow brood. After deep cogitation, East and his chum had spliced a knife on to the end of a fishing-rod; and having watched Martin out, had, after half-an-hour's severe sawing, cut the string by which the basket was suspended, and tumbled it on to the pavement below, with hideous remonstrance-from the occupants. Poor Martin, returning from his short absence, collected the fragments and replaced his brood (except one whose neck had been broken in the descent) in their old location, suspending them this time by string and wire twisted together, defiant of any sharp instrument which his persecutors could command. But, like the Russian engineers at Sebastopol, East and his chum had an answer for every move of the adversary; and the next day had mounted a gun in the shape of a pea-shooter upon the ledge of their window, trained so as to bear exactly upon the spot which Martin had to occupy while tending his nurselings. The moment he began to feed they began to shoot; in vain did the enemy himself invest in a pea-shooter, and endeavour to answer the fire while he fed the young birds with his other hand; his attention was divided, and his shots flew wild, while every one of theirs told on his face and hands, and drove him into howlings and imprecations. He had been driven to ensconce the nest in a corner of his already too well-filled den.

His door was barricaded by a set of ingenious bolts of his own invention, for the sieges were frequent by the neighbours when any unusually ambrosial odour spread itself from the den to the neighbouring studies. The door panels were in a normal state of smash, but the frame of the door resisted all besiegers, and behind it the owner carried on his varied pursuits; much in the same state of mind, I should fancy, as a border-farmer lived in, in the days of the old moss-troopers, when his hold might be summoned or his cattle carried off at any minute of night or day.

'Open, Martin, old boy—it's only I, Tom Brown.'

'Oh, very well, stop a moment.' One bolt went back. 'You're sure East isn't there?'

'No, no, hang it, open.' Tom gave a kick, the other bolt creaked, and he entered the den.

Den indeed it was, about five feet six inches long by five wide, and seven feet high. About six tattered school-books, and a few chemical books, Taxidermy, Stanley on Birds, and an odd volume of Bewick, the latter in much better preservation, occupied the top shelves. The other shelves, where they had not been cut away and used by the owner for other purposes, were fitted up for the abiding places of birds, beasts, and reptiles. There was no attempt at carpet or curtain. The table was entirely occupied by the great work of Martin, the electric machine, which was covered carefully with the remains of his tablecloth. The jackdaw cage occupied one wall, and the other was adorned by a small hatchet, a pair of climbing irons, and his tin candle-box, in which he was for the time being endeavouring to raise a hopeful young family of field-mice. As nothing should be let to lie useless, it was well that the candle-box was thus occupied, for candles Martin never had. A pound was issued to him weekly as to the other boys, but as candles were available capital, and easily exchangeable for birds' eggs or young birds, Martin's pound invariably found its way in a few hours to Howlett's the bird-fancier's, in the Bilton Road, who would give a hawk's or nightingale's egg or young linnet in exchange. Martin's ingenuity was therefore for ever on the rack to supply himself with a light; just now he had hit upon a grand invention, and the den was lighted by a flaring cotton-wick issuing from a ginger-beer bottle full of some doleful composition. When light altogether failed him, Martin would loaf about by the fires in the passages or hall, after the manner of Diggs, and try to do his verses or learn his lines by the fire-light.

'Well, old boy, you haven't got any sweeter in the den this half. How that stuff in the bottle stinks. Never mind, I ain't going to stop, but you come up after prayers to our study; you know young Arthur, we've got Gray's study. We'll have a good supper and talk about bird's-nesting.'

Martin was evidently highly pleased at the invitation, and promised to be up without fail.

As soon as prayers were over, and the sixth and fifth form boys had withdrawn to the aristocratic seclusion of their own room, and the rest, or democracy, had sat down to their supper in the Hall, Tom and Arthur, having secured their allowances of bread and cheese, started on their feet to catch the eye of the praepostor of the week, who remained in charge during supper, walking up and down the Hall. He happened to be an easy-going fellow, so they got a pleasant nod to their 'Please may I go out?' and away they scrambled to prepare for Martin a sumptuous banquet. This Tom had insisted on, for he was in great delight on the occasion; the reason of which delight must be expounded. The fact was that this was the first attempt at a friendship of his own which Arthur had made, and Tom hailed it as a grand step. The ease with which he himself became hail fellow-well-met with anybody, and blundered into and out of twenty friendships a half-year, made him sometimes sorry and sometimes angry at Arthur's reserve and loneliness. True, Arthur was always pleasant, and even jolly, with any boys who came with Tom to their study; but Tom felt that it was only through him, as it were, that his chum associated with others, and that but for him Arthur would have been dwelling in a wilderness. This increased his consciousness of responsibility; and though he hadn't reasoned it out and made it clear to himself, yet somehow he knew that this responsibility, this trust which he had taken on him without thinking about it, head-over-heels in fact, was the centre and turning-point of his school-life, that which was to make him or mar him; his appointed work and trial for the time being. And Tom was becoming a new boy, though with frequent tumbles in the dirt and perpetual hard battle with himself, and was daily growing in manfulness and thoughtfulness, as every high-couraged and well-principled boy must, when he finds himself for the first time consciously at grips with self and the devil. Already he could turn almost without a sigh, from the school-gates, from which had just scampered off East and three or four others of his particular set, bound for some jolly lark not quite according to law, and involving probably a row with louts, keepers, or farm-labourers, the skipping dinner or calling over, some of Phoebe Jennings' beer, and a very possible flogging at the end of all as relish. He had quite got over the stage in which he would grumble to himself, 'Well, hang it, it's very hard of the Doctor to have saddled me with Arthur. Why couldn't he have chummed him with Fogey, or Thomkin, or any of the fellows who never do anything but walk round the close, and finish their copies the first day they're set?' But although all this was past, he often longed, and felt that he was right in longing, for more time for the legitimate pastimes of cricket, fives, bathing, and fishing within bounds, in which Arthur could not yet be his companion, and he felt that when the young 'un (as he now generally called him) had found a pursuit and some other friend for himself, he should be able to give more time to the education of his own body with a clear conscience.

And now what he so wished for had come to pass; he almost hailed it as a special providence (as indeed it was, but not for the reasons he gave for it—what providences are?) that Arthur should have singled out Martin of all fellows for a friend. 'The old Madman is the very fellow,' thought he; 'he will take him scrambling over half the country after birds' eggs and flowers, make him run and swim and climb like an Indian, and not teach him a word of anything bad, or keep him from his lessons. What luck," And so, with more than his usual heartiness, he dived into his cupboard, and hauled out an old knuckle-bone of ham, and two or three bottles of beer, together with the solemn pewter only used on state occasions; while Arthur, equally elated at the easy accomplishment of his first act of volition in the joint establishment, produced from his side a bottle of pickles and a pot of jam, and cleared the table. In a minute or two the noise of the boys coming up from supper was heard, and Martin knocked and was admitted, bearing his bread and cheese, and the three fell to with hearty good will upon the viands, talking faster than they ate, for all shyness disappeared in a moment before Tom's bottled-beer and hospitable ways. 'Here's Arthur a regular young town-mouse, with a natural taste for the woods, Martin, longing to break his neck climbing trees, and with a passion for young snakes.'

'Well, I say,' sputtered out Martin eagerly, 'will you come to-morrow, both of you, to Caldecott's Spinney then, for I know of a kestrel's nest, up a fir-tree—I can't get at it without help; and, Brown, you can climb against any one.'

'Oh yes, do let us go,' said Arthur; 'I never saw a hawk's nest or a hawk's egg.'

'You just come down to my study then, and I'll show you five sorts,' said Martin.

'Aye, the old Madman has got the best collection in the house, out-and-out,' said Tom; and then Martin, warming with unaccustomed good cheer and the chance of a convert, launched out into a proposed birds'-nesting campaign, betraying all manner of important secrets; a golden-crested wren's nest near Butlin's Mound, a moorhen who was sitting on fourteen eggs in a pond down the Barby Road, and a kingfisher's nest in a corner of the old canal above Brownsover Mill. He had heard, he said, that no one had ever got a kingfisher's nest out perfect, and that the British Museum, or the Government, or somebody, had offered £100 to any one who could bring them a nest and eggs not damaged. In the middle of which astounding announcement, to which the others were listening with open ears, and already considering the application of the £100, a knock came to the door, and East's voice was heard craving admittance.

'There's Harry,' said Tom; 'we'll let him in—I'll keep him steady, Martin. I thought the old boy would smell out the supper.'

The fact was that Tom's heart had already smitten him for not asking his 'fidus Achates' to the feast, although only an extempore affair; and though prudence and the desire to get Martin and Arthur together alone at first, had overcome his scruples, he was now heartily glad to open the door, broach another bottle of beer, and hand over the old ham-knuckle to the searching of his old friend's pocket-knife.

'Ah, you greedy vagabonds,' said East, with his mouth full, 'I knew there was something going on when I saw you cut off out of Hall so quick with your suppers. What a stunning tap, Tom! you are a wunner for bottling the swipes.'

'I've had practice enough for the sixth in my time, and it's hard if I haven't picked up a wrinkle or two for my own benefit.'

'Well, old Madman, and how goes the birds'-nesting campaign? How's Howlett? I expect the young rooks'll be out in another fortnight, and then my turn comes.'

'There'll be no young rooks fit for pies for a month yet: shows how much you know about it,' rejoined Martin, who, though very good friends with East, regarded him with considerable suspicion for his propensity to practical jokes.

'Scud knows nothing and cares for nothing but grub and mischief,' said Tom; 'but young rook pie, specially when you've had to climb for them, is very pretty eating. However, I say, Scud, we're all going after a hawk's nest to-morrow, in Caldecott's Spinney, and if you'll come and behave yourself, we'll have a stunning climb.'

'And a bathe in Aganippe. Hooray! I'm your man.'

'No, no; no bathing in Aganippe; that's where our betters go.'

'Well, well, never mind. I'm for the hawk's nest and anything that turns up.'

And the bottled-beer being finished, and his hunger appeased, East departed to his study, 'that sneak Jones,' as he informed them, who had just got into the sixth and occupied the next study, having instituted a nightly visitation upon East and his chum, to their no small discomfort.

When he was gone, Martin rose to follow, but Tom stopped him. 'No one goes near New-row,' said he, 'so you may just as well stop here and do your verses, and then we'll have some more talk. We'll be no end quiet; besides no praepostor comes here now—we haven't been visited once this half.'

So the table was cleared, the cloth restored, and the three fell to work with Gradus and dictionary upon the morning's vulgus.

They were three very fair examples of the way in which such tasks were done at Rugby, in the consulship of Plancus. And doubtless the method is little changed, for there is nothing new under the sun, especially at schools.

Now be it known unto all you boys who are at schools which do not rejoice in the time-honoured institution of the Vulgus (commonly supposed to have been established by William of Wykeham at Winchester, and imported to Rugby by Arnold, more for the sake of the lines which were learnt by heart with it, than for its own intrinsic value, as I've always understood), that it is a short exercise, in Greek or Latin verse, on a given subject, the minimum number of lines being fixed for each form. The master of the form gave out at fourth lesson on the previous day the subject for each morning's vulgus, and at first lesson each boy had to bring his vulgus ready to be looked over; and with the vulgus, a certain number of lines from one of the Latin or Greek poets then being construed in the form had to be got by heart. The master at first lesson called up each boy in the form in order, and put him on in the lines. If he couldn't say them, or seem to say them, by reading them off the master's or some other boy's book who stood near, he was sent back, and went below all the boys who did so say or seem to say them; but in either case his vulgus was looked over by the master, who gave and entered in his book, to the credit or discredit of the boy, so many marks as the composition merited. At Rugby vulgus and lines were the first lesson every other day in the week, on Tuesdays, Thursdays, and Saturdays; and as there were thirty-eight weeks in the school year, it is obvious to the meanest capacity that the master of each form had to set one hundred and fourteen subjects every year, two hundred and twenty-eight every two years, and so on. Now to persons of moderate invention this was a considerable task, and human nature being prone to repeat itself, it will not be wondered that the masters gave the same subjects sometimes over again after a certain lapse of time. To meet and rebuke this bad habit of the masters, the School-boy mind, with its accustomed ingenuity, had invented an elaborate system of tradition. Almost every boy kept his own vulgus written out in a book, and these books were duly handed down from boy to boy, till (if the tradition has gone on till now) I suppose the popular boys, in whose hands bequeathed vulgus-books have accumulated, are prepared with three or four vulguses on any subject in heaven or earth, or in 'more worlds than one', which an unfortunate master can pitch upon. At any rate, such lucky fellows generally had one for themselves and one for a friend in my time. The only objection to the traditionary method of doing your vulgus was, the risk that the successions might have become confused, and so that you and another follower of tradition should show up the same identical vulgus some fine morning; in which case, when it happened, considerable grief was the result—but when did such risk hinder boys or men from short cuts and pleasant paths?

Now in the study that night. Tom was the upholder of the traditionary method of vulgus doing. He carefully produced two large vulgus-books, and began diving into them, and picking out a line here, and an ending there (tags as they were vulgarly called), till he had gotten all that he thought he could make fit. He then proceeded to patch his tags together with the help of his Gradus, producing an incongruous and feeble result of eight elegiac lines, the minimum quantity for his form, and finishing up with two highly moral lines extra, making ten in all, which he cribbed entire from one of his books, beginning 'O genus humanum', and which he himself must have used a dozen times before, whenever an unfortunate or wicked hero, of whatever nation or language under the sun, was the subject. Indeed he began to have great doubts whether the master wouldn't remember them, and so only threw them in as extra lines, because in any case they would call off attention from the other tags, and if detected, being extra lines, he wouldn't be sent back to do two more in their place, while if they passed muster again he would get marks for them.

The second method pursued by Martin may be called the dogged, or prosaic method. He, no more than Tom, took any pleasure in the task, but having no old vulgus-books of his own, or any one's else, could not follow the traditionary method, for which too, as Tom remarked, he hadn't the genius. Martin then proceeded to write down eight lines in English, of the most matter-of-fact kind, the first that came into his head; and to convert these, line by line, by main force of Gradus and dictionary, into Latin that would scan. This was all he cared for, to produce eight lines with no false quantities or concords: whether the words were apt, or what the sense was, mattered nothing; and, as the article was all new, not a line beyond the minimum did the followers of the dogged method ever produce.

The third, or artistic method was Arthur's. He considered first what point in the character or event which was the subject could most neatly be brought out within the limits of a vulgus, trying always to get his idea into the eight lines, but not binding himself to ten or even twelve lines if he couldn't do this. He then set to work, as much as possible without Gradus or other help, to clothe his idea in appropriate Latin or Greek, and would not be satisfied till he had polished it well up with the aptest and most poetic words and phrases he could get at.

A fourth method indeed was used in the school, but of too simple a kind to require comment. It may be called the vicarious method, obtained amongst big boys of lazy or bullying habits, and consisted simply in making clever boys whom they could thrash do their whole vulgus for them, and construe it to them afterwards; which latter is a method not to be encouraged, and which I strongly advise you all not to practise. Of the others you will find the traditionary most troublesome, unless you can steal your vulguses whole (experto crede), and that the artistic method pays the best both in marks and other ways.

The vulguses being finished by nine o'clock, and Martin having rejoiced above measure in the abundance of light, and of Gradus and dictionary, and other conveniences almost unknown to him for getting through the work, and having been pressed by Arthur to come and do his verses there whenever he liked, the three boys went down to Martin's den, and Arthur was initiated into the lore of birds' eggs to his great delight. The exquisite colouring and forms astonished and charmed him who had scarcely ever seen any but a hen's egg or an ostrich's, and by the time he was lugged away to bed he had learned the names of at least twenty sorts, and dreamt of the glorious perils of tree-climbing, and that he had found a roc's egg in the island as big as Sindbad's and clouded like a tit-lark's, in blowing which Martin and he had nearly been drowned in the yolk.

CHAPTER 4

THE BIRD-FANCIERS

'I have found out a gift for my fair,
   I have found where the wood-pigeons breed;
But let me the plunder forbear.
   She would say 'twas a barbarous deed.'
                —ROWE

'And now, my lad, take them five shilling,
   And on my advice in future think;
So Billy pouched them all so willing.
   And got that night disguised in drink.'
            —MS. BALLAD

The next morning at first lesson Tom was turned back in his lines, and so had to wait till the second round, while Martin and Arthur said theirs all right and got out of school at once. When Tom got out and ran down to breakfast at Harrowell's they were missing, and Stumps informed him that they had swallowed down their breakfasts and gone off together, where he couldn't say. Tom

168

hurried over his own breakfast, and went first to Martin's study and then to his own, but no signs of the missing boys were to be found. He felt half angry and jealous of Martin—where could they be gone? He learnt second lesson with East and the rest in no very good temper, and then went out into the quadrangle. About ten minutes before school Martin and Arthur arrived in the quadrangle breathless; and, catching sight of him, Arthur rushed up all excitement and with a bright glow on his face.

'Oh Tom, look here,' cried he, holding out three moorhen's eggs; 'we've been down the Barby Road to the pool Martin told us of last night, and just see what we've got.'

Tom wouldn't be pleased, and only looked out for something to find fault with.

'Why, young 'un,' said he, 'what have you been after? You don't mean to say you've been wading?'

The tone of reproach made poor little Arthur shrink up in a moment and look piteous, and Tom with a shrug of his shoulders turned his anger on Martin.

'Well, I didn't think, Madman, that you'd have been such a muff as to let him be getting wet through at this time of day. You might have done the wading yourself.'

'So I did, of course; only he would come in too to see the nest. We left eleven eggs in; they'll be hatched in a day or two.'

'Hang the eggs!' said Tom; 'a fellow can't turn his back for a moment but all his work's undone. He'll be laid up for a week for this precious lark, I'll be bound.'

'Indeed, Tom, now,' pleaded Arthur, 'my feet ain't wet, for Martin made me take off my shoes and stockings and trousers.'

'But they are wet and dirty too—can't I see?' answered Tom; 'and you'll be called up and floored when the master sees what a state you're in. You haven't looked at second lesson, you know.' Oh Tom, you old humbug! you to be upbraiding any one with not learning their lessons. If you hadn't been floored yourself now at first lesson, do you mean to say you wouldn't have been with them? and you've taken away all poor little Arthur's joy and pride in his first birds' eggs, and he goes and puts them down in the study, and takes down his books with a sigh, thinking he has done something horribly wrong, whereas he has learnt on in advance much more than will be done at second lesson.

But the old Madman hasn't, and gets called up and makes some frightful shots, losing about ten places, and all but getting floored. This somewhat appeases Tom's wrath, and by the end of the lesson he has regained his temper. And afterwards in their study he begins to get right again, as he watches Arthur's intense joy at seeing Martin blowing the eggs and glueing them carefully on to bits of cardboard, and notes the anxious loving looks which the little fellow casts sidelong at him. And then he thinks, 'What an ill-tempered beast I am! Here's just what I was wishing for last night come about, and I'm spoiling it all,' and in another five minutes has swallowed the last mouthful of his bile, and is repaid by seeing his little sensitive plant expand again, and sun itself in his smiles.

After dinner the Madman is busy with the preparations for their expedition, fitting new straps on to his climbing-irons, filling large pill-boxes with cotton-wool, and sharpening East's small axe. They carry all their munitions into calling-over, and directly afterwards, having dodged such praepostors as are on the look-out for fags at cricket, the four set off at a smart trot down the Lawford footpath straight for Caldecott's Spinney and the hawk's nest.

Martin leads the way in high feather; it is quite a new sensation to him getting companions, and he finds it very pleasant, and means to show them all manner of proofs of his science and skill. Brown and East may be better at cricket and football and games, thinks he, but out in the fields and woods see if I can't teach them something. He has taken the leadership already, and strides away in front with his climbing-irons strapped under one arm, his pecking-bag under the other, and his pockets and hat full of pill-boxes, cotton-wool, and other etceteras. Each of the others carries a pecking-bag, and East his hatchet.

When they had crossed three or four fields without a check, Arthur began to lag, and Tom seeing this shouted to Martin to pull up a bit: 'We ain't out Hare-and-hounds—what's the good of grinding on at this rate?'

'There's the spinney,' said Martin, pulling up on the brow of a slope at the bottom of which lay Lawford brook, and pointing to the top of the opposite slope; 'the nest is in one of those high fir-trees at this end. And down by the brook there, I know of a sedgebird's nest; we'll go and look at it coming back.'

'Oh, come on, don't let us stop,' said Arthur, who was getting excited at the sight of the wood; so they broke into a trot again, and were soon across the brook, up the slope, and into the spinney.

Here they advanced as noiselessly as possible, lest keepers or other enemies should be about, and stopped at the foot of a tall fir, at the top of which Martin pointed out with pride the kestrel's nest, the object of their quest.

'Oh where! which is it?' asks Arthur, gaping up in the air, and having the most vague idea of what it would be like.

'There, don't you see?' said East, pointing to a lump of mistletoe in the next tree, which was a beech: he saw that Martin and Tom were busy with the climbing-irons, and couldn't resist the temptation of hoaxing. Arthur stared and wondered more than ever.

'Well, how curious! it doesn't look a bit like what I expected,' said he.

'Very odd birds, kestrels,' said East, looking waggishly at his victim, who was still star-gazing.

'But I thought it was in a fir-tree?' objected Arthur.

'Ah, don't you know? that's a new sort of fir which old Caldecott brought from the Himalayas.'

'Really!' said Arthur; 'I'm glad I know that—how unlike our firs they are. They do very well too here, don't they? the spinney's full of them.'

'What's that humbug he's telling you?' cried Tom, looking up, having caught the word Himalayas, and suspecting what East was after.

'Only about this fir,' said Arthur, putting his hand on the stem of the beech.

'Fir!' shouted Tom, 'why, you don't mean to say, young 'un, you don't know a beech when you see one?'

Poor little Arthur looked terribly ashamed, and East exploded in laughter which made the wood ring.

'I've hardly ever seen any trees,' faltered Arthur.

'What a shame to hoax him, Scud!' cried Martin. 'Never mind, Arthur, you shall know more about trees than he does in a week or two.'

'And isn't that the kestrel's nest, then?' asked Arthur.

'That! why, that's a piece of mistletoe. There's the nest, that lump of small sticks up this fir.'

'Don't believe him, Arthur,' struck in the incorrigible East; 'I just saw an old magpie go out of it.'

Martin did not deign to reply to this sally, except by a grunt, as he buckled the last buckle of his climbing-irons; and Arthur looked reproachfully at East without speaking.

But now came the tug of war. It was a very difficult tree to climb until the branches were reached, the first of which was some fourteen feet up, for the trunk was too large at the bottom to be swarmed; in fact neither of the boys could reach more than half round it with their arms. Martin and Tom, both of whom had irons on, tried it without success at first; the fir bark broke away where they stuck the irons in as soon as they leant any weight on their feet, and the grip of their arms wasn't enough to keep them up; so after getting up three or four feet, down they came slithering to the ground, barking their arms and faces. They were furious, and East sat by laughing and shouting at each failure, 'Two to one on the old magpie!'

'We must try a pyramid,' said Tom at last. 'Now, Scud, you lazy rascal, stick yourself against the tree!'

'I dare say! and have you standing on my shoulders with the irons on: what do you think my skin's made of?' However, up he got and leant against the tree, putting his head down and clasping it with his arms as far as he could. 'Now then, Madman,' said Tom, 'you next.'

'No, I'm lighter than you; you go next.' So Tom got on East's shoulders and grasped the tree above, and then Martin scrambled up on to Tom's shoulders, amidst the totterings and groanings of the pyramid, and with a spring which sent his supporters howling to the ground, clasped the stem some ten feet up, and remained clinging. For a moment or two they thought he couldn't get up, but then, holding on with arms and teeth, he worked first one iron, then the other firmly into the bark, got another grip with his arms, and in another minute had hold of the lowest branch.

'All up with the old magpie now,' said East; and after a minute's rest, up went Martin, hand over hand, watched by Arthur with fearful eagerness.

'Isn't it very dangerous?' said he.

'Not a bit,' answered Tom; 'you can't hurt if you only get good hand-hold. Try every branch with a good pull before you trust it, and then up you go.'

Martin was now amongst the small branches close to the nest, and away dashed the old bird and soared up above the trees watching the intruder.

'All right—four eggs!' shouted he.

'Take 'em all!' shouted East; 'that'll be one apiece.'

'No, no! leave one, and then she won't care,' said Tom.

We boys had an idea that birds couldn't count, and were quite content as long as you left one egg. I hope it is so.

Martin carefully put one egg into each of his boxes and the third into his mouth, the only other place of safety, and came down like a lamplighter. All went well till he was within ten feet of the ground, when, as the trunk enlarged, his hold got less and less firm, and at last down he came with a run, tumbling on to his back on the turf, spluttering and spitting out the remains of the great egg, which had broken by the jar of his fall.

'Ugh, ugh! something to drink—ugh! it was addled,' spluttered he, while the wood rang again with the merry laughter of East and Tom.

Then they examined the prizes, gathered up their things, and went off to the brook, where Martin swallowed huge draughts of water to get rid of the taste; and they visited the sedgebird's nest, and from thence struck across the country in high glee, beating the hedges and brakes as they went along; and Arthur at last, to his intense delight, was allowed to climb a small hedgerow oak for a magpie's nest with Tom, who kept all round him like a mother, and showed him where to hold and how to throw his weight; and though he was in a great fright didn't show it, and was applauded by all for his lissomness.

They crossed a road soon afterwards, and there close to them lay a heap of charming pebbles.

'Look here,' shouted East, 'here's luck! I've been longing for some good honest pecking this half-hour. Let's fill the bags, and have no more of this foozling birds'-nesting.'

No one objected, so each boy filled the fustian bag he carried full of stones: they crossed into the next field, Tom and East taking one side of the hedges and the other two the other side. Noise enough they made certainly, but it was too early in the season for the young birds, and the old birds were too strong on the wing for our young marksmen, and flew out of shot after the first discharge. But it was great fun, rushing along the hedgerows and discharging stone after stone at blackbirds and chaffinches, though no result in the shape of slaughtered birds was obtained; and Arthur soon entered into it, and rushed to head back the birds, and shouted, and threw, and tumbled into ditches and over and through hedges, as wild as the Madman himself.

Presently the party, in full cry after an old blackbird (who was evidently used to the thing and enjoyed the fun, for he would wait till they came close to him and then fly on for forty yards or so, and with an impudent flicker of his tail dart into the depths of the quickset), came beating down a high double hedge, two on each side.

'There he is again,' 'head him,' 'let drive,' 'I had him there,' 'take care where you're throwing Madman,' the shouts might have been heard a quarter-of-a-mile off. They were heard some two hundred yards off by a farmer and two of his shepherds, who were doctoring sheep in a fold in the next field.

Now the farmer in question rented a house and yard situate at the end of the field in which the young bird-fanciers had arrived, which house and yard he didn't occupy or keep any one else in. Nevertheless, like a brainless and unreasoning Briton, he persisted in maintaining on the premises a large stock of cocks, hens, and other poultry. Of course all sorts of depredators visited the place from time to time: foxes and gipsies wrought havoc in the night; while in the daytime I regret to have to confess that visits from the Rugby boys, and consequent disappearances of ancient and respectable fowls, were not unfrequent. Tom and East had during the period of their outlawry visited the barn in question for felonious purposes, and on one occasion had conquered and slain a duck there, and borne away the carcase triumphantly, hidden in their handkerchiefs. However, they were sickened of the practice by the trouble and anxiety which the wretched duck's body caused them. They carried it to Sally Harrowell's in hopes of a good supper, but she after examining it made a long face and refused to dress or have anything to do with it. Then they took it into their study, and began plucking it themselves; but what to do with the feathers, where to hide them?

'Good gracious, Tom, what a lot of feathers a duck has!' groaned East, holding a bag full in his hand, and looking disconsolately at the carcase not yet half plucked.

'And I do think he's getting high too, already,' said Tom, smelling at him cautiously, 'so we must finish him up soon.'

'Yes, all very well, but how are we to cook him? I'm sure I ain't going to try it on in the hall or passages; we can't afford to be roasting ducks about, our character's too bad.'

174

'I wish we were rid of the brute,' said Tom, throwing him on the table in disgust. And after a day or two more it became clear, that got rid of he must be; so they packed him and sealed him up in brown paper, and put him in the cupboard of an unoccupied study, where he was found in the holidays by the matron, a gruesome body.

They had never been duck-hunting there since, but others had, and the bold yeoman was very sore on the subject, and bent on making an example of the first boys he could catch. So he and his shepherds crouched behind the hurdles, and watched the party who were approaching all unconscious.

Why should that old guinea-fowl be lying out in the hedge just at this particular moment of all the year? Who can say? Guinea-fowls always are—so are all other things, animals, and persons, requisite for getting one into scrapes, always ready when any mischief can come of them. At any rate, just under East's nose popped out the old guinea-hen, scuttling along and shrieking 'come back, come back,' at the top of her voice. Either of the other three might perhaps have withstood the temptation, but East first lets drive the stone he has in his hand at her, and then rushes to turn her into the hedge again. He succeeds, and then they are all at it for dear life, up and down the hedge in full cry, the 'come back, come back,' getting shriller and fainter every minute.

Meantime the farmer and his men steal over the hurdles and creep down the hedge towards the scene of action. They are almost within a stone's throw of Martin, who is pressing the unlucky chase hard, when Tom catches sight of them and sings out, 'Louts, 'ware louts, your side! Madman, look ahead!' and then catching hold of Arthur, hurries him away across the field towards Rugby as hard as they can tear. Had he been by himself he would have stayed to see it out with the others, but now his heart sinks and all his pluck goes. The idea of being led up to the Doctor with Arthur for bagging fowls, quite unmans and takes half the run out of him.

However, no boys are more able to take care of themselves than East and Martin; they dodge the pursuers, slip through a gap, and come pelting after Tom and Arthur, whom they catch up in no time; the farmer and his men are making good running about a field behind. Tom wishes to himself that they had made off in any other direction, but now they are all in for it together, and must see it out. 'You won't leave the young 'un, will you?' says he, as they haul poor little Arthur, already losing wind from the fright, through the next hedge. 'Not we,' is the answer from both. The next hedge is a stiff one; the pursuers gain horribly on them, and they only just pull Arthur through with two great rents in his trousers, as the foremost shepherd comes up on the other side. As they start into the next field they are aware of two figures walking down the footpath in the middle of it, and recognize Holmes and Diggs taking a constitutional. Those good-natured fellows immediately shout 'On.' 'Let's go to them and surrender,' pants Tom.—Agreed.—And in another minute the four boys, to the great astonishment of those worthies, rush breathless up to Holmes and Diggs, who pull up to see what is the matter, and then the whole is explained by the appearance of the farmer and his men, who unite their forces and bear down on the knot of boys.

There is no time to explain, and Tom's heart beats frightfully quick, as he ponders, 'Will they stand by us?'

The farmer makes a rush at East and collars him; and that young gentleman, with unusual discretion, instead of kicking his shins looks appealingly at Holmes, and stands still.

'Hullo there, not so fast,' says Holmes, who is bound to stand up for them till they are proved in the wrong. 'Now what's all this about?'

'I've got the young varmint at last, have I,' pants the farmer; 'why they've been a skulking about my yard and stealing my fowls, that's where 'tis; and if I doan't have they flogged for it, every one on 'em, my name ain't Thompson.'

Holmes looks grave, and Diggs's face falls. They are quite ready to fight, no boys in the School more so; but they are praepostors, and understand their office, and can't uphold unrighteous causes.

'I haven't been near his old barn this half,' cries East. 'Nor I,' 'nor I,' chime in Tom and Martin.

'Now, Willum, didn't you see 'em there last week?'

'Ees, I seen 'em sure enough,' says Willum, grasping a prong he carried, and preparing for action.

The boys deny stoutly, and Willum is driven to admit that, 'if it worn't they 'twas chaps as like 'em as two peas'n;' and 'leastways he'll swear he see'd them two in the yard last Martinmas,' indicating East and Tom.

Holmes has had time to meditate. 'Now, sir,' says he to Willum, 'you see you can't remember what you have seen, and I believe the boys.'

'I doan't care,' blusters the farmer; 'they was arter my fowls today, that's enough for I. Willum, you catch hold o' t'other chap. They've been a sneaking about this two hours, I tells 'ee,' shouted he, as Holmes stands between Martin and Willum, 'and have druv a matter of a dozen young pullets pretty nigh to death.'

'Oh, there's a whacker!' cried East; 'we haven't been within a hundred yards of his barn; we haven't been up here above ten minutes, and we've seen nothing but a tough old guinea-hen, who ran like a greyhound.'

'Indeed that's all true, Holmes, upon my honour,' added Tom; 'we weren't after his fowls; guinea-hen ran out of the hedge under our feet, and we've seen nothing else.'

'Drat their talk. Thee catch hold o' t'other, Willum, and come along wi' un.'

'Farmer Thompson,' said Holmes, warning off Willum and the prong with his stick, while Diggs faced the other shepherd, cracking his fingers like pistol shots, 'now listen to reason——the boys haven't been after your fowls, that's plain.'

'Tells 'ee I seed 'em. Who be you, I should like to know?'

'Never you mind, Farmer,' answered Holmes. 'And now I'll just tell you what it is——you ought to be ashamed of yourself for leaving all that poultry about with no one to watch it so near the School. You deserve to have it all stolen. So if you choose to come up to the Doctor with them, I shall go with you and tell him what I think of it.'

The farmer began to take Holmes for a master; besides, he wanted to get back to his flock. Corporal punishment was out of the question, the odds were too great; so he began to hint at paying for the damage. Arthur jumped at this, offering to pay anything, and the farmer immediately valued the guinea-hen at half-a-sovereign.

'Half-a-sovereign!' cried East, now released from the farmer's grip; 'well, that is a good one! the old hen ain't hurt a bit, and she's seven years old, I know, and as tough as whipcord; she couldn't lay another egg to save her life.'

It was at last settled that they should pay the farmer two shillings and his man one shilling, and so the matter ended, to the unspeakable relief of Tom, who hadn't been able to say a word, being sick at heart at the idea of what the Doctor would think of him: and now the whole party of boys marched off down the footpath towards Rugby. Holmes, who was one of the best boys in the school, began to improve the occasion. 'Now, you youngsters,' said he, as he marched along in the middle of them, 'mind this, you're very well out of this scrape. Don't you go near Thompson's barn again, do you hear?'

Profuse promises from all, especially East.

'Mind I don't ask questions,' went on Mentor, 'but I rather think some of you have been there before this after his chickens. Now knocking over other people's chickens, and running off with them, is stealing. It's a nasty word, but that's the plain English of it. If the chickens were dead and lying in a shop you wouldn't take them, I know that, any more than you would apples out of Griffith's basket; but there's no real difference between chickens running about and apples on a tree, and the same articles in a shop. I wish our morals were sounder in such matters. There's nothing so mischievous as these school distinctions, which jumble up right and wrong, and justify things in us for which poor boys would be sent to prison.' And good old Holmes delivered his soul on the walk home of many wise sayings, and as the song says—

Gee'd 'em a sight of good advice.

Which same sermon sank into them all more or less, and very penitent they were for several hours. But truth compels me to admit that East at any rate forgot it all in a week, but remembered the insult which had been put upon him by farmer. Thompson, and with the Tadpole and other hare-brained youngsters, committed a raid on the barn soon afterwards, in which they were caught by the shepherds and severely handled, besides having to pay eight shillings, all the money they had in the world, to escape being taken up to the Doctor.

Martin became a constant inmate in the joint study from this time, and Arthur took to him so kindly that Tom couldn't resist slight fits of jealousy, which, however, he managed to keep to himself. The kestrel's eggs had not been broken, strange to say, and formed the nucleus of Arthur's collection, at which Martin worked heart and soul; and introduced Arthur to Howlett the bird-fancier, and instructed him in the rudiments of the art of stuffing. In token of his gratitude, Arthur allowed Martin to tattoo a small anchor on one of his wrists, which decoration, however, he carefully concealed from Tom. Before the end of the half-year he had trained into a bold climber and good runner, and, as Martin had foretold, knew twice as much about trees, birds, flowers, and many other things, as our good-hearted and facetious young friend Harry East.

CHAPTER 5

THE FIGHT

'Surgebat Macnevisius
Et mox jactabat ultro,
Pugnabo tuâ gratiâ
Feroci hoc Mactwoltro.'
—*Etonian*

There is a certain sort of fellow, we who are used to studying boys all know him well enough, of whom you can predicate with almost positive certainty, after he has been a month at school, that he is sure to have a fight, and with almost equal certainty that he will have but one. Tom Brown was one of these; and as it is our well-weighed intention to give a full, true, and correct account of Tom's only single combat with a school-fellow in the manner of our old friend Bell's Life, let those young persons whose stomachs are not strong, or who think a good set-to with the weapons which God has given us all, an uncivilized, unchristian, or ungentlemanly affair, just skip this chapter at once, for it won't be to their taste.

It was not at all usual in those days for two Schoolhouse boys to have a fight. Of course there were exceptions, when some cross-grained hard-headed fellow came up, who would never be happy unless he was quarrelling with his nearest neighbours, or when there was some class-dispute, between the fifth-form and the fags for instance, which required bloodletting; and a champion was picked out on each side tacitly, who settled the matter by a good hearty mill. But for the most part, the constant use of those surest keepers of the peace, the boxing-gloves, kept the Schoolhouse boys from fighting one another. Two or three nights in every week the gloves were brought out, either in the hall or fifth-form room; and every boy who was ever likely to fight at all knew all his neighbours' prowess perfectly well, and could tell to a nicety what chance he would have in a stand-up fight with any other boy in the house. But of course no such experience could be gotten as regarded boys in other houses; and as most of the other houses were more or less jealous of the Schoolhouse, collisions were frequent.

After all, what would life be without fighting, I should like to know? From the cradle to the grave, fighting, rightly understood, is the business, the real, highest, honestest business of every son of man. Every one who is worth his salt has his enemies; who must be beaten, be they evil thoughts and habits in himself, or spiritual wickedness in high places, or Russians, or Border-ruffians, or Bill, Tom, or Harry, who will not let him live his life in quiet till he has thrashed them.

It is no good for Quakers, or any other body of men, to uplift their voices against fighting. Human nature is too strong for them, and they don't follow their own precepts. Every soul of them is doing his own piece of fighting, somehow and somewhere. The world might be a better world without fighting for anything I know, but it wouldn't be our world; and therefore I am dead against crying peace when there is no peace, and isn't meant to be. I'm as sorry as any man to see folk fighting the wrong people and the wrong things, but I'd a deal sooner see them doing that, than that they should have no fight in them. So having recorded, and being about to record, my hero's fights of all sorts, with all sorts of enemies, I shall now proceed to give an account of his passage-at-arms with the only one of his school-fellows whom he ever had to encounter in this manner.

It was drawing towards the close of Arthur's first half-year, and the May evenings were lengthening out. Locking-up was not till eight o'clock, and everybody was beginning to talk about what he would do in the holidays. The shell, in which form all our dramatis personae now are, were reading amongst other things the last book of Homer's Iliad, and had worked through it as far as the speeches of the women over Hector's body. It is a whole school-day, and four or five of the Schoolhouse boys (amongst whom are Arthur, Tom, and East) are preparing third lesson together. They have finished the regulation forty lines, and are for the most part getting very tired, notwithstanding the exquisite pathos of Helen's lamentation. And now several long four-syllabled words come together, and the boy with the dictionary strikes work.

'I am not going to look out any more words,' says he; 'we've done the quantity. Ten to one we shan't get so far. Let's go out into the close.'

'Come along boys,' cries East, always ready to leave the grind, as he called it; 'our old coach is laid up, you know, and we shall have one of the new masters, who's sure to go slow and let us down easy.'

So an adjournment to the close was carried *nem. con.*, little Arthur not daring to uplift his voice; but, being deeply interested in what they were reading, stayed quietly behind, and learnt on for his own pleasure.

As East had said, the regular master of the form was unwell, and they were to be heard by one of the new masters, quite a young man, who had only just left the University. Certainly it would be hard lines, if, by dawdling as much as possible in coming in and taking their places, entering into long-winded explanations of what was the usual course of the regular master of the form, and others of the stock contrivances of boys for wasting time in school, they could not spin out the lesson so that he should not work them through more than the forty lines; as to which quantity there was a perpetual fight going on between the master and his form, the latter insisting, and enforcing by passive resistance, that it was the prescribed quantity of Homer for a shell lesson, the former that there was no fixed quantity, but that they must always be ready to go on to fifty or sixty lines if there were time within the hour. However, notwithstanding all their efforts, the new master got on horribly quick; he seemed to have the bad taste to be really interested in the lesson, and to be trying to work them up into something like appreciation of it, giving them good spirited English words, instead of the wretched bald stuff into which they rendered poor old Homer; and construing over each piece himself to them, after each boy, to show them how it should be done.

Now the clock strikes the three-quarters; there is only a quarter-of-an-hour more; but the forty lines are all but done. So the boys, one after another, who are called up, stick more and more, and make balder and ever more bald work of it. The poor young master is pretty near beat by this time, and feels ready to knock his head against the wall, or his fingers against somebody else's head. So he gives up altogether the lower and middle parts of the form, and looks round in despair at the boys on the top bench, to see if there is one out of whom he can strike a spark or two, and who will be too chivalrous to murder the most beautiful utterances of the most beautiful woman of the old world. His eye rests on Arthur, and he calls him up to finish construing Helen's speech. Whereupon all the other boys draw long breaths, and begin to stare about and take it easy. They are all safe; Arthur is the head of the form and sure to be able to construe, and that will tide on safely till the hour strikes.

Arthur proceeds to read out the passage in Greek before construing it, as the custom is. Tom who isn't paying much attention, is suddenly caught by the falter in his voice as he reads the two lines—

ἀλλὰ σὺ τόν γ᾽ ἐπέεσσι παραιφάμενος κατέρυκες
Σῇ τ᾽ ἀγανοφροσύνῃ καὶ σοῖς ἀγανοῖς ἐπέεσσιν.

He looks up at Arthur. 'Why, bless us,' thinks he, 'what can be the matter with the young 'un? He's never going to get floored. He's sure to have learnt to the end.' Next moment he is reassured by the spirited tone in which Arthur begins construing, and betakes himself to drawing dogs' heads in his note-book, while the master, evidently enjoying the change, turns his back on the middle bench and stands before Arthur, beating a sort of time with his hand and foot, and saying, 'Yes, yes,' 'very well,' as Arthur goes on.

But as he nears the fatal two lines, Tom catches that falter again and looks up. He sees that there is something the matter, Arthur can hardly get on at all. What can it be?

Suddenly at this point Arthur breaks down altogether, and fairly bursts out crying, and dashes the cuff of his jacket across his eyes, blushing up to the roots of his hair, and feeling as if he should like to go down suddenly through the floor. The whole form are taken aback, most of them stare stupidly at him, while those who are gifted with presence of mind find their places and look steadily at their books, in hopes of not catching the master's eye and getting called up in Arthur's place.

The master looks puzzled for a moment, and then seeing, as the fact is, that the boy is really affected to tears by the most touching thing in Homer, perhaps in all profane poetry put together, steps up to him and lays his hand kindly on his shoulder, saying, 'Never mind, my little man, you've construed very well. Stop a minute, there's no hurry.'

Now as luck would have it, there sat next above Tom on that day, in the middle bench of the form, a big boy, by name Williams, generally supposed to be the cock of the shell, therefore of all the school below the fifths. The small boys, who are great speculators on the prowess of their elders, used to hold forth to one another about Williams's great strength, and to discuss whether East or Brown would take a licking from him. He was called Slogger Williams, from the force with which it was supposed he could hit. In the main he was a rough good-natured fellow enough, but very much alive to his own dignity. He reckoned himself the king of the form, and kept up his position with the strong hand, especially in the matter of forcing boys not to construe more than the legitimate forty lines. He had already grunted and grumbled to himself, when Arthur went on reading beyond the forty lines. But now that he had broken down just in the middle of all the long words, the Slogger's wrath was fairly roused.

'Sneaking little brute,' muttered he, regardless of prudence, 'clapping on the waterworks just in the hardest place; see if I don't punch his head after fourth lesson.'

'Whose?' said Tom, to whom the remark seemed to be addressed.

'Why, that little sneak Arthur's,' replied Williams.

'No, you shan't,' said Tom.

'Hullo!' exclaimed Williams, looking at Tom with great surprise for a moment, and then giving him a sudden dig in the ribs with his elbow, which sent Tom's books flying on to the floor, and called the attention of the master, who turned suddenly round, and seeing the state of things, said—

'Williams, go down three places, and then go on.'

The Slogger found his legs very slowly, and proceeded to go below Tom and two other boys with great disgust, and then turning round and facing the master, said, 'I haven't learnt any more, sir; our lesson is only forty lines.'

'Is that so?' said the master, appealing generally to the top bench. No answer.

'Who is the head boy of the form?' said he, waxing wroth.

'Arthur, sir,' answered three or four boys indicating our friend.

'Oh, your name's Arthur. Well now, what is the length of your regular lesson?'

Arthur hesitated a moment, and then said, 'We call it only forty lines, sir.'

'How do you mean, you call it?'

'Well, sir, Mr Graham says we ain't to stop there when there's time to construe more.'

'I understand,' said the master. 'Williams, go down three more places, and write me out the lesson in Greek and English. And now, Arthur, finish construing.'

'Oh! would I be in Arthur's shoes after fourth lesson,' said the little boys to one another; but Arthur finished Helen's speech without any further catastrophe, and the clock struck four, which ended third lesson.

Another hour was occupied in preparing and saying fourth lesson, during which Williams was bottling up his wrath; and when five struck and the lessons for the day were over, he prepared to take summary vengeance on the innocent cause of his misfortune.

Tom was detained in school a few minutes after the rest, and on coming out into the quadrangle, the first thing he saw was a small ring of boys, applauding Williams, who was holding Arthur by the collar.

'There, you young sneak,' said he, giving Arthur a cuff on the head with his other hand, 'what made you say that—'

'Hullo!' said Tom, shouldering into the crowd, 'you drop that, Williams; you shan't touch him.'

'Who'll stop me?' said the Slogger, raising his hand again.

'I,' said Tom; and suiting the action to the word, struck the arm which held Arthur's collar so sharply, that the Slogger dropped it with a start, and turned the full current of his wrath on Tom.

'Will you fight?'

'Yes, of course.'

'Huzza, there's going to be a fight between Slogger Williams and Tom Brown.'

The news ran like wild-fire about, and many boys who were on their way to tea at their several houses turned back, and sought the back of the chapel, where the fights come off.

'Just run and tell East to come and back me,' said Tom to a small Schoolhouse boy, who was off like a rocket to Harrowell's, just stopping for a moment to poke his head into the Schoolhouse hall, where the lower boys were already at tea, and sing out, 'Fight! Tom Brown and Slogger Williams.'

Up start half the boys at once, leaving bread, eggs, butter, sprats, and all the rest, to take care of themselves. The greater part of the remainder follow in a minute, after swallowing their tea, carrying their food in their hands to consume as they go. Three or four only remain, who steal the butter of the more impetuous, and make to themselves an unctuous feast.

In another minute East and Martin tear through the quadrangle, carrying a sponge, and arrive at the scene of action just as the combatants are beginning to strip.

Tom felt he had got his work cut out for him, as he stripped off his jacket, waistcoat, and braces. East tied his handkerchief round his waist, and rolled up his shirt-sleeves for him: 'Now, old boy, don't you open your mouth to say a word, or try to help yourself a bit, we'll do all that; you keep all your breath and strength for the Slogger.' Martin meanwhile folded the clothes, and put them under the chapel rails; and now Tom, with East to handle him and Martin to give him a knee, steps out on the turf, and is ready for all that may come: and here is the Slogger too, all stripped, and thirsting for the fray.

It doesn't look a fair match at first glance: Williams is nearly two inches taller, and probably a long year older than his opponent, and he is very strongly made about the arms and shoulders; 'peels well', as the little knot of big fifth-form boys, the amateurs, say; who stand outside the ring of little boys, looking complacently on, but taking no active part in the proceedings. But down below he is not so good by any means; no spring from the loins, and feebleish, not to say shipwrecky, about the knees. Tom on the contrary, though not half so strong in the arms, is good all over, straight, hard, and springy, from neck to ankle, better perhaps in his legs than anywhere. Besides, you can see by the clear white of his eye and fresh bright look of his skin, that he is in tip-top training, able to do all he knows; while the Slogger looks rather sodden, as if he didn't take much exercise and ate too much tuck. The timekeeper is chosen, a large ring made, and the two stand up opposite one another for a moment, giving us time just to make our little observations.

'If Tom'll only condescend to fight with his head and heels,' as East mutters to Martin, 'we shall do.'

But seemingly he won't, for there he goes in, making play with both hands. Hard all, is the word; the two stand to one another like men; rally follows rally in quick succession, each fighting as if he thought to finish the whole thing out of hand. 'Can't last at this rate,' say the knowing ones, while the partisans of each make the air ring with their shouts and counter-shouts, of encouragement, approval and defiance.

'Take it easy, take it easy—keep away, let him come after you,' implores East, as he wipes Tom's face after the first round with wet sponge, while he sits back on Martin's knee, supported by the Madman's long arms, which tremble a little from excitement.

'Time's up,' calls the timekeeper.

'There he goes again, hang it all!' growls East, as his man is at it again as hard as ever. A very severe round follows, in which Tom gets out-and-out the worst of it, and is at last hit clean off his legs, and deposited on the grass by a right-hander from the Slogger.

Loud shouts rise from the boys of Slogger's house, and the Schoolhouse are silent and vicious, ready to pick quarrels anywhere.

'Two to one in half-crowns on the big 'un,' says Rattle, one of the amateurs, a tall fellow, in thunder-and-lightning waistcoat, and puffy good-natured face.

'Done!' says Grove, another amateur of quieter look, taking out his note-book to enter it, for our friend Rattle sometimes forgets these little things.

Meantime East is freshening up Tom with the sponges for next round, and has set two other boys to rub his hands.

'Tom, old boy,' whispers he, 'this may be fun for you, but it's death to me. He'll hit all the fight out of you in another five minutes, and then I shall go and drown myself in the island ditch. Feint him—use your legs! draw him about! he'll lose his wind then in no time, and you can go into him. Hit at his body too; we'll take care of his frontispiece by-and-by.'

Tom felt the wisdom of the counsel, and saw already that he couldn't go in and finish the Slogger off at mere hammer and tongs, so changed his tactics completely in the third round. He now fights cautious, getting away from and parrying the Slogger's lunging hits, instead of trying to counter, and leading his enemy a dance all round the ring after him. 'He's funking; go in, Williams,' 'Catch him up,' 'Finish him off,' scream the small boys of the Slogger party.

'Just what we want,' thinks East, chuckling to himself, as he sees Williams, excited by these shouts and thinking the game in his own hands, blowing himself in his exertions to get to close quarters again, while Tom is keeping away with perfect ease.

They quarter over the ground again and again, Tom always on the defensive.

The Slogger pulls up at last for a moment, fairly blown.

'Now then, Tom,' sings out East, dancing with delight. Tom goes in in a twinkling, and hits two heavy body blows, and gets away again before the Slogger can catch his wind; which when he does he rushes with blind fury at Tom, and being skilfully parried and avoided, over-reaches himself and falls on his face, amidst terrific cheers from the Schoolhouse boys.

'Double your two to one?' says Grove to Rattle, note-book in hand.

'Stop a bit,' says that hero, looking uncomfortably at Williams, who is puffing away on his second's knee, winded enough, but little the worse in any other way.

After another round the Slogger too seems to see that he can't go in and win right off, and has met his match or thereabouts. So he too begins to use his head, and tries to make Tom lose patience, and come in before his time. And so the fight sways on, now one and now the other getting a trifling pull.

Tom's face begins to look very one-sided—there are little queer bumps on his forehead, and his mouth is bleeding; but East keeps the wet sponges going so scientifically, that he comes up looking as fresh and bright as ever. Williams is only slightly marked in the face, but by the nervous movement of his elbows you can see that Tom's body blows are telling. In fact half the vice of the slogger's hitting is neutralized, for he daren't lunge out freely for fear of exposing his sides. It is too interesting by this time for much shouting, and the whole ring is very quiet.

'All right, Tommy,' whispers East; 'hold on's the horse that's to win. We've got the last. Keep your head, old boy.'

But where is Arthur all this time? Words cannot paint the poor little fellow's distress. He couldn't muster courage to come up to the ring, but wandered up and down from the great fives'—court to the corner of the chapel rails. Now trying to make up his mind to throw himself between them, and try to stop them; then thinking of running in and telling his friend Mary, who he knew would instantly report to the Doctor. The stories he had heard of men being killed in prize-fights rose up horribly before him.

Once only, when the shouts of 'Well done, Brown!' Huzza for the Schoolhouse!' rose higher than ever, he ventured up to the ring, thinking the victory was won. Catching sight of Tom's face in the state I have described, all fear of consequences vanishing out of his mind, he rushed straight off to the matron's room, beseeching her to get the fight stopped, or he shall die.

But it's time for us to get back to the close. What is this fierce tumult and confusion? The ring is broken, and high and angry words are being bandied about; 'It's all fair', 'It isn't', 'No hugging'; the fight is stopped. The combatants, however, sit there quietly, tended by their seconds, while their adherents wrangle in the middle. East can't help shouting challenges to two or three of the other side, though he never leaves Tom for a moment, and plies the sponges as fast as ever.

The fact is, that at the end of the last round, Tom seeing a good opening had closed with his opponent, and after a moment's struggle had thrown him heavily, by help of the fall he had learnt from his village rival in the Vale of White Horse. Williams hadn't the ghost of a chance with Tom at wrestling; and the conviction broke at once on the Slogger faction, that if this were allowed their man must be licked. There was a strong feeling in the school against catching hold and throwing, though it was generally ruled all fair within certain limits; so the ring was broken and the fight stopped.

The Schoolhouse are over-ruled—the fight is on again, but there is to be no throwing; and East in high wrath threatens to take his man away after next round (which he don't mean to do by the way), when suddenly young Brooke comes through the small gate at the end of the chapel. The Schoolhouse faction rush to him. 'Oh, hurra! now we shall get fair play.'

'Please, Brooke, come up, they won't let Tom Brown throw him.'

'Throw whom?' says Brooke, coming up to the ring. 'Oh! Williams, I see. Nonsense! of course he may throw him if he catches him fairly above the waist.'

Now, young Brooke, you're in the sixth, you know, and you ought to stop all fights. He looks hard at both boys. 'Anything wrong?' says he to East, nodding at Tom.

'Not a bit.'

'Not beat at all?'

'Bless you, no! heaps of fight in him. Ain't there, Tom?'

Tom looks at Brooke and grins.

'How's he?' nodding at Williams.

'So, so; rather done, I think, since his last fall. He won't stand above two more.'

'Time's up!' the boys rise again and face one another. Brooke can't find it in his heart to stop them just yet, so the round goes on, the Slogger waiting for Tom, and reserving all his strength to hit him out should he come in for the wrestling dodge again, for he feels that that must be stopped, or his sponge will soon go up in the air.

And now another new-comer appears on the field, to wit the under-porter, with his long brush and great wooden receptacle for dust under his arm. He has been sweeping out the schools.

'You'd better stop gentlemen,' he says; 'the Doctor knows that Brown's fighting—he'll be out in a minute.'

'You go to Bath, Bill,' is all that that excellent servitor gets by his advice. And being a man of his hands, and a staunch upholder of the Schoolhouse, can't help stopping to look on for a bit, and see Tom Brown, their pet craftsman, fight a round.

It is grim earnest now, and no mistake. Both boys feel this, and summon every power of head, hand, and eye to their aid. A piece of luck on either side, a foot slipping, a blow getting well home, or another fall, may decide it. Tom works slowly round for an opening, he has all the legs, and can choose his own time; the Slogger waits for the attack, and hopes to finish it by some heavy right-handed blow. As they quarter slowly over the ground, the evening sun comes out from behind a cloud and falls full on Williams' face. Tom darts in, the heavy right-hand is delivered, but only grazes his head. A short rally at close quarters, and they close; in another moment the Slogger is thrown again heavily for the third time.

'I'll give you three to two on the little one in half-crowns,' says Grove to Rattle.

'No thank'ee,' answers the other, diving his hands further into his coat-tails.

Just at this stage of the proceedings the door of the turret which leads to the Doctor's library suddenly opens, and he steps into the close, and makes straight for the ring, in which

Brown and the Slogger are both seated on their seconds' knees for the last time.

'The Doctor! the Doctor!' shouts some small boy who catches sight of him, and the ring melts away in a few seconds, the small boys tearing off, Tom collaring his jacket and waistcoat and slipping through the little gate by the chapel, and round the corner to Harrowell's with his backers, as lively as need be. Williams and his backers making off not quite so fast across the close. Grove, Rattle, and the other bigger fellows trying to combine dignity and prudence in a comical manner, and walking off fast enough, they hope, not to be recognized, and not fast enough to look like running away.

Young Brooke alone remains on the ground by the time the Doctor gets there, and touches his hat, not without a slight inward qualm.

'Hah! Brooke. I am surprised to see you here. Don't you know that I expect the sixth to stop fighting?'

Brooke felt much more uncomfortable than he had expected, but he was rather a favourite with the Doctor for his openness and plainness of speech; so blurted out, as he walked by the Doctor's side, who had already turned back—

'Yes, sir, generally. But I thought you wished us to exercise a discretion in the matter too—not to interfere too soon.'

'But they have been fighting this half-hour and more,' said the Doctor.

'Yes, sir; but neither was hurt. And they're the sort of boys who'll be all the better friends now, which they wouldn't have been if they had been stopped any earlier—before it was so equal.'

'Who was fighting with Brown?' said the Doctor.

'Williams, sir, of Thompson's. He is bigger than Brown, and had the best of it at first, but not when you came up, sir. There's a good deal of jealousy between our house and Thompson's, and there would have been more fights if this hadn't been let go on, or if either of them had had much the worst of it.'

'Well but, Brooke,' said the Doctor, 'doesn't this look a little as if you exercised your discretion by only stopping a fight when the Schoolhouse boy is getting the worst of it?'

Brooke, it must be confessed, felt rather gravelled.

'Now remember,' added the Doctor, as he stopped at the turret-door, 'this fight is not to go on—you'll see to that. And I expect you to stop all fights in future at once.'

190

'Very well, sir,' said young Brooke, touching his hat, and not sorry to see the turret-door close behind the Doctor's back.

Meantime Tom and the staunchest of his adherents had reached Harrowell's, and Sally was bustling about to get them a late tea, while Stumps had been sent off to Tew the butcher, to get a piece of raw beef for Tom's eye, which was to be healed off-hand so that he might show well in the morning. He was not a bit the worse except a slight difficulty in his vision, a singing in his ears, and a sprained thumb, which he kept in a cold-water bandage, while he drank lots of tea, and listened to the Babel of voices talking and speculating of nothing but the fight, and how Williams would have given in after another fall (which he didn't in the least believe), and how on earth the Doctor could have got to know of it, such bad luck! He couldn't help thinking to himself that he was glad he hadn't won; he liked it better as it was, and felt very friendly to the Slogger. And then poor little Arthur crept in and sat down quietly near him, and kept looking at him and the raw beef with such plaintive looks, that Tom at last burst out laughing.

'Don't make such eyes, young 'un,' said he, 'there's nothing the matter.'

'Oh but, Tom, are you much hurt? I can't bear thinking it was all for me.'

'Not a bit of it, don't flatter yourself. We were sure to have had it out sooner or later.'

'Well, but you won't go on, will you? You'll promise me you won't go on?'

'Can't tell about that—all depends on the houses. We're in the hands of our countrymen, you know. Must fight for the Schoolhouse flag, if so be.'

However, the lovers of the science were doomed to disappointment this time. Directly after locking-up, one of the night fags knocked at Tom's door.

'Brown, young Brooke wants you in the sixth-form room.'

Up went Tom to the summons, and found the magnates sitting at their supper.

'Well, Brown,' said young Brooke, nodding to him, 'how do you feel?'

'Oh, very well, thank you, only I've sprained my thumb, I think.'

'Sure to do that in a fight. Well, you hadn't the worst of it, I could see. Where did you learn that throw?'

'Down in the country, when I was a boy.'

'Hullo! why what are you now? Well, never mind, you're a plucky fellow. Sit down and have some supper.'

Tom obeyed, by no means loth. And the fifth-form boy next him filled him a tumbler of bottled-beer, and he ate and drank, listening to the pleasant talk, and wondering how soon he should be in the fifth, and one of that much envied society.

As he got up to leave, Brooke said, 'You must shake hands tomorrow morning; I shall come and see that done after first lesson.'

And so he did. And Tom and the Slogger shook hands with great satisfaction and mutual respect. And for the next year or two, whenever fights were being talked of, the small boys who had been present shook their heads wisely, saying, 'Ah! but you should just have seen the fight between Slogger Williams and Tom Brown!'

And now, boys all, three words before we quit the subject. I have put in this chapter on fighting of malice prepense, partly because I want to give you a true picture of what every-day school life was in my time, and not a kid-glove and go-to-meeting-coat picture; and partly because of the cant and twaddle that's talked of boxing and fighting with fists now-a-days. Even Thackeray has given in to it; and only a few weeks ago there was some rampant stuff in *The Times* on the subject, in an article on field sports.

Boys will quarrel, and when they quarrel will sometimes fight. Fighting with fists is the natural and English way for English boys to settle their quarrels. What substitute for it is there, amongst any nation under the sun? What would you like to see take its place?

Learn to box then, as you learn to play cricket and football. Not one of you will be the worse, but very much the better for learning to box well. Should you never have to use it in earnest, there's no exercise in the world so good for the temper, and for the muscles of the back and legs.

As to fighting, keep out of it if you can, by all means. When the time comes, if it ever should, that you have to say 'Yes' or 'No' to a challenge to fight, say 'No' if you can—only take care you make it clear to yourselves why you say 'No'. It's a proof of the highest courage, if done from true Christian motives. It's quite right and justifiable, if done from a simple aversion to physical pain and danger. But don't say 'No' because you fear a licking, and say or think it's because you fear God, for that's neither Christian nor honest. And if you do fight, fight it out; and don't give in while you can stand and see.

CHAPTER 6

FEVER IN THE SCHOOL

'This our hope for all that's mortal
And we too shall burst the bond;
Death keeps watch beside the portal,
But 'tis life that dwells beyond.'
—JOHN STERLING

Two years have passed since the events recorded in the last chapter, and the end of the summer half-year is again drawing on. Martin has left and gone on a cruise in the South Pacific, in one of his uncle's ships; the old magpie, as disreputable as ever, his last bequest to Arthur, lives in the joint study. Arthur is nearly sixteen, and at the head of the twenty, having gone up the school at the rate of a form a half-year. East and Tom have been much more deliberate in their progress, and are only a little way up the fifth form. Great strapping boys they are, but still thorough boys, filling about the same place in the house that young Brooke filled when they were new boys, and much the same sort of fellows. Constant intercourse with Arthur has done much for both of them, especially for Tom; but much remains yet to be done, if they are to get all the good out of Rugby which is to be got there in these times. Arthur is still frail and delicate, with more spirit than body; but, thanks to his intimacy with them and Martin, has learned to swim, and run, and play cricket, and has never hurt himself by too much reading.

One evening, as they were all sitting down to supper in the fifth-form room, some one started a report that a fever had broken out at one of the boarding-houses; 'they say,' he added, 'that Thompson is very ill, and that Dr Robertson has been sent for from Northampton.'

'Then we shall all be sent home,' cried another. 'Hurrah! five weeks' extra holidays, and no fifth-form examination!'

'I hope not,' said Tom; 'there'll be no Marylebone match then at the end of the half.'

Some thought one thing, some another, many didn't believe the report; but the next day, Tuesday, Dr Robertson arrived, and stayed all day, and had long conferences with the Doctor.

On Wednesday morning, after prayers, the Doctor addressed the whole School. There were several cases of fever in different houses, he said, but Dr Robertson after the most careful examination had assured him that it was not infectious, and that if proper care were taken there could be no reason for stopping the school work at present. The examinations were just coming on, and it would be very unadvisable to break-up now. However, any boys who chose to do so were at liberty to write home, and, if their parents wished it, to leave at once. He should send the whole School home if the fever spread.

The next day Arthur sickened, but there was no other case. Before the end of the week thirty or forty boys had gone, but the rest stayed on. There was a general wish to please the Doctor, and a feeling that it was cowardly to run away.

On the Saturday Thompson died, in the bright afternoon, while the cricket-match was going on as usual on the big-side ground; the Doctor, coming from his death-bed, passed along the gravel-walk at the side of the close, but no one knew what had happened till the next day. At morning lecture it began to be rumoured, and by afternoon chapel was known generally; and a feeling of seriousness and awe at the actual presence of death among them, came over the whole School. In all the long years of his ministry the Doctor perhaps never spoke words which sank deeper than some of those in that day's sermon. 'When I came yesterday from visiting all but the very death-bed of him who has been taken from us, and looked around upon all the familiar objects and scenes within our own ground, where your common amusements were going on, with your common cheerfulness and activity, I felt there was nothing painful in witnessing that; it did not seem in any way shocking or out of tune with those feelings which the sight of a dying Christian must be supposed to awaken. The unsuitableness in point of natural feeling between scenes of mourning and scenes of liveliness did not at all present itself. But I did feel that if at that moment any of those faults had been brought before me which sometimes occur amongst us; had I heard that any of you had been guilty of falsehood, or of drunkenness, or of any other such sin; had I heard from any quarter the language of profaneness, or of unkindness, or of indecency; had I heard or seen any signs of that wretched folly, which courts the laugh of fools by affecting not to dread evil and not to care for good, then the unsuitableness of any of these things with the scene I had just quitted would indeed have been most intensely painful. And why? Not because such things would really have been worse than at any other time, but because at such a moment the eyes are opened really to know good and evil, because we then feel what it is so to live as that death becomes an infinite blessing, and what it is so to live also, that it were good for us if we had never been born.'

Tom had gone into chapel in sickening anxiety about Arthur, but he came out cheered and strengthened by those grand words, and walked up alone to their study. And when he sat down and looked round, and saw Arthur's straw-hat and cricket-jacket hanging on their pegs, and marked all his little neat arrangements, not one of which had been disturbed, the tears indeed rolled down his cheeks, but they were calm and blessed tears, and he repeated to himself, 'Yes, Geordie's eyes are opened—he knows what it is so to live as that death becomes an infinite blessing. But do I? Oh, God, can I bear to lose him?'

The week passed mournfully away. No more boys sickened, but Arthur was reported worse each day, and his mother arrived early in the week. Tom made many appeals to be allowed to see him, and several times tried to get up to the sick-room; but the housekeeper was always in the way, and at last spoke to the Doctor, who kindly but peremptorily, forbade him.

Thompson was buried on the Tuesday, and the burial service, so soothing and grand always, but beyond all words solemn when read over a boy's grave to his companions, brought him much comfort, and many strange new thoughts and longings. He went back to his regular life, and played cricket and bathed as usual: it seemed to him that this was the right thing to do, and the new thoughts and longings became more brave and healthy for the effort. The crisis came on Saturday, the day week that Thompson had died; and during that long afternoon Tom sat in his study reading his Bible, and going every half-hour to the housekeeper's room, expecting each time to hear that the gentle and brave little spirit had gone home. But God had work for Arthur to do: the crisis passed—on Sunday evening he was declared out of danger; on Monday he sent a message to Tom that he was almost well, had changed his room, and was to be allowed to see him the next day.

It was evening when the housekeeper summoned him to the sick room. Arthur was lying on the sofa by the open window, through which the rays of the western sun stole gently, lighting up his white face and golden hair. Tom remembered a German picture of an angel which he knew; often had he thought how transparent and golden and spirit-like it was; and he shuddered to think how like it Arthur looked, and felt a shock as if his blood had all stopped short, as he realized how near the other world his friend must have been to look like that. Never till that moment had he felt how his little chum had twined himself round his heart-strings; and as he stole gently across the room and knelt down, and put his arm round Arthur's head on the pillow, felt ashamed and half angry at his own red and brown face, and the bounding sense of health and power which filled every fibre of his body, and made every moment of mere living a joy to him. He needn't have troubled himself, it was this very strength and power so different from his own which drew Arthur so to him.

Arthur laid his thin white hand, on which the blue veins stood out so plainly, on Tom's great brown fist, and smiled at him; and then looked out of the window again, as if he couldn't bear to lose a moment of the sunset, into the tops of the great feathery elms, round which the rooks were circling and clanging, returned in flocks from their evening's foraging parties. The elms rustled, the sparrows in the ivy just outside the window chirped and fluttered about, quarrelling and making it up again; the rooks young and old talked in chorus, and the merry shouts of the boys, and the sweet click of the cricketbats, came up cheerily from below.

'Dear George,' said Tom, 'I am so glad to be let up to see you at last. I've tried hard to come so often, but they wouldn't let me before.'

'Oh, I know, Tom; Mary has told me every day about you, and how she was obliged to make the Doctor speak to you to keep you away. I'm very glad you didn't get up, for you might have caught it, and you couldn't stand being ill with all the matches going on. And you're in the eleven too, I hear—I'm so glad.'

'Yes, ain't it jolly?' said Tom proudly; 'I'm ninth too. I made forty at the last pie-match, and caught three fellows out. So I was put in above Jones and Tucker. Tucker's so savage, for he was head of the twenty-two.'

'Well, I think you ought to be higher yet,' said Arthur, who was as jealous for the renown of Tom in games, as Tom was for his as a scholar.

'Never mind, I don't care about cricket or anything now you're getting well, Geordie; and I shouldn't have hurt, I know, if they'd have let me come up—nothing hurts me. But you'll get about now directly, won't you? You won't believe how clean I've kept the study. All your things are just as you left them; and I feed the old magpie just when you used, though I have to come in from big-side for him, the old rip. He won't look pleased, all I can do, and sticks his head first on one side and then on the other, and blinks at me before he'll begin to eat, till I'm half inclined to box his ears. And whenever East comes in, you should see him hop off to the window, dot and go one, though Harry wouldn't touch a feather of him now.'

Arthur laughed. 'Old Gravey has a good memory, he can't forget the sieges of poor Martin's den in old times.' He paused a moment, and then went on. 'You can't think how often I've been thinking of old Martin since I've been ill; I suppose one's mind gets restless, and likes to wander off to strange unknown places. I wonder what queer new pets the old boy has got; how he must be revelling in the thousand new birds, beasts, and fishes.'

Tom felt a pang of jealousy, but kicked it out in a moment. 'Fancy him on a South-sea island, with the Cherokees or Patagonians, or some such wild niggers;' (Tom's ethnology and geography were faulty, but sufficient for his needs;) 'they'll make the old Madman cock medicine-man, and tattoo him all over. Perhaps he's cutting about now all blue, and has a squaw and a wigwam. He'll improve their boomerangs, and be able to throw them too, without having old Thomas sent after him by the Doctor to take them away.'

Arthur laughed at the remembrance of the boomerang story, but then looked grave again, and said, 'He'll convert all the Island, I know.'

'Yes, if he don't blow it up first.'

'Do you remember, Tom, how you and East used to laugh at him and chaff him, because he said he was sure the rooks all had calling-over, or prayers, or something of the sort, when the locking-up bell rang? Well, I declare,' said Arthur, looking up seriously into Tom's laughing eyes, 'I do think he was right. Since I've been lying here I've watched them every night; and do you know, they really do come, and perch all of them just about locking-up time; and then first there's a regular chorus of caws, and then they stop a bit, and one old fellow, or perhaps two or three in different trees, caw solos, and then off they all go again, fluttering about and cawing anyhow till they roost.'

'I wonder if the old blackies do talk,' said Tom, looking up at them. 'How they must abuse me and East, and pray for the Doctor for stopping the slinging.'

'There! look, look!' cried Arthur, 'don't you see the old fellow without a tail coming up? Martin used to call him "the clerk". He can't steer himself. You never saw such fun as he is in a high wind, when he can't steer himself home, and gets carried right past the trees, and has to bear up again and again before he can perch.'

The locking-up bell began to toll, and the two boys were silent and listened to it. The sound soon carried Tom off to the river and the woods, and he began to go over in his mind the many occasions on which he had heard that toll coming faintly down the breeze, and had to pack up his rod in a hurry and make a run for it, to get in before the gates were shut. He was roused with a start from his memories by Arthur's voice, gentle and weak from his late illness.

'Tom, will you be angry if I talk to you very seriously?'

'No, dear old boy, not I. But ain't you faint, Arthur, or ill? What can I get for you? Don't say anything to hurt yourself now, you are very weak; let me come up again.'

'No, no, I shan't hurt myself: I'd sooner speak to you now, if you don't mind. I've asked Mary to tell the Doctor that you are with me, so you needn't go down to calling-over; and I mayn't have another chance, for I shall most likely have to go home for change of air to get well, and mayn't come back this half.'

'Oh, do you think you must go away before the end of the half? I'm so sorry. It's more than five weeks yet to the holidays, and all the fifth-form examination and half the cricket-matches to come yet. And what shall I do all that time alone in our study? Why, Arthur, it will be more than twelve weeks before I see you again. Oh, hang it, I can't stand that. Besides, who's to keep me up to working at the examination books? I shall come out bottom of the form, as sure as eggs is eggs.'

Tom was rattling on, half in joke, half in earnest, for he wanted to get Arthur out of his serious vein, thinking it would do him harm; but Arthur broke in—

'Oh please, Tom, stop, or you'll drive all I had to say out of my head. And I'm already horribly afraid I'm going to make you angry.'

'Don't gammon, young 'un,' rejoined Tom (the use of the old name, dear to him from old recollections, made Arthur start and smile, and feel quite happy); 'you know you ain't afraid, and you've never made me angry since the first month we chummed together. Now I'm going to be quite sober for a quarter of an hour, which is more than I am once in a year, so make the most of it; heave ahead, and pitch into me right and left.'

'Dear Tom, I ain't going to pitch into you,' said Arthur piteously; 'and it seems so cocky in me to be advising you, who've been my backbone ever since I've been at Rugby, and have made the school a paradise to me. Ah, I see I shall never do it, unless I go head-over-heels at once, as you said when you taught me to swim. Tom, I want you to give up using vulgusbooks and cribs.'

Arthur sank back on to his pillow with a sigh, as if the effort had been great; but the worst was now over, and he looked straight at Tom, who was evidently taken aback. He leant his elbows on his knees and stuck his hands into his hair, whistled a verse of Billy Taylor, and then was quite silent for another minute. Not a shade crossed his face, but he was clearly puzzled. At last he looked up and caught Arthur's anxious look, took his hand, and said simply—

'Why, young 'un?'

'Because you're the honestest boy in Rugby and that ain't honest.'

'I don't see that.'

'What were you sent to Rugby for?'

'Well, I don't know exactly—nobody ever told me. I suppose because all boys are sent to a public school in England.'

'But what do you think yourself? What do you want to do here, and to carry away?'

Tom thought a minute. 'I want to be A1 at cricket and football and all the other games, and to make my hands keep my head against any fellow, lout or gentleman. I want to get into the sixth before I leave, and to please the Doctor; and I want to carry away just as much Latin and Greek as will take me through Oxford respectably.

There now, young 'un, I never thought of it before, but that's pretty much about my figure. Ain't it all on the square? What have you got to say to that?'

'Why, that you're pretty sure to do all that you want, then.'

'Well, I hope so. But you've forgot one thing, what I want to leave behind me. I want to leave behind me,' said Tom, speaking slow and looking much moved, 'the name of a fellow who never bullied a little boy, or turned his back on a big one.'

Arthur pressed his hand, and after a moment's silence went on: 'You say, Tom, you want to please the Doctor. Now do you want to please him by what he thinks you do, or by what you really do?'

'By what I really do, of course.'

'Does he think you use cribs and vulgus-books?'

Tom felt at once that his flank was turned, but he couldn't give in. 'He was at Winchester himself,' said he, 'he knows all about it.'

'Yes, but does he think *you* use them? Do you think he approves of it?'

'You young villain,' said Tom, shaking his fist at Arthur, half vexed and half pleased, 'I never think about it. Hang it—there, perhaps he don't. Well, I suppose he don't.'

Arthur saw that he had got his point; he knew his friend well, and was wise in silence as in speech. He only said, 'I would sooner have the Doctor's good opinion of me as I really am, than any man's in the world.'

After another minute Tom began again: 'Look here, young 'un, how on earth am I to get time to play the matches this half, if I give up cribs? We're in the middle of that long crabbed chorus in the Agamemnon. I can only just make head or tail of it with the crib. Then there's Pericles' speech coming on in Thucydides, and 'The Birds' to get up for the examination, besides the Tacitus.' Tom groaned at the thought of his accumulated labours. 'I say, young 'un, there's only five weeks or so left to holidays, mayn't I go on as usual for this half? I'll tell the Doctor about it some day, or you may.'

Arthur looked out of window; the twilight had come on, and all was silent. He repeated in a low voice, 'In this thing the Lord pardon thy servant, that when my master goeth into the house of Rimmon to worship there, and he leaneth on my hand, and I bow down myself in the house of Rimmon, when I bow down myself in the house of Rimmon, the Lord pardon thy servant in this thing.'

Not a word more was said on the subject, and the boys were again silent. One of those blessed short silences, in which the resolves which colour a life are so often taken.

Tom was the first to break it. 'You've been very ill indeed, haven't you, Geordie?' said he, with a mixture of awe and curiosity, feeling as if his friend had been in some strange place or scene, of which he could form no idea, and full of the memory of his own thoughts during the last week.

'Yes, very. I'm sure the Doctor thought I was going to die. He gave me the Sacrament last Sunday, and you can't think what he is when one is ill. He said such brave, and tender, and gentle things to me, I felt quite light and strong after it, and never had any more fear. My mother brought our old medical man, who attended me when I was a poor sickly child; he said my constitution was quite changed, and that I'm fit for anything now. If it hadn't, I couldn't have stood three days of this illness. That's all thanks to you, and the games you've made me fond of.'

'More thanks to old Martin,' said Tom; 'he's been your real friend.'

'Nonsense, Tom, he never could have done for me what you have.'

'Well, I don't know, I did little enough. Did they tell you—you won't mind hearing it now, I know—that poor Thompson died last week? The other three boys are getting quite round, like you.'

'Oh, yes, I heard of it.'

Then Tom, who was quite full of it, told Arthur of the burial service in the chapel, and how it had impressed him, and, he believed, all the other boys. 'And though the Doctor never said a word about it,' said he, 'and it was a half-holiday and match day, there wasn't a game played in the close all the afternoon, and the boys all went about as if it were Sunday.'

'I'm very glad of it,' said Arthur. 'But, Tom, I've had such strange thoughts about death lately. I've never told a soul of them, not even my mother. Sometimes I think they're wrong, but, do you know, I don't think in my heart I could be sorry at the death of any of my friends.'

Tom was taken quite aback. 'What in the world is the young 'un after now?' thought he; 'I've swallowed a good many of his crotchets, but this altogether beats me. He can't be quite right in his head.' He didn't want to say a word, and shifted about uneasily in the dark; however Arthur seemed to be waiting for an answer, so at last he said, 'I don't think I quite see what you mean, Geordie. One's told so often to think about death, that I've tried it on sometimes, especially this last week. But we won't talk of it now. I'd better go—you're getting tired, and I shall do you harm.'

'No, no, indeed I ain't, Tom; you must stop till nine, there's only twenty minutes. I've settled you shall stop till nine. And oh! do let me talk to you—I must talk to you. I see it's just as I feared. You think I'm half mad—don't you now?'

'Well, I did think it odd what you said, Geordie, as you ask me.'

Arthur paused a moment, and then said quickly, 'I'll tell you how it all happened. At first, when I was sent to the sick-room and found I had really got the fever, I was terribly frightened. I thought I should die, and I could not face it for a moment. I don't think it was sheer cowardice at first, but I thought how hard it was to be taken away from my mother and sisters and you all, just as I was beginning to see my way to many things, and to feel that I might be a man and do a man's work. To die without having fought, and worked, and given one's life away, was too hard to bear. I got terribly impatient, and accused God of injustice, and strove to justify myself; and the harder I strove the deeper I sank. Then the image of my dear father often came across me, but I turned from it. Whenever it came, a heavy numbing throb seemed to take hold of my heart, and say, dead—dead—dead. And I cried out, "The living, the living shall praise Thee, O God; the dead cannot praise Thee. There is no work in the grave; in the night no man can work. But I can work. I can do great things. I *will* do great things. Why wilt Thou slay me," And so I struggled and plunged, deeper and deeper, and went down into a living black tomb. I was alone there, with no power to stir or think; alone with myself; beyond the reach of all human fellowship; beyond Christ's reach, I thought, in my nightmare. You, who are brave and bright and strong, can have no idea of that agony. Pray to God you never may. Pray as for your life.'

Arthur stopped—from exhaustion Tom thought; but what between his fear lest Arthur should hurt himself, his awe, and longing for him to go on, he couldn't ask or stir to help him.

Presently he went on, but quite calm and slow. 'I don't know how long I was in that state. For more than a day, I know, for I was quite conscious, and lived my outer life all the time, and took my medicines, and spoke to my mother, and heard what they said. But I didn't take much note of time, I thought time was over for me, and that that tomb was what was beyond Well, on last Sunday morning, as I seemed to lie in that tomb, alone, as I thought, for ever and ever, the black dead wall was cleft in two, and I was caught up and borne through into the light by some great power, some living mighty spirit. Tom, do you remember the living creatures and the wheels in Ezekiel? It was just like that; "when they went I heard the noise of their wings, like the noise of great waters, as the voice of the Almighty, the voice of speech, as the noise of an host; when they stood they let down their wings"—"and they went every one straight forward; whither the spirit was to go they went, and they turned not when they went." And we rushed through the bright air, which was full of myriads of living creatures, and paused on the brink of a great river. And the power held me up, and I knew that that great river was the grave, and death dwelt there; but not the death I had met in the black tomb, that I felt was gone for ever. For on the other bank of the great river I saw men and women and children rising up pure and bright, and the tears were wiped from their eyes, and they put on glory and strength, and all weariness and pain fell away. And beyond were a multitude which no man could number, and they worked at some great work; and they who rose from the river went on and joined in the work. They all worked, and each worked in a different way, but all at the same work. And I saw there my father, and the men in the old town whom I knew when I was a child; many a hard stern man, who never came to church, and whom they called atheist and infidel. There they were, side by side with my father, whom I had seen toil and die for them, and women and little children, and the seal was on the foreheads of all. And I longed to see what the work was, and could not; so I tried to plunge in the river, for I thought I would join them, but I could not. Then I looked about to see how they got into the river. And this I could not see, but I saw myriads on this side, and they too worked, and I knew that it was the same work; and the same seal was on their foreheads. And though I saw that there was toil and anguish in the work of these, and the most that were working were blind and feeble, yet, I longed no more to plunge into the river,

203

but more and more to know what the work was. And as I looked I saw my mother and my sisters, and I saw the Doctor, and you, Tom, and hundreds more whom I knew; and at last I saw myself too, and I was toiling and doing ever so little a piece of the great work. Then it all melted away, and the power left me, and as it left me I thought I heard a voice say, "The vision is for an appointed time; though it tarry, wait for it, for in the end it shall speak and not lie, it shall surely come, it shall not tarry." It was early morning I know then, it was so quiet and cool, and my mother was fast asleep in the chair by my bedside; but it wasn't only a dream of mine. I know it wasn't a dream. Then I fell into a deep sleep, and only woke after afternoon chapel; and the Doctor came and gave me the Sacrament, as I told you. I told him and my mother I should get well—I knew I should; but I couldn't tell them why. Tom,' said Arthur gently, after another minute, 'do you see why I could not grieve now to see my dearest friend die? It can't be—it isn't all fever or illness. God would never have let me see it so clear if it wasn't true. I don't understand it all yet—it will take me my life and longer to do that—to find out what the work is.'

When Arthur stopped there was a long pause. Tom could not speak, he was almost afraid to breathe, lest he should break the train of Arthur's thoughts. He longed to hear more, and to ask questions. In another minute nine o'clock struck, and a gentle tap at the door called them both back into the world again. They did not answer however for a moment, and so the door opened, and a lady came in carrying a candle.

She went straight to the sofa, and took hold of Arthur's hand, and then stooped down and kissed him.

'My dearest boy, you feel a little feverish again. Why didn't you have lights? You've talked too much and excited yourself in the dark.'

'Oh no, mother, you can't think how well I feel. I shall start with you tomorrow for Devonshire. But, mother, here's my friend, here's Tom Brown—you know him?'

'Yes, indeed, I've known him for years,' she said, and held out her hand to Tom, who was now standing up behind the sofa. This was Arthur's mother. Tall and slight and fair, with masses of golden hair drawn back from the broad white forehead, and the calm blue eye meeting his so deep and open—the eye that he knew so well, for it was his friend's over again, and the lovely tender mouth that trembled while he looked. She stood there a woman of thirty-eight, old enough to be his mother, and one whose face showed the lines which must be written on the faces of good men's wives and widows—but he thought he had never seen anything so beautiful. He couldn't help wondering if Arthur's sisters were like her.

Tom held her hand, and looked on straight in her face; he could neither let it go nor speak.

'Now, Tom,' said Arthur, laughing, 'where are your manners? you'll stare my mother out of countenance.' Tom dropped the little hand with a sigh. 'There, sit down, both of you. Here, dearest mother, there's room here,' and he made a place on the sofa for her. 'Tom you needn't go; I'm sure you won't be called up at first lesson.' Tom felt that he would risk being floored at every lesson for the rest of his natural school life, sooner than go; so sat down. 'And now,' said Arthur, 'I have realized one of the dearest wishes of my life—to see you two together.'

And then he led away the talk to their home in Devonshire, and the red bright earth, and the deep green combes, and the peat streams like cairn-gorm pebbles, and the wild moor with its high cloudy Tors for a giant background to the picture—till Tom got jealous, and stood up for the clear chalk streams, and the emerald water meadows and great elms and willows of the dear old Royal county, as he gloried to call it. And the mother sat on quiet and loving, rejoicing in their life. The quarter-to-ten struck, and the bell rang for bed, before they had well begun their talk as it seemed.

Then Tom rose with a sigh to go.

'Shall I see you in the morning, Geordie?' said he, as he shook his friend's hand. 'Never mind though; you'll be back next half, and I shan't forget the house of Rimmon.'

Arthur's mother got up and walked with him to the door, and there gave him her hand again, and again his eyes met that deep loving look, which was like a spell upon him. Her voice trembled slightly as she said, 'Good night—you are one who knows what our Father has promised to the friend of the widow and the fatherless. May He deal with you as you have dealt with me and mine!'

Tom was quite upset; he mumbled something about owing everything good in him to Geordie—looked in her face again, pressed her hand to his lips, and rushed down the stairs to his study, where he sat till old Thomas came kicking at the door, to tell him his allowance would be stopped if he didn't go off to bed. (It would have been stopped anyhow, but that he was a great favourite with the old gentleman, who loved to come out in the afternoons into the close to Tom's wicket, and bowl slow twisters to him, and talk of the glories of by-gone Surrey heroes, with whom he had played in former generations.) So Tom roused himself and took up his candle to go to bed; and then for the first time was aware of a beautiful new fishing-rod, with old Eton's mark on it, and a splendidly bound Bible, which lay on his table, on the title page of which was written—'TOM BROWN, from his affectionate and grateful friends, Frances Jane Arthur; George Arthur.'

I leave you all to guess how he slept, and what he dreamt of.

CHAPTER 7

HARRY EAST'S DILEMMAS
AND DELIVERANCES

'The Holy Supper is kept indeed,
In whatso we share with another's need—
Not that which we give, but what we share,
For the gift without the giver is bare:
Who bestows himself with his alms feeds three,
Himself, his hungering neighbour, and Me.'
The Vision of Sir Launfal—LOWELL, p. 11

The next morning after breakfast, Tom, East, and Gower met as usual to learn their second lesson together. Tom had been considering how to break his proposal of giving up the crib to the others, and having found no better way, (as indeed none better can ever be found by man or boy), told them simply what had happened; how he had been to see Arthur, who had talked to him upon the subject, and what he had said, and for his part he had made up his mind and wasn't going to use cribs any more. And not being quite sure of his ground, took the high and pathetic tone, and was proceeding to say, 'how that having learnt his lessons with them for so many years, it would grieve him much to put an end to the arrangement, and he hoped at any rate that if they wouldn't go on with him, they should still be just as good friends, and respect one another's motives—but—'

Here the other boys, who had been listening with open eyes and ears, burst in—

'Stuff and nonsense!' cried Gower. 'Here, East, get down the crib and find the place.'

'Oh, Tommy, Tommy!' said East, proceeding to do as he was bidden, 'that it should ever have come to this. I knew Arthur'd be the ruin of you some day, and you of me. And now the time's come'—and he made a doleful face.

'I don't know about ruin,' answered Tom; 'I know that you and I would have had the sack long ago, if it hadn't been for him. And you know it as well as I.'

'Well, we were in a baddish way before he came, I own, but this new crotchet of his is past a joke.'

'Let's give it a trial, Harry; come—you know how often he has been right and we wrong.'

'Now don't you two be jawing away about young Squaretoes,' struck in Gower. 'He's no end of a sucking wiseacre, I dare say, but we've no time to lose, and I've got the fives'-court at half-past nine.'

'I say, Gower,' said Tom appealingly, 'be a good fellow, and let's try if we can't get on without the crib.'

'What! in this chorus? Why we shan't get through ten lines.'

'I say, Tom,' cried East, having hit on a new idea, 'don't you remember, when we were in the upper fourth, and old Momus caught me construing off the leaf of a crib which I'd torn out and put in my book, and which would float out on to the floor; he sent me up to be flogged for it?'

'Yes, I remember it very well.'

'Well, the Doctor, after he'd flogged me, told me himself that he didn't flog me for using a translation, but for taking it into lesson, and using it there when I hadn't learnt a word before I came in. He said there was no harm in using a translation to get a clue to hard passages, if you'd tried all you could first to make them out without.'

'Did he though?' said Tom; 'then Arthur must be wrong.'

'Of course he is,' said Gower, 'the little prig. We'll only use the crib when we can't construe without it. Go ahead, East.'

And on this agreement they started. Tom satisfied with having made his confession, and not sorry to have a locus poenitentiae, and not be deprived altogether of the use of his old and faithful friend.

The boys went on as usual, each taking a sentence in turn, and the crib being handed to the one whose turn it was to construe. Of course Tom couldn't object to this, as, was it not simply lying there to be appealed to in case the sentence should prove too hard altogether for the construer? But it must be owned that Gower and East did not make very tremendous exertions to conquer their sentences before having recourse to its help. Tom however with the most heroic virtue and gallantry rushed into his sentence, searching in a high-minded manner for nominative and verb, and turning over his dictionary frantically for the first hard word which stopped him. But in the meantime Gower, who was bent on getting to fives, would peep quietly into the crib, and then suggest, 'Don't you think this is the meaning?' 'I think you must take it this way, Brown;' and as Tom didn't see his way to not profiting by these suggestions, the lesson went on about as quickly as usual, and Gower was able to start for the fives'-court within five minutes of the half-hour.

When Tom and East were left face to face, they looked at one another for a minute, Tom puzzled, and East chock-full of fun, and then burst into a roar of laughter.

'Well, Tom,' said East, recovering himself, 'I don't see any objection to the new way. It's about as good as the old one, I think; besides, the advantage it gives one of feeling virtuous, and looking down on one's neighbours.'

Tom shoved his hand into his back hair. 'I ain't so sure,' said he; 'you two fellows carried me off my legs: I don't think we really tried one sentence fairly. Are you sure you remember what the Doctor said to you?'

'Yes. And I'll swear I couldn't make out one of my sentences today. No, nor never could. I really don't remember,' said East, speaking slowly and impressively, 'to have come across one Latin or Greek sentence this half, that I could go and construe by the light of nature. Whereby I am sure Providence intended cribs to be used.'

'The thing to find out,' said Tom meditatively, 'is, how long one ought to grind at a sentence without looking at the crib. Now I think if one fairly looks out all the words one don't know, and then can't hit it, that's enough.'

'To be sure, Tommy,' said East demurely, but with a merry twinkle in his eye. 'Your new doctrine too, old fellow,' added he, 'when one comes to think of it, is a cutting at the root of all school morality. You'll take away mutual help, brotherly love, or in the vulgar tongue giving construes, which I hold to be one of our highest virtues. For how can you distinguish between getting a construe from another boy, and using a crib? Hang it, Tom, if you're going to deprive all our school-fellows of the chance of exercising Christian benevolence and being good Samaritans, I shall cut the concern.'

'I wish you wouldn't joke about it, Harry; it's hard enough to see one's way, a precious sight harder than I thought last night. But I suppose there's a use and an abuse of both, and one'll get straight enough somehow. But you can't make out anyhow that one has a right to use old vulgus-books and copybooks.'

'Hullo, more heresy! how fast a fellow goes down hill when he once gets his head before his legs. Listen to me, Tom. Not use old vulgus-books—why you Goth! ain't we to take the benefit of the wisdom, and admire and use the work of past generations? Not use old copybooks! Why you might as well say we ought to pull down Westminster Abbey, and put up a go-to-meeting shop with churchwarden windows; or never read Shakespeare, but only Sheridan Knowles. Think of all the work and labour that our predecessors have bestowed on these very books, and are we to make their work of no value?'

'I say, Harry, please don't chaff; I'm really serious.'

'And then, is it not our duty to consult the pleasure of others rather than our own, and above all that of our masters? Fancy then the difference to them in looking over a vulgus which has been carefully touched and retouched by themselves and others, and which must bring them a sort of dreamy pleasure, as if they'd met the thought or expression of it somewhere or another—before they were born perhaps; and that of cutting up, and making picture-frames round all your and my false quantities, and other monstrosities. Why, Tom, you wouldn't be so cruel as never to let old Momus hum over the "O genus humanum" again, and then look up doubtingly through his spectacles, and end by smiling and giving three extra marks for it; just for old sake's sake, I suppose.'

'Well,' said Tom, getting up in something as like a huff as he was capable of, 'it's deuced hard that when a fellow's really trying to do what he ought, his best friends'll do nothing but chaff him and try to put him down.' And he stuck his books under his arm and his hat on his head, preparatory to rushing out into the quadrangle, to testify with his own soul of the faithlessness of friendships.

'Now don't be an ass, Tom,' said East, catching hold of him, 'you know me well enough by this time; my bark's worse than my bite. You can't expect to ride your new crotchet without anybody's trying to stick a nettle under his tail and make him kick you off: especially as we shall all have to go on foot still. But now sit down and let's go over it again. I'll be as serious as a judge.'

Then Tom sat himself down on the table, and waxed eloquent about all the righteousnesses and advantages of the new plan, as was his wont whenever he took up anything; going into it as if his life depended upon it, and sparing no abuse which he could think of of the opposite method, which he denounced as ungentlemanly, cowardly, mean, lying, and no one knows what besides. 'Very cool of Tom,' as East thought, but didn't say, 'seeing as how he only came out of Egypt himself last night at bed-time.'

'Well, Tom,' said he at last, 'you see when you and I came to school there were none of these sort of notions. You may be right—I dare say you are. Only what one has always felt about the masters is, that it's a fair trial of skill, and last between us and them—like a match at football, or a battle. We're natural enemies in school, that's the fact. We've got to learn so much Latin and Greek and do so many verses, and they've got to see that we do it. If we can slip the collar and do so much less without getting caught, that's one to us. If they can get more out of us, or catch us shirking, that's one to them. All's fair in war, but lying. If I run my luck against theirs and go into school without looking at my lessons, and don't get called up, why am I a snob or a sneak? I don't tell the master I've learnt it. He's got to find out whether I have or not: what's he paid for? If he calls me up and I get floored, he makes me write it out in Greek and English. Very good, he's caught me, and I don't grumble. I grant you, if I go and snivel to him, and tell him I've really tried to learn it but found it so hard without a translation, or say I've had a toothache or any humbug of that kind, I'm a snob. That's my school morality; it's served me, and you too, Tom, for the matter of that, these five years. And it's all clear and fair, no mistake about it. We understand it, and they understand it, and I don't know what we're to come to with any other.'

Tom looked at him, pleased, and a little puzzled. He had never heard East speak his mind seriously before, and couldn't help feeling how completely he had hit his own theory and practice up to that time.

'Thank you, old fellow,' said he. 'You're a good old brick to be serious, and not put out with me. I said more than I meant, I dare say, only you see I know I'm right: whatever you and Gower and the rest do, I shall hold on—I must. And as it's all new and an up-hill game, you see, one must hit hard and hold on tight at first.'

'Very good,' said East; 'hold on and hit away, only don't hit under the line.'

'But I must bring you over, Harry, or I shan't be comfortable. Now I allow all you've said. We've always been honourable enemies with the masters. We found a state of war when we came, and went into it of course. Only don't you think things are altered a good deal? I don't feel as I used to the masters. They seem to me to treat one quite differently.'

'Yes, perhaps they do,' said East; 'there's a new set you see mostly, who don't feel sure of themselves yet. They don't want to fight till they know the ground.'

'I don't think it's only that,' said Tom. 'And then the Doctor, he does treat one so openly, and like a gentleman, and as if one was working with him.'

'Well, so he does,' said East; 'he's a splendid fellow, and when I get into the sixth I shall act accordingly. Only you know he has nothing to do with our lessons now, except examining us. I say though,' looking at his watch, 'it's just the quarter. Come along.'

As they walked out they got a message to say, 'that Arthur was just starting and would like to say good-bye'; so they went down to the private entrance of the Schoolhouse, and found an open carriage, with Arthur propped up with pillows in it, looking already better, Tom thought.

They jumped up on to the steps to shake hands with him, and Tom mumbled thanks for the presents he had found in his study, and looked round anxiously for Arthur's mother.

East, who had fallen back into his usual humour, looked quaintly at Arthur, and said—

'So you've been at it again, through that hot-headed convert of yours there. He's been making our lives a burthen to us all the

211

morning about using cribs. I shall get floored to a certainty at second lesson, if I'm called up.'

Arthur blushed and looked down. Tom struck in—

'Oh, it's all right. He's converted already; he always comes through the mud after us, grumbling and spluttering.'

The clock struck and they had to go off to school, wishing Arthur a pleasant holiday; Tom lingering behind a moment to send his thanks and love to Arthur's mother.

Tom renewed the discussion after second lesson, and succeeded so far as to get East to promise to give the new plan a fair trial.

Encouraged by his success, in the evening, when they were sitting alone in the study, where East lived now almost, 'vice Arthur on leave,' after examining the new fishing-rod, which both pronounced to be the genuine article ('play enough to throw a midge tied on a single hair against the wind, and strength enough to hold a grampus'), they naturally began talking about Arthur. Tom, who was still bubbling over with last night's scene and all the thoughts of the last week, and wanting to clinch and fix the whole in his own mind, which he could never do without first going through the process of belabouring somebody else with it all, suddenly rushed into the subject of Arthur's illness, and what he had said about death.

East had given him the desired opening, after a serio-comic grumble, 'that life wasn't worth having now they were tied to a young beggar who was always "raising his standard"; and that he, East, was like a prophet's donkey, who was obliged to struggle on after the donkey-man who went after the prophet; that he had none of the pleasure of starting the new crotchets, and didn't half understand them, but had to take the kicks and carry the luggage as if he had all the fun,' he threw his legs up on to the sofa, and put his hands behind his head, and said—

'Well, after all, he's the most wonderful little fellow I ever came across. There ain't such a meek, humble boy in the school. Hanged if I don't think now really, Tom, that he believes himself a much worse fellow than you or I, and that he don't think he has more influence in the house than Dot Bowles, who came last quarter, and ain't ten yet. But he turns you and me round his little finger, old boy—there's no mistake about that.' And East nodded at Tom sagaciously.

'Now or never!' thought Tom; so shutting his eyes and hardening his heart, he went straight at it, repeating all that Arthur had said, as near as he could remember it, in the very words, and all he had himself thought. The life seemed to ooze out of it as he went on, and several times he felt inclined to stop, give it all up, and change the subject. But somehow he was borne on, he had a necessity upon him to speak it all out, and did so. At the end he looked at East with some anxiety, and was delighted to see that that young gentleman was thoughtful and attentive. The fact is, that in the stage of his inner life at which Tom had lately arrived, his intimacy with and friendship for East could not have lasted if he had not made him aware of, and a sharer in, the thoughts that were beginning to exercise him. Nor indeed could the friendship have lasted if East had shown no sympathy with these thoughts; so that it was a great relief to have unbosomed himself, and to have found that his friend could listen.

Tom had always had a sort of instinct that East's levity was only skin-deep, and his instinct was a true one. East had no want of reverence for anything he felt to be real: but his was one of those natures that burst into what is generally called recklessness and impiety the moment they feel that anything is being poured upon them for their good, which does not come home to their inborn sense of right, or which appeals to anything like self-interest in them. Daring and honest by nature, and outspoken to an extent which alarmed all respectabilities, with a constant fund of animal health and spirits which he did not feel bound to curb in any way, he had gained for himself with the steady part of the school (including as well those who wished to appear steady as those who really were so), the character of a boy whom it would be dangerous to be intimate with; while his own hatred of everything cruel, or underhand, or false, and his hearty respect for what he could see to be good and true, kept off the rest.

Tom, besides being very like East in many points of character, had largely developed in his composition the capacity for taking the weakest side. This is not putting it strongly enough; it was a necessity with him, he couldn't help it any more than he could eating or drinking. He could never play on the strongest side with any heart at football or cricket, and was sure to make friends with any boy who was unpopular, or down on his luck.

Now though East was not what is generally called unpopular, Tom felt more and more every day, as their characters developed, that he stood alone, and did not make friends among their contemporaries; and therefore sought him out. Tom was himself much more popular, for his power of detecting humbug was much less acute, and his instincts were much more sociable. He was at this period of his life, too, largely given to taking people for what they gave themselves out to be; but his singleness of heart, fearlessness, and honesty were just what East appreciated, and thus the two had been drawn into great intimacy.

This intimacy had not been interrupted by Tom's guardianship of Arthur.

East had often, as has been said, joined them in reading the Bible; but their discussion had almost always turned upon the characters of the men and women of whom they read, and not become personal to themselves. In fact, the two had shrunk from personal religious discussion, not knowing how it might end; and fearful of risking a friendship very dear to both, and which they felt somehow, without quite knowing why, would never be the same, but either tenfold stronger or sapped at its foundation, after such a communing together.

What a bother all this explaining is! I wish we could get on without it. But we can't. However, you'll all find, if you haven't found it out already, that a time comes in every human friendship, when you must go down into the depths of yourself, and lay bare what is there to your friend, and wait in fear for his answer. A few moments may do it; and, it may be (most likely will be, as you are English boys) that you never do it but once. But done it must be, if the friendship is to be worth the name. You must find what is there, at the very root and bottom of one another's hearts; and it you are at one there, nothing on earth can, or at least ought to sunder you.

East had remained lying down until Tom finished speaking, as if fearing to interrupt him; he now sat up at the table and leant his head on one hand, taking up a pencil with the other and working little holes with it in the table-cover. After a bit he looked up, stopped the pencil, and said, 'Thank you very much, old fellow; there's no other boy in the house would have done it for me but you or Arthur. I can see well enough,' he went on after a pause, 'all the best big fellows look on me with suspicion; they think I'm a devil-may-care reckless young scamp—So I am—eleven hours out of twelve—but not the twelfth. Then all of our contemporaries worth knowing follow suit, of course; we're very good friends at games and all that, but not a soul of them but you and Arthur ever tried to break through the crust, and see whether there was anything at the bottom of me; and then the bad ones I won't stand, and they know that.'

'Don't you think that's half fancy, Harry?'

'Not a bit of it,' said East bitterly, pegging away with his pencil. 'I see it all plain enough. Bless you, you think everybody's as straightforward and kind-hearted as you are.'

'Well, but what's the reason of it? There must be a reason. You can play all the games as well as any one, and sing the best song, and are the best company in the house. You fancy you're not liked, Harry. It's all fancy.'

'I only wish it was, Tom. I know I could be popular enough with all the bad ones, but that I won't have, and the good ones won't have me.'

'Why not?' persisted Tom; 'you don't drink or swear, or get out at night; you never bully, or cheat at lessons. If you only showed you liked it, you'd have all the best fellows in the house running after you.'

'Not I,' said East. Then with an effort he went on, 'I'll tell you what it is. I never stop the Sacrament. I can see from the Doctor downwards, how that tells against me.'

'Yes, I've seen that,' said Tom, 'and I've been very sorry for it, and Arthur and I have talked about it. I've often thought of speaking to you, but it's so hard to begin on such subjects. I'm very glad you've opened it. Now, why don't you?'

'I've never been confirmed!' said East.

'Not been confirmed!' said Tom, in astonishment. 'I never thought of that. Why weren't you confirmed with the rest of us nearly three years ago? I always thought you'd been confirmed at home.'

'No,' answered East sorrowfully; 'you see this was how it happened. Last Confirmation was soon after Arthur came, and you were so taken up with him, I hardly saw either of you. Well, when the Doctor sent round for us about it, I was living mostly with Green's set—you know the sort. They all went in—I daresay it was all right, and they got good by it; I don't want to judge them. Only all I could see of their reasons drove me just the other way. 'Twas, "because the doctor liked it;" "no boy got on who didn't stay the Sacrament;" it was "the correct thing," in fact, like having a good hat to wear on Sundays. I couldn't stand it. I didn't feel that I wanted to lead a different life, I was very well content as I was, and I wasn't going to sham religious to curry favour with the Doctor, or any one else.'

East stopped speaking, and pegged away more diligently than ever with his pencil. Tom was ready to cry. He felt half sorry at first that he had been confirmed himself. He seemed to have deserted his earliest friend, to have left him by himself at his worst need for those long years. He got up and went and sat by East, and put his arm over his shoulder.

'Dear old boy,' he said, 'how careless and selfish I've been. But why didn't you come and talk to Arthur and me?'

'I wish to heaven I had,' said East, 'but I was a fool. It's too late talking of it now.'

'Why too late? You want to be confirmed now, don't you?'

'I think so,' said East. 'I've thought about it a good deal: only often I fancy I must be changing, because I see it's to do me good here, just what stopped me last time. And then I go back again.'

'I'll tell you now how 'twas with me,' said Tom warmly. 'If it hadn't been for Arthur, I should have done just as you did. I hope I should. I honour you for it. But then he made it out just as if it was taking the weak side before all the world—going in once for all against everything that's strong and rich and proud and respectable, a little band of brothers against the whole world. And the Doctor seemed to say so too, only he said a great deal more.'

'Ah!' groaned East, 'but there again, that's just another of my difficulties whenever I think about the matter. I don't want to be one of your saints, one of your elect, whatever the right phrase is. My sympathies are all the other way; with the many, the poor devils who run about the streets and don't go to church. Don't stare, Tom; mind, I'm telling you all that's in my heart—as far as I know it—but it's all a muddle. You must be gentle with me if you want to land me. Now I've seen a deal of this sort of religion, I was bred up in it, and I can't stand it. If nineteen-twentieths of the world are to be left to uncovenanted mercies, and that sort of thing, which means in plain English to go to hell, and the other twentieth are to rejoice at it all, why—'

'Oh! but, Harry, they ain't, they don't,' broke in Tom, really shocked. 'Oh, how I wish Arthur hadn't gone! I'm such a fool about these things. But it's all you want too, East; it is indeed. It cuts both ways somehow, being confirmed and taking the Sacrament. It makes you feel on the side of all the good and all the bad too, of everybody in the world. Only there's some great dark strong power, which is crushing you and everybody else. That's what Christ conquered, and we've got to fight. What a fool I am! I can't explain. If Arthur were only here!'

'I begin to get a glimmering of what you mean,' said East.

'I say now,' said Tom eagerly, 'do you remember how we both hated Flashman?'

'Of course I do,' said East; 'I hate him still. What then?'

'Well, when I came to take the Sacrament, I had a great struggle about that. I tried to put him out of my head; and when I couldn't do that, I tried to think of him as evil, as something that the Lord who was loving me hated, and which I might hate too. But it wouldn't do. I broke down; I believe Christ himself broke me down; and when the Doctor gave me the bread and wine, and leant over me praying, I prayed for poor Flashman as if it had been you or Arthur.'

East buried his face in his hands on the table. Tom could feel the table tremble. At last he looked up, 'Thank you again, Tom.' said he; 'you don't know what you may have done for me tonight. I think I see now how the right sort of sympathy with poor devils is got at.'

'And you'll stop the Sacrament next time, won't you?' said Tom.

'Can I, before I'm confirmed?'

'Go and ask the Doctor.'

'I will.'

That very night, after prayers, East followed the Doctor and the old Verger bearing the candle, upstairs. Tom watched, and saw the Doctor turn round when he heard footsteps following him closer than usual, and say, 'Hah, East! Do you want to speak to me, my man?'

'If you please, sir;' and the private door closed, and Tom went to his study in a state of great trouble of mind.

It was almost an hour before East came back; then he rushed in breathless.

'Well, it's all right,' he shouted, seizing Tom by the hand. 'I feel as if a ton weight were off my mind.'

'Hurra,' said Tom; 'I knew it would be, but tell us all about it.'

'Well, I just told him all about it. You can't think how kind and gentle he was, the great grim man, whom I've feared more than anybody on earth. When I stuck, he lifted me, just as if I'd been a little child. And he seemed to know all I'd felt, and to have gone through it all. And I burst out crying—more than I've done this five years, and he sat down by me, and stroked my head; and I went blundering on, and told him all; much worse things than I've told you. And he wasn't shocked a bit, and didn't snub me, or tell me I was a fool, and it was all nothing but pride or wickedness, tho' I daresay it was. And he didn't tell me not to follow out my thoughts, and he didn't give me any cut-and-dried explanation. But when I'd done he just talked a bit—I can hardly remember what he said, yet; but it seemed to spread round me like healing, and strength, and light; and to bear me up, and plant me on a rock, where I could hold my footing and fight for myself. I don't know what to do, I feel so happy. And it's all owing to you, dear old boy!' and he seized Tom's hand again.

'And you're to come to the Communion?' said Tom.

'Yes, and to be confirmed in the holidays.'

Tom's delight was as great as his friend's. But he hadn't yet had out all his own talk, and was bent on improving the occasion: so he proceeded to propound Arthur's theory about not being sorry for his friends' deaths, which he had hitherto kept in the background, and by which he was much exercised; for he didn't feel it honest to take what pleased him and throw over the rest, and was trying vigorously to persuade himself that he should like all his best friends to die off-hand.

But East's powers of remaining serious were exhausted, and in five minutes he was saying the most ridiculous things he could think of, till Tom was almost getting angry again.

Despite of himself, however, he couldn't help laughing and giving it up, when East appealed to him with 'Well, Tom, you ain't going to punch my head, I hope, because I insist upon being sorry when you got to earth?'

And so their talk finished for that time, and they tried to learn first lesson; with very poor success, as appeared next morning, when they were called up and narrowly escaped being floored, which ill-luck however did not sit heavily on either of their souls.

CHAPTER 8

TOM BROWN'S LAST MATCH

'Heaven grant the manlier heart, that timely, ere
Youth fly, with life's real tempest would be coping;
    The fruit of dreamy hoping
    Is, waking, blank despair.'
                    —CLOUGH. *Ambarvalia*

The curtain now rises upon the last act of our little drama—for hard-hearted publishers warn me that a single volume must of necessity have an end. Well, well! the pleasantest things must come to an end. I little thought last long vacation, when I began these pages to help while away some spare time at a watering-place, how vividly many an old scene, which had lain hid away for years in some dusty old corner of my brain, would come back again, and stand before me as clear and bright as if it had happened yesterday. The book has been a most grateful task to me, and I only hope that all you, my dear young friends who read it (friends assuredly you must be, if you get as far as this) will be half as sorry to come to the last stage as I am.

Not but what there has been a solemn and a sad side to it. As the old scenes became living, and the actors in them became living too, many a grave in the Crimea and distant India, as well as in the quiet church-yards of our dear old country, seemed to open and send forth their dead, and their voices and looks and ways were again in one's ears and eyes, as in the old School-days. But this was not sad; how should it be, if we believe as our Lord has taught us? How should it be, when one more turn of the wheel, and we shall be by their sides again, learning from them again, perhaps, as we did when we were new boys?

Then there were others of the old faces so dear to us once, who had somehow or another just gone clean out of sight—are they dead or living? We know not, but the thought of them brings no sadness

219

with it. Wherever they are, we can well believe they are doing God's work and getting His wages.

But are there not some, whom we still see sometimes in the streets, whose haunts and homes we know, whom we could probably find almost any day in the week if we were set to do it, yet from whom we are really farther than we are from the dead, and from those who have gone out of our ken? Yes, there are and must be such; and therein lies the sadness of old School memories. Yet of these our old comrades, from whom more than time and space separate us, there are some, by whose sides we can feel sure that we shall stand again when time shall be no more. We may think of one another now as dangerous fanatics or narrow bigots, with whom no truce is possible, from whom we shall only sever more and more to the end of our lives, whom it would be our respective duties to imprison or hang, if we had the power. We must go our way, and they theirs, as long as flesh and spirit hold together; but let our own Rugby poet speak words of healing for this trial:

> To veer how vain! on, onward strain,
>   Brave barks! in light, in darkness too;
> Through winds and tides one compass guides,
>   To that, and your own selves, be true.
>
> But, o blithe breeze! and O great seas,
>   Though ne'er that earliest parting past,
> On your wide plain they join again,
>   Together lead them home at last.
>
> One port, methought, alike they sought,
>   One purpose hold, where'er they fare.
> O bounding breeze, O rushing seas!
>   At last, at last, unite them there!

This is not mere longing, it is prophecy. So over these too, our old friends who are friends no more, we sorrow not as men without hope. It is only for those who seem to us to have lost compass and purpose, and to be drifting helplessly on rocks and quicksands; whose lives are spent in the service of the world, the flesh, and the devil; for self alone, and not for their fellow-men, their country, or their God, that we must mourn and pray without sure hope and without light; trusting only that He, in whose hands they as well as we are, who has died for them as well as for us, who sees all His creatures

> With larger other eyes than ours,
> To make allowance for us all,

will, in His own way and at His own time, lead them also home.

Another two years have passed, and it is again the end of the summer half-year at Rugby; in fact the School has broken up. The fifth-form examinations were over last week, and upon them have followed the speeches, and the sixth-form examinations for exhibitions; and they too are over now. The boys have gone to all the winds of heaven, except the town boys and the eleven, and the few enthusiasts besides who have asked leave to stay in their houses to see the result of the cricket matches. For this year the Wellesburn return match and the Marylebone match are played at Rugby, to the great delight of the town and neighbourhood, and the sorrow of those aspiring young cricketers who have been reckoning for the last three months on showing off at Lords' ground.

The Doctor started for the Lakes yesterday morning, after an interview with the captain of the eleven, in the presence of Thomas, at which he arranged in what School the cricket dinners were to be, and all other matters necessary for the satisfactory carrying out of the festivities; and warned them as to keeping all spirituous liquors out of the close, and having the gates closed by nine o'clock.

The Wellesburn match was played out with great success yesterday, the School winning by three wickets; and today the great event of the cricketing year, the Marylebone match, is being played. What a match it has been! The London eleven came down by an afternoon train yesterday, in time to see the end of the Wellesburn match; and as soon as it was over, their leading men and umpire inspected the ground, criticizing it rather unmercifully. The captain of the School eleven, and one or two others, who had played the Lords' match before and knew old Mr Aislebie and several of the Lords' men, accompanied them; while the rest of the eleven looked on from under the Three Trees with admiring eyes, and asked one another the names of the illustrious strangers, and recounted how many runs each of them had made in the late matches in Bell's Life. They looked such hard-bitten, wiry, whiskered fellows, that their young adversaries felt rather desponding as to the result of the morrow's match. The ground was at last chosen, and two men set to work upon it to water and roll; and then, there being yet some half-hour of daylight, some one had suggested a dance on the turf. The close was half full of citizens and their families, and the idea was hailed with enthusiasm. The cornopean player was still on the ground; in five minutes the eleven and half-a-dozen of the Wellesburn and Marylebone men got partners somehow or another, and a merry country dance was going on, to which every one flocked, and new couples joined in every minute, till there were a hundred of them going down the middle and up again—and the long line of School buildings looked gravely down on them, every window glowing with the last rays of the western sun, and the rooks clanged about in the tops of the old elms, greatly excited and resolved on having their country dance too, and the great flag flapped lazily in the gentle western breeze. Altogether it was a sight which would have made glad the heart of our brave old founder, Lawrence Sheriff, if he were half as good a fellow as I take him to have been. It was a cheerful sight to see; but what made it so valuable in the sight of the Captain of the School eleven was, that he there saw his young hands shaking off their shyness and awe of the Lords' men, as they crossed hands and capered about on the grass together; for the strangers entered into it all, and threw away their cigars, and danced and shouted like boys; while old Mr Aislebie stood by looking on in his white hat, leaning on a bat, in benevolent enjoyment. 'This hop will be worth thirty runs to us tomorrow, and will be the making of Raggles and Johnson,' thinks the young leader, as he revolves many things in his mind, standing by the side of Mr Aislebie, whom he will not leave for a minute, for he feels that the character of the School for courtesy is resting on his shoulders.

But when a quarter to nine struck, and he saw old Thomas beginning to fidget about with the keys in his hand, he thought of the Doctor's parting monition, and stopped the cornopean at once, notwithstanding the loud-voiced remonstrances from all sides; and the crowd scattered away from the close, the eleven all going into the School-house, where supper and beds were provided for them by the Doctor's orders.

Deep had been the consultations at supper as to the order of going in, who should bowl the first over, whether it would be best to play steady or freely; and the youngest hands declared that they shouldn't be a bit nervous, and praised their opponents as the jolliest fellows in the world, except perhaps their old friends the Wellesburn men. How far a little good-nature from their elders will go with the right sort of boys!

The morning had dawned bright and warm, to the intense relief of many an anxious youngster, up betimes to mark the signs of the weather. The eleven went down in a body before breakfast, for a plunge in the cold bath in the corner of the close. The ground was in splendid order, and soon after ten o'clock, before spectators had arrived, all was ready, and two of the Lords' men took their places at the wicket; the School, with the usual liberality of young hands, having put their adversaries in first. Old Bailey stepped up to the wicket, and called play, and the match has begun.

'Oh, well bowled! well bowled, Johnson!' cries the Captain, catching up the ball and sending it high above the rook trees, while the third Marylebone man walks away from the wicket, and old Bailey gravely sets up the middle stumps again and puts the bails on.

'How many runs?' Away scamper three boys to the scoring table, and are back again in a minute amongst the rest of the eleven, who are collected together in a knot between wicket. 'Only eighteen runs, and three wickets down!' 'Huzza, for old Rugby!' sings out Jack Raggles the long-stop, toughest and burliest of boys, commonly called 'Swiper Jack'; and forthwith stands on his head, and brandishes his legs in the air in triumph, till the next boy catches hold of his heels and throws him over on to his back.

'Steady there, don't be such an ass, Jack,' says the Captain, 'we haven't got the best wicket yet. Ah, look out now at cover-point,' adds he, as he sees a long-armed, bare-headed, slashing looking player coming to the wicket. 'And, Jack, mind your hits; he steals more runs than any man in England.'

And they all find that they have got their work to do now; the new comer's off-hitting is tremendous, and his running like a flash of lightning. He is never in his ground, except when his wicket is down. Nothing in the whole game so trying to boys; he has stolen three byes in the first ten minutes, and Jack Raggles is furious, and begins throwing over savagely to the further wicket, until he is sternly stopped by the Captain. It is all that young gentleman can do to keep his team steady, but he knows that everything depends on it, and faces his work bravely. The score creeps up to fifty, the boys begin to look blank, and the spectators, who are now mustering strong, are very silent. The ball flies off his bat to all parts of the field, and he gives no rest and no catches to any one. But cricket is full of glorious chances, and the goddess who presides over it loves to bring down the most skilful players. Johnson the young bowler is getting wild, and bowls a ball almost wide to the off; the batter steps out and cuts it beautifully to where cover-point is standing very deep, in fact almost off the ground. The ball comes skimming and twisting along about three feet from the ground; he rushes at it, and it sticks somehow or other in the fingers of his left hand, to the utter astonishment of himself and the whole field. Such a catch hasn't been made in the close for years, and the cheering is maddening. 'Pretty cricket,' says the Captain, throwing himself on the ground by the deserted wicket with a long breath; he feels that a crisis has passed.

I wish I had space to describe the whole match; how the Captain stumped the next man off a leg-shooter, and bowled slow cobs to old Mr Aislebie, who came in for the last wicket. How the Lords' men were out by half-past twelve o'clock for ninety-eight runs. How the Captain of the School eleven went in first to give his men pluck, and scored twenty-five in beautiful style; how Rugby was only four behind in the first innings. What a glorious dinner they had in the fourth-form School, and how the cover-point hitter sang the most topping comic songs, and old Mr Aislebie made the best speeches that ever were heard, afterwards. But I haven't space, that's the fact, and so you must fancy it all, and carry yourselves on to half-past seven o'clock, when the School are again in, with five wickets down and only thirty-two runs to make to win. The Marylebone men played carelessly in their second innings, but they are working like horses now to save the match.

There is much healthy, hearty, happy life scattered up and down the close; but the group to which I beg to call your special attention is there, on the slope of the island, which looks towards the cricket-ground. It consists of three figures; two are seated on a bench, and one on the ground at their feet. The first, a tall, slight, and rather gaunt man, with a bushy eyebrow, and a dry humorous smile, is evidently a clergyman. He is carelessly dressed, and looks rather used up, which isn't much to be wondered at, seeing that he has just finished six weeks of examination work; but there he basks, and spreads himself out in the evening sun, bent on enjoying life, though he doesn't quite know what to do with his arms and legs. Surely it is our friend the young Master, whom we have had glimpses of before, but his face has gained a great deal since we last came across him.

And by his side, in white flannel shirt and trousers, straw hat, the Captain's belt, and the untanned yellow cricket shoes, which all the eleven wear, sits a strapping figure, near six feet high, with ruddy tanned face and whiskers, curly brown hair, and a laughing dancing eye. He is leaning forward with his elbows resting on his knees, and dandling his favourite bat, with which he has made thirty or forty runs today, in his strong brown hands. It is Tom Brown, grown into a young man nineteen years old, a praepostor and captain of the eleven, spending his last day as a Rugby boy, and let us hope as much wiser as he is bigger, since we last had the pleasure of coming across him.

And at their feet on the warm dry ground, similarly dressed, sits Arthur, Turkish fashion, with his bat across his knees. He too is no longer a boy, less of a boy in fact than Tom, if one may judge from the thoughtfulness of his face, which is some-what paler too than one could wish; but his figure though slight is well knit and active, and all his old timidity has disappeared, and is replaced by silent quaint fun, with which his face twinkles all over, as he listens to the broken talk between the other two, in which he joins every now and then.

All three are watching the game eagerly, and joining in the cheering which follows every good hit. It is pleasing to see the easy friendly footing which the pupils are on with their master, perfectly respectful, yet with no reserve and nothing forced in their intercourse. Tom has clearly abandoned the old theory of 'natural enemies' in this case at any rate.

But it is time to listen to what they are saying, and see what we can gather out of it.

'I don't object to your theory,' says the master, 'and I allow you have made a fair case for yourself. But now, in such books as Aristophanes for instance, you've been reading a play this half with the Doctor, haven't you?'

'Yes, the Knights,' answered Tom.

'Well, I'm sure you would have enjoyed the wonderful humour of it twice as much if you had taken more pains with your scholarship.'

'Well, sir, I don't believe any boy in the form enjoyed the sets-to between Cleon and the Sausage-seller more than I did—eh, Arthur?' said Tom, giving him a stir with his foot.

'Yes I must say he did,' said Arthur. 'I think, sir, you've hit upon the wrong book there.'

'Not a bit of it,' said the master. 'Why, in those very passages of arms, how can you thoroughly appreciate them unless you are master of the weapons? and the weapons are the language which you, Brown, have never half worked at; and so, as I say, you must have lost all the delicate shades of meaning which make the best part of the fun.'

'Oh! well played—bravo, Johnson!' shouted Arthur, dropping his bat and clapping furiously, and Tom joined in with a 'bravo Johnson!' which might have been heard at the chapel.

'Eh! what was it? I didn't see,' inquired the master; 'they only got one run, I thought?'

'No, but such a ball, three-quarters length and coming straight for his leg bail. Nothing but that turn of the wrist could have saved him, and he drew it away to leg for a safe one. Bravo, Johnson!'

'How well they are bowling though,' said Arthur; 'they don't mean to be beat, I can see.'

'There now,' struck in the master, 'you see that's just what I have been preaching this half-hour. The delicate play is the true thing. I don't understand cricket, so I don't enjoy those fine draws which you tell me are the best play, though when you or Raggles hit a ball hard away for six I am as delighted as any one. Don't you see the analogy?'

'Yes, sir,' answered Tom, looking up roguishly, 'I see; only the question remains whether I should have got most good by understanding Greek particles or cricket thoroughly. I'm such a thick, I never should have had time for both.'

'I see you are an incorrigible,' said the master with a chuckle, 'but I refute you by an example. Arthur there has taken in Greek and cricket too.'

'Yes, but no thanks to him; Greek came natural to him. Why, when he first came I remember he used to read Herodotus for pleasure as I did Don Quixote, and couldn't have made a false

226

concord if he'd tried ever so hard—and then I looked after his cricket.'

'Out! Bailey has given him out—do you see, Tom?' cries Arthur. 'How foolish of them to run so hard.'

'Well, it can't be helped, he has played very well. Whose turn is it to go in?'

'I don't know; they've got your list in the tent.'

'Let's go and see,' said Tom, rising; but at this moment Jack Raggles and two or three more come running to the island moat.

'Oh, Brown, mayn't I go in next?' shouts the Swiper.

'Whose name is next on the list?' says the Captain.

'Winter's, and then Arthur's,' answers the boy who carries it; 'but there are only twenty-six runs to get, and no time to lose. I heard Mr Aislebie say that the stumps must be drawn at a quarter-past eight exactly.'

'Oh, do let the Swiper go in,' chorus the boys; so Tom yields against his better judgement.

'I daresay now I've lost the match by this nonsense,' he says as he sits down again; 'they'll be sure to get Jack's wicket in three or four minutes; however, you'll have the chance, sir, of seeing a hard hit or two,' adds he, smiling and turning to the master.

'Come, none of your irony, Brown,' answers the master. 'I'm beginning to understand the game scientifically. What a noble game it is too!'

'Isn't it? But it's more than a game. It's an institution,' said Tom.

'Yes,' said Arthur, 'the birthright of British boys old and young, as *habeas corpus* and trial by jury are of British men.'

'The discipline and reliance on one another which it teaches is so valuable, I think,' went on the master, 'it ought to be such an unselfish game. It merges the individual in the eleven; he doesn't play that he may win, but that his side may.'

'That's very true,' said Tom, 'And that's why football and cricket, now one comes to think of it, are such much better games than fives' or hare-and-hounds, or any others where the object is to come in first or to win for oneself, and not that one's side may win.'

'And then the Captain of the eleven!' said the master, 'what a post is his in our School-word! almost as hard as the Doctor's; requiring skill and gentleness and firmness, and I know not what other rare qualities.'

'Which don't he wish he may get?' said Tom laughing: 'at any rate he hasn't got them yet, or he wouldn't have been such a flat tonight as to let Jack Raggles go in out of his turn.'

'Ah! the Doctor never would have done that,' said Arthur, demurely. 'Tom, you've a great deal to learn yet in the art of ruling.'

'Well, I wish you'd tell the Doctor so, then, and get him to let me stop till I'm twenty. I don't want to leave, I'm sure.'

'What a sight it is,' broke in the master, 'the Doctor as a ruler. Perhaps ours is the only little corner of the British Empire which is thoroughly wisely and strongly ruled just now. I'm more and more thankful every day of my life that I came here to be under him.'

'So am I, I'm sure,' said Tom; 'and more and more sorry that I've got to leave.'

'Every place and thing one sees here reminds one of some wise act of his,' went on the master. 'This island now—you remember the time, Brown, when it was laid out in small gardens, and cultivated by frost-bitten fags in February and March?'

'Of course I do,' said Tom; 'didn't I hate spending two hours in the afternoons grubbing in the tough dirt with the stump of a fives' bat? But turf-cart was good fun enough.'

'I daresay it was, but it was always leading to fights with the townspeople; and then the stealing flowers out of all the gardens in Rugby for the Easter show was abominable.'

'Well, so it was,' said Tom, looking down, 'but we fags couldn't help ourselves. But what has that to do with the Doctor's ruling?'

'A great deal, I think,' said the master; 'what brought island-fagging to an end?'

'Why, the Easter Speeches were put off till Mid-summer,' said Tom, 'and the sixth had the gymnastic poles put up here.'

'Well, and who changed the time of the Speeches, and put the idea of gymnastic poles into the heads of their worships the sixth form?' said the master.

'The Doctor, I suppose,' said Tom. 'I never thought of that.'

'Of course you didn't,' said the master, 'or else, fag as you were, you would have shouted with the whole school against putting down old customs. And that's the way that all the Doctor's reforms have been carried out when he has been left to himself—quietly and naturally, putting a good thing in the place of a bad, and letting the bad die out; no wavering and no hurry—the best thing that could be done for the time being, and patience for the rest.'

'Just Tom's own way,' chimed in Arthur, nudging Tom with his elbow, 'driving a nail where it will go'; to which allusion Tom answered by a sly kick.

'Exactly so,' said the master, innocent of the allusion and bye-play.

Meantime Jack Raggles, with his sleeves tucked up above his great brown elbows, scorning pads and gloves, has presented himself at the wicket; and having run one for a forward drive of Johnson's, is about to receive his first ball. There are only twenty-four runs to make, and four wickets to go down, a winning match if they play decently steady. The ball is a very swift one, and rises fast, catching Jack on the outside of the thigh, and bounding away as if from india-rubber, while they run two for a leg-bye amidst great applause, and shouts from Jack's many admirers. The next ball is a beautifully pitched ball for the outer stump, which the reckless and unfeeling Jack catches hold of, and hits right round to leg for five, while the applause becomes deafening: only seventeen runs to get with four wickets—the game is all but ours!

It is over now, and Jack walks swaggering about his wicket, with the bat over his shoulder, while Mr Aislebie holds a short parley with his men. Then the cover-point hitter, that cunning man, goes on to bowl slow twisters. Jack waves his hand triumphantly towards the tent, as much as to say, 'See if I don't finish it all off now in three hits.'

Alas, my son Jack! the enemy is too old for thee. The first ball of the over Jack steps out and meets, swiping with all his force. If he had only allowed for the twist! but he hasn't, and so the ball goes spinning up straight into the air, as if it would never come down again. Away runs Jack, shouting and trusting to the chapter of accidents, but the bowler runs steadily under it, judging every spin, and calling out 'I have it,' catches it, and playfully pitches it on to the back of the stalwart Jack, who is departing with a rueful countenance.

'I knew how it would be,' says Tom, rising. 'Come along, the game's getting very serious.'

So they leave the island and go to the tent, and after deep consultation Arthur is sent in, and goes off to the wicket with a last exhortation from Tom, to play steady and keep his bat straight.

To the suggestions that Winter is the best bat left, Tom only replies, 'Arthur is the steadiest, and Johnson will make the runs if the wicket is only kept up.'

'I am surprised to see Arthur in the eleven,' said the master, as they stood together in front of the dense crowd, which was now closing in round the ground.

'Well, I'm not quite sure that he ought to be in for his play,' said Tom, 'but I couldn't help putting him in. It will do him so much good, and you can't think what I owe him.'

The master smiled. The clock strikes eight, and the whole field becomes fevered with excitement. Arthur, after two narrow escapes, scores one; and Johnson gets the ball. The bowling and fielding are superb, and Johnson's batting worthy the occasion. He makes here a two and there a one, managing to keep the ball to himself, and Arthur backs up and runs perfectly: only eleven runs to make now, and the crowd scarcely breathe. At last Arthur gets the ball again, and actually drives it forward for two, and feels prouder than when he got the three best prizes, at hearing Tom's shout of joy, 'Well played, well played, young 'un!'

But the next ball is too much for a young hand, and his bails fly different ways. Nine runs to make, and two wickets to go down—it is too much for human nerves.

Before Winter can get in, the omnibus which is to take the Lords' men to the train pulls up at the side of the close, and Mr Aislebie and Tom consult, and give out that the stumps will be drawn after the next over. And so ends the great match. Winter and Johnson carry out their bats, and, it being a one day's match, the Lords' men are declared the winners, they having scored the most in the first innings.

But such a defeat is a victory: so think Tom and all the School eleven, as they accompany their conquerors to the omnibus, and send them off with three ringing cheers, after Mr Aislebie has shaken hands all round, saying to Tom, 'I must compliment you, sir, on your eleven, and I hope we shall have you for a member if you come up to town.'

As Tom and the rest of the eleven were turning back into the close, and everybody was beginning to cry out for another country dance, encouraged by the success of the night before, the young master, who was just leaving the close, stopped him, and asked him to come up to tea at half-past eight, adding, 'I won't keep you more than half-an-hour, and ask Arthur to come up too.'

'I'll come up with you directly if you'll let me,' said Tom, 'for I feel rather melancholy, and not quite up to the country dance and supper with the rest.'

'Do by all means,' said the master; 'I'll wait here for you.'

So Tom went off to get his boots and things from the tent, to tell Arthur of the invitation, and to speak to his second in command about stopping the dancing and shutting up the close as soon as it grew dusk. Arthur promised to follow as soon as he had had a dance. So Tom handed his things over to the man in charge of the tent, and walked quietly away to the gate where the master was waiting, and the two took their way together up the Hill-morton road.

Of course they found the master's house locked up, and all the servants away in the close, about this time no doubt footing it away on the grass with extreme delight to themselves, and in utter oblivion of the unfortunate bachelor their master, whose one enjoyment in the shape of meals was his 'dish of tea' (as our grandmothers called it) in the evening; and the phrase was apt in his case, for he always poured his out into the saucer before drinking. Great was the good man's horror at finding himself shut out of his own house. Had he been alone he would have treated it as a matter of course, and would have strolled contentedly up and down his gravel-walk until some one came home; but he was hurt at the stain on his character of host, especially as the guest was a pupil. However, the guest seemed to think it a great joke, and presently, as they poked about round the house, mounted a wall from which he could reach a passage window: the window, as it turned out, was not bolted, so in another minute Tom was in the house and down at the front door, which he opened from inside. The master chuckled grimly at this burglarious entry, and insisted on leaving the hall-door and two of the front windows open, to frighten the truants on their return; and then the two set about foraging for tea, in which operation the master was much at fault, having the faintest possible idea of where to find anything, and being moreover wondrously short-sighted; but Tom by a sort of instinct knew the right cupboards in the kitchen and pantry, and soon managed to place on the snuggery table better materials for a meal than had appeared there probably during the reign of his tutor, who was then and there initiated, amongst other things, into the excellence of that mysterious condiment, a dripping cake. The cake was newly baked, and all rich and flaky; Tom had found it reposing in the cook's private cupboard, awaiting her return; and as a warning to her they finished it to the last crumb. The kettle sang away merrily on the hob of the snuggery, for, notwithstanding the time of year, they lighted a fire, throwing both the windows wide open at the same time; the heap of books and papers were pushed away to the other end of the table, and the great solitary engraving of King's College Chapel over the mantel-piece looked less stiff than usual, as they settled themselves down in the twilight to the serious drinking of tea.

After some talk on the match, and other indifferent subjects, the conversation came naturally back to Tom's approaching departure, over which he began again to make his moan.

'Well, we shall all miss you quite as much as you will miss us,' said the master. 'You are the Nestor of the School now, are you not?'

'Yes, ever since East left,' answered Tom.

'Bye-the-bye, have you heard from him?'

'Yes, I had a letter in February, just before he started for India to join his regiment.'

'He will make a capital officer.'

'Aye, won't he!' said Tom, brightening; 'no fellow could handle boys better, and I suppose soldiers are very like boys. And he'll never tell them to go where he won't go himself. No mistake about that—a braver fellow never walked.'

'His year in the sixth will have taught him a good deal that will be useful to him now.'

'So it will,' said Tom, staring into the fire. 'Poor dear Harry,' he went on, 'how well I remember the day we were put out of the twenty. How he rose to the situation, and burnt his cigar-cases, and gave away his pistols, and pondered on the constitutional authority of the sixth, and his new duties to the Doctor, and the fifth form, and the fags. Aye, and no fellow ever acted up to them better, though he was always a people's man—for the fags, and against constituted authorities. He couldn't help that, you know. I'm sure the Doctor must have liked him?' said Tom, looking up inquiringly.

'The Doctor sees the good in every one, and appreciates it,' said the master dogmatically; 'but I hope East will get a good colonel.

He won't do if he can't respect those above him. How long it took him even here, to learn the lesson of obeying.'

'Well, I wish I were alongside of him,' said Tom. 'If I can't be at Rugby I want to be at work in the world, and not dawdling away three years at Oxford.'

'What do you mean by "at work in the world"?' said the master, pausing, with his lips close to his saucerful of tea, and peering at Tom over it.

'Well, I mean real work; one's profession; whatever one will have really to do, and make one's living by. I want to be doing some real good, feeling that I am not only at play in the world,' answered Tom, rather puzzled to find out himself what he really did mean.

'You are mixing up two very different things in your head, I think, Brown,' said the master, putting down his empty saucer, 'and you ought to get clear about them. You talk of "working to get your living," and "doing some real good in the world," in the same breath. Now you may be getting a very good living in a profession, and yet doing no good at all in the world, but quite the contrary, at the same time. Keep the latter before you as your one object, and you will be right, whether you make a living or not; but if you dwell on the other, you'll very likely drop into mere money-making, and let the world take care of itself for good or evil. Don't be in a hurry about finding your work in the world for yourself; you are not old enough to judge for yourself yet, but just look about you in the place you find yourself in, and try to make things a little better and honester there. You'll find plenty to keep your hand in at Oxford, or wherever else you go. And don't be led away to think this part of the world important, and that unimportant. Every corner of the world is important. No man knows whether this part or that is most so, but every man may do some honest work in his own corner.' And then the good man went on to talk wisely to Tom of the sort of work which he might take up as an undergraduate; and warned him of the prevalent University sins, and explained to him the many and great differences between University and School life; till the twilight changed into darkness, and they heard the truant servants stealing in by the back entrance.

'I wonder where Arthur can be,' said Tom at last, looking at his watch; 'why, it's nearly half-past nine already.'

'Oh, he is comfortably at supper with the eleven, forgetful of his oldest friends,' said the master. 'Nothing has given me greater pleasure,' he went on, 'than your friendship for him, it has been the making of you both.'

'Of me, at any rate,' answered Tom; 'I should never have been here now but for him. It was the luckiest chance in the world that sent him to Rugby, and made him my chum.'

'Why do you talk of lucky chances?' said the master; 'I don't know that there are any such things in the world; at any rate there was neither luck nor chance in that matter.'

Tom looked at him inquiringly, and he went on. 'Do you remember when the Doctor lectured you and East at the end of one half-year, when you were in the shell, and had been getting into all sorts of scrapes?'

'Yes, well enough,' said Tom, 'it was the half-year before Arthur came.'

'Exactly so,' answered the master. 'Now I was with him a few minutes afterwards, and he was in great distress about you two. And, after some talk, we both agreed that you in particular wanted some object in the School beyond games and mischief, for it was quite clear that you never would make the regular school work your first object. And so the Doctor, at the beginning of the next half-year, looked out the best of the new boys, and separated you and East, and put the young boy into your study, in the hope that when you had somebody to lean on you, you would begin to stand a little steadier yourself, and get manliness and thoughtfulness. And I can assure you, he has watched the experiment ever since with great satisfaction. Ah! not one of you boys will ever know the anxiety you have given him, or the care with which he has watched over every step in your school lives.'

Up to this time Tom had never wholly given in to, or understood the Doctor. At first he had thoroughly feared him. For some years, as I have tried to show, he had learnt to regard him with love and respect, and to think him a very great and wise and good man. But, as regarded his own position in the School, of which he was no little proud, Tom had no idea of giving any one credit for it but himself; and, truth to tell, was a very self-conceited young gentleman on the subject. He was wont to boast that he had fought his own way fairly up the School, and had never made up to, or been taken up by any big fellow or master, and that it was now quite a different place from what it was when he first came. And indeed, though he didn't actually boast of it, yet in his secret soul he did to a great extent believe, that the great reform in the School had been owing quite as much to himself as to any one else. Arthur, he acknowledged, had done him good, and taught him a good deal, so had other boys in different ways; but they had not had the same means of influence on the School in general; and as for the Doctor, why he was a splendid master; but every one knew that masters could do very little out of school hours. In short, he felt on terms of equality with his chief, so far as the social state of the School was concerned, and thought that the Doctor would find it no easy matter to get on without him. Moreover, his school Toryism was still strong, and he looked still with some jealousy on the Doctor, as somewhat of a fanatic in the matter of change; and thought it very desirable for the School that he should have some wise person (such as himself) to look sharply after vested School-rights, and see that nothing was done to the injury of the republic without due protest.

It was a new light to him to find, that besides teaching the sixth, and governing and guiding the whole School, editing classics, and writing histories, the great Head-master had found time in those busy years to watch over the career, even of him, Tom Brown, and his particular friends—and, no doubt, of fifty other boys at the same time; and all this without taking the least credit to himself, or seeming to know, or let any one else know, that he ever thought particularly of any boy at all.

However, the Doctor's victory was complete from that moment over Tom Brown at any rate. He gave way at all points, and the enemy marched right over him, cavalry, infantry, and artillery, the land transport corps, and the camp followers. It had taken eight long years to do it, but now it was done thoroughly, and there wasn't a corner of him left which didn't believe in the Doctor. Had he returned to school again, and the Doctor begun the half-year by abolishing fagging, and football, and the Saturday half-holiday, or all or any of the most cherished school institutions, Tom would have supported him with the blindest faith. And so, after a half confession of his previous short comings, and sorrowful adieus to his tutor, from whom he received two beautifully-bound volumes of the Doctor's Sermons as a parting present, he marched down to the School-house, a hero-worshipper, who would have satisfied the soul of Thomas Carlyle himself.

There he found the eleven at high jinks after supper, Jack Raggles shouting comic songs, and performing feats of strength; and was greeted by a chorus of mingled remonstrance at his desertion, and joy at his reappearance. And falling in with the humour of the evening, was soon as great a boy as all the rest; and at ten o'clock was chaired round the quadrangle, on one of the hall benches borne aloft by the eleven, shouting in chorus, 'For he's a jolly good fellow,' while old Thomas in a melting mood, and the other Schoolhouse servants stood looking on.

And the next morning after breakfast he squared up all the cricketing accounts, went round to his tradesmen and other acquaintances, and said his hearty good-byes; and by twelve o'clock was in the train, and away for London, no longer a schoolboy, and divided in his thoughts between hero-worship, honest regrets over the long stage of his life which was now slipping out of sight behind him, and hopes and resolves for the next stage, upon which he was entering with all the confidence of a young traveller.

CHAPTER 9

FINIS

'Strange friend, past, present, and to be:
Loved deeplier, darklier understood;
Behold, I dream a dream of good,
And mingle all the world with thee.'
TENNYSON

In the summer of 1842, our hero stopped once again at the well-known station; and, leaving his bag and fishing-rod with a porter, walked slowly and sadly up towards the town. It was now July. He had rushed away from Oxford the moment that term was over, for a fishing ramble in Scotland with two college friends, and had been for three weeks living on oatcake, mutton-hams, and whiskey, in the wildest parts of Skye. They had descended one sultry evening on the little inn at Kyle Rhea ferry, and while Tom and another of the party put their tackle together and began exploring the stream for a sea-trout for supper, the third strolled into the house to arrange for their entertainment. Presently he came out in a loose blouse and slippers, a short pipe in his mouth, and an old newspaper in his hand, and threw himself on the heathery scrub which met the shingle, within easy hail of the fishermen. There he lay, the picture of free-and-easy, loafing, hand-to-mouth young England, 'improving his mind,' as he shouted to them, by the perusal of the fortnight-old weekly paper, soiled with the marks of toddy-glasses and tobacco ashes, the legacy of the last traveller, which he had hunted out from the kitchen of the little hostelry, and being a youth of a communicative turn of mind, began imparting the contents to the fishermen as he went on.

'What a bother they are making about these wretched corn laws; here's three or four columns full of nothing but sliding scales and fixed duties.—Hang this tobacco, it's always going out!—Ah, here's something better—a splendid match between Kent and England, Brown! Kent winning by three wickets. Felix fifty-six runs without a chance, and not out!'

Tom, intent on a fish which had risen at him twice, answered only with a grunt.

'Anything about the Goodwood?' called out the third man.

'Rory-o-more drawn. Butterfly colt amiss,' shouted the student.

'Just my luck,' grumbled the inquirer, jerking his flies off the water, and throwing again with a heavy sullen splash, and frightening Tom's fish.

'I say, can't you throw lighter over there? we ain't fishing for grampuses,' shouted Tom across the stream.

'Hullo, Brown! here's something for you,' called out the reading man next moment. 'Why, your old master, Arnold of Rugby, is dead.'

Tom's hand stopped half-way in his cast, and his line and flies went all tangling round and round his rod; you might have knocked him over with a feather. Neither of his companions took any notice of him luckily; and with a violent effort he set to work mechanically to disentangle his line. He felt completely carried off his moral and intellectual legs, as if he had lost his standing-point in the invisible world besides which, the deep loving loyalty which he felt for his old leader made the shock intensely painful. It was the first great wrench of his life, the first gap which the angel Death had made in his circle, and he felt numbed, and beaten down, and spiritless. Well, well! I believe it was good for him and for many others in like case; who had to learn by that loss, that the soul of man cannot stand or lean upon any human prop, however strong, and wise, and good; but, that He upon whom alone it can stand and lean will knock away all such props in His own wise and merciful way, until there is no ground or stay left but Himself, the Rock of Ages, upon whom alone a sure foundation for every soul of man is laid.

As he wearily laboured at his line, the thought struck him, 'It may all be false, a mere newspaper lie,' and he strode up to the recumbent smoker.

'Let me look at the paper,' said he.

'Nothing else in it,' answered the other, handing it up to him listlessly—'Hullo, Brown! what's the matter, old fellow—ain't you well?'

'Where is it?' said Tom, turning over the leaves, his hands trembling, and his eyes swimming, so that he could not read.

'What? What are you looking for?' said his friend, jumping up and looking over his shoulder.

'That—about Arnold,' said Tom.

'Oh here,' said the other, putting his finger on the paragraph. Tom read it over and over again; there could be no mistake of identity, though the account was short enough.

'Thank you,' said he at last, dropping the paper. 'I shall go for a walk: don't you and Herbert wait supper for me.' And away he strode, up over the moor at the back of the house, to be alone, and master his grief if possible.

His friend looked after him, sympathizing and wondering, and knocking the ashes out of his pipe, walked over to Herbert. After a short parley they walked together up to the house.

'I'm afraid that confounded newspaper has spoiled Brown's fun for this trip.'

'How odd that he should be so fond of his old master,' said Herbert. Yet they also were both public-school men.

The two, however, notwithstanding Tom's prohibition, waited supper for him, and had everything ready when he came back some half-an-hour afterwards. But he could not join in their cheerful talk, and the party was soon silent, notwithstanding the efforts of all three. One thing only had Tom resolved, and that was that he couldn't stay in Scotland any longer; he felt an irresistible longing to get to Rugby, and then home, and soon broke it to the others, who had too much tact to oppose.

So by daylight the next morning he was marching through Ross-shire, and in the evening hit the Caledonian canal, took the next steamer, and travelled as fast as boat and railway could carry him to the Rugby station.

As he walked up to the town he felt shy and afraid of being seen, and took the back streets; why, he didn't know, but he followed his instinct. At the School-gates he made a dead pause; there was not a soul in the quadrangle—all was lonely, and silent, and sad. So with another effort he strode through the quadrangle, and into the School-house offices.

He found the little matron in her room in deep mourning; shook her hand, tried to talk, and moved nervously about; she was evidently thinking of the same subject as he, but he couldn't begin talking.

'Where shall I find Thomas?' said he at last, getting desperate.

'In the servants' hall, I think, sir. But won't you take anything?' said the matron, looking rather disappointed.

'No, thank you,' said he, and strode off again to find the old Verger, who was sitting in his little den as of old, puzzling over hieroglyphics.

He looked up through his spectacles, as Tom seized his hand and wrung it.

'Ah! you've heard all about it, sir, I see,' said he.

Tom nodded, and then sat down on the shoe-board, while the old man told his tale, and wiped his spectacles, and fairly flowed over with quaint, homely, honest sorrow.

By the time he had done Tom felt much better.

'Where is he buried, Thomas?' said he at last.

'Under the altar in the chapel, sir,' answered Thomas. 'You'd like to have the key, I daresay.'

'Thank you, Thomas—Yes, I should very much.' And the old man fumbled among his bunch, and then got up, as though he would go with him; but after a few steps stopped short, and said, 'Perhaps you'd like to go by yourself, sir?'

Tom nodded, and the bunch of keys were handed to him, with an injunction to be sure and lock the door after him, and bring them back before eight o'clock.

He walked quickly through the quadrangle and out into the close. The longing which had been upon him and driven him thus far, like the gad-fly in the Greek legends, giving him no rest in mind or body, seemed all of a sudden not to be satisfied, but to shrivel up, and pall. 'Why should I go on? It's no use,' he thought, and threw himself at full length on the turf, and looked vaguely and listlessly at all the well-known objects. There were a few of the town boys playing cricket, their wicket pitched on the best piece in the middle of the big-side ground, a sin about equal to sacrilege in the eyes of a captain of the eleven. He was very nearly getting up to go and send them off. 'Pshaw! they won't remember me. They've more right there than I,' he muttered. And the thought that his sceptre had departed, and his mark was wearing out, came home to him for the first time, and bitterly enough. He was lying on the very spot where the fights came off; where he himself had fought six years ago his first and last battle. He conjured up the scene till he could almost hear the shouts of the ring, and East's whisper in his ear; and looking across the close to the Doctor's private door, half expected to see it open, and the tall figure in cap and gown come striding under the elm-trees towards him.

No, no! that sight could never be seen again. There was no flag flying on the round tower; the School-house windows were all shuttered up: and when the flag went up again, and the shutters came down, it would be to welcome a stranger. All that was left on earth of him whom he had honoured, was lying cold and still under the chapel floor. He would go in and see the place once more, and then leave it once for all. New men and new methods might do for other people; let those who would worship the rising star, he at least would be faithful to the sun which had set. And so he got up, and walked to the chapel door and unlocked it, fancying himself the only mourner in all the broad land, and feeding on his own selfish sorrow.

He passed through the vestibule, and then paused for a moment to glance over the empty benches. His heart was still proud and high, and he walked up to the seat which he had last occupied as a sixth-form boy, and sat himself down there to collect his thoughts.

And, truth to tell, they needed collecting and setting in order not a little. The memories of eight years were all dancing through his brain, and carrying him about whither they would; while beneath them all, his heart was throbbing with the dull sense of a loss that could never be made up to him. The rays of the evening sun came solemnly through the painted windows above his head and fell in gorgeous colours on the opposite wall, and the perfect stillness soothed his spirit by little and little. And he turned to the pulpit, and looked at it, and then leaning forward with his head on his hands, groaned aloud. 'If he could only have seen the Doctor again for one five minutes, to have told him all that was in his heart, what he owed to him, how he loved and reverenced him, and would by God's help follow his steps in life and death, he could have borne it all without a murmur. But that he should have gone away for ever without knowing it all, was too much to bear'—'But am I sure that he does not know it all?'—the thought made him start—'May he not even now be near me, in this very chapel? If he be, am I sorrowing as he would have me sorrow—as I shall wish to have sorrowed when I shall meet him again?'

He raised himself up and looked round; and after a minute rose and walked humbly down to the lowest bench, and sat down on the very seat which he had occupied on his first Sunday at Rugby. And then the old memories rushed back again, but softened and subdued, and soothing him as he let himself be carried away by them. And he looked up at the great painted window above the altar, and remembered how when a little boy he used to try not to look through it at the elm-trees and the rooks, before the painted glass came—and the subscription for the painted glass, and the letter he wrote home for money to give to it. And there, down below, was the very name of the boy who sat on his right hand on that first day, scratched rudely in the oak panelling.

And then came the thought of all his old school-fellows; and form after form of boys, nobler, and braver, and purer than he, rose up and seemed to rebuke him. Could he not think of them, and what they had felt and were feeling, they who had honoured and loved from the first, the man whom he had taken years to know and love? Could he not think of those yet dearer to him who was gone, who bore his name and shared his blood, and were now without a husband or a father? Then the grief which he began to share with others became gentle and holy, and he rose up once more, and walked up the steps to the altar; and while the tears flowed freely down his cheeks, knelt down humbly and hopefully, to lay down there his share of a burden which had proved itself too heavy for him to bear in his own strength.

Here let us leave him—where better could we leave him, than at the altar, before which he had first caught a glimpse of the glory of his birthright, and felt the drawing of the bond which links all living souls together in one brotherhood—at the grave beneath the altar of him, who had opened his eyes to see that glory, and softened his heart till it could feel that bond.

And let us not be hard on him, if at that moment his soul is fuller of the tomb and him who lies there, than of the altar and Him of whom it speaks. Such stages have to be gone through, I believe, by all young and brave souls, who must win their way through hero-worship, to the worship of Him who is the King and Lord of heroes. For it is only through our mysterious human relationships, through the love and tenderness and purity of mothers, and sisters, and wives, through the strength and courage and wisdom of fathers, and brothers, and teachers, that we can come to the knowledge of Him, in whom alone the love, and the tenderness, and the purity, and the strength, and the courage, and the wisdom of all these dwell for ever and ever in perfect fulness.

The Call of the Wild

JACK LONDON

The Call
of the Wild

PARRAGON

The Call of the Wild
A Parragon Classic

This is a Siena Book
Siena is an imprint of Parragon

First published in 1903

This edition published in 1999 by
Parragon
13 Whiteladies Road
Clifton
Bristol BS8 1PB

Printed and bound in the UK

CHAPTER 1

INTO THE PRIMITIVE

Old longings nomadic leap,
  Chafing at custom's chain;
Again from its brumal sleep
  Wakens the ferine strain

Buck did not read the newspapers, or he would have known that trouble was brewing, not alone for himself, but for every tide-water dog, strong of muscle and with warm, long hair, from Puget Sound to San Diego. Because men, groping in the Arctic darkness, had found a yellow metal, and because steamship and transportation companies were booming the find, thousands of men were rushing into the Northland. These men wanted dogs, and the dogs they wanted were heavy dogs, with strong muscles by which to toil, and furry coats to protect them from the frost.

Buck lived at a big house in the sun-kissed Santa Clara Valley. Judge Miller's place, it was called. It stood back from the road, half hidden among the trees, through which glimpses could be caught of the wide cool veranda that ran around its four sides. The house was approached by gravelled driveways which wound about through wide-spreading lawns and under the interlacing boughs of tall poplars. At the rear things were on even a more spacious scale than at the front. There were great stables, where a dozen grooms and boys held forth, rows of vine-clad servants' cottages, an

5

endless and orderly array of outhouses, long grape arbours, green pastures, orchards, and berry patches. Then there was the pumping plant for the artesian well, and the big cement tank where Judge Miller's boys took their morning plunge and kept cool in the hot afternoon.

And over this great demesne Buck ruled. Here he was born, and here he had lived the four years of his life. It was true, there were other dogs. There could not but be other dogs on so vast a place, but they did not count. They came and went, resided in the populous kennels, or lived obscurely in the recesses of the house after the fashion of Toots, the Japanese pug, or Ysabel, the Mexican hairless—strange creatures that rarely put nose out of doors or set foot to ground. On the other hand, there were the fox terriers, a score of them at least, who yelped fearful promises at Toots and Ysabel looking out of the windows at them and protected by a legion of housemaids armed with brooms and mops.

But Buck was neither house-dog nor kennel-dog. The whole realm was his. He plunged into the swimming tank or went hunting with the Judge's sons; he escorted Mollie and Alice, the Judge's daughters, on long twilight or early morning rambles; on wintry nights he lay at the Judge's feet before the roaring library fire; he carried the Judge's grandsons on his back, or rolled them in the grass, and guarded their footsteps through wild adventures down to the fountain in the stable yard, and even beyond, where the paddocks were, and the berry patches. Among the terriers he stalked imperiously, and Toots and Ysabel he utterly ignored, for he was king— king over all creeping, crawling, flying things of Judge Miller's place, humans included.

His father, Elmo, a huge St. Bernard, had been the Judge's inseparable companion, and Buck did fair to follow in the way of his father. He was not so large—he weighed only one hundred and forty pounds—for his mother, Shep, had been a Scotch shepherd dog. Nevertheless, one hundred and forty pounds, to which was added the dignity that comes of good living and universal respect, enabled him to carry himself in right royal fashion. During the four years since his puppyhood he had lived the life of a sated aristocrat; he had a fine pride in himself, was ever a trifle egotistical, as country gentlemen sometimes become because of their insular situation. But he had saved himself by not becoming a mere pampered house-dog. Hunting and kindred outdoor delights had kept down the fat and hardened his muscles; and to him, as to the cold-tubbing races, the love of water had been a tonic and a health preserver.

And this was the manner of dog Buck in the fall of 1897, when the Klondike strike dragged men from all the world into the frozen North. But Buck did not read the newspapers, and he did not know that Manuel, one of the gardener's helpers, was an undesirable acquaintance. Manuel had one besetting sin. He loved to play Chinese lottery. Also, in his gambling, he had one besetting weakness—faith in a system; and this made his damnation certain. For to play a system requires money, while the wages of a gardener's helper do not lap over the needs of a wife and numerous progeny.

The Judge was at a meeting of the Raisin Growers' Association, and the boys were busy organizing an athletic club, on the memorable night of Manuel's treachery. No one saw him and Buck go off through the orchard on what Buck imagined was merely a stroll. And with the exception of a solitary man, no one saw them arrive at the little flag station known as College Park. This man talked with Manuel, and money chinked between them.

'You might wrap up the goods before you deliver 'm,' the stranger said gruffly, and Manuel doubled a piece of stout rope around Buck's neck under the collar.

'Twist it, an' you'll choke 'm plentee,' said Manuel, and the stranger grunted a ready affirmative.

Buck had accepted the rope with quiet dignity. To be sure, it was an unwonted performance: but he had learned to trust in men he knew, and to give them credit for a wisdom that outreached his own. But when the ends of the rope were placed in the stranger's hands, he growled menacingly. He had merely intimated his displeasure, in his pride believing that to intimate was to command. But to his surprise the rope tightened around his neck, shutting off his breath. In quick rage he sprang at the man, who met him halfway, grappled him close by the throat, and with a deft twist threw him over on his back. Then the rope tightened mercilessly, while Buck struggled in a fury, his tongue lolling out of his mouth and his great chest panting futilely. Never in all his life had he been so vilely treated, and never in all his life had he been so angry. But his strength ebbed, his eyes glazed, and he knew nothing when the train was flagged and the two men threw him into the baggage car.

The next he knew, he was dimly aware that his tongue was hurting and that he was being jolted along in some kind of a conveyance. The hoarse shriek of a locomotive whistling a crossing told him where he was. He had travelled too often with the Judge not to know the sensation of riding in a baggage car. He opened his eyes, and into them came the unbridled anger of a kidnapped king. The man sprang for his throat, but Buck was too quick for him. His jaws closed on the hand, nor did they relax till his senses were choked out of him once more.

'Yep, has fits,' the man said, hiding his mangled hand from the baggageman, who had been attracted by the sounds of struggle. "I'm takin' 'm up for the boss to 'Frisco. A crack dog-doctor there thinks that he can cure 'm.'

Concerning that night's ride, the man spoke most eloquently for himself, in a little shed back of a saloon on the San Francisco water front.

'All I get is fifty for it,' he grumbled; 'an' I wouldn't do it over for a thousand, cold cash.'

His hand was wrapped in a bloody handkerchief, and the right trouser leg was ripped from knee to ankle.

'How much did the other mug get?' the saloon-keeper demanded.

'A hundred,' was the reply. 'Wouldn't take a sou less, so help me.'

'That makes a hundred and fifty,' the saloon-keeper calculated; 'and he's worth it, or I'm a squarehead.'

The kidnapper undid the bloody wrappings and looked at his lacerated hand. 'If I don't get the hydrophoby—'

'It'll be because you was born to hang,' laughed the saloon-keeper. 'Here, lend me a hand before you pull your freight,' he added.

Dazed, suffering intolerable pain from throat and tongue, with the life half throttled out of him, Buck attempted to face his tormentors. But he was thrown down and choked repeatedly, till they succeeded in filing the heavy brass collar from off his neck. Then the rope was removed, and he was flung into a cagelike crate.

There he lay for the remainder of the weary night, nursing his wrath and wounded pride. He could not understand what it all meant. What did they want with him, these strange men? Why were they keeping him pent up in this narrow crate? He did not know why, but he felt oppressed by the vague sense of impending calamity. Several times during the night he sprang to his feet when the shed door rattled open, expecting to see the Judge, or the boys at least. But each time it was the bulging face of the saloon-keeper that peered in at him by the sickly light of a tallow candle. And each time the joyful bark that trembled in Buck's throat was twisted into a savage growl.

But the saloon-keeper let him alone, and in the morning four men entered and picked up the crate. More tormentors, Buck decided, for they were evil-looking creatures, ragged and unkempt; and he stormed and raged at them through the bars. They only laughed and poked sticks at him, which he promptly assailed with his teeth till he realized that that was what they wanted. Whereupon he lay down sullenly and allowed the crate to be lifted into a wagon. Then, he, and the crate in which he was imprisoned, began a passage through many hands. Clerks in the express office took charge of him; he was carted about in another wagon; a truck carried him, with an assortment of boxes and parcels, upon a ferry steamer; he was trucked off the steamer into a great railway depot, and finally he was deposited in an express car.

For two days and nights this express car was dragged along at the tail of shrieking locomotives; and for two days and nights Buck neither ate nor drank. In his anger he had met the first advances of the express messengers with growls, and they had retaliated by teasing him. When he flung himself against the bars, quivering and frothing, they laughed at him and taunted him. They growled and barked like detestable dogs, mewed, and flapped their arms and crowed. It was all very silly, he knew; but therefore the more outrage to his dignity, and his anger waxed and waxed. He did not mind the hunger so much, but the lack of water caused him severe suffering and fanned his wrath to fever-pitch. For that matter, high-strung and finely sensitive, the ill treatment had flung him into a fever, which was fed by the inflammation of his parched and swollen throat and tongue.

He was glad for one thing: the rope was off his neck. That had given them an unfair advantage; but now that it was off, he would show them. They would never get another rope around his neck. Upon that he was resolved. For two days and nights he neither ate nor drank, and during those two days and nights of torment, he accumulated a fund of wrath that boded ill for whoever first fell foul of him. His eyes turned blood-shot, and he was metamorphosed into a raging fiend. So changed was he that the Judge himself would not have recognized him; and the express messengers breathed with relief when they bundled him off the train at Seattle.

Four men gingerly carried the crate from the wagon into a small, high-walled back yard. A stout man, with a red sweater that sagged generously at the neck, came out and signed the book for the driver. That was the man, Buck divined, the next tormentor, and he hurled himself savagely against the bars. The man smiled grimly, and brought a hatchet and a club.

'You ain't going to take him out now?' the driver asked.

'Sure,' the man replied, driving the hatchet into the crate for a pry.

There was an instantaneous scattering of the four men who had carried it in, and from safe perches on top the wall they prepared to watch the performance.

Buck rushed at the splintering wood, sinking his teeth into it, surging and wrestling with it. Wherever the hatchet fell on the outside, he was there on the inside, snarling and growling, as furiously anxious to get out as the man in the red sweater was calmly intent on getting him out.

"Now, you red-eyed devil," he said, when he had made an opening sufficient for the passage of Buck's body. At the same time he dropped the hatchet and shifted the club to his right hand.

And Buck was truly a red-eyed devil, as he drew himself together for the spring, hair bristling, mouth foaming, a mad glitter in his blood-shot eyes. Straight at the man he launched his one hundred and forty pounds of fury, surcharged with the pent passion of two days and nights. In mid air, just as his jaws were about to close on the man, he received a shock that checked his body and brought his teeth together with an agonizing clip. He whirled over, fetching the ground on his back and side. He had never been struck by a club in his life, and did not understand. With a snarl that was part bark and more scream he was again on his feet and launched into the air. And again the shock came and he was brought crushingly to the ground. This time he was aware that it was the club, but his madness knew no caution. A dozen times he charged, and as often the club broke the charge and smashed him down.

After a particularly fierce blow, he crawled to his feet, too dazed to rush. He staggered limply about, the blood flowing from nose and mouth and ears, his beautiful coat sprayed and flecked with bloody slaver. Then the man advanced and deliberately dealt him a frightful blow on the nose. All the pain he had endured was as nothing compared with the exquisite agony of this. With a roar that was almost lionlike in its ferocity, he again hurled himself at the man. But the man, shifting the club from right to left, coolly caught him by the under jaw, at the same time wrenching downward and backward. Buck described a complete circle in the air, and half of another, then crashed to the ground on his head and chest.

For the last time he rushed. The man struck the shrewd blow he had purposely withheld for so long, and Buck crumpled up and went down, knocked utterly senseless.

'He's no slouch at dog-breakin', that's wot I say,' one of the men on the wall cried enthusiastically.

13

'Druther break cayuses any day, and twice on Sundays,' was the reply of the driver, as he climbed on the wagon and started the horses.

Buck's senses came back to him, but not his strength. He lay where he had fallen, and from there he watched the man in the red sweater.

'"Answers to the name of Buck,'" the man soliloquized, quoting from the saloon-keeper's letter which had announced the consignment of the crate and contents. 'Well, Buck, my boy,' he went on in a genial voice, 'we've had our little ruction, and the best thing we can do is to let it go at that. You've learned your place, and I know mine. Be a good dog and all 'll go well and the goose hang high. Be a bad dog, and I'll whale the stuffin' outa you. Understand?'

As he spoke he fearlessly patted the head he had so mercilessly pounded, and though Buck's hair involuntarily bristled at touch of the hand, he endured it without protest. When the man brought him water he drank eagerly, and later bolted a generous meal of raw meat, chunk by chunk, from the man's hand.

He was beaten (he knew that); but he was not broken. He saw, once for all, that he stood no chance against a man with a club. He had learned the lesson, and in all his after life he never forgot it. That club was a revelation. It was his introduction to the reign of primitive law, and he met the introduction half-way. The facts of life took on a fiercer aspect; and while he faced that aspect uncowed, he faced it with all the latent cunning of his nature aroused. As the days went by, other dogs came, in crates and at the ends of ropes, some docilely, and some raging and roaring as he had come; and, one and

14

all, he watched them pass under the dominion of the man in the red sweater. Again and again, as he looked at each brutal performance, the lesson was driven home to Buck: a man with a club was a lawgiver, a master to be obeyed, though not necessarily conciliated. Of this last Buck was never guilty, though he did see beaten dogs that fawned upon the man, and wagged their tails, and licked his hand. Also he saw one dog, that would neither conciliate nor obey, finally killed in the struggle for mastery.

Now and again men came, strangers, who talked excitedly, wheedlingly, and in all kinds of fashions to the man in the red sweater. And at such times that money passed between them the strangers took one or more of the dogs away with them. Buck wondered where they went, for they never came back; but the fear of the future was strong upon him, and he was glad each time when he was not selected.

Yet his time came, in the end, in the form of a little weazened man who spat broken English and many strange and uncouth exclamations which Buck could not understand.

'Sacredam!' he cried, when his eyes lit upon Buck. 'Dat one dam bully dog! Eh? How moch?'

'Three hundred, and a present at that,' was the prompt reply of the man in the red sweater. 'And seein' it's government money, you ain't got no kick coming, eh, Perrault?'

Perrault grinned. Considering that the price of dogs had been boomed skyward by the unwonted demand, it was not an unfair sum for so fine an animal. The Canadian Government would be no loser, nor would its

15

despatches travel the slower. Perrault knew dogs, and when he looked at Buck he knew that he was one in a thousand—'One in ten t'ousand,' he commented mentally.

Buck saw money pass between them, and was not surprised when Curly, a good-natured Newfoundland, and he were led away by the little weazened man. That was the last he saw of the man in the red sweater, and as Curly and he looked at receding Seattle from the deck of the *Narwhal*, it was the last he saw of the warm Southland. Curly and he were taken below by Perrault and turned over to a black-faced giant called François. Perrault was a French-Canadian, and swarthy; but François was a French-Canadian half-breed, and twice as swarthy. They were a new kind of men to Buck (of which he was destined to see many more), and while he developed no affection for them, he none the less grew honestly to respect them. He speedily learned that Perrault and François were fair men, calm and impartial in administering justice, and too wise in the way of dogs to be fooled by dogs.

In the 'tween-decks of the *Narwhal*, Buck and Curly joined two other dogs. One of them was a big, snow-white fellow from Spitzbergen who had been brought away by a whaling captain, and who had later accompanied a Geological Survey into the Barrens. He was friendly, in a treacherous sort of way, smiling into one's face the while he meditated some underhand trick, as, for instance, when he stole from Buck's food at the first meal. As Buck sprang to punish him, the lash of François's whip sang through the air, reaching the culprit first; and nothing remained to Buck but to

16

recover the bone. That was fair of François, he decided, and the half-breed began to rise in Buck's estimation.

The other dog made no advances, nor received any; also, he did not attempt to steal from the newcomers. He was a gloomy, morose fellow, and he showed Curly plainly that all he desired was to be left alone, and further, that there would be trouble if he were not left alone. 'Dave' he was called, and he ate and slept, or yawned between times, and took interest in nothing, not even when the *Narwhal* crossed Queen Charlotte Sound and rolled and pitched and bucked like a thing possessed. When Buck and Curly grew excited, half wild with fear, he raised his head as though annoyed, favoured them with an incurious glance, yawned, and went to sleep again.

Day and night the ship throbbed to the tireless pulse of the propeller, and though one day was very like another, it was apparent to Buck that the weather was steadily growing colder. At last, one morning, the propeller was quiet, and the *Narwhal* was pervaded with an atmosphere of excitement. He felt it, as did the other dogs, and knew that a change was at hand. François leashed them and brought them on deck. At the first step upon the cold surface, Buck's feet sank into a white mushy something very like mud. He sprang back with a snort. More of this white stuff was falling through the air. He shook himself, but more of it fell upon him. He sniffed it curiously, then licked some up on his tongue. It bit like fire, and the next instant was gone. This puzzled him. He tried it again, with the same result. The onlookers laughed uproariously, and he felt ashamed, he knew not why, for it was his first snow.

CHAPTER 2

THE LAW OF CLUB AND FANG

Buck's first day on the Dyea beach was like a nightmare. Every hour was filled with shock and surprise. He had been suddenly jerked from the heart of civilization and flung into the heart of things primordial. No lazy, sun-kissed life was this, with nothing to do but loaf and be bored. Here was neither peace, nor rest, nor a moment's safety. All was confusion and action, and every moment life and limb were in peril. There was imperative need to be constantly alert; for these dogs and men were not town dogs and men. They were savages, all of them, who knew no law but the law of club and fang.

He had never seen dogs fight as these wolfish creatures fought, and his first experience taught him an unforgettable lesson. It is true, it was a vicarious experience, else he would not have lived to profit by it. Curly was the victim. They were camped near the log store, where she, in her friendly way, made advances to a husky dog the size of a full-grown wolf, though not half so large as she. There was no warning, only a leap in like a flash, a metallic clip of teeth, a leap out equally swift, and Curly's face was ripped open from eye to jaw.

It was the wolf manner of fighting, to strike and leap away; but there was more to it than this. Thirty or forty huskies ran to the spot and surrounded the combatants in an intent and silent circle. Buck did not comprehend that silent intentness, or the eager way with which they were licking their chops. Curly rushed her antagonist, who struck again and leaped aside. He met her next rush with his chest, in a peculiar fashion that tumbled her off her feet. She never regained them. This was what the onlooking huskies had waited for. They closed in upon her, snarling and yelping, and she was buried, screaming with agony, beneath the bristling mass of bodies.

So sudden was it, and so unexpected, that Buck was taken aback. He saw Spitz run out his scarlet tongue in a way he had of laughing; and he saw François, swinging an axe, spring into the mess of dogs. Three men with clubs were helping him to scatter them. It did not take long. Two minutes from the time Curly went down, the last of her assailants were clubbed off. But she lay there limp and lifeless in the bloody, trampled snow, almost literally torn to pieces, the swart half-breed standing over her and cursing horribly. The scene often came back to Buck to trouble him in his sleep. So that was the way. No fair play. Once down, that was the end of you. Well, he would see to it that he never went down. Spitz ran out his tongue and laughed again, and from that moment Buck hated him with a bitter and deathless hatred.

Before he had recovered from the shock caused by the tragic passing of Curly, he received another shock. François fastened upon him an arrangement of straps and buckles. It was a harness, such as he had seen the grooms put on the horses at home. And as he had seen horses work, so he was set to work, hauling François on a sled to the forest that fringed the valley, and returning with a load of firewood. Though his dignity was sorely hurt by thus being made a draught animal, he was too wise to rebel. He buckled down with a will and did his best, though it was all new and strange. François was stern, demanding instant obedience, and by virtue of his whip receiving instant obedience; while Dave, who was an experienced wheeler, nipped Buck's hind quarters whenever he was in error. Spitz was the leader, likewise experienced, and while he could not always get at Buck, he growled sharp reproof now and again, or cunningly threw his weight in the traces to jerk Buck into the way he should go. Buck learned easily, and under the combined tuition of his two mates and François made remarkable progress. Ere they returned to camp he knew enough to stop at 'ho,' to go ahead at 'mush,' to swing wide on the bends, and to keep clear of the wheeler when the loaded sled shot downhill at their heels.

'T'ree vair' good dogs,' François told Perrault. 'Dat Buck, heem pool lak hell. I tich heem queek as anyt'ing.'

By afternoon, Perrault, who was in a hurry to be on the trail with his despatches, returned with two more dogs. 'Billee' and 'Joe' he called them, two brothers, and true huskies both. Sons of the one mother though they were, they were as different as day and night. Billee's one fault was his excessive good nature, while Joe was the very opposite, sour and introspective, with a perpetual snarl and a malignant eye. Buck received them in comradely fashion, Dave ignored them, while Spitz proceeded to thrash first one and then the other. Billee wagged his tail appeasingly, turned to run when he saw that appeasement was of no avail, and cried (still appeasingly) when Spitz's sharp teeth scored his flank.

21

But no matter how Spitz circled, Joe whirled around on his heels to face him, mane bristling, ears laid back, lips writhing and snarling, jaws clipping together as fast as he could snap, and eyes diabolically gleaming—the incarnation of belligerent fear. So terrible was his appearance that Spitz was forced to forego disciplining him; but to cover his own discomfiture he turned upon the inoffensive and wailing Billee and drove him to the confines of the camp.

By evening Perrault secured another dog, an old husky, long and lean and gaunt, with a battle-scarred face and a single eye which flashed a warning of prowess that commanded respect. He was called Sol-leks, which means the Angry One. Like Dave, he asked nothing, gave nothing, expected nothing; and when he marched slowly and deliberately into their midst, even Spitz left him alone. He had one peculiarity which Buck was unlucky to .discover. He did not like to be approached on his blind side. Of this offence Buck was unwittingly guilty, and the first knowledge he had of his indiscretion was when Sol-leks whirled upon him and slashed his shoulder to the bone for three inches up and down. Forever after Buck avoided his blind side, and to the last of their comradeship had no more trouble. His only apparent ambition, like Dave's, was to be left alone; though, as Buck was afterward to learn, each of them possessed one other and even more vital ambition.

That night Buck faced the great problem of sleeping. The tent, illumined by a candle, glowed warmly in the midst of the white plain; and when he, as a matter of course, entered it, both Perrault and François bombarded him with curses and cooking utensils, till he recovered from his consternation and fled ignominiously into the outer cold. A chill wind was blowing that nipped him sharply and bit with especial venom into his wounded shoulder. He lay down on the snow and attempted to sleep, but the frost soon drove him shivering to his feet. Miserable and disconsolate, he wandered about among the many tents, only to find that one place was as cold as another. Here and there savage dogs rushed upon him, but he bristled his neck-hair and snarled (for he was learning fast), and they let him go his way unmolested.

Finally an idea came to him. He would return and see how his own team-mates were making out. To his astonishment, they had disappeared. Again he wandered about through the great camp, looking for them, and again he returned. Were they in the tent? No, that could not be, else he would not have been driven out. Then where could they possibly be? With drooping tail and shivering body, very forlorn indeed, he aimlessly circled the tent. Suddenly the snow gave way beneath his fore legs and he sank down. Something wriggled under his feet. He sprang back, bristling and snarling, fearful of the unseen and unknown. But a friendly little yelp reassured him, and he went back to investigate. A whiff of warm air ascended to his nostrils, and there, curled up under the snow in a snug ball, lay Billee. He whined placatingly, squirmed and wriggled to show his good will and intentions, and even ventured, as a bribe for peace, to lick Buck's face with his warm wet tongue.

Another lesson. So that was the way they did it, eh? Buck confidently selected a spot and with much fuss and waste effort proceeded to dig a hole for himself. In a trice the heat from his body filled the confined space and he was asleep. The day had been long and arduous, and he slept soundly and comfortably, though he growled and barked and wrestled with bad dreams.

Nor did he open his eyes till roused by the noises of the waking camp. At first he did not know where he was. It had snowed during the night and he was completely buried. The snow walls pressed him on every side, and a great surge of fear swept through him—the fear of the wild thing for the trap. It was a token that he was harking back through his own life to the lives of his forbears; for he was a civilized dog, an unduly civilized dog, and of his own experience knew no trap and so could not of himself fear it. The muscles of his whole body contracted spasmodically and instinctively, the hair on his neck and shoulders stood on end, and with a ferocious snarl he bounded straight up into the blinding day, the snow flying about him in a flashing cloud. Ere he landed on his feet, he saw the white camp spread out before him and knew where he was and remembered all that had passed from the time he went for a stroll with Manuel to the hole he had dug for himself the night before.

A shout from François hailed his appearance. 'Wot I say?' the dog-driver cried to Perrault. 'Dat Buck for sure learn queek as anyt'ing.'

Perrault nodded gravely. As courier for the Canadian Government, bearing important despatches, he was anxious to secure the best dogs, and he was particularly gladdened by the possession of Buck.

Three more huskies were added to the team inside an hour, making a total of nine and before another quarter of an hour had passed they were in harness and swinging up the trail toward the Dyea Canon. Buck was glad to be gone, and though the work was hard he found he did not particularly despise it. He was surprised at the eagerness which animated the whole team and which was communicated to him; but still more surprising was the change wrought in Dave and Sol-leks. They were new dogs, utterly transformed by the harness. All passiveness and unconcern had dropped from them. They were alert and active, anxious that the work should go well, and fiercely irritable with whatever, by delay or confusion, retarded that work. The toil of the traces seemed the supreme expression of their being, and all that they lived for and the only thing in which they took delight.

Dave was wheeler or sled dog, pulling in front of him was Buck, then came Sol-leks; the rest of the team was strung out ahead, single file, to the leader, which position was filled by Spitz.

Buck had been purposely placed between Dave and Sol-leks so that he might receive instruction. Apt scholar that he was, they were equally apt teachers, never allowing him to linger long in error, and enforcing their teaching with their sharp teeth. Dave was fair and very wise. He never nipped Buck without cause, and he never failed to nip him when he stood in need of it. As François's whip backed him up, Buck found it to be cheaper to mend his ways than to retaliate. Once, during a brief halt, when he got tangled in the traces and delayed the start, both Dave and Sol-leks flew at him and administered a sound trouncing. The resulting tangle was even worse, but Buck took good care to keep the traces clear thereafter; and ere the day was done, so well had he mastered his work, his mates about ceased nagging him. François's whip snapped less frequently, and Perrault even honored Buck by lifting up his feet and carefully examining them.

It was a hard day's run, up the Cañon, through Sheep Camp, past the Scales and the timber line, across glaciers and snowdrifts hundreds of feet deep, and over the great Chilcoot Divide, which stands between the salt water and the fresh and guards forbiddingly the sad and lonely North. They made good time down the chain of lakes which fills the craters of extinct volcanoes, and late that night pulled into the huge camp at the head of Lake Bennett, where thousands of gold-seekers were building boats against the break-up of the ice in the spring. Buck made his hole in the snow and slept the sleep of the exhausted just, but all too early was routed out in the cold darkness and harnessed with his mates to the sled.

That day they made forty miles, the trail being packed; but the next day, and for many days to follow, they broke their own trail, worked harder, and made poorer time. As a rule, Perrault travelled ahead of the team, packing the snow with webbed shoes to make it easier for them. François, guiding the sled at the gee-pole, sometimes exchanged places with him, but not often. Perrault was in a hurry, and he prided himself on his knowledge of ice, which knowledge was indispensable, for the fall ice was very thin, and where there was swift water, there was no ice at all.

Day after day, for days unending, Buck toiled in the traces. Always, they broke camp in the dark, and the first grey of dawn found them hitting the trail with fresh miles reeled off behind them. And always they pitched camp after dark, eating their bit of fish, and crawling to sleep into the snow. Buck was ravenous. The pound and a half of sun-dried salmon, which was his ration for each day, seemed to go nowhere. He never had enough, and suffered from perpetual hunger pangs. Yet the other dogs, because they weighed less and were born to the life, received a pound only of the fish and managed to keep in good condition.

He swiftly lost the fastidiousness which had characterized his old life. A dainty eater, he found that his mates, finishing first, robbed him of his unfinished ration. There was no defending it. While he was fighting off two or three, it was disappearing down the throats of the others. To remedy this, he ate as fast as they; and, so greatly did hunger compel him, he was not above taking what did not belong to him. He watched and learned. When he saw Pike, one of the new dogs, a clever malingerer and thief, slyly steal a slice of bacon when Perrault's back was turned, he duplicated the performance the following day, getting away with the whole chunk. A great uproar was raised, but he was unsuspected; while Dub, an awkward blunderer who was always getting caught, was punished for Buck's misdeed.

This first theft marked Buck as fit to survive in the hostile Northland environment. It marked his adaptability, his capacity to adjust himself to changing conditions, the lack of which would have meant swift and terrible death. It marked, further, the decay or going to pieces of his moral nature, a vain thing and a handicap in the ruthless struggle for existence. It was all well enough in the Southland, under the law of love and fellowship, to respect private property and personal feelings; but in the Northland, under the law of club and fang, whoso took such things into account was a fool, and in so far as he observed them he would fail to prosper.

Not that Buck reasoned it out. He was fit, that was all, and unconsciously he accommodated himself to the new mode of life. All his days, no matter what the odds, he had never run from a fight. But the club of the man in the red sweater had beaten into him a more fundamental and primitive code. Civilized, he could have died for a moral consideration, say the defence of Judge Miller's riding-whip; but the completeness of his decivilization was now evidenced by his ability to flee from the defence of a moral consideration and to save his hide. He did not steal for joy of it, but because of the clamour of his stomach. He did not rob openly, but stole secretly and cunningly, out of respect for club and fang. In short, the things he did were done because it was easier to do them than not to do them.

His development (or retrogression) was rapid. His muscles became hard as iron, and he grew callous to all ordinary pain. He achieved an internal as well as external economy. He could eat anything, no matter how loathsome or indigestible; and, once eaten, the juices of his stomach extracted the last least particle of nutriment; and his blood carried it to the farthest reaches of his body, building it into the toughest and stoutest of tissues. Sight and scent became remarkably keen, while his hearing developed such acuteness that in his sleep he heard the faintest sound and knew whether it heralded peace or peril. He learned to bite the ice out with his teeth when it collected between his toes; and when he was thirsty and there was a thick scum of ice over the water hole, he would break it by rearing and striking it with stiff fore legs. His most conspicuous trait was an ability to scent the wind and forecast it a night in advance. No matter how breathless the air when he dug his nest by tree or bank, the wind that later blew inevitably found him to leeward, sheltered and snug.

And not only did he learn by experience, but instincts long dead became alive again. The domesticated generations fell from him. In vague ways he remembered back to the youth of the breed, to the time the wild dogs ranged in packs through the primeval forest and killed their meat as they ran it down. It was no task for him to learn to fight with cut and slash and the quick wolf snap. In this manner had fought forgotten ancestors. They quickened the old life within him, and the old tricks which they had stamped into the heredity of the breed were his tricks. They came to him without effort or discovery, as though they had been his always. And when, on the still cold nights, he pointed his nose at a star and howled long and wolflike, it was his ancestors, dead and dust, pointing nose at star and howling down through the centuries and through him. And his cadences were their cadences, the cadences which voiced their woe and what to them was the meaning of the stillness, and the cold, and dark.

Thus, as token of what a puppet thing life is, the ancient song surged through him and he came into his own again; and he came because men had found a yellow metal in the North, and because Manuel was a gardener's helper whose wages did not lap over the needs of his wife and divers small copies of himself.

CHAPTER 3

THE DOMINANT PRIMORDIAL
BEAST

The dominant primordial beast was strong in Buck, and under the fierce conditions of trail life it grew and grew. Yet it was a secret growth. His new-born cunning gave him poise and control. He was too busy adjusting himself to the new life to feel at ease, and not only did he not pick fights, but he avoided them whenever possible. A certain deliberateness characterized his attitude. He was not prone to rashness and precipitate action; and in the bitter hatred between him and Spitz he betrayed no impatience, shunned all offensive acts.

On the other hand, possibly because he divined in Buck a dangerous rival, Spitz never lost an opportunity of showing his teeth. He even went out of his way to bully Buck, striving constantly to start the fight which could end only in the death of one or the other. Early in the trip this might have taken place had it not been for an unwonted accident. At the end of this day they made a bleak and miserable camp on the shore of Lake Le Barge. Driving snow, a wind that cut like a white-hot knife, and darkness, had forced them to grope for a camping place. They could hardly have fared worse. At their backs rose a perpendicular wall of rock, and Perrault and François were compelled to make their fire and spread their sleeping robes on the ice of the lake itself. The tent they had discarded at Dyea in order to travel light. A few sticks of driftwood furnished them with a fire that thawed down through the ice and left them to eat supper in the dark.

Close in under the sheltering rock Buck made his nest. So snug and warm was it that he was loath to leave it when François distributed the fish which he had first thawed over the fire. But when Buck finished his ration and returned, he found his nest occupied. A warning snarl told him that the trespasser was Spitz. Till now Buck had avoided trouble with his enemy, but this was too much. The beast in him roared. He sprang upon Spitz with a fury which surprised them both, and Spitz particularly, for his whole experience with Buck had gone to teach him that his rival was an unusually timid dog, who managed to hold his own only because of his great weight and size.

François was surprised, too, when they shot out in a tangle from the disrupted nest and he divined the cause of the trouble. 'A-a-ah!' he cried to Buck. 'Gif it to heem, by Gar! Gif it to heem, the dirty t'eef!'

Spitz was equally willing. He was crying with sheer rage and eagerness as he circled back and forth for a chance to spring in. Buck was no less eager, and no less cautious, as he likewise circled back and forth for the advantage. But it was then that the unexpected happened, the thing which projected their struggle for supremacy far into the future, past many a weary mile of trail and toil.

An oath from Perrault, the resounding impact of a club upon a bony frame, and a shrill yelp of pain, heralded the breaking forth of pandemonium. The camp was suddenly discovered to be alive with skulking furry forms—starving huskies, four or five score of them, who had scented the camp from some Indian village. They had crept in while Buck and Spitz were fighting, and when the two men sprang among them with stout clubs they showed their teeth and fought back. They were crazed by the smell of the food. Perrault found one with head buried in the grub-box. His club landed heavily on the gaunt ribs, and the grub-box was capsized on the ground. On the instant a score of the famished brutes were scrambling for the bread and bacon. The clubs fell upon them unheeded. They yelped and howled under the rain of blows, but struggled none the less madly till the last crumb had been devoured.

In the meantime the astonished team-dogs had burst out of their nests only to be set upon by the fierce invaders. Never had Buck seen such dogs. It seemed as though their bones would burst through their skins. They were mere skeletons, draped loosely in draggled hides, with blazing eyes and slavered fangs. But the hunger-madness made them terrifying, irresistible. There was no opposing them. The team-dogs were swept back against the cliff at the first onset. Buck was beset by three huskies, and in a trice his head and shoulders were ripped and slashed. The din was frightful. Billee was crying as usual. Dave and Sol-leks, dripping blood from a score of wounds, were fighting bravely side by side. Joe was snapping like a demon. Once, his teeth closed on the fore leg of a husky, and he crunched down through the bone. Pike, the malingerer, leaped upon the crippled animal, breaking its neck with a quick flash of teeth and a jerk. Buck got a frothing adversary by the throat, and was sprayed with blood when his

33

teeth sank through the jugular. The warm taste of it in his mouth goaded him to greater fierceness. He flung himself upon another, and at the same time felt teeth sink into his own throat. It was Spitz, treacherously attacking from the side.

Perrault and François, having cleaned out their part of the camp, hurried to save their sled-dogs. The wild wave of famished beasts rolled back before them, and Buck shook himself free. But it was only for a moment. The two men were compelled to run back to save the grub, upon which the huskies returned to the attack on the team. Billee, terrified into bravery, sprang through the savage circle and fled away over the ice. Pike and Dub followed on his heels, with the rest of the team behind. As Buck drew himself together to spring after them, out of the tail of his eye he saw Spitz rush upon him with the evident intention of overthrowing him. Once off his feet and under that mass of huskies, there was no hope for him. But he braced himself to the shock of Spitz's charge, then joined the flight out on the lake.

Later, the nine team-dogs gathered together and sought shelter in the forest. Though unpursued, they were in a sorry plight. There was not one who was not wounded in four or five places, while some were wounded grievously. Dub was badly injured in a hind leg; Dolly, the last husky added to the team at Dyea, had a badly torn throat; Joe had lost an eye; while Billee, the good-natured, with an ear chewed and rent to ribbons, cried and whimpered throughout the night. At daybreak they limped warily back to camp, to find the marauders gone and the two men in bad tempers. Fully half their grub supply was gone. The huskies had chewed through the sled lashings and canvas coverings. In fact, nothing, no matter how remotely eatable had escaped them. They had eaten a pair of Perrault's moose-hide moccasins, chunks out of the leather traces, and even two feet of lash from the end of François's whip. He broke from a mournful contemplation of it to look over his wounded dogs.

'Ah, my frien's,' he said softly, 'mebbe it mek you mad dog, dose many bites. Mebbe all mad dog, sacredam! Wot you t'ink, eh, Perrault?'

The courier shook his head dubiously. With four hundred miles of trail still between him and Dawson, he could ill afford to have madness break out among his dogs. Two hours of cursing and exertion got the harnesses into shape, and the wound-stiffened team was under way, struggling painfully over the hardest part of the trail they had yet encountered, and for that matter, the hardest between them and Dawson.

The Thirty Mile River was wide open. Its wild water defied the frost, and it was in the eddies only and in the quiet places that the ice held at all. Six days of exhausting toil were required to cover those thirty terrible miles. And terrible they were, for every foot of them was accomplished at the risk of life to dog and man. A dozen times, Perrault, nosing the way, broke through the ice bridges, being saved by the long pole he carried, which he so held that it fell each time across the hole made by his body. But a cold snap was on, the thermometer registering fifty below zero, and each time he broke through he was compelled for very life to build a fire and dry his garments.

Nothing daunted him. It was because nothing daunted him that he had been chosen for government courier. He took all manner of risks, resolutely thrusting his little weazened face into the frost and struggling on from dim dawn to dark. He skirted the frowning shores on rim ice that bent and crackled under foot and upon which they dared not halt. Once, the sled broke through, with Dave and Buck, and they were half-frozen and all but drowned by the time they were dragged out. The usual fire was necessary to save them. They were coated solidly with ice, and the two men kept them on the run around the fire, sweating and thawing, so close that they were singed by the flames.

At another time Spitz went through, dragging the whole team after him up to Buck, who strained backward with all his strength, his fore paws on the slippery edge and the ice quivering and snapping all around. But behind him was Dave, likewise straining backward, and behind the sled was François, pulling till his tendons cracked.

Again, the rim ice broke away before and behind, and there was no escape except up the cliff. Perrault scaled it by a miracle, while François prayed for just that miracle; and with every thong and sled lashing and the last bit of harness rove into a long rope, the dogs were hoisted, one by one, to the cliff crest. François came up last, after the sled and load. Then came the search for a place to descend, which descent was ultimately made by the aid of the rope, and night found them back on the river with a quarter of a mile to the day's credit.

By the time they made the Hootalinqua and good ice, Buck was played out. The rest of the dogs were in like condition; but Perrault, to make up lost time, pushed them late and early. The first day they covered thirty-five miles to the Big Salmon; the next day thirty-five more to the Little Salmon; the third day forty miles, which brought them well up toward the Five Fingers.

Buck's feet were not so compact and hard as the feet of the huskies. His had softened during the many generations since the day his last wild ancestor was tamed by a cave-dweller or river man. All day long he limped in agony, and camp once made, lay down like a dead dog. Hungry as he was, he would not move to receive his ration of fish, which François had to bring to him. Also, the dog-driver rubbed Buck's feet for half an hour each night after supper, and sacrificed the tops of his own moccasins to make four moccasins for Buck. This was a great relief, and Buck caused even the weazened face of Perrault to twist itself into a grin one morning, when François forgot the moccasins and Buck lay on his back, his four feet waving appealingly in the air, and refused to budge without them. Later his feet grew hard to the trail, and the worn-out foot-gear was thrown away.

At the Pelly one morning, as they were harnessing up, Dolly, who had never been conspicuous for anything, went suddenly mad. She announced her condition by a long, heartbreaking wolf howl that sent every dog bristling with fear, then sprang straight for Buck. He had never seen a dog go mad, nor did he have any reason to fear madness; yet he knew that here was horror, and fled away from it in a panic. Straight away he raced, with Dolly, panting and frothing, one leap behind; nor could she gain on him, so great was his terror, nor could he leave her, so great was her madness. He plunged through the wooded breast of the island, flew down to the lower end, crossed a back channel filled with rough ice to another island, gained a third island, curved back to the main river, and in desperation started to cross it. And all the time, though he did not look, he could hear her snarling just one leap behind. François called to him a quarter of a mile away and he doubled back, still one leap ahead, gasping painfully for air and putting all his faith in that François would save him. The dog-driver held the axe poised in his hand, and as Buck shot past him the axe crashed down upon mad Dolly's head.

Buck staggered over against the sled, exhausted, sobbing for breath, helpless. This was Spitz's opportunity. He sprang upon Buck, and twice his teeth sank into his unresisting foe and ripped and tore the flesh to the bone. Then François's lash descended, and Buck had the satisfaction of watching Spitz receive the worst whipping as yet administered to any of the team.

'One devil, dat Spitz,' remarked Perrault. 'Some dam day heem keel dat Buck.'

'Dat Buck two devils,' was François's rejoinder. 'All de tam I watch dat Buck I know for sure. Lissen: some darn fine day heem get mad lak hell an' den heem chew dat Spitz all up an' spit heem out on de snow. Sure. I know.'

From then on it was war between them. Spitz, as lead-dog and acknowledged master of the team, felt his supremacy threatened by this strange Southland dog. And strange Buck was to him, for of the many Southland dogs he had known, not one had shown up worthily in camp and on trail. They were all too soft, dying under the toil, the frost, and starvation. Buck was the exception. He alone endured and prospered, matching the husky in strength, savagery, and cunning. Then he was a masterful dog, and what made him dangerous was the fact that the club of the man in the red sweater had knocked all blind pluck and rashness out of his desire for mastery. He was preeminently cunning, and could bide his time with a patience that was nothing less than primitive.

It was inevitable that the clash for leadership should come. Buck wanted it. He wanted it because it was his nature, because he had been gripped tight by that nameless, incomprehensible pride of the trail and trace—that pride which holds dogs in the toil to the last gasp, which lures them to die joyfully in the harness, and breaks their hearts if they are cut out of the harness. This was the pride of Dave as wheel-dog, of Sol-leks as he pulled with all his strength; the pride that laid hold of them at break of camp, transforming them from sour and sullen brutes into straining, eager, ambitious creatures; the pride that spurred them on all day and dropped them at pitch of camp at night, letting them fall back into gloomy unrest and uncontent. This was the pride that bore up Spitz and made him thrash the sled-dogs who blundered and shirked in the traces or hid away at harness-up time in the morning. Likewise it was this pride that made him fear Buck as a possible lead-dog. And this was Buck's pride, too.

He openly threatened the other's leadership. He came between him and the shirks he should have punished. And he did it deliberately. One night there was a heavy snowfall, and in the morning Pike, the malingerer, did not appear. He was securely hidden in his nest under a foot of snow. François called him and sought him in vain. Spitz was wild with wrath. He raged through the camp, smelling and digging in every likely place, snarling so frightfully that Pike heard and shivered in his hiding-place.

But when he was at last unearthed, and Spitz flew at him to punish him, Buck flew, with equal rage, in between. So unexpected was it, and so shrewdly managed, that Spitz was hurled backward and off his feet. Pike, who had been trembling abjectly, took heart at this open mutiny, and sprang upon his overthrown leader. Buck, to whom fairplay was a forgotten code, likewise sprang upon Spitz. But François, chuckling at the incident while unswerving in the administration of justice, brought his lash down upon Buck with all his might. This failed to drive Buck from his prostrate rival, and the butt of the whip was brought into play. Half-stunned by the blow, Buck was knocked backward and the lash laid upon him again and again, while Spitz soundly punished the many times offending Pike.

In the days that followed, as Dawson grew closer and closer, Buck still continued to interfere between Spitz and the culprits; but he did it craftily, when François was not around. With the covert mutiny of Buck, a general insubordination sprang up and increased. Dave and Sol-leks were unaffected, but the rest of the team went from bad to worse. Things no longer went right. There was continual bickering and jangling. Trouble was always afoot, and at the bottom of it was Buck. He kept François busy, for the dog-driver was in constant apprehension of the life-and-death struggle between the two which he knew must take place sooner or later; and on more than one night the sounds of quarrelling and strife among the other dogs turned him out of his sleeping robe, fearful that Buck and Spitz were at it.

But the opportunity did not present itself, and they pulled into Dawson one dreary afternoon with the great fight still to come. Here were many men, and countless dogs, and Buck found them all at work. It seemed the ordained order of things that dogs should work. All day they swung up and down the main street in long teams, and in the night their jingling bells still went by. They hauled cabin logs and firewood, freighted up to the mines, and did all manner of work that horses did in the Santa Clara Valley. Here and there Buck met Southland dogs, but in the main they were the wild wolf husky breed. Every night, regularly, at nine, at twelve, at three, they lifted a nocturnal song, a weird and eerie chant, in which it was Buck's delight to join.

With the aurora borealis flaming coldly overhead, or the stars leaping in the frost dance, and the land numb and frozen under its pall of snow, this song of the huskies might have been the defiance of life, only it was pitched in minor key, with long-drawn wailings and half-sobs, and was more the pleading of life, the articulate travail of existence. It was an old song, old as the breed itself—one of the first songs of the younger world in a day when songs were sad. It was invested with the woe of unnumbered generations, this plaint by which Buck was so strangely stirred. When he moaned and sobbed, it was with the pain of living that was of old the pain of his wild fathers, and the fear and mystery of the cold and dark that was to them fear and mystery. And that he should be stirred by it marked the completeness

41

with which he harked back through the ages of fire and roof to the raw beginnings of life in the howling ages.

Seven days from the time they pulled into Dawson, they dropped down the steep bank by the Barracks to the Yukon Trail, and pulled for Dyea and Salt Water. Perrault was carrying despatches if anything more urgent than those he had brought in; also, the travel pride had gripped him, and he purposed to make the record trip of the year. Several things favoured him in this. The week's rest had recuperated the dogs and put them in thorough trim. The trail they had broken into the country was packed hard by later journeyers. And further, the police had arranged in two or three places deposits of grub for dog and man, and he was travelling light.

They made Sixty Mile, which is a fifty-mile run, on the first day; and the second day saw them booming up the Yukon well on their way to Pelly. But such splendid running was achieved not without great trouble and vexation on the part of François. The insidious revolt led by Buck had destroyed the solidarity of the team. It no longer was as one dog leaping in the traces. The encouragement Buck gave the rebels led them into all kinds of petty misdemeanors. No more was Spitz a leader greatly to be feared. The old awe departed, and they grew equal to challenging his authority. Pike robbed him of half a fish one night, and gulped it down under the protection of Buck. Another night Dub and Joe fought Spitz and made him forego the punishment they deserved. And even Billee, the good-natured, was less good-natured, and whined not half so placatingly as in former days. Buck never came near Spitz without snarling and bristling menacingly. In fact, his conduct approached that of a bully, and he was given to swaggering up and down before Spitz's very nose.

The breaking down of discipline likewise affected the dogs in their relations with one another. They quarrelled and bickered more than ever among themselves, till at times the camp was a howling bedlam. Dave and Solleks alone were unaltered, though they were made irritable by the unending squabbling. François swore strange barbarous oaths, and stamped the snow in futile rage, and tore his hair. His lash was always singing among the dogs, but it was of small avail. Directly his back was turned they were at it again. He backed up Spitz with his whip, while Buck backed up the remainder of the team. François knew he was behind all the trouble, and Buck knew he knew; but Buck was too clever ever again to be caught red-handed. He worked faithfully in the harness, for the toil had become a delight to him; yet it was a greater delight slyly to precipitate a fight amongst his mates and tangle the traces.

At the mouth of the Tahkeena, one night after supper, Dub turned up a snowshoe rabbit, blundered it, and missed. In a second the whole team was in full cry. A hundred yards away was a camp of the Northwest Police, with fifty dogs, huskies all, who joined the chase. The rabbit sped down the river, turned off into a small creek, up the frozen bed of which it held steadily. It ran lightly on the surface of the snow, while the dogs ploughed through by main strength. Buck led the pack, sixty strong, around bend after bend, but he could not gain. He lay down low to the race, whining eagerly, his splendid body flashed forward, leap by leap, in the wan white moonlight. And leap by leap, like some pale frost wraith, the snowshoe rabbit flashed on ahead.

All that stirring of old instincts which at stated periods drives men out from the sounding cities to forest and plain to kill things by chemically propelled leaden pellets, the blood lust, the joy to kill—all this was Buck's, only it was infinitely more intimate. He was ranging at the head of the pack, running the wild thing down, the living meat, to kill with his own teeth and wash his muzzle to the eyes in warm blood.

There is an ecstasy that marks the summit of life, and beyond which life cannot rise. And such is the paradox of living, this ecstasy comes when one is most alive, and it comes as a complete forgetfulness that one is alive. This ecstasy, this forgetfulness of living, comes to the artist, caught up and out of himself in a sheet of flame; it comes to the soldier, war-mad on a stricken field and refusing quarter; and it came to Buck, leading the pack, sounding the old wolf-cry, straining after the food that was alive and that fled swiftly before him through the moonlight. He was sounding the deeps of his nature, and of the parts of his nature that were deeper than he, going back into the womb of Time. He was mastered by the sheer surging of life, the tidal wave of being, the perfect joy of each separate muscle, joint, and sinew in that it was everything that was not death, that it was aglow and rampant, expressing itself in movement, flying exultantly under the stars and over the face of dead matter that did not move.

But Spitz, cold and calculating even in his supreme moods, left the pack and cut across a narrow neck of land where the creek made a long bend around. Buck did not know of this, and as he rounded the bend, the frost wraith of a rabbit still flitting before him, he saw another and larger frost wraith leap from the overhanging bank into the immediate path of the rabbit. It was Spitz. The rabbit could not turn, and as the white teeth broke its back in mid air it shrieked as loudly as a stricken man may shriek. At sound of this, the cry of Life plunging down from Life's apex in the grip of Death, the full pack at Buck's heels raised a hell's chorus of delight.

Buck did not cry out. He did not check himself, but drove in upon Spitz, shoulder to shoulder, so hard that he missed the throat. They rolled over and over in the powdery snow. Spitz gained his feet almost as though he had not been overthrown, slashing Buck down the shoulder and leaping clear. Twice his teeth clipped together, like the steel jaws of a trap, as he backed away for better footing, with lean and lifting lips that writhed and snarled.

In a flash Buck knew it. The time had come. It was to the death. As they circled about, snarling, ears laid back, keenly watchful for the advantage, the scene came to Buck with a sense of familiarity. He seemed to remember it all—the white woods, and earth, and moonlight, and the thrill of battle. Over the whiteness and silence brooded a ghostly calm. There was not a faintest whisper of air—nothing moved, not a leaf quivered, the visible breaths of the dogs rising slowly and lingering in the frosty air. They had made short work of the snowshoe rabbit, these dogs that were ill-tamed wolves; and they were now drawn up in an expectant circle. They, too, were silent, their eyes only gleaming and their breaths drifting slowly upward. To Buck it was nothing new or strange, this scene of old time. It was as though it had always been, the wonted way of things.

Spitz was a practised fighter. From Spitzbergen through the Arctic, and across Canada and the Barrens, he had held his own with all manner of dogs and achieved to mastery over them. Bitter rage was his, but never blind rage. In passion to rend and destroy, he never forgot that his enemy was in like passion to rend and destroy. He never rushed till he was prepared to receive a rush; never attacked till he had first defended that attack.

In vain Buck strove to sink his teeth in the neck of the big white dog. Wherever his fangs struck for the softer flesh, they were countered by the fangs of Spitz. Fang clashed fang, and lips were cut and bleeding, but Buck could not penetrate his enemy's guard. Then he warmed up and enveloped Spitz in a whirlwind of rushes. Time and time again he tried for the snow-white throat, where life bubbled near to the surface, and each time and every time Spitz slashed him and got away. Then Buck took to rushing, as though for the throat, when, suddenly drawing back his head and curving in from the side, he would drive his shoulder at the shoulder of Spitz, as a ram by which to overthrow him. But instead, Buck's shoulder was slashed down each time as Spitz leaped lightly away.

Spitz was untouched, while Buck was streaming with blood and panting hard. The fight was growing desperate. And all the while the silent and wolfish circle waited to finish off whichever dog went down. As Buck grew winded, Spitz took to rushing, and he kept him staggering for footing. Once Buck went over, and the whole circle of sixty dogs started up; but he recovered himself, almost in mid air, and the circle sank down again and waited.

But Buck possessed a quality that made for greatness— imagination. He fought by instinct, but he could fight by head as well. He rushed, as though attempting the old shoulder trick, but at the last instant swept low to the snow and in. His teeth closed on Spitz's left fore leg. There was a crunch of breaking bone, and the white dog faced him on three legs. Thrice he tried to knock him over, then repeated the trick and broke the right fore leg. Despite the pain and helplessness, Spitz struggled madly to keep up. He saw the silent circle, with gleaming eyes, lolling tongues, and silvery breaths drifting upward, closing in upon him as he had seen similar circles close in upon beaten antagonists in the past. Only this time he was the one who was beaten.

There was no hope for him. Buck was inexorable. Mercy was a thing reserved for gentler climes. He manoeuvred for the final rush. The circle had tightened till he could feel the breaths of the huskies on his flanks. He could see them, beyond Spitz and to either side, half crouching for the spring, their eyes fixed upon him. A pause seemed to fall. Every animal was motionless as though turned to stone. Only Spitz quivered and bristled as he staggered back and forth, snarling with horrible menace, as though to frighten off impending death. Then Buck sprang in and out; but while he was in, shoulder had at last squarely met shoulder. The dark circle became a dot on the moon-flooded snow as Spitz disappeared from view. Buck stood and looked on, the successful champion, the dominant primordial beast who had made his kill and found it good.

CHAPTER 4

WHO HAS WON TO MASTERSHIP

'Eh? Wot I say? I spik true w'en I say dat Buck two devils.' This was François's speech next morning when he discovered Spitz missing and Buck covered with wounds. He drew him to the fire and by its light pointed them out.

'Dat Spitz fight lak hell,' said Perrault, as he surveyed the gaping rips and cuts.

'An' dat Buck fight lak two hells,' was François's answer. 'An' now we make good time. No more Spitz, no more trouble, sure.'

While Perrault packed the camp outfit and loaded the sled, the dog-driver proceeded to harness the dogs. Buck trotted up to the place Spitz would have occupied as leader; but François, not noticing him, brought Sol-leks to the coveted position. In his judgment, Sol-leks was the best lead-dog left. Buck sprang upon Sol-leks in a fury, driving him back and standing in his place.

'Eh? eh?' François cried, slapping his thighs gleefully. 'Look at dat Buck. Heem keel dat Spitz, heem t'ink to take de job.'

'Go 'way, Chook!' he cried, but Buck refused to budge.

He took Buck by the scruff of the neck, and though the dog growled threateningly, dragged him to one side and replaced Sol-leks. The old dog did not like it, and showed plainly that he was afraid of Buck. François was obdurate, but when he turned his back Buck again displaced Sol-leks, who was not at all unwilling to go.

François was angry. 'Now, by Gar, I feex you!' he cried, coming back with a heavy club in his hand.

Buck remembered the man in the red sweater, and retreated slowly; nor did he attempt to charge in when Sol-leks was once more brought forward. But he circled just beyond the range of the club, snarling with bitterness and rage; and while he circled he watched the club so as to dodge it if thrown by François, for he was become wise in the way of clubs.

The driver went about his work, and he called to Buck when he was ready to put him in his old place in front of Dave. Buck retreated two or three steps. François followed him up, whereupon he again retreated. After some time of this, François threw down the club, thinking that Buck feared a thrashing. But Buck was in open revolt. He wanted, not to escape a clubbing, but to have the leadership. It was his by right. He had earned it, and he would not be content with less.

Perrault took a hand. Between them they ran him about for the better part of an hour. They threw clubs at him. He dodged. They cursed him, and his fathers and mothers before him, and all his seed to come after him down to the remotest generation, and every hair on his body and drop of blood in his veins; and he answered curse with snarl and kept out of their reach. He did not try to run away, but retreated around and around the camp, advertising plainly that when his desire was met, he would come in and be good.

François sat down and scratched his head. Perrault looked at his watch and swore. Time was flying, and they should have been on the trail an hour gone. François scratched his head again. He shook it and grinned sheepishly at the courier, who shrugged his shoulders in sign that they were beaten. Then François went up to where Sol-leks stood and called to Buck. Buck laughed as dogs laugh, yet kept his distance. François unfastened Sol-lek's traces and put him back in his old place. The team stood harnessed to the sled in an unbroken line, ready for the trail. There was no place for Buck save at the front. Once more François called, and once more Buck laughed and kept away.

'T'row down de club,' Perrault commanded.

François complied, whereupon Buck trotted in, laughing triumphantly, and swung around into position at the head of the team. His traces were fastened, the sled broken out, and with both men running they dashed out on to the river trail.

Highly as the dog-driver had forevalued Buck, with his two devils, he found, while the day was yet young, that he had undervalued. At a bound Buck took up the duties of leadership; and where judgment was required, and quick thinking and quick acting, he showed himself the superior even of Spitz, of whom François had never seen an equal.

But it was in giving the law and making his mates live up to it, that Buck excelled. Dave and Sol-leks did not mind the change in leadership. It was none of their business. Their business was to toil, and toil mightily, in the traces. So long as that were not interfered with, they did not care what happened. Billee, the good-natured, could lead for all they cared, so long as he kept order. The rest of the team, however, had grown unruly during

51

the last days of Spitz, and their surprise was great now that Buck proceeded to lick them into shape.

Pike, who pulled at Buck's heels, and who never put an ounce more of his weight against the breast-band than he was compelled to do, was swiftly and repeatedly shaken for loafing; and ere the first day was done he was pulling more than ever before in his life. The first night in camp, Joe, the sour one, was punished roundly—a thing that Spitz had never succeeded in doing. Buck simply smothered him by virtue of superior weight, and cut him up till he ceased snapping and began to whine for mercy.

The general tone of the team picked up immediately. It recovered its old-time solidarity, and once more the dogs leaped as one dog in the traces. At the Rink Rapids two native huskies, Teek and Koona, were added; and the celerity with which Buck broke them in took away François's breath.

'Nevaire such a dog as dat Buck!' he cried. 'No, nevaire! Heem worth one t'ousan' dollair, by Gar! Eh? Wot you say, Perrault?'

And Perrault nodded. He was ahead of the record then, and gaining day by day. This trail was in excellent condition, well packed and hard, and there was no new-fallen snow with which to contend. It was not too cold. The temperature dropped to fifty below zero and remained there the whole trip. The men rode and ran by turn, and the dogs were kept on the jump, with but infrequent stoppages.

The Thirty Mile River was comparatively coated with ice, and they covered in one day going out what had taken them ten days coming in. In one run they made a sixty-mile dash from the foot of Lake Le Barge to the White Horse Rapids. Across Marsh, Tagish, and Bennett (seventy miles of lakes), they flew so fast that the man whose turn it was to run towed behind the sled at the end of a rope. And on the last night of the second week they topped White Pass and dropped down the sea slope with the lights of Skaguay and of the shipping at their feet.

It was a record run. Each day for fourteen days they had averaged forty miles. For three days Perrault and François threw chests up and down the main street of Skaguay and were deluged with invitations to drink, while the team was the constant centre of a worshipful crowd of dog-busters and mushers. Then three or four western bad men aspired to clean out the town, were riddled like pepperboxes for their pains, and public interest turned to other idols. Next came official orders. François called Buck to him, threw his arms round him, wept over him. And that was the last of François and Perrault. Like other men, they passed out of Buck's life for good.

A Scotch half-breed took charge of him and his mates, and in company with a dozen other dog-teams he started back over the weary trail to Dawson. It was no light running now, nor record time, but heavy toil each day, with a heavy load behind; for this was the mail train, carrying word from the world to the men who sought gold under the shadow of the Pole.

Buck did not like it, but he bore up well to the work, taking pride in it after the manner of Dave and Sol-leks, and seeing that his mates, whether they prided in it or not, did their fair share. It was a monotonous life, operating with machine-like regularity. One day was very like another. At a certain time each morning the cooks turned out, fires were built, and breakfast was eaten. Then, while some broke camp, others harnessed the dogs, and they were under way an hour or so before the darkness fell which gave warning of dawn. At night, camp was made. Some pitched the flies, others cut firewood and pine boughs for the beds, and still others carried water or ice for the cooks. Also, the dogs were fed. To them, this was the one feature of the day, though it was good to loaf around, after the fish was eaten, for an hour or so with the other dogs, of which there were fivescore and odd. There were fierce fighters among them, but three battles with the fiercest brought Buck to mastery, so that when he bristled and showed his teeth they got out of his way.

Best of all, perhaps, he loved to lie near the fire, hind legs crouched under him, fore legs stretched out in front, head raised, and eyes blinking dreamily at the flames. Sometimes he thought of Judge Miller's big house in the sun-kissed Santa Clara Valley, and of the cement swimming-tank, and Ysabel, the Mexican hairless, and Toots, the Japanese pug; but oftener he remembered the man in the red sweater, the death of Curly, the great fight with Spitz, and the good things he had eaten or would like to eat. He was not homesick. The Sunland was very dim and distant, and such memories had no power over him. Far more potent were the memories of his heredity that gave things he had never seen before a seeming familiarity; the instincts (which were but the memories of his ancestors become habits) which had lapsed in later days, and still later, in him, quickened and become alive again.

Sometimes as he crouched there, blinking dreamily at the flames, it seemed that the flames were of another fire, and that as he crouched by this other fire he saw another and different man from the half-breed cook before him. This other man was shorter of leg and longer of arm, with muscles that were stringy and knotty rather than rounded and swelling. The hair of this man was long and matted, and his head slanted back under it from the eyes. He uttered strange sounds, and seemed very much afraid of the darkness, into which he peered continually, clutching in his hand, which hung midway between knee and foot, a stick with a heavy stone made fast to the end. He was all but naked, a ragged and fire-scorched skin hanging part way down his back, but on his body there was much hair. In some places, across the chest and shoulders and down the outside of the arms and thighs, it was matted into almost a thick fur. He did not stand erect, but with trunk inclined forward from the hips, on legs that bent at the knees. About his body there was a peculiar springiness, or resiliency, almost catlike, and a quick alertness as of one who lived in perpetual fear of things seen and unseen.

At other times this hairy man squatted by the fire with head between his legs and slept. On such occasions his elbows were on his knees, his hands clasped above his head as though to shed rain by the hairy arms. And beyond that fire, in the circling darkness, Buck could see many gleaming coals, two by two, always two by two, which he knew to be the eyes of great beasts of prey. And he could hear the crashing of their bodies through the undergrowth, and the noises they made in the night. And dreaming there by the Yukon bank, with lazy eyes blinking at the fire, these sounds and sights of another world would make the hair to rise along his back and stand on end across his shoulders and up his neck, till he whimpered low and suppressedly, or growled softly, and the half-breed cook shouted at him, 'Hey, you Buck, wake up!' Whereupon the other world would vanish and the real world come into his eyes, and he would get up and yawn and stretch as though he had been asleep.

It was a hard trip, with the mail behind them, and the heavy work wore them down. They were short of weight and in poor condition when they made Dawson, and should have had a ten days' or a week's rest at least. But in two days' time they dropped down the Yukon bank from the Barracks, loaded with letters for the outside. The dogs were tired, the drivers grumbling, and to make matters worse, it snowed every day. This meant a soft trail, greater friction on the runners, and heavier pulling for the dogs; yet the drivers were fair through it all, and did their best for the animals.

Each night the dogs were attended to first. They ate before the drivers ate, and no man sought his sleeping-robe till he had seen to the feet of the dogs he drove. Still, their strength went down. Since the beginning of the winter they had travelled eighteen hundred miles, dragging sleds the whole weary distance; and eighteen hundred miles will tell upon life of the toughest. Buck stood it, keeping his mates up to their work and maintaining discipline, though he, too, was very tired. Billee cried and whimpered regularly in his sleep each night. Joe was sourer than ever, and Sol-leks was unapproachable, blind side or other side.

But it was Dave who suffered most of all. Something had gone wrong with him. He became more morose and irritable, and when camp was pitched at once made his nest, where his driver fed him. Once out of the harness and down, he did not get on his feet again till harness-up time in the morning. Sometimes, in the traces, when jerked by a sudden stoppage of the sled, or by straining to start it, he would cry out with pain. The driver examined him, but could find nothing. All the drivers became interested in his case. They talked it over at meal-time, and over their last pipes before going to bed, and one night they held a consultation. He was brought from his nest to the fire and was pressed and prodded till he cried out many times. Something was wrong inside, but they could locate no broken bones, could not make it out.

By the time Cassiar Bar was reached, he was so weak that he was falling repeatedly in the traces. The Scotch half-breed called a halt and took him out of the team, making the next dog, Sol-leks, fast to the sled. His intention was to rest Dave, letting him run free behind the sled. Sick as he was, Dave resented being taken out, grunting and growling while the traces were unfastened, and whimpering broken-heartedly when he saw Sol-leks in the position he had held and served so long. For the pride of trace and trail was his, and, sick unto death, he could not bear that another dog should do his work.

When the sled started, he floundered in the soft snow alongside the beaten trail, attacking Sol-leks with his teeth, rushing against him and trying to thrust him off into the soft snow on the other side, striving to leap inside his traces and get between him and the sled, and all the while whining and yelping and crying with grief and pain. The half-breed tried to drive him away with the whip; but he paid no heed to the stinging lash, and the man had not the heart to strike harder. Dave refused to run quietly on the trail behind the sled, where the going was easy, but continued to flounder alongside in the soft snow, where the going was most difficult, till exhausted. Then he fell, and lay where he fell, howling lugubriously as the long train of sleds churned by.

With the last remnant of his strength he managed to stagger along behind till the train made another stop, when he floundered past the sleds to his own, where he stood alongside Sol-leks. His driver lingered a moment to get a light for his pipe from the man behind. Then he returned and started his dogs. They swung out on the trail with remarkable lack of exertion, turned their heads uneasily, and stopped in surprise. The driver was surprised, too; the sled had not moved. He called his comrades to witness the sight. Dave had bitten through both of Sol-leks's traces, and was standing directly in front of the sled in his proper place.

He pleaded with his eyes to remain there. The driver was perplexed. His comrades talked of how a dog could break its heart through being denied the work that killed it, and recalled instances they had known, where dogs, too old for the toil, or injured, had died because they were cut out of the traces. Also, they held it a mercy, since Dave was to die anyway, that he should die in the traces, heart-easy and content. So he was harnessed in again, and proudly he pulled as of old, though more than once he cried out involuntarily from the bite of his inward hurt. Several times he fell down and was dragged in the traces, and once the sled ran upon him so that he limped thereafter in one of his hind legs.

But he held out till camp was reached, when his driver made a place for him by the fire. Morning found him too weak to travel. At harness-up time he tried to crawl to his driver. By convulsive efforts he got on his feet, staggered, and fell. Then he wormed his way forward slowly toward where the harnesses were being put on his mates. He would advance his fore legs and drag up his body with a sort of hitching movement, when he would advance his fore legs and hitch ahead again for a few more inches. His strength left him, and the last his mates saw of him he lay gasping in the snow and yearning toward them. But they could hear him mournfully howling till they passed out of sight behind a belt of river timber.

Here the train was halted. The Scotch half-breed slowly retraced his steps to the camp they had left. The men ceased talking. A revolver-shot rang out. The man came back hurriedly. The whips snapped, the bells tinkled merrily, the sleds churned along the trail; but Buck knew, and every dog knew, what had taken place behind the belt of river trees.

CHAPTER 5

THE TOIL OF TRACE AND TRAIL

Thirty days from the time it left Dawson, the Salt Water Mail, with Buck and his mates at the fore, arrived at Skaguay. They were in a wretched state, worn out and worn down. Buck's one hundred and forty pounds had dwindled to one hundred and fifteen. The rest of his mates, though lighter dogs, had relatively lost more weight then he. Pike, the malingerer, who, in his lifetime of deceit, had often successfully feigned a hurt leg, was now limping in earnest. Sol-leks was limping, and Dub was suffering from a wrenched shoulder-blade.

They were all terribly footsore. No spring or rebound was left in them. Their feet fell heavily on the trail, jarring their bodies and doubling the fatigue of a day's travel. There was nothing the matter with them except that they were dead tired. It was not the dead-tiredness that comes through brief and excessive effort, from which recovery is a matter of hours; but it was the dead-tiredness that comes through the slow and prolonged strength drainage of months of toil. There was no power of recuperation left, no reserve strength to call upon. It had been all used, the last least bit of it. Every muscle, every fibre, every cell, was tired, dead tired. And there was reason for it. In less than five months they had travelled twenty-five hundred miles, during the last eighteen hundred of which they had had but five days' rest. When they arrived at Skaguay they were apparently on their last legs. They could barely keep the traces taut, and on the down grades just managed to keep out of the way of the sled.

'Mush on, poor sore feets,' the driver encouraged them as they tottered down the main street of Skaguay. 'Dis is de las'. Den we get one long res'. Eh? For sure. One bully long res'.'

The drivers confidently expected a long stopover. Themselves, they had covered twelve hundred miles with two days' rest, and in the nature of reason and common justice they deserved an interval of loafing. But so many were the men who had rushed into the Klondike, and so many were the sweethearts, wives, and kin that had not rushed in, that the congested mail was taking on Alpine proportions; also, there were official orders. Fresh batches of Hudson Bay dogs were to take the places of those worthless for the trail. The worthless ones were to be got rid of, and, since dogs count for little against dollars, they were to be sold.

Three days passed, by which time Buck and his mates found how really tired and weak they were. Then, on the morning of the fourth day, two men from the States came along and bought them, harness and all, for a song. The men addressed each other as 'Hal' and 'Charles'. Charles was a middle-aged, lightish-coloured man, with weak and watery eyes and a moustache that twisted fiercely and vigorously up, giving the lie to the limply drooping lip it concealed. Hal was a youngster of nineteen or twenty, with a big Colt's revolver and a hunting-knife strapped about him on a belt that fairly bristled with cartridges. This belt was the most salient thing about him. It advertised his callowness–a callowness sheer and unutterable. Both men were manifestly out of place, and why such as they should adventure the North is part of the mystery of things that passes understanding.

Buck heard the chaffering, saw the money pass between the man and the Government agent, and knew that the Scotch half-breed and the mail-train drivers were passing out of his life on the heels of Perrault and François and the others who had gone before. When driven with his mates to the new owners' camp, Buck saw a slipshod and slovenly affair, tent half stretched, dishes unwashed, everything in disorder; also, he saw a woman. "Mercedes" the men called her. She was Charles's wife and Hal's sister—a nice family party.

Buck watched them apprehensively as they proceeded to take down the tent and load the sled. There was a great deal of effort about their manner, but no businesslike method. The tent was rolled into an awkward bundle three times as large as it should have been. The tin dishes were packed away unwashed. Mercedes continually fluttered in the way of her men and kept up an unbroken chattering of remonstrance and advice. When they put a clothes-sack on the front of the sled, she suggested it should go on the back; and when they had put it on the back, and covered it over with a couple of other bundles, she discovered overlooked articles which could abide nowhere else but in that very sack, and they unloaded again.

Three men from a neighbouring tent came out and looked on, grinning and winking at one another.

'You've got a right smart load as it is,' said one of them; 'and it's not me should tell you your business, but I wouldn't tote that tent along if I was you.'

'Undreamed of!' cried Mercedes, throwing up her hands in dainty dismay. 'However in the world could I manage without a tent?'

'It's springtime, and you won't get any more cold weather,' the man replied.

She shook her head decidedly, and Charles and Hal put the last odds and ends on top the mountainous load.

'Think it'll ride?' one of the men asked.

'Why shouldn't it?' Charles demanded rather shortly.

'Oh, that's all right, that's all right,' the man hastened meekly to say. 'I was just a-wonderin', that is all. It seemed a mite top-heavy.'

Charles turned his back and drew the lashings down as well as he could, which was not in the least well.

'An' of course the dogs can hike along all day with that contraption behind them,' affirmed a second of the men.

'Certainly,' said Hal, with freezing politeness, taking hold of the gee-pole with one hand and swinging his whip from the other. 'Mush!' he shouted. 'Mush on there!'

The dogs sprang against the breast-bands, strained hard for a few moments, then relaxed. They were unable to move the sled.

'The lazy brutes, I'll show them,' he cried, preparing to lash out at them with the whip.

But Mercedes interfered, crying, 'Oh, Hal, you mustn't,' as she caught hold of the whip and wrenched it from him. 'The poor dears! Now you must promise you won't be harsh with them for the rest of the trip, or I won't go a step.'

'Precious lot you know about dogs,' her brother sneered; 'and I wish you'd leave me alone. They're lazy, I tell you, and you've got to whip them to get anything out of them. That's their way. You ask any one. Ask one of those men.'

Mercedes looked at them imploringly, untold repugnance at sight of pain written in her pretty face.

'They're weak as water, if you want to know,' came the reply from one of the men. 'Plum tuckered out, that's what's the matter. They need a rest.'

'Rest be blanked,' said Hal, with his beardless lips; and Mercedes said, 'Oh!' in pain and sorrow at the oath.

But she was a clannish creature, and rushed at once to the defence of her brother. 'Never mind that man,' she said pointedly. 'You're driving our dogs, and you do what you think best with them.'

Again Hal's whip fell upon the dogs. They threw themselves against the breast-bands, dug their feet into the packed snow, got down low to it, and put forth all their strength. The sled held as though it were an anchor. After two efforts, they stood still, panting. The whip was whistling savagely, when once more Mercedes interfered. She dropped on her knees before Buck, with tears in her eyes, and put her arms around his neck.

'You poor, poor dears,' she cried sympathetically, 'why don't you pull hard?—then you wouldn't be whipped.' Buck did not like her, but he was feeling too miserable to resist her, taking it as part of the day's miserable work.

One of the onlookers, who had been clenching his teeth to suppress hot speech, now spoke up:—

'It's not that I care a whoop what becomes of you, but for the dogs' sakes I just want to tell you, you can help them a mighty lot by breaking out that sled. The runners are froze fast. Throw your weight against the gee-pole, right and left, and break it out.'

A third time the attempt was made, but this time, following the advice, Hal broke out the runners which had been frozen to the snow. The overloaded and unwieldy sled forged ahead, Buck and his mates struggling frantically under the rain of blows. A hundred yards ahead the path turned and sloped steeply into the main street. It would have required an experienced man to keep the top-heavy sled upright, and Hal was not such a man. As they swung on the turn the sled went over, spilling half its load through the loose lashings. The dogs never stopped. The lightened sled bounded on its side behind them. They were angry because of the ill treatment they had received and the unjust load. Buck was raging. He broke into a run, the team following his lead. Hal cried 'Whoa! whoa!' but they gave no heed. He tripped and was pulled off his feet. The capsized sled ground over him, and the dogs dashed on up the street, adding to the gaiety of Skaguay as they scattered the remainder of the outfit along§lg its chief thoroughfare.

Kind-hearted citizens caught the dogs and gathered up the scattered belongings. Also, they gave advice. Half the load and twice the dogs, if they ever expected to reach Dawson, was what was said. Hal and his sister and brother-in-law listened unwillingly, pitched tent, and overhauled the outfit. Canned goods were turned out that made men laugh, for canned goods on the Long

Trail is a thing to dream about. 'Blankets for a hotel,' quoth one of the men who laughed and helped. 'Half as many is too much; get rid of them. Throw away that tent, and all those dishes,—who's going to wash them, anyway? Good Lord, do you think you're travelling on a Pullman?'

And so it went, the inexorable elimination of the superfluous. Mercedes cried when her clothes-bags were dumped on the ground and article after article was thrown out. She cried in general, and she cried in particular over each discarded thing. She clasped hands about knees, rocking back and forth broken-heartedly. She averred she would not go an inch, not for a dozen Charleses. She appealed to everybody and to everything, finally wiping her eyes and proceeding to cast out even articles of apparel that were imperative necessaries. And in her zeal, when she had finished with her own, she attacked the belongings of her men and went through them like a tornado.

This accomplished, the outfit, though cut in half, was still a formidable bulk. Charles and Hal went out in the evening and bought six Outside dogs. These, added to the six of the original team, and Teek and Koona, the huskies obtained at the Rink Rapids on the record trip, brought the team up to fourteen. But the Outside dogs, though practically broken in since their landing, did not amount to much. Three were short-haired pointers, one was a Newfoundland, and the other two were mongrels of indeterminate breed. They did not seem to know anything, these newcomers. Buck and his comrades looked upon them with disgust, and though he speedily taught them their places and what not to do, he could not teach them what to do. They did not take kindly to trace and trail. With the exception of the two mongrels, they were bewildered and spirit-broken by the strange savage environment in which they found themselves and by the ill treatment they had received. The two mongrels were without spirit at all; bones were the only things breakable about them.

With the newcomers hopeless and forlorn, and the old team worn out by twenty-five hundred miles of continuous trail, the outlook was anything but bright. The two men, however, were quite cheerful. And they were proud, too. They were doing the thing in style, with fourteen dogs. They had seen other sleds depart over the Pass for Dawson, or come in from Dawson, but never had they seen a sled with so many as fourteen dogs. In the nature of Arctic travel there was a reason why fourteen dogs should not drag one sled, and that was that one sled could not carry the food for fourteen dogs. But Charles and Hal did not know this. They had worked the trip out with a pencil, so much to a dog, so many dogs, so many days, Q.E.D. Mercedes looked over their shoulders and nodded comprehensively, it was all so very simple.

Late next morning Buck led the long team up the street. There was nothing lively about it, no snap or go in him and his fellows. They were starting dead weary. Four times he had covered the distance between Salt Water and Dawson, and the knowledge that, jaded and tired, he was facing the same trail once more, made him bitter. His heart was not in the work, nor was the heart of any dog. The Outsides were timid and frightened, the Insides without confidence in their masters.

Buck felt vaguely that there was no depending upon these two men and the woman. They did not know how to do anything, and as the days went by it became apparent that they could not learn. They were slack in all things, without order or discipline. It took them half the night to pitch a slovenly camp, and half the morning to break that camp and get the sled loaded in fashion so slovenly that for the rest of the day they were occupied in stopping and rearranging the load. Some days they did not make ten miles. On other days they were unable to get started at all. And on no day did they succeed in making more than half the distance used by the men as a basis in their dog-food computation.

It was inevitable that they should go short on dog-food. But they hastened it by overfeeding, bringing the day nearer when underfeeding would commence. The Outside dogs, whose digestions had not been trained by chronic famine to make the most of little, had voracious appetites. And when, in addition to this, the worn-out huskies pulled weakly, Hal decided that the orthodox ration was too small. He doubled it. And to cap it all, when Mercedes, with tears in her pretty eyes and a quaver in her throat, could not cajole him into giving the dogs still more, she stole from the fish-sacks and fed them slyly. But it was not food that Buck and the huskies needed, but rest. And though they were making poor time, the heavy load they dragged sapped their strength severely.

Then came the underfeeding. Hal awoke one day to the fact that his dog-food was half gone and the distance only quarter covered; further, that for love or money no additional dog-food was to be obtained. So he cut down even the orthodox ration and tried to increase the day's travel. His sister and brother-in-law seconded him; but they were frustrated by their heavy outfit and their own incompetence. It was a simple matter to give the dogs less food; but it was impossible to make the dogs travel faster, while their own inability to get under way earlier in the morning prevented them from travelling longer hours. Not only did they not know how to work dogs, but they did not know how to work themselves.

The first to go was Dub. Poor blundering thief that he was, always getting caught and punished, he had none the less been a faithful worker. His wrenched shoulder-blade, untreated and unrested, went from bad to worse, till finally Hal shot him with the big Colt's revolver. It is a saying of the country that an Outside dog starves to death on the ration of the husky, so the six Outside dogs under Buck could do no less than die on half the ration of the husky. The Newfoundland went first, followed by the three short-haired pointers, the two mongrels hanging more grittily on to life, but going in the end.

By this time all the amenities and gentlenesses of the Southland had fallen away from the three people. Shorn of its glamour and romance, Arctic travel became to them a reality too harsh for their manhood and woman-hood. Mercedes ceased weeping over the dogs, being too occupied with weeping over herself and with quarrelling with her husband and brother. To quarrel was the one thing they were never too weary to do. Their irritability arose out of their misery, increased with it, doubled upon it, outdistanced it. The wonderful patience of the trail which comes to men who toil hard and suffer sore, and remain sweet of speech and kindly, did not come to these two men and the woman. They had no inkling of such a patience. They were stiff and in pain; their muscles ached, their bones ached, their very hearts ached; and because of this they became sharp of speech, and hard words were first on their lips in the morning and last at night.

Charles and Hal wrangled whenever Mercedes gave them a chance. It was the cherished belief of each that he did more than his share of the work, and neither forbore to speak this belief at every opportunity. Sometimes Mercedes sided with her husband, sometimes with her brother. The result was a beautiful and unending family quarrel. Starting from a dispute as to which should chop a few sticks for the fire (a dispute which concerned only Charles and Hal), presently would be lugged in the rest of the family, fathers, mothers, uncles, cousins, people thousands of miles away, and some of them dead. That Hal's views on art, or the sort of society plays his mother's brother wrote, should have anything to do with the chopping of a few sticks of firewood, passes comprehension; nevertheless the quarrel was as likely to tend in that direction as in the direction of Charles's political prejudices. And that Charles's sister's tale-bearing tongue should be relevant to the building of a Yukon fire, was apparent only to Mercedes, who disburdened herself of copious opinions upon that topic, and incidentally upon a few other traits unpleasantly peculiar to her husband's family. In the meantime the fire remained unbuilt, the camp half pitched, and the dogs unfed.

Mercedes nursed a special grievance—the grievance of sex. She was pretty and soft, and had been chival-

71

rously treated all her days. But the present treatment by her husband and brother was everything save chivalrous. It was her custom to be helpless. They complained. Upon which impeachment of what to her was her most essential sex-prerogative, she made their lives unendurable. She no longer considered the dogs, and because she was sore and tired, she persisted in riding on the sled. She was pretty and soft, but she weighed one hundred and twenty pounds—a lusty last straw to the load dragged by the weak and starving animals. She rode for days, till they fell in the traces and the sled stood still. Charles and Hal begged her to get off and walk, pleaded with her, entreated, the while she wept and importuned Heaven with a recital of their brutality.

On one occasion they took her off the sled by main strength. They never did it again. She let her legs go limp like a spoiled child, and sat down on the trail. They went on their way, but she did not move. After they had travelled three miles they unloaded the sled, came back for her, and by main strength put her on the sled again.

In the excess of their own misery they were callous to the suffering of their animals. Hal's theory, which he practised on others, was that one must get hardened. He had started out preaching it to his sister and brother-in-law. Failing there, he hammered it into the dogs with a club. At the Five Fingers the dog-food gave out, and a toothless old squaw offered to trade them a few pounds of frozen horse-hide for the Colt's revolver that kept the big hunting-knife company at Hal's hip. A poor substitute for food was this hide, just as it had been stripped from the starved horses of the cattlemen six months back. In its frozen state it was more like strips of galvanized iron, and when a dog wrestled it into his stomach it thawed into thin and innutritious leathery strings and into a mass of short hair, irritating and indigestible.

And through it all Buck staggered along at the head of the team as in a nightmare. He pulled when he could; when he could no longer pull, he fell down and remained down till blows from whip or club drove him to his feet again. All the stiffness and gloss had gone out of his beautiful furry coat. The hair hung down, limp and draggled, or matted with dried blood where Hal's club had bruised him. His muscles had wasted away to knotty strings, and the flesh pads had disappeared, so that each rib and every bone in his frame were outlined cleanly through the loose hide that was wrinkled in folds of emptiness. It was heartbreaking, only Buck's heart was unbreakable. The man in the red sweater had proved that.

As it was with Buck, so was it with his mates. They were perambulating skeletons. There were seven all together, including him. In their very great misery they had become insensible to the bite of the lash or the bruise of the club. The pain of the beating was dull and distant, just as the things their eyes saw and their ears heard seemed dull and distant. They were not half living, or quarter living. They were simply so many bags of bones in which sparks of life fluttered faintly. When a halt was made, they dropped down in the traces like dead dogs, and the spark dimmed and paled and seemed to go out. And when the club or whip fell upon them, the spark fluttered feebly up, and they tottered to their feet and staggered on.

There came a day when Billee, the good-natured, fell and could not rise. Hal had traded off his revolver, so he took the axe and knocked Billee on the head as he lay in the traces, then cut the carcass out of the harness and dragged it to one side. Buck saw, and his mates saw, and they knew that this thing was very close to them. On the next day Koona went, and but five of them remained: Joe, too far gone to be malignant; Pike, crippled and limping, only half conscious and not conscious enough longer to malinger; Sol-leks, the one-eyed, still faithful to the toil of trace and trail, and mournful in that he had so little strength with which to pull; Teek, who had not travelled so far that winter and who was now beaten more than the others because he was fresher; and Buck, still at the head of the team, but no longer enforcing discipline or striving to enforce it, blind with weakness half the time and keeping the trail by the loom of it and by the dim feel of his feet.

It was beautiful spring weather, but neither dogs nor humans were aware of it. Each day the sun rose earlier and set later. It was dawn by three in the morning, and twilight lingered till nine at night. The whole long day was a blaze of sunshine. The ghostly winter silence had given way to the great spring murmur of awakening life. This murmur arose from all the land, fraught with the joy of living. It came from the things that lived and moved again, things which had been as dead and which had not moved during the long months of frost. The sap was rising in the pines. The willows and aspens were bursting out in young buds. Shrubs and vines were putting on fresh garbs of green. Crickets sang in the nights, and in the days all manner of creeping, crawling things rustled forth into the sun. Partridges and woodpeckers were booming and knocking in the forest. Squirrels were chattering, birds singing, and overhead honked the wild-fowl driving up from the south in cunning wedges that split the air.

From every hill slope came the trickle of running water, the music of unseen fountains. All things were thawing, bending, snapping. The Yukon was straining to break loose the ice that bound it down. It ate away from beneath; the sun ate from above. Air-holes formed, fissures sprang and spread apart, while thin sections of ice fell through bodily into the river. And amid all this bursting, rending, throbbing of awakening life, under the blazing sun and through the soft-sighing breezes, like wayfarers to death, staggered the two men, the woman, and the huskies.

With the dogs falling, Mercedes weeping and riding, Hal swearing innocuously, and Charles's eyes wistfully watering, they staggered into John Thornton's camp at the mouth of White River. When they halted, the dogs dropped down as though they had all been struck dead. Mercedes dried her eyes and looked at John Thornton. Charles sat down on a log to rest. He sat down very slowly and painstakingly what of his great stiffness. Hal did the talking. John Thornton was whittling the last touches on an axe-handle he had made from a stick of birch. He whittled and listened, gave monosyllabic replies, and, when it was asked, terse advice. He knew the breed, and he gave his advice in the certainty that it would not be followed.

'They told us up above that the bottom was dropping out of the trail and that the best thing for us to do was to lay over,' Hal said in response to Thornton's warning to take no more chances on the rotten ice. 'They told us we couldn't make White River, and here we are.' This last with a sneering ring of triumph in it.

'And they told you true,' John Thornton answered. 'The bottom's likely to drop out at any moment. Only fools, with the blind luck of fools, could have made it. I tell you straight, I wouldn't risk my carcass on that ice for all the gold in Alaska.'

'That's because you're not a fool, I suppose,' said Hal. 'All the same, we'll go on to Dawson.' He uncoiled his whip. 'Get up there, Buck! Hi! Get up there! Mush on!'

Thornton went on whittling. It was idle, he knew, to get between a fool and his folly; while two or three fools more or less would not alter the scheme of things.

But the team did not get up at the command. It had long since passed into the stage where blows were required to rouse it. The whip flashed out, here and there, on its merciless errands. John Thornton compressed his lips. Sol-leks was the first to crawl to his feet. Teek followed. Joe came next, yelping with pain. Pike made painful efforts. Twice he fell over, when half up, and on the third attempt managed to rise. Buck made no effort. He lay quietly where he had fallen. The lash bit into him again and again, but he neither whined nor struggled. Several times Thornton started, as though to speak, but changed his mind. A moisture came into his eyes, and, as the whipping continued, he rose and walked irresolutely up and down.

This was the first time Buck had failed, in itself a sufficient reason to drive Hal into a rage. He exchanged the whip for the customary club. Buck refused to move under the rain of heavier blows which now fell upon him. Like his mates, he was barely able to get up, but, unlike them, he had made up his mind not to get up. He had a vague feeling of impending doom. This had been strong upon him when he pulled in to the bank, and it had not departed from him. What of the thin and rotten ice he had felt under his feet all day, it seemed that he sensed disaster close at hand, out there ahead on the ice where his master was trying to drive him. He refused to stir. So greatly had he suffered, and so far gone was he, that the blows did not hurt much. And as they continued to fall upon him, the spark of life within flickered and went down. It was nearly out. He felt strangely numb. As though from a great distance, he was aware that he was being beaten. The last sensations of pain left him. He no longer felt anything, though very faintly he could hear the impact of the club upon his body. But it was no longer his body, it seemed so far away.

And then, suddenly, without warning, uttering a cry that was inarticulate and more like the cry of an animal, John Thornton sprang upon the man who wielded the club. Hal was hurled backward, as though struck by a falling tree. Mercedes screamed. Charles looked on wistfully, wiped his watery eyes, but did not get up because of his stiffness.

John Thornton stood over Buck, struggling to control himself, too convulsed with rage to speak.

'If you strike that dog again, I'll kill you,' he at last managed to say in a choking voice.

'It's my dog,' Hal replied, wiping the blood from his

mouth as he came back. 'Get out of my way, or I'll fix you. I'm going to Dawson.'

Thornton stood between him and Buck, and evinced no intention of getting out of the way. Hal drew his long hunting-knife. Mercedes screamed, cried, laughed, and manifested the chaotic abandonment of hysteria. Thornton rapped Hal's knuckles with the axe-handle, knocking the knife to the ground. He rapped his knuckles again as he tried to pick it up. Then he stooped, picked it up himself, and with two strokes cut Buck's traces.

Hal had no fight left in him. Besides, his hands were full with his sister, or his arms, rather; while Buck was too near dead to be of further use in hauling the sled. A few minutes later they pulled out from the bank and down the river. Buck heard them go and raised his head to see. Pike was leading, Sol-leks was at the wheel, and between were Joe and Teek. They were limping and staggering. Mercedes was riding the loaded sled. Hal guided at the gee-pole, and Charles stumbled along in the rear.

As Buck watched them, Thornton knelt beside him and with rough, kindly hands searched for broken bones. By the time his search had disclosed nothing more than many bruises and a state of terrible starvation, the sled was a quarter of a mile away. Dog and man watched it crawling along over the ice. Suddenly, they saw its back end drop down, as into a rut, and the gee-pol, with Hal clinging to it, jerk into the air. Mercedes's scream came to their ears. They saw Charles turn and make one step to run back, and then a whole section of ice give way and dogs and humans disappear. A yawning hole was all that was to be seen. The bottom had dropped out of the trail.

John Thornton and Buck looked at each other.

'You poor devil,' said John Thornton, and Buck licked his hand.

CHAPTER 6

FOR THE LOVE OF A MAN

When John Thornton froze his feet in the previous December, his partners had made him comfortable and left him to get well, going on themselves up the river to get out a raft of saw-logs for Dawson. He was still limping slightly at the time he rescued Buck, but with the continued warm weather even the slight limp left him. And here, lying by the river bank through the long spring days, watching the running water, listening lazily to the songs of birds and the hum of nature, Buck slowly won back his strength.

A rest comes very good after one has travelled three thousand miles, and it must be confessed that Buck waxed lazy as his wounds healed, his muscles swelled out, and the flesh came back to cover his bones. For that matter, they were all loafing,—Buck, John Thornton, and Skeet and Nig,— waiting for the raft to come that was to carry them down to Dawson. Skeet was a little Irish setter who early made friends with Buck, who, in a dying condition, was unable to resent her first advances. She had the doctor trait which some dogs possess; and as a mother cat washes her kittens, so she washed and cleaned Buck's wounds. Regularly, each morning after he had finished his breakfast, she performed her self-appointed task, till he came to look for her ministrations as much as he did for Thornton's. Nig, equally friendly, though less demonstrative, was a huge black dog, half bloodhound and half deerhound, with eyes that laughed and a boundless good nature.

To Buck's surprise these dogs manifested no jealousy toward him. They seemed to share the kindliness and largeness of John Thornton. As Buck grew stronger they enticed him into all sorts of ridiculous games, in which Thornton himself could not forbear to join; and in this fashion Buck romped through his convalescence and into a new existence. Love, genuine passionate love, was his for the first time. This he had never experienced at Judge Miller's down in the sun-kissed Santa Clara Valley. With the Judge's sons, hunting and tramping, it had been a working partnership; with the Judge's grand-sons, a sort of pompous guardianship; and with the Judge himself, a stately and dignified friendship. But love that was feverish and burning, that was adoration, that was madness, it had taken John Thornton to arouse.

This man had saved his life, which was something; but, further, he was the ideal master. Other men saw to the welfare of their dogs from a sense of duty and business expediency; he saw to the welfare of his as if they were his own children, because he could not help it. And he saw further. He never forgot a kindly greet-ing or a cheering word, and to sit down for a long talk with them ('gas' he called it) was as much his delight as theirs. He had a way of taking Buck's head roughly between his hands, and resting his own head upon Buck's, of shaking him back and forth, the while calling him ill names that to Buck were love names. Buck knew no greater joy than that rough embrace and the sound of murmured oaths, and at each jerk back and forth it seemed that his heart would be shaken out of his body so great was its ecstasy. And when, released, he sprang to his feet, his mouth laughing, his eyes eloquent, his throat vibrant with unuttered sound, and in that fashion remained without movement, John Thornton would reverently exclaim, 'God! you can all but speak!'

Buck had a trick of love expression that was akin to hurt. He would often seize Thornton's hand in his mouth and close so fiercely that the flesh bore the impress of his teeth for some time afterward. And as Buck understood the oaths to be love words, so the man understood this feigned bite for a caress.

For the most part, however, Buck's love was expressed in adoration. While he went wild with happiness when Thornton touched him or spoke to him, he did not seek these tokens. Unlike Skeet, who was wont to shove her nose under Thornton's hand and nudge and nudge till petted, or Nig, who would stalk up and rest his great head on Thornton's knee, Buck was content to adore at a distance. He would lie by the hour, eager, alert, at Thornton's feet, looking up into his face, dwelling upon it, studying it, following with keenest interest each fleeting expression, every movement or change of feature. Or, as chance might have it, he would lie farther away, to the side or rear, watching the outlines of the man and the occasional movements of his body. And often, such was the communion in which they lived, the strength of Buck's gaze would draw John Thornton's head around, and he would return the gaze, without speech, his heart shining out of his eyes as Buck's heart shone out.

For a long time after his rescue, Buck did not like Thornton to get out of his sight. From the moment he left the tent to when he entered it again, Buck would follow at his heels. His transient masters since he had come into the Northland had bred in him a fear that no master could be permanent. He was afraid that Thornton would pass out of his life as Perrault and François and the Scotch half-breed had passed out. Even in the night, in his dreams, he was haunted by this fear. At such times he would shake off sleep and creep through the chill to the flap of the tent, where he would stand and listen to the sound of his master's breathing.

But in spite of this great love he bore John Thornton, which seemed to bespeak the soft civilizing influence, the strain of the primitive, which the Northland had aroused in him, remained alive and active. Faithfulness and devotion, things born of fire and roof, were his, yet he retained his wildness and wiliness. He was a thing of the wild, come in from the wild to sit by John Thornton's fire, rather than a dog of the soft Southland stamped with the marks of generations of civilization. Because of his very great love, he could not steal from this man, but from any other man, in any other camp, he did not hesitate an instant; while the cunning with which he stole enabled him to escape detection.

His face and body were scored by the teeth of many dogs, and he fought as fiercely as ever and more shrewdly. Skeet and Nig were too good-natured for quarrelling—besides, they belonged to John Thornton; but the strange dog, no matter what the breed or valour, swiftly acknowledged Buck's supremacy or found himself struggling for life with a terrible antagonist. And Buck was merciless. He had learned well the law of club and fang, and he never forewent an advantage or drew back from a foe he had started on the way to Death. He had lessoned from Spitz, and from the chief fighting dogs of the police and mail, and knew there was no middle course. He must master or be mastered; while to show mercy was a weakness. Mercy did not exist in the primordial life. It was misunderstood for fear, and such misunderstandings made for death. Kill or be killed, eat or be eaten, was the law; and this mandate, down out of the depths of Time, he obeyed.

He was older than the days he had seen and the breaths he had drawn. He linked the past with the present, and the eternity behind him throbbed through him in a mighty rhythm to which he swayed as the tides and seasons swayed. He sat by John Thornton's fire, a broad-breasted dog, white-fanged and long-furred; but behind him were the shades of all manner of dogs, half-wolves and wild wolves, urgent and prompting, tasting the savour of the meat he ate, thirsting for the water he drank, scenting the wind with him, listening with him and telling him the sounds made by the wild life in the forest, dictating his moods, directing his actions, lying down to sleep with him when he lay down, and dreaming with him and beyond him and becoming themselves the stuff of his dreams.

So peremptorily did these shades beckon him, that each day mankind and the claims of mankind slipped farther from him. Deep in the forest a call was sounding, and as often as he heard this call, mysteriously thrilling and luring, he felt compelled to turn his back upon the fire and the beaten earth around it, and to plunge into the forest, and on and on, he knew not where or why; nor did he wonder where or why, the call sounding imperiously, deep in the forest. But as often as he gained the soft unbroken earth and the green shade, the love for John Thornton drew him back to the fire again.

Thornton alone held him. The rest of mankind was as nothing. Chance travellers might praise or pet him; but he was cold under it all, and from a too demonstrative man he would get up and walk away. When Thornton's partners, Hans and Pete, arrived on the long-expected raft, Buck refused to notice them till he learned they were close to Thornton; after that he tolerated them in a passive sort of way, accepting favours from them as though he favoured them by accepting. They were of the same large type as Thornton, living close to the earth, thinking simply and seeing clearly; and ere they swung the raft into the big eddy by the saw-mill at Dawson, they understood Buck and his ways, and did not insist upon an intimacy such as obtained with Skeet and Nig.

For Thornton, however, his love seemed to grow and grow. He, alone among men, could put a pack upon Buck's back in the summer travelling. Nothing was too great for Buck to do, when Thornton commanded. One day (they had grub-staked themselves from the proceeds of the raft and left Dawson for the head-waters of the Tanana) the men and dogs were sitting on the crest of a cliff which fell away, straight down, to naked bed-rock three hundred feet below. John Thornton was sitting near the edge, Buck at his shoulder. A thoughtless whim seized Thornton, and he drew the attention of Hans and Pete to the experiment he had in mind. 'Jump, Buck!' he commanded, sweeping his arm out and over the chasm.

The next instant he was grappling with Buck on the extreme edge, while Hans and Pete were dragging them back into safety.

'It's uncanny,' Pete said, after it was over and they had caught their speech.

Thornton shook his head. 'No, it is splendid, and it is terrible, too. Do you know, it sometimes makes me afraid.'

'I'm not hankering to be the man that lays hands on you while he's around,' Pete announced conclusively, nodding his head toward Buck.

'Py Jingo!' was Hans's contribution. 'Not mineself either.'

It was at Circle City, ere the year was out, that Pete's apprehensions were realized. 'Black' Burton, a man evil-tempered and malicious, had been picking a quarrel with a tenderfoot at the bar, when Thornton stepped good-naturedly between. Buck, as was his custom, was lying in a corner, head on paws, watching his master's every action. Burton struck out, without warning, straight from the shoulder. Thornton was sent spinning, and saved himself from falling only by clutching the rail of the bar.

Those who were looking on heard what was neither bark nor yelp, but a something which is best described as a roar, and they saw Buck's body rise up in the air as he left the floor for Burton's throat. The man saved his life by instinctively throwing out his arm, but was hurled backward to the floor with Buck on top of him. Buck loosed his teeth from the flesh of the arm and drove in again for the throat. This time the man succeeded only in partly blocking, and his throat was torn open. Then the crowd was upon Buck, and he was driven off; but while a surgeon checked the bleeding, he prowled up and down, growling furiously, attempting to rush in, and being forced back by an array of hostile clubs. A 'miners' meeting,' called on the spot, decided that the dog had sufficient provocation, and Buck was discharged. But his reputation was made, and from that day his name spread through every camp in Alaska.

Later on, in the fall of the year, he saved John Thornton's life in quite another fashion. The three partners were lining a long and narrow poling-boat down a bad stretch of rapids on the Forty-Mile Creek. Hans and Pete moved along the bank, snubbing with a thin Manila rope from tree to tree, while Thornton remained in the boat, helping its descent by means of a pole, and shouting directions to the shore. Buck, on the bank, worried and anxious, kept abreast of the boat, his eyes never off his master.

At a particularly bad spot, where a ledge of barely submerged rocks jutted out into the river, Hans cast off the rope, and, while Thornton poled the boat out into the stream, ran down the bank with the end in his hand to snub the boat when it had cleared the ledge. This it did, and was flying down-stream in a current as swift as a mill-race, when Hans checked it with the rope and checked too suddenly. The boat flirted over and snubbed in to the bank bottom up, while Thornton, flung sheer out of it, was carried down-stream toward the worst part of the rapids, a stretch of wild water in which no swimmer could live.

Buck had sprung in on the instant; and at the end of

three hundred yards, amid a mad swirl of water, he overhauled Thornton. When he felt him grasp his tail, Buck headed for the bank, swimming with all his splendid strength. But the progress shoreward was slow; the progress down-stream amazingly rapid. From below came the fatal roaring where the wild current went wilder and was rent in shreds and spray by the rocks which thrust through like the teeth of an enormous comb. The suck of the water as it took the beginning of the last steep pitch was frightful, and Thornton knew that the shore was impossible. He scraped furiously over a rock, bruised across a second, and struck a third with crushing force. He clutched its slippery top with both hands, releasing Buck, and over the roar of the churning water shouted: 'Go, Buck! Go!'

Buck could not hold his own, and swept on downstream, struggling desperately, but unable to win back. When he heard Thornton's command repeated, he partly reared out of the water, throwing his head high, as though for a last look, then turned obediently toward the bank. He swam powerfully and was dragged ashore by Pete and Hans at the very point where swimming ceased to be possible and destruction began.

They knew that the time a man could cling to a slippery rock in the face of that driving current was a matter of minutes, and they ran as fast as they could up the bank to a point far above where Thornton was hanging on. They attached the line with which they had been snubbing the boat to Buck's neck and shoulders, being careful that it should neither strangle him nor impede his swimming, and launched him into the stream. He struck out boldly, but not straight enough into the stream. He discovered the mistake too late, when Thornton was abreast of him and a bare half-dozen strokes away while he was being carried helplessly past.

Hans promptly snubbed with the rope, as though Buck were a boat. The rope thus tightening on him in the sweep of the current, he was jerked under the surface, and under the surface he remained till his body struck against the bank and he was hauled out. He was half drowned, and Hans and Pete threw themselves upon him, pounding the breath into him and the water out of him. He staggered to his feet and fell down. The faint sound of Thornton's voice came to them, and though they could not make out the words of it, they knew that he was in his extremity. His master's voice acted on Buck like an electric shock. He sprang to his feet and ran up the bank ahead of the men to the point of his previous departure.

Again the rope was attached and he was launched, and again he struck out, but this time straight into the stream. He had miscalculated once, but he would not be guilty of it a second time. Hans paid out the rope, permitting no slack, while Pete kept it clear of coils. Buck held on till he was on a line straight above Thornton; then he turned, and with the speed of an express train headed down upon him. Thornton saw him coming, and, as Buck struck him like a battering ram, with the whole force of the current behind him, he reached up and closed both arms around the shaggy neck. Hans snubbed the rope around the tree, and Buck and Thornton were jerked under the water. Strangling, suffocating, sometimes one uppermost and sometimes the other, dragging over the jagged bottom, smashing against rocks and snags, they veered in to the bank.

Thornton came to, belly downward and being violently propelled back and forth across a drift log by Hans and Pete. His first glance was for Buck, over whose limp and apparently lifeless body Nig was setting up a howl, while Skeet was licking the wet face and closed eyes. Thornton was himself bruised and battered, and he went carefully over Buck's body, when he had been brought around, finding three broken ribs.

"That settles it," he announced. "We camp right here." And camp they did, till Buck's ribs knitted and he was able to travel.

That winter, at Dawson, Buck performed another exploit, not so heroic, perhaps, but one that put his name many notches higher on the totem-pole of Alaskan fame. This exploit was particularly gratifying to the three men; for they stood in need of the outfit which it furnished, and were enabled to make a long-desired trip into the virgin East, where miners had not yet appeared. It was brought about by a conversation in the Eldorado Saloon, in which men waxed boastful of their favourite dogs. Buck, because of his record, was the target for these men, and Thornton was driven stoutly to defend him. At the end of half an hour one man stated that his dog could start a sled with five hundred pounds and walk off with it; a second bragged six hundred for his dog; and a third, seven hundred.

'Pooh! pooh!' said John Thornton; 'Buck can start a thousand pounds.'

'And break it out? and walk off with it for a hundred yards?' demanded Matthewson, a Bonanza King, he of the seven hundred vaunt.

'And break it out, and walk off with it for a hundred yards,' John Thornton said coolly.

'Well,' Matthewson said, slowly and deliberately, so that all could hear, 'I've got a thousand dollars that says he can't. And there it is.' So saying, he slammed a sack of gold dust of the size of a bologna sausage down upon the bar.

Nobody spoke. Thornton's bluff, if bluff it was, had been called. He could feel a flush of warm blood creeping up his face. His tongue had tricked him. He did not know whether Buck could start a thousand pounds. Half a ton! The enormousness of it appalled him. He had great faith in Buck's strength and had often thought him capable of starting such a load; but never, as now, had he faced the possibility of it, the eyes of a dozen men fixed upon him, silent and waiting. Further, he had no thousand dollars; nor had Hans or Pete.

'I've got a sled standing outside now, with twenty fifty-pound sacks of flour on it,' Matthewson went on with brutal directness; 'so don't let that hinder you.'

Thornton did not reply. He did not know what to say. He glanced from face to face in the absent way of a man who has lost the power of thought and is seeking somewhere to find the thing that will start it going again. The face of Jim O'Brien, a Mastodon King and old-time comrade, caught his eyes. It was as a cue to him, seeming to rouse him to do what he would never have dreamed of doing.

'Can you lend me a thousand?' he asked, almost in a whisper.

'Sure,' answered O'Brien, thumping down a plethoric sack by the side of Matthewson's. 'Though it's little faith I'm having, John, that the beast can do the trick.'

The Eldorado emptied its occupants into the street to see the test. The tables were deserted, and the dealers and gamekeepers came forth to see the outcome of the wager and to lay odds. Several hundred men, furred and mittened, banked around the sled within easy distance. Matthewson's sled, loaded with a thousand pounds of flour, had been standing for a couple of hours, and in the intense cold (it was sixty below zero) the runners had frozen fast to the hard-packed snow. Men offered odds of two to one that Buck could not budge the sled. A quibble arose concerning the phrase 'break out'. O'Brien contended it was Thornton's privilege to knock the runners loose, leaving Buck to 'break it out' from a dead standstill. Matthewson insisted that the phrase included breaking the runners from the frozen grip of the snow. A majority of the men who had witnessed the making of the bet decided in his favour, whereat the odds went up to three to one against Buck.

There were no takers. Not a man believed him capable of the feat. Thornton had been hurried into the wager, heavy with doubt; and now that he looked at the sled itself, the concrete fact, with the regular team of ten dogs curled up in the snow before it, the more impossible the task appeared. Matthewson waxed jubilant.

'Three to one!' he proclaimed. 'I'll lay you another thousand at that figure, Thornton. What d'ye say?'

Thornton's doubt was strong in his face, but his fighting spirit was aroused—the fighting spirit that soars above odds, fails to recognize the impossible, and is deaf to all save the clamour for battle. He called Hans and

Pete to him. Their sacks were slim, and with his own the three partners could rake together only two hundred dollars. In the ebb of their fortunes, this sum was their total capital; yet they laid it unhesitatingly against Matthewson's six hundred.

The team of ten dogs was unhitched, and Buck, with his own harness, was put into the sled. He had caught the contagion of the excitement, and he felt that in some way he must do a great thing for John Thornton. Murmurs of admiration at his splendid appearance went up. He was in perfect condition, without an ounce of superfluous flesh, and the one hundred and fifty pounds that he weighed were so many pounds of grit and virility. His furry coat shone with the sheen of silk. Down the neck and across the shoulders, his mane, in repose as it was, half bristled and seemed to lift with every movement, as though excess of vigour made each particular hair alive and active. The great breast and heavy fore legs were no more than in proportion with the rest of the body, where the muscles showed in tight rolls underneath the skin. Men felt these muscles and proclaimed them hard as iron, and the odds went down to two to one.

'Gad, sir! Gad, sir!' stuttered a member of the latest dynasty, a king of the Skookum Benches. 'I offer you eight hundred for him, sir, before the test, sir; eight hundred just as he stands.'

Thornton shook his head and stepped to Buck's side.

'You must stand off from him,' Matthewson protested. 'Free play and plenty of room.'

The crowd fell silent; only could be heard the voices of the gamblers vainly offering two to one. Everybody acknowledged Buck a magnificent animal, but twenty fifty-pound sacks of flour bulked too large in their eyes for them to loosen their pouch-strings.

Thornton knelt down by Buck's side. He took his head in his two hands and rested cheek on cheek. He did not playfully shake him, as was his wont, or murmur soft love curses; but whispered in his ear. 'As you love me, Buck. As you love me,' was what he whispered. Buck whined with suppressed eagerness.

The crowd was watching curiously. The affair was growing mysterious. It seemed like a conjuration. As Thornton got to his feet, Buck seized his mittened hand between his jaws, pressing in with his teeth and releasing slowly, half- reluctantly. It was the answer, in terms, not of speech, but of love. Thornton stepped well back.

'Now, Buck,' he said.

Buck tightened the traces, then slacked them for a matter of several inches. It was the way he had learned.

'Gee!' Thornton's voice rang out, sharp in the tense silence.

Buck swung to the right, ending the movement in a plunge that took up the slack and with a sudden jerk arrested his one hundred and fifty pounds. The load quivered, and from under the runners arose a crisp crackling.

'Haw!' Thornton commanded.

Buck duplicated the manoeuvre, this time to the left. The crackling turned into a snapping, the sled pivoting and the runners slipping and grating several inches to the side. The sled was broken out. Men were holding their breaths, intensely unconscious of the fact.

'Now, MUSH!'

Thornton's command cracked out like a pistol-shot. Buck threw himself forward, tightening the traces with a jarring lunge. His whole body was gathered compactly together in the tremendous effort, the muscles writhing and knotting like live things under the silky fur. His great chest was low to the ground, his head forward and down, while his feet were flying like mad, the claws scarring the hard-packed snow in parallel grooves. The sled swayed and trembled, half-started forward. One of his feet slipped, and one man groaned aloud. Then the sled lurched ahead in what appeared a rapid succession of jerks, though it never really came to a dead stop again . . . half an inch . . . an inch . . . two inches. . . . The jerks perceptibly diminished; as the sled gained momentum, he caught them up, till it was moving steadily along.

Men gasped and began to breathe again, unaware that for a moment they had ceased to breathe. Thornton was running behind, encouraging Buck with short, cheery words. The distance had been measured off, and as he neared the pile of firewood which marked the end of the hundred yards, a cheer began to grow and grow, which burst into a roar as he passed the firewood and halted at command. Every man was tearing himself loose, even Matthewson. Hats and mittens were flying in the air. Men were shaking hands, it did not matter with whom, and bubbling over in a general incoherent babel.

But Thornton fell on his knees beside Buck. Head was against head, and he was shaking him back and forth. Those who hurried up heard him cursing Buck, and he cursed him long and fervently, and softly and lovingly.

'Gad, sir! Gad, sir!' spluttered the Skookum Bench king. 'I'll give you a thousand for him, sir, a thousand, sir—twelve hundred, sir.'

Thornton rose to his feet. His eyes were wet. The tears were streaming frankly down his cheeks. 'Sir,' he said to the Skookum Bench king, 'no, sir. You can go to hell, sir. It's the best I can do for you, sir.'

Buck seized Thornton's hand in his teeth. Thornton shook him back and forth. As though animated by a common impulse, the onlookers drew back to a respectful distance; nor were they again indiscreet enough to interrupt.

CHAPTER 7

THE SOUNDING OF THE CALL

When Buck earned sixteen hundred dollars in five minutes for John Thornton, he made it possible for his master to pay off certain debts and to journey with his partners into the East after a fabled lost mine, the history of which was as old as the history of the country. Many men had sought it; few had found it; and more than a few there were who had never returned from the quest. This lost mine was steeped in tragedy and shrouded in mystery. No one knew of the first man. The oldest tradition stopped before it got back to him. From the beginning there had been an ancient and ramshackle cabin. Dying men had sworn to it, and to the mine the site of which it marked, clinching their testimony with nuggets that were unlike any known grade of gold in the Northland.

But no living man had looted this treasure house, and the dead were dead; wherefore John Thornton and Pete and Hans, with Buck and half a dozen other dogs, faced into the East on an unknown trail to achieve where men and dogs as good as themselves had failed. They sledded seventy miles up the Yukon, swung to the left into the Stewart River, passed the Mayo and the McQuestion, and held on until the Stewart itself became a streamlet, threading the upstanding peaks which marked the backbone of the continent.

John Thornton asked little of man or nature. He was unafraid of the wild. With a handful of salt and a rifle he could plunge into the wilderness and fare wherever he pleased and as long as he pleased. Being in no haste, Indian fashion, he hunted his dinner in the course of the day's travel; and if he failed to find it, like the Indian, he kept on travelling, secure in the knowledge that sooner or later he would come to it. So, on this great journey into the East, straight meat was the bill of fare, ammunition and tools principally made up the load on the sled, and the time-card was drawn upon the limitless future.

To Buck it was boundless delight, this hunting, fishing, and indefinite wandering through strange places. For weeks at a time they would hold on steadily, day after day; and for weeks upon end they would camp, here and there, the dogs loafing and the men burning holes through frozen muck and gravel and washing countless pans of dirt by the heat of the fire. Sometimes they went hungry, sometimes they feasted riotously, all according to the abundance of game and the fortune of hunting. Summer arrived, and dogs and men packed on their backs, rafted across blue mountain lakes, and descended or ascended unknown rivers in slender boats whipsawed from the standing forest.

The months came and went, and back and forth they twisted through the uncharted vastness, where no men were and yet where men had been if the Lost Cabin were true. They went across divides in summer blizzards, shivered under the midnight sun on naked mountains between the timber line and the eternal snows, dropped into summer valleys amid swarming gnats and flies, and in the shadows of glaciers picked strawberries and flowers as ripe and fair as any the Southland could boast. In the fall of the year they penetrated a weird lake country, sad and silent, where wild-fowl had been, but where then there was no life nor sign of life—only the blowing of chill winds, the forming of ice in sheltered places, and the melancholy rippling of waves on lonely beaches.

And through another winter they wandered on the obliterated trails of men who had gone before. Once, they came upon a path blazed through the forest, an ancient path, and the Lost Cabin seemed very near. But the path began nowhere and ended nowhere, and it remained mystery, as the man who made it and the reason he made it remained mystery. Another time they chanced upon the time-graven wreckage of a hunting lodge, and amid the shreds of rotted blankets John Thornton found a long-barrelled flint-lock. He knew it for a Hudson Bay Company gun of the young days in the Northwest, when such a gun was worth its height in beaver skins packed flat. And that was all—no hint as to the man who in an early day had reared the lodge and left the gun among the blankets.

Spring came on once more, and at the end of all their wandering the found, not the Lost Cabin, but a shallow placer in a broad valley where the gold showed like yellow butter across the bottom of the washing-pan. They sought no farther. Each day they worked earned them thousands of dollars in clean dust and nuggets, and they worked every day. The gold was sacked in moose-hide bags, fifty pounds to the bag, and piled like so much firewood outside the spruce-bough lodge. Like giants they toiled, days flashing on the heels of days like dreams as they heaped the treasure up.

There was nothing for the dogs to do, save the hauling in of meat now and again that Thornton killed, and Buck spent long hours musing by the fire. The vision of the short-legged hairy man came to him more frequently, now that there was little work to be done; and often, blinking by the fire, Buck wandered with him in that other world which he remembered.

The salient thing of this other world seemed fear. When he watched the hairy man sleeping by the fire, head between his knees and hands clasped above, Buck saw that he slept restlessly, with many starts and awakenings, at which times he would peer fearfully into the darkness and fling more wood upon the fire. Did they walk by the beach of a sea, where the hairy man gathered shell-fish and ate them as he gathered, it was with eyes that roved everywhere for hidden danger and with legs prepared to run like the wind at its first appearance. Through the forest they crept noiselessly, Buck at the hairy man's heels; and they were alert and vigilant, the pair of them, ears twitching and moving and nostrils quivering, for the man heard and smelled as keenly as Buck. The hairy man could spring up into the trees and travel ahead as fast as on the ground, swinging by the arms from limb to limb, sometimes a dozen feet apart, letting go and catching, never falling, never missing his grip. In fact, he seemed as much at home among the trees as on the ground; and Buck had memories of nights of vigil spent beneath trees wherein the hairy man roosted, holding on tightly as he slept.

And closely akin to the visions of the hairy man was the call still sounding in the depths of the forest. It filled him with a great unrest and strange desires. It caused him to feel a vague, sweet gladness, and he was aware of wild yearnings and stirrings for he knew not what. Sometimes he pursued the call into the forest, looking for it as though it were a tangible thing, barking softly or defiantly, as the mood might dictate. He would thrust his nose into the cool wood moss, or into the black soil where long grasses grew, and snort with joy at the fat earth smells; or he would crouch for hours, as if in concealment, behind fungus-covered trunks of fallen trees, wide-eyed and wide-eared to all that moved and sounded about him. It might be, lying thus, that he hoped to surprise this call he could not understand. But he did not know why he did these various things. He was impelled to do them, and did not reason about them at all.

Irresistible impulses seized him. He would be lying in camp, dozing lazily in the heat of the day, when suddenly his head would lift and his ears cock up, intent and listening, and he would spring to his feet and dash away, and on and on, for hours, through the forest aisles and across the open spaces where the niggerheads bunched. He loved to run down dry watercourses, and to creep and spy upon the bird life in the woods. For a day at a time he would lie in the underbrush where he could watch the partridges drumming and strutting up and down. But especially he loved to run in the dim twilight of the summer midnights, listening to the subdued and sleepy murmurs of the forest, reading signs and sounds as man may read a book, and seeking

103

for the mysterious something that called—called, waking or sleeping, at all times, for him to come.

One night he sprang from sleep with a start, eager-eyed, nostrils quivering and scenting, his mane bristling in recurrent waves. From the forest came the call (or one note of it, for the call was many noted), distinct and definite as never before—a long-drawn howl, like, yet unlike, any noise made by husky dog. And he knew it, in the old familiar way, as a sound heard before. He sprang through the sleeping camp and in swift silence dashed through the woods. As he drew closer to the cry he went more slowly, with caution in every movement, till he came to an open place among the trees, and looking out saw, erect on haunches, with nose pointed to the sky, a long, lean, timber wolf.

He had made no noise, yet it ceased from its howling and tried to sense his presence. Buck stalked into the open, half crouching, body gathered compactly together, tail straight and stiff, feet falling with unwonted care. Every movement advertised commingled threatening and overture of friendliness. It was the menacing truce that marks the meeting of wild beasts that prey. But the wolf fled at sight of him. He followed, with wild leapings, in a frenzy to overtake. He ran him into a blind channel, in the bed of the creek, where a timber jam barred the way. The wolf whirled about, pivoting on his hind legs after the fashion of Joe and of all cornered husky dogs, snarling and bristling, clipping his teeth together in a continuous and rapid succession of snaps.

Buck did not attack, but circled him about and hedged him in with friendly advances. The wolf was suspicious and afraid; for Buck made three of him in weight, while his head barely reached Buck's shoulder. Watching his chance, he darted away, and the chase was resumed. Time and again he was cornered, and the thing repeated, though he was in poor condition or Buck could not so easily have overtaken him. He would run till Buck's head was even with his flank when he would whirl around at bay, only to dash away again at the first opportunity.

But in the end Buck's pertinacity was rewarded; for the wolf, finding that no harm was intended, finally sniffed noses with him. Then they became friendly, and played about in the nervous, half-coy way with which fierce beasts belie their fierceness. After some time of this the wolf started off at an easy lope in a manner that plainly showed he was going somewhere. He made it clear to Buck that he was to come, and they ran side by side through the sombre twilight, straight up the creek bed, into the gorge from which it issued, and across the bleak divide where it took its rise.

On the opposite slope of the watershed they came down into a level country where were great stretches of forest and many streams, and through these great stretches they ran steadily, hour after hour, the sun rising higher and the day growing warmer. Buck was wildly glad. He knew he was at last answering the call, running by the side of his wood brother toward the place from where the call surely came. Old memories were coming upon him fast, and he was stirring to them as of old he stirred to the realities of which they were the shadows. He had done this thing before, somewhere in that other and dimly remembered world, and he was doing it again, now, running free in the open, the unpacked earth underfoot, the wide sky overhead.

They stopped by a running stream to drink, and, stopping, Buck remembered John Thornton. He sat down. The wolf started on toward the place from where the call surely came, then returned on him, sniffing noses and making actions as though to encourage him. But Buck turned about and started slowly on the back track. For the better part of an hour the wild brother ran by his side, whining softly. Then he sat down, pointed his nose upward, and howled. It was a mournful howl, and as Buck held steadily on his way he heard it grow faint and fainter until it was lost in the distance.

John Thornton was eating dinner when Buck dashed into camp and sprang upon him in a frenzy of affection, overturning him, scrambling upon him, licking his face, biting his hand—'playing the general tom-fool,' as John Thornton characterized it, the while he shook Buck back and forth and cursed him lovingly.

For two days and nights Buck never left camp, never let Thornton out of his sight. He followed him about at his work, watched him while he ate, saw him into his blankets at night and out of them in the morning. But after two days the call in the forest began to sound more imperiously than ever. Buck's restlessness came back on him, and he was haunted by recollections of the wild brother, and of the smiling land beyond the divide and the run side by side through the wide forest stretches. Once again he took to wandering in the woods, but the wild brother came no more; and though he listened through long vigils, the mournful howl was never raised.

He began to sleep out at night, staying away from camp for days at a time; and once he crossed the divide at the head of the creek and went down into the land of timber and streams. There he wandered for a week, seeking vainly for fresh sign of the wild brother, killing his meat as he travelled and travelling with the long easy lope that seems never to tire. He fished for salmon in a broad stream that emptied somewhere into the sea, and by this stream he killed a large black bear, blinded by the mosquitoes while likewise fishing, and raging through the forest helpless and terrible. Even so, it was a hard fight, and it aroused the last latent remnants of Buck's ferocity. And two days later, when he returned to his kill and found a dozen wolverenes quarrelling over the spoil, he scattered them like chaff; and those that fled left two behind who would quarrel no more.

The blood-longing became stronger than ever before. He was a killer, a thing that preyed, living on the things that lived, unaided, alone, by virtue of his own strength and prowess, surviving triumphantly in a hostile environment where only the strong survived. Because of all this he became possessed of a great pride in himself, which communicated itself like a contagion to his physical being. It advertised itself in all his movements, was apparent in the play of every muscle, spoke plainly as speech in the way he carried himself, and made his glorious furry coat if anything more glorious. But for the stray brown on his muzzle and above his eyes, and for the splash of white hair that ran midmost down his chest, he might well have been mistaken for a gigantic wolf, larger than the largest of the breed. From his St. Bernard father he had inherited size and weight, but it was his shepherd mother who had given shape to that size and weight. His muzzle was the long wolf muzzle, save that it was larger than the muzzle of any wolf; and his head, somewhat broader, was the wolf head on a massive scale.

His cunning was wolf cunning, and wild cunning; his intelligence, shepherd intelligence and St. Bernard intelligence; and all this, plus an experience gained in the fiercest of schools, made him as formidable a creature as any that roamed the wild. A carnivorous animal, living on a straight meat diet, he was in full flower, at the high tide of his life, overspilling with vigour and virility. When Thornton passed a caressing hand along his back, a snapping and crackling followed the hand, each hair discharging its pent magnetism at the contact. Every part, brain and body, nerve tissue and fibre, was keyed to the most exquisite pitch; and between all the parts there was a perfect equilibrium or adjustment. To sights and sounds and events which required action, he responded with lightning-like rapidity. Quickly as a husky dog could leap to defend from attack or to attack, he could leap twice as quickly. He saw the movement, or heard sound, and responded in less time than another dog required to compass the mere seeing or hearing. He perceived and determined and responded in the same instant. In point of fact the three actions of perceiving, determining, and responding were sequential; but so infinitesimal were the intervals of time between them that they appeared simultaneous. His muscles were surcharged with vitality, and snapped into play sharply, like steel springs. Life streamed through him in splendid flood, glad and rampant, until it seemed that it would burst him asunder in sheer ecstasy and pour forth generously over the world.

'Never was there such a dog,' said John Thornton one day, as the partners watched Buck marching out of camp.

'When he was made, the mould was broke,' said Pete.

'Py jingo! I t'ink so mineself,' Hans affirmed.

They saw him marching out of camp, but they did not see the instant and terrible transformation which took place as soon as he was within the secrecy of the forest. He no longer marched. At once he became a thing of the wild, stealing along softly, cat-footed, a passing shadow that appeared and disappeared among the shadows. He knew how to take advantage of every cover, to crawl on his belly like a snake, and like a snake to leap and strike. He could take a ptarmigan from its nest, kill a rabbit as it slept, and snap in mid air the little chipmunks fleeing a second too late for the trees. Fish, in open pools, were not too quick for him; nor were beaver, mending their dams, too wary. He killed to eat, not from wantonness; but he preferred to eat what he killed himself. So a lurking humour ran through his deeds, and it was his delight to steal upon the squirrels, and, when he all but had them, to let them go, chattering in mortal fear to the tree-tops.

As the fall of the year came on, the moose appeared in greater abundance, moving slowly down to meet the winter in the lower and less rigorous valleys. Buck had already dragged down a stray part-grown calf; but he wished strongly for larger and more formidable quarry, and he came upon it one day on the divide at the head of the creek. A band of twenty moose had crossed over from the land of streams and timber, and chief among them was a great bull. He was in a savage temper, and, standing over six feet from the ground, was as formidible an antagonist as even Buck could desire. Back and forth the bull tossed his great palmated antlers, branching to fourteen points and embracing seven feet within the tips. His small eyes burned with a vicious and bitter light, while he roared with fury at sight of Buck.

From the bull's side, just forward of the flank, protruded a feathered arrow-end, which accounted for his savageness. Guided by that instinct which came from the old hunting days of the primordial world, Buck proceeded to cut the bull out from the herd. It was no slight task. He would bark and dance about in front of the bull, just out of reach of the great antlers and of the terrible splay hoofs which could have stamped his life out with a single blow. Unable to turn his back on the fanged danger and go on, the bull would be driven into paroxysms of rage. At such moments he charged Buck, who retreated craftily, luring him on by a simulated inability to escape. But when he was thus separated from his fellows, two or three of the younger bulls would charge back upon Buck and enable the wounded bull to rejoin the herd.

There is a patience of the wild—dogged, tireless, persistent as life itself—that holds motionless for endless hours the spider in its web, the snake in its coils, the panther in its ambuscade; this patience belongs peculiarly to life when it hunts its living food; and it belonged to Buck as he clung to the flank of the herd, retarding its march, irritating the young bulls, worrying the cows with their half-grown calves, and driving the wounded bull mad with helpless rage. For half a day this continued. Buck multiplied himself, attacking from all sides, enveloping the herd in a whirlwind of menace, cutting out his victim as fast as it could rejoin its mates, wearing out the patience of creatures preyed upon, which is a lesser patience than that of creatures preying.

As the day wore along and the sun dropped to its bed in the northwest (the darkness had come back and the fall nights were six hours long), the young bulls retraced their steps more and more reluctantly to the aid of their beset leader. The down-coming winter was harrying them on to the lower levels, and it seemed they could never shake off this tireless creature that held them back. Besides, it was not the life of the herd, or of the young bulls, that was threatened. The life of only one member was demanded, which was a remoter interest than their lives, and in the end they were content to pay the toll.

As twilight fell the old bull stood with lowered head, watching his mates—the cows he had known, the calves he had fathered, the bulls he had mastered—as they shambled on at a rapid pace through the fading light. He could not follow, for before his nose leaped the merciless fanged terror that would not let him go. Three hundredweight more than half a ton he weighed; he had lived a long, strong life, full of fight and struggle, and at the end he faced death at the teeth of a creature whose head did not reach beyond his great knuckled knees.

From then on, night and day, Buck never left his prey, never gave it a moment's rest, never permitted it to browse the leaves of trees or the shoots of young birch and willow. Nor did he give the wounded bull opportunity to slake his burning thirst in the slender trickling streams they crossed. Often, in desperation, he burst into long stretches of flight. At such times Buck did not attempt to stay him, but loped easily at his heels, satisfied with the way the game was played, lying down when the moose stood still, attacking him fiercely when he strove to eat or drink.

The great head drooped more and more under its tree of horns, and the shambling trot grew weaker and weaker. He took to standing for long periods, with nose to the ground and dejected ears dropped limply; and Buck found more time in which to get water for himself and in which to rest. At such moments, panting with red lolling tongue and with eyes fixed upon the big bull, it appeared to Buck that a change was coming over the face of things. He could feel a new stir in the land. As the moose were coming into the land, other kinds of life were coming in. Forest and stream and air seemed palpitant with their presence. The news of it was borne in upon him, not by sight, or sound, or smell, but by some other and subtler sense. He heard nothing, saw nothing, yet knew that the land was somehow different; that through it strange things were afoot and ranging; and he resolved to investigate after he had finished the business in hand.

At last, at the end of the fourth day, he pulled the great moose down. For a day and a night he remained by the kill, eating and sleeping, turn and turn about. Then, rested, refreshed and strong, he turned his face toward camp and John Thornton. He broke into the long easy lope, and went on, hour after hour, never at loss for the tangled way, heading straight home through strange country with a certitude of direction that put man and his magnetic needle to shame.

As he held on he became more and more conscious of the new stir in the land. There was life abroad in it different from the life which had been there throughout the summer. No longer was this fact borne in upon him in some subtle, mysterious way. The birds talked of it, the squirrels chattered about it, the very breeze whispered of it. Several times he stopped and drew in the fresh morning air in great sniffs, reading a message which made him leap on with greater speed. He was oppressed with a sense of calamity happening, if it were not calamity already happened; and as he crossed the last watershed and dropped down into the valley toward camp, he proceeded with greater caution.

Three miles away he came upon a fresh trail that sent his neck hair rippling and bristling. It led straight toward camp and John Thornton. Buck hurried on, swiftly and stealthily, every nerve straining and tense, alert to the multitudinous details which told a story—all but the end. His nose gave him a varying description of the passage of the life on the heels of which he was travelling. He remarked the pregnant silence of the forest. The bird life had flitted. The squirrels were in hiding. One only he saw,—a sleek grey fellow, flattened against a grey dead limb so that he seemed a part of it, a woody excrescence upon the wood itself.

As Buck slid along with the obscureness of a gliding shadow, his nose was jerked suddenly to the side as though a positive force had gripped and pulled it. He followed the new scent into a thicket and found Nig. He was lying on his side, dead where he had dragged himself, an arrow protruding, head and feathers, from either side of his body.

A hundred yards farther on, Buck came upon one of the sled-dogs Thornton had bought in Dawson. This dog was thrashing about in a death-struggle, directly on the trail, and Buck passed around him without stopping. From the camp came the faint sound of many voices, rising and falling in a sing-song chant. Bellying forward to the edge of the clearing, he found Hans, lying on his face, feathered with arrows like a porcupine. At the same instant Buck peered out where the spruce-bough lodge had been and saw what made his hair leap straight up on his neck and shoulders. A gust of overpowering rage swept over him. He did not know that he growled, but he growled aloud with a terrible ferocity. For the last time in his life he allowed passion to usurp cunning and reason, and it was because of his great love for John Thornton that he lost his head.

The Yeehats were dancing about the wreckage of the spruce-bough lodge when they heard a fearful roaring and saw rushing upon them an animal the like of which they had never seen before. It was Buck, a live hurricane of fury, hurling himself upon them in a frenzy to destroy. He sprang at the foremost man (it was the chief of the Yeehats), ripping the throat wide open till the rent jugular spouted a fountain of blood. He did not pause to worry the victim, but ripped in passing, with the next bound tearing wide the throat of a second man. There was no withstanding him. He plunged about in their very midst, tearing, rending, destroying, in constant and terrific motion which defied the arrows they discharged at him. In fact, so

114

inconceivably rapid were his movements, and so closely were the Indians tangled together, that they shot one another with the arrows; and one young hunter, hurling a spear at Buck in mid air, drove it through the chest of another hunter with such force that the point broke through the skin of the back and stood out beyond. Then a panic seized the Yeehats, and they fled in terror to the woods, proclaiming as they fled the advent of the Evil Spirit.

And truly Buck was the Fiend incarnate, raging at their heels and dragging them down like deer as they raced through the trees. It was a fateful day for the Yeehats. They scattered far and wide over the country, and it was not till a week later that the last of the survivors gathered together in a lower valley and counted their losses. As for Buck, wearying of the pursuit, he returned to the desolated camp. He found Pete where he had been killed in his blankets in the first moment of surprise. Thornton's desperate struggle was fresh-written on the earth, and Buck scented every detail of it down to the edge of a deep pool. By the edge, head and fore feet in the water, lay Skeet, faithful to the last. The pool itself, muddy and discoloured from the sluice boxes, effectually hid what it contained, and it contained John Thornton; for Buck followed his trace into the water, from which no trace led away.

All day Buck brooded by the pool or roamed restlessly about the camp. Death, as a cessation of movement, as a passing out and away from the lives of the living, he knew, and he knew John Thornton was dead. It left a great void in him, somewhat akin to hunger, but a void which ached and ached, and which food could not fill. At times, when he paused to contemplate the carcasses of the Yeehats, he forgot the pain of it; and at such times he was aware of a great pride in himself—a pride greater than any he had yet experienced. He had killed man, the noblest game of all, and he had killed in the face of the law of club and fang. He sniffed the bodies curiously. They had died so easily. It was harder to kill a husky dog than them. They were no match at all, were it not for their arrows and spears and clubs. Thenceforward he would be unafraid of them except when they bore in their hands their arrows, spears, and clubs.

Night came on, and a full moon rose high over the trees into the sky, lighting the land till it lay bathed in ghostly day. And with the coming of the night, brooding and mourning by the pool, Buck became alive to a stirring of the new life in the forest other than that which the Yeehats had made. He stood up, listening and scenting. From far away drifted a faint, sharp yelp, followed by a chorus of similar sharp yelps. As the moments passed the yelps grew closer and louder. Again Buck knew them as things heard in that other world which persisted in his memory. He walked to the centre of the open space and listened. It was the call, the many-noted call, sounding more luringly and compelling than ever before. And as never before, he was ready to obey. John Thornton was dead. The last tie was broken. Man and the claims of man no longer bound him.

Hunting their living meat, as the Yeehats were hunting it, on the flanks of the migrating moose, the wolf pack had at last crossed over from the land of streams and timber and invaded Buck's valley. Into the clearing where the moonlight streamed, they poured in a silvery flood; and in the centre of the clearing stood Buck, motionless as a statue, waiting their coming. They were awed, so still and large he stood, and a moment's pause fell, till the boldest one leaped straight for him. Like a flash Buck struck, breaking the neck. Then he stood, without movement, as before, the stricken wolf rolling in agony behind him. Three others tried it in sharp succession; and one after the other they drew back, streaming blood from slashed throats or shoulders.

This was sufficient to fling the whole pack forward, pell-mell, crowded together, blocked and confused by its eagerness to pull down the prey. Buck's marvellous quickness and agility stood him in good stead. Pivoting on his hind legs, and snapping and gashing, he was everywhere at once, presenting a front which was apparently unbroken so swiftly did he whirl and guard from side to side. But to prevent them from getting behind him, he was forced back, down past the pool and into the creek bed, till he brought up against a high gravel bank. He worked along to a right angle in the bank which the men had made in the course of mining, and in this angle he came to bay, protected on three sides and with nothing to do but face the front.

And so well did he face it, that at the end of half an hour the wolves drew back discomfited. The tongues of all were out and lolling, the white fangs showing cruelly white in the moonlight. Some were lying down with heads raised and ears pricked forward; others stood on their feet, watching him; and still others were lapping water from the pool. One wolf, long and lean and grey, advanced cautiously, in a friendly manner, and Buck recognized the wild brother with whom he had run for a night and a day. He was whining softly, and, as Buck whined, they touched noses.

Then an old wolf, gaunt and battle-scarred, came forward. Buck writhed his lips into the preliminary of a snarl, but sniffed noses with him. Whereupon the old wolf sat down, pointed nose at the moon, and broke out the long wolf howl. The others sat down and howled. And now the call came to Buck in unmistakable accents. He, too, sat down and howled. This over, he came out of his angle and the pack crowded around him, sniffing in half-friendly, half-savage manner. The leaders lifted the yelp of the pack and sprang away into the woods. The wolves swung in behind, yelping in chorus. And Buck ran with them, side by side with the wild brother, yelping as he ran.

And here may well end the story of Buck. The years were not many when the Yeehats noted a change in the breed of timber wolves; for some were seen with splashes of brown on head and muzzle, and with a rift of white centring down the chest. But more remarkable than this, the Yeehats tell of a Ghost Dog that runs at the head of the pack. They are afraid of the Ghost Dog, for it has cunning greater than they, stealing from their camps in fierce winters, robbing their traps, slaying their dogs, and defying their bravest hunters.

Nay, the tale grows worse. Hunters there are who fail to return to the camp, and hunters there have been whom their tribesmen found with throats slashed cruelly open and with wolf prints about them in the snow greater than the prints of any wolf. Each fall, when the Yeehats follow the movement of the moose, there is a certain valley which they never enter. And women there are who become sad when the word goes over the fire of how the Evil Spirit came to select that valley for an abiding-place.

In the summers there is one visitor, however, to that valley, of which the Yeehats do not know. It is a great, gloriously coated wolf, like, and yet unlike, all other wolves. He crosses alone from the smiling timber land and comes down into an open space among the trees. Here a yellow stream flows from rotted moose-hide sacks and sinks into the ground, with long grasses growing through it and vegetable mould overrunning it and hiding its yellow from the sun; and here he muses for a time, howling once, long and mournfully, ere he departs.

But he is not always alone. When the long winter nights come on and the wolves follow their meat into the lower valleys, he may be seen running at the head of the pack through the pale moonlight or glimmering borealis, leaping gigantic above his fellows, his great throat a-bellow as he sings a song of the younger world, which is the song of the pack.